BRANDON SANDERSON

OATHBRINGER

PART ONE

Book Three of

THE STORMLIGHT ARCHIVE

This edition first published in Great Britain in 2019 by Gollancz

First published in Great Britain in 2017 by Gollancz
an imprint of the Orion Publishing Group Ltd
Carmelite House, 50 Victoria Embankment
London EC4Y 0DZ

An Hachette UK Company

13 15 17 19 20 18 16 14 12

Illustrations preceding chapters 39 and 58 by Dan dos Santos
Illustrations preceding chapters 8, 15, 25, 27, 33, 67, 99, 108 and 116
by Ben McSweeney
Illustrations preceding chapters 77 and 94 by Miranda Meeks
Illustrations preceding chapters 44 and 104 by Kelley Harris
Maps and illustrations preceding chapters 1, 5, 53, 61, 89 and 120 by Isaac Stewart
Viewpoint icons by Isaac Stewart, Ben McSweeney and Howard Lyon

A CIP catalogue record for this book is
available from the British Library.

ISBN 978 0 575 09336 2

Typeset by Input Data Services Ltd, Somerset

Printed in Great Britain by Clays Ltd, Elcograf S.p.A.

www.brandonsanderson.com
www.gollancz.co.uk

For Alan Layton
   Who was cheering for Dalinar
      (And me)
   Before Stormlight even existed.

PREFACE AND ACKNOWLEDGMENTS

Welcome to *Oathbringer*! It's been a long road, creating this book. I thank you for your patience. Stormlight books are a huge undertaking – which you might be able to infer from the large list of people below.

If you haven't had the chance to read *Edgedancer* – a separate Stormlight novella taking place between books two and three – I'd recommend it to you now. Find it sold on its own, or in the story collection *Arcanum Unbounded*, which has novellas and novelettes from all across the Cosmere. (The universe in which this series, *Mistborn, Elantris, Warbreaker*, and others take place.)

That said, as always, every series is written so it can be read and enjoyed on its own, without knowledge of these other series or books. If you're intrigued, you can find a longer explanation I've written at brandonsanderson.com/cosmere.

Now, on to the parade of names! As I often say, though my name goes on the cover, there are tons of people involved in bringing you these books. They deserve my most hearty of thanks, and yours as well, for their tireless work across the three years it took to write this novel.

My main agent for these books (and everything else) is the wonderful Joshua Bilmes, of JABberwocky. Others at the agency who worked on them include Brady McReynolds, Krystyna Lopez, and Rebecca Eskildsen. Special thanks also go to John Berlyne, my UK agent, of Zeno – along with all of the sub-agents who work with us around the world.

My editor at Tor on this project was the ever-brilliant Moshe Feder. Special thanks to Tom Doherty, who has believed in the Stormlight project for years, and Devi Pillai, who provided essential publishing and editorial aid during the course of the novel's creation.

Others at Tor who provided help include Robert Davis, Melissa Singer, Rachel Bass, and Patty Garcia. Karl Gold was our Production Manager and Nathan Weaver the Managing Editor, with Meryl Gross and Rafal Gibek in trade production. Irene Gallo was our Art Director, Michael Whelan the cover designer, Greg Collins the interior designer, and Carly Sommerstein our proofreader.

At Gollancz/Orion (my UK publisher) thanks goes to Gillian Redfearn, Stevie Finegan, and Charlotte Clay.

Our copyeditor on this book was Terry McGarry, who has done excellent work on many of my novels. The ebook was prepared by Victoria Wallis and Caitlin Buckley at Macmillan.

Many people at my own company worked long hours to produce this book. A Stormlight novel is 'crunch time' for us here at Dragonsteel, and so make sure to give the team a thumbs-up (or, in Peter's case, a block of cheese) next time you meet them. Our manager and Chief Operations Officer is my lovely wife, Emily Sanderson. Vice President and Editorial Director is the Insistent Peter Ahlstrom. Art Director is Isaac Stewart.

Our shipping manager (and the one who ships you all our signed books and T-shirts via the brandonsanderson.com store) is Kara Stewart. Continuity editor – and holy keeper of our internal continuity wiki – is Karen Ahlstrom. Adam Horne is my executive assistant and publicity/marketing director. Emily's assistant is Kathleen Dorsey Sanderson and our executive minion is Emily 'Mem' Grange.

The audiobook was read by my personal favorite audiobook narrators, Michael Kramer and Kate Reading. Thanks again, guys, for making time in your schedule for this!

Oathbringer continues the tradition of filling The Stormlight Archive with beautiful art. We again have a fantastic cover illustration by Michael Whelan, whose attention to detail has given us an incredibly accurate rendition of Jasnah Kholin. I love that she gets a place to shine on the cover of this book, and I continue to feel honored and grateful that Michael takes time away from his gallery work to paint the world of Roshar.

It takes a variety of artists to recreate the styles found in the ephemera of another world, so this time around we've worked with even more artists than before. Dan dos Santos and Howard Lyon are responsible for the paintings of the Heralds on the front and back endpapers. I wanted these to have a style evoking classical paintings of the Renaissance and the later Romantic era, and both Dan and Howard exceeded expectations. These pieces are not only great art for a book, they are great art period, deserving of a place in any gallery.

I should note that Dan and Howard also contributed their talents to the interior art, for which I'm also grateful. Dan's fashion pieces are good enough to be cover art, and Howard's linework for some of the new chapter icons is something I hope to see more of in future volumes.

Ben McSweeney joins us again, providing nine pieces of art from Shallan's sketchbook. Between a cross-continent move, a demanding day job, and the needs of a growing family, Ben has been ever consistent in delivering top-notch illustrations. He is a great artist and a quality human being.

Also lending their talents to this volume with full-page illustrations are Miranda Meeks and Kelley Harris. Both have done fantastic work for us in the past, and I think you'll love their contributions this time around.

In addition, a variety of wonderful people helped behind the scenes as consultants or facilitated other aspects of the art in this book: The David Rumsey Map Collection, Brent at Woodsounds Flutes, Angie and Michelle at Two Tone Press, Emily Dunlay, David and Doris Stewart, Shari Lyon, Payden McRoberts, and Greg Davidson.

My writing group for *Oathbringer* (and they often read submissions each week at 5–8x the normal size) included Karen Ahlstrom, Peter Ahlstrom, Emily Sanderson, Eric James Stone, Darci Stone, Ben Olsen, Kaylynn ZoBell, Kathleen Dorsey Sanderson, Alan 'Leyten from Bridge Four' Layton, Ethan 'Skar from Bridge Four' Skarstedt, and Ben 'Don't put me in Bridge Four' Olsen.

Special thanks go to Chris 'Jon' King for feedback on some particularly tricky scenes involving Teft, Will Hoyum for some advice on paraplegics, and Mi'chelle Walker for some special advisement on passages involving specific mental health issues.

Beta readers included (take a deep breath) Aaron Biggs, Aaron Ford, Adam Hussey, Austin Hussey, Alice Arneson, Alyx Hoge, Aubree Pham, Bao Pham, Becca Horn Reppert, Bob Kluttz, Brandon Cole, Darci Cole, Brian T. Hill, Chris 'Jon' King, Chris Kluwe, Cory Aitchison, David Behrens, Deana Covel Whitney, Eric Lake, Gary Singer, Ian McNatt, Jessica Ashcraft, Joel Phillips, Jory Phillips, Josh Walker, Mi'chelle Walker, Kalyani Poluri, Rahul Pantula, Kellyn Neumann, Kristina Kugler, Lyndsey 'Lyn' Luther, Mark Lindberg, Marnie Peterson, Matt Wiens, Megan Kanne, Nathan 'Natam' Goodrich, Nikki Ramsay, Paige Vest, Paul Christopher, Randy MacKay, Ravi Persaud, Richard Fife, Ross Newberry, Ryan 'Drehy' Dreher Scott, Sarah 'Saphy' Hansen, Sarah Fletcher, Shivam Bhatt, Steve Godecke, Ted Herman, Trae Cooper, and William Juan.

Our beta reader comment coordinators were Kristina Kugler and Kellyn Neumann.

Our gamma readers included many of the beta readers again, plus: Benjamin R. Black, Chris 'Gunner' McGrath, Christi Jacobsen, Corbett Rubert, Richard Rubert, Dr Daniel Stange, David Han-Ting Chow, Donald Mustard III, Eric Warrington, Jared Gerlach, Jareth Greeff, Jesse Y. Horne, Joshua Combs, Justin Koford, Kendra Wilson, Kerry Morgan, Lindsey Andrus, Lingting Xu, Loggins Merrill, Marci Stringham, Matt Hatch, Scott Escujuri, Stephen Stinnett, and Tyson Thorpe.

As you can see, a book like this is a *huge* undertaking. Without the efforts of these many people, you'd be holding a far, far inferior book.

As always, some final thanks go to my family: Emily Sanderson, Joel Sanderson, Dallin Sanderson, and Oliver Sanderson. They put up with a husband/father who is often off in another world, thinking about highstorms and Knights Radiant.

Finally, thanks to you all, for your support of these books! They don't always come out as quickly as I'd like, but that is in part because I want them to be as perfect as they can get. You hold in your hands a volume I've been preparing and outlining for almost two decades. May you enjoy your time in Roshar.

Journey before destination.

CONTENTS

Book Three Oathbringer

Prologue: To Weep   3

Part One: United   11

Interludes   365

Part Two: New Beginnings   371

Interludes   609

ILLUSTRATIONS

NOTE: *Many illustrations, titles included, contain spoilers for material that comes before them in the book. Look ahead at your own risk.*

Map of Roshar   xii-xiii

Map of the Oathgate Locations   12

Map of Alethkar   55

Shallan's Sketchbook: The Tower   84

Shallan's Sketchbook: Corridor   160

Shallan's Sketchbook: Horses   266

Shallan's Sketchbook: Spren in the Wall   292

Shallan's Sketchbook: Urithiru   372

Folio: The Vorin Havah   446

Navani's Notebook: Ship Designs   488

Alethi Glyphs Page 1   569

ROSHAR

ENDLESS OCEAN

Rall Elorim

RESHI

Kasitor

IRI

RIRA

Kurth

Reshi

oEila

The Misted Mountains

BABATHARNAM

MARABETHIA

Panatham

The Purelake

SHINOVAR

Aimian Sea

YULAY

Fu Namir

DESH

AZIR

AIMIA

ALM

UEZTER

Azimir

Urithiru
The Valley

Yeddaw

EMUL

GREATER
HEXI

STEEN

LIAFOR

TASHIKK

Sesemalex Dar

Icewater

TUKAR

MARAT

N

LEEWARD

STORMWARD

S

SOUTHERN DEPTHS

STEAMWATER OCEAN

ISLES

Sea

Northgrip

HERDAZ

AKAK

Mourn's
Vault

Varikev

Ru Parat

Elanar

JAH KEVED

Kholinar

UNCLAIMED HILLS

TU

BAYLA

Valath

Horneater Peaks

Shulin

ALETHKAR

BAVLAND

Rathalas

Dawn's
Shadow

Silnasen

TU

TRIAX

Vedenar

Dumadari

Karanak

Shattered
Plain

TU

FALLI

Tarat Sea

Kharbranth

FROSTLANDS

New Natanan

Longbrow's

Thaylen City

Kina

The Shallow Crypts

THAYLENAH

OCEAN OF ORIGINS

FOR HIS ROYAL MAJESTY KING GAVILAR KHOLIN
BY HIS ROYAL HIGH CARTOGRAPHER
ISASIK SHULIN
1167

BOOK

THREE

❖

OATHBRINGER

PROLOGUE

TO WEEP

SIX YEARS AGO

Eshonai had always told her sister that she was certain something wonderful lay over the next hill. Then one day, she'd crested a hill and found *humans*.

She'd always imagined humans – as sung of in the songs – as dark, formless monsters. Instead they were wonderful, bizarre creatures. They spoke with no discernible rhythm. They wore clothing more vibrant than carapace, but couldn't grow their own armor. They were so terrified of the storms that even when traveling they hid inside vehicles.

Most remarkably, they had only *one form*.

She first assumed the humans must have forgotten their forms, much as the listeners once had. That built an instant kinship between them.

Now, over a year later, Eshonai hummed to the Rhythm of Awe as she helped unload drums from the cart. They'd traveled a great distance to see the human homeland, and each step had overwhelmed her further. That experience culminated here, in this incredible city of Kholinar and its magnificent palace.

This cavernous unloading dock on the western side of the palace was so large, two hundred listeners had packed in here after their first arrival, and still hadn't filled the place. Indeed, most of the listeners couldn't attend the feast upstairs – where the treaty between their two peoples was being witnessed – but the Alethi had seen to their refreshment anyway, providing mountains of food and drink for the group down here.

She stepped out of the wagon, looking around the loading dock, humming to Excitement. When she'd told Venli she was determined to map the world, she'd imagined a place of natural discovery. Canyons and hills, forests and laits overgrown with life. Yet all along, *this* had been out here. Waiting just beyond their reach.

Along with more listeners.

When Eshonai had first met the humans, she'd seen the little listeners they had with them. A hapless tribe who were trapped in dullform. Eshonai had assumed the humans were taking care of the poor souls without songs.

Oh, how innocent those first meetings had been.

Those captive listeners had not been merely some small tribe, but instead representative of an enormous population. And the humans had not been caring for them.

The humans owned them.

A group of these parshmen, as they were called, clustered around the outside of Eshonai's ring of workers.

'They keep trying to help,' Gitgeth said to Curiosity. He shook his head, his beard sparkling with ruby gemstones that matched the prominent red colors of his skin. 'The little rhythmless ones want to be near us. They sense that something is wrong with their minds, I tell you.'

Eshonai handed him a drum from the back of the cart, then hummed to Curiosity herself. She hopped down and approached the group of parshmen.

'You aren't needed,' she said to Peace, spreading her hands. 'We would prefer to handle our own drums.'

The ones without songs looked at her with dull eyes.

'Go,' she said to Pleading, waving toward the nearby festivities, where listeners and human servants laughed together, despite the language barrier. Humans clapped along to listeners singing the old songs. 'Enjoy yourselves.'

A few looked toward the singing and cocked their heads, but they didn't move.

'It won't work,' Brianlia said to Skepticism, resting her arms across a drum nearby. 'They simply can't *imagine* what it is to live. They're pieces of property, to be bought and sold.'

What to make of this idea? Slaves? Klade, one of the Five, had gone to the slavers in Kholinar and purchased a person to see if it truly was possible. He hadn't even bought a parshman; there had been *Alethi* for sale. Apparently the parshmen were expensive, and considered high-quality slaves. The listeners had been told this, as if it were supposed to make them proud.

She hummed to Curiosity and nodded to the side, looking toward the others. Gitgeth smiled and hummed to Peace, waving for her to go. Everyone was used to Eshonai wandering off in the middle of jobs. It wasn't that she was unreliable. . . . Well, perhaps she was, but at least she was consistent.

Regardless, she'd be wanted at the king's celebration soon anyway; she was one of the best among the listeners at the dull human tongue, which she'd taken to naturally. It was an advantage that had earned her a place on this expedition, but it was also a problem. Speaking the human tongue made her important, and people who grew too important couldn't be allowed to go off chasing the horizon.

She left the unloading bay and walked up the steps into the palace proper, trying to take in the ornamentation, the artistry, the sheer overwhelming *wonder* of the building. Beautiful and terrible. People who were bought and sold maintained this place, but was that what freed the humans to create great works like the carvings on the pillars she passed, or the inlaid marble patterns on the floor?

She passed soldiers wearing their artificial carapace. Eshonai didn't have armor of her own at the moment; she wore workform instead of warform, as she liked its flexibility.

Humans didn't have a choice. They hadn't lost their forms as she'd first assumed; they *only had one.* Forever in mateform, workform, and warform all at once. And they wore their emotions on their faces far more than listeners. Oh, Eshonai's people would smile, laugh, cry. But not like these Alethi.

The lower level of the palace was marked by broad hallways and galleries, lit by carefully cut gemstones that made light sparkle. Chandeliers hung above her, broken suns spraying light everywhere. Perhaps the plain appearance of the human bodies – with their bland skin that was various shades of tan – was another reason they sought to ornament everything, from their clothing to these pillars.

Could we do this? she thought, humming to Appreciation. *If we knew the right form for creating art?*

The upper floors of the palace were more like tunnels. Narrow stone corridors, rooms like bunkers dug into a mountainside. She made her way toward the feast hall to check if she was needed, but stopped here and there to glance into rooms. She'd been told she could wander as she pleased, that the palace was open to her save for areas with guards at the doors.

She passed a room with paintings on all the walls, then one with a bed and furniture. Another door revealed an indoor privy with running water, a marvel that she still didn't understand.

She poked through a dozen rooms. As long as she reached the king's celebration in time for the music, Klade and the others of the Five wouldn't complain. They were as familiar with her ways as everyone else. She was always wandering off, poking into things, peeking into doors . . .

And finding the king?

Eshonai froze, the door cracked open, allowing her to see into a lush room with a thick red rug and bookshelves lining the walls. So much information just lying around, casually ignored. More surprisingly, King Gavilar himself stood pointing at something on a table, surrounded by five others: two officers, two women in long dresses, and one old man in robes.

Why wasn't Gavilar at the feast? Why weren't there guards at the door? Eshonai attuned Anxiety and pulled back, but not before one of the women prodded Gavilar and pointed toward Eshonai. Anxiety pounding in her head, she pulled the door closed.

A moment later a tall man in uniform stepped out. 'The king would like to see you, Parshendi.'

She feigned confusion. 'Sir? Words?'

'Don't be coy,' the soldier said. 'You're one of the interpreters. Come in. You aren't in trouble.'

Anxiety shaking her, she let him lead her into the den.

'Thank you, Meridas,' Gavilar said. 'Leave us for a moment, all of you.'

They filed out, leaving Eshonai at the door attuning Consolation and humming it loudly – even though the humans wouldn't understand what it meant.

'Eshonai,' the king said. 'I have something to show you.'

6

He knew her name? She stepped farther into the small, warm room, holding her arms tightly around her. She didn't understand this man. It was more than his alien, dead way of speaking. More than the fact that she couldn't anticipate what emotions might be swirling in there, as warform and mateform contested within him.

More than any human, this man baffled her. Why *had* he offered them such a favorable treaty? At first it had seemed an accommodation between tribes. That was before she'd come here, seen this city and the Alethi armies. Her people had once possessed cities of their own, and armies to envy. They knew that from the songs.

That had been long ago. They were a fragment of a lost people. Traitors who had abandoned their gods to be free. This man could have crushed the listeners. They'd once assumed that their Shards – weapons they had so far kept hidden from the humans – would be enough to protect them. But she'd now seen over a dozen Shardblades and suits of Shardplate among the Alethi.

Why did he smile at her like that? What was he hiding, by not singing to the rhythms to calm her?

'Sit, Eshonai,' the king said. 'Oh, don't be frightened, little scout. I've been wanting to speak to you. Your mastery of our language is unique!'

She settled on a chair while Gavilar reached down and removed something from a small satchel. It glowed with red Stormlight, a construction of gemstones and metal, crafted in a beautiful design.

'Do you know what this is?' he asked, gently pushing it toward her.

'No, Your Majesty.'

'It's what we call a fabrial, a device powered by Stormlight. This one makes warmth. Just a smidge, unfortunately, but my wife is confident her scholars can create one that will heat a room. Wouldn't that be wonderful? No more smoky fires in hearths.'

It seemed lifeless to Eshonai, but she didn't say so. She hummed to Praise so he'd feel happy telling her of this, and handed it back.

'Look closely,' King Gavilar said. 'Look deep into it. Can you see what's moving inside? It's a spren. That is how the device works.'

Captive like in a gemheart, she thought, attuning Awe. *They've built devices that mimic how we apply the forms?* The humans did so much with their limitations!

'The chasmfiends aren't your gods, are they?' he asked.

7

'What?' she asked, attuning Skepticism. 'Why ask that?' What a strange turn in the conversation.

'Oh, it's merely something I've been thinking about.' He took the fabrial back. 'My officers feel so superior, as they think they have you figured out. They think you're savages, but they are so wrong. You're not savages. You're an enclave of memories. A window into the past.'

He leaned forward, the light from the ruby leaking between his fingers. 'I need you to deliver a message to your leaders. The Five? You're close to them, and I'm being watched. I need their help to achieve something.'

She hummed to Anxiety.

'Now, now,' he said. 'I'm going to help you, Eshonai. Did you know, I've discovered how to bring your gods back?'

No. She hummed to the Rhythm of the Terrors. *No ...*

'My ancestors,' he said, holding up the fabrial, 'first learned how to hold a spren inside a gemstone. And with a very special gemstone, you can hold even a god.'

'Your Majesty,' she said, daring to take his hand in hers. He couldn't feel the rhythms. He didn't know. 'Please. We no longer worship those gods. We left them, *abandoned* them.'

'Ah, but this is for your good, and for ours.' He stood up. 'We live without honor, for your gods once brought ours. Without them, we have no *power*. This world is trapped, Eshonai! Stuck in a dull, lifeless state of transition.' He looked toward the ceiling. 'Unite them. I need a threat. Only danger will unite them.'

'What ...' she said to Anxiety. 'What are you saying?'

'Our enslaved parshmen were once like you. Then we somehow robbed them of their ability to undergo the transformation. We did it by capturing a spren. An ancient, *crucial* spren.' He looked at her, green eyes alight. 'I've seen how that can be reversed. A new storm that will bring the Heralds out of hiding. A new war.'

'Insanity.' She rose to her feet. 'Our gods tried to destroy you.'

'The old Words must be spoken again.'

'You can't ...' She trailed off, noticing for the first time that a map covered the table nearby. Expansive, it showed a land bounded by oceans – and the artistry of it put her own attempts to shame.

She rose and stepped to the table, gaping, the Rhythm of Awe playing

8

in her mind. *This is gorgeous.* Even the grand chandeliers and carved walls were nothing by comparison. This was knowledge *and* beauty, fused into one.

'I thought you'd be pleased to hear that we are allies in seeking the return of your gods,' Gavilar said. She could almost hear the Rhythm of Reprimand in his dead words. 'You claim to fear them, but why fear that which made you live? My people need to be united, and I need an empire that won't simply turn to infighting once I am gone.'

'So you seek for *war*?'

'I seek for an end to something that we never finished. My people were Radiant once, and your people – the parshmen – were vibrant. Who is served by this drab world where my people fight each other in endless squabbles, without light to guide them, and your people are as good as corpses?'

She looked back at the map. 'Where . . . where is the Shattered Plains? This portion here?'

'That is all of Natanatan you gesture toward, Eshonai! This is the Shattered Plains.' He pointed at a spot not much bigger than his thumbnail, when the entire map was as large as the table.

It gave her a sudden dizzying perspective. This was the world? She'd assumed that in traveling to Kholinar, they'd crossed almost as far as the land could go. Why hadn't they shown her this before!

Her legs weakened, and she attuned Mourning. She dropped back into her seat, unable to stand.

So vast.

Gavilar removed something from his pocket. A sphere? It was dark, yet somehow still glowed. As if it had . . . an aura of blackness, a phantom light that was not light. Faintly violet. It seemed to suck in the light around it.

He set it on the table before her. 'Take that to the Five and explain what I told you. Tell them to remember what your people once were. *Wake up,* Eshonai.'

He patted her on the shoulder, then left the room. She stared at that terrible light, and – from the songs – knew it for what it was. The forms of power had been associated with a dark light, a light from the king of gods.

She plucked the sphere off the table and went running.

When the drums were set up, Eshonai insisted on joining the drummers. An outlet for her anxiety. She beat to the rhythm in her head, banging as hard as she could, trying with each beat to banish the things the king had said.

And the things she'd just done.

The Five sat at the high table, the remnants of their final course uneaten.

He intends to bring back our gods, she'd told the Five.

Close your eyes. Focus on the rhythms.

He can do it. He knows so much.

Furious beats pulsing through her soul.

We have to do something.

Klade's slave was an assassin. Klade claimed that a *voice* – speaking to the rhythms – had led him to the man, who had confessed his skills when pressed. Venli had apparently been with Klade, though Eshonai hadn't seen her sister since earlier in the day.

After a frantic debate, the Five had agreed this was a sign of what they were to do. Long ago, the listeners had summoned the courage to adopt dullform in order to escape their gods. They'd sought freedom at any cost.

Today, the cost of maintaining that freedom would be high.

She played the drums. She felt the rhythms. She wept softly, and didn't look as the strange assassin – wearing flowing white clothing provided by Klade – left the room. She'd voted with the others for this course of action.

Feel the peace of the music. As her mother always said. *Seek the rhythms. Seek the songs.*

She resisted as the others pulled her away. She wept to leave the music behind. Wept for her people, who might be destroyed for tonight's action. Wept for the world, which might never know what the listeners had done for it.

Wept for the king, whom she had consigned to death.

The drums cut off around her, and dying music echoed through the halls.

PART

ONE

United

DALINAR • SHALLAN •
KALADIN • ADOLIN

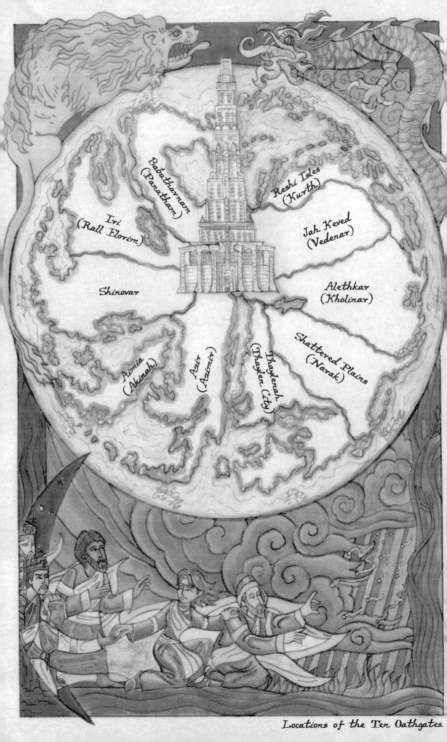

Iri
(Rall Elorim)

Babatharnam
(Panatham)

Reshi Isles
(Kurth)

Jah Keved
(Vedenar)

Shinovar

Alethkar
(Kholinar)

Shattered Plains
(Narak)

Aimia
(Akinah)

Azir
(Azimir)

Thaylenah
(Thaylen City)

Locations of the Ten Oathgates

I

BROKEN AND DIVIDED

I'm certain some will feel threatened by this record. Some few may feel liberated. Most will simply feel that it should not exist.

—From *Oathbringer*, preface

D alinar Kholin appeared in the vision standing beside the memory of a dead god.

It had been six days since his forces had arrived at Urithiru, legendary holy tower city of the Knights Radiant. They had escaped the arrival of a new devastating storm, seeking refuge through an ancient portal. They were settling into their new home hidden in the mountains.

And yet, Dalinar felt as if he knew nothing. He didn't understand the force he fought, let alone how to defeat it. He barely understood the storm, and what it meant in returning the Voidbringers, ancient enemies of men.

So he came here, into his visions. Seeking to pull secrets from the god – named Honor, or the Almighty – who had left them. This particular vision was the first that Dalinar had ever experienced. It began with him standing next to an image of the god in human form, both perched atop a cliff overlooking Kholinar: Dalinar's home, seat of the government. In the vision, the city had been destroyed by some unknown force.

The Almighty started speaking, but Dalinar ignored him. Dalinar had become a Knight Radiant by bonding the Stormfather himself – soul of the highstorm, most powerful spren on Roshar – and Dalinar had discovered he could now have these visions replayed for him at will. He'd already heard this monologue three times, and had repeated it word for word to Navani for transcription.

This time, Dalinar instead walked to the edge of the cliff and knelt to look out upon the ruins of Kholinar. The air smelled dry here, dusty and warm. He squinted, trying to extract some meaningful detail from the chaos of broken buildings. Even the windblades – once magnificent, sleek rock formations exposing countless strata and variations – had been shattered.

The Almighty continued his speech. These visions were like a diary, a set of immersive messages the god had left behind. Dalinar appreciated the help, but right now he wanted details.

He searched the sky and discovered a ripple in the air, like heat rising from distant stone. A shimmer the size of a building.

'Stormfather,' he said. 'Can you take me down below, into the rubble?'

You are not supposed to go there. That is not part of the vision.

'Ignore what I'm supposed to do, for the moment,' Dalinar said. 'Can you do it? Can you transport me to those ruins?'

The Stormfather rumbled. He was a strange being, somehow connected to the dead god, but not exactly the same thing as the Almighty. At least today he wasn't using a voice that rattled Dalinar's bones.

In an eyeblink, Dalinar was transported. He no longer stood atop the cliff, but was on the plains down before the ruins of the city.

'Thank you,' Dalinar said, striding the short remaining distance to the ruins.

Only six days had passed since their discovery of Urithiru. Six days since the awakening of the Parshendi, who had gained strange powers and glowing red eyes. Six days since the arrival of the new storm – the Everstorm, a tempest of dark thunderheads and red lightning.

Some in his armies thought that it was finished, the storm over as one catastrophic event. Dalinar knew otherwise. The Everstorm would return, and would soon hit Shinovar in the far west. Following that, it would course across the land.

Nobody believed his warnings. Monarchs in places like Azir and

Thaylenah admitted that a strange storm had appeared in the east, but they didn't believe it would return.

They couldn't guess how destructive this storm's return would be. When it had first appeared, it had clashed with the highstorm, creating a unique cataclysm. Hopefully it would not be as bad on its own – but it would still be a storm blowing the wrong way. And it would awaken the world's parshman servants and make them into Voidbringers.

What do you expect to learn? the Stormfather said as Dalinar reached the rubble of the city. *This vision was constructed to draw you to the ridge to speak with Honor. The rest is backdrop, a painting.*

'Honor put this rubble here,' Dalinar said, waving toward the broken walls heaped before him. 'Backdrop or not, his knowledge of the world and our enemy couldn't help but affect the way he made this vision.'

Dalinar hiked up the rubble of the outer walls. Kholinar had been . . . storm it, Kholinar *was* . . . a grand city, like few in the world. Instead of hiding in the shadow of a cliff or inside a sheltered chasm, Kholinar trusted in its enormous walls to buffer it from highstorm winds. It *defied* the winds, and did not bow to the storms.

In this vision, something had destroyed it anyway. Dalinar crested the detritus and surveyed the area, trying to imagine how it had felt to settle here so many millennia ago. Back when there had been no walls. It had been a hardy, stubborn lot who had grown this place.

He saw scrapes and gouges on the stones of the fallen walls, like those made by a predator in the flesh of its prey. The windblades had been smashed, and from up close he could see claw marks on one of those as well.

'I've seen creatures that could do this,' he said, kneeling beside one of the stones, feeling the rough gash in the granite surface. 'In my visions, I witnessed a stone monster that ripped itself free of the underlying rock.

'There are no corpses, but that's probably because the Almighty didn't populate the city in this vision. He just wanted a symbol of the coming destruction. He didn't think Kholinar would fall to the Everstorm, but to the Voidbringers.'

Yes, the Stormfather said. *The storm will be a catastrophe, but not nearly on the scale of what follows. You can find refuge from storms, Son of Honor. Not so with our enemies.*

Now that the monarchs of Roshar had refused to listen to Dalinar's warning that the Everstorm would soon strike them, what else could Dalinar do? The real Kholinar was reportedly consumed by riots – and the queen had gone silent. Dalinar's armies had limped away from their first confrontation with the Voidbringers, and even many of his own highprinces hadn't joined him in that battle.

A war was coming. In awakening the Desolation, the enemy had rekindled a millennia-old conflict of ancient creatures with inscrutable motivations and unknown powers. Heralds were supposed to appear and lead the charge against the Voidbringers. The Knights Radiant should have already been in place, prepared and trained, ready to face the enemy. They were supposed to be able to trust in the guidance of the Almighty.

Instead, Dalinar had only a handful of new Radiants, and there was no sign of help from the Heralds. And beyond that, the Almighty – God himself – was dead.

Somehow, Dalinar was supposed to save the world anyway.

The ground started to tremble; the vision was ending with the land falling away. Atop the cliff, the Almighty would have just concluded his speech.

A final wave of destruction rolled across the land like a highstorm. A metaphor designed by the Almighty to represent the darkness and devastation that was coming upon humankind.

Your legends say that you won, he had said. *But the truth is that we lost. And we are losing. . . .*

The Stormfather rumbled. *It is time to go.*

'No,' Dalinar said, standing atop the rubble. 'Leave me.'

But—

'Let me feel it!'

The wave of destruction struck, crashing against Dalinar, and he shouted defiance. He had not bowed before the highstorm; he would not bow before this! He faced it head-on, and in the blast of power that ripped apart the ground, he saw something.

A golden light, brilliant yet terrible. Standing before it, a dark figure in black Shardplate. The figure had nine shadows, each spreading out in a different direction, and its eyes glowed a brilliant red.

Dalinar stared deep into those eyes, and felt a chill wash through him. Though the destruction raged around him, vaporizing rocks, those *eyes* frightened him more. He saw something terribly familiar in them.

This was a danger far beyond even the storms.

This was the enemy's champion. And he was coming.

UNITE THEM. QUICKLY.

Dalinar gasped as the vision shattered. He found himself sitting beside Navani in a quiet stone room in the tower city of Urithiru. Dalinar didn't need to be bound for visions any longer; he had enough control over them that he had ceased acting them out while experiencing them.

He breathed deeply, sweat trickling down his face, his heart racing. Navani said something, but for the moment he couldn't hear her. She seemed distant compared to the rushing in his ears.

'What was that light I saw?' he whispered.

I saw no light, the Stormfather said.

'It was brilliant and golden, but terrible,' Dalinar whispered. 'It bathed everything in its heat.'

Odium, the Stormfather rumbled. *The enemy.*

The god who had killed the Almighty. The force behind the Desolations.

'Nine shadows,' Dalinar whispered, trembling.

Nine shadows? The Unmade. His minions, ancient spren.

Storms. Dalinar knew of them from legend only. Terrible spren who twisted the minds of men.

Still, those eyes haunted him. As frightening as it was to contemplate the Unmade, he feared that figure with the red eyes the most. Odium's champion.

Dalinar blinked, looking to Navani, the woman he loved, her face painfully concerned as she held his arm. In this strange place and stranger time, she was something real. Something to hold on to. A mature beauty – in some ways the picture of a perfect Vorin woman: lush lips, light violet eyes, silvering black hair in perfect braids, curves accentuated by the tight silk havah. No man would ever accuse Navani of being scrawny.

'Dalinar?' she asked. 'Dalinar, what happened? Are you well?'

'I'm . . .' He drew in a deep breath. 'I'm well, Navani. And I know what we must do.'

Her frown deepened. 'What?'

'I have to unite the world against the enemy faster than he can destroy it.'

He had to find a way to make the other monarchs of the world listen to him. He had to prepare them for the new storm and the Voidbringers. And, barring that, he had to help them survive the effects.

But if he succeeded, he wouldn't have to face the Desolation alone. This was not a matter of one nation against the Voidbringers. He needed the kingdoms of the world to join him, and he needed to find the Knights Radiant who were being created among their populations.

Unite them.

'Dalinar,' she said, 'I think that's a worthy goal ... but storms, what of ourselves? This mountainside is a wasteland – what are we going to feed our armies?'

'The Soulcasters—'

'Will run out of gemstones eventually,' Navani said. 'And they can create only the basic necessities. Dalinar, we're half frozen up here, broken and divided. Our command structure is in disarray, and it—'

'Peace, Navani,' Dalinar said, rising. He pulled her to her feet. 'I know. We have to fight anyway.'

She embraced him. He held to her, feeling her warmth, smelling her perfume. She preferred a less floral scent than other women – a fragrance with spice to it, like the aroma of newly cut wood.

'We can do this,' he told her. 'My tenacity. Your brilliance. Together, we *will* convince the other kingdoms to join with us. They'll see when the storm returns that our warnings were right, and they'll unite against the enemy. We can use the Oathgates to move troops and to support each other.'

The Oathgates. Ten portals, ancient fabrials, were gateways to Urithiru. When a Knight Radiant activated one of the devices, those people standing upon its surrounding platform were brought to Urithiru, appearing on a similar device here at the tower.

They only had one pair of Oathgates active now – the ones that moved people back and forth between Urithiru and the Shattered Plains. Nine more could theoretically be made to work – but unfortunately, their research determined that a mechanism inside each of them had to be unlocked from *both* sides before they'd work.

If he wanted to travel to Vedenar, Thaylen City, Azimir, or any of the other locations, they'd first need to get one of their Radiants to the city and unlock the device.

'All right,' she said. 'We'll do it. Somehow we'll make them listen – even if they've got their fingers planted firmly in their ears. Makes one wonder how they manage it, with their heads rammed up their own backsides.'

He smiled, and suddenly thought himself foolish for idealizing her just earlier. Navani Kholin was not some timid, perfect ideal – she was a sour storm of a woman, set in her ways, stubborn as a boulder rolling down a mountain and increasingly impatient with things she considered foolish.

He loved her the most for that. For being open and genuine in a society that prided itself on secrets. She'd been breaking taboos, and hearts, since their youth. At times, the idea that she loved him back seemed as surreal as one of his visions.

A knock came at the door to his room, and Navani called for the person to enter. One of Dalinar's scouts poked her head in through the door. Dalinar turned, frowning, noting the woman's nervous posture and quick breathing.

'What?' he demanded.

'Sir,' the woman said, saluting, face pale. 'There's . . . been an incident. A corpse discovered in the corridors.'

Dalinar felt something building, an energy in the air like the sensation of lightning about to strike. 'Who?'

'Highprince Torol Sadeas, sir,' the woman said. 'He's been murdered.'

2

ONE PROBLEM SOLVED

I needed to write it anyway.

—From *Oathbringer*, preface

S top! What do you think you're doing?' Adolin Kholin strode over to a group of workers in crem-stained work outfits who were unloading boxes from the back of a wagon. Their chull twisted, trying to search out rockbuds to munch on. Fruitlessly. They were deep within the tower, for all the fact that this cavern was as large as a small town.

The workers had the decency to look chagrined, though they probably didn't know what for. A flock of scribes trailing Adolin checked the contents of the wagon. Oil lamps on the ground did little to push back the darkness of the enormous room, which had a ceiling that went up four stories.

'Brightlord?' one of the workers asked, scratching at his hair beneath his cap. 'I was just unloadin'. That's what I think I was doin'.'

'Manifest says beer,' Rushu – a young ardent – told Adolin.

'Section two,' Adolin said, rapping the knuckles of his left hand against the wagon. 'Taverns are being set up along the central corridor with the lifts, six crossroads inward. My aunt *expressly* told your highlords this.'

The men just stared at him blankly.

'I can have a scribe show you. Pick these boxes back up.'

The men sighed, but started reloading their wagon. They knew better than to argue with the son of a highprince.

Adolin turned to survey the deep cavern, which had become a dumping ground for both supplies and people. Children ran past in groups. Workers set up tents. Women gathered water at the well in the center. Soldiers carried torches or lanterns. Even axehounds raced this way and that. Four entire warcamps full of people had frantically crossed the Shattered Plains to Urithiru, and Navani had struggled to find the right spot for them all.

For all the chaos, though, Adolin was glad to have these people. They were fresh; they hadn't suffered the battle with the Parshendi, the attack of the Assassin in White, and the terrible clash of two storms.

The Kholin soldiers were in terrible shape. Adolin's own sword hand was wrapped and still throbbing, his wrist broken during the fighting. His face had a nasty bruise, and he was one of the more lucky ones.

'Brightlord,' Rushu said, pointing at another wagon. 'That looks like wines.'

'Delightful,' Adolin said. Was *nobody* paying attention to Aunt Navani's directives?

He dealt with this wagon, then had to break up an argument among men who were angry they had been set to hauling water. They claimed that was parshman work, beneath their nahn. Unfortunately, there were no parshmen any longer.

Adolin soothed them and suggested they could start a water haulers' guild if forced to continue. Father would approve that for certain, though Adolin worried. Would they have the funds to pay all these people? Wages were based on a man's rank, and you couldn't just make slaves of men for no reason.

Adolin was glad for the assignment, to distract him. Though he didn't have to see to each wagon himself – he was here to supervise – he threw himself into the details of the work. He couldn't exactly spar, not with his wrist in this shape, but if he sat alone too long he started thinking about what had happened the day before.

Had he really done that?

Had he really *murdered* Torol Sadeas?

It was almost a relief when at long last a runner came for him, whispering that something had been discovered in the corridors of the third floor.

Adolin was certain he knew what it was.

⁂

Dalinar heard the shouts long before he arrived. They echoed down the tunnels. He knew that tone. Conflict was near.

He left Navani and broke into a run, sweating as he burst into a wide intersection between tunnels. Men in blue, lit by the harsh light of lanterns, faced off against others in forest green. Angerspren grew from the floor like pools of blood.

A corpse with a green jacket draped over the face lay on the ground.

'Stand down!' Dalinar bellowed, charging into the space between the two groups of soldiers. He pulled back a bridgeman who had gotten right up in the face of one of Sadeas's soldiers. 'Stand down, or I'll have you all in the stockade, every man!'

His voice hit the men like stormwinds, drawing eyes from both sides. He pushed the bridgeman toward his fellows, then shoved back one of Sadeas's soldiers, praying the man would have the presence of mind to resist attacking a highprince.

Navani and the scout stopped at the fringes of the conflict. The men from Bridge Four finally backed down one corridor, and Sadeas's soldiers retreated up the one opposite. Just far enough that they could still glare at one another.

'You'd better be ready for Damnation's own thunder,' Sadeas's officer shouted at Dalinar. 'Your men *murdered* a highprince!'

'We found him like this!' Teft of Bridge Four shouted back. 'Probably tripped on his own knife. Serves him well, the storming bastard.'

'Teft, *stand down!*' Dalinar shouted at him.

The bridgeman looked abashed, then saluted with a stiff gesture.

Dalinar knelt, pulling the jacket back from Sadeas's face. 'That blood is dried. He's been lying here for some time.'

'We've been looking for him,' said the officer in green.

'Looking for him? You *lost* your highprince?'

'The tunnels are confusing!' the man said. 'They don't go natural directions. We got turned about and . . .'

'Thought he might have returned to another part of the tower,' a man said. 'We spent last night searching for him there. Some people said they thought they'd seen him, but they were wrong, and . . .'

And a highprince was left lying here in his own gore for half a day, Dalinar thought. *Blood of my fathers.*

'We couldn't find him,' the officer said, 'because your men murdered him and moved the body—'

'That blood has been pooling there for hours. Nobody moved the body.' Dalinar pointed. 'Place the highprince in that side room there and send for Ialai, if you haven't. I want to have a better look.'

.⋅.

Dalinar Kholin was a connoisseur of death.

Even since his youth, the sight of dead men had been a familiar thing to him. You stay on the battlefield long enough, and you become familiar with its master.

So Sadeas's bloodied, ruined face didn't shock him. The punctured eye, smashed up into the socket by a blade that had been rammed into the brain. Fluid and blood had leaked out, then dried.

A knife through the eye was the sort of wound that killed an armored man wearing a full helm. It was a maneuver you practiced to use on the battlefield. But Sadeas had not been wearing armor and had not been on a battlefield.

Dalinar leaned down, inspecting the body lit by flickering oil lanterns as it lay on the table.

'Assassin,' Navani said, clicking her tongue and shaking her head. 'Not good.'

Behind him, Adolin and Renarin gathered with Shallan and a few of the bridgemen. Across from Dalinar stood Kalami; the thin, orange-eyed woman was one of his more senior scribes. They'd lost her husband, Teleb, in the battle against the Voidbringers. He hated to call upon her in her time of grief, but she insisted that she remain on duty.

Storms, he had so few high officers left. Cael had fallen in the clash between Everstorm and highstorm, almost making it to safety. He'd lost Ilamar and Perethom to Sadeas's betrayal at the Tower. The only highlord he had left was Khal, who was still recuperating from a wound he'd taken during the clash with the Voidbringers – one he'd kept to himself until everyone else was safe.

Even Elhokar, the king, had been wounded by assassins in his palace while the armies were fighting at Narak. He'd been recuperating ever since. Dalinar wasn't certain if he would come to see Sadeas's body or not.

Either way, Dalinar's lack of officers explained the room's other occupants: Highprince Sebarial and his mistress, Palona. Likable or not, Sebarial was one of the two living highprinces who had responded to Dalinar's call to march for Narak. Dalinar had to rely on someone, and he didn't trust most of the highprinces farther than the wind could blow them.

Sebarial, along with Aladar – who had been summoned but had not yet arrived – would have to form the foundation of a new Alethkar. Almighty help them all.

'Well!' said Palona, hands on hips as she regarded Sadeas's corpse. 'I guess that's one problem solved!'

Everyone in the room turned toward her.

'What?' she said. 'Don't tell me you weren't all thinking it.'

'This is going to look bad, Brightlord,' Kalami said. 'Everyone is going to act like those soldiers outside and assume you had him assassinated.'

'Any sign of the Shardblade?' Dalinar asked.

'No, sir,' one of the bridgemen said. 'Whoever killed him probably took it.'

Navani rubbed Dalinar on the shoulder. 'I wouldn't have put it as Palona did, but he *did* try to have you killed. Perhaps this is for the best.'

'No,' Dalinar said, voice hoarse. 'We needed him.'

'I know you're desperate, Dalinar,' Sebarial said. 'My presence here is sufficient proof of *that*. But surely we haven't sunk so far as to be better off with Sadeas among us. I agree with Palona. Good riddance.'

Dalinar looked up, inspecting those in the room. Sebarial and Palona. Teft and Sigzil, the lieutenants from Bridge Four. A handful of other soldiers, including the young scout woman who had fetched him. His sons, steady Adolin and impenetrable Renarin. Navani, with her hand on his shoulder. Even the aging Kalami, hands clasped before her, meeting his eyes and nodding.

'You all agree, don't you?' Dalinar asked.

Nobody objected. Yes, this murder was inconvenient for Dalinar's reputation, and they certainly wouldn't have gone so far as to kill Sadeas themselves. But now that he was gone . . . well, why shed any tears?

Memories churned inside Dalinar's head. Days spent with Sadeas, listening to Gavilar's grand plans. The night before Dalinar's wedding, when he'd shared wine with Sadeas at a rowdy feast that Sadeas had organized in his name.

It was hard to reconcile that younger man, that *friend*, with the thicker, older face on the slab before him. The adult Sadeas had been a murderer whose treachery had caused the deaths of better men. For those men, abandoned during the battle at the Tower, Dalinar could feel only satisfaction at finally seeing Sadeas dead.

That troubled him. He knew *exactly* how the others were feeling. 'Come with me.'

He left the body and strode out of the room. He passed Sadeas's guards, who hurried back in. They would deal with the corpse; hopefully he'd defused the situation enough to prevent an impromptu clash between his forces and theirs. For now, the best thing to do was get Bridge Four away from here.

Dalinar's retinue followed him through the halls of the cavernous tower, bearing oil lamps. The walls were twisted with lines – natural strata of alternating earthy colors, like those made by crem drying in layers. He didn't blame the soldiers for losing track of Sadeas; it was strikingly easy to get lost in this place, with its endless passageways all leading into darkness.

Fortunately, he had an idea of where they were, and led his people to the outer rim of the tower. Here he strode through an empty chamber and stepped out onto a balcony, one of many similar ones that were like wide patios.

Above him rose the enormous tower city of Urithiru, a strikingly high structure built up against the mountains. Created from a sequence of ten ringlike tiers – each containing eighteen levels – the tower city was adorned with aqueducts, windows, and balconies like this one.

The bottom floor also had wide sections jutting out at the perimeter: large stone surfaces, each a plateau in its own right. They had stone railings at their edges, where the rock fell away into the depths of the chasms between mountain peaks. At first, these wide flat sections of stone had baffled them. But the furrows in the stone, and planter boxes on the inner edges, had revealed their purpose. Somehow, these were *fields*. Like the large spaces for gardens atop each tier of the tower, this area had been farmed, despite the cold. One of these fields extended below this balcony, two levels down.

Dalinar strode up to the edge of the balcony and rested his hands on the smooth stone retaining wall. The others gathered behind him. Along the way they'd picked up Highprince Aladar, a distinguished bald Alethi with dark tan skin. He was accompanied by May, his daughter: a short, pretty woman in her twenties with tan eyes and a round face, her jet-black Alethi hair worn short and curving around her face. Navani whispered to them the details of Sadeas's death.

Dalinar swept his hand outward in the chill air, pointing away from the balcony. 'What do you see?'

The bridgemen gathered to look off the balcony. Their number included the Herdazian, who now had two arms after regrowing the one with Stormlight. Kaladin's men had begun manifesting powers as Windrunners – though apparently they were merely 'squires.' Navani said it was a type of apprentice Radiant that had once been common: men and women whose abilities were tied to their master, a full Radiant.

The men of Bridge Four had not bonded their own spren, and – though they had started manifesting powers – had lost their abilities when Kaladin had flown to Alethkar to warn his family of the Everstorm.

'What do I see?' the Herdazian said. 'I see clouds.'

'*Lots* of clouds,' another bridgeman added.

'Some mountains too,' another said. 'They look like teeth.'

'Nah, horns,' the Herdazian argued.

'We,' Dalinar interrupted, 'are above the storms. It's going to be easy to forget the tempest the rest of the world is facing. The Everstorm will return, bringing the Voidbringers. We have to assume that this city – our armies – will soon be the only bastion of order left in the world. It is our calling, our *duty*, to take the lead.'

'Order?' Aladar said. 'Dalinar, have you *seen* our armies? They fought an impossible battle only six days ago, and despite being rescued, we technically *lost*. Roion's son is woefully underprepared for dealing with the remnants of his princedom. Some of the strongest forces – those of Thanadal and Vamah – *stayed behind* in the warcamps!'

'The ones who did come are already squabbling,' Palona added. 'Old Torol's death back there will only give them something else to dissent about.'

Dalinar turned around, gripping the top of the stone wall with both hands, fingers cold. A chill wind blew against him, and a few windspren passed like little translucent people riding on the breeze.

'Brightness Kalami,' Dalinar said. 'What do you know of the Desolations?'

'Brightlord?' she asked, hesitant.

'The Desolations. You've done scholarly work on Vorin theory, yes? Can you tell us of the Desolations?'

Kalami cleared her throat. 'They were destruction made manifest, Brightlord. Each one was so profoundly devastating that humankind was left broken. Populations ruined, society crippled, scholars dead. Humankind was forced to spend generations rebuilding after each one. Songs tell of how the losses compounded upon one another, causing us to slide farther each time, until the Heralds left a people with swords and fabrials and returned to find them wielding sticks and stone axes.'

'And the Voidbringers?' Dalinar asked.

'They came to annihilate,' Kalami said. 'Their goal was to wipe humankind from Roshar. They were specters, formless – some say they are spirits of the dead, others spren from Damnation.'

'We will have to find a way to stop this from happening again,' Dalinar said softly, turning back to the group. 'We are the ones this world must be able to look to. We must provide stability, a rallying point.

'This is why I cannot rejoice to find Sadeas dead. He was a thorn in my side, but he was a capable general and a brilliant mind. We needed him. Before this is through, we'll need everyone who can fight.'

'Dalinar,' Aladar said. 'I used to bicker. I used to be like the other highprinces. But what I saw on that battlefield ... those red eyes ... Sir, I'm with you. I will follow you to the ends of the storms themselves. What do you want me to do?'

'Our time is short. Aladar, I name you our new Highprince of Information, in command of the judgment and law of this city. Establish order in Urithiru and make sure that the highprinces have clearly delineated realms of control within it. Build a policing force, and patrol these hallways. Keep the peace, and prevent clashes between soldiers like the one we avoided earlier.

'Sebarial, I name you Highprince of Commerce. Account our supplies and establish marketplaces in Urithiru. I want this tower to become a functioning city, not just a temporary waystop.

'Adolin, see that the armies are put into a training regimen. Count the troops we have, from all the highprinces, and convey to them that their spears will be required for the defense of Roshar. So long as they remain here, they are under my authority as Highprince of War. We'll crush their squabbling beneath a weight of training. We control the Soulcasters, and we control the food. If they want rations, they'll have to listen.'

'And us?' the scruffy lieutenant of Bridge Four asked.

'Continue to explore Urithiru with my scouts and scribes,' Dalinar said. 'And let me know the moment your captain returns. Hopefully he will bring good news from Alethkar.'

He took a deep breath. A voice echoed in the back of his mind, as if distant. *Unite them.*

Be ready for when the enemy's champion arrives.

'Our ultimate goal is the preservation of all Roshar,' Dalinar said softly. 'We've seen the cost of division in our ranks. Because of it, we failed to stop the Everstorm. But that was just the trial run, the sparring before the real fight. To face the Desolation, I will find a way to do what my ancestor the Sunmaker failed to do through conquest. I *will* unify Roshar.'

Kalami gasped softly. No man had ever united the entire continent – not during the Shin invasions, not during the height of the Hierocracy, not during the Sunmaker's conquest. This was his task, he was increasingly certain. The enemy would unleash his worst terrors: the Unmade and the Voidbringers. That phantom champion in the dark armor.

Dalinar would resist them with a unified Roshar. Such a shame he hadn't found a way to somehow convince Sadeas to join in his cause.

Ah, Torol, he thought. *What we could have done together, if we hadn't been so divided. . . .*

'Father?' A soft voice drew his attention. Renarin, who stood beside Shallan and Adolin. 'You didn't mention us. Me and Brightness Shallan. What is our task?'

'To practice,' Dalinar said. 'Other Radiants will be coming to us, and you two will need to lead them. The knights were once our greatest weapon against the Voidbringers. They will need to be so again.'

'Father, I . . .' Renarin stumbled over the words. 'It's just . . . Me? I can't. I don't know how to . . . let alone . . .'

'Son,' Dalinar said, stepping over. He took Renarin by the shoulder. 'I trust you. The Almighty and the spren have granted you powers to defend and protect this people. Use them. *Master* them, then report back to me what you can do. I think we're all curious to find out.'

Renarin exhaled softly, then nodded.

3

MOMENTUM

THIRTY-FOUR YEARS AGO

Rockbuds crunched like skulls beneath Dalinar's boots as he charged across the burning field. His elites pounded after him, a handpicked force of soldiers both lighteyed and dark. They weren't an honor guard. Dalinar didn't need *guards*. These were simply the men he considered competent enough not to embarrass him.

Around him, rockbuds smoldered. Moss – dried from the summer heat and long days between storms this time of year – flared up in waves, setting the rockbud shells alight. Flamespren danced among them. And, like a spren himself, Dalinar charged through the smoke, trusting in his padded armor and thick boots to protect him.

The enemy – pressed on the north by his armies – had pulled back into this town just ahead. With some difficulty Dalinar had waited, so he could bring his elites in as a flanking force.

He hadn't expected the enemy to fire this plain, desperately burning their own crops to block the southern approach. Well, the fires could go to Damnation. Though some of his men were overwhelmed by the smoke or heat, most stayed with him. They'd crash into the enemy, pressing them back against the main army.

Hammer and anvil. His favorite kind of tactic: the type that didn't allow his enemies to get away from him.

As Dalinar burst from the smoky air, he found a few lines of spearmen hastily forming ranks on the southern edge of the town. Anticipations-pren – like red streamers growing from the ground and whipping in the wind – clustered around them. The low town wall had been torn down in a contest a few years back, so the soldiers had only rubble as a fortification – though a large ridge to the east made a natural windbreak against the storms, which had allowed this place to sprawl almost like a real city.

Dalinar bellowed at the enemy soldiers, beating his sword – just an ordinary longsword – against his shield. He wore a sturdy breastplate, an open-fronted helm, and iron-reinforced boots. The spearmen ahead of him wavered as his elites roared from amid the smoke and flame, shouting a bloodthirsty cacophony.

A few of the spearmen dropped their weapons and ran. Dalinar grinned. He didn't need Shards to intimidate.

He hit the spearmen like a boulder rolling through a grove of saplings, his sword tossing blood into the air. A good fight was about *momentum.* Don't stop. Don't think. Drive forward and convince your enemies that they're as good as dead already. That way, they'll fight you less as you send them to their pyres.

The spearmen thrust their spears frantically – less to try to kill, more to try to push away this madman. Their ranks collapsed as too many of them turned their attention toward him.

Dalinar laughed, slamming aside a pair of spears with his shield, then disemboweling one man with a blade deep in the gut. The man dropped his spear in agony, and his neighbors backed away at the horrific sight. Dalinar came in with a roar, killing them with a sword that bore their friend's blood.

Dalinar's elites struck the now-broken line, and the real slaughter began. He pushed forward, keeping momentum, shearing through the ranks until he reached the back, then breathed deeply and wiped ashen sweat from his face. A young spearman wept on the ground nearby, screaming for his mother as he crawled across the stone, trailing blood. Fearspren mixed with orange, sinewy painspren all around. Dalinar shook his head and rammed his sword down into the boy's back as he passed.

Men often cried for their parents as they died. Didn't matter how old they were. He'd seen greybeards do it, same as kids like this one. *He's not much younger than me,* Dalinar thought. Maybe seventeen. But then, Dalinar had never felt young, regardless of his age.

His elites carved the enemy line in two. Dalinar danced, shaking off his bloodied blade, feeling alert, excited, but not yet *alive*. Where was it?

Come on. . . .

A larger group of enemy soldiers was jogging down the street toward him, led by several officers in white and red. From the way they suddenly pulled up, he guessed they were alarmed to find their spearmen falling so quickly.

Dalinar charged. His elites knew to watch, so he was rapidly joined by fifty men – the rest had to finish off the unfortunate spearmen. Fifty would do. The crowded confines of the town would mean Dalinar shouldn't need more.

He focused his attention on the one man riding a horse. The fellow wore plate armor obviously meant to resemble Shardplate, though it was only of common steel. It lacked the beauty, the power, of true Plate. He still looked like he was the most important person around. Hopefully that would mean he was the best.

The man's honor guard rushed to engage, and Dalinar felt something stir inside him. Like a thirst, a physical need.

Challenge. He needed a *challenge*!

He engaged the first member of the guard, attacking with a swift brutality. Fighting on a battlefield wasn't like dueling in an arena; Dalinar didn't dance around the fellow, testing his abilities. Out here, that sort of thing got you stabbed in the back by someone else. Instead, Dalinar slammed his sword down against the enemy, who raised his shield to block. Dalinar struck a series of quick, powerful blows, like a drummer pounding out a furious beat. *Bam, bam, bam, bam!*

The enemy soldier clutched his shield over his head, leaving Dalinar squarely in control. Dalinar raised his own shield before him and shoved it against the man, forcing him back until he stumbled, giving Dalinar an opening.

This man didn't get a chance to cry for his mother.

The body dropped before him. Dalinar let his elites handle the others; the way was open to the brightlord. Who was he? The highprince fought to the north. Was this some other important lighteyes? Or . . . didn't Dalinar remember hearing something about a son during Gavilar's endless planning meetings?

Well, this man certainly looked grand on that white mare, watching the battle from within his helm's visor, cape streaming around him. The foe raised his sword to his helm toward Dalinar in a sign of challenge accepted.

Idiot.

Dalinar raised his shield arm and pointed, counting on at least one of his strikers to have stayed with him. Indeed, Jenin stepped up, unhooked the shortbow from his back, and – as the brightlord shouted his surprise – shot the horse in the chest.

'Hate shooting horses,' Jenin grumbled as the beast reared in pain. 'Like throwing a thousand broams into the storming ocean, Brightlord.'

'I'll buy you two when we finish this,' Dalinar said as the brightlord tumbled off his horse. Dalinar dodged around flashing hooves and squeals of pain, seeking out the fallen man. He was pleased to find the enemy rising.

They engaged, sweeping at one another, frantic. Life was about *momentum*. Pick a direction and don't let anything – man or storm – turn you aside. Dalinar battered at the brightlord, driving him backward, furious and persistent.

He felt like he was winning the contest, controlling it, right up until he slammed his shield at the enemy and – in the moment of stress – felt something *snap*. One of the straps that held the shield to his arm had broken.

The enemy reacted immediately. He shoved the shield, twisting it around Dalinar's arm, snapping the other strap. The shield tumbled free.

Dalinar staggered, sweeping with his sword, trying to parry a blow that didn't come. The brightlord instead lunged in close and rammed Dalinar with his shield.

Dalinar ducked the blow that followed, but the backhand hit him solidly on the side of the head, sending him stumbling. His helm twisted, bent metal biting into his scalp, drawing blood. He saw double, his vision swimming.

He's coming in for the kill.

Dalinar roared, swinging his blade up in a lurching, wild parry that connected with the brightlord's weapon and swept it completely out of his hands.

The man instead punched Dalinar in the face with a gauntlet. His nose crunched.

Dalinar fell to his knees, sword slipping from his fingers. His foe was breathing deeply, cursing between breaths, winded by the short, frantic contest. He reached to his belt for a knife.

An emotion stirred inside Dalinar.

It was a fire that filled the pit within. It washed through him and awakened him, bringing clarity. The sounds of his elites fighting the brightlord's honor guard faded, metal on metal becoming clinks, grunts becoming merely a distant humming.

Dalinar smiled. Then the smile became a toothy grin. His vision returned as the brightlord – knife in hand – looked up and started, stumbling back. He seemed horrified.

Dalinar roared, spitting blood and throwing himself at the enemy. The swing that came at him seemed pitiful and Dalinar ducked it, ramming his shoulder against his foe's lower body. Something thrummed inside Dalinar, the pulse of the battle, the rhythm of killing and dying.

The Thrill.

He knocked his opponent off balance, then went searching for his sword. Dym, however, hollered Dalinar's name and tossed him a poleaxe, with a hook on one side and a broad, thin axe blade on the other. Dalinar seized it from the air and spun, hooking the brightlord around the ankle with the axehead, then yanked.

The brightlord fell in a clatter of steel. Before Dalinar could capitalize on this, two men of the honor guard managed to extricate themselves from Dalinar's men and come to the defense of their brightlord.

Dalinar swung and buried the axehead into one guard's side. He ripped it free and spun again – smashing the weapon down on the rising brightlord's helm and sending him to his knees – before coming back and barely catching the remaining guard's sword on the haft of the poleaxe.

Dalinar pushed upward, holding the poleaxe in two hands, sweeping the guard's blade into the air over his head. Dalinar stepped forward until he was face-to-face with the fellow. He could feel the man's breath.

He spat blood draining from his nose into the guard's eyes, then kicked him in the stomach. He turned toward the brightlord, who was trying to flee. Dalinar growled, full of the Thrill. He swung the poleaxe with one hand, hooking the spike into the brightlord's side, and yanked, dropping him yet again.

The brightlord rolled over. He was greeted by the sight of Dalinar slamming his poleaxe down with both hands, driving the spike right through the breastplate and into his chest. It made a satisfying crunch, and Dalinar pulled it out bloodied.

As if that blow had been a signal, the honor guard finally broke before his elites. Dalinar grinned as he watched them go, gloryspren popping up around him as glowing golden spheres. His men unhooked shortbows and shot a good dozen of the fleeing enemy in the back. Damnation, it felt good to best a force larger than your own.

Nearby, the fallen brightlord groaned softly. 'Why ...' the man said from within his helm. 'Why us?'

'Don't know,' Dalinar said, tossing the poleaxe back to Dym.

'You ... you *don't know?*' the dying man said.

'My brother chooses,' Dalinar said. 'I just go where he points me.' He gestured toward the dying man, and Dym rammed a sword into the armored man's armpit, finishing the job. The fellow had fought reasonably well; no need to extend his suffering.

Another soldier approached, handing Dalinar his sword. It had a chip the size of a thumb right in the blade. Looked like it had bent as well. 'You're supposed to stick it into the squishy parts, Brightlord,' Dym said, 'not pound it against the hard parts.'

'I'll keep that in mind,' Dalinar said, tossing the sword aside as one of his men selected a replacement from among the fallen.

'You ... all right, Brightlord?' Dym asked.

'Never been better,' Dalinar said, voice faintly distorted by the clogged nose. Hurt like Damnation itself, and he drew a small flock of painspren – like little sinewy hands – up from the ground.

His men formed up around him, and Dalinar led the way farther down the street. Before too long, he could make out the bulk of the enemy still fighting ahead, harried by his army. He halted his men, considering his options.

Thakka, captain of the elites, turned to him. 'Orders, sir?'

'Raid those buildings,' Dalinar said, pointing at a line of homes. 'Let's see how well they fight while they watch us rounding up their families.'

'The men will want to loot,' Thakka said.

'What is there to loot in hovels like these? Soggy hogshide and old rockbud bowls?' He pulled off his helm to wipe the blood from his face.

'They can loot afterward. Right now I need hostages. There are civilians somewhere in this storming town. Find them.'

Thakka nodded, shouting the orders. Dalinar reached for some water. He'd need to meet up with Sadeas, and—

Something slammed into Dalinar's shoulder. He caught only a brief sight of it, a black blur that hit with the force of a roundhouse kick. It threw him down, and pain flared up from his side.

He blinked as he found himself lying on the ground. A storming *arrow* sprouted from his right shoulder, with a long, thick shaft. It had gone straight through the chain mail, just to the side of where his cuirass met his arm.

'Brightlord!' Thakka said, kneeling, shielding Dalinar with his body. 'Kelek! Brightlord, are you—'

'Who in Damnation shot that?' Dalinar demanded.

'Up there,' one of his men said, pointing at the ridge above the town.

'That's got to be over *three hundred yards,*' Dalinar said, shoving Thakka aside and standing. 'That can't—'

He was watching, so he was able to jump out of the way of the next arrow, which dropped a mere foot from him, cracking against the stone ground. Dalinar stared at it, then started shouting. 'Horses! Where are the storming horses!'

A small group of soldiers came trotting forward, bringing all eleven horses, which they'd guided carefully across the field. Dalinar had to dodge *another* arrow as he seized the reins of Fullnight, his black gelding, and heaved himself into the saddle. The arrow in his arm was a cutting pain, but he felt something more pressing drawing him forward. Helping him focus.

He galloped back the way they'd come in, getting out of the archer's sight, trailed by ten of his best men. There had to be a way up that slope. . . . There! A rocky set of switchbacks, shallow enough that he didn't mind running Fullnight up them.

Dalinar worried that by the time he reached the top, his quarry would have escaped. However, when he eventually burst onto the top of the ridge, an arrow slammed into his *left* breast, going straight through the breastplate near the shoulder, nearly throwing him from the saddle.

Damnation! Dalinar hung on somehow, clenching the reins in one hand, and leaned low, peering ahead as the archer – still a distant figure

– stood upon a rocky knob and launched another arrow. And another. Storms, the fellow was quick!

He jerked Fullnight to one side, then the other, feeling the thrumming sense of the Thrill surge within him. It drove away the pain, let him focus.

Ahead, the archer finally seemed to grow alarmed, and leaped from his perch to flee.

Dalinar charged Fullnight over that knob a moment later. The archer turned out to be a man in his twenties wearing rugged clothing, with arms and shoulders that looked like they could have lifted a chull. Dalinar had the option of running him down, but instead galloped Fullnight past and kicked the man in the back, sending him sprawling.

As Dalinar pulled up his horse, the motion sent a spike of pain through his arm. He forced it down, eyes watering, and turned toward the archer, who lay in a heap amid spilled black arrows.

Dalinar lurched from the saddle, an arrow sprouting from each shoulder, as his men caught up. He seized the archer and hauled the fellow to his feet, noting the blue tattoo on his cheek. The archer gasped and stared at Dalinar. He expected he was quite a sight, covered in soot from the fires, his face a mask of blood from the nose and the cut scalp, stuck with not one but *two* arrows.

'You waited until my helm was off,' Dalinar demanded. 'You are an assassin. You were set here *specifically* to kill me.'

The man winced, then nodded.

'Amazing!' Dalinar said, letting go of the fellow. 'Show me that shot again. How far *is* that, Thakka? I'm right, aren't I? Over three hundred yards?'

'Almost four,' Thakka said, pulling over his horse. 'But with a height advantage.'

'Still,' Dalinar said, stepping up to the lip of the ridge. He looked back at the befuddled archer. 'Well? Grab your bow!'

'My . . . bow?' the archer said.

'Are you deaf, man?' Dalinar snapped. 'Go get it!'

The archer regarded the ten elites on horseback, grim-faced and dangerous, before wisely deciding to obey. He picked up an arrow, then his bow – which was made of a sleek black wood Dalinar didn't recognize.

'Went right through my storming armor,' Dalinar muttered, feeling at the arrow that had hit him on the left. That one didn't seem too bad – it had punctured the steel, but had lost most of its momentum in doing so. The one on his right, though, had cut through the chain and was sending blood down his arm.

He shook his head, shading his eyes with his left hand, inspecting the battlefield. To his right, the armies clashed, and his main body of elites had come up to press at the flank. The rearguard had found some civilians and was shoving them into the street.

'Pick a corpse,' Dalinar said, pointing toward an empty square where a skirmish had happened. 'Stick an arrow in one down there, if you can.'

The archer licked his lips, still seeming confused. Finally, he took a spyglass off his belt and studied the area. 'The one in blue, near the over-turned cart.'

Dalinar squinted, then nodded. Nearby, Thakka had climbed off his horse and had slid out his sword, resting it on his shoulder. A not-so-subtle warning. The archer drew his bow and launched a single black-fletched arrow. It flew true, sticking into the chosen corpse.

A single awespren burst around Dalinar, like a ring of blue smoke. 'Stormfather! Thakka, before today, I'd have bet you half the princedom that such a shot wasn't possible.' He turned to the archer. 'What's your name, assassin?'

The man raised his chin, but didn't reply.

'Well, in any case, welcome to my elites,' Dalinar said. 'Someone get the fellow a horse.'

'What?' the archer said. 'I tried to *kill* you!'

'Yes, from a distance. Which shows remarkably good judgment. I can make use of someone with your skills.'

'We're enemies!'

Dalinar nodded toward the town below, where the beleaguered enemy army was – at long last – surrendering. 'Not anymore. Looks like we're all allies now!'

The archer spat to the side. 'Slaves beneath your brother, the tyrant.'

Dalinar let one of his men help him onto his horse. 'If you'd rather be killed, I can respect that. Alternatively, you can join me and name your price.'

'The life of my brightlord Yezriar,' the archer said. 'The heir.'

'Is that the fellow . . . ?' Dalinar said, looking to Thakka.

'. . . That you killed down below? Yes, sir.'

'He's got a hole in his chest,' Dalinar said, looking back to the assassin. 'Tough break.'

'You . . . you monster! Couldn't you have captured him?'

'Nah. The other princedoms are digging in their heels. Refuse to recognize my brother's crown. Games of catch-me with the high lighteyes just encourage people to fight back. If they know we're out for blood, they'll think twice.' Dalinar shrugged. 'How about this? Join with me, and we won't pillage the town. What's left of it, anyway.'

The man looked down at the surrendering army.

'You in or not?' Dalinar said. 'I promise not to make you shoot anyone you like.'

'I . . .'

'Great!' Dalinar said, turning his horse and trotting off.

A short time later, when Dalinar's elites rode up to him, the sullen archer was on a horse with one of the other men. The pain surged in Dalinar's right arm as the Thrill faded, but it was manageable. He'd need surgeons to look at the arrow wound.

Once they reached the town again, he sent orders to stop the looting. His men would hate that, but this town wasn't worth much anyway. The riches would come once they started into the centers of the princedoms.

He let his horse carry him in a leisurely gait through the town, passing soldiers who had settled down to water themselves and rest from the protracted engagement. His nose still smarted, and he had to forcibly prevent himself from snorting up blood. If it was well and truly broken, that wouldn't turn out well for him.

Dalinar kept moving, fighting off the dull sense of . . . nothingness that often followed a battle. This was the worst time. He could still remember being alive, but now had to face a return to mundanity.

He'd missed the executions. Sadeas already had the local highprince's head – and those of his officers – up on spears. Such a showman, Sadeas was. Dalinar passed the grim line, shaking his head, and heard a muttered curse from his new archer. He'd have to talk to the man, reinforce that in striking at Dalinar earlier, he'd shot an arrow at an enemy. That was to be respected. If he tried something against Dalinar or Sadeas now, it would be different. Thakka would already be searching out the fellow's family.

'Dalinar?' a voice called.

He stilled his horse, turning toward the sound. Torol Sadeas

– resplendent in golden yellow Shardplate that had already been washed clean – pushed through a cluster of officers. The red-faced young man looked far older than he had a year ago. When they'd started all this, he'd still been a gangly youth. No longer.

'Dalinar, are those *arrows*? Stormfather, man, you look like a thornbush! What happened to your face?'

'A fist,' Dalinar said, then nodded toward the heads on spears. 'Nice work.'

'We lost the crown prince,' Sadeas said. 'He'll mount a resistance.'

'That would be impressive,' Dalinar said, 'considering what I did to him.'

Sadeas relaxed visibly. 'Oh, Dalinar. What would we do without you?'

'Lose. Someone get me something to drink and a pair of surgeons. In that order. Also, Sadeas, I promised we wouldn't pillage the city. No looting, no slaves taken.'

'You *what*?' Sadeas demanded. 'Who did you promise?'

Dalinar thumbed over his shoulder at the archer.

'Another one?' Sadeas said with a groan.

'He's got amazing aim,' Dalinar said. 'Loyal, too.' He glanced to the side, where Sadeas's soldiers had rounded up some weeping women for Sadeas to pick from.

'I was looking forward to tonight,' Sadeas noted.

'And I was looking forward to breathing through my nose. We'll live. More than can be said for the kids we fought today.'

'Fine, fine,' Sadeas said, sighing. 'I suppose we could spare one town. A symbol that we are not without mercy.' He looked over Dalinar again. 'We need to get you some Shards, my friend.'

'To protect me?'

'Protect you? Storms, Dalinar, at this point I'm not certain a *rockslide* could kill you. No, it just makes the rest of us look bad when you accomplish what you do while practically unarmed!'

Dalinar shrugged. He didn't wait for the wine or the surgeons, but instead led his horse back to gather his elites and reinforce the orders to guard the city from looting. Once finished, he walked his horse across smoldering ground to his camp.

He was done living for the day. It would be weeks, maybe months, before he got another opportunity.

4

OATHS

I know that many women who read this will see it only as further proof that I am the godless heretic everyone claims.

—From *Oathbringer*, preface

Two days after Sadeas was found dead, the Everstorm came again. Dalinar walked through his chambers in Urithiru, pulled by the unnatural storm. Bare feet on cold rock. He passed Navani – who sat at the writing desk working on her memoirs again – and stepped onto his balcony, which hung straight out over the cliffs beneath Urithiru.

He could feel something, his ears popping, cold – even more cold than usual – blowing in from the west. And something else. An inner chill.

'Is that you, Stormfather?' Dalinar whispered. 'This feeling of dread?'

This thing is not natural, the Stormfather said. *It is unknown.*

'It didn't come before, during the earlier Desolations?'

No. It is new.

As always, the Stormfather's voice was far off, like very distant thunder. The Stormfather didn't always reply to Dalinar, and didn't remain near him. That was to be expected; he was the soul of the storm. He could not – should not – be contained.

And yet, there was an almost childish petulance to the way he sometimes ignored Dalinar's questions. It seemed that sometimes he did so

41

merely because he didn't want Dalinar to think that he would come whenever called.

The Everstorm appeared in the distance, its black clouds lit from within by crackling red lightning. It was low enough in the sky that – fortunately – its top wouldn't reach Urithiru. It surged like a cavalry, trampling the calm, ordinary clouds below.

Dalinar forced himself to watch that wave of darkness flow around Urithiru's plateau. Soon it seemed as if their lonely tower were a lighthouse looking over a dark, deadly sea.

It was hauntingly silent. Those red lightning bolts didn't rumble with thunder in the proper way. He heard the occasional *crack*, stark and shocking, like a hundred branches snapping at once. But the sounds didn't seem to match the flashes of red light that rose from deep within.

The storm was so quiet, in fact, that he was able to hear the telltale rustle of cloth as Navani slipped up behind him. She wrapped her arms around him, pressing against his back, resting her head against his shoulder. His eyes flickered down, and he noticed that she'd removed the glove from her safehand. It was barely visible in the dark: slender, gorgeous fingers – delicate, with the nails painted a blushing red. He saw it by the light of the first moon above, and by the intermittent flashes of the storm beneath.

'Any further word from the west?' Dalinar whispered. The Everstorm was slower than a highstorm, and had hit Shinovar many hours before. It did not recharge spheres, even if you left them out during the entire Everstorm.

'The spanreeds are abuzz. The monarchs are delaying a response, but I suspect that soon they'll realize they *have* to listen to us.'

'I think you underestimate the stubbornness a crown can press into a man or woman's mind, Navani.'

Dalinar had been out during his share of highstorms, particularly in his youth. He'd watched the chaos of the stormwall pushing rocks and refuse before it, the sky-splitting lightning, the claps of thunder. Highstorms were the ultimate expression of nature's power: wild, untamed, sent to remind man of his insignificance.

However, highstorms never seemed hateful. This storm was different. It felt *vengeful*.

Staring into that blackness below, Dalinar thought he could see what it had done. A series of impressions, thrown at him in anger. The storm's experiences as it had slowly crossed Roshar.

Houses ripped apart, screams of the occupants lost to the tempest.

People caught in their fields, running in a panic before the unpredicted storm.

Cities blasted with lightning. Towns cast into shadow. Fields swept barren.

And vast seas of glowing red eyes, coming awake like spheres suddenly renewed with Stormlight.

Dalinar hissed out a long, slow breath, the impressions fading. 'Was that real?' he whispered.

Yes, the Stormfather said. *The enemy rides this storm. He's aware of you, Dalinar.*

Not a vision of the past. Not some possibility of the future. His kingdom, his people, his entire *world* was being attacked. He drew a deep breath. At the very least, this wasn't the singular tempest that they'd experienced when the Everstorm had clashed with the highstorm for the first time. This seemed less powerful. It wouldn't tear down cities, but it did rain destruction upon them – and the winds would attack in bursts, hostile, even *deliberate*.

The enemy seemed more interested in preying upon the small towns. The fields. The people caught unaware.

Though it was not as destructive as he'd feared, it would still leave thousands dead. It would leave cities broken, particularly those without shelter to the west. More importantly, it would steal the parshmen laborers and turn them into Voidbringers, loosed on the public.

All in all, this storm would exact a price in blood from Roshar that hadn't been seen since . . . well, since the Desolations.

He lifted his hand to grasp Navani's, as she in turn held to him. 'You did what you could, Dalinar,' she whispered after a time watching. 'Don't insist on carrying this failure as a burden.'

'I won't.'

She released him and turned him around, away from the sight of the storm. She wore a dressing gown, not fit to go about in public, but also not precisely immodest.

Save for that hand, with which she caressed his chin. 'I,' she whispered, 'don't believe you, Dalinar Kholin. I can read the truth in the tightness of your muscles, the set of your jaw. I know that you, while being crushed beneath a boulder, would insist that you've got it under control and ask to see field reports from your men.'

The scent of her was intoxicating. And those entrancing, brilliant violet eyes.

'You need to relax, Dalinar,' she said.

'Navani . . .' he said.

She looked at him, questioning, so beautiful. Far more gorgeous than when they'd been young. He'd swear it. For how could anyone be as beautiful as she was now?

He seized her by the back of the head and pulled her mouth to his own. Passion woke within him. She pressed her body to his, breasts pushing against him through the thin gown. He drank of her lips, her mouth, her scent. Passionspren fluttered around them like crystal flakes of snow.

Dalinar stopped himself and stepped back.

'Dalinar,' she said as he pulled away. 'Your stubborn refusal to get seduced is making me question my feminine wiles.'

'Control is important to me, Navani,' he said, his voice hoarse. He gripped the stone balcony wall, white knuckled. 'You know how I was, what I became, when I was a man with no control. I will not surrender now.'

She sighed and sidled up to him, pulling his arm free of the stone, then slipping under it. 'I won't push you, but I need to know. Is this how it's going to continue? Teasing, dancing on the edge?'

'No,' he said, staring out over the darkness of the storm. 'That would be an exercise in futility. A general knows not to set himself up for battles he cannot win.'

'Then what?'

'I'll find a way to do it right. With oaths.'

The oaths were vital. The promise, the act of being bound together.

'How?' she said, then poked him in the chest. 'I'm as religious as the next woman – more than most, actually. But Kadash turned us down, as did Ladent, even Rushu. She squeaked when I mentioned it and *literally* ran away.'

'Chanada,' Dalinar said, speaking of the senior ardent of the warcamps. 'She spoke to Kadash, and had him go to each of the ardents. She probably did it the moment she heard we were courting.'

'So no ardent will marry us,' Navani said. 'They consider us siblings. You're stretching to find an impossible accommodation; continue with this, and it's going to leave a lady wondering if you actually care.'

'Have you ever thought that?' Dalinar said. 'Sincerely.'

'Well . . . no.'

'You are the woman I love,' Dalinar said, pulling her tight. 'A woman I have always loved.'

'Then who cares?' she said. 'Let the ardents hie to Damnation, with ribbons around their ankles.'

'Blasphemous.'

'I'm not the one telling everyone that God is dead.'

'Not *everyone*,' Dalinar said. He sighed, letting go of her – with reluctance – and walked back into his rooms, where a brazier of coal radiated welcome warmth, as well as the room's only light. They had recovered his fabrial heating device from the warcamps, but didn't yet have the Stormlight to run it. The scholars had discovered long chains and cages, apparently used for lowering spheres down into the storms, so they'd be able to renew their spheres – if the highstorms ever returned. In other parts of the world, the Weeping had restarted, then fitfully stopped. It might start again. Or the proper storms might start up. Nobody knew, and the Stormfather refused to enlighten him.

Navani entered and pulled the thick drapings closed over the doorway, tying them tightly in place. This room was heaped with furniture, chairs lining the walls, rolled rugs stacked atop them. There was even a standing mirror. The images of twisting windspren along its sides bore the distinctly rounded look of something that had been carved first from weevilwax, then Soulcast into hardwood.

They had deposited all this here for him, as if worried about their highprince living in simple stone quarters. 'Let's have someone clear this out for me tomorrow,' Dalinar said. 'There's room enough for it in the chamber next door, which we can turn into a sitting room or a common room.'

Navani nodded as she settled onto one of the sofas – he saw her reflected in the mirror – her hand still casually uncovered, gown dropping to the side, exposing neck, collarbone, and some of what was beneath. She wasn't trying to be seductive right now; she was merely comfortable around him. Intimately familiar, past the point where she felt embarrassed for him to see her uncovered.

It was good that one of them was willing to take the initiative in the relationship. For all his impatience to advance on the battlefield, this was one area in which he'd always needed encouragement. Same as it had been all those years ago . . .

'When I married last,' Dalinar said softly, 'I did many things wrong. I *started* wrong.'

'I wouldn't say that. You married *Shshshsh* for her Shardplate, but many marriages are for political reasons. That doesn't mean you were wrong. If you'll recall, we all encouraged you to do it.'

As always, when he heard his dead wife's name, the word was replaced to his hearing with a breezy sound of rushing air – the name couldn't gain purchase in his mind, any more than a man could hold to a gust of wind.

'I'm not trying to replace her, Dalinar,' Navani said, suddenly sounding concerned. 'I know you still have affection for *Shshshsh*. It's all right. I can share you with her memory.'

Oh, how little they all understood. He turned toward Navani, set his jaw against the pain, and said it.

'I don't remember her, Navani.'

She looked to him with a frown, as if she thought she hadn't heard him correctly.

'I can't remember my wife at all,' he said. 'I don't know her face. Portraits of her are a fuzzy smudge to my eyes. Her name is taken from me whenever spoken, like someone has plucked it away. I don't remember what she and I said when we first met; I can't even remember seeing her at the feast that night when she first arrived. It's all a blur. I can remember some events surrounding my wife, but nothing of the actual details. It's all just . . . gone.'

Navani raised her safehand fingers to her mouth, and from the way her brow knit with concern, he figured he must look like he was in agony.

He slumped down in a chair across from her.

'The alcohol?' she asked softly.

'Something more.'

She breathed out. 'The Old Magic. You said you knew both your boon and your curse.'

He nodded.

'Oh, Dalinar.'

'People glance at me when her name comes up,' Dalinar continued, 'and they give me these looks of pity. They see me keeping a stiff expression, and they assume I'm being stoic. They infer hidden pain, when really I'm just trying to keep up. It's hard to follow a conversation where half of it keeps slipping away from your brain.

'Navani, maybe I did grow to love her. I can't remember. Not one moment of intimacy, not one fight, not a *single word* she ever said to me. She's gone, leaving debris that mars my memory. I can't remember how she died. That one gets to me, because there are parts of that day I *know* I should remember. Something about a city in rebellion against my brother, and my wife being taken hostage?'

That . . . and a long march alone, accompanied only by hatred and the Thrill. He remembered those emotions vividly. He'd brought vengeance to those who had taken his wife from him.

Navani settled down on the seat beside Dalinar, resting her head on his shoulder. 'Would that I could create a fabrial,' she whispered, 'to take away this kind of pain.'

'I think . . . I think losing her must have hurt me terribly,' Dalinar whispered, 'because of what it drove me to do. I am left with only the scars. Regardless, Navani, I want it to be *right* with us. No mistakes. Done properly, with oaths, spoken to you before someone.'

'Mere words.'

'Words are the most important things in my life right now.'

She parted her lips, thoughtful. 'Elhokar?'

'I wouldn't want to put him in that position.'

'A foreign priest? From the Azish, maybe? They're *almost* Vorin.'

'That would be tantamount to declaring myself a heretic. It goes too far. I will not defy the Vorin church.' He paused. 'I might be willing to sidestep it though. . . .'

'What?' she asked.

He looked upward, toward the ceiling. 'Maybe we go to someone with authority greater than theirs.'

'You want a *spren* to marry us?' she said, sounding amused. 'Using a foreign priest would be heretical, but not a spren?'

'The Stormfather is the largest remnant of Honor,' Dalinar said. 'He's a sliver of the Almighty himself – and is the closest thing to a god we have left.'

'Oh, I'm not objecting,' Navani said. 'I'd let a confused dishwasher marry us. I just think it's a little unusual.'

'It's the best we're going to get, assuming he is willing.' He looked to Navani, then raised his eyebrows and shrugged.

'Is that a proposal?'

'. . . Yes?'

'Dalinar Kholin,' she said. 'Surely you can do better.'

He rested his hand on the back of her head, touching her black hair, which she had left loose. 'Better than you, Navani? No, I don't think that I could. I don't think that any man has ever had a chance better than this.'

She smiled, and her only reply was a kiss.

∴

Dalinar was surprisingly nervous as, several hours later, he rode one of Urithiru's strange fabrial lifts toward the roof of the tower. The lift resembled a balcony, one of many that lined a vast open shaft in the middle of Urithiru – a columnar space as wide as a ballroom, which stretched up from the first floor to the last one.

The tiers of the city, despite looking circular from the front, were actually more half-circles, with the flat sides facing east. The edges of the lower levels melded into the mountains to either side, but the very center was open to the east. The rooms up against that flat side had windows there, providing a view toward the Origin.

And here, in this central shaft, those windows made up one wall. A pure, single unbroken pane of glass hundreds of feet tall. In the day, that lit the shaft with brilliant sunlight. Now, it was dark with the gloom of night.

The balcony crawled steadily along a vertical trench in the wall; Adolin and Renarin rode with him, along with a few guards and Shallan Davar. Navani was already up above. The group stood on the other side of the balcony, giving him space to think. And to be nervous.

Why should he be nervous? He could hardly keep his hands from shaking. Storms. You'd think he was some silk-covered virgin, not a general well into his middle years.

He felt a rumbling deep within him. The Stormfather was being responsive at the moment, for which he was grateful.

'I'm surprised,' Dalinar whispered to the spren, 'you agreed to this so willingly. Grateful, but still surprised.'

I respect all oaths, the Stormfather responded.

'What about foolish oaths? Made in haste, or in ignorance?'

There are no foolish oaths. All are the mark of men and true spren over beasts and subspren. The mark of intelligence, free will, and choice.

Dalinar chewed on that, and found he was not surprised by the extreme opinion. Spren *should* be extreme; they were forces of nature. But was this how Honor himself, the Almighty, had thought?

The balcony ground its inexorable way toward the top of the tower. Only a handful of the dozens of lifts worked; back when Urithiru flourished, they all would have been going at once. They passed level after level of unexplored space, which bothered Dalinar. Making this his fortress was like camping in an unknown land.

The lift finally reached the top floor, and his guards scrambled to open the gates. Those were from Bridge Thirteen these days – he'd assigned Bridge Four to other responsibilities, considering them too important for simple guard duty, now that they were close to becoming Radiants.

Increasingly anxious, Dalinar led the way past several pillars designed with representations of the orders of Radiants. A set of steps took him up through a trapdoor onto the very roof of the tower.

Although each tier was smaller than the one below it, this roof was still over a hundred yards wide. It was cold up here, but someone had set up braziers for warmth and torches for light. The night was strikingly clear, and high above, starspren swirled and made distant patterns.

Dalinar wasn't sure what to make of the fact that no one – not even his sons – had questioned him when he'd announced his intent to marry in the middle of the night, on the roof of the tower. He searched out Navani, and was shocked to see that she'd found a traditional bridal crown. The intricate headdress of jade and turquoise complemented her wedding gown. Red for luck, it was embroidered with gold and shaped in a much looser style than the havah, with wide sleeves and a graceful drape.

Should Dalinar have found something more traditional to wear himself? He suddenly felt like a dusty, empty frame hung beside the gorgeous painting that was Navani in her wedding regalia.

Elhokar stiffly stood at her side wearing a formal golden coat and loose takama underskirt. He was paler than normal, following the failed assassination attempt during the Weeping, where he'd nearly bled to death. He'd been resting a great deal lately.

Though they'd decided to forgo the extravagance of a traditional Alethi wedding, they had invited some others. Brightlord Aladar and his daughter, Sebarial and his mistress. Kalami and Teshav to act as witnesses. He felt relieved to see them there – he'd feared Navani would be unable to find women willing to notarize the wedding.

A smattering of Dalinar's officers and scribes filled out the small procession. At the very back of the crowd gathered between the braziers, he spotted a surprising face. Kadash, the ardent, had come as requested. His scarred, bearded face didn't look pleased, but he *had* come. A good sign. Perhaps with everything else happening in the world, a highprince marrying his widowed sister-in-law wouldn't cause too much of a stir.

Dalinar stepped up to Navani and took her hands, one shrouded in a sleeve, the other warm to his touch. 'You look amazing,' he said. 'How did you find that?'

'A lady must be prepared.'

Dalinar looked to Elhokar, who bowed his head to Dalinar. *This will further muddy the relationship between us,* Dalinar thought, reading the same sentiment on his nephew's features.

Gavilar would not appreciate how his son had been handled. Despite his best intentions, Dalinar had trodden down the boy and seized power. Elhokar's time recuperating had worsened the situation, as Dalinar had grown accustomed to making decisions on his own.

However, Dalinar would be lying to himself if he said that was where it had begun. His actions had been done for the good of Alethkar, for the good of Roshar itself, but that didn't deny the fact that – step by step – he'd usurped the throne, despite claiming all along he had no intention of doing so.

Dalinar let go of Navani with one hand and rested it on his nephew's shoulder. 'I'm sorry, son,' he said.

'You always are, Uncle,' Elhokar said. 'It doesn't stop you, but I don't suppose that it should. Your life is defined by deciding what you want, then seizing it. The rest of us could learn from that, if only we could figure out how to keep up.'

Dalinar winced. 'I have things to discuss with you. Plans that you might appreciate. But for tonight, I simply ask your blessing, if you can find it to give.'

'This will make my mother happy,' Elhokar said. 'So, fine.' Elhokar kissed his mother on the forehead, then left them, striding across the rooftop. At first Dalinar worried the king would stalk down below, but he stopped beside one of the more distant braziers, warming his hands.

'Well,' Navani said. 'The only one missing is your spren, Dalinar. If he's going to—'

A strong breeze struck the top of the tower, carrying with it the scent of recent rainfall, of wet stone and broken branches. Navani gasped, pulling against Dalinar.

A presence emerged in the sky. The Stormfather encompassed everything, a face that stretched to both horizons, regarding the men imperiously. The air became strangely still, and everything but the tower's top seemed to fade. It was as if they had slipped into a place outside of time itself.

Lighteyes and guards alike murmured or cried out. Even Dalinar, who had been expecting this, found himself taking a step backward – and he had to fight the urge to cringe down before the spren.

OATHS, the Stormfather rumbled, ARE THE SOUL OF RIGHTEOUSNESS. IF YOU ARE TO SURVIVE THE COMING TEMPEST, OATHS MUST GUIDE YOU.

'I am comfortable with oaths, Stormfather,' Dalinar called up to him. 'As you know.'

YES. THE FIRST IN MILLENNIA TO BIND ME. Somehow, Dalinar felt the spren's attention shifting to Navani. AND YOU. DO OATHS HOLD MEANING TO YOU?

'The right oaths,' Navani said.

AND YOUR OATH TO THIS MAN?

'I swear it to him, and to you, and any who care to listen. Dalinar Kholin is mine, and I am his.'

YOU HAVE BROKEN OATHS BEFORE.

'All people have,' Navani said, unbowed. 'We're frail and foolish. This one I will not break. I vow it.'

The Stormfather seemed content with this, though it was far from a traditional Alethi wedding oath. BONDSMITH? he asked.

'I swear it likewise,' Dalinar said, holding to her. 'Navani Kholin is mine, and I am hers. I love her.'

SO BE IT.

Dalinar had anticipated thunder, lightning, some kind of celestial trump of victory. Instead, the timelessness ended. The breeze passed. The Stormfather vanished. All through the gathered guests, smoky blue awespren rings burst out above heads. But not Navani's. Instead she was ringed by gloryspren, the golden lights rotating above her head. Nearby, Sebarial rubbed his temple – as if trying to understand what he'd seen. Dalinar's new guards sagged, looking suddenly exhausted.

Adolin, being Adolin, let out a whoop. He ran over, trailing joyspren in the shape of blue leaves that hurried to keep up with him. He gave Dalinar – then Navani – enormous hugs. Renarin followed, more reserved but – judging from the wide grin on his face – equally pleased.

The next part became a blur, shaking hands, speaking words of thanks. Insisting that no gifts were needed, as they'd skipped that part of the traditional ceremony. It seemed that the Stormfather's pronouncement had been dramatic enough that everyone accepted it. Even Elhokar, despite his earlier pique, gave his mother a hug and Dalinar a clasp on the shoulder before going below.

That left only Kadash. The ardent waited to the end. He stood with hands clasped before him as the rooftop emptied.

To Dalinar, Kadash had always looked wrong in those robes. Though he wore the traditional squared beard, it was not an ardent that Dalinar saw. It was a soldier, with a lean build, dangerous posture, and keen light violet eyes. He had a twisting old scar running up to and around the top of his shaved head. Kadash's life might now be one of peace and service, but his youth had been spent at war.

Dalinar whispered a few words of promise to Navani, and she left him to go to the level below, where she'd ordered food and wine to be set up. Dalinar stepped over to Kadash, confident. The pleasure of having finally done what he'd postponed for so long surged through him. He was *married* to Navani. This was a joy that he'd assumed lost to him since his youth, an outcome he hadn't even allowed himself to *dream* would be his.

He would not apologize for it, or for her.

'Brightlord,' Kadash said quietly.

'Formality, old friend?'

'I wish I could only be here as an old friend,' Kadash said softly. 'I have to report this, Dalinar. The ardentia will not be pleased.'

'Surely they cannot deny my marriage if the Stormfather himself blessed the union.'

'A spren? You expect us to accept the authority of a *spren*?'

'A remnant of the Almighty.'

'Dalinar, that's *blasphemy*,' Kadash said, voice pained.

'Kadash. You know I'm no heretic. You've fought by my side.'

'That's supposed to reassure me? Memories of what we did together, Dalinar? I appreciate the man you have become; you should avoid reminding me of the man you once were.'

Dalinar paused, and a memory swirled up from the depths inside him – one he hadn't thought of in years. One that surprised him. Where had it come from?

He remembered Kadash, bloodied, kneeling on the ground having retched until his stomach was empty. A hardened soldier who had encountered something so vile that even he was shaken.

He'd left to become an ardent the next day.

'The Rift,' Dalinar whispered. 'Rathalas.'

'Dark times need not be dredged up,' Kadash said. 'This isn't about … that day, Dalinar. It's about today, and what you've been spreading among the scribes. Talk of these things you've seen in visions.'

'Holy messages,' Dalinar said, feeling cold. 'Sent by the Almighty.'

'Holy messages claiming the Almighty is *dead*?' Kadash said. 'Arriving on the eve of the return of the Voidbringers? Dalinar, can't you see how this looks? I'm your ardent, technically your *slave*. And yes, perhaps still your friend. I've tried to explain to the councils in Kharbranth and Jah Keved that you mean well. I tell the ardents of the Holy Enclave that you're looking back toward when the Knights Radiant were pure, rather than their eventual corruption. I tell them that you have no control over these visions.

'But Dalinar, that was before you started teaching that the Almighty was dead. They're angry enough over that, and now you've gone and defied convention, spitting in the eyes of the ardents! I personally don't think it matters if you marry Navani. That prohibition is outdated to be sure. But what you've done tonight …'

Dalinar reached to place a hand on Kadash's shoulder, but the man pulled away.

'Old friend,' Dalinar said softly, 'Honor might be dead, but I have felt . . . something else. Something beyond. A warmth and a light. It is not that God has died, it is that the Almighty was *never* God. He did his best to guide us, but he was an impostor. Or perhaps only an agent. A being not unlike a spren – he had the power of a god, but not the pedigree.'

Kadash looked at him, eyes widening. 'Please, Dalinar. Don't ever repeat what you just said. I think I can explain away what happened tonight. Maybe. But you don't seem to realize you're aboard a ship barely afloat in a storm, while you insist on doing a jig on the prow!'

'I will not hold back truth if I find it, Kadash,' Dalinar said. 'You just saw that I am *literally* bound to a spren of oaths. I don't dare lie.'

'I don't think you would lie, Dalinar,' Kadash said. 'But I do think you can make mistakes. Do not forget that I was there. You are *not* infallible.'

There? Dalinar thought as Kadash backed up, bowed, then turned and left. *What does he remember that I cannot?*

Dalinar watched him go. Finally, he shook his head, and went to join the midnight feast, intent on being done with it as soon as was seemly. He needed time with Navani.

His wife.

Annotated for your convenience.

5

HEARTHSTONE

I can point to the moment when I decided for certain this record had to be written. I hung between realms, seeing into Shadesmar – the realm of the spren – and beyond.

—From *Oathbringer*, preface

Kaladin trudged through a field of quiet rockbuds, fully aware that he was too late to prevent a disaster. His failure pressed down on him with an almost physical sensation, like the weight of a bridge he was forced to carry all on his own.

After so long in the eastern part of the stormlands, he had nearly forgotten the sights of a fertile landscape. Rockbuds here grew almost as big as barrels, with vines as thick as his wrist spilling out and lapping water from the pools on the stone. Fields of vibrant green grass pulled back into burrows before him, easily three feet tall when standing at height. The field was dappled with glowing lifespren, like motes of green dust.

The grass back near the Shattered Plains had barely reached as high as his ankle, and had mostly grown in yellowish patches on the leeward side of hills. He was surprised to find that he distrusted this taller, fuller grass. An ambusher could hide in that, by crouching down and waiting for the grass to rise back up. How had Kaladin never noticed? He'd run through fields like this playing catch-me with his brother, trying to see who was quick enough to grab handfuls of grass before it hid.

Kaladin felt drained. Used up. Four days ago, he'd traveled by Oathgate to the Shattered Plains, then flown to the northwest at speed. Filled to bursting with Stormlight – and carrying a wealth more in gemstones – he'd been determined to reach his home, Hearthstone, before the Everstorm returned.

After just half a day, he'd run out of Stormlight somewhere in Aladar's princedom. He'd been walking ever since. Perhaps he could have flown all the way to Hearthstone if he'd been more practiced with his powers. As it was, he'd traveled over a thousand miles in half a day, but this last bit – ninety or so miles – had taken an excruciating *three days*.

He hadn't beaten the Everstorm. It had arrived earlier in the day, around noon.

Kaladin noticed a bit of debris peeking out of the grass, and he trudged toward it. The foliage obligingly pulled back before him, revealing a broken wooden churn, the kind used for turning sow's milk into butter. Kaladin crouched and rested fingers on the splintered wood, then glanced toward another chunk of wood peeking out over the tops of the grass.

Syl zipped down as a ribbon of light, passing his head and spinning around the length of wood.

'It's the edge of a roof,' Kaladin said. 'The lip that hangs down on the leeward side of a building.' Probably from a storage shed, judging by the other debris.

Alethkar wasn't in the harshest of the stormlands, but neither was this some soft-skinned Western land. Buildings here were built low and squat, sturdy sides pointed eastward toward the Origin, like the shoulder of a man set and ready to take the force of an impact. Windows would only be on the leeward – the westward – side. Like the grass and the trees, humankind had learned to weather the storms.

That depended on storms always blowing in the same direction. Kaladin had done what he could to prepare the villages and towns he passed for the coming Everstorm, which would blow in the wrong direction and transform parshmen into destructive Voidbringers. Nobody in those towns had possessed working spanreeds, however, and he'd been unable to contact his home.

He hadn't been fast enough. Earlier today, he'd spent the Everstorm within a tomb he'd hollowed out of rock using his Shardblade – Syl herself, who could manifest as any weapon he desired. In truth, the storm hadn't been nearly as bad as the one where he'd fought the Assassin in White. But the debris he found here proved that this one had been bad enough.

The mere memory of that red storm outside his hollow made panic rise inside him. The Everstorm was so *wrong*, so unnatural – like a baby born with no face. Some things just should not be.

He stood up and continued on his way. He had changed uniforms before leaving – his old uniform had been bloodied and tattered. He now wore a spare generic Kholin uniform. It felt wrong not to bear the symbol of Bridge Four.

He crested a hill and spotted a river to his right. Trees sprouted along its banks, hungry for the extra water. That would be Hobble's Brook. So if he looked directly west . . .

Hand shading his eyes, he could see hills that had been stripped of grass and rockbuds. They'd soon be slathered with seed-crem, and lavis polyps would start to bud. That hadn't started yet; this was *supposed* to be the Weeping. Rain should be falling right now in a constant, gentle shower.

Syl zipped up in front of him, a ribbon of light. 'Your eyes are brown again,' she noted.

It took a few hours without summoning his Shardblade. Once he did that, his eyes would bleed to a glassy light blue, almost glowing. Syl found the variation fascinating; Kaladin still hadn't decided how he felt about it.

'We're close,' Kaladin said, pointing. 'Those fields belong to Hobbleken. We're maybe two hours from Hearthstone.'

'Then you'll be home!' Syl said, her ribbon of light spiraling and taking the shape of a young woman in a flowing havah, tight and buttoning above the waist, with safehand covered.

Kaladin grunted, walking down the slope, longing for Stormlight. Being without it now, after holding so much, was an echoing hollowness within him. Was this what it would be like every time he ran dry?

The Everstorm hadn't recharged his spheres, of course. Neither with Stormlight nor some other energy, which he'd feared might happen.

'Do you like the new dress?' Syl asked, wagging her covered safehand as she stood in the air.

'Looks strange on you.'

'I'll have you know I put a *ton* of thought into it. I spent positively hours thinking of just how – Oh! What's that?'

She turned into a little stormcloud that shot toward a lurg clinging to a stone. She inspected the fist-size amphibian on one side, then the other, before squealing in joy and turning into a perfect imitation of the thing – except pale white-blue. This startled the creature away, and she giggled, zipping back toward Kaladin as a ribbon of light.

'What were we saying?' she asked, forming into a young woman and resting on his shoulder.

'Nothing important.'

'I'm *sure* I was scolding you. Oh, yes, you're home! Yay! Aren't you *excited*?'

She didn't see it – didn't realize. Sometimes, for all her curiosity, she could be oblivious.

'But . . . it's your home . . .' Syl said. She huddled down. 'What's wrong?'

'The Everstorm, Syl,' Kaladin said. 'We were supposed to beat it here.' He'd *needed* to beat it here.

Surely someone would have survived, right? The fury of the storm, and then the worse fury after? The murderous rampage of servants turned into monsters?

Oh, Stormfather. Why hadn't he been *faster*?

He forced himself into a double march again, pack slung over his shoulder. The weight was still heavy, dreadfully so, but he found that he had to know. Had to see.

Someone had to witness what had happened to his home.

⁘

The rain resumed about an hour out of Hearthstone, so at least the weather patterns hadn't been *completely* ruined. Unfortunately, this meant he had to hike the rest of the way wet. He splashed through puddles where rainspren grew, blue candles with eyes on the very tip.

'It will be all right, Kaladin,' Syl promised from his shoulder. She'd created an umbrella for herself, and still wore the traditional Vorin dress instead of her usual girlish skirt. 'You'll see.'

The sky had darkened by the time he finally crested the last lavis hill and looked down on Hearthstone. He braced himself for the destruction, but it shocked him nonetheless. Some of the buildings he remembered were simply ... gone. Others stood without roofs. He couldn't see the entire town from his vantage, not in the gloom of the Weeping, but many of the structures he could make out were hollow and ruined.

He stood for a long time as night fell. He didn't spot a glimmer of light in the town. It was empty.

Dead.

A part of him scrunched up inside, huddling into a corner, tired of being whipped so often. He'd embraced his power; he'd taken the path of a Radiant. Why hadn't it been enough?

His eyes immediately sought out his own home on the outskirts of town. But no. Even if he'd been able to see it in the rainy evening gloom, he didn't want to go there. Not yet. He couldn't face the death he might find.

Instead, he rounded Hearthstone on the northwestern side, where a hill led up to the citylord's manor. The larger rural towns like this served as a kind of hub for the small farming communities around them. Because of that, Hearthstone was cursed with the presence of a lighteyed ruler of some status. Brightlord Roshone, a man whose greedy ways had ruined far more than one life.

Moash ... Kaladin thought as he trudged up the hill toward the manor, shivering in the chill and the darkness. He'd have to face his friend's betrayal – and near assassination of Elhokar – at some point. For now, he had more pressing wounds that needed tending.

The manor was where the town's parshmen had been kept; they'd have begun their rampage here. He was pretty sure that if he ran across Roshone's broken corpse, he wouldn't be too heartbroken.

'Wow,' Syl said. '*Gloomspren.*'

Kaladin looked up and noted an unusual spren whipping about. Long, grey, like a tattered streamer of cloth in the wind. It wound around him, fluttering. He'd seen its like only once or twice before.

'Why are they so rare?' Kaladin asked. 'People feel gloomy all the time.'

'Who knows?' Syl said. 'Some spren are common. Some are uncommon.' She tapped his shoulder. 'I'm pretty sure one of my aunts liked to hunt these things.'

'*Hunt* them?' Kaladin asked. 'Like, try to spot them?'

'No. Like you hunt greatshells. Can't remember her name …' Syl cocked her head, oblivious to the fact that rain was falling through her form. 'She wasn't really my aunt. Just an honorspren I referred to that way. What an odd memory.'

'More seems to be coming back to you.'

'The longer I'm with you, the more it happens. Assuming you don't try to kill me again.' She gave him a sideways look. Though it was dark, she glowed enough for him to make out the expression.

'How often are you going to make me apologize for that?'

'How many times have I done it so far?'

'At least fifty.'

'Liar,' Syl said. 'Can't be more than twenty.'

'I'm sorry.'

Wait. Was that light up ahead?

Kaladin stopped on the path. It *was* light, coming from the manor house. It flickered unevenly. Fire? Was the manor burning? No, it seemed to be candles or lanterns inside. Someone, it appeared, had survived. Humans or Voidbringers?

He needed to be careful, though as he approached, he found that he didn't want to be. He wanted to be reckless, angry, destructive. If he found the creatures that had taken his home from him …

'Be ready,' he mumbled to Syl.

He stepped off the pathway, which was kept free of rockbuds and other plants, and crept carefully toward the manor. Light shone between boards that had been pounded across the building's windows, replacing glass that the Everstorm undoubtedly broke. He was surprised the manor had survived as well as it had. The porch had been ripped free, but the roof remained.

The rain masked other sounds and made it difficult to see much beyond that, but someone, or something, *was* inside. Shadows moved in front of the lights.

Heart pounding, Kaladin rounded toward the northern side of the building. The servants' entrance would be here, along with the quarters for the parshmen. An unusual amount of noise came from inside the manor house. Thumping. Motion. Like a nest full of rats.

He had to feel his way through the gardens. The parshmen had been housed in a small structure built in the manor's shadow, with a single open chamber and benches for sleeping. Kaladin reached it by touch and felt at a large hole ripped in the side.

Scraping came from behind him.

Kaladin spun as the back door of the manor opened, its warped frame grinding against stone. He dove for cover behind a shalebark mound, but light bathed him, cutting through the rain. A lantern.

Kaladin stretched his hand to the side, prepared to summon Syl, yet the person who stepped from the manor was no Voidbringer, but instead a human guardsman in an old helm spotted by rust.

The man held up his lantern. 'Here now,' he shouted at Kaladin, fumbling at the mace on his belt. 'Here now! You there!' He pulled free the weapon and held it out in a quivering hand. 'What are you? Deserter? Come here into the light and let me see you.'

Kaladin stood up warily. He didn't recognize the soldier – but either someone had survived the Voidbringer assault, or this man was part of an expedition investigating the aftermath. Either way, it was the first hopeful sign Kaladin had seen since arriving.

He held his hands up – he was unarmed save for Syl – and let the guard bully him into the building.

6

FOUR LIFETIMES

I thought that I was surely dead. Certainly, some who saw farther than I did thought I had fallen.

—From *Oathbringer*, preface

Kaladin stepped into Roshone's manor, and his apocalyptic visions of death and loss started to fade as he recognized people. He passed Toravi, one of the town's many farmers, in the hallway. Kaladin remembered the man as being enormous, with thick shoulders. In actuality, he was shorter than Kaladin by half a hand, and most of Bridge Four could have outmatched him for muscles.

Toravi didn't seem to recognize Kaladin. The man stepped into a side chamber, which was packed with darkeyes sitting on the floor.

The soldier walked Kaladin along the candlelit hallway. They passed through the kitchens, and Kaladin noted dozens of other familiar faces. The townspeople filled the manor, packing every room. Most sat on the floor in family groups, and while they looked tired and disheveled, they were alive. Had they rebuffed the Voidbringer assault, then?

My parents, Kaladin thought, pushing through a small group of townspeople and moving more quickly. Where were his parents?

'Whoa, there!' said the soldier behind, grabbing Kaladin by the shoulder. He shoved his mace into the small of Kaladin's back. 'Don't make me down you, son.'

Kaladin turned on the guardsman, a clean-shaven fellow with brown eyes that seemed set a little too close together. That rusted cap was a disgrace.

'Now,' the soldier said, 'we're just going to go find Brightlord Roshone, and you're going to explain why you were skulking round the place. Act real nice, and maybe he won't hang you. Understand?'

The townspeople in the kitchens noticed Kaladin finally, and pulled away. Many whispered to one another, eyes wide, fearful. He heard the words 'deserter,' 'slave brands,' 'dangerous.'

Nobody said his name.

'They don't recognize you?' Syl asked as she walked across a kitchen countertop.

Why would they recognize this man he had become? Kaladin saw himself reflected in a pan hanging beside the brick oven. Long hair with a curl to it, the tips resting against his shoulders. A rough uniform that was a shade too small for him, face bearing a scruffy beard from several weeks without shaving. Soaked and exhausted, he looked like a vagabond.

This wasn't the homecoming he'd imagined during his first months at war. A glorious reunion where he returned as a hero wearing the knots of a sergeant, his brother delivered safe to his family. In his fancies, people had praised him, slapped him on the back and accepted him.

Idiocy. These people had never treated him or his family with any measure of kindness.

'Let's go,' the soldier said, shoving him on the shoulder.

Kaladin didn't move. When the man shoved harder, Kaladin rolled his body with the push, and the shift of weight sent the guard stumbling past him. The man turned, angry. Kaladin met his gaze. The guard hesitated, then took a step back and gripped his mace more firmly.

'Wow,' Syl said, zipping up to Kaladin's shoulder. 'That is *quite* the glare you gave.'

'Old sergeant's trick,' Kaladin whispered, turning and leaving the kitchens. The guard followed behind, barking an order that Kaladin ignored.

Each step through this manor was like walking through a memory. There was the dining nook where he'd confronted Rillir and Laral on the night he'd discovered his father was a thief. This hallway beyond, hung with portraits of people he didn't know, had been where he'd played as a child. Roshone hadn't changed the portraits.

He'd have to talk to his parents about Tien. It was why he hadn't tried to contact them after being freed from slavery. Could he face them? Storms, he hoped they lived. But could he *face them*?

He heard a moan. Soft, underneath the sounds of people talking, still he picked it out.

'There were wounded?' he asked, turning on his guard.

'Yeah,' the man said. 'But—'

Kaladin ignored him and strode down the hallway, Syl flying along beside his head. Kaladin shoved past people, following the sounds of the tormented, and eventually stumbled into the doorway of the parlor. It had been transformed into a surgeon's triage room, with mats laid out on the floor bearing wounded.

A figure knelt by one of the pallets carefully splinting a broken arm. Kaladin had known as soon as he'd heard those moans of pain where he'd find his father.

Lirin glanced at him. Storms. Kaladin's father looked weathered, bags underneath his dark brown eyes. The hair was greyer than Kaladin remembered, the face gaunter. But he was the same. Balding, diminutive, thin, bespectacled . . . and amazing.

'What's this?' Lirin asked, turning back to his work. 'Did the high-prince's house send soldiers already? That was faster than expected. How many did you bring? We can certainly use . . .' Lirin hesitated, then looked back at Kaladin.

Then his eyes opened wide.

'Hello, Father,' Kaladin said.

The guardsman finally caught up, shouldering past gawking towns-people and waving his mace toward Kaladin like a baton. Kaladin sidestepped absently, then pushed the man so he stumbled farther down the hallway.

'It *is* you,' Lirin said. Then he scrambled over and caught Kaladin in an embrace. 'Oh, Kal. My boy. My little boy. Hesina! *HESINA!*'

Kaladin's mother appeared in the doorway a moment later, bearing a tray of freshly boiled bandages. She probably thought that Lirin needed her help with a patient. Taller than her husband by a few fingers, she wore her hair tied back with a kerchief just as Kaladin remembered.

She raised her gloved safehand to her lips, gaping, and the tray slipped down in her other hand, tumbling bandages to the floor. Shockspren, like pale yellow triangles breaking and re-forming, appeared behind her. She dropped the tray and reached to the side of Kaladin's face with a soft touch. Syl zipped around in a ribbon of light, laughing.

Kaladin couldn't laugh. Not until it had been said. He took a deep breath, choked on it the first time, then finally forced it out.

'I'm sorry, Father, Mother,' he whispered. 'I joined the army to protect him, but I could barely protect myself.' He found himself shaking, and he put his back to the wall, letting himself sink down until he was seated. 'I let Tien die. I'm sorry. It's my fault. . . .'

'Oh, Kaladin,' Hesina said, kneeling down beside him and pulling him into an embrace. 'We got your letter, but over a year ago they told us you had died as well.'

'I should have saved him,' Kaladin whispered.

'You shouldn't have gone in the first place,' Lirin said. 'But now . . . Almighty, now you're back.' Lirin stood up, tears leaking down his cheeks. 'My son! My son is *alive*!'

⁂

A short time later, Kaladin sat among the wounded, holding a cup of warm soup in his hands. He hadn't had a hot meal since . . . when?

'That's *obviously* a slave's brand, Lirin,' a soldier said, speaking with Kaladin's father near the doorway into the room. '*Sas* glyph, so it happened here in the princedom. They probably told you he'd died to save you the shame of the truth. And then the *shash* brand – you don't get that for mere insubordination.'

Kaladin sipped his soup. His mother knelt beside him, one hand on his shoulder, protective. The soup tasted of home. Boiled vegetable broth with steamed lavis stirred in, spiced as his mother always made it.

He hadn't spoken much in the half hour since he'd arrived. For now, he just wanted to be here with them.

Strangely, his memories had turned fond. He remembered Tien laughing, brightening the dreariest of days. He remembered hours spent studying medicine with his father, or cleaning with his mother.

Syl hovered before his mother, still wearing her little havah, invisible to everyone but Kaladin. The spren had a perplexed look on her face.

'The wrong-way highstorm did break many of the town's buildings,' Hesina explained to him softly. 'But our home still stands. We had to dedicate your spot to something else, Kal, but we can make space for you.'

Kaladin glanced at the soldier. Captain of Roshone's guard; Kaladin thought he remembered the man. He almost seemed too pretty to be a soldier, but then, he *was* lighteyed.

'Don't worry about that,' Hesina said. 'We'll deal with it, whatever the ... trouble is. With all these wounded pouring in from the villages around, Roshone will need your father's skill. Roshone won't go making a storm and risk Lirin's discontent – and you *won't* be taken from us again.'

She talked to him as if he were a child.

What a surreal sensation, being back here, being treated like he was still the boy who had left for war five years ago. Three men bearing their son's name had lived and died in that time. The soldier who had been forged in Amaram's army. The slave, so bitter and angry. His parents had never met Captain Kaladin, bodyguard to the most powerful man in Roshar.

And then ... there was the next man, the man he was becoming. A man who owned the skies and spoke ancient oaths. Five years had passed. And four lifetimes.

'He's a runaway slave,' the guard captain hissed. 'We can't just *ignore* that, surgeon. He probably stole the uniform. And even if for some reason he was allowed to hold a spear despite his brands, he's a deserter. Look at those haunted eyes and tell me you don't see a man who has done terrible things.'

'He's my *son*,' Lirin said. 'I'll buy his writ of slavery. You're *not* taking him. Tell Roshone he can either let this slide, or he can go without a surgeon. Unless he assumes Mara can take over after just a few years of apprenticeship.'

Did they think they were speaking softly enough that he couldn't hear?

Look at the wounded people in this room, Kaladin. You're missing something.

The wounded ... they displayed fractures. Concussions. Very few lacerations. This was not the aftermath of a battle, but of a natural disaster. So what had happened to the Voidbringers? Who had fought them off?

'Things have gotten better since you left,' Hesina promised Kaladin, squeezing his shoulder. 'Roshone isn't as bad as he once was. I think he feels guilty. We can rebuild, be a family again. And there's something else you need to know about. We—'

'Hesina,' Lirin said, throwing his hands into the air.

'Yes?'

'Write a letter to the highprince's administrators,' Lirin said. 'Explain the situation; see if we can get a forbearance, or at least an explanation.' He looked to the soldier. 'Will *that* satisfy your master? We can wait upon a higher authority, and in the meantime I can have my son back.'

'We'll see,' the soldier said, folding his arms. 'I'm not sure how much I like the idea of a *shash*-branded man running around my town.'

Hesina rose to join Lirin. The two had a hushed exchange as the guard settled back against the doorway, pointedly keeping an eye on Kaladin. Did he know how little like a soldier he looked? He didn't walk like a man acquainted with battle. He stepped too hard, and stood with his knees too straight. There were no dents in his breastplate, and his sword's scabbard knocked against things as he turned.

Kaladin sipped his soup. Was it any wonder that his parents still thought of him as a child? He'd come in looking ragged and abandoned, then had started sobbing about Tien's death. Being home brought out the child in him, it seemed.

Perhaps it was time, for once, to stop letting the rain dictate his mood. He couldn't banish the seed of darkness inside him, but Stormfather, he didn't need to let it rule him either.

Syl walked up to him in the air. 'They're like I remember them.'

'Remember them?' Kaladin whispered. 'Syl, you never knew me when I lived here.'

'That's true,' she said.

'So how can you remember them?' Kaladin said, frowning.

'Because I do,' Syl said, flitting around him. 'Everyone is connected, Kaladin. Every*thing* is connected. I didn't know you then, but the winds did, and I am of the winds.'

'You're honorspren.'

'The winds are of Honor,' she said, laughing as if he'd said something ridiculous. 'We are kindred blood.'

'You don't have blood.'

'And you don't have an imagination, it appears.' She landed in the air before him and became a young woman. 'Besides, there was . . . another voice. Pure, with a song like tapped crystal, distant yet demanding . . .' She smiled, and zipped away.

Well, the world might have been upended, but Syl was as impenetrable as ever. Kaladin set aside his soup and climbed to his feet. He stretched to one side, then the other, feeling satisfying *pops* from his joints. He walked toward his parents. Storms, but everyone in this town seemed smaller than he remembered. He hadn't been *that* much shorter when he'd left Hearthstone, had he?

A figure stood right outside the room, speaking with the guard with the rusty helmet. Roshone wore a lighteyes' coat that was several seasons out of fashion – Adolin would have shaken his head at that. The citylord wore a wooden foot on his right leg, and had lost weight since Kaladin had last seen him. His skin drooped on his figure like melted wax, bunching up at his neck.

That said, Roshone had the same imperious bearing, the same angry expression – his light yellow eyes seemed to blame everyone and everything in this insignificant town for his banishment. He'd once lived in Kholinar, but had been involved in the deaths of some citizens – Moash's grandparents – and had been shipped out here as punishment.

He turned toward Kaladin, lit by candles on the walls. 'So, *you're* alive. They didn't teach you to keep yourself in the army, I see. Let me have a look at those brands of yours.' He reached over and held up the hair in front of Kaladin's forehead. 'Storms, boy. What did you do? Hit a lighteyes?'

'Yes,' Kaladin said.

Then punched him.

He bashed Roshone right in the face. A solid hit, exactly like Hav had taught him. Thumb outside of his fist, he connected with the first two knuckles of his hand across Roshone's cheekbone, then followed through to slide across the front of the face. Rarely had he delivered such a perfect punch. It barely even hurt his fist.

Roshone dropped like a felled tree.

'That,' Kaladin said, 'was for my friend Moash.'

I did not die.
I experienced something worse.

—From *Oathbringer*, preface

'K aladin!' Lirin exclaimed, grabbing him by the shoulder. 'What are you *doing*, son?'

Roshone sputtered on the ground, his nose bleeding. 'Guards, take him! You hear me!'

Syl landed on Kaladin's shoulder, hands on her hips. She tapped her foot. 'He probably deserved that.'

The darkeyed guard scrambled to help Roshone to his feet while the captain leveled his sword at Kaladin. A third joined them, running in from another room.

Kaladin stepped one foot back, falling into a guard position.

'Well?' Roshone demanded, holding his handkerchief to his nose. 'Strike him down!' Angerspren boiled up from the ground in pools.

'Please, no,' Kaladin's mother cried, clinging to Lirin. 'He's just distraught. He—'

Kaladin held out a hand toward her, palm forward, in a quieting motion. 'It's all right, Mother. That was only payment for a little unsettled debt between Roshone and me.'

He met the eyes of the guards, each in turn, and they shuffled uncertainly. Roshone blustered. Unexpectedly, Kaladin felt in complete control of the situation – and . . . well, more than a little embarrassed.

Suddenly, the perspective of it crashed down on him. Since leaving Hearthstone, Kaladin had met true evil, and Roshone hardly compared. Hadn't he sworn to protect even those he didn't like? Wasn't the whole *point* of what he had learned to keep him from doing things like this? He glanced at Syl, and she nodded to him.

Do better.

For a short time, it had been nice to just be Kal again. Fortunately, he wasn't that youth any longer. He was a new person – and for the first time in a long, *long* while, he was happy with that person.

'Stand down, men,' Kaladin said to the soldiers. 'I promise not to hit your brightlord again. I apologize for that; I was momentarily distracted by our previous history. Something he and I both need to forget. Tell me, what happened to the parshmen? Did they not attack the town?'

The soldiers shifted, glancing toward Roshone.

'I said *stand down*,' Kaladin snapped. 'For storm's sake, man. You're holding that sword like you're going to chop a stumpweight. And you? *Rust* on your cap? I know Amaram recruited most of the able-bodied men in the region, but I've seen messenger boys with more battle poise than you.'

The soldiers looked to one another. Then, red-faced, the lighteyed one slid his sword back into its sheath.

'What are you doing?' Roshone demanded. 'Attack him!'

'Brightlord, sir,' the man said, eyes down. 'I may not be the best soldier around, but . . . well, sir, trust me on this. We should just pretend that punch never happened.' The other two soldiers nodded their heads in agreement.

Roshone sized Kaladin up, dabbing at his nose, which wasn't bleeding badly. 'So, they *did* make something out of you in the army, did they?'

'You have no idea. We need to talk. Is there a room here that isn't clogged full of people?'

'Kal,' Lirin said. 'You're speaking foolishness. Don't give orders to Brightlord Roshone!'

Kaladin pushed past the soldiers and Roshone, walking farther down the hallway. 'Well?' he barked. 'Empty room?'

'Up the stairs, sir,' one of the soldiers said. 'Library is empty.'

'Excellent.' Kaladin smiled to himself, noting the 'sir.' 'Join me up there, men.'

Kaladin started toward the stairs. Unfortunately, an authoritative bearing could only take a man so far. Nobody followed, not even his parents.

'I gave you people an order,' Kaladin said. 'I'm not fond of repeating myself.'

'And what,' Roshone said, 'makes you think you can order anyone around, boy?'

Kaladin turned back and swept his arm before him, summoning Syl. A bright, dew-covered Shardblade formed from mist into his hand. He spun the Blade and rammed her down into the floor in one smooth motion. He held the grip, feeling his eyes bleed to blue.

Everything grew still. Townspeople froze, gaping. Roshone's eyes bulged. Curiously, Kaladin's father just lowered his head and closed his eyes.

'Any other questions?' Kaladin asked.

⁘

'They were gone when we went back to check on them, um, Brightlord,' said Aric, the short guard with the rusty helm. 'We'd locked the door, but the side was ripped clean open.'

'They didn't attack a soul?' Kaladin asked.

'No, Brightlord.'

Kaladin paced through the library. The room was small, but neatly organized with rows of shelves and a fine reading stand. Each book was exactly flush with the others; either the maids were extremely meticulous, or the books were not often moved. Syl perched on one shelf, her back to a book, swinging her legs girlishly over the edge.

Roshone sat on one side of the room, periodically pushing both hands along his flushed cheeks toward the back of his head in an odd nervous gesture. His nose had stopped bleeding, though he'd have a nice bruise. That was a fraction of the punishment the man deserved, but Kaladin found he had no passion for abusing Roshone. He had to be better than that.

'What did the parshmen look like?' Kaladin asked of the guardsmen. 'They changed, following the unusual storm?'

'Sure did,' Aric said. 'I peeked when I heard them break out, after the storm passed. They looked like Voidbringers, I tell you, with big bony bits jutting from their skin.'

'They were taller,' the guard captain added. 'Taller than me, easily as tall as you are, Brightlord. With legs thick as stumpweights and hands that could have strangled a whitespine, I tell you.'

'Then why didn't they attack?' Kaladin asked. They could have easily taken the manor; instead, they'd run off into the night. It spoke of a more disturbing goal. Perhaps Hearthstone was too small to be bothered with.

'I don't suppose you tracked their direction?' Kaladin said, looking toward the guards, then Roshone.

'Um, no, Brightlord,' the captain said. 'Honestly, we were just worried about surviving.'

'Will you tell the king?' Aric asked. 'That storm ripped away *four* of our silos. We'll be starving afore too long, with all these refugees and no food. When the highstorms start coming again, we won't have half as many homes as we need.'

'I'll tell Elhokar.' But Stormfather, the rest of the kingdom would be just as bad.

He needed to focus on the Voidbringers. He couldn't report back to Dalinar until he had the Stormlight to fly home, so for now it seemed his most useful task would be to find out where the enemy was gathering, if he could. What were the Voidbringers planning? Kaladin hadn't experienced their strange powers himself, though he'd heard reports of the Battle of Narak. Parshendi with glowing eyes and lightning at their command, ruthless and terrible.

'I'll need maps,' he said. 'Maps of Alethkar, as detailed as you have, and some way to carry them through the rain without ruining them.' He grimaced. 'And a horse. Several of them, the finest you have.'

'So you're robbing me now?' Roshone asked softly, staring at the floor.

'Robbing?' Kaladin said. 'We'll call it renting instead.' He pulled a handful of spheres from his pocket and dropped them on the table. He glanced toward the soldiers. 'Well? Maps? Surely Roshone keeps survey maps of the nearby areas.'

Roshone was not important enough to have stewardship over any of the highprince's lands – a distinction Kaladin had never realized while he

73

lived in Hearthstone. Those lands would be watched over by much more important lighteyes; Roshone would only be a first point of contact with surrounding villages.

'We'll want to wait for the lady's permission,' the guard captain said. 'Sir.'

Kaladin raised an eyebrow. They'd disobey Roshone for him, but not the manor's lady? 'Go to the house ardents and tell them to prepare the things I request. Permission will be forthcoming. And locate a spanreed connected to Tashikk, if any of the ardents have one. Once I have the Stormlight to use it, I'll want to send word to Dalinar.'

The guards saluted and left.

Kaladin folded his arms. 'Roshone, I'm going to need to chase those parshmen and see if I can figure out what they're up to. I don't suppose any of your guards have tracking experience? Following the creatures would be hard enough without the rain swamping everything.'

'Why do they matter so much?' Roshone asked, still staring at the floor.

'Surely you've guessed,' Kaladin said, nodding to Syl as her ribbon of light flitted over to his shoulder. 'Weather in turmoil and terrors transformed from common servants? That storm with the red lightning, blowing the wrong direction? The Desolation is here, Roshone. The Voidbringers have returned.'

Roshone groaned, leaning forward, arms wrapped around himself as if he were going to be sick.

'Syl?' Kaladin whispered. 'I might need you again.'

'You sound apologetic,' she replied, cocking her head.

'I am. I don't like the idea of swinging you about, smashing you into things.'

She sniffed. 'Firstly, I *don't* smash into things. I am an *elegant* and *graceful* weapon, stupid. Secondly, why would you be bothered?'

'It doesn't feel right,' Kaladin replied, still whispering. 'You're a woman, not a weapon.'

'Wait . . . so this is about me being a girl?'

'No,' Kaladin said immediately, then hesitated. 'Maybe. It just feels strange.'

She sniffed. 'You don't ask your other weapons how they feel about being swung about.'

'My other weapons aren't people.' He hesitated. 'Are they?'

She looked at him with head cocked and eyebrows raised, as if he'd said something very stupid.

Everything has a spren. His mother had taught him that from an early age.

'So . . . some of my spears have been women, then?' he asked.

'Female, at least,' Syl said. 'Roughly half, as these things tend to go.' She flitted up into the air in front of him. 'It's your fault for personifying us, so no complaining. Of course, some of the old spren have four genders instead of two.'

'What? Why?'

She poked him in the nose. 'Because humans didn't imagine those ones, silly.' She zipped out in front of him, changing into a field of mist. When he raised his hand, the Shardblade appeared.

He strode to where Roshone sat, then stooped down and held the Shardblade before the man, point toward the floor.

Roshone looked up, transfixed by the weapon's blade, as Kaladin had anticipated. You couldn't be near one of these things and *not* be drawn by it. They had a magnetism.

'How did you get it?' Roshone asked.

'Does it matter?'

He didn't reply, but they both knew the truth. Owning a Shardblade was enough – if you could claim it, and not have it taken from you, it was yours. With one in his possession, the brands on his head were meaningless. No man, not even Roshone, would imply otherwise.

'You,' Kaladin said, 'are a cheat, a rat, and a murderer. But as much as I hate it, we don't have time to oust Alethkar's ruling class and set up something better. We are under attack by an enemy we do not understand, and which we could not have anticipated. So you're going to have to stand up and lead these people.'

Roshone stared at the blade, looking at his reflection.

'We're not powerless,' Kaladin said. 'We can and will fight back – but first we need to survive. The Everstorm will return. Regularly, though I don't know the interval yet. I need you to prepare.'

'How?' Roshone whispered.

'Build homes with slopes in both directions. If there's not time for that, find a sheltered location and hunker down. I can't stay. This crisis is bigger than one town, one people, even if it's *my* town and *my* people. I have to rely on you. Almighty preserve us, you're all we have.'

Roshone slumped down farther in his seat. Great. Kaladin stood and dismissed Syl.

'We'll do it,' a voice said from behind him.

Kaladin froze. Laral's voice sent a shiver down his spine. He turned slowly, and found a woman who did not at all match the image in his head. When he'd last seen her, she'd been wearing a perfect lighteyed dress, beautiful and young, yet her pale green eyes had seemed hollow. She'd lost her betrothed, Roshone's son, and had instead become engaged to the father – a man more than twice her age.

The woman he confronted was no longer a youth. Her face was firm, lean, and her hair was pulled back in a no-nonsense tail of black peppered with blonde. She wore boots and a utilitarian havah, damp from the rain.

She looked him up and down, then sniffed. 'Looks like you went and grew up, Kal. I was sorry to hear the news of your brother. Come now. You need a spanreed? I've got one to the queen regent in Kholinar, but that one hasn't been responsive lately. Fortunately, we do have one to Tashikk, as you asked about. If you think that the king will respond to you, we can go through an intermediary.'

She walked back out the doorway.

'Laral . . .' he said, following.

'I hear you stabbed my floor,' she noted. 'That's good hardwood, I'll have you know. Honestly. Men and their weapons.'

'I dreamed of coming back,' Kaladin said, stopping in the hallway outside the library. 'I imagined returning here a war hero and challenging Roshone. I wanted to save you, Laral.'

'Oh?' She turned back to him. 'And what made you think I needed saving?'

'You can't tell me,' Kaladin said softly, waving backward toward the library, 'that you've been happy with *that*.'

'Becoming a lighteyes does not grant a man any measure of decorum, it appears,' Laral said. 'You will stop insulting my husband, Kaladin. Shard-bearer or not, another word like that, and I'll have you thrown from my home.'

'Laral—'

'I *am* quite happy here. Or I was, until the winds started blowing the wrong direction.' She shook her head. 'You take after your father. Always feeling like you need to save everyone, even those who would rather you mind your own business.'

'Roshone brutalized my family. He sent my brother to his death and did everything he could to destroy my father!'

'And your father spoke against my husband,' Laral said, 'disparaging him in front of the other townspeople. How would you feel, as a new brightlord exiled far from home, only to find that the town's most important citizen is openly critical of you?'

Her perspective was skewed, of course. Lirin had tried to befriend Roshone at first, hadn't he? Still, Kaladin found little passion to continue the argument. What did he care? He intended to see his parents moved from this city anyway.

'I'll go set up the spanreed,' she said. 'It might take some time to get a reply. In the meantime, the ardents should be fetching your maps.'

'Great,' Kaladin said, pushing past her in the hallway. 'I'm going to go speak with my parents.'

Syl zipped over his shoulder as he started down the steps. 'So, that's the girl you were going to marry.'

'No,' Kaladin whispered. 'That's a girl I was never going to marry, no matter what happened.'

'I like her.'

'You would.' He reached the bottom of the steps and looked back up. Roshone had joined Laral at the top of the stairs, carrying the gems Kaladin had left on the table. How much had that been?

Five or six ruby broams, he thought, and maybe a sapphire or two. He did the calculations in his head. Storms ... That was a ridiculous sum – more money than the goblet full of spheres that Roshone and Kaladin's father had spent years fighting over back in the day. That was now mere pocket change to Kaladin.

He'd always thought of all lighteyes as rich, but a minor brightlord in an insignificant town ... well, Roshone was actually poor, just a different kind of poor.

Kaladin searched back through the house, passing people he'd once known – people who now whispered 'Shardbearer' and got out of his way with alacrity. So be it. He'd accepted his place the moment he'd seized Syl from the air and spoken the Words.

Lirin was back in the parlor, working on the wounded again. Kaladin stopped in the doorway, then sighed and knelt beside Lirin. As the man reached toward his tray of tools, Kaladin picked it up and held it at the ready. His old position as his father's surgery assistant. The new apprentice was helping with wounded in another room.

Lirin eyed Kaladin, then turned back to the patient, a young boy who had a bloodied bandage around his arm. 'Scissors,' Lirin said.

Kaladin proffered them, and Lirin took the tool without looking, then carefully cut the bandage free. A jagged length of wood had speared the boy's arm. He whimpered as Lirin palpated the flesh nearby, covered in dried blood. It didn't look good.

'Cut out the shaft,' Kaladin said, 'and the necrotic flesh. Cauterize.'

'A little extreme, don't you think?' Lirin asked.

'Might want to remove it at the elbow anyway. That's going to get infected for sure – look how dirty that wood is. It will leave splinters.'

The boy whimpered again. Lirin patted him. 'You'll be fine. I don't see any rotspren yet, and so we're not going to take the arm off. Let me talk to your parents. For now, chew on this.' He gave the boy some bark as a relaxant.

Together, Lirin and Kaladin moved on; the boy wasn't in immediate danger, and Lirin would want to operate after the anesthetic took effect.

'You've hardened,' Lirin said to Kaladin as he inspected the next patient's foot. 'I was worried you'd never grow calluses.'

Kaladin didn't reply. In truth, his calluses weren't as deep as his father might have wanted.

'But you've also become one of them,' Lirin said.

'My eye color doesn't change a thing.'

'I wasn't speaking of your eye color, son. I don't give two chips whether a man is lighteyed or not.' He waved a hand, and Kaladin passed him a rag to clean the toe, then started preparing a small splint.

'What you've become,' Lirin continued, 'is a killer. You solve problems with the fist and the sword. I had hoped that you would find a place among the army's surgeons.'

'I wasn't given much choice,' Kaladin said, handing over the splint, then preparing some bandages to wrap the toe. 'It's a long story. I'll tell you sometime.' *The less soul-crushing parts of it, at least.*

'I don't suppose you're going to stay.'

'No. I need to follow those parshmen.'

'More killing, then.'

'And you honestly think we shouldn't fight the *Voidbringers*, Father?'

Lirin hesitated. 'No,' he whispered. 'I know that war is inevitable. I just didn't want *you* to have to be a part of it. I've seen what it does to men. War flays their souls, and those are wounds I can't heal.' He secured the splint, then turned to Kaladin. 'We're surgeons. Let others rend and break; *we* must not harm others.'

'No,' Kaladin said. 'You're a surgeon, Father, but I'm something else. A watcher at the rim.' Words spoken to Dalinar Kholin in a vision. Kaladin stood up. 'I will protect those who need it. Today, that means hunting down some Voidbringers.'

Lirin looked away. 'Very well. I am . . . glad you returned, son. I'm glad you're safe.'

Kaladin rested his hand on his father's shoulder. 'Life before death, Father.'

'See your mother before you leave,' Lirin said. 'She has something to show you.'

Kaladin frowned, but made his way out of the healing chamber to the kitchens. The entire place was lit only by candles, and not many of them. Everywhere he went, he saw shadows and uncertain light.

He filled his canteen with fresh water and found a small umbrella. He'd need that for reading maps in this rain. From there, he went hiking up to check on Laral in the library. Roshone had retreated to his room, but she was sitting at a writing table with a spanreed before her.

Wait. The spanreed was *working*. Its ruby glowed.

'Stormlight!' Kaladin said, pointing.

'Well, of course,' she said, frowning at him. 'Fabrials require it.'

'How do you have *infused* spheres?'

'The highstorm,' Laral said. 'Just a few days back.'

During the clash with the Voidbringers, the Stormfather had summoned an irregular highstorm to match the Everstorm. Kaladin had flown before its stormwall, fighting the Assassin in White.

'That storm was unexpected,' Kaladin said. 'How in the world did you know to leave your spheres out?'

'Kal,' she said, 'it's not so hard to hang some spheres out once a storm starts blowing!'

'How many do you have?'

'Some,' Laral said. 'The ardents have a few – I wasn't the only one to think of it. Look, I've got someone in Tashikk willing to relay a message to Navani Kholin, the king's mother. Wasn't that what you implied you wanted? You really think she'll respond to you?'

The answer, blessedly, came as the spanreed started writing. ' "Captain?" ' Laral read. ' "This is Navani Kholin. Is it really you?" '

Laral blinked, then looked up at him.

'It is,' Kaladin said. 'The last thing I did before leaving was speak with Dalinar at the top of the tower.' Hopefully that would be enough to authenticate him.

Laral jumped, then wrote it.

' "Kaladin, this is Dalinar," ' Laral read as the message came back. ' "What is your status, soldier?" '

'Better than expected, sir,' Kaladin said. He outlined what he'd discovered, in brief. He ended by noting, 'I'm worried that they left because Hearthstone wasn't important enough to bother destroying. I've ordered horses and some maps. I figure I can do a little scouting and see what I can find about the enemy.'

' "Careful," ' Dalinar responded. ' "You don't have any Stormlight left?" '

'I might be able to find a little. I doubt it will be enough to get me home, but it will help.'

It took a few minutes before Dalinar replied, and Laral took the opportunity to change the paper on the spanreed board.

' "Your instincts are good, Captain," ' Dalinar finally sent. ' "I feel blind in this tower. Get close enough to discover what the enemy is doing, but don't take unnecessary risks. Take the spanreed. Send us a glyph each evening to know you are safe." '

'Understood, sir. Life before death.'

' "Life before death." '

Laral looked to him, and he nodded that the conversation was over. She packed up the spanreed for him without a word, and he took it gratefully, then hurried out of the room and down the steps.

His activities had drawn quite a crowd of people, who had gathered in the small entry hall before the steps. He intended to ask if anyone had infused spheres, but was interrupted by the sight of his mother. She was speaking with several young girls, and held a toddler in her arms. What was she doing with . . .

Kaladin stopped at the foot of the steps. The little boy was perhaps a year old, chewing on his hand and babbling around his fingers.

'Kaladin, meet your brother,' Hesina said, turning toward him. 'Some of the girls were watching him while I helped with the triage.'

'A brother,' Kaladin whispered. It had never occurred to him. His mother would be forty-one this year, and . . .

A brother.

Kaladin reached out. His mother let him take the little boy, hold him in hands that seemed too rough to be touching such soft skin. Kaladin trembled, then pulled the child tight against him. Memories of this place had not broken him, and seeing his parents had not overwhelmed him, but this . . .

He could not stop the tears. He felt like a fool. It wasn't as if this changed anything – Bridge Four were his brothers now, as close to him as any blood relative.

And yet he wept.

'What's his name?'

'Oroden.'

'Child of peace,' Kaladin whispered. 'A good name. A very good name.'

Behind him, an ardent approached with a scroll case. Storms, was that Zeheb? Still alive, it seemed, though she'd always seemed older than the stones themselves. Kaladin handed little Oroden back to his mother, then wiped his eyes and took the scroll case.

People crowded at the edges of the room. He was quite the spectacle: the surgeon's son turned slave turned Shardbearer. Hearthstone wouldn't see this much excitement for another hundred years.

At least not if Kaladin had any say about it. He nodded to his father – who had stepped out of the parlor room – then turned to the crowd. 'Does anyone here have infused spheres? I will trade you, two chips for one. Bring them forth.'

Syl buzzed around him as a collection was made, and Kaladin's mother made the trades for him. What he ended up with was only a pouch's worth, but it seemed vast riches. At the very least, he wasn't going to need those horses any longer.

He tied the pouch closed, then looked over his shoulder as his father stepped up. Lirin took a small glowing diamond chip from his pocket, then handed it toward Kaladin.

Kaladin accepted it, then glanced at his mother and the little boy in her arms. His *brother*.

'I want to take you to safety,' he said to Lirin. 'I need to leave now, but I'll be back soon. To take you to—'

'No,' Lirin said.

'Father, it's the *Desolation*,' Kaladin said.

Nearby, people gasped softly, their eyes haunted. Storms; Kaladin should have done this in private. He leaned in toward Lirin. 'I know of a place that is safe. For you, Mother. For little Oroden. Please don't be stubborn, for once in your life.'

'You can take them, if they'll go,' Lirin said. 'But I'm staying here. Particularly if . . . what you just said is true. These people will need me.'

'We'll see. I'll return as soon as I can.' Kaladin set his jaw, then walked to the front door of the manor. He pulled it open, letting in the sounds of rain, the scents of a drowned land.

He paused, looked back at the room full of dirtied townspeople, home-less and frightened. They'd overheard him, but they'd known already. He'd heard them whispering. Voidbringers. The Desolation.

He couldn't leave them like this.

'You heard correctly,' Kaladin said loudly to the hundred or so people gathered in the manor's large entry hall – including Roshone and Laral, who stood on the steps up to the second floor. 'The Voidbringers have returned.'

Murmurs. Fright.

Kaladin sucked in some of the Stormlight from his pouch. Pure, lumi-nescent smoke began to rise from his skin, distinctly visible in the dim room. He Lashed himself upward so he rose into the air, then added a Lashing downward, leaving him to hover about two feet above the floor, glowing. Syl formed from mist as a Shardspear in his hand.

'Highprince Dalinar Kholin,' Kaladin said, Stormlight puffing before his lips, 'has refounded the Knights Radiant. And this time, we will *not* fail you.'

The expressions in the room ranged from adoring to terrified. Kaladin found his father's face. Lirin's jaw had dropped. Hesina clutched her infant child in her arms, and her expression was one of pure delight, an awespren bursting around her head in a blue ring.

You I will protect, little one, Kaladin thought at the child. *I will protect them all.*

He nodded to his parents, then turned and Lashed himself outward, streaking away into the rain-soaked night. He'd stop at Stringken, about half a day's walk – or a short flight – to the south and see if he could trade spheres there.

Then he'd hunt some Voidbringers.

A POWERFUL LIE

That moment notwithstanding, I can honestly say this book has been brewing in me since my youth.

—From *Oathbringer*, preface

Shallan drew.

She scraped her drawing pad with agitated, bold streaks. She twisted the charcoal stick in her fingers every few lines, seeking the sharpest points to make the lines a deep black.

'Mmm ...' Pattern said from near her calves, where he adorned her skirt like embroidery. 'Shallan?'

She kept drawing, filling the page with black strokes.

'Shallan?' Pattern asked. 'I understand why you hate me, Shallan. I did not mean to help you kill your mother, but it is what I did. It is what I did. ...'

Shallan set her jaw and kept sketching. She sat outside at Urithiru, her back against a cold chunk of stone, her toes frigid, coldspren growing up like spikes around her. Her frazzled hair whipped past her face in a gust of air, and she had to pin the paper of her pad down with her thumbs, one trapped in her left sleeve.

'Shallan ...' Pattern said.

'It's all right,' Shallan said in a hushed voice as the wind died down. 'Just . . . just let me draw.'

'Mmm . . .' Pattern said. 'A powerful lie . . .'

A simple landscape; she should be able to draw a simple, calming landscape. She sat on the edge of one of the ten Oathgate platforms, which rose ten feet higher than the main plateau. Earlier in the day, she'd activated this Oathgate, bringing forth a few hundred more of the thousands who were waiting at Narak. That would be it for a while: each use of the device used an incredible amount of Stormlight. Even with the gemstones that the newcomers had brought, there wasn't much to go around.

Plus, there wasn't much of *her* to go around. Only an active, full Knight Radiant could work the control buildings at the center of each platform, initiating the swap. For now, that meant only Shallan.

It meant she had to summon her Blade each time. The Blade she'd used to kill her mother. A truth she'd spoken as an Ideal of her order of Radiants.

A truth that she could no longer, therefore, stuff into the back of her mind and forget.

Just draw.

The city dominated her view. It stretched impossibly high, and she struggled to contain the enormous tower on the page. Jasnah had searched this place out in the hope of finding books and records here of ancient date; so far, they hadn't found anything like that. Instead, Shallan struggled to *understand* the tower.

If she locked it down into a sketch, would she finally be able to grasp its incredible size? She couldn't get an angle from which to view the entire tower, so she kept fixating on the little things. The balconies, the shapes of the fields, the cavernous openings – maws to engulf, consume, overwhelm.

She ended up with a sketch not of the tower itself, but instead a criss-crossing of lines on a field of softer charcoal. She stared at the sketch, a windspren passing and troubling the pages. She sighed, dropping her charcoal into her satchel and getting out a damp rag to wipe her freehand fingers.

Down on the plateau, soldiers ran drills. The thought of them all living in that place disturbed Shallan. Which was stupid. It was just a *building*.

But it was one she couldn't sketch.

'Shallan . . .' Pattern said.

'We'll work it out,' she said, eyes forward. 'It's not *your* fault my parents are dead. You didn't cause it.'

'You can hate me,' Pattern said. 'I understand.'

Shallan closed her eyes. She didn't *want* him to understand. She wanted him to convince her she was wrong. She needed to be *wrong*.

'I don't hate you, Pattern,' Shallan said. 'I hate the sword.'

'But—'

'The sword isn't you. The sword is me, my father, the life we led, and the way it got twisted all about.'

'I . . .' Pattern hummed softly. 'I don't understand.'

I'd be shocked if you did, Shallan thought. *Because I sure don't.* Fortunately, she had a distraction coming her way in the form of a scout climbing up the ramp to the platform where Shallan perched. The darkeyed woman wore white and blue, with trousers beneath a runner's skirt, and had long, dark Alethi hair.

'Um, Brightness Radiant?' the scout asked after bowing. 'The high-prince has requested your presence.'

'Bother,' Shallan said, while inwardly relieved to have something to do. She handed the scout her sketchbook to hold while she packed up her satchel.

Dun spheres, she noted.

While three of the highprinces had joined Dalinar on his expedition to the center of the Shattered Plains, the greater number had remained behind. When the unexpected highstorm had come, Hatham had received word via spanreed from scouts out along the plains.

His warcamp had been able to get out most of their spheres for re-charging before the storm hit, giving him a huge amount of Stormlight compared to the rest of them. He was becoming a wealthy man as Dalinar traded for infused spheres to work the Oathgate and bring in supplies.

Compared to that, providing spheres to her to practice her Lightweav-ing wasn't a terrible expense – but she still felt guilty to see that she'd drained two of them by consuming Stormlight to help her with the chill air. She'd have to be careful about that.

She got everything packed, then reached back for the sketchbook and found the scout woman flipping through the pages with wide eyes. 'Brightness . . .' she said. 'These are amazing.'

Several were sketches as if looking up from the base of the tower, catching a vague sense of Urithiru's stateliness, but more giving a sense of vertigo. With dissatisfaction, Shallan realized she'd enhanced the surreal nature of the sketches with impossible vanishing points and perspective.

'I've been trying to draw the tower,' Shallan said, 'but I can't get it from the right angle.' Maybe when Brightlord Brooding-Eyes returned, he could fly her to another peak along the mountain chain.

'I've never seen anything like these,' the scout said, flipping pages. 'What do you call it?'

'Surrealism,' Shallan said, taking the large sketchbook back and tucking it under her arm. 'It was an old artistic movement. I guess I defaulted to it when I couldn't get the picture to look how I wanted. Hardly anyone bothers with it anymore except students.'

'It made my eyes make my brain think it forgot to wake up.'

Shallan gestured, and the scout led the way back down and across the plateau. Here, Shallan noticed that more than a few soldiers on the field had stopped their drills and were watching her. Bother. She would never again return to being just Shallan, the insignificant girl from a backwater town. She was now 'Brightness Radiant,' ostensibly from the Order of Elsecallers. She'd persuaded Dalinar to pretend – in public, at least – that Shallan was from an order that couldn't make illusions. She needed to keep that secret from spreading, or her effectiveness would be weakened.

The soldiers stared at her as if they expected her to grow Shardplate, shoot gouts of flame from her eyes, and fly off to tear down a mountain or two. *Probably should try to act more composed,* Shallan thought to herself. *More . . . knightly?*

She glanced at a soldier who wore the gold and red of Hatham's army. He immediately looked down and rubbed at the glyphward prayer tied around his upper right arm. Dalinar was determined to recover the reputation of the Radiants, but storms, you couldn't change an entire nation's perspective in a matter of a few months. The ancient Knights Radiant had betrayed humankind; while many Alethi seemed willing to give the orders a fresh start, others weren't so charitable.

Still, she tried to keep her head high, her back straight, and to walk more like her tutors had always instructed. Power was an illusion of perception, as Jasnah had said. The first step to being in control was to see yourself as capable of being in control.

The scout led her into the tower and up a flight of stairs, toward Dalinar's secure section. 'Brightness?' the woman asked as they walked. 'Can I ask you a question?'

'As that was a question, apparently you can.'

'Oh, um. Huh.'

'It's fine. What did you want to know?'

'You're ... a Radiant.'

'That one was actually a statement, and that's making me doubt my previous assertion.'

'I'm sorry. I just ... I'm curious, Brightness. How does it work? Being a Radiant? You have a Shardblade?'

So that was where this was going. 'I assure you,' Shallan said, 'it is quite possible to remain properly feminine while fulfilling my duties as a knight.'

'Oh,' the scout said. Oddly, she seemed *disappointed* by that response. 'Of course, Brightness.'

Urithiru seemed to have been crafted straight from the rock of a mountain, like a sculpture. Indeed, there weren't seams at the corners of rooms, nor were there distinct bricks or blocks in the walls. Much of the stone exposed thin lines of strata. Beautiful lines of varied hue, like layers of cloth stacked in a merchant's shop.

The corridors often twisted about in strange curves, rarely running straight toward an intersection. Dalinar suggested that perhaps this was to fool invaders, like a castle fortification. The sweeping turns and lack of seams made the corridors feel like tunnels.

Shallan didn't need a guide – the strata that cut through the walls had distinctive patterns. Others seemed to have trouble telling those apart, and talked of painting the floors with guidelines. Couldn't they distinguish the pattern here of wide reddish strata alternating with smaller yellow ones? Just go in the direction where the lines were sloping slightly upward, and you'd head toward Dalinar's quarters.

They soon arrived, and the scout took up duty at the door in case her services were needed again. Shallan entered a room that only a day before had been empty, but was now arrayed with furniture, creating a large meeting place right outside Dalinar and Navani's private rooms.

Adolin, Renarin, and Navani sat before Dalinar, who stood with hands on hips, contemplating a map of Roshar on the wall. Though the place was stuffed with rugs and plush furniture, the finery fit this bleak chamber like a lady's havah fit a pig.

'I don't know how to approach the Azish, Father,' Renarin was saying as she entered. 'Their new emperor makes them unpredictable.'

'They're *Azish*,' Adolin said, giving Shallan a wave with his unwounded hand. 'How can they *not* be predictable? Doesn't their government mandate how to peel your fruit?'

'That's a stereotype,' Renarin said. He wore his Bridge Four uniform, but had a blanket over his shoulders and was holding a cup of steaming tea, though the room wasn't particularly cold. 'Yes, they have a large bureaucracy. A change in government is still going to cause upheaval. In fact, it might be *easier* for this new Azish emperor to change policy, since policy is well defined enough to change.'

'I wouldn't worry about the Azish,' Navani said, tapping her notepad with a pen, then writing something in it. 'They'll listen to reason; they always do. What about Tukar and Emul? I wouldn't be surprised if that war of theirs is enough to distract them even from the return of the Desolations.'

Dalinar grunted, rubbing his chin with one hand. 'There's that warlord in Tukar. What's his name?'

'Tezim,' Navani said. 'Claims he's an aspect of the Almighty.'

Shallan sniffed as she slipped into the seat beside Adolin, setting her satchel and drawing pad on the floor. 'Aspect of the Almighty? At least he's humble.'

Dalinar turned toward her, then clasped his hands behind his back. Storms. He always seemed so . . . *large*. Bigger than any room he was in, brow perpetually furrowed by the deepest of thoughts. Dalinar Kholin could make choosing what to have for breakfast look like the most important decision in all of Roshar.

'Brightness Shallan,' he said. 'Tell me, how would you deal with the Makabaki kingdoms? Now that the storm has come as we warned, we have an opportunity to approach them from a position of strength. Azir is the most important, but just faced a succession crisis. Emul and Tukar are, of course, at war, as Navani noted. We could certainly use Tashikk's information networks, but they're so isolationist. That leaves Yezier and

Liafor. Perhaps the weight of their involvement would persuade their neighbors?'

He turned toward her expectantly.

'Yes, yes . . .' Shallan said, thoughtful. 'I *have* heard of several of those places.'

Dalinar drew his lips to a line, and Pattern hummed in concern on her skirts. Dalinar did not seem the type of man you joked with.

'I'm sorry, Brightlord,' Shallan continued, leaning back in her chair. 'But I'm confused as to why you want *my* input. I know of those kingdoms, of course – but my knowledge is an academic thing. I could probably name their primary export for you, but as to foreign policy . . . well, I'd never even spoken to someone from *Alethkar* before leaving my homeland. And we're neighbors!'

'I see,' Dalinar said softly. 'Does your spren offer some counsel? Could you bring him out to speak to us?'

'Pattern? He's not particularly knowledgeable about our kind, which is sort of why he's here in the first place.' She shifted in her seat. 'And to be frank, Brightlord, I think he's scared of you.'

'Well, he's obviously not a fool,' Adolin noted.

Dalinar shot his son a glance.

'Don't be like that, Father,' Adolin said. 'If anyone would be able to go about intimidating forces of nature, it would be you.'

Dalinar sighed, turning and resting his hand on the map. Curiously, it was Renarin who stood up, setting aside his blanket and cup, then walked over to put his hand on his father's shoulder. The youth looked even more spindly than normal when standing beside Dalinar, and though his hair wasn't as blond as Adolin's, it was still patched with yellow. He seemed such a strange contrast to Dalinar, cut from almost entirely different cloth.

'It's just so big, son,' Dalinar said, looking at the map. 'How can I unite all of Roshar when I've never even *visited* many of these kingdoms? Young Shallan spoke wisdom, though she might not have recognized it. We don't know these people. Now I'm expected to be responsible for them? I wish I could *see* it all. . . .'

Shallan shifted in her seat, feeling as if she'd been forgotten. Perhaps he'd sent for her because he'd wanted to seek the aid of his Radiants, but the Kholin dynamic had always been a family one. In that, she was an intruder.

Dalinar turned and walked to fetch a cup of wine from a warmed pitcher near the door. As he passed Shallan, she felt something unusual. A leaping within her, as if part of her were being *pulled* by him.

He walked past again, holding a cup, and Shallan slipped from her seat, following him toward the map on the wall. She breathed in as she walked, drawing Stormlight from her satchel in a shimmering stream. It infused her, glowing from her skin.

She rested her freehand against the map. Stormlight poured off her, illuminating the map in a swirling tempest of Light. She didn't exactly understand what she was doing, but she rarely did. Art wasn't about understanding, but about *knowing*.

The Stormlight streamed off the map, passing between her and Dalinar in a rush, causing Navani to scramble off her seat and back away. The Light swirled in the chamber and became another, larger map – floating at about table height – in the center of the room. Mountains grew up like furrows in a piece of cloth pressed together. Vast plains shone green from vines and fields of grass. Barren stormward hillsides grew splendid shadows of life on the leeward sides. Stormfather . . . as she watched, the topography of the landscape became *real*.

Shallan's breath caught. Had *she* done that? How? Her illusions usually required a previous drawing to imitate.

The map stretched to the sides of the room, shimmering at the edges. Adolin stood up from his seat, crashing through the middle of the illusion somewhere near Kharbranth. Wisps of Stormlight broke around him, but when he moved, the image swirled and neatly re-formed behind him.

'How . . .' Dalinar leaned down near their section, which detailed the Reshi Isles. 'The detail is amazing. I can almost see the cities. What did you do?'

'I don't know if I did *anything*,' Shallan said, stepping into the illusion, feeling the Stormlight swirl around her. Despite the detail, the perspective was still from very far away, and the mountains weren't even as tall as one of her fingernails. 'I couldn't have created this, Brightlord. I don't have the knowledge.'

'Well *I* didn't do it,' Renarin said. 'The Stormlight quite certainly came from you, Brightness.'

'Yes, well, your father was tugging on me at the time.'

'Tugging?' Adolin asked.

'The Stormfather,' Dalinar said. 'This is his influence – this is what he sees each time a storm blows across Roshar. It wasn't me or you, but *us*. Somehow.'

'Well,' Shallan noted, 'you *were* complaining about not being able to take it all in.'

'How much Stormlight did this take?' Navani asked, rounding the outside of the new, vibrant map.

Shallan checked her satchel. 'Um . . . all of it.'

'We'll get you more,' Navani said with a sigh.

'I'm sorry for—'

'No,' Dalinar said. 'Having my Radiants practice with their powers is among the most valuable resources I could purchase right now. Even if Hatham makes us pay through the nose for spheres.'

Dalinar strode through the image, disrupting it in a swirl around him. He stopped near the center, beside the location of Urithiru. He looked from one side of the room to the other in a long, slow survey.

'Ten cities,' he whispered. 'Ten kingdoms. Ten Oathgates connecting them from long ago. This is how we fight it. This is how we begin. We don't start by saving the world – we start with this simple step. We protect the cities with Oathgates.

'The Voidbringers are everywhere, but we can be more mobile. We can shore up capitals, deliver food or Soulcasters quickly between kingdoms. We can make those ten cities bastions of light and strength. But we must be quick. He's coming. The man with nine shadows . . .'

'What's this?' Shallan said, perking up.

'The enemy's champion,' Dalinar said, eyes narrowing. 'In the visions, Honor told me our best chance of survival involved forcing Odium to accept a contest of champions. I've seen the enemy's champion – a creature in black armor, with red eyes. A parshman perhaps. It had nine shadows.'

Nearby, Renarin had turned toward his father, eyes wide, jaw dropping. Nobody else seemed to notice.

'Azimir, capital of Azir,' Dalinar said, stepping from Urithiru to the center of Azir to the west, 'is home to an Oathgate. We need to open it and gain the trust of the Azish. They will be important to our cause.'

He stepped farther to the west. 'There's an Oathgate hidden in

Shinovar. Another in the capital of Babatharnam, and a fourth in far-off Rall Elorim, City of Shadows.'

'Another in Rira,' Navani said, joining him. 'Jasnah thought it was in Kurth. A sixth was lost in Aimia, the island that was destroyed.'

Dalinar grunted, then turned toward the map's eastern section. 'Vedenar makes seven,' he said, stepping into Shallan's homeland. 'Thaylen City is eight. Then the Shattered Plains, which we hold.'

'And the last one is in Kholinar,' Adolin said softly. 'Our home.'

Shallan approached and touched him on the arm. Spanreed communication into the city had stopped working. Nobody knew the status of Kholinar; their best clue had come via Kaladin's spanreed message.

'We start small,' Dalinar said, 'with a few of the most important to holding the world. Azir. Jah Keved. Thaylenah. We'll contact other nations, but our focus is on these three powerhouses. Azir for its organization and political clout. Thaylenah for its shipping and naval prowess. Jah Keved for its manpower. Brightness Davar, any insight you could offer into your homeland – and its status following the civil war – would be appreciated.'

'And Kholinar?' Adolin asked.

A knock at the door interrupted Dalinar's response. He called admittance, and the scout from before peeked in. 'Brightlord,' she said, looking concerned. 'There's something you need to see.'

'What is it, Lyn?'

'Brightlord, sir. There's . . . there's been another murder.'

THE THREADS OF A SCREW

The sum of my experiences has pointed at this moment. This decision.

—From *Oathbringer*, preface

One benefit of having become 'Brightness Radiant' was that for once, Shallan was *expected* to be a part of important events. Nobody questioned her presence during the rush through the corridors, lit by oil lanterns carried by guards. Nobody thought she was out of place; nobody even considered the propriety of leading a young woman to the scene of a brutal murder. What a welcome change.

From what she overheard the scout telling Dalinar, the corpse had been a lighteyed officer named Vedekar Perel. He was from Sebarial's army, but Shallan didn't know him. The body had been discovered by a scouting party in a remote part of the tower's second level.

As they drew nearer, Dalinar and his guards jogged the rest of the distance, outpacing Shallan. Storming Alethi long legs. She tried to suck in some Stormlight – but she'd used it all on that blasted map, which had disintegrated into a puff of Light as they'd left.

That left her exhausted and annoyed. Ahead of her, Adolin stopped and looked back. He danced a moment, as if impatient, then hurried to her instead of running ahead.

'Thanks,' Shallan said as he fell into step beside her.

'It's not like he can get more dead, eh?' he said, then chuckled awkwardly. Something about this had him seriously disturbed.

He reached for her hand with his hurt one, which was still splinted, then winced. She took his arm instead, and he held up his oil lantern as they hurried on. The strata here spiraled, twisting around the floor, ceiling, and walls like the threads of a screw. It was striking enough that Shallan took a Memory of it for later sketching.

Shallan and Adolin finally caught up to the others, passing a group of guards maintaining a perimeter. Though Bridge Four had discovered the body, they'd sent for Kholin reinforcements to secure the area.

They protected a medium-sized chamber now lit by a multitude of oil lamps. Shallan paused in the doorway right before a ledge that surrounded a wide square depression, perhaps four feet deep, cut into the stone floor of the room. The wall strata here continued their curving, twisting medley of oranges, reds, and browns – ballooning out across the sides of this chamber in wide bands before coiling back into narrow stripes to continue down the hall that led out the other side.

The dead man lay at the bottom of the cavity. Shallan steeled herself, but even so found the sight nauseating. He lay on his back, and had been stabbed right through the eye. His face was a bloody mess, his clothing disheveled from what looked to have been an extended fight.

Dalinar and Navani stood on the ledge above the pit. His face was stiff, a stone. She stood with her safehand raised to her lips.

'We found him just like this, Brightlord,' said Peet the bridgeman. 'We sent for you immediately. Storm me if it doesn't look exactly the same as what happened to Highprince Sadeas.'

'He's even lying in the same position,' Navani said, grabbing her skirts and descending a set of steps into the lower area. It made up almost the entire room. In fact . . .

Shallan looked toward the upper reaches of the chamber, where several stone sculptures – like the heads of horses – extended from the walls with their mouths open. *Spouts*, she thought. *This was a bathing chamber.*

Navani knelt beside the body, away from the blood running toward a drain on the far side of the basin. 'Remarkable . . . the positioning, the puncturing of the eye . . . It's *exactly* like what happened to Sadeas. This has to be the same killer.'

Nobody tried to shelter Navani from the sight – as if it were completely proper for the king's mother to be poking at a corpse. Who knew? Maybe in Alethkar, ladies were expected to do this sort of thing. It was still odd to Shallan how temerarious the Alethi were about towing their women into battle to act as scribes, runners, and scouts.

She looked to Adolin to get his read on the situation, and found him staring, aghast, mouth open and eyes wide. 'Adolin?' Shallan asked. 'Did you know him?'

He didn't seem to hear her. 'This is impossible,' he muttered. '*Impossible.*'

'Adolin?'

'I . . . No, I didn't know him, Shallan. But I'd assumed . . . I mean, I figured the death of Sadeas was an isolated crime. You know how he was. Probably got himself into trouble. Any number of people could have wanted him dead, right?'

'Looks like it was something more than that,' Shallan said, folding her arms as Dalinar walked down the steps to join Navani, trailed by Peet, Lopen, and – remarkably – Rlain of Bridge Four. That one drew attention from the other soldiers, several of whom positioned themselves subtly to protect Dalinar from the Parshendi. They considered him a danger, regardless of which uniform he wore.

'Colot?' Dalinar said, looking toward the lighteyed captain who led the soldiers here. 'You're an archer, aren't you? Fifth Battalion?'

'Yes, sir!'

'We have you scouting the tower with Bridge Four?' Dalinar asked.

'The Windrunners needed extra feet, sir, and access to more scouts and scribes for maps. My archers are mobile. Figured it was better than doing parade drills in the cold, so I volunteered my company.'

Dalinar grunted. 'Fifth Battalion . . . who was your policing force?'

'Eighth Company,' Colot said. 'Captain Tallan. Good friend of mine. He . . . didn't make it, sir.'

'I'm sorry, Captain,' Dalinar said. 'Would you and your men withdraw for a moment so I can consult with my son? Maintain that perimeter until I tell you otherwise, but do inform King Elhokar of this and send a messenger to Sebarial. I'll visit and tell him about this in person, but he'd best get a warning.'

'Yes, sir,' the lanky archer said, calling orders. The soldiers left, including the bridgemen. As they moved, Shallan felt something prickle at the back of her neck. She shivered, and couldn't help glancing over her shoulder, hating how this unfathomable building made her feel.

Renarin was standing right behind her. She jumped, letting out a pathetic squeak. Then she blushed furiously; she'd forgotten he was even with them. A few shamespren faded into view around her, floating white and red flower petals. She'd rarely attracted those, which was a wonder. She'd have thought they would take up permanent residence nearby.

'Sorry,' Renarin mumbled. 'Didn't mean to sneak up on you.'

Adolin walked down into the room's basin, still looking distracted. Was he *that* upset by finding a murderer among them? People tried to kill him practically every day. Shallan grabbed the skirt of her havah and followed him down, staying clear of the blood.

'This is troubling,' Dalinar said. 'We face a terrible threat that would wipe our kind from Roshar like leaves before the stormwall. I don't have time to worry about a murderer slinking through these tunnels.' He looked up at Adolin. 'Most of the men I'd have assigned to an investigation like this are dead. Niter, Malan . . . the King's Guard is no better, and the bridgemen – for all their fine qualities – have no experience with this sort of thing. I'll need to leave it to you, son.'

'*Me?*' Adolin said.

'You did well investigating the incident with the king's saddle, even if that turned out to be something of a wind chase. Aladar is Highprince of Information. Go to him, explain what happened, and set one of his policing teams to investigate. Then work with them as my liaison.'

'You want me,' Adolin said, 'to investigate who killed Sadeas.'

Dalinar nodded, squatting down beside the corpse, though Shallan had no idea what he expected to see. The fellow was very dead. 'Perhaps if I put my son on the job, it will convince people I'm serious about finding the killer. Perhaps not – they might just think I've put someone in charge who can keep the secret. Storms, I miss Jasnah. She would have known how to spin this, to keep opinion from turning against us in court.

'Either way, son, stay on this. Make sure the remaining highprinces at least know that we consider these murders a priority, and that we are dedicated to finding the one who committed them.'

Adolin swallowed. 'I understand.'

Shallan narrowed her eyes. What had gotten into him? She glanced toward Renarin, who still stood up above, on the walkway around the empty pool. He watched Adolin with unblinking sapphire eyes. He was *always* a little strange, but he seemed to know something she didn't.

On her skirt, Pattern hummed softly.

Dalinar and Navani eventually left to speak with Sebarial. Once they were gone, Shallan seized Adolin by the arm. 'What's wrong?' she hissed. 'You knew that dead man, didn't you? Do you know who killed him?'

He looked her in the eyes. 'I have no idea who did this, Shallan. But I *am* going to find out.'

She held his light blue eyes, weighing his gaze. Storms, what was she thinking? Adolin was a wonderful man, but he was about as deceitful as a newborn.

He stalked off, and Shallan hurried after him. Renarin remained in the room, looking down the hall after them until Shallan got far enough away that – over her shoulder – she could no longer see him.

Perhaps my heresy stretches back to those days in my childhood,
where these ideas began.

—From *Oathbringer*, preface

Kaladin leaped from a hilltop, preserving Stormlight by Lashing
himself upward just enough to give him some lift.

He soared through the rain, angled toward another hilltop.
Beneath him, the valley was clogged with vivim trees, which wound
their spindly branches together to create an almost impenetrable wall of
forestation.

He landed lightly, skidding across the wet stone past rainspren like
blue candles. He dismissed his Lashing, and as the force of the ground
reasserted itself, he stepped into a quick march. He'd learned to march
before learning the spear or shield. Kaladin smiled. He could almost
hear Hav's voice barking commands from the back of the line, where
he helped stragglers. Hav had always said that once men could march
together, learning to fight was easy.

'Smiling?' Syl said. She'd taken the shape of a large raindrop streaking
through the air beside him, falling the wrong way. It was a natural shape,
but also completely wrong. Plausible impossibility.

'You're right,' Kaladin said, rain dribbling down his face. 'I should be more solemn. We're chasing down Voidbringers.' Storms, how odd it sounded to say that.

'I didn't intend it as a reprimand.'

'Hard to tell with you sometimes.'

'And what was *that* supposed to mean?'

'Two days ago, I found that my mother is still alive,' Kaladin said, 'so the position is not, in fact, vacant. You can stop trying to fill it.'

He Lashed himself upward slightly, then let himself slide down the wet stone of the steep hill, standing sideways. He passed open rockbuds and wiggling vines, glutted and fat from the constant rainfall. Following the Weeping, they'd often find as many dead plants around the town as they did after a strong highstorm.

'Well, I'm not trying to mother you,' Syl said, still a raindrop. Talking to her could be a surreal experience. 'Though perhaps I chide you on occasion, when you're being sullen.'

He grunted.

'Or when you're being uncommunicative.' She transformed into the shape of a young woman in a havah, seated in the air and holding an umbrella as she moved along beside him. 'It is my solemn and important duty to bring *happiness, light,* and *joy* into your world when you're being a dour idiot. Which is most of the time. So there.'

Kaladin chuckled, holding a little Stormlight as he ran up the side of the next hill, then skidded down into the next valley. This was prime farmland; there was a reason why the Akanny region was prized by Sadeas. It might be a cultural backwater, but these rolling fields probably fed half the kingdom with their lavis and tallew crops. Other villages focused on raising large passels of hogs for leather and meat. Gumfrems, a kind of chull-like beast, were less common pasture animals harvested for their gemhearts, which – though small – allowed Soulcasting of meat.

Syl turned into a ribbon of light and zipped in front of him, making loops. It was difficult not to feel uplifted, even in the gloomy weather. He'd spent the entire sprint to Alethkar worrying – and then assuming – that he'd be too late to save Hearthstone. To find his parents alive . . . well, it was an unexpected blessing. The type his life had been severely lacking.

So he gave in to the urging of the Stormlight. Run. *Leap.* Though he'd spent two days chasing the Voidbringers, Kaladin's exhaustion had faded. There weren't many empty beds to be found in the broken villages he passed, but he had been able to find a roof to keep him dry and something warm to eat.

He'd started at Hearthstone and worked his way outward in a spiral – visiting villages, asking after the local parshmen, then warning people that the terrible storm would return. So far, he hadn't found a single town or village that had been attacked.

Kaladin reached the next hilltop and pulled to a stop. A weathered stone post marked a crossroads. During his youth, he'd never gotten this far from Hearthstone, though he wasn't more than a few days' walk away.

Syl zipped up to him as he shaded his eyes from the rain. The glyphs and simple map on the stone marker would indicate the distance to the next town – but he didn't need that. He could make it out as a smudge in the gloom. A fairly large town, by local standards.

'Come on,' he said, starting down the hillside.

'I think,' Syl said, landing on his shoulder and becoming a young woman, 'I would make a *wonderful* mother.'

'And what inspired this topic?'

'You're the one who brought it up.'

In comparing Syl to his mother for nagging him? 'Are you even capable of having children? Baby spren?'

'I have no idea,' Syl proclaimed.

'You call the Stormfather . . . well, Father. Right? So he birthed you?'

'Maybe? I think so? Helped shape me, is more like it. Helped us find our voices.' She cocked her head. 'Yes. He made some of us. Made me.'

'So maybe you could do that,' Kaladin said. 'Find little, uh, bits of the wind? Or of Honor? Shape them?'

He used a Lashing to leap over a snarl of rockbuds and vines, and startled a pack of cremlings as he landed, sending them scuttling away from a nearly clean mink skeleton. Probably the leavings of a larger predator.

'Hmmm,' Syl said. 'I *would* be an excellent mother. I'd teach the little spren to fly, to coast the winds, to harass you. . . .'

Kaladin smiled. 'You'd get distracted by an interesting beetle and fly off, leaving them in a drawer somewhere.'

'Nonsense! Why would I leave my babies in a drawer? Far too boring. A highprince's shoe though . . .'

He flew the remaining distance to the village, and the sight of broken buildings at the western edge dampened his mood. Though the destruction continued to be less than he'd feared, every town or village had lost people to the winds or the terrible lightning.

This village – Hornhollow, the map called it – was in what once would have been considered an ideal location. The land here dipped into a depression, and a hill to the east cut the brunt of the highstorms. It held about two dozen structures, including two large storm sanctuaries where travelers could stay – but there were also many outer buildings. This was the highprince's land, and an industrious darkeyes of high enough nahn could get a commission to work an unused hill out by itself, then keep a portion of the crop.

A few sphere lanterns gave light to the square, where people had gathered for a town meeting. That was convenient. Kaladin dropped toward the lights and held his hand to the side. Syl formed there by unspoken command, taking the shape of a Shardblade: a sleek, beautiful sword with the symbol of the Windrunners prominent on the center, with lines sweeping off it toward the hilt – grooves in the metal that looked like flowing tresses of hair. Though Kaladin preferred a spear, the Blade was a symbol.

Kaladin hit the ground in the center of the village, near its large central cistern, used to catch rainwater and filter away the crem. He rested the Sylblade on his shoulder and stretched out his other hand, preparing his speech. *People of Hornhollow. I am Kaladin, of the Knights Radiant. I have come—*

'Lord Radiant!' A portly lighteyed man stumbled out of the crowd, wearing a long raincloak and a wide-brimmed hat. He looked ridiculous, but it was the Weeping. Constant rain didn't exactly encourage heights of fashion.

The man clapped his hands in an energetic motion, and a pair of ardents stumbled up beside him, bearing goblets full of glowing spheres. Around the perimeter of the square, people hissed and whispered, anticipation-spren flapping in an unseen wind. Several men held up small children to get a better look.

'Great,' Kaladin said softly. 'I've become a menagerie act.'

In his mind, he heard Syl giggle.

Well, best to put on a good show of it. He lifted the Sylblade high overhead, prompting a cheer from the crowd. He would have bet that most of the people in this square used to curse the name of the Radiants, but none of that was manifest now in the people's enthusiasm. It was hard to believe that centuries of mistrust and vilification would be forgotten so quickly. But with the sky breaking and the land in turmoil, people would look to a symbol.

Kaladin lowered his Blade. He knew all too well the danger of symbols. Amaram had been one to him, long ago.

'You knew of my coming,' Kaladin said to the citylord and the ardents. 'You've been in contact with your neighbors. Have they told you what I've been saying?'

'Yes, Brightlord,' the lighteyed man said, gesturing eagerly for him to take the spheres. As he did so – replacing them with spent ones he'd traded for previously – the man's expression fell noticeably.

Expected me to pay two for one as I did at the first few towns, did you? Kaladin thought with amusement. Well, he dropped a few extra dun spheres in. He'd rather be known as generous, particularly if it helped word spread, but he couldn't halve his spheres each time he went through them.

'This is good,' Kaladin said, fishing out a few small gemstones. 'I can't visit every holding in the area. I need you to send messages to each nearby village, carrying words of comfort and command from the king. I will pay for the time of your runners.'

He looked out at the sea of eager faces, and couldn't help but remember a similar day in Hearthstone where he and the rest of the townspeople had waited, eager to catch a glimpse of their new citylord.

'Of course, Brightlord,' the lighteyed man said. 'Would you wish to rest now, and take a meal? Or would you rather visit the location of the attack immediately?'

'*Attack?*' Kaladin said, feeling a spike of alarm.

'Yes, Brightlord,' the portly lighteyes said. 'Isn't that why you're here? To see where the rogue parshmen assaulted us?'

Finally! 'Take me there. *Now.*'

⁖

They'd attacked a grain storage just outside town. Squashed between two hills and shaped like a dome, it had weathered the Everstorm without so much as a loosed stone. That made it a particular shame that the Void-bringers had ripped open the door and pillaged what was inside.

Kaladin knelt within, flipping over a broken hinge. The building smelled of dust and tallew, but was too wet. Townspeople who would suffer a dozen leaks in their bedroom would go to great expense to keep their grain dry.

It felt odd to not have the rain on his head, though he could still hear it pattering outside.

'May I continue, Brightlord?' the ardent asked him. She was young, pretty, and nervous. Obviously she didn't know where he fit into the scheme of her religion. The Knights Radiant had been founded by the Heralds, but they were also traitors. So . . . he was either a divine being of myth or a cretin one step above a Voidbringer.

'Yes, please,' Kaladin said.

'Of the five eyewitnesses,' the ardent said, 'four, um, independently counted the number of attackers at . . . fifty or so? Anyway, it's safe to say that they've got large numbers, considering how many sacks of grain they were able to carry away in such a short time. They, um, didn't look exactly like parshmen. Too tall, and wearing armor. The sketch I made . . . Um . . .'

She tried showing him her sketch again. It wasn't much better than a child's drawing: a bunch of scribbles in vaguely humanoid shapes.

'Anyway,' the young ardent continued, oblivious to the fact that Syl had landed on her shoulder and was inspecting her face. 'They attacked right after first moonset. They had the grain out by middle of second moon, um, and we didn't hear anything until the change of guard happened. Sot raised the alarm, and that chased the creatures off. They only left four sacks, which we moved.'

Kaladin took a crude wooden cudgel off the table next to the ardent. The ardent glanced at him, then quickly looked back to her paper, blushing. The room, lit by oil lamps, was depressingly hollow. This grain should have gotten the village to the next harvest.

To a man from a farming village, nothing was more distressing than an empty silo at planting time.

'The men who were attacked?' Kaladin said, inspecting the cudgel, which the Voidbringers had dropped while fleeing.

'They've both recovered, Brightlord,' the ardent said. 'Though Khem has a ringing in his ear he says won't go away.'

Fifty parshmen in warform – which was what the descriptions sounded most like to him – could easily have overrun this town and its handful of militia guards. They could have slaughtered everyone and taken whatever they wished; instead, they'd made a surgical raid.

'The red lights,' Kaladin said. 'Describe them again.'

The ardent started; she'd been looking at him. 'Um, all five witnesses mentioned the lights, Brightlord. There were several small glowing red lights in the darkness.'

'Their eyes.'

'Maybe?' the ardent said. 'If those were eyes, it was only a few. I went and asked, and none of the witnesses specifically saw eyes glowing – and Khem got a look right in one of the parshmen's faces as they struck him.'

Kaladin dropped the cudgel and dusted off his palms. He took the sheet with the picture on it out of the young ardent's hands and inspected it, just for show, then nodded to her. 'You did well. Thank you for the report.'

She sighed, grinning stupidly.

'Oh!' Syl said, still on the ardent's shoulder. 'She thinks you're pretty!'

Kaladin drew his lips to a line. He nodded to the woman and left her, striking back into the rain toward the center of town.

Syl zipped up to his shoulder. 'Wow. She must be *desperate* living out here. I mean, look at you. Hair that hasn't been combed since you flew across the continent, uniform stained with crem, and that *beard*.'

'Thank you for the boost of confidence.'

'I guess when there's nobody about but farmers, your standards really drop.'

'She's an ardent,' Kaladin said. 'She'd have to marry another ardent.'

'I don't think she was thinking about marriage, Kaladin . . .' Syl said, turning and looking backward over her shoulder. 'I know you've been busy lately fighting guys in white clothing and stuff, but *I've* been doing research. People lock their doors, but there's plenty of room to get in underneath. I figured, since you don't seem inclined to do any learning yourself, I should study. So if you have questions . . .'

'I'm well aware of what is involved.'

'You sure?' Syl asked. 'Maybe we could have that ardent draw you a picture. She seems like she'd be really eager.'

'Syl . . .'

'I just want you to be happy, Kaladin,' she said, zipping off his shoulder and running a few rings around him as a ribbon of light. 'People in relationships are happier.'

'That,' Kaladin said, 'is demonstrably false. Some might be. I know a lot who aren't.'

'Come on,' Syl said. 'What about that Lightweaver? You seemed to like her.'

The words struck uncomfortably close to the truth. 'Shallan is engaged to Dalinar's son.'

'So? You're better than him. I don't trust him one bit.'

'You don't trust anyone who carries a Shardblade, Syl,' Kaladin said with a sigh. 'We've been over this. It's not a mark of bad character to have bonded one of the weapons.'

'Yes, well, let's have someone swing around the corpse of *your* sisters by the feet, and we'll see whether you consider it a "mark of bad character" or not. This is a distraction. Like that Lightweaver could be for you . . .'

'Shallan's a lighteyes,' Kaladin said. 'That's the end of the conversation.'

'But—'

'End,' he said, stepping into the home of the village lighteyes. Then he added under his breath, 'And stop spying on people when they're being intimate. It's creepy.'

The way she spoke, she expected to be *there* when Kaladin . . . Well, he'd never considered that before, though she went with him everywhere else. Could he convince her to wait outside? She'd still listen, if not sneak in to watch. Stormfather. His life just kept getting stranger. He tried – unsuccessfully – to banish the image of lying in bed with a woman, Syl sitting on the headboard and shouting out encouragement and advice. . . .

'Lord Radiant?' the citylord asked from inside the front room of the small home. 'Are you well?'

'Painful memory,' Kaladin said. 'Your scouts are certain of the direction the parshmen went?'

The citylord looked over his shoulder at a scraggly man in leathers, bow on his back, standing by the boarded-up window. Trapper, with a writ from the local highlord to catch mink on his lands. 'Followed them half a day out, Brightlord. They never deviated. Straight toward Kholinar, I'd swear to Kelek himself.'

'Then that's where I'm going as well,' Kaladin said.

'You want me to lead you, Brightlord Radiant?' the trapper asked.

Kaladin drew in Stormlight. 'Afraid you'd just slow me down.' He nodded to the men, then stepped out and Lashed himself upward. People clogged the road and cheered from rooftops as he left the town behind.

⁘

The scents of horses reminded Adolin of his youth. Sweat, and manure, and hay. Good scents. *Real* scents.

He'd spent many of those days, before he was fully a man, on campaign with his father during border skirmishes with Jah Keved. Adolin had been afraid of horses back then, though he'd never have admitted it. So much faster, more intelligent, than chulls.

So alien. Creatures all covered in hair – which made him shiver to touch – with big glassy eyes. And those hadn't even been *real* horses. For all their pedigree breeding, the horses they'd rode on campaign had just been ordinary Shin Thoroughbreds. Expensive, yes. But by definition, therefore, not *priceless.*

Not like the creature before him now.

They were housing the Kholin livestock in the far northwest section of the tower, on the ground floor, near where winds from outside blew along the mountains. Some clever constructions in the hallways by the royal engineers had ventilated the scents away from the inner corridors, though that left the region quite chilly.

Gumfrems and hogs clogged some rooms, while conventional horses stabled in others. Several even contained Bashin's axehounds, animals who never got to go on hunts anymore.

Such accommodations weren't good enough for the Blackthorn's horse. No, the massive black Ryshadium stallion had been given his own field. Large enough to serve as a pasture, it was open to the sky and in an enviable spot, if you discounted the scents of the other animals.

As Adolin emerged from the tower, the black monster of a horse came galloping over. Big enough to carry a Shardbearer without looking small, Ryshadium were often called the 'third Shard.' Blade, Plate, and Mount.

That didn't do them justice. You couldn't earn a Ryshadium simply by defeating someone in combat. They chose their riders.

But, Adolin thought as Gallant nuzzled his hand, *I suppose that was how it used to be with Blades too. They were spren who chose their bearers.*

'Hey,' Adolin said, scratching the Ryshadium's snout with his left hand.

'A little lonely out here, isn't it? I'm sorry about that. Wish you weren't alone any –' He cut off as his voice caught in his throat.

Gallant stepped closer, towering over him, but somehow still gentle. The horse nuzzled Adolin's neck, then blew out sharply.

'Ugh,' Adolin said, turning the horse's head. 'That's a scent I could do without.' He patted Gallant's neck, then reached with his right hand into his shoulder pack – before a sharp pain from his wrist reminded him yet again of his wound. He reached in with the other hand and took out some sugar lumps, which Gallant consumed eagerly.

'You're as bad as Aunt Navani,' Adolin noted. 'That's why you came running, isn't it? You smelled treats.'

The horse turned his head, looking at Adolin with one watery blue eye, rectangular pupil at the center. He almost seemed . . . offended.

Adolin often had felt he could read his own Ryshadium's emotions. There had been a . . . bond between him and Sureblood. More delicate and indefinable than the bond between man and sword, but still there.

Of course, Adolin *was* the one who talked to his sword sometimes, so he had a habit of this sort of thing.

'I'm sorry,' Adolin said. 'I know the two of you liked to run together. And . . . I don't know if Father will be able to get down as much to see you. He'd already been withdrawing from battle before he got all these new responsibilities. I thought I'd stop by once in a while.'

The horse snorted loudly.

'Not to *ride* you,' Adolin said, reading indignation in the Ryshadium's motions. 'I just thought it might be nice for both of us.'

The horse poked his snout at Adolin's satchel until he dug out another sugar cube. It seemed like agreement to Adolin, who fed the horse, then leaned back against the wall and watched him gallop through the pasture.

Showing off, Adolin thought with amusement as Gallant pranced past him. Maybe Gallant would let him brush his coat. That would feel good, like the evenings he'd spent with Sureblood in the dark calm of the stables. At least, that was what he'd done before everything had gotten busy, with Shallan and the duels and everything else.

He'd ignored the horse right up until he'd needed Sureblood in battle. And then, in a flash of light, he was gone.

Adolin took a deep breath. Everything seemed insane these days. Not just Sureblood, but what he'd done to Sadeas, and now the investigation . . .

Watching Gallant seemed to help a little. Adolin was still there, leaning against the wall, when Renarin arrived. The younger Kholin poked his head through the doorway, looking around. He didn't shy away when Gallant galloped past, but he did regard the stallion with wariness.

'Hey,' Adolin said from the side.

'Hey. Bashin said you were down here.'

'Just checking on Gallant,' Adolin said. 'Because Father's been so busy lately.'

Renarin approached. 'You could ask Shallan to draw Sureblood,' Renarin said. 'I bet, um, she'd be able to do a good job. To remember.'

It wasn't a bad suggestion, actually. 'Were you looking for me, then?'

'I . . .' Renarin watched Gallant as the horse pranced by again. 'He's excited.'

'He likes an audience.'

'They don't fit, you know.'

'Don't fit?'

'Ryshadium have stone hooves,' Renarin said, 'stronger than ordinary horses'. Never need to be shod.'

'And that makes them not fit? I'd say that makes them fit better. . . .' Adolin eyed Renarin. 'You mean ordinary horses, don't you?'

Renarin blushed, then nodded. People had trouble following him sometimes, but that was merely because he tended to be so thoughtful. He'd be thinking about something deep, something brilliant, and then would only mention a part. It made him seem erratic, but once you got to know him, you realized he wasn't trying to be esoteric. His lips just sometimes failed to keep up with his brain.

'Adolin,' he said softly. 'I . . . um . . . I have to give you back the Shardblade you won for me.'

'Why?' Adolin said.

'It hurts to hold,' Renarin said. 'It always has, to be honest. I thought it was just me, being strange. But it's all of us.'

'Radiants, you mean.'

He nodded. 'We can't use the dead Blades. It's not right.'

'Well, I suppose I could find someone else to use it,' Adolin said, running through options. 'Though you should really be the one to choose. By right of bestowal, the Blade is yours, and you should pick the successor.'

'I'd rather you do it. I've given it to the ardents already, for safekeeping.'

'Which means you'll be unarmed,' Adolin said.

Renarin glanced away.

'Or not,' Adolin said, then poked Renarin in the shoulder. 'You've got a replacement already, don't you.'

Renarin blushed again.

'You mink!' Adolin said. 'You've managed to create a Radiant Blade? Why didn't you tell us?'

'It just happened. Glys wasn't certain he could do it ... but we need more people to work the Oathgate ... so ...'

He took a deep breath, then stretched his hand to the side and summoned a long glowing Shardblade. Thin, with almost no crossguard, it had waving folds to the metal, like it had been forged.

'Gorgeous,' Adolin said. 'Renarin, it's fantastic!'

'Thanks.'

'So why are you embarrassed?'

'I'm ... not?'

Adolin gave him a flat stare.

Renarin dismissed the Blade. 'I simply ... Adolin, I was starting to *fit in*. With Bridge Four, with being a Shardbearer. Now, I'm in the darkness again. Father expects me to be a Radiant, so I can help him unite the world. But how am I supposed to learn?'

Adolin scratched his chin with his good hand. 'Huh. I assumed that it just kind of came to you. It hasn't?'

'Some has. But it ... frightens me, Adolin.' He held up his hand, and it started to glow, wisps of Stormlight trailing off it, like smoke from a fire. 'What if I hurt someone, or ruin things?'

'You're not going to,' Adolin said. 'Renarin, that's the power of the Almighty himself.'

Renarin only stared at that glowing hand, and didn't seem convinced. So Adolin reached out with his good hand and took Renarin's, holding it.

'This is good,' Adolin said to him. 'You're not going to hurt anyone. You're here to save us.'

Renarin looked to him, then smiled. A pulse of Radiance washed through Adolin, and for an instant he saw himself *perfected*. A version of himself that was somehow complete and whole, the man he could be.

It was gone in a moment, and Renarin pulled his hand free and murmured an apology. He mentioned again the Shardblade needing to be given away, then fled back into the tower.

Adolin stared after him. Gallant trotted up and nudged him for more sugar, so he reached absently into his satchel and fed the horse.

Only after Gallant trotted off did Adolin realize he'd used his right hand. He held it up, amazed, moving his fingers.

His wrist had been completely healed.

II

THE RIFT

THIRTY-THREE YEARS AGO

Dalinar danced from one foot to the other in the morning mist, feeling a new power, an *energy* in every step. Shardplate. His *own* Shardplate.

The world would never be the same place. They'd all expected he would someday have his own Plate or Blade, but he'd never been able to quiet the whisper of uncertainty from the back of his mind. What if it never happened?

But it had. Stormfather, it *had*. He'd won it himself, in combat. Yes, that combat had involved kicking a man off a cliff, but he'd defeated a Shardbearer regardless.

He couldn't help but bask in how grand it felt.

'Calm, Dalinar,' Sadeas said from beside him in the mist. Sadeas wore his own golden Plate. 'Patience.'

'It won't do any good, Sadeas,' Gavilar – clad in bright blue Plate – said from Dalinar's other side. All three of them wore their faceplates up for the moment. 'The Kholin boys are chained axehounds, and we smell blood. We can't go into battle breathing calming breaths, centered and serene, as the ardents teach.'

Dalinar shifted, feeling the cold morning fog on his face. He wanted to dance with the anticipationspren whipping in the air around him. Behind, the army waited in disciplined ranks, their footsteps, clinkings, coughs, and murmured banter rising through the fog.

He almost felt as if he didn't need that army. He wore a massive hammer on his back, so heavy an unaided man – even the strongest of them – wouldn't be able to lift it. He barely noticed the weight. Storms, this *power*. It felt remarkably like the Thrill.

'Have you given thought to my suggestion, Dalinar?' Sadeas asked.

'No.'

Sadeas sighed.

'If Gavilar commands me,' Dalinar said, 'I'll marry.'

'Don't bring me into this,' Gavilar said. He summoned and dismissed his Shardblade repeatedly as they talked.

'Well,' Dalinar said, 'until you say something, I'm staying single.' The only woman he'd ever wanted belonged to Gavilar. They'd married – storms, they had a child now. A little girl.

His brother must never know how Dalinar felt.

'But think of the *benefit,* Dalinar,' Sadeas said. 'Your wedding could bring us alliances, Shards. Perhaps you could win us a princedom – one we wouldn't have to storming drive to the brink of collapse before they join us!'

After two years of fighting, only four of the ten princedoms had accepted Gavilar's rule – and two of those, Kholin and Sadeas, had been easy. The result was a united Alethkar: *against* House Kholin.

Gavilar was convinced that he could play them off one another, that their natural selfishness would lead them to stab one another in the back. Sadeas, in turn, pushed Gavilar toward greater brutality. He claimed that the fiercer their reputation, the more cities would turn to them willingly rather than risk being pillaged.

'Well?' Sadeas asked. 'Will you at least consider a union of political necessity?'

'Storms, you still on that?' Dalinar said. 'Let me fight. You and my brother can worry about politics.'

'You can't escape this forever, Dalinar. You realize that, right? We'll have to worry about feeding the darkeyes, about city infrastructure, about ties with other kingdoms. *Politics.*'

'You and Gavilar,' Dalinar said.

'All of us,' Sadeas said. 'All three.'

'Weren't you trying to get me to relax?' Dalinar snapped. Storms.

The rising sun finally started to disperse the fog, and that let him see their target: a wall about twelve feet high. Beyond that, nothing. A flat rocky expanse, or so it appeared. The chasm city was difficult to spot from this direction. Named Rathalas, it was also known as the Rift: an entire city that had been built inside a rip in the ground.

'Brightlord Tanalan is a Shardbearer, right?' Dalinar asked.

Sadeas sighed, lowering his faceplate. 'We only went over this *four* times, Dalinar.'

'I was drunk. Tanalan. Shardbearer?'

'Blade only, Brother,' Gavilar said.

'He's mine,' Dalinar whispered.

Gavilar laughed. 'Only if you find him first! I've half a mind to give that Blade to Sadeas. At least *he* listens in our meetings.'

'All right,' Sadeas said. 'Let's do this carefully. Remember the plan. Gavilar, you—'

Gavilar gave Dalinar a grin, slammed his faceplate down, then took off running to leave Sadeas midsentence. Dalinar whooped and joined him, Plated boots grinding against stone.

Sadeas cursed loudly, then followed. The army remained behind for the moment.

Rocks started falling; catapults from behind the wall hurled solitary boulders or sprays of smaller rocks. Chunks slammed down around Dalinar, shaking the ground, causing rockbud vines to curl up. A boulder struck just ahead, then bounced, spraying chips of stone. Dalinar skidded past it, the Plate lending a spring to his motion. He raised his arm before his eye slit as a hail of arrows darkened the sky.

'Watch the ballistas!' Gavilar shouted.

Atop the wall, soldiers aimed massive crossbowlike devices mounted to the stone. One sleek bolt – the size of a spear – launched directly at Dalinar, and it proved far more accurate than the catapults. He threw himself to the side, Plate grinding on stone as he slid out of the way. The bolt hit the ground with such force that the wood shattered.

Other shafts trailed netting and ropes, hoping to trip a Shardbearer and render him prone for a second shot. Dalinar grinned, feeling the Thrill awaken within him, and recovered his feet. He leaped over a bolt trailing netting.

Tanalan's men delivered a storm of wood and stone, but it wasn't nearly enough. Dalinar took a stone in the shoulder and lurched, but quickly regained his momentum. Arrows were useless against him, the boulders too random, and the ballistas too slow to reload.

This was how it should be. Dalinar, Gavilar, Sadeas. Together. Other responsibilities didn't matter. Life was about the *fight*. A good battle in the day – then at night, a warm hearth, tired muscles, and a good vintage of wine.

Dalinar reached the squat wall and *leaped*, propelling himself in a mighty jump. He gained just enough height to grab one of the crenels of the wall's top. Men raised hammers to pound his fingers, but he hurled himself over the lip and onto the wall walk, crashing down amid panicked defenders. He jerked the release rope on his hammer – dropping it on an enemy behind – then swung out with his fist, sending men broken and screaming.

This was almost too easy! He seized his hammer, then brought it up and swung it in a wide arc, tossing men from the wall like leaves before a gust of wind. Just beyond him, Sadeas kicked over a ballista, destroying the device with a casual blow. Gavilar attacked with his Blade, dropping corpses by the handful, their eyes burning. Up here, the fortification worked against the defenders, leaving them cramped and clumped up – perfect for Shardbearers to destroy.

Dalinar surged through them, and in a few moments likely killed more men than he had in his entire life. At that, he felt a surprising yet profound dissatisfaction. This was not about his skill, his momentum, or even his reputation. You could have replaced him with a toothless gaffer and produced practically the same result.

He gritted his teeth against that sudden useless emotion. He dug deeply within, and found the Thrill waiting. It filled him, driving away dissatisfaction. Within moments he was roaring his pleasure. Nothing these men did could touch him. He was a destroyer, a conqueror, a glorious maelstrom of death. A *god*.

Sadeas was saying something. The silly man gestured in his golden Shardplate. Dalinar blinked, looking out over the wall. He could see the Rift proper from this vantage, a deep chasm in the ground that hid an entire city, built up the sides of either cliff.

'Catapults, Dalinar!' Sadeas said. 'Bring down those catapults!'

Right. Gavilar's armies had started to charge the walls. Those catapults

– near the way down into the Rift proper – were still launching stones, and would drop hundreds of men.

Dalinar leaped for the edge of the wall and grabbed a rope ladder to swing down. The ropes, of course, immediately snapped, sending him toppling to the ground. He struck with a crash of Plate on stone. It didn't hurt, but his pride took a serious blow. Above, Sadeas looked at him over the edge. Dalinar could practically hear his voice.

Always rushing into things. Take some time to think once in a while, won't you?

That had been a flat-out greenvine mistake. Dalinar growled and climbed to his feet, searching for his hammer. Storms! He'd bent the handle in his fall. How had he done *that*? It wasn't made of the same strange metal as Blades and Plate, but it was still good steel.

Soldiers guarding the catapults swarmed toward him while the shadows of boulders passed overhead. Dalinar set his jaw, the Thrill saturating him, and reached for a stout wooden door set into the wall nearby. He ripped it free, the hinges popping, and stumbled. It came off more easily than he'd expected.

There was more to this armor than he'd ever imagined. Maybe he wasn't any better with the Plate than some old gaffer, but he would change that. At that moment, he determined that he'd never be surprised again. He'd wear this Plate morning and night – he'd *sleep* in the storming stuff – until he was more comfortable in it than out.

He raised the wooden door and swung it like a bludgeon, sweeping soldiers away and opening a path to the catapults. Then he dashed forward and grabbed the side of one catapult. He ripped its wheel off, splintering wood and sending the machine teetering. He stepped onto it, grabbing the catapult's arm and breaking it free.

Only ten more to go. He stood atop the wrecked machine when he heard a distant voice call his name. 'Dalinar!'

He looked toward the wall, where Sadeas reached back and heaved his Shardbearer's hammer. It spun in the air before slamming into the catapult next to Dalinar, wedging itself into the broken wood.

Sadeas raised a hand in salute, and Dalinar waved back in gratitude, then grabbed the hammer. The destruction went a lot faster after that. He pounded the machines, leaving behind shattered wood. Engineers – many of them women – scrambled away, screaming, 'Blackthorn, Blackthorn!'

By the time he neared the last catapult, Gavilar had secured the gates and opened them to his soldiers. A flood of men entered, joining those who had scaled the walls. The last of the enemies near Dalinar fled down into the city, leaving him alone. He grunted and kicked the final broken catapult, sending it rolling backward across the stone toward the edge of the Rift.

It tipped, then fell over. Dalinar stepped forward, walking onto a kind of observation post, a section of rock with a railing to prevent people from slipping over the side. From this vantage, he got his first good look down at the city.

'The Rift' was a fitting name. To his right, the chasm narrowed, but here at the middle he'd have been hard-pressed to throw a stone across to the other side, even with Shardplate. And within it, there was life. Gardens bobbing with lifespren. Buildings built practically on top of one another down the V-shaped cliff sides. The place teemed with a network of stilts, bridges, and wooden walkways.

Dalinar turned and looked back at the wall that ran in a wide circle around the opening of the Rift on all sides except the west, where the canyon continued until it opened up below at the shores of the lake.

To survive in Alethkar, you had to find shelter from the storms. A wide cleft like this one was perfect for a city. But how did you protect it? Any attacking enemy would have the high ground. Many cities walked a risky line between security from storms and security from men.

Dalinar shouldered Sadeas's hammer as groups of Tanalan's soldiers flooded down from the walls, forming up to flank Gavilar's army on both right and left. They'd try to press against the Kholin troops from both sides, but with three Shardbearers to face, they were in trouble. Where was Highlord Tanalan himself?

Behind, Thakka approached with a small squad of elites, joining Dalinar on the stone viewing platform. Thakka put his hands on the railing, whistling softly.

'Something's going on with this city,' Dalinar said.

'What?'

'I don't know. . . .' Dalinar might not pay attention to the grand plans Gavilar and Sadeas made, but he was a soldier. He knew battlefields like a woman knew her mother's recipes: he might not be able to give you measurements, but he could taste when something was off.

The fighting continued behind him, Kholin soldiers clashing with Tanalan's defenders. Tanalan's armies didn't fare well; demoralized by the advancing Kholin army, the enemy ranks quickly broke and scrambled into a retreat, clogging the ramps down into the city. Gavilar and Sadeas didn't give chase; they had the high ground now. No need to rush into a potential ambush.

Gavilar clomped across the stone, Sadeas beside him. They'd want to survey the city and rain arrows upon those below – maybe even use stolen catapults, if Dalinar had left any functional. They'd siege this place until it broke.

Three Shardbearers, Dalinar thought. *Tanalan has to be planning to deal with us somehow. . . .*

This viewing platform was the best vantage for looking into the city. And they'd situated the catapults right next to it – machines that the Shardbearers were certain to attack and disable. Dalinar glanced to the sides, and saw cracks in the stone floor of the viewing platform.

'No!' Dalinar shouted to Gavilar. 'Stay back! It's a—'

The enemy must have been watching, for the moment he shouted, the ground fell out from beneath him. Dalinar caught a glimpse of Gavilar – held back by Sadeas – looking on in horror as Dalinar, Thakka, and a handful of other elites were toppled into the Rift.

Storms. The entire section of stone where they'd been standing – the lip hanging out over the Rift – had broken free! As the large section of rock tumbled down into the first buildings, Dalinar was flung into the air above the city. Everything spun around him.

A moment later, he crashed into a building with an awful *crunch*. Something hard hit his arm, an impact so powerful he heard his armor there shatter.

The building failed to stop him. He tore right through the wood and continued, helm grinding against stone as he somehow came in contact with the side of the Rift.

He hit another surface with a loud crunch, and blessedly here he finally stopped. He groaned, feeling a sharp pain from his left hand. He shook his head, and found himself staring upward some fifty feet through a shattered section of the near-vertical wooden city. The large section of falling rock had torn a swath through the city along the steep incline, smashing homes and walkways. Dalinar had been flung just to the north, and had eventually come to rest on the wooden roof of a building.

He didn't see signs of his men. Thakka, the other elites. But without Shardplate . . . He growled, angerspren boiling around him like pools of blood. He shifted on the rooftop, but the pain in his hand made him wince. His armor all down his left arm had shattered, and in falling he appeared to have broken a few fingers.

His Shardplate leaked glowing white smoke from a hundred fractures, but the only pieces he'd lost completely were from his left arm and hand.

He gingerly pried himself from the rooftop, but as he shifted, he broke through and fell into the home. He grunted as he hit, members of a family screaming and pulling back against the wall. Tanalan apparently hadn't told the people of his plan to crush a section of his own city in a desperate attempt to deal with the enemy Shardbearers.

Dalinar got to his feet, ignoring the cowering people, and shoved open the door – breaking it with the strength of his push – and stepped out onto a wooden walkway that ran before the homes on this tier of the city.

A hail of arrows immediately fell on him. He turned his right shoulder toward them, growling, shielding his eye slit as best he could while he inspected the source of the attack. Fifty archers were set up on a garden platform on the other storming side of the Rift from him. Wonderful.

He recognized the man leading the archers. Tall, with an imperious bearing and stark white plumes on his helm. Who put chicken feathers on their helms? Looked ridiculous. Well, Tanalan was a fine enough fellow. Dalinar had beat him once at pawns, and Tanalan had paid the bet with a hundred glowing bits of ruby, each dropped into a corked bottle of wine. Dalinar had always found that amusing.

Reveling in the Thrill, which rose in him and drove away pain, Dalinar charged along the walkway, ignoring arrows. Above, Sadeas was leading a force down one of the ramps outside the path of the rockfall, but it would be slow going. By the time they arrived, Dalinar intended to have a new Shardblade.

He charged onto one of the bridges that crossed the Rift. Unfortunately, he knew exactly what *he* would do if preparing this city for an assault. Sure enough, a pair of soldiers hurried down the other side of the Rift, then used axes to attack the support posts to Dalinar's bridge. It had Soulcast metal ropes holding it up, but if they could get those posts down – dropping the lines – his weight would surely cause the entire thing to fall.

The bottom wash of the Rift was easily another hundred feet below. Growling, Dalinar made the only choice he could. He threw himself over the side of his walkway, dropping a short distance to one below. It looked sturdy enough. Even so, one foot smashed through the wooden planks, nearly followed by his entire body.

He heaved himself up and continued running across. Two more soldiers reached the posts holding up this bridge, and they began frantically hacking away.

The walkway shook beneath Dalinar's feet. Stormfather. He didn't have much time, but there were no more walkways within jumping distance. Dalinar pushed himself to a run, roaring, his footfalls cracking boards.

A single black arrow fell from above, swooping like a skyeel. It dropped one of the soldiers. Another arrow followed, hitting the second soldier even as he gawked at his fallen ally. The walkway stopped shaking, and Dalinar grinned, pulling to a stop. He turned, spotting a man standing near the sheared-off section of stone above. He lifted a black bow toward Dalinar.

'Teleb, you storming miracle,' Dalinar said.

He reached the other side and plucked an axe from the hands of a dead man. Then he charged up a ramp toward where he'd seen Highlord Tanalan.

He found the place easily, a wide wooden platform built on struts connected to parts of the wall below, and draped with vines and blooming rockbuds. Lifespren scattered as Dalinar reached it.

Centered in the garden, Tanalan waited with a force of some fifty soldiers. Puffing inside his helm, Dalinar stepped up to confront them. Tanalan was armored in simple steel, no Shardplate, though a brutal-looking Shardblade – wide, with a hooked tip – appeared in his grasp.

Tanalan barked for his soldiers to stand back and lower their bows. Then he strode toward Dalinar, holding the Shardblade with both hands.

Everyone always fixated upon Shardblades. Specific weapons had lore dedicated to them, and people traced which kings or brightlords had carried which sword. Well, Dalinar had used both Blade and Plate, and if given the choice of one, he'd pick Plate every time. All he needed to do was get in one solid hit on Tanalan, and the fight would be over. The highlord, however, had to contend with a foe who could resist his blows.

The Thrill thrummed inside Dalinar. Standing between two squat trees, he set his stance, keeping his exposed left arm pointed away from the highlord while gripping the axe in his gauntleted right hand. Though it was a war axe, it felt like a child's plaything.

'You should not have come here, Dalinar,' Tanalan said. His voice bore a distinctively nasal accent common to this region. The Rifters always had considered themselves a people apart. 'We had no quarrel with you or yours.'

'You refused to submit to the king,' Dalinar said, armor plates clinking as he rounded the highlord while trying to keep an eye on the soldiers. He wouldn't put it past them to attack him once he was distracted by the duel. It was what he himself would have done.

'The king?' Tanalan demanded, angerspren boiling up around him. 'There hasn't been a throne in Alethkar for generations. Even if we *were* to have a king again, who is to say the Kholins deserve the mantle?'

'The way I see it,' Dalinar said, 'the people of Alethkar deserve a king who is the strongest and most capable of leading them in battle. If only there were a way to prove that.' He grinned inside his helm.

Tanalan attacked, sweeping in with his Shardblade and trying to leverage his superior reach. Dalinar danced back, waiting for his moment. The Thrill was a heady rush, a lust to prove himself.

But he needed to be cautious. Ideally Dalinar would prolong this fight, relying on his Plate's superior strength and the stamina it provided. Unfortunately, that Plate was still leaking, and he had all these guards to deal with. Still, he tried to play it as Tanalan would expect, dodging attacks, acting as if he were going to drag out the fight.

Tanalan growled and came in again. Dalinar blocked the blow with his arm, then made a perfunctory swing with his axe. Tanalan dodged back easily. Stormfather, that Blade was long. Almost as tall as Dalinar was.

Dalinar maneuvered, brushing against the foliage of the garden. He couldn't even feel the pain of his broken fingers anymore. The Thrill called to him.

Wait. Act like you're drawing this out as long as possible. . . .

Tanalan advanced again, and Dalinar dodged backward, faster because of his Plate. And then when Tanalan tried his next strike, Dalinar ducked *toward him.*

He deflected the Shardblade with his arm again, but this blow hit hard, shattering the arm plate. Still, Dalinar's surprise rush let him lower his shoulder and slam it against Tanalan. The highlord's armor *clanged,* bending before the force of the Shardplate, and the highlord tripped.

Unfortunately, Dalinar was off balance just enough from his rush to fall alongside the highlord. The platform shook as they hit the ground, the wood cracking and groaning. Damnation! Dalinar had *not* wanted to go to the ground while surrounded by foes. Still, he had to stay inside the reach of that Blade.

Dalinar dropped off his right gauntlet – without the arm piece connecting it to the rest of the armor, it was dead weight – as the two of them twisted in a heap. He'd lost the axe, unfortunately. The highlord battered against Dalinar with the pommel of his sword, to no effect. But with one hand broken and the other lacking the power of Plate, Dalinar couldn't get a good hold on his foe.

Dalinar rolled, finally positioning himself above Tanalan, where the weight of the Shardplate would keep his foe pinned. At that moment though, the other soldiers attacked. Just as he'd expected. Honorable duels like this – on a battlefield at least – always lasted only until your lighteyes was losing.

Dalinar rolled free. The soldiers obviously weren't ready for how quickly he responded. He got to his feet and scooped up his axe, then lashed out. His right arm still had the pauldron down to the elbow brace, so when he swung, he had *power* – a strange mix of Shard-enhanced strength and frailty from his exposed arms. He had to be careful not to snap his own wrist.

He dropped three men with a flurry of axe slices. The others backed away, blocking him with polearms as their fellows helped Tanalan to his feet.

'You speak of the people,' Tanalan said hoarsely, gauntleted hand feeling at his chest where the cuirass had been bent significantly by Dalinar's rush. He seemed to be having trouble breathing. 'As if this were about *them.* As if it were for their good that you loot, you pillage, you *murder.* You're an uncivilized brute.'

'You can't civilize war,' Dalinar said. 'There's no painting it up and making it pretty.'

'You don't have to pull sorrow behind you like a sledge on the stones, scraping and crushing those you pass. You're a *monster*.'

'I'm a soldier,' Dalinar said, eyeing Tanalan's men, many of whom were preparing their bows.

Tanalan coughed. 'My city is lost. My plan has failed. But I can do Alethkar one last service. I can take you down, you bastard.'

The archers started to loose.

Dalinar roared and threw himself to the ground, hitting the platform with the weight of Shardplate. The wood cracked around him, weakened by the fighting earlier, and he broke through it, shattering struts underneath.

The entire platform came crashing down around him, and together they fell toward the tier below. Dalinar heard screams, and he hit the next walkway hard enough to daze him, even with Shardplate.

Dalinar shook his head, groaning, and found his helm cracked right down the front, the uncommon vision granted by the armor spoiled. He pulled the helm free with one hand and gasped for breath. Storms, his good arm hurt too. He glanced at it and found splinters piercing his skin, including one chunk as long as a dagger.

He grimaced. Below, the few remaining soldiers who had been positioned to cut down bridges came charging up toward him.

Steady, Dalinar. Be ready!

He got to his feet, dazed, exhausted, but the two soldiers didn't come for him. They huddled around Tanalan's body where it had fallen from the platform above. The soldiers grabbed him, then fled.

Dalinar roared and awkwardly gave pursuit. His Plate moved slowly, and he stumbled through the wreckage of the fallen platform, trying to keep up with the soldiers.

The pain from his arms made him mad with rage. But the Thrill, the *Thrill* drove him forward. He would not be beaten. He would not stop! Tanalan's Shardblade had not appeared beside his body. That meant his foe still lived. Dalinar had *not yet won*.

Fortunately, most of the soldiers had been positioned to fight on the other side of the city. This side was practically empty, save for huddled townspeople – he caught glimpses of them hiding in their homes.

Dalinar limped up ramps along the side of the Rift, following the men dragging their brightlord. Near the top, the two soldiers set their burden down beside an exposed portion of the chasm's rock wall. They did something that caused a portion of that wall to open inward, revealing a hidden door. They towed their fallen brightlord into it, and two other soldiers – responding to their frantic calls – rushed out to meet Dalinar, who arrived moments later.

Helmless, Dalinar saw red as he engaged them. They bore weapons; he did not. They were fresh, and he had wounds nearly incapacitating both arms.

The fight still ended with the two soldiers on the ground, broken and bleeding. Dalinar kicked open the hidden door, Plated legs functioning enough to smash it down.

He lurched into a small tunnel with diamond spheres glowing on the walls. That door was covered in hardened crem on the outside, making it seem like a part of the wall. If he hadn't seen them enter, it would have taken days, maybe weeks to locate this place.

At the end of a short walk, he found the two soldiers he'd followed. Judging by the blood trail, they'd deposited their brightlord in the closed room behind them.

They rushed Dalinar with the fatalistic determination of men who knew they were probably dead. The pain in Dalinar's arms and head seemed nothing before the Thrill. He had rarely felt it so strong as he did now, a beautiful clarity, such a *wonderful* emotion.

He ducked forward, supernaturally quick, and used his shoulder to crush one soldier against the wall. The other fell to a well-placed kick, then Dalinar burst through the door beyond them.

Tanalan lay on the ground here, blood surrounding him. A beautiful woman was draped across him, weeping. Only one other person was in the small chamber: a young boy. Six, perhaps seven. Tears streaked the child's face, and he struggled to lift his father's Shardblade in two hands.

Dalinar loomed in the doorway.

'You can't have my daddy,' the boy said, words distorted by his sorrow. Painspren crawled around the floor. 'You *can't*. You . . . you . . .' His voice fell to a whisper. 'Daddy said . . . we fight monsters. And with faith, we will win. . . .'

⁜

A few hours later, Dalinar sat on the edge of the Rift, his legs swinging over the broken city below. His new Shardblade rested across his lap, his Plate – deformed and broken – in a heap beside him. His arms were bandaged, but he'd chased away the surgeons.

He stared out at what seemed an empty plain, then flicked his eyes toward the signs of human life below. Dead bodies in heaps. Broken buildings. Splinters of civilization.

Gavilar eventually walked up, trailed by two bodyguards from Dalinar's elites, Kadash and Febin today. Gavilar waved them back, then groaned as he settled down beside Dalinar, removing his helm. Exhaustionspren spun overhead, though – despite his fatigue – Gavilar looked thoughtful. With those keen, pale green eyes, he'd always seemed to know so much. Growing up, Dalinar had simply assumed that his brother would always be right in whatever he said or did. Aging hadn't much changed his opinion of the man.

'Congratulations,' Gavilar said, nodding toward the Blade. 'Sadeas is irate it wasn't his.'

'He'll find one of his own eventually,' Dalinar said. 'He's too ambitious for me to believe otherwise.'

Gavilar grunted. 'This attack nearly cost us too much. Sadeas is saying we need to be more careful, not risk ourselves and our Shards in solitary assaults.'

'Sadeas is smart,' Dalinar said. He reached gingerly with his right hand, the less mangled one, and raised a mug of wine to his lips. It was the only drug he cared about for the pain – and maybe it would help with the shame too. Both feelings seemed stark, now that the Thrill had receded and left him deflated.

'What do we do with them, Dalinar?' Gavilar asked, waving down toward the crowds of civilians the soldiers were rounding up. 'Tens of thousands of people. They won't be cowed easily; they won't like that you killed their highlord *and* his heir. Those people will resist us for years. I can feel it.'

Dalinar took a drink. 'Make soldiers of them,' he said. 'Tell them we'll spare their families if they fight for us. You want to stop doing a Shardbearer rush at the start of battles? Sounds like we'll need some expendable troops.'

Gavilar nodded, considering. 'Sadeas is right about other things too, you know. About us. And what we're going to have to become.'

'Don't talk to me about that.'

'Dalinar ...'

'I lost half my elites today, my captain included. I've got enough problems.'

'Why are we here, fighting? Is it for honor? Is it for Alethkar?'

Dalinar shrugged.

'We can't just keep acting like a bunch of thugs,' Gavilar said. 'We can't rob every city we pass, feast every night. We need discipline; we need to hold the land we have. We need bureaucracy, order, laws, *politics*.'

Dalinar closed his eyes, distracted by the shame he felt. What if Gavilar found out?

'We're going to have to grow up,' Gavilar said softly.

'And become soft? Like these highlords we kill? *That's* why we started, isn't it? Because they were all lazy, fat, corrupt?'

'I don't know anymore. I'm a father now, Dalinar. That makes me wonder about what we do once we have it all. How do we make a kingdom of this place?'

Storms. A kingdom. For the first time in his life, Dalinar found that idea horrifying.

Gavilar eventually stood up, responding to some messengers who were calling for him. 'Could you,' he said to Dalinar, 'at least try to be a *little* less foolhardy in future battles?'

'This coming from you?'

'A thoughtful me,' Gavilar said. 'An ... exhausted me. Enjoy Oathbringer. You earned it.'

'Oathbringer?'

'Your sword,' Gavilar said. 'Storms, didn't you listen to *anything* last night? That's Sunmaker's old sword.'

Sadees, the Sunmaker. He had been the last man to unite Alethkar, centuries ago. Dalinar shifted the Blade in his lap, letting the light play off the pristine metal.

'It's yours now,' Gavilar said. 'By the time we're done, I'll have it so that nobody even thinks of Sunmaker anymore. Just House Kholin and Alethkar.'

He walked away. Dalinar rammed the Shardblade into the stone and leaned back, closing his eyes again and remembering the sound of a brave boy crying.

I ask not that you forgive me. Nor that you even understand.

—From *Oathbringer*, preface

Dalinar stood beside the glass windows in an upper-floor room of Urithiru, hands clasped behind his back. He could see his reflection hinted in the window, and beyond it vast openness. The sky cloud-free, the sun burning white.

Windows as tall as he was – he'd never seen anything like them. Who would dare build something of glass, so brittle, and face it *toward* the storms? But of course, this city was above the storms. These windows seemed a mark of defiance, a symbol of what the Radiants had meant. They had stood above the pettiness of world politics. And because of that height, they could see so far. . . .

You idealize them, said a distant voice in his head, like rumbling thunder. *They were men like you. No better. No worse.*

'I find that encouraging,' Dalinar whispered back. 'If they were like us, then it means we can be like them.'

They eventually betrayed us. Do not forget that.

'Why?' Dalinar asked. 'What happened? What changed them?'

The Stormfather fell silent.

'Please,' Dalinar said. 'Tell me.'

Some things are better left forgotten, the voice said to him. *You of all men should understand this, considering the hole in your mind and the person who once filled it.*

Dalinar drew in a sharp breath, stung by the words.

'Brightlord,' Brightness Kalami said from behind. 'The emperor is ready for you.'

Dalinar turned. Urithiru's upper levels held several unique rooms, including this amphitheater. Shaped like a half-moon, the room had windows at the top – the straight side – then rows of seats leading down to a speaking floor below. Curiously, each seat had a small pedestal beside it. For the Radiant's spren, the Stormfather told him.

Dalinar started down the steps toward his team: Aladar and his daughter, May. Navani, wearing a bright green havah, sitting in the front row with feet stretched out before her, shoes off and ankles crossed. Elderly Kalami to write, and Teshav Khal – one of Alethkar's finest political minds – to advise. Her two senior wards sat beside her, ready to provide research or translation if needed.

A small group, prepared to change the world.

'Send my greetings to the emperor,' Dalinar instructed.

Kalami nodded, writing. Then she cleared her throat, reading the response that the spanreed – writing as if on its own – relayed. 'You are greeted by His Imperial Majesty Ch.V.D. Yanagawn the First, Emperor of Makabak, King of Azir, Lord of the Bronze Palace, Prime Aqasix, grand minister and emissary of Yaezir.'

'An imposing title,' Navani noted, 'for a fifteen-year-old boy.'

'He supposedly raised a child from the dead,' Teshav said, 'a miracle that gained him the support of the viziers. Local word is that they had trouble finding a new Prime after the last two were murdered by our old friend the Assassin in White. So the viziers picked a boy with questionable lineage and made up a story about him saving someone's life in order to demonstrate a divine mandate.'

Dalinar grunted. 'Making things up doesn't sound very Azish.'

'They're fine with it,' Navani said, 'as long as you can find witnesses willing to fill out affidavits. Kalami, thank His Imperial Majesty for meeting with us, and his translators for their efforts.'

Kalami wrote, and then she looked up at Dalinar, who began to pace the center of the room. Navani stood to join him, eschewing her shoes, walking in socks.

'Your Imperial Majesty,' Dalinar said, 'I speak to you from the top of Urithiru, city of legend. The sights are breathtaking. I invite you to visit me here and tour the city. You are welcome to bring any guards or retinue you see fit.'

He looked to Navani, and she nodded. They'd discussed long how to approach the monarchs, and had settled on a soft invitation. Azir was first, the most powerful country in the west and home to what would be the most central and important of the Oathgates to secure.

The response took time. The Azish government was a kind of beautiful mess, though Gavilar had often admired it. Layers of clerics filled all levels – where both men and women wrote. Scions were kind of like ardents, though they weren't slaves, which Dalinar found odd. In Azir, being a priest-minister in the government was the highest honor to which one could aspire.

Traditionally, the Azish Prime claimed to be emperor of all Makabak – a region that included over a half-dozen kingdoms and princedoms. In reality, he was king over only Azir, but Azir did cast a long, long shadow.

As they waited, Dalinar stepped up beside Navani, resting his fingers on one of her shoulders, then drew them across her back, the nape of her neck, and let them linger on the other shoulder.

Who would have thought a man his age could feel so giddy?

'"Your Highness,"' the reply finally came, Kalami reading the words. '"We thank you for your warning about the storm that blew from the wrong direction. Your timely words have been noted and recorded in the official annals of the empire, recognizing you as a friend to Azir."'

Kalami waited for more, but the spanreed stopped moving. Then the ruby flashed, indicating that they were done.

'That wasn't much of a response,' Aladar said. 'Why didn't he reply to your invitation, Dalinar?'

'Being noted in their official records is a great honor to the Azish,' Teshav said, 'so they've paid you a compliment.'

'Yes,' Navani said, 'but they are trying to dodge the offer we made. Press them, Dalinar.'

'Kalami, please send the following,' Dalinar said. 'I am honored, though I wish my inclusion in your annals could have been due to happier circumstances. Let us discuss the future of Roshar together, here. I am eager to make your personal acquaintance.'

They waited as patiently as they could for a response. It finally came, in Alethi. ' "We of the Azish crown are saddened to share mourning for the fallen with you. As your noble brother was killed by the Shin destroyer, so were beloved members of our court. This creates a bond between us." '

That was all.

Navani clicked her tongue. 'They're not going to be pushed into an answer.'

'They could at least explain themselves!' Dalinar snapped. 'It feels like we're having two different conversations!'

'The Azish,' Teshav said, 'do not like to give offense. They're almost as bad as the Emuli in that regard, particularly with foreigners.'

It wasn't only an Azish attribute, in Dalinar's estimation. It was the way of politicians worldwide. Already this conversation was starting to feel like his efforts to bring the highprinces to his side, back in the warcamps. Half answer after half answer, mild promises with no bite to them, laughing eyes that mocked him even while they pretended to be perfectly sincere.

Storms. Here he was again. Trying to unite people who didn't want to listen to him. He couldn't afford to be bad at this, not any longer.

There was a time, he thought, *when I united in a different way.* He smelled smoke, heard men screaming in pain. Remembered bringing blood and ash to those who defied his brother.

Those memories had become particularly vivid lately.

'Another tactic maybe?' Navani suggested. 'Instead of an invitation, try an offer of aid.'

'Your Imperial Majesty,' Dalinar said. 'War is coming; surely you have seen the changes in the parshmen. The Voidbringers have returned. I would have you know that the Alethi are your allies in this conflict. We would share information regarding our successes and failures in resisting this enemy, with hope that you will report the same to us. Mankind must be unified in the face of the mounting threat.'

The reply eventually came: ' "We agree that aiding one another in this new age will be of the utmost importance. We are glad to exchange information. What do you know of these transformed parshmen?" '

'We engaged them on the Shattered Plains,' Dalinar said, relieved to make some kind of headway. 'Creatures with red eyes, and similar in many ways to the parshmen we found on the Shattered Plains – only more dangerous. I will have my scribes prepare reports for you detailing all we have learned in fighting the Parshendi over the years.'

' "Excellent," ' the reply finally came. ' "This information will be extremely welcome in our current conflict." '

'What is the status of your cities?' Dalinar asked. 'What have the parshmen been doing there? Do they seem to have a goal beyond wanton destruction?'

Tensely, they waited for word. So far they'd been able to discover blessed little about the parshmen the world over. Captain Kaladin sent reports using scribes from towns he visited, but knew next to nothing. Cities were in chaos, and reliable information scarce.

' "Fortunately," ' came the reply, ' "our city stands, and the enemy is not actively attacking any longer. We are negotiating with the hostiles." '

'Negotiating?' Dalinar said, shocked. He turned to Teshav, who shook her head in wonder.

'Please clarify, Your Majesty,' Navani said. 'The Voidbringers are willing to *negotiate* with you?'

' "Yes," ' came the reply. ' "We are exchanging contracts. They have very detailed demands, with outrageous stipulations. We hope that we can forestall armed conflict in order to gather ourselves and fortify the city." '

'They can write?' Navani pressed. 'The Voidbringers themselves are sending you *contracts*?'

' "The average parshman cannot write, so far as we can tell," ' the reply came. ' "But some are different – stronger, with strange powers. They do not speak like the others." '

'Your Majesty,' Dalinar said, stepping up to the spanreed writing table, speaking more urgently – as if the emperor and his ministers could hear his passion through the written word. 'I need to talk to you directly. I can come myself, through the portal we wrote of earlier. We must get it working again.'

Silence. It stretched so long that Dalinar found himself grinding his teeth, itching to summon a Shardblade and dismiss it, over and over, as had been his habit as a youth. He'd picked it up from his brother.

A response finally came. ' "We regret to inform you that the device you mention," ' Kalami read, ' "is not functional in our city. We have investigated it, and have found that it was destroyed long ago. We cannot come to you, nor you to us. Many apologies."'

'He's telling us this now?' Dalinar said. 'Storms! That's information we could have used as soon as he learned it!'

'It's a lie,' Navani said. 'The Oathgate on the Shattered Plains functioned after centuries of storms and crem buildup. The one in Azimir is a monument in the Grand Market, a large dome in the center of the city.'

Or so she'd determined from maps. The one in Kholinar had been incorporated into the palace structure, while the one in Thaylen City was some kind of religious monument. A beautiful relic like this wouldn't simply be destroyed.

'I agree with Brightness Navani's assessment,' Teshav said. 'They are worried about the idea of you or your armies visiting. This is an excuse.' She frowned, as if the emperor and his ministers were little more than spoiled children disobeying their tutors.

The spanreed started writing again.

'What does it say?' Dalinar said, anxious.

'It's an affidavit,' Navani said, amused. 'That the Oathgate is not functional, signed by imperial architects and stormwardens.' She read further. 'Oh, this is delightful. Only the Azish would assume you'd want *certification* that something is broken.'

'Notably,' Kalami added, 'it only certifies that the device "does not function as a portal." But of course it would not, not unless a Radiant were to visit and work it. This affidavit basically says that when turned off, the device doesn't work.'

'Write this, Kalami,' Dalinar said. 'Your Majesty. You ignored me once. Destruction caused by the Everstorm was the result. Please, this time listen. You cannot negotiate with the Voidbringers. We *must* unify, share information, and protect Roshar. Together.'

She wrote it and Dalinar waited, hands pressed against the table.

' "We misspoke when we mentioned negotiations," ' Kalami read. ' "It was a mistake of translation. We agree to share information, but time is short right now. We will contact you again to further discuss. Farewell, Highprince Kholin." '

'Bah!' Dalinar said, pushing himself back from the table. 'Fools, idiots! Storming lighteyes and *Damnation's* own politics!' He stalked across the room, wishing he had something to kick, before forcing his temper under control.

'That's more of a stonewall than I expected,' Navani said, folding her arms. 'Brightness Khal?'

'In my experiences with the Azish,' Teshav said, 'they are extremely proficient at saying very little in as many words as possible. This is not an unusual example of communication with their upper ministers. Don't be put off; it will take time to accomplish anything with them.'

'Time during which Roshar burns,' Dalinar said. 'Why did they pull back regarding their claim to have had negotiations with the Voidbringers? Are they thinking of allying themselves to the enemy?'

'I hesitate to guess,' Teshav said. 'But I would say that they simply decided they'd given away more information than intended.'

'We *need* Azir,' Dalinar said. 'Nobody in Makabak will listen to us unless we have Azir's blessing, not to mention that Oathgate. . . .' He trailed off as a different spanreed on the table started blinking.

'It's the Thaylens,' Kalami said. 'They're early.'

'You want to reschedule?' Navani asked.

Dalinar shook his head. 'No, we can't afford to wait another few days before the queen can spare time again.' He took a deep breath. Storms, talking to politicians was more exhausting than a hundred-mile march in full armor. 'Proceed, Kalami. I'll contain my frustration.'

Navani settled down on one of the seats, though Dalinar remained standing. Light poured in through the windows, pure and bright. It flowed down, bathing him. He breathed in, almost feeling as if he could taste the sunlight. He'd spent too many days inside the twisting stone corridors of Urithiru, lit by the frail light of candles and lamps.

' "Her Royal Highness,"' Kalami read, ' "Brightness Fen Rnamdi, queen of Thaylenah, writes to you."' Kalami paused. 'Brightlord . . . pardon the interruption, but that indicates that the queen holds the spanreed herself rather than using a scribe.'

To another woman, that would have been intimidating. To Kalami, it was merely one of many footnotes – which she added copiously to the bottom of the page before preparing the reed to relay Dalinar's words.

'Your Majesty,' Dalinar said, clasping his hands behind his back and pacing the stage at the center of the seats. *Do better. Unite them.* 'I send you greetings from Urithiru, holy city of the Knights Radiant, and extend to you our humblest invitation. This tower is truly a sight to behold, matched only by the glory of a sitting monarch. I would be honored to present it for you to experience.'

The spanreed quickly scribbled a reply. Queen Fen was writing directly in Alethi. ' "Kholin," ' Kalami read, ' "you old brute. Quit spreading chull scat. What do you really want?" '

'I always *did* like her,' Navani noted.

'I'm being sincere, Your Majesty,' Dalinar said. 'My only desire is for us to meet in person, and to talk to you and show you what we've discovered. The world is changing around us.'

' "Oh," ' came the reply, ' "the world is changing, is it? What led you to this incredible conclusion? Was it the fact that our slaves suddenly became Voidbringers, or was it perhaps the storm that blew the *wrong way*," ' – She wrote that twice as large as the line around it, Brightlord – ' "ripping our cities apart?" '

Aladar cleared his throat. 'Her Majesty seems to be having a bad day.'

'She's insulting us,' Navani said. 'For Fen, that actually implies a good day.'

'She's always been perfectly civil the few times I've met her,' Dalinar said with a frown.

'She was being queenly then,' Navani said. 'You've got her talking to you directly. Trust me, it's a good sign.'

'Your Majesty,' Dalinar said, 'please tell me of your parshmen. The transformation came upon them?'

' "Yes," ' she replied. ' "Storming monsters stole our best ships – almost everything in the harbor from single-masted sloops on up – and escaped the city." '

'They ... sailed?' Dalinar said, again shocked. 'Confirm. They didn't attack?'

' "There were some scuffles," ' Fen wrote, ' "but most everyone was too busy dealing with the effects of the storm. By the time we got things somewhat sorted out, they were sailing away in a grand fleet of royal warships and private trading vessels alike." '

Dalinar drew a breath. *We don't know half as much about the Voidbringers as we assumed.* 'Your Majesty,' he continued. 'You might remember that we *warned* you about the imminent arrival of that storm.'

' "I believed you," ' Fen said. ' "If only because we got word from New

Natanan confirming it. We tried to prepare, but a nation cannot upend four millennia worth of tradition at a snap of the fingers. Thaylen City is a shambles, Kholin. The storm broke our aqueducts and sewer systems, and ripped apart our docks – flattened the entire outer market! We have to fix all our cisterns, reinforce our buildings to withstand storms, and rebuild society – all without any parshman laborers and in the middle of the storming Weeping. I don't have *time* for sightseeing."'

'It's hardly sightseeing, Your Majesty,' Dalinar said. 'I am aware of your problems, and dire though they are, we cannot ignore the Voidbringers. I intend to convene a grand conference of kings to fight this threat.'

' "Led by you," ' Fen wrote in reply. ' "Of course." '

'Urithiru is the natural location for a meeting,' Dalinar said. 'Your Majesty, the Knights Radiant have returned – we speak again their ancient oaths, and bind the Surges of nature to us. If we can restore your Oathgate to functionality, you can be here in an afternoon, then return the same evening to direct the needs of your city.'

Navani nodded at this tactic, though Aladar folded his arms, looking thoughtful.

'What?' Dalinar asked him as Kalami wrote.

'We need a Radiant to travel to the city to activate their Oathgate, right?' Aladar asked.

'Yes,' Navani said. 'A Radiant needs to unlock the gate on this side – which we can do at any moment – then one has to travel to the destination city and undo the lock there as well. That done, a Radiant can initiate a transfer from either location.'

'Then the only one we have that can theoretically get to Thaylen City is the Windrunner,' Aladar said. 'But what if it takes him months to get back here? Or what if he's captured by the enemy? Can we even make good on our promises, Dalinar?'

A troubling problem, but one that Dalinar thought he might have an answer to. There was a weapon that he'd decided to keep hidden for now. It might work as well as a Radiant's Shardblade in opening the Oathgates – and might let someone reach Thaylen City by flight.

That was moot for the time being. First he needed a willing ear on the other side of the spanreed.

Fen's reply came. ' "I will admit that my merchants are intrigued by these Oathgates. We have lore surrounding them here, that the one most

Passionate could cause the portal of worlds to open again. I think every girl in Thaylenah dreams of being the one to invoke it."'

'The Passions,' Navani said with a downward turn of her lips. The Thaylens had a pagan pseudo-religion, and that had always been a curious aspect in dealing with them. They would praise the Heralds one moment, then speak of the Passions the next.

Well, Dalinar wasn't one to fault another for unconventional beliefs.

' "If you want to send me what you know about these Oathgates, well, that sounds great," ' Fen continued. ' "But I'm not interested in some grand conference of kings. You let me know what you boys come up with, because I'm going to be here frantically trying to rebuild my city." '

'Well,' Aladar said, 'at least we finally got an honest response.'

'I'm not convinced this is honest,' Dalinar said. He rubbed his chin, thinking. He'd only met this woman a few times, but something seemed *off* about her responses.

'I agree, Brightlord,' Teshav said. 'I think any Thaylen would jump at the chance to come pull strings at a meeting of monarchs, if only to see if she can find a way to get trade deals out of them. She is most certainly hiding something.'

'Offer troops,' Navani said, 'to help her rebuild.'

'Your Majesty,' Dalinar said, 'I am deeply grieved to hear of your losses. I have many soldiers here who are currently unoccupied. I would gladly send you a battalion to help repair your city.'

The reply was slow in coming. ' "I'm not sure what I think of having Alethi troops on my stone, well intentioned or not." '

Aladar grunted. 'She's worried about invasion? Everyone knows Alethi and ships don't mix.'

'She's not worried about us arriving on ships,' Dalinar said. 'She's worried about an army of troops suddenly materializing in the center of her city.'

A very rational worry. If Dalinar had the inclination, he could send a Windrunner to secretly open a city's Oathgate, and invade in an unprecedented assault that appeared right behind enemy lines.

He needed allies, not subjects, so he wouldn't do it – at least not to a potentially friendly city. Kholinar, however, was another story. They still didn't have reliable word of what was happening in the Alethi capital. But if the rioting was still going on, he'd been thinking that there might be a way to get armies in and restore order.

For now, he needed to focus on Queen Fen. 'Your Majesty,' he said, nodding for Kalami to write, 'consider my offer of troops, please. And as you do, might I suggest that you begin searching among your people for budding Knights Radiant? They are the key to working Oathgates.

'We have had a number of Radiants manifest near the Shattered Plains. They are formed through an interaction with certain spren, who seem to be searching for worthy candidates. I can only assume this is happening worldwide. It is entirely likely that among the people of your city, someone has already spoken the oaths.'

'You're giving up quite an advantage, Dalinar,' Aladar noted.

'I'm planting a seed, Aladar,' Dalinar said. 'And I'll plant it on any hill I can find, regardless of who owns it. We must fight as a unified people.'

'I don't dispute that,' Aladar said, standing up and stretching. 'But your knowledge of the Radiants is a bargaining point, one that can perhaps draw people to you – force them to work *with* you. Give up too much, and you might find a "headquarters" for the Knights Radiant in every major city across Roshar. Rather than working together, you'll have them competing to recruit.'

He was right, unfortunately. Dalinar hated turning knowledge into bargaining chips, but what if this was why he'd always failed in his negotiations with the highprinces? He wanted to be honest, straightforward, and let the pieces fall where they may. But it seemed that someone better at the game – and more willing to break the rules – always snatched the pieces from the air as he dropped them, then set them down the way they wanted.

'And,' he said quickly for Kalami to add, 'we would be happy to send our Radiants to train those you discover, then introduce them to the system and fraternity of Urithiru, to which each of them has a right by nature of their oaths.'

Kalami added this, then twisted the spanreed to indicate they were done and waiting for a reply.

' "We will consider this," ' Kalami read as the spanreed scribbled across the page. ' "The crown of Thaylenah thanks you for your interest in our people, and we will consider negotiations regarding your offer of troops. We have sent some of our few remaining cutters to track down the fleeing parshmen, and will inform you of what we discover. Until we speak again, Highprince."'

'Storms,' Navani said. 'She reverted to queenspeak. We lost her somewhere in there.'

Dalinar sat down in the seat next to her and let out a long sigh.

'Dalinar . . .' she said.

'I'm fine, Navani,' he said. 'I can't expect glowing commitments to cooperation on my first attempt. We'll just have to keep trying.'

The words were more optimistic than he felt. He wished he could talk to these people in person, instead of over spanreed.

They talked to the princess of Yezier next, followed by the prince of Tashikk. They didn't have Oathgates, and were less essential to his plan, but he wanted to at least open lines of communication with them.

Neither gave him more than vague answers. Without the Azish emperor's blessing, he wouldn't be able to get any of the smaller Makabaki kingdoms to commit. Perhaps the Emuli or the Tukari would listen, but he'd only ever get one of those two, considering their long-standing feud.

At the end of the last conference, Aladar and his daughter excusing themselves, Dalinar stretched, feeling worn down. And this wasn't the end of it. He would have discussions with the monarchs of Iri – it had three, strangely. The Oathgate at Rall Elorim was in their lands, making them important – and they held sway over nearby Rira, which had another Oathgate.

Beyond that, of course, there were the Shin to deal with. They hated using spanreeds, so Navani had poked at them through a Thaylen merchant who had been willing to relay information.

Dalinar's shoulder protested as he stretched. He had found middle age to be like an assassin – quiet, creeping along behind him. Much of the time he would go about his life as he always had, until an unexpected ache or pain gave warning. He was not the youth he had once been.

And bless the Almighty for that, he thought idly, bidding farewell to Navani – who wanted to sift through information reports from various spanreed stations around the world. Aladar's daughter and scribes were gathering them in bulk for her.

Dalinar collected several of his guards, leaving others for Navani should she need some extra hands, and climbed up along the rows of seats to the room's exit at the top. Hovering just outside the doorway – like an axehound banished from the warmth of the fire – stood Elhokar.

'Your Majesty?' Dalinar said, starting. 'I'm glad you could make the meeting. Are you feeling better?'

'Why do they refuse you, Uncle?' Elhokar asked, ignoring the question. 'Do they think perhaps you will try to usurp their thrones?'

Dalinar drew in his breath sharply, and his guards looked embarrassed to be standing nearby. They backed up to give him and the king privacy.

'Elhokar . . .' Dalinar said.

'You likely think I say this in spite,' the king said, poking his head into the room, noting his mother, then looking back at Dalinar. 'I don't. You *are* better than I am. A better soldier, a better person, and certainly a better king.'

'You do yourself a disservice, Elhokar. You must—'

'Oh, save your platitudes, Dalinar. For once in your life, just be *honest* with me.'

'You think I haven't been?'

Elhokar raised his hand and lightly touched his own chest. 'Perhaps you have been, at times. Perhaps the liar here is me – lying to tell myself I could do this, that I could be a fraction of the man my father was. No, don't interrupt me, Dalinar. Let me have my say. Voidbringers? Ancient cities full of wonder? The *Desolations*?' Elhokar shook his head. 'Perhaps . . . perhaps I'm a fine king. Not extraordinary, but not an abject failure. But in the face of these events, the world needs better than fine.'

There seemed a fatalism to his words, and that sent a worried shiver through Dalinar. 'Elhokar, what are you saying?'

Elhokar strode into the chamber and called down to those at the bottom of the rows of seats. 'Mother, Brightness Teshav, would you witness something for me?'

Storms, no, Dalinar thought, hurrying after Elhokar. 'Don't do this, son.'

'We all must accept the consequences of our actions, Uncle,' Elhokar said. 'I've been learning this very slowly, as I can be as dense as a stone.'

'But—'

'Uncle, am I your king?' Elhokar demanded.

'Yes.'

'Well, I shouldn't be.' He knelt, shocking Navani and causing her to pull to a stop three-quarters of the way up the steps. 'Dalinar Kholin,' Elhokar said in a loud voice, 'I swear to you now. There are princes and highprinces. Why not kings and highkings? I give an oath, immutable and witnessed, that I accept you as my monarch. As Alethkar is to me, I am to you.'

Dalinar breathed out, looking to Navani's aghast face, then down to his nephew, kneeling as a vassal on the floor.

'You *did* ask for this, Uncle,' Elhokar said. 'Not specifically in words, but it is the only place we could have gone. You have slowly been taking command ever since you decided to trust those visions.'

'I've tried to include you,' Dalinar said. Silly, impotent words. He should be better than that. 'You are right, Elhokar. I'm sorry.'

'Are you?' Elhokar asked. 'Are you really?'

'I'm sorry,' Dalinar said, 'for your pain. I'm sorry that I didn't handle this better. I'm sorry that this . . . this must be. Before you make this oath, tell me what you expect that it entails?'

'I've already said the words,' Elhokar said, growing red faced. 'Before witnesses. It is done. I've—'

'Oh, stand up,' Dalinar said, grabbing him by the arm and hauling him to his feet. 'Don't be dramatic. If you really want to swear this oath, I'll let you. But let's not pretend you can sweep into a room, shout a few words, and assume it's a legal contract.'

Elhokar pulled his arm free and rubbed it. 'Won't even let me abdicate with dignity.'

'You're *not* abdicating,' Navani said, joining them. She shot a glare at the guards, who stood watching with slack jaws, and they grew white at the glare. She pointed at them as if to say, *Not a word of this to anyone else.* 'Elhokar, you intend to shove your uncle into a position above you. He's right to ask. What will this mean for Alethkar?'

'I . . .' Elhokar swallowed. 'He should give up his lands to his heir. Dalinar is a king of somewhere else, after all. Dalinar, Highking of Urithiru, maybe the Shattered Plains.' He stood straighter, speaking more certainly. 'Dalinar must stay out of the direct management of my lands. He can give me commands, but *I* decide how to see them accomplished.'

'It sounds reasonable,' Navani said, glancing at Dalinar.

Reasonable, but gut-wrenching. The kingdom he'd fought for – the kingdom he'd forged in pain, exhaustion, and blood – now rejected him.

This is my land now, Dalinar thought. *This tower covered in coldspren.* 'I can accept these terms, though at times I might need to give commands to your highprinces.'

'As long as they're in your domain,' Elhokar said, a hint of stubbornness to his voice, 'I consider them under your authority. While they visit Urithiru or the Shattered Plains, command as you wish. When they return to my kingdom, you must go through me.' He looked to Dalinar, and then glanced down, as if embarrassed to be making demands.

'Very well,' Dalinar said. 'Though we need to work this out with scribes before we make the change officially. And before we go too far, we should make certain there is still an Alethkar for you to rule.'

'I've been thinking the same thing. Uncle, I want to lead our forces to Alethkar and recapture our homeland. Something is wrong in Kholinar. More than these riots or my wife's supposed behavior, more than the spanreeds going still. The enemy is doing something in the city. I'll take an army to stop it, and save the kingdom.'

Elhokar? Leading troops? Dalinar had been imagining himself leading a force, cutting through the Voidbringer ranks, sweeping them from Alethkar and marching into Kholinar to restore order.

Truth was, though, it didn't make sense for either of them to lead such an assault. 'Elhokar,' Dalinar said, leaning in. 'I've been considering something. The Oathgate is attached to the *palace itself.* We don't need to march an army all the way to Alethkar. All we need to do is restore that device! Once it works, we can transport our forces into the city to secure the palace, restore order, and fend off the Voidbringers.'

'Get into the city,' Elhokar said. 'Uncle, to do that we might *need* an army in the first place!'

'No,' Dalinar said. 'A small team could reach Kholinar far faster than an army. As long as there was a Radiant with them, they could sneak in, restore the Oathgate, and open the way for the rest of us.'

Elhokar perked up. 'Yes! I'll do it, Uncle. I'll take a team and reclaim our home. Aesudan is there; if the rioting is still happening, she's fighting against it.'

That wasn't what the reports – before they'd cut off – had suggested to Dalinar. If anything, the queen was the *cause* of the riots. And he certainly hadn't been intending Elhokar to go on this mission himself.

Consequences. The lad was earnest, as he'd always been. Besides, Elhokar seemed to have learned something from his near death at the hands of assassins. He was certainly humbler now than he'd been in years past.

'It is fitting,' Dalinar said, 'that their king should be the one who saves them. I will see that you have whatever resources you need, Elhokar.'

Glowing gloryspren orbs burst around Elhokar. He grinned at them. 'I only seem to see those when I'm around you, Uncle. Funny. For all that I should resent you, I don't. It's hard to resent a man who is doing his best. I'll do it. I'll save Alethkar. I need one of your Radiants. The hero, preferably.'

'The hero?'

'The bridgeman,' Elhokar said. 'The soldier. He needs to go with me, so if I screw up and fail, someone will be there to save the city anyway.'

Dalinar blinked. 'That's very . . . um . . .'

'I've had ample chances to reflect lately, Uncle,' Elhokar said. 'The Almighty has preserved me, despite my stupidity. I'll bring the bridgeman with me, and I'll observe him. Figure out why he's so special. See if he'll teach me to be like him. And if I fail . . .' He shrugged. 'Well, Alethkar is in safe hands regardless, right?'

Dalinar nodded, bemused.

'I need to make plans,' Elhokar said. 'I've only just recovered from my wounds. But I can't leave until the hero returns anyway. Could he fly me and my chosen team to the city? That would certainly be the fastest way. I will want every report we've had from Kholinar, and I need to study the Oathgate device in person. Yes, and have drawings done comparing it to the one in the city. And . . .' He beamed. 'Thank you, Uncle. Thank you for believing in me, if only this small amount.'

Dalinar nodded to him, and Elhokar retreated, a spring in his step. Dalinar sighed, feeling overwhelmed by the exchange. Navani hovered by his side as he settled down in one of the seats for the Radiants, beside a pedestal for a little spren.

On one side, he had a king swearing to him an oath he didn't want. On the other, he had an entire group of monarchs who wouldn't listen to his most rational of suggestions. Storms.

'Dalinar?' Kalami said. 'Dalinar!'

He leaped to his feet, and Navani spun. Kalami was watching one of the spanreeds, which had started writing. What was it now? What terrible news awaited him?

' "Your Majesty," ' Kalami read from the page, ' "I consider your offer generous, and your advice wise. We have located the device you call an Oathgate. One of my people has come forward, and – remarkably – claims to be Radiant. Her spren directed her to speak with me; we plan to use her Shardblade to test the device.

' "If it works, I will come to you in all haste. It is well that someone is attempting to organize a resistance to the evils that befall us. The nations of Roshar must put aside their squabbles, and the reemergence of the holy city of Urithiru is proof to me that the Almighty guides your hand. I look forward to counseling with you and adding my forces to yours in a joint operation to protect these lands."' She looked up at him, amazed. 'It was sent by Taravangian, king of Jah Keved and Kharbranth.'

Taravangian? Dalinar hadn't expected him to reply so quickly. He was said to be a kindly, if somewhat simple man. Perfect for ruling a small city-state with the help of a governing council. His elevation to king of Jah Keved was widely seen as an act of spite from the former king, who hadn't wanted to give the throne to any of his rivals' houses.

The words still warmed Dalinar. Someone had listened. Someone was willing to join him. Bless that man, *bless him*.

If Dalinar failed everywhere else, at least he would have King Taravangian at his side.

13

CHAPERONE

I ask only that you read or listen to these words.

—From *Oathbringer*, preface

Shallan breathed out Stormlight and stepped through it, feeling it envelop her, transform her.

She'd been moved, upon request, to Sebarial's section of Urithiru, in part because he'd promised her a room with a balcony. Fresh air and a view of the mountain peaks. If she couldn't be completely free of this building's shadowed depths, then at least she could have a home on the borders.

She pulled at her hair, pleased to see it had turned black. She had become Veil, a disguise she'd been working on for some time.

Shallan held up hands that were callused and worked – even the safehand. Not that Veil was unfeminine. She kept her nails filed, and liked to dress nicely, keep her hair brushed. She simply didn't have time for frivolities. A good sturdy coat and trousers suited Veil better than a flowing havah. And she had *no* time for an extended sleeve covering her safehand. She'd wear a glove, thank you very much.

At the moment she was dressed in her nightgown; she'd change later, once she was ready to sneak out into Urithiru's halls. She needed some practice first. Though she felt bad about the use of Stormlight when everyone else was scrimping, Dalinar *had* told her to train with her powers.

She strode through her chamber, adopting Veil's gait – confident and sturdy, never prim. You couldn't balance a book on Veil's head as she walked, but she'd happily balance one on your face after she knocked you unconscious.

She circled the room several times, crossing the patch of evening light from the window. Her room was ornamented by bright circular patterns of strata on the walls. The stone was smooth to the touch, and a knife couldn't scratch it.

There wasn't much furniture, though Shallan was hopeful that the latest scavenging expeditions to the warcamps would return with something she could appropriate from Sebarial. For now she did what she could with some blankets, a single stool, and – blessedly – a hand mirror. She'd hung it on the wall, tied to a stone knob that she assumed was for hanging pictures.

She checked her face in the mirror. She wanted to get to the point where she could become Veil at a moment's notice, without needing to review sketches. She prodded at her features, but of course as the more angular nose and pronounced forehead were a result of Lightweaving, she couldn't feel them.

When she frowned, Veil's face mimicked the motion perfectly. 'Something to drink, please,' she said. No, rougher. 'Drink. Now.' Too strong?

'Mmm,' Pattern said. 'The voice becomes a good lie.'

'Thank you. I've been working on sounds.' Veil's voice was deeper than Shallan's, rougher. She'd started to wonder, how far could she go in changing how things sounded?

For now, she wasn't sure she'd gotten the lips right in the illusion. She sauntered over to her art supplies and flipped open her sketchbook, looking for renditions of Veil she'd drawn instead of going to dinner with Sebarial and Palona.

The first page of the sketchbook was of the corridor with the twisting strata she'd passed through the other day: lines of madness curling toward darkness. She flipped to the next, a picture of one of the tower's budding markets. Thousands of merchants, washwomen, prostitutes, innkeepers, and craftsmen of all varieties were setting up in Urithiru. Shallan knew well how many – she'd been the one to bring them all through the Oathgate.

In her sketch, the black upper reaches of the large market cavern loomed over tiny figures scurrying between tents, holding fragile lights. The next was another tunnel into darkness. And the next. Then a room where the strata coiled about one another in a mesmerizing manner. She hadn't realized she'd done so many. She flipped twenty pages before she found her sketches of Veil.

Yes, the lips were right. The build was wrong, however. Veil had a lean strength, and that wasn't coming through in the nightgown. It looked too much like Shallan's figure beneath.

Someone knocked on the wooden plate hung outside her rooms. She had just a cloth draping the doorway right now. Many of the tower's doors had warped over the years; hers had been ripped out, and she was still waiting on a replacement.

The one knocking would be Palona, who had once again noticed that Shallan had skipped dinner. Shallan sucked in a breath, destroying the image of Veil, recovering some of the Stormlight from her Lightweaving. 'Come,' she said. Honestly, it didn't seem to matter to Palona that Shallan was a storming *Knight Radiant* now, she'd still mother her all the—

Adolin stepped in, carrying a large plate of food in one hand, some books under the other arm. He saw her and stumbled, nearly dropping it all.

Shallan froze, then yelped and tucked her bare safehand behind her back. Adolin didn't even have the decency to blush at finding her practically naked. He balanced the food in his hand, recovering from his stumble, and then grinned.

'Out!' Shallan said, waving her freehand at him. 'Out, out, out!'

He backed away awkwardly, through the draped cloth over the doorway. Stormfather! Shallan's blush was probably so bright they could have used her as a signal to send the army to war. She pulled on a glove, then wrapped that in a safepouch, then threw on the blue dress she had draped over the back of her chair and did up the sleeve. She didn't have the presence of mind to pull on her bodice vest first, not that she really needed one anyway. She kicked it under a blanket instead.

'In my defense,' Adolin said from outside, 'you *did* invite me in.'

'I thought you were Palona!' Shallan said, doing up the buttons on the side of her dress – which proved difficult, with three layers covering her safehand.

'You know, you could *check* to see who is at your door.'

'Don't make this my fault,' Shallan said. 'You're the one slipping into young ladies' bedrooms practically unannounced.'

'I knocked!'

'The knock was feminine.'

'It was . . . Shallan!'

'Did you knock with one hand or two?'

'I'm carrying a storming platter of food – for *you*, by the way. Of course the knock was one-handed. And seriously, who knocks with *two*?'

'It was quite feminine, then. I'd have thought that imitating a woman to catch a glimpse of a young lady in her undergarments was beneath you, Adolin Kholin.'

'Oh, for Damnation's sake, Shallan. Can I come in *now*? And just so we're clear, I'm a *man* and your betrothed, my name is Adolin Kholin, I was born under the sign of the nine, I have a birthmark on the back of my left thigh, and I had crab curry for breakfast. Anything else you need to know?'

She poked her head out, pulling the cloth tight around her neck. 'Back of your left thigh, eh? What's a girl got to do to sneak a glimpse of *that*?'

'Knock like a man, apparently.'

She gave him a grin. 'Just a sec. This dress is being a pain.' She ducked back into the room.

'Yes, yes. Take your time. I'm not standing out here holding a heavy platter of food, smelling it after having skipped dinner so I could dine with you.'

'It's good for you,' Shallan said. 'Builds strength, or something. Isn't that the sort of thing you do? Strangle rocks, stand on your head, throw boulders around.'

'Yes, I have quite my share of murdered rocks stuffed under my bed.'

Shallan grabbed her dress with her teeth at the neck to pull it tight, helping with the buttons. Maybe.

'What *is* it with women and their undergarments anyway?' Adolin said, the platter clinking as some of the plates slid against one another. 'I mean, that shift covers basically the same parts as a formal dress.'

'It's the decency of it,' Shallan said around a mouthful of fabric. 'Besides, certain things have a tendency to poke out through a shift.'

'Still seems arbitrary to me.'

'Oh, and men aren't arbitrary about clothing? A uniform is basically the same as any other coat, right? Besides, aren't you the one who spends his afternoons searching through fashion folios?'

He chuckled and started a reply, but Shallan, finally dressed, swept back the sheet on her doorway. Adolin stood up from leaning against the wall of the corridor and took her in – frazzled hair, dress that she had missed two buttons on, cheeks flushed. Then he grinned a dopey grin.

Ash's eyes ... he actually thought she was pretty. This wonderful, princely man actually *liked* being with her. She'd traveled to the ancient city of the Knights Radiant, but compared to Adolin's affection, all the sights of Urithiru were dun spheres.

He liked her. *And* he brought her food.

Do not *find a way to screw this up,* Shallan thought to herself as she took the books from under his arm. She stepped aside, letting him enter and set the platter on the floor. 'Palona said you hadn't eaten,' he said, 'and then she found out I'd skipped dinner. So, uh ...'

'So she sent you with a lot,' Shallan said, inspecting the platter piled high with dishes, flatbreads, and shellfood.

'Yeah,' Adolin said, standing and scratching at his head. 'I think it's a Herdazian thing.'

Shallan hadn't realized how hungry she was. She'd been intending to get something at one of the taverns later tonight while prowling about wearing Veil's face. Those taverns had set up in the main market, despite Navani's attempts to send them elsewhere, and Sebarial's merchants had quite the stock to sell.

Now that this was all before her ... well, she didn't worry much about decorum as she settled down on the ground and started to spoon herself up a thin, watery curry with vegetables.

Adolin remained standing. He *did* look sharp in that blue uniform, though admittedly she'd never really seen him in anything else. *Birthmark on the thigh, eh ...*

'You'll have to sit on the ground,' Shallan said. 'No chairs yet.'

'I just realized,' he said, 'this is your bedroom.'

'And my drawing room, and my sitting room, and my dining room, and my "Adolin says obvious things" room. It's quite versatile, this room – singular – of mine. Why?'

'I'm just wondering if it's proper,' he said, then actually blushed – which was adorable. 'For us to be in here alone.'

'*Now* you're worried about propriety?'

'Well, I did recently get lectured about it.'

'That wasn't a lecture,' Shallan said, taking a bite of food. The succulent tastes overwhelmed her mouth, bringing on that delightful sharp pain and mixing of flavor that you only got from the first bite of something sweet. She closed her eyes and smiled, savoring it.

'So ... not a lecture?' Adolin said. 'Was there to be more to that quip?'

'Sorry,' she said, opening her eyes. 'It wasn't a lecture, it was a creative application of my tongue to keep you distracted.' Looking at his lips, she could think of some other creative applications for her tongue. . . .

Right. She took a deep breath.

'It *would* be inappropriate,' Shallan said, 'if we were alone. Fortunately, we are not.'

'Your ego doesn't count as a separate individual, Shallan.'

'Ha! Wait. You think I have an ego?'

'It just sounded good – I don't mean ... Not that ... Why are you grinning?'

'Sorry,' Shallan said, making two fists before herself and shivering in glee. She'd spent so *long* feeling timid, it was so satisfying to hear a reference to her confidence. It was working! Jasnah's teaching about practicing and acting like she was in control. It was *working*.

Well, except for that whole part about having to admit to herself that she'd killed her mother. As soon as she thought of it, she instinctively tried to shove the memory away, but it wouldn't budge. She'd spoken it to Pattern as a truth – which were the odd Ideals of the Lightweavers.

It was stuck in her mind, and every time she thought about it, the gaping wound flared up with pain again. Shallan had killed her mother. Her father had covered it up, pretended he'd murdered his wife, and the event had destroyed his life – driving him to anger and destruction.

Until eventually Shallan had killed him too.

'Shallan?' Adolin asked. 'Are you well?'

No.

'Sure. Fine. Anyway, we *aren't* alone. Pattern, come here please.' She held out her hand, palm up.

He reluctantly moved down from the wall where he'd been watching. As always, he made a ripple in whatever he crossed, be it cloth or stone – like there was something under the surface. His complex, fluctuating pattern of lines was always changing, melding, vaguely circular but with surprising tangents.

He crossed up her dress and onto her hand, then split out from beneath her skin and rose into the air, expanding fully into three dimensions. He hovered there, a black, eye-bending network of shifting lines – some patterns shrinking while others expanded, rippling across his surface like a field of moving grass.

She would *not* hate him. She could hate the sword she'd used to kill her mother, but not him. She managed to push aside the pain for now – not forgetting it, but hopefully not letting it spoil her time with Adolin.

'Prince Adolin,' Shallan said, 'I believe you've heard my spren's voice before. Let me introduce you formally. This is Pattern.'

Adolin knelt, reverent, and stared at the mesmerizing geometries. Shallan didn't blame him; she'd lost herself more than once in that network of lines and shapes that almost seemed to repeat, but never quite did.

'Your spren,' Adolin said. 'A Shallanspren.'

Pattern sniffed in annoyance at that.

'He's called a Cryptic,' she said. 'Every order of Radiant bonds a different variety of spren, and that bond lets me do what I do.'

'Craft illusions,' Adolin said softly. 'Like that one with the map the other day.'

Shallan smiled and – realizing she had just a smidge of Stormlight left from her illusion earlier – was unable to resist showing off. She raised her sleeved safehand and breathed out, sending a shimmering patch of Stormlight above the blue cloth. It formed into a small image of Adolin from her sketches of him in his Shardplate. This one remained frozen, Shardblade on his shoulder, faceplate up – like a little doll.

'This is an incredible talent, Shallan,' Adolin said, poking at the version of himself – which fuzzed, offering no resistance. He paused, then poked at Pattern, who shied back. 'Why do you insist on hiding this, pretending that you're a different order than you are?'

'Well,' she said, thinking fast and closing her hand, dismissing the image of Adolin. 'I just think it might give us an edge. Sometimes secrets are important.'

Adolin nodded slowly. 'Yeah. Yeah, they are.'

'Anyway,' Shallan said. 'Pattern, you're to be our chaperone tonight.'

'What,' Pattern said with a hum, 'is a chaperone?'

'That is someone who watches two young people when they are together, to make certain they don't do anything inappropriate.'

'Inappropriate?' Pattern said. 'Such as ... dividing by zero?'

'What?' Shallan asked, looking to Adolin, who shrugged. 'Look, just keep an eye on us. It will be all right.'

Pattern hummed, melting down into his two-dimensional form and taking up residence on the side of a bowl. He seemed content there, like a cremling snuggled into its crack.

Unable to wait any longer, Shallan dug into her meal. Adolin settled down across from her and attacked his own food. For a time, Shallan ignored her pain and savored the moment – good food, good company, the setting sun casting ruby and topaz light across the mountains and into the room. She felt like drawing this scene, but knew it was the type of moment she couldn't capture on a page. It wasn't about content or composition, but the pleasure of living.

The trick to happiness wasn't in freezing every momentary pleasure and clinging to each one, but in ensuring one's life would produce many future moments to anticipate.

Adolin – after finishing an entire plate of stranna haspers steamed in the shell – picked out a few chunks of pork from a creamy red curry, then put them on a plate and handed them in her direction. 'Wanna try a bite?'

Shallan made a gagging noise.

'Come on,' he said, wagging the plate. 'It's delicious.'

'It would burn my lips off, Adolin Kholin,' Shallan said. 'Don't think I didn't notice you picking the absolute *spiciest* concoction Palona sent. Men's food is dreadful. How can you taste anything beneath all that spice?'

'Keeps it from being bland,' Adolin said, stabbing one of the chunks and popping it in his mouth. 'There's nobody here but us. You can try it.'

She eyed it, remembering the times as a child when she'd sneaked tastes of men's food – though not this specific dish.

Pattern buzzed. 'Is this the inappropriate thing I'm supposed to stop you from doing?'

'No,' Shallan said, and Pattern settled back down. *Perhaps a chaperone*, she thought, *who believes basically everything I tell him isn't going to be the most effective.*

Still, with a sigh, she grabbed a chunk of the pork in some flatbread. She *had* left Jah Keved hunting new experiences, after all.

She tried a bite, and was given immediate reason to regret her decisions in life.

Eyes brimming with tears, she scrambled for the cup of water Adolin, insufferably, had picked up to hand toward her. She gulped that down, though it didn't seem to do anything. She followed it by wiping her tongue with a napkin – in the most feminine way possible, of course.

'I hate you,' she said, drinking *his* water next.

Adolin chuckled.

'Oh!' Pattern said suddenly, bursting up from the bowl to hover in the air. 'You were talking about *mating*! I'm to make sure you don't accidentally mate, as mating is forbidden by human society until you have first performed appropriate rituals! Yes, yes. Mmmm. Dictates of custom require following certain patterns before you copulate. I've been studying this!'

'Oh, Stormfather,' Shallan said, covering her eyes with her freehand. A few shamespren even peeked in for a glimpse before vanishing. Twice in one week.

'Very well, you two,' Pattern said. 'No mating. *NO MATING.*' He hummed to himself, as if pleased, then sank down onto a plate.

'Well, that was humiliating,' Shallan said. 'Can we maybe talk about those books you brought? Or ancient Vorin theology, or strategies for counting grains of sand? Anything other than what just happened? Please?'

Adolin chuckled, then reached for a slim notebook that was on top of the pile. 'May Aladar sent teams to question Vedekar Perel's family and friends. They discovered where he was before he died, who last saw him, and wrote down anything suspicious. I thought we could read the report.'

'And the rest of the books?'

'You seemed lost when Father asked you about Makabaki politics,' Adolin said, pouring some wine, merely a soft yellow. 'So I asked around, and it seems that some of the ardents hauled their entire libraries out here. I was able to get a servant to locate you a few books I'd enjoyed on the Makabaki.'

'Books?' Shallan said. 'You?'

'I don't spend *all* my time hitting people with swords, Shallan,' Adolin said. 'Jasnah and Aunt Navani made very certain that my youth was filled with interminable periods spent listening to ardents lecture me on politics and trade. Some of it stuck in my brain, against my natural inclinations. Those three books are the best of the ones I remember having read to me, though the last one is an updated version. I thought it might help.'

'That's thoughtful,' she said. 'Really, Adolin. Thank you.'

'I figured, you know, if we're going to move forward with the betrothal . . .'

'Why wouldn't we?' Shallan said, suddenly panicked.

'I don't know. You're a *Radiant*, Shallan. Some kind of half-divine being from mythology. And all along I was thinking we were giving *you* a favorable match.' He stood up and started pacing. 'Damnation. I didn't mean to say it like that. I'm sorry. I just . . . I keep worrying that I'm going to screw this up somehow.'

'You worry *you're* going to screw it up?' Shallan said, feeling a warmth inside that wasn't completely due to the wine.

'I'm not good with relationships, Shallan.'

'Is there anyone who actually is? I mean, is there *really* someone out there who looks at relationships and thinks, "You know what, I've got this"? Personally, I rather think we're all collectively idiots about it.'

'It's worse for me.'

'Adolin, dear, the last man *I* had a romantic interest in was not only an ardent – forbidden to court me in the first place – but also turned out to be an assassin who was merely trying to obtain my favor so he could get close to Jasnah. I think you overestimate everyone else's capability in this regard.'

He stopped pacing. 'An assassin.'

'Seriously,' Shallan said. 'He almost killed me with a loaf of poisoned bread.'

'Wow. I have to hear this story.'

'Fortunately, I just told it to you. His name was Kabsal, and he was so incredibly sweet to me that I can almost forgive him for trying to kill me.'

Adolin grinned. 'Well, it's nice to hear that I don't have a high bar to jump – all I have to do is *not* poison you. Though you shouldn't be telling me about past lovers. You'll make me jealous.'

'Please,' Shallan said, dipping her bread in some leftover sweet curry. Her tongue *still* hadn't recovered. 'You've courted, like, half the warcamps.'

'It's not that bad.'

'Isn't it? From what I hear, I'd have to go to Herdaz to find an eligible woman you haven't pursued.' She held out her hand to him, to help her to her feet.

'Are you mocking my failings?'

'No, I'm *lauding* them,' she said, standing up beside him. 'You see, Adolin dear, if you hadn't wrecked all those other relationships, you wouldn't be here. With me.' She pulled close. 'And so, in reality, you're the *greatest* at relationships there ever was. You ruined only the wrong ones, you see.'

He leaned down. His breath smelled of spices, his uniform of the crisp, clean starch Dalinar required. His lips touched hers, and her heart fluttered. So warm.

'No mating!'

She started, pulling out of the kiss to find Pattern hovering beside them, pulsing quickly through shapes.

Adolin bellowed a laugh, and Shallan couldn't help joining in at the ridiculousness of it. She stepped back from him, but kept hold on his hand. 'Neither of us is going to mess this up,' she said to him, squeezing his hand. 'Despite what might at times seem like our best efforts otherwise.'

'Promise?' he asked.

'I promise. Let's look at this notebook of yours and see what it says about our murderer.'

In this record, I hold nothing back. I will try not to shy away from difficult topics, or paint myself in a dishonestly heroic light.

—From *Oathbringer*, preface

Kaladin crept through the rains, sidling in a wet uniform across the rocks until he was able to peek through the trees at the Voidbringers. Monstrous terrors from the mythological past, enemies of all that was right and good. Destroyers who had laid waste to civilization countless times.

They were playing cards.

What in Damnation's depths? Kaladin thought. The Voidbringers had posted a single guard, but the creature had simply been sitting on a tree stump, easy to avoid. A decoy, Kaladin had assumed, figuring he would find the true guard watching from the heights of the trees.

If there was a hidden guard though, Kaladin had missed spotting them – and they'd missed Kaladin in equal measure. The dim light served him well, as he was able to settle between some bushes right at the edge of the Voidbringer camp. Between trees they had stretched tarps, which leaked horribly. In one place they'd made a proper tent, fully enclosed with walls – and he couldn't see what was inside.

There wasn't enough shelter, so many sat out in the rain. Kaladin spent a torturous few minutes expecting to be spotted. All they had to do was notice that these bushes had drawn in their leaves at his touch.

Nobody looked, fortunately. The leaves timidly peeked back out, obscuring him. Syl landed on his arm, hands on her hips as she surveyed the Voidbringers. One of them had a set of wooden Herdazian cards, and he sat at the edge of the camp – directly before Kaladin – using a flat surface of stone as a table. A female sat opposite him.

They looked different from what he expected. For one thing, their skin was a different shade – many parshmen here in Alethkar had marbled white and red skin, rather than the deep red on black like Rlain from Bridge Four. They didn't wear warform, though neither did they wear some terrible, powerful form. Though they were squat and bulky, their only carapace ran along the sides of their forearms and jutted out at their temples, leaving them with full heads of hair.

They still wore their simple slave smocks, tied at the waists with strings. No red eyes. Did that change, perhaps, like his own eyes?

The male – distinguished by a dark red beard, the hairs each unnaturally thick – finally placed a card on the rock next to several others.

'Can you *do* that?' the female asked.

'I think so.'

'You said squires can't capture.'

'Unless another card of mine is touching yours,' the male said. He scratched at his beard. 'I think?'

Kaladin felt cold, like the rainwater was seeping in through his skin, penetrating all the way to his blood and washing through him. They spoke like Alethi. Not a hint of an accent. With his eyes closed, he wouldn't have been able to tell these voices from those of common darkeyed villagers from Hearthstone, save for the fact that the female had a deeper voice than most human women.

'So . . .' the female said. 'You're saying you don't know how to play the game after all.'

The male began gathering up the cards. 'I *should* know, Khen. How many times did I watch them play? Standing there with my tray of drinks. I should be an expert at this, shouldn't I?'

'Apparently not.'

The female stood and walked over to another group, who were trying to build a fire under a tarp without much success. It took a special kind of luck to be able to get flames going outside during the Weeping. Kaladin, like most in the military, had learned to live with the constant dampness.

They had the stolen sacks of grain – Kaladin could see them piled underneath one of the tarps. The grain had swollen, splitting several of the sacks. Several were eating soggy handfuls, since they had no bowls.

Kaladin wished he didn't immediately taste the mushy, awful stuff in his own mouth. He'd been given unspiced, boiled tallow on many occasions. Often he'd considered it a blessing.

The male who'd been speaking continued to sit on his rock, holding up a wooden card. They were a lacquered set, durable. Kaladin had occasionally seen their like in the military. Men would save for months to get a set like this, that wouldn't warp in the rain.

The parshman looked so forlorn, staring down at his card, shoulders slumped.

'This is wrong,' Kaladin whispered to Syl. 'We've been so *wrong*. . . .' Where were the destroyers? What had happened to the beasts with the red eyes that had tried to crush Dalinar's army? The terrible, haunting figures that Bridge Four had described to him?

We thought we understood what was going to happen, Kaladin thought. *I was so sure. . . .*

'Alarm!' a sudden, shrill voice called. 'Alarm! You fools!'

Something zipped through the air, a glowing yellow ribbon, a streak of light in the dim afternoon shade.

'He's there,' the shrill voice said. 'You're being watched! Beneath those shrubs!'

Kaladin burst up through the underbrush, ready to suck in Stormlight and be away. Though fewer towns had any now, as it was running out again, he had a little left.

The parshmen seized cudgels made from branches or the handles of brooms. They bunched together and held the sticks like frightened villagers, no stance, no control.

Kaladin hesitated. *I could take them all in a fight even without Stormlight.* He'd seen men hold weapons like that many times before. Most recently, he'd seen it inside the chasms, when training the bridgemen.

These were no warriors.

Syl flitted up to him, prepared to become a Blade. 'No,' Kaladin whispered to her. Then he held his hands to the sides, speaking more loudly. 'I surrender.'

15

BRIGHTNESS RADIANT

I will express only direct, even brutal, truth. You must know what I have done, and what those actions cost me.

—From *Oathbringer*, preface

'Brightlord Perel's body was found in the same area as Sadeas's,' Shallan said, pacing back and forth in her room as she flipped through pages of the report. 'That *can't* be a coincidence. This tower is far too big. So we know where the murderer is prowling.'

'Yeah, I suppose,' Adolin said. He lounged with his back against the wall, coat unbuttoned while tossing a small leather ball filled with dried grain into the air and catching it again. 'I just think the murders could have been done by two different people.'

'Same *exact* method of murder,' Shallan said. 'Body positioned the same way.'

'Nothing else connecting them,' Adolin said. 'Sadeas was slime, widely hated, and usually accompanied by guards. Perel was quiet, well-liked, and known for his administrative prowess. He was less a soldier than a manager.'

The sun had fully set by now, and they'd set out spheres on the floor for light. The remnants of their meal had been carted away by a servant, and Pattern hummed happily on the wall near Adolin's head. Adolin glanced at him occasionally, looking uncomfortable, which she fully understood. She'd grown used to Pattern, but his lines *were* strange.

Wait until Adolin sees a Cryptic in Shadesmar form, she thought, *with a full body but twisting shapes for his head.*

Adolin tossed the little stitched ball into the air and caught it with his right hand – the one that Renarin, amazingly, had healed. She wasn't the only one practicing with her powers. She was especially glad someone else had a Shardblade now. When the highstorms returned, and they began working the Oathgate in earnest, she'd have help.

'These reports,' Shallan said, tapping the notebook against her hand, 'are both informative and useless. Nothing connects Perel and Sadeas save their both being lighteyes – that and the part of the tower they were in. Perhaps mere *opportunity* drove the killer's choice of victims.'

'You're saying someone happened to kill a highprince,' Adolin said, 'by accident? Like . . . a back-alley murder outside a pub?'

'Maybe. Brightness Aladar suggests in here that your father lay down some rules on people moving alone through empty parts of the tower.'

'I still think there might be two murderers,' Adolin said. 'You know . . . like someone saw Sadeas dead, and figured they could get away with killing someone else, blaming it on the first fellow.'

Oh, Adolin, Shallan thought. He'd arrived at a theory he liked, and now wouldn't let it go. It was a common mistake warned of in her scientific books.

Adolin did have one point – a highprince being murdered was unlikely to be random chance. There were no signs of Sadeas's Shardblade, Oath-bringer, being used by anyone, not even a rumor of it.

Maybe the second death is a kind of decoy? Shallan thought, riffling through the report again. *An attempt to make it seem like random attacks?* No, that was too convoluted – and she had no more evidence for it than Adolin had for his theory.

That did leave her thinking. Maybe everyone was paying attention to these two deaths because they'd happened to important lighteyes. Could there be other deaths they hadn't noticed because they'd happened to less prominent individuals? If a beggar had been found in Adolin's proverbial back alley behind a pub, would anyone have remarked upon it – even if he'd been stabbed through the eye?

I need to get out there among them and see what I can find. She opened her mouth to tell him she should probably turn in, but he was already standing, stretching.

'I think we've done what we can with that,' he said, nodding toward the report. 'At least for tonight.'

'Yeah,' Shallan said, feigning a yawn. 'Probably.'

'So ...' Adolin said, then took a deep breath. 'There's ... something else.'

Shallan frowned. Something else? Why did he suddenly look like he was preparing to do something difficult?

He's going to break off our betrothal! a part of her mind thought, though she pounced on that emotion and shoved it back behind the curtains where it belonged.

'Okay, this isn't easy,' Adolin said. 'I don't want to offend, Shallan. But ... you know how I had you eat that man's food?'

'Um, yes. If my tongue is particularly spicy in the coming days, I blame you.'

'Shallan, there's something similar that we need to talk about. Something about you we can't just ignore.'

'I ...' *I killed my parents. I stabbed my mother through the chest and I strangled my father while singing to him.*

'You,' Adolin said, 'have a Shardblade.'

I didn't want to kill her. I had to. I had *to.*

Adolin grabbed her by the shoulders and she started, focusing on him. He was ... grinning?

'You have a *Shardblade,* Shallan! A *new* one. That's incredible. I dreamed for years of earning my Blade! So many men spend their lives with that very dream and never see it fulfilled. And here you have one!'

'And that's a good thing, right?' she said, held in his grip with arms pulled tight against her body.

'Of course it is!' Adolin said, letting go of her. 'But, I mean, you're a woman.'

'Was it the makeup that tipped you off, or the dress? Oh, it was the breasts, wasn't it? Always giving us away.'

'Shallan, this is serious.'

'I know,' she said, calming her nerves. 'Yes, Pattern can become a Shardblade, Adolin. I don't see what this has to do with anything. I can't

163

give it away. . . . Stormfather. You want to teach me how to use it, don't you?'

He grinned. 'You said that Jasnah was a Radiant too. Women, gaining Shardblades. It's weird, but it's not like we can *ignore* it. What about Plate? Do you have that hidden somewhere too?'

'Not that I know of,' she said. Her heart was beating quickly, her skin growing cold, her muscles tense. She fought against the sensation. 'I don't know where Plate comes from.'

'I know it's not feminine, but who cares? You've got a sword; you should know how to use it, and custom can go to Damnation. There, I said it.' He took a deep breath. 'I mean, the bridgeboy can have one, and he's *darkeyed*. Well, he was. Anyway, it's not so different from that.'

Thank you, Shallan thought, *for ranking all women as something equivalent to peasants.* But she held her tongue. This was obviously an important moment for Adolin, and he *was* trying to be broad-minded.

But . . . thinking of what she'd done pained her. Holding the weapon would be worse. So much worse.

She wanted to hide. But she couldn't. This truth refused to budge from her mind. Could she explain? 'So, you're right, but—'

'Great!' Adolin said. 'Great. I brought the Blade guards so we won't hurt each other. I stashed them back at the guard post. I'll go fetch them.'

He was out the door a moment later. Shallan stood with her hand stretched toward him, objections dying on her lips. She curled her fingers up and brought her hand to her breast, her heart thundering within.

'Mmmm,' Pattern said. 'This is good. This needs to be done.'

Shallan scrambled through the room to the small mirror she'd hung from the wall. She stared at herself, eyes wide, hair an utter mess. She'd started breathing in sharp, quick gasps. 'I can't –' she said. 'I can't be this person, Pattern. I can't just wield the sword. Some brilliant knight on a tower, pretending she should be followed.'

Pattern hummed softly a tone she'd come to recognize as confusion. The bewilderment of one species trying to comprehend the mind of another.

Sweat trickled down Shallan's face, running beside her eye as she stared at herself. What did she expect to see? The thought of breaking down in front of Adolin heightened her tension. Her every muscle grew taut, and the corners of her vision started to darken. She could see only before herself, and she wanted to run, go somewhere. *Be away.*

No. No, just be *someone else.*

Hands shaking, she scrambled over and dug out her drawing pad. She ripped pages, flinging them out of the way to reach an empty one, then seized her charcoal pencil.

Pattern moved over to her, a floating ball of shifting lines, buzzing in concern. 'Shallan? Please. What is wrong?'

I can hide, Shallan thought, drawing at a frenzied pace. *Shallan can flee and leave someone in her place.*

'It's because you hate me,' Pattern said softly. 'I can die, Shallan. I can go. They will send you another to bond.'

A high-pitched whine started to rise in the room, one Shallan didn't immediately recognize as coming from the back of her own throat. Pattern's words were like knives to her side. *No, please. Just draw.*

Veil. Veil would be fine holding a sword. She didn't have Shallan's broken soul, and hadn't killed her parents. She'd be able to do this.

No. No, what would Adolin do if he returned and found a completely different woman in the room? He couldn't know of Veil. The lines she sketched, ragged and unrefined from the shaking pencil, quickly took the shape of her own face. But hair in a bun. A poised woman, not as flighty as Shallan, not as unintentionally silly.

A woman who hadn't been sheltered. A woman hard enough, strong enough, to wield this sword. A woman like . . . like Jasnah.

Yes, Jasnah's subtle smile, composure, and self-confidence. Shallan outlined her own face with these ideals, creating a harder version of it. Could . . . could she be this woman?

I have to be, Shallan thought, drawing in Stormlight from her satchel, then breathing it out in a puff around her. She stood up as the change took hold. Her heartbeat slowed, and she wiped the sweat from her brow, then calmly undid her safehand sleeve, tossed aside the foolish extra pouch she'd tied around her hand inside, then rolled the sleeve back to expose her still-gloved hand.

Good enough. Adolin couldn't possibly expect her to put on sparring clothing. She pulled her hair back into a bun and fixed it in place with hairspikes from her satchel.

When Adolin returned to the room a moment later, he found a poised, calm woman who wasn't *quite* Shallan Davar. *Brightness Radiant is her name,* she thought. *She will go only by title.*

Adolin carried two long, thin pieces of metal that somehow could meld to the front of Shardblades and make them less dangerous for use in sparring. Radiant inspected them with a critical eye, then held her hand to the side, summoning Pattern. The Blade formed – a long, thin weapon nearly as tall as she was.

'Pattern,' she said, 'can modulate his shape, and will dull his edge to safe levels. I shan't need such a clunky device.' Indeed, Pattern's edge rippled, dulling.

'Storms, that's handy. I'll still need one though.' Adolin summoned his own Blade, a process that took him ten heartbeats – during which he turned his head, looking at her.

Shallan glanced down, realizing that she'd enhanced her bust in this guise. Not for him, of course. She'd just been making herself look more like Jasnah.

Adolin's sword finally appeared, with a thicker blade than her own, sinuous along the sharp edge, with delicate crystalline ridges along the back. He put one of the guards on the sword's edge.

Radiant put one foot forward, Blade lifted high in two hands beside her head.

'Hey,' Adolin said. 'That's not bad.'

'Shallan *did* spend quite a lot of time drawing you all.'

Adolin nodded thoughtfully. He approached and reached toward her with a thumb and two fingers. She thought he was going to adjust her grip, but instead he pressed his fingers against her collarbone and shoved lightly.

Radiant stumbled backward, almost tripping.

'A stance,' Adolin said, 'is about more than just looking great on the battlefield. It's about footing, center of balance, and control of the fight.'

'Noted. So how do I make it better?'

'I'm trying to decide. Everyone I've worked with before had been using a sword since their youth. I'm wondering how Zahel would have changed my training if I'd never even *picked up* a weapon.'

'From what I've heard of him,' Radiant said, 'it will depend on where there are any convenient rooftops nearby to jump off.'

'That's how he trained with Plate,' Adolin said. 'This is Blade. Should I teach you dueling? Or should I teach you how to fight in an army?'

'I shall settle,' Radiant said, 'for knowing how to avoid cutting off any of my own appendages, Brightlord Kholin.'

'Brightlord Kholin?'

Too formal. Right. That was how Radiant would act, of course – but she could allow herself some familiarity. Jasnah had done that.

'I was merely,' Radiant said, 'attempting to show the respect due a master from his humble pupil.'

Adolin chuckled. 'Please. We don't need that. But here, let's see what we can do about that stance. . . .'

Over the next hour, Adolin positioned her hands, her feet, and her arms a dozen times over. He picked a basic stance for her that she could eventually adapt into several of the formal stances – the ones like Windstance, which Adolin said wouldn't rely on strength or reach as much as mobility and skill.

She wasn't certain why he'd bothered fetching the metal sparring sleeves, as the two of them didn't exchange any blows. Other than correcting her stance ten thousand times, he spoke about the art of the duel. How to treat your Shardblade, how to think of an opponent, how to show respect to the institutions and traditions of the duel itself.

Some of it was very practical. Shardblades were dangerous weapons, which explained the demonstrations on how to hold hers, how to walk with it, how to take care not to slice people or things while casually turning.

Other parts of his monologue were more . . . mystical.

'The Blade is part of you,' Adolin said. 'The Blade is more than your tool; it is your life. Respect it. It will not fail you – if you are bested, it is because you failed the sword.'

Radiant stood in what felt like a very stiff pose, Blade held before herself in two hands. She'd only scraped Pattern on the ceiling two or three times; fortunately, most of the rooms in Urithiru had high ceilings.

Adolin gestured for her to perform a simple strike, as they'd been practicing. Radiant raised both arms, tilting the sword, then took a step forward while bringing it down. The entire angle of movement couldn't have been more than ninety degrees – barely a strike at all.

Adolin smiled. 'You're catching it. A few thousand more of those, and it will start to feel natural. We'll have to work on your breathing though.'

'My breathing?'

He nodded absently.

'Adolin,' Radiant said, 'I assure you, I have been breathing – without fail – my entire life.'

'Yeah,' he said. 'That's why you're going to have to unlearn it.'

'How I stand, how I think, how I breathe. I have trouble distinguishing what is actually relevant, and what is part of the subculture and superstition of swordsmen.'

'It's all relevant,' Adolin said.

'Eating chicken before a match?'

Adolin grinned. 'Well, maybe some things are personal quirks. But the swords *are* part of us.'

'I know mine is part of me,' Radiant said, resting the Blade at her side and setting her gloved safehand on it. 'I've bonded it. I suspect this is the origin of the tradition among Shardbearers.'

'So academic,' Adolin said, shaking his head. 'You need to *feel* this, Shallan. *Live* it.'

That would not have been a difficult task for Shallan. Radiant, however, preferred not to feel things she hadn't considered in depth beforehand.

'Have you considered,' she said, 'that your Shardblade was once a living spren, wielded by one of the Knights Radiant? Doesn't that change how you look at it?'

Adolin glanced toward his Blade, which he'd left summoned, strapped with the sheath and set across her blankets. 'I've always *kind of* known. Not that it was alive. That's silly. Swords aren't alive. I mean . . . I've always known there was something special about them. It's part of being a duelist, I think. We all know it.'

She let the matter drop. Swordsmen, from what she'd seen, were superstitious. As were sailors. As were . . . well, basically everyone but scholars like Radiant and Jasnah. It *was* curious to her how much of Adolin's rhetoric about Blades and dueling reminded her of religion.

How strange that these Alethi often treated their actual religion so flippantly. In Jah Keved, Shallan had spent hours painting lengthy passages from the Arguments. You'd speak the words out loud over and over, committing them to memory while kneeling or bowing, before finally burning the paper. The Alethi instead preferred to let the ardents deal with the Almighty, like he was some annoying parlor guest who could be safely distracted by servants offering a particularly tasty tea.

Adolin let her do some more strikes, perhaps sensing that she was growing tired of having her stance constantly adjusted. As she was swinging, he grabbed his own Blade and fell in beside her, modeling the stance and the strikes.

After a short time of that she dismissed her Blade, then picked up her sketchbook. She quickly flipped past the drawing of Radiant, and started to sketch Adolin in his stance. She was forced to let some of Radiant bleed away.

'No, stand there,' Shallan said, pointing at Adolin with her charcoal. 'Yes, like that.'

She sketched out the stance, then nodded. 'Now strike, and hold the last position.'

He did so. By now he'd removed his jacket, standing in only shirt and trousers. She did like how that tight shirt fit him. Even Radiant would admire that. She wasn't *dead*, just pragmatic.

She looked over the two sketches, then resummoned Pattern and fell into position.

'Hey, *nice*,' Adolin said as Radiant performed the next few strikes. 'Yeah, you've got it.'

He again fell in beside her. The simple attack he'd taught her was obviously a poor test of his skills, but he executed it with precision nonetheless, then grinned and started talking about the first few lessons he'd had with Zahel long ago.

His blue eyes were alight, and Shallan loved seeing that glow from him. Almost like Stormlight. She knew that passion – she'd felt what it was to be alive with interest, to be consumed by something so fully that you lost yourself in the wonder of it. For her it was art, but watching him, she thought that the two of them weren't so different.

Sharing these moments with him and drinking of his excitement felt special. Intimate. Even more so than their closeness had been earlier in the evening. She let herself be Shallan in some of the moments, but whenever the pain of holding the sword started to spike – whenever she really *thought* about what she was doing – she was able to become Radiant and avoid it.

She was genuinely reluctant to see the time end, so she let it stretch into the late evening, well past when she should have called a halt. At long last, Shallan bade a tired, sweaty farewell to Adolin and watched him trot down the strata-lined hallway outside, a spring to his step, a lamp in his hands, blade guards held on his shoulder.

Shallan would have to wait another night to visit taverns and hunt for answers. She trailed back into her room – strangely contented for all that the world might be in the middle of ending. That night she slept, for once, in peace.

16

WRAPPED
THREE TIMES

For in this comes the lesson.

—From *Oathbringer*, preface

A legend rested on the stone slab before Dalinar. A weapon pulled from the ancient mists of time, and said to have been forged during the shadowdays by the hand of God himself. The Blade of the Assassin in White, claimed by Kaladin Stormblessed during their clash above the storm.

Upon cursory inspection, it was indistinguishable from an ordinary Shardblade. Elegant, relatively small – in that it was barely five feet long – it was thin and curved like a tusk. It had patterns only at the base of the blade near the hilt.

He'd lit it with four diamond broams, placed at the corners of the altar-like stone slab. This small room had no strata or paintings on the walls, so the Stormlight lit only him and that alien Blade. It did have one oddity.

There was no gemstone.

Gemstones were what allowed men to bond to Shardblades. Often affixed at the pommel, though occasionally at the spot where hilt met blade, the gem would flash when you first touched it, initiating the process. Keep the Blade with you for a week, and the Blade became yours – dismissible and returnable in time with your heartbeat.

This Blade didn't have one. Dalinar hesitantly reached out and rested his fingers on its silvery length. It was warm to the touch, like something alive.

'It doesn't scream when I touch it,' he noted.

The knights, the Stormfather said in his head, *broke their oaths. They abandoned everything they'd sworn, and in so doing killed their spren. Other Blades are the corpses of those spren, which is why they scream at your touch. This weapon, instead, was made directly from Honor's soul, then given to the Heralds. It is also the mark of an oath, but a different type – and does not have the mind to scream on its own.*

'And Shardplate?' Dalinar asked.

Related, but different, the Stormfather rumbled. *You haven't spoken the oaths required to know more.*

'You cannot break oaths,' Dalinar said, fingers still resting on the Honorblade. 'Right?'

I cannot.

'What of the thing we fight? Odium, the origin of the Voidbringers and their spren. Can he break oaths?'

No, the Stormfather said. *He is far greater than I, but the power of ancient Adonalsium permeates him. And controls him. Odium is a force like pressure, gravitation, or the movement of time. These things cannot break their own rules. Nor can he.*

Dalinar tapped the Honorblade. A fragment of Honor's own soul, crystallized into metallic form. In a way, the death of their god gave him hope – for if Honor had fallen, surely Odium could as well.

In visions, Honor had left Dalinar with a task. *Vex Odium, convince him that he can lose, and appoint a champion. He will take that chance instead of risking defeat again, as he has suffered so often. This is the best advice I can give you.*

'I've seen that the enemy is preparing a champion,' Dalinar said. 'A dark creature with red eyes and nine shadows. Will Honor's suggestion work? Can I make Odium agree to a decisive contest between me and that champion?'

Of course Honor's suggestion would work, the Stormfather said. *He spoke it.*

'I mean,' Dalinar said, '*why* would it work? Why would this Odium ever agree to a contest of champions? It seems too momentous a matter to risk on something so small and inferior as the prowess and will of men.'

Your enemy is not a man like you, the Stormfather replied, voice rumbling, thoughtful. Even ... frightened. *He does not age. He feels. He is angry. But this does not change, and his rage does not cool. Epochs can pass, and he will remain the same.*

To fight directly might coax out forces that could hurt him, as he has been hurt before. Those scars do not heal. To pick a champion, then lose, will only cost him time. He has that in plenitude. He still will not agree easily, but it is possible he will *agree. If presented with the option in the right moment, the right way. Then he will be bound.*

'And we win ...'

Time, the Stormfather said. *Which, though dross to him, is the most valuable thing a man can have.*

Dalinar slipped the Honorblade off the slab. At the side of the room, a shaft cut into the ground. Two feet wide, it was one of many strange holes, corridors, and hidden corners they'd found in the tower city. This one was probably part of a sewage system; judging by the rust on the edges of the hole, there had once been a metal pipe here connecting the stone hole in the floor to one in the ceiling.

One of Navani's primary concerns was figuring out how all this worked. For now, they'd gotten by using wooden frames to turn certain large, communal rooms with ancient baths into privies. Once they had more Stormlight, their Soulcasters could deal with the waste, as they'd done in the warcamps.

Navani found the system inelegant. Communal privies with sometimes long lines made for an inefficient city, and she claimed that these tubes indicated a widespread piping and sanitation system. It was exactly the sort of large-scale civic project that engaged her – he'd never known anyone to get as excited by sewage as Navani Kholin.

For now, this tube was empty. Dalinar knelt and lowered the sword into the hole, sliding it into a stone sheath he'd cut in the side. The upper lip of the hole shielded the protruding hilt from sight; you'd have to reach down and feel in the hole to find the Honorblade.

He stood up, then gathered his spheres and made his way out. He hated leaving it there, but he could think of nothing safer. His rooms didn't feel secure enough yet – he had no vault, and a crowd of guards would only draw attention. Beyond Kaladin, Navani, and the Stormfather himself, nobody even knew that Dalinar had this. If he masked his movements, there was virtually no chance of the Blade being discovered in this vacant portion of the tower.

What will you do with it? the Stormfather asked as Dalinar entered the empty corridors. *It is a weapon beyond parallel. The gift of a god. With it, you would be a Windrunner unoathed. And more. More that men do not understand, and cannot. Like a Herald, nearly.*

'All the more reason,' Dalinar said, 'to think very carefully before using it. Though I wouldn't mind if you kept an eye on it for me.'

The Stormfather actually laughed. *You think I can see all things?*

'I kind of assumed . . . The map we made . . .'

I see what is left out in the storms, and that darkly. I am no god, Dalinar Kholin. No more than your shadow on the wall is you.

Dalinar reached the steps downward, then wound around and around, holding a broam for light. If Captain Kaladin didn't return soon, the Honorblade would provide another means of Windrunning – a way to get to Thaylen City or Azir at speed. Or to get Elhokar's team to Kholinar. The Stormfather had also confirmed it could work Oathgates, which might prove handy.

Dalinar reached more inhabited sections of the tower, which bustled with movement. A chef's assistants hauling supplies from the storage dump right inside the tower gates, a couple of men painting lines on the floor to guide, families of soldiers in a particularly wide hallway, sitting on boxes along the wall and watching children roll wooden spheres down a slope into a room that had probably been another bath.

Life. Such an odd place to make a home, yet they'd transformed the barren Shattered Plains into one. This tower wouldn't be so different, assuming they could keep farming operations going on the Shattered Plains. And assuming they had enough Stormlight to keep those Oathgates working.

He was the odd man out, holding a sphere. Guards patrolled with lanterns. The cooks worked by lamp oil, but their stores were starting to run low. The women watching children and darning socks used only the light of a few windows along the wall here.

Dalinar passed near his rooms. Today's guards, spearmen from Bridge Thirteen, waited outside. He waved for them to follow him.

'Is all well, Brightlord?' one asked, catching up quickly. He spoke with a slow drawl – a Koron accent, from near the Sunmaker Mountains in central Alethkar.

'Fine,' Dalinar said tersely, trying to determine the time. How long had he spent speaking with the Stormfather?

'Good, good,' the guard said, spear held lightly to his shoulder. 'Wouldn't want anything ta have happened ta you. While you were out. Alone. In the corridors. When you said nobody should be going about alone.'

Dalinar eyed the man. Clean-shaven, he was a little pale for an Alethi and had dark brown hair. Dalinar vaguely thought the man had shown up among his guards several times during the last week or so. He liked to roll a sphere across his knuckles in what Dalinar found to be a distracting way.

'Your name?' Dalinar asked as they walked.

'Rial,' the man said. 'Bridge Thirteen.' The soldier raised a hand and gave a precise salute, so careful it could have been given by one of Dalinar's finest officers, except he maintained the same lazy expression.

'Well, Sergeant Rial, I was *not* alone,' Dalinar said. 'Where did you get this habit of questioning officers?'

'It isn't a habit if you only do it once, Brightlord.'

'And you've only ever done it once?'

'Ta you?'

'To anyone.'

'Well,' Rial said, 'those don't count, Brightlord. I'm a new man. Reborn in the bridge crews.'

Lovely. 'Well, Rial, do you know what time it is? I have trouble telling in these storming corridors.'

'You could use the clock device Brightness Navani sent you, sir,' Rial said. 'I think that's what they're for, you know.'

Dalinar affixed him with another glare.

'Wasn't questioning you, sir,' Rial said. 'It wasn't a question, see....'

Dalinar finally turned and stalked back down the corridor to his rooms. Where was that package Navani had given him? He found it on an end table, and from inside it removed a leather bracer somewhat like what an archer would wear. It had two clock faces set into the top. One showed the time with three hands – even seconds, as if that mattered. The other was a stormclock, which could be set to wind down to the next projected highstorm.

How did they get it all so small? he wondered, shaking the device. Set into the leather, it also had a painrial – a gemstone fabrial that would take pain from him if he pressed his hand on it. Navani had been working on various forms of pain-related fabrials for use by surgeons, and had mentioned using him as a test subject.

He strapped the device to his forearm, right above the wrist. It felt conspicuous there, wrapping around the outside of his uniform sleeve, but it *had* been a gift. In any case, he had an hour until his next scheduled meeting. Time to work out some of his restless energy. He collected his two guards, then made his way down a level to one of the larger chambers near where he housed his soldiers.

The room had black and grey strata on the walls, and was filled with men training. They all wore Kholin blue, even if just an armband. For now both lighteyes and dark practiced in the same chamber, sparring in rings with padded cloth mats.

As always, the sounds and smells of sparring warmed Dalinar. Sweeter than the scent of flatbread baking was that of oiled leather. More welcoming than the sound of flutes was that of practice swords rapping against one another. Wherever he was, and whatever station he obtained, a place like this would always be home.

He found the swordmasters assembled at the back wall, seated on cushions and supervising their students. Save for one notable exception, they all had squared beards, shaved heads, and simple, open-fronted robes that tied at the waist. Dalinar owned ardents who were experts in all manner of specialties, and per tradition any man or woman could come to them and be apprenticed in a new skill or trade. The swordmasters, however, were his pride.

Five of the six men rose and bowed to him. Dalinar turned to survey the room again. The smell of sweat, the clang of weapons. They were the signs of preparation. The world might be in chaos, but Alethkar prepared.

Not Alethkar, he thought. *Urithiru. My kingdom.* Storms, it was going to be difficult to accustom himself to that. He would always be Alethi, but once Elhokar's proclamation came out, Alethkar would no longer be his. He still hadn't figured out how to present that fact to his armies. He wanted to give Navani and her scribes time to work out the exact legalities.

'You've done well here,' Dalinar said to Kelerand, one of the swordmasters. 'Ask Ivis if she'd look at expanding the training quarters into adjacent chambers. I want you to keep the troops busy. I'm worried about them getting restless and starting more fights.'

'It will be done, Brightlord,' Kelerand said, bowing.

'I'd like a spar myself,' Dalinar said.

'I shall find someone suitable, Brightlord.'

'What about you, Kelerand?' Dalinar said. The swordmaster bested Dalinar two out of three times, and though Dalinar had given up delusions of someday becoming the better swordsman – he was a soldier, not a duelist – he liked the challenge.

'I will,' Kelerand said stiffly, 'of course do as my highprince commands, though if given a choice, I shall pass. With all due respect, I don't feel that I would make a suitable match for you today.'

Dalinar glanced toward the other standing swordmasters, who lowered their eyes. Swordmaster ardents weren't generally like their more religious counterparts. They could be formal at times, but you could laugh with them. Usually.

They were still ardents though.

'Very well,' Dalinar said. 'Find me someone to fight.'

Though he'd intended it only as a dismissal of Kelerand, the other four joined him, leaving Dalinar. He sighed, leaning back against the wall, and glanced to the side. One man still lounged on his cushion. He wore a scruffy beard and clothing that seemed an afterthought – not dirty, but ragged, belted with rope.

'Not offended by my presence, Zahel?' Dalinar asked.

'I'm offended by everyone's presence. You're no more revolting than the rest, Mister Highprince.'

Dalinar settled down on a stool to wait.

'You didn't expect this?' Zahel said, sounding amused.

'No. I thought . . . well, they're *fighting* ardents. Swordsmen. Soldiers, at heart.'

'You're dangerously close to threatening them with a decision, Brightlord: choose between God and their highprince. The fact that they like you doesn't make the decision easier, but more difficult.'

'Their discomfort will pass,' Dalinar said. 'My marriage, though it seems dramatic now, will eventually be a mere trivial note in history.'

'Perhaps.'

'You disagree?'

'Every moment in our lives seems trivial,' Zahel said. 'Most are forgotten while some, equally humble, become the points upon which history pivots. Like white on black.'

'White . . . on black?' Dalinar asked.

'Figure of speech. I don't really care what you did, Highprince. Lighteyed self-indulgence or serious sacrilege, either way it doesn't affect me. But there *are* those who are asking how far you're going to end up straying.'

Dalinar grunted. Honestly, had he expected *Zahel* of all people to be helpful? He stood up and began to pace, annoyed at his own nervous energy. Before the ardents could return with someone for him to duel, he stalked back into the middle of the room, looking for soldiers he recognized. Men who wouldn't feel inhibited sparring with a highprince.

He eventually located one of General Khal's sons. Not the Shardbearer, Captain Halam Khal, but the next oldest son – a beefy man with a head that had always seemed a little too small for his body. He was stretching after some wrestling matches.

'Aratin,' Dalinar said. 'You ever sparred with a highprince?'

The younger man turned, then immediately snapped to attention. 'Sir?'

'No need for formality. I'm just looking for a match.'

'I'm not equipped for a proper duel, Brightlord,' he said. 'Give me some time.'

'No need,' Dalinar said. 'I'm fine for a wrestling match. It's been too long.'

Some men would rather not spar with a man as important as Dalinar, for fear of hurting him. Khal had trained his sons better than that. The young man grinned, displaying a prominent gap in his teeth. 'Fine with me, Brightlord. But I'll have you know, I've not lost a match in months.'

'Good,' Dalinar said. 'I need a challenge.'

The swordmasters finally returned as Dalinar, stripped to the waist, was pulling on a pair of sparring leggings over his undershorts. The tight leggings came down only to his knees. He nodded to the swordmasters – ignoring the gentlemanly lighteyes they'd sought out for him to spar – and stepped into the wrestling ring with Aratin Khal. His guards gave the swordmasters a kind of apologetic shrug, then Rial counted off a start to the wrestling match. Dalinar immediately lunged forward and slammed into Khal, grabbing him under the arms, struggling to hold his feet back and force his opponent off balance. The wrestling match would eventually go to the ground, but you wanted to be the one who controlled when and how that happened.

There was no grabbing the leggings in a traditional vehah match, and of course no grabbing hair, so Dalinar twisted, trying to get his opponent into a sturdy hold while preventing the man from shoving him over. Dalinar scrambled, his muscles taut, his fingers slipping on his opponent's skin.

For those frantic moments, he could focus only on the match. His strength against that of his opponent. Sliding his feet, twisting his weight, straining for purchase. There was a purity to the contest, a simplicity that he hadn't experienced in what seemed like ages.

Aratin pulled Dalinar tight, then managed to twist, tripping Dalinar over his hip. They went to the mat, and Dalinar grunted, raising his arm to his neck to prevent a chokehold, turning his head. Old training prompted him to twist and writhe before the opponent could get a good grip on him.

Too slow. It had been years since he'd done this regularly. The other man moved with Dalinar's twist, forgoing the attempt at a chokehold, instead getting Dalinar under the arms from behind and pressing him down, face against the mat, his weight on top of Dalinar.

Dalinar growled, and by instinct reached out for that extra reserve he'd always had. The pulse of the fight, the edge.

The Thrill. Soldiers spoke of it in the quiet of the night, over campfires. That battle rage unique to the Alethi. Some called it the power of their ancestors, others the true mindset of the soldier. It had driven the Sun-maker to glory. It was the open secret of Alethi success.

No. Dalinar stopped himself from reaching for it, but he needn't have worried. He couldn't remember feeling the Thrill in months – and the longer he'd been apart from it, the more he'd begun to recognize that there was something profoundly *wrong* about the Thrill.

So he gritted his teeth and struggled – cleanly and fairly – with his opponent.

And got pinned.

Aratin was younger, more practiced at this style of fight. Dalinar didn't make it easy, but he was on the bottom, lacked leverage, and simply wasn't as young as he'd once been. Aratin twisted him over, and before too long Dalinar found himself pressed to the mat, shoulders down, completely immobilized.

Dalinar knew he was beaten, but couldn't bring himself to tap out. Instead he strained against the hold, teeth gritted and sweat pouring down the sides of his face. He became aware of something. Not the Thrill . . . but Stormlight in the pocket of his uniform trousers, lying beside the ring.

Aratin grunted, arms like steel. Dalinar smelled his own sweat, the rough cloth of the mat. His muscles protested the treatment.

He knew he could seize the Stormlight power, but his sense of fairness protested at the mere thought. Instead he arched his back, holding his breath and heaving with everything he had, then twisted, trying to get back on his face for the leverage to escape.

His opponent shifted. Then groaned, and Dalinar felt the man's grip slipping . . . slowly. . . .

'Oh, for storm's sake,' a feminine voice said. 'Dalinar?'

Dalinar's opponent let go immediately, backing away. Dalinar twisted, puffing from exertion, to find Navani standing outside the ring with arms folded. He grinned at her, then stood up and accepted a light takama overshirt and towel from an aide. As Aratin Khal retreated, Dalinar raised a fist to him and bowed his head – a sign that Dalinar considered Aratin the victor. 'Well played, son.'

'An honor, sir!'

Dalinar threw on the takama, turning to Navani and wiping his brow with the towel. 'Come to watch me spar?'

'Yes, what every wife loves,' Navani said. 'Seeing that in his spare time, her husband likes to roll around on the floor with half-naked, sweaty men.' She glanced at Aratin. 'Shouldn't you be sparring with men closer to your own age?'

'On the battlefield,' Dalinar said, 'I don't have the luxury of choosing the age of my opponent. Best to fight at a disadvantage here to prepare.' He hesitated, then said more softly, 'I think I almost had him anyway.'

'Your definition of "almost" is particularly ambitious, gemheart.'

Dalinar accepted a waterskin from an aide. Though Navani and her aides weren't the only women in the room, the others were ardents. Navani in her bright yellow gown still stood out like a flower on a barren stone field.

As Dalinar scanned the chamber, he found that many of the ardents – not just the swordmasters – failed to meet his gaze. And there was Kadash, his former comrade-in-arms, speaking with the swordmasters.

Nearby, Aratin was receiving congratulations from his friends. Pinning the Blackthorn was considered quite the accomplishment. The young man accepted their praise with a grin, but he held his shoulder and winced when someone slapped him on the back.

I should have tapped out, Dalinar thought. Pushing the contest had endangered them both. He was annoyed at himself. He'd specifically chosen someone younger and stronger, then became a poor loser? Getting older was something he needed to accept, and he was kidding himself if he actually thought this would help him on the battlefield. He'd given away his armor, no longer carried a Shardblade. When exactly did he expect to be fighting in person again?

The man with nine shadows.

The water suddenly tasted stale in his mouth. He'd been expecting to fight the enemy's champion himself, assuming he could even make the contest happen to their advantage. But wouldn't assigning the duty to someone like Kaladin make far more sense?

'Well,' Navani said, 'you might want to throw on a uniform. The Iriali queen is ready.'

'The meeting isn't for a few hours.'

'She wants to do it now. Apparently, her court tidereader saw something in the waves that means an earlier meeting is better. She should be contacting us any minute.'

Storming Iriali. Still, they had an Oathgate – two, if you counted the one in the kingdom of Rira, which Iri had sway over. Among Iri's three monarchs, currently two kings and a queen, the latter had authority over foreign policy, so she was the one they needed to talk to.

'I'm fine with moving up the time,' Dalinar said.

'I'll await you in the writing chamber.'

'Why?' Dalinar said, waving a hand. 'It's not like she can see me. Set up here.'

'Here,' Navani said flatly.

'Here,' Dalinar said, feeling stubborn. 'I've had enough of cold chambers, silent save for the scratching of reeds.'

Navani raised an eyebrow at him, but ordered her assistants to get out their writing materials. A worried ardent came over, perhaps to try to dissuade her – but after a few firm orders from Navani, he went running to get her a bench and table.

Dalinar smiled and went to select two training swords from a rack near the swordmasters. Common longswords of unsharpened steel. He tossed one to Kadash, who caught it smoothly, but then placed it in front of him with point down, resting his hands on the pommel.

'Brightlord,' Kadash said, 'I would prefer to give this task to another, as I don't particularly feel—'

'Tough,' Dalinar said. 'I need some practice, Kadash. As your master, I demand you give it to me.'

Kadash stared at Dalinar for a protracted moment, then let out an annoyed huff and followed Dalinar to the ring. 'I won't be much of a match for you, Brightlord. I have dedicated my years to scripture, not the sword. I was only here to—'

'—check up on me. I know. Well, maybe I'll be rusty too. I haven't fought with a common longsword in decades. I always had something better.'

'Yes. I remember when you first got your Blade. The world itself trembled on that day, Dalinar Kholin.'

'Don't be melodramatic,' Dalinar said. 'I was merely one in a long line of idiots given the ability to kill people too easily.'

Rial hesitantly counted the start to the match, and Dalinar rushed in swinging. Kadash rebuffed him competently, then stepped to the side of the ring. 'Pardon, Brightlord, but you *were* different from the others. You were much, much better at the killing part.'

I always have been, Dalinar thought, rounding Kadash. It was odd to remember the ardent as one of his elites. They hadn't been close then; they'd only become so during Kadash's years as an ardent.

Navani cleared her throat. 'Hate to interrupt this stick-wagging,' she said, 'but the queen is ready to speak with you, Dalinar.'

'Great,' he said, not taking his eyes off Kadash. 'Read me what she says.'

'While you're sparring?'

'Sure.'

He could practically feel Navani roll her eyes. He grinned, coming in at Kadash again. She thought he was being silly. Perhaps he was.

He was also failing. One at a time, the world's monarchs were shutting him out. Only Taravangian of Kharbranth – known to be slow witted – had agreed to listen to him. Dalinar was doing something wrong. In an extended war campaign, he'd have forced himself to look at his problems from a new perspective. Bring in new officers to voice their ideas. Try to approach battles from different terrain.

Dalinar clashed blades with Kadash, smashing metal against metal.

' "Highprince," ' Navani read as he fought, ' "it is with wondrous awe at the grandeur of the One that I approach you. The time for the world to undergo a glorious new experience has arrived." '

'Glorious, Your Majesty?' Dalinar said, swiping at Kadash's leg. The man dodged back. 'Surely you can't *welcome* these events?'

' "All experience is welcome," ' came the reply. ' "We are the One experiencing itself – and this new storm is glorious even if it brings pain." '

Dalinar grunted, blocking a backhand from Kadash. Swords rang loudly.

'I hadn't realized,' Navani noted, 'that she was so religious.'

'Pagan superstition,' Kadash said, sliding back across the mat from Dalinar. 'At least the Azish have the decency to worship the Heralds, although they blasphemously place them above the Almighty. The Iriali are no better than Shin shamans.'

'I remember, Kadash,' Dalinar said, 'when you weren't nearly so judgmental.'

'I've been informed that my laxness might have served to encourage you.'

'I always found your perspective to be refreshing.' He stared right at Kadash, but spoke to Navani. 'Tell her: Your Majesty, as much as I welcome a challenge, I fear the suffering these new . . . experiences will bring. We must be unified in the face of the coming dangers.'

'Unity,' Kadash said softly. 'If that is your goal, Dalinar, then why do you seek to rip apart your own people?'

Navani started writing. Dalinar drew closer, passing his longsword from one hand to the other. 'How do you know, Kadash? How do you *know* the Iriali are the pagans?'

Kadash frowned. Though he wore the square beard of an ardent, that scar on his head wasn't the only thing that set him apart from his fellows. They treated swordplay like just another art. Kadash had the haunted eyes of a soldier. When he dueled, he kept watch to the sides, in case someone tried to flank him. An impossibility in a solo duel, but all too likely on a battlefield.

'How can you ask that, Dalinar?'

'Because it should be asked,' Dalinar said. 'You claim the Almighty is God. Why?'

'Because he simply *is*.'

'That isn't good enough for me,' Dalinar said, realizing for the first time it was true. 'Not anymore.'

The ardent growled, then leaped in, attacking with real determination this time. Dalinar danced backward, fending him off, as Navani read – loudly.

' "Highprince, I will be frank. The Iriali Triumvirate is in agreement. Alethkar has not been relevant in the world since the Sunmaker's fall. The power of the ones who control the new storm, however, is undeniable. They offer gracious terms." '

Dalinar stopped in place, dumbfounded. 'You'd side with the *Voidbringers*?' he asked toward Navani, but then was forced to defend himself from Kadash, who hadn't let up.

'What?' Kadash said, clanging his blade against Dalinar's. 'Surprised someone is willing to side with evil, Dalinar? That someone would pick darkness, superstition, and heresy instead of the Almighty's light?'

'I am *not* a heretic.' Dalinar slapped Kadash's blade away – but not before the ardent scored a touch on Dalinar's arm. The hit was hard, and though the swords were blunted, that would bruise for certain.

'You just *told* me you doubted the Almighty,' Kadash said. 'What is left, after that?'

'I don't know,' Dalinar said. He stepped closer. 'I don't know, and that *terrifies* me, Kadash. But Honor spoke to me, confessed that he was beaten.'

'The princes of the Voidbringers,' Kadash said, 'were said to be able to blind the eyes of men. To send them lies, Dalinar.'

He rushed in, swinging, but Dalinar danced back, retreating around the rim of the dueling ring.

' "My people," ' Navani said, reading the reply from the queen of Iri, ' "do not want war. Perhaps the way to prevent another Desolation is to let the Voidbringers take what they wish. From our histories, sparse though they are, it seems that this was the one option men never explored. An experience from the One we rejected."'

Navani looked up, obviously as surprised to read the words as Dalinar was to hear them. The pen kept writing. ' "Beyond that,"' she added, ' "we have reasons to distrust the word of a thief, Highprince Kholin."'

Dalinar groaned. So *that* was what this was all about – Adolin's Shardplate. Dalinar glanced at Navani. 'Find out more, try to console them?'

She nodded, and started writing. Dalinar gritted his teeth and charged Kadash again. The ardent caught his sword, then grabbed his takama with his free hand, pulling him close, face to face.

'The Almighty is *not dead*,' Kadash hissed.

'Once, you'd have counseled me. Now you glare at me. What happened to the ardent I knew? A man who had lived a real life, not just watched the world from high towers and monasteries?'

'He's frightened,' Kadash said softly. 'That he's somehow failed in his most solemn duty to a man he deeply admires.'

They met eyes, their swords still locked, but neither one actually trying to push the other. For a moment, Dalinar saw in Kadash the man he'd always been. The gentle, understanding model of everything good about the Vorin church.

'Give me something to take back to the curates of the church,' Kadash pled. 'Recant your insistence that the Almighty is dead. If you do that, I can make them accept the marriage. Kings have done worse and retained Vorin support.'

Dalinar set his jaw, then shook his head.

'Dalinar . . .'

'Falsehoods serve nobody, Kadash,' Dalinar said, pulling back. 'If the Almighty is dead, then pretending otherwise is pure stupidity. We need real hope, not faith in lies.'

Around the room, more than a few men had stopped their bouts to watch or listen. The swordmasters had stepped up behind Navani, who was still exchanging some politic words with the Iriali queen.

'Don't throw out everything we've believed because of a few dreams, Dalinar,' Kadash said. 'What of our society, what of *tradition*?'

'Tradition?' Dalinar said. 'Kadash, did I ever tell you about my first sword trainer?'

'No,' Kadash said, frowning, glancing at the other ardents. 'Was it Rembrinor?'

Dalinar shook his head. 'Back when I was young, our branch of the Kholin family didn't have grand monasteries and beautiful practice grounds. My father found a teacher for me from two towns over. His name was Harth. Young fellow, not a true swordmaster – but good enough.

'He was very focused on proper procedure, and wouldn't let me train until I'd learned how to put on a takama the right way.' Dalinar gestured at the takama shirt he was wearing. 'He wouldn't have stood for me fighting like this. You put on the skirt, then the overshirt, then you wrap your cloth belt around yourself three times and tie it.

'I always found that annoying. The belt was too tight, wrapped three times – you had to pull it hard to get enough slack to tie the knot. The first time I went to duels at a neighboring town, I felt like an idiot. Everyone else had long drooping belt ends at the front of their takamas.

'I asked Harth why we did it differently. He said it was the right way, the *true* way. So, when my travels took me to Harth's hometown, I searched out his master, a man who had trained with the ardents in Kholinar. He insisted that this was the right way to tie a takama, as he'd learned from his master.'

By now, they'd drawn an even larger crowd. Kadash frowned. 'And the point?'

'I found my master's master's master in Kholinar after we captured it,' Dalinar said. 'The ancient, wizened ardent was eating curry and flatbread, completely uncaring of who ruled the city. I asked him. Why tie your belt three times, when everyone else thinks you should do it twice?

'The old man laughed and stood up. I was shocked to see that he was terribly short. 'If I only tie it twice,' he exclaimed, 'the ends hang down so low, I trip!''

The chamber fell silent. Nearby, one soldier chuckled, but quickly cut himself off – none of the ardents seemed amused.

'I love tradition,' Dalinar said to Kadash. 'I've *fought* for tradition. I make my men follow the codes. I uphold Vorin virtues. But merely being tradition does not make something worthy, Kadash. We can't just assume that because something is *old* it is *right*.'

He turned to Navani.

'She's not listening,' Navani said. 'She insists you are a thief, not to be trusted.'

'Your Majesty,' Dalinar said. 'I am led to believe that you would let nations fall, and men be slaughtered, because of a petty grievance from the past. If my relations with the kingdom of Rira are prompting you to consider supporting the enemies of all humankind, then perhaps we could discuss a personal reconciliation first.'

Navani nodded at that, though she glanced at the people watching and cocked an eyebrow. She thought all this should have been done in private. Well, perhaps she was right. At the same time, Dalinar felt he'd needed this. He couldn't explain why.

He raised his sword to Kadash in a sign of respect. 'Are we done here?'

In response, Kadash came running at him, sword raised. Dalinar sighed, then let himself get touched on the left, but ended the exchange with his weapon leveled at Kadash's neck.

'That's not a valid dueling strike,' the ardent said.

'I'm not much of a duelist these days.'

The ardent grunted, then shoved away Dalinar's weapon and lunged at him. Dalinar, however, caught Kadash's arm, then spun the man with his own momentum. He slammed Kadash down to the ground and held him there.

'The world is ending, Kadash,' Dalinar said. 'I can't simply rely on tradition. I need to know *why*. Convince me. Offer me proof of what you say.'

'You shouldn't *need* proof in the Almighty. You sound like your niece!'

'I'll take that as a compliment.'

'What . . . what of the Heralds?' Kadash said. 'Do you deny *them*, Dalinar? They were servants of the Almighty, and their existence proved his. They had *power*.'

'Power?' Dalinar said. 'Like this?'

He sucked in Stormlight. Murmuring rose from those watching as Dalinar began to glow, then did . . . something else. Commanded the Light. When he rose, he left Kadash stuck to the ground in a pool of Radiance that held him fast, binding him to the stone. The ardent wriggled, helpless.

'The Knights Radiant have returned,' Dalinar said. 'And yes, I accept the authority of the Heralds. I accept that there was a being, once, named Honor – the Almighty. He helped us, and I would welcome his help again. If you can prove to me that Vorinism as it currently stands is what the Heralds taught, we will speak again.'

He tossed his sword aside and stepped up to Navani.

'Nice show,' she said softly. 'That was for the room, not just Kadash, I assume?'

'The soldiers need to know where I stand in relation to the church. What does our queen say?'

'Nothing good,' she muttered. 'She says you can contact her with arrangements for the return of the stolen goods, and she'll consider.'

'Storming woman,' Dalinar said. 'She's after Adolin's Shardplate. How valid is her claim?'

'Not very,' Navani said. 'You got that through marriage, and to a light-eyes from Rira, not Iri. Yes, the Iriali claim their sister nation as a vassal, but even if the claim weren't disputed, the queen doesn't have any actual relation to Evi or her brother.'

Dalinar grunted. 'Rira was never strong enough to try to claim the Plate back. But if it will bring Iri to our side, then I'd consider it. Maybe I can agree to . . .' He trailed off. 'Wait. What did you say?'

'Hum?' Navani said. 'About . . . oh, right. You can't hear her name.'

'Say it again,' Dalinar whispered.

'What?' Navani said. 'Evi?'

Memories blossomed in Dalinar's head. He staggered, then slumped against the writing table, feeling as if he'd been struck by a hammer to the head. Navani called for physicians, implying his dueling had overtaxed him.

That wasn't it. Instead, it was the burning in his mind, the sudden shock of a word spoken.

Evi. He could *hear his wife's name*.

And he suddenly remembered her face.

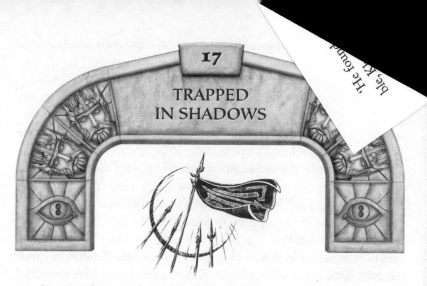

17

TRAPPED
IN SHADOWS

*It is not a lesson I claim to be able to teach. Experience herself is the
great teacher, and you must seek her directly.*

—From *Oathbringer*, preface

'I still think we should kill him,' Khen – the parshwoman who had been
playing cards – said to the others.

Kaladin sat tied and bound to a tree. He'd spent the night there.
They'd let him up several times to use the latrine today, but otherwise kept him bound. Though their knots were good, they always
posted guards, even though he'd turned himself in to them in the first
place.

His muscles were stiff, and the posture was uncomfortable, but he had
endured worse as a slave. Almost the entire afternoon had passed so far
– and they were still arguing about him.

He didn't see that yellow-white spren again, the one that had been a
ribbon of light. He almost thought he'd imagined it. At least the rain had
finally stopped. Hopefully that meant the highstorms – and Stormlight
– were close to returning.

'Kill him?' another of the parshmen said. 'Why? What danger is he to
us?'

'He'll tell others where we are.'

us easily enough on his own. I doubt others will have trou-
_.en.'

The parshmen didn't seem to have a specific leader. Kaladin could hear
them talking from where they stood, huddled together beneath a tarp.
The air smelled wet, and the clump of trees shivered when a gust of wind
blew through. A shower of water drops came down on top of him, somehow more cold than the Weeping itself.

Soon, blessedly, this would all dry up and he could finally see the sun
again.

'So we let him go?' Khen asked. She had a gruff voice, angry.

'I don't know. Would you actually do it, Khen? Bash his head in yourself?'

The tent fell silent.

'If it means they can't take us again?' she said. 'Yes, I'd kill him. I won't
go back, Ton.'

They had simple, darkeyed Alethi names – matched by their uncomfortably familiar accents. Kaladin didn't worry for his safety; though
they'd taken his knife, spanreed, and spheres, he could summon Syl at a
moment's notice. She flitted nearby on gusts of wind, dodging between
the branches of trees.

The parshmen eventually left their conference, and Kaladin dozed. He
was later roused by the noise of them gathering up their meager belong-
ings: an axe or two, some waterskins, the nearly ruined bags of grain. As
the sun set, long shadows stretched across Kaladin, plunging the camp
into darkness again. It seemed that the group moved at night.

The tall male who had been playing cards the night before approached
Kaladin, who recognized the pattern of his skin. He untied the ropes
binding Kaladin to the tree, the ones around his ankles – but left the
bonds on Kaladin's hands.

'You *could* capture that card,' Kaladin noted.

The parshman stiffened.

'The card game,' Kaladin said. 'The squire can capture if supported by
an allied card. So you were right.'

The parshman grunted, yanking on the rope to tow Kaladin to his
feet. He stretched, working stiff muscles and painful cramps, as the other
parshmen broke down the last of the improvised tarp tents: the one that
had been fully enclosed. Earlier in the day, though, Kaladin had gotten a
look at what was inside.

Children.

There were a dozen of them, dressed in smocks, of various ages from toddler to young teenager. The females wore their hair loose, and the males wore theirs tied or braided. They hadn't been allowed to leave the tent except at a few carefully supervised moments, but he had heard them laughing. He'd first worried they were captured human children.

As the camp broke, they scattered about, excited to finally be released. One younger girl scampered across the wet stones and seized the empty hand of the man leading Kaladin. Each of the children bore the distinctive look of their elders – the not-quite-Parshendi appearance with the armored portions on the sides of their heads and forearms. For the children, the color of the carapace was a light orange-pink.

Kaladin couldn't define why this sight seemed so strange to him. Parshmen did breed, though people often spoke of them *being bred,* like animals. And, well, that wasn't far from the truth, was it? Everyone knew it.

What would Shen – Rlain – think if Kaladin had said those words out loud?

The procession moved out of the trees, Kaladin led by his ropes. They kept talk to a minimum, and as they crossed through a field in the darkness, Kaladin had a distinct impression of familiarity. Had he been here before, done this before?

'What about the king?' his captor said, speaking in a soft voice, but turning his head to direct the question at Kaladin.

Elhokar? What . . . *Oh, right. The cards.*

'The king is one of the most powerful cards you can place,' Kaladin said, struggling to remember all the rules. 'He can capture any other card except another king, and can't be captured himself unless touched by three enemy cards of knight or better. Um . . . and he is immune to the Soulcaster.' *I think.*

'When I watched men play, they used this card rarely. If it is so powerful, why delay?'

'If your king gets captured, you lose,' Kaladin said. 'So you only play him if you're desperate or if you are certain you can defend him. Half the times I've played, I left him in my barrack all game.'

The parshman grunted, then looked to the girl at his side, who tugged on his arm and pointed. He gave her a whispered response, and she ran on tiptoes toward a patch of flowering rockbuds, visible by the light of the first moon.

The vines pulled back, blossoms closing. The girl, however, knew to squat at the side and wait, hands poised, until the flowers reopened – then she snatched one in each hand, her giggles echoing across the plain. Joyspren followed her like blue leaves as she returned, giving Kaladin a wide berth.

Khen, walking with a cudgel in her hands, urged Kaladin's captor to keep moving. She watched the area with the nervousness of a scout on a dangerous mission.

That's it, Kaladin thought, remembering why this felt familiar. *Sneaking away from Tasinar.*

It had happened after he'd been condemned by Amaram, but before he'd been sent to the Shattered Plains. He avoided thinking of those months. His repeated failures, the systematic butchering of his last hints of idealism . . . well, he'd learned that dwelling on such things took him to dark places. He'd failed so many people during those months. Nalma had been one of those. He could remember the touch of her hand in his: a rough, callused hand.

That had been his most successful escape attempt. It had lasted five days.

'You're not monsters,' Kaladin whispered. 'You're not soldiers. You're not even the seeds of the void. You're just . . . runaway slaves.'

His captor spun, yanking on Kaladin's rope. The parshman seized Kaladin by the front of his uniform, and his daughter hid behind his leg, dropping one of her flowers and whimpering.

'Do you *want* me to kill you?' the parshman asked, pulling Kaladin's face close to his own. 'You insist on reminding me how your kind see us?'

Kaladin grunted. 'Look at my forehead, parshman.'

'And?'

'Slave brands.'

'What?'

Storms . . . parshmen weren't branded, and they didn't mix with other slaves. Parshmen were actually too valuable for that. 'When they make a human into a slave,' Kaladin said, 'they brand him. I've been here. Right where you are.'

'And you think that makes you understand?'

'Of course it does. I'm one—'

'*I* have spent my entire *life* living in a fog,' the parshman yelled at him. 'Every day knowing I should say something, do *something* to stop this! Every night clutching my daughter, wondering why the world seems to move around us in the light – while we are trapped in shadows. They sold her mother. *Sold her.* Because she had birthed a healthy child, which made her good breeding stock.

'Do you understand *that*, human? Do you understand watching your family be torn apart, and knowing you should object – knowing deep in your soul that something is *profoundly* wrong? Can you know that feeling of being unable to say a *single storming word* to stop it?'

The parshman pulled him even closer. 'They may have taken your freedom, but they took our *minds.*'

He dropped Kaladin and whirled, gathering up his daughter and holding her close as he jogged to catch up to the others, who had turned back at the outburst. Kaladin followed, yanked by his rope, stepping on the little girl's flower in his forced haste. Syl zipped past, and when Kaladin tried to catch her attention, she just laughed and flew higher on a burst of wind.

His captor suffered several quiet chastisements when they caught up; this column couldn't afford to draw attention. Kaladin walked with them, and remembered. He did understand a little.

You were never free while you ran; you felt as if the open sky and the endless fields were a torment. You could feel the pursuit following, and each morning you awoke expecting to find yourself surrounded.

Until one day you were right.

But parshmen? He'd accepted Shen into Bridge Four, yes. But accepting that a sole parshman could be a bridgeman was starkly different from accepting the entire people as . . . well, human.

As the column stopped to distribute waterskins to the children, Kaladin felt at his forehead, tracing the scarred shape of the glyphs there.

They took our minds. . . .

They'd tried to take his mind too. They'd beaten him to the stones, stolen everything he loved, and murdered his brother. Left him unable to think straight. Life had become a blur until one day he'd found himself standing over a ledge, watching raindrops die and struggling to summon the motivation to end his life.

Syl soared past in the shape of a shimmering ribbon.

'Syl,' Kaladin hissed. 'I need to talk to you. This isn't the time for—'

'Hush,' she said, then giggled and zipped around him before flitting over and doing the same to his captor.

Kaladin frowned. She was acting so carefree. Too carefree? Like she'd been back before they forged their bond?

No. It couldn't be.

'Syl?' he begged as she returned. 'Is something wrong with the bond? Please, I didn't—'

'It's not that,' she said, speaking in a furious whisper. 'I think parshmen might be able to see me. Some, at least. And that other spren is still here too. A higher spren, like me.'

'Where?' Kaladin asked, twisting.

'He's invisible to you,' Syl said, becoming a group of leaves and blowing around him. 'I think I've fooled him into thinking I'm just a windspren.'

She zipped away, leaving a dozen unanswered questions on Kaladin's lips. *Storms . . . is that spren how they know where to go?*

The column started again, and Kaladin walked for a good hour in silence before Syl next decided to come back to him. She landed on his shoulder, becoming the image of a young woman in her whimsical skirt. 'He's gone ahead for a little bit,' she said. 'And the parshmen aren't looking.'

'The spren is guiding them,' Kaladin said under his breath. 'Syl, this spren must be . . .'

'From *him*,' she whispered, wrapping her arms around herself and growing small – actively shrinking to about two-thirds her normal size. 'Voidspren.'

'There's more,' Kaladin said. 'These parshmen . . . how do they know how to talk, how to act? Yes, they've spent their lives around society – but to be this, well, normal after such a long time half asleep?'

'The Everstorm,' Syl said. 'Power has filled the holes in their souls, bridging the gaps. They didn't just wake, Kaladin. They've been healed, Connection refounded, Identity restored. There's more to this than we ever realized. Somehow when you conquered them, you stole their ability to change forms. You literally ripped off a piece of their souls and locked it away.' She turned sharply. 'He's coming back. I will stay nearby, in case you need a Blade.'

She left, zipping straight into the air as a ribbon of light. Kaladin continued to shuffle behind the column, chewing on her words, before speeding up and stepping beside his captor.

'You're being smart, in some ways,' Kaladin said. 'It's good to travel at night. But you're following the riverbed over there. I know it makes for more trees, and more secure camping, but this is literally the first place someone would look for you.'

Several of the other parshmen gave him glances from nearby. His captor didn't say anything.

'The big group is an issue too,' Kaladin added. 'You should break into smaller groups and meet up each morning, so if you get spotted you'll seem less threatening. You can say you were sent somewhere by a lighteyes, and travelers might let you go. If they run across all seventy of you together, there's no chance of that. This is all assuming, of course, you don't want to fight – which you don't. If you fight, they'll call out the highlords against you. For now they've got bigger problems.'

His captor grunted.

'I can help you,' Kaladin said. 'I might not understand what you've been through, but I *do* know what it feels like to run.'

'You think I'd trust you?' the parshman finally said. 'You will *want* us to be caught.'

'I'm not sure I do,' Kaladin said, truthful.

His captor said nothing more and Kaladin sighed, dropping back into position behind. Why had the Everstorm not granted these parshmen powers like those on the Shattered Plains? What of the stories of scripture and lore? The Desolations?

They eventually stopped for another break, and Kaladin found himself a smooth rock to sit against, nestled into the stone. His captor tied the rope to a nearby lonely tree, then went to confer with the others. Kaladin leaned back, lost in thought until he heard a sound. He was surprised to find his captor's daughter approaching. She carried a waterskin in two hands, and stopped right beyond his reach.

She didn't have shoes, and the walk so far had not been kind to her feet, which – though tough with calluses – were still scored by scratches and scrapes. She timidly set the waterskin down, then backed away. She didn't flee, as Kaladin might have expected, when he reached for the water.

'Thank you,' he said, then took a mouthful. It was pure and clear

– apparently the parshmen knew how to settle and scoop their water. He ignored the rumbling of his stomach.

'Will they really chase us?' the girl asked.

By Mishim's pale green light, he decided this girl was not as timid as he had assumed. She was nervous, but she met his eyes with hers.

'Why can't they just let us go?' she asked. 'Could you go back and tell them? We don't want trouble. We just want to go away.'

'They'll come,' Kaladin said. 'I'm sorry. They have a lot of work to do in rebuilding, and they'll want the extra hands. You are a . . . resource they can't simply ignore.'

The humans he'd visited hadn't known to expect some terrible Void-bringer force; many thought their parshmen had merely run off in the chaos.

'But why?' she said, sniffling. 'What did we do to them?'

'You tried to destroy them.'

'No. We're nice. We've always been nice. I never hit anyone, even when I was mad.'

'I didn't mean you specifically,' Kaladin said. 'Your ancestors – the people like you from long ago. There was a war, and . . .'

Storms. How did you explain slavery to a seven-year-old? He tossed the waterskin to her, and she scampered back to her father – who had only just noticed her absence. He stood, a stark silhouette in the night, studying Kaladin.

'They're talking about making camp,' Syl whispered from nearby. She had crawled into a crack in the rock. 'The Voidspren wants them to march on through the day, but I don't think they're going to. They're worried about their grain spoiling.'

'Is that spren watching me right now?' Kaladin asked.

'No.'

'Then let's cut this rope.'

He turned and hid what he was doing, then quickly summoned Syl as a knife to cut himself free. That would change his eye color, but in the darkness, he hoped the parshmen wouldn't notice.

Syl puffed back into a spren. 'Sword now?' she said. 'The spheres they took from you have all run out, but they'll scatter at seeing a Blade.'

'No.' Kaladin instead picked up a large stone. The parshmen hushed, noticing his escape. Kaladin carried his rock a few steps, then dropped it, crushing a rockbud. He was surrounded a few moments later by angry parshmen carrying cudgels.

Kaladin ignored them, picking through the wreckage of the rockbud. He held up a large section of shell.

'The inside of this,' he said, turning it over for them, 'will still be dry, despite the rainfall. The rockbud needs a barrier between itself and the water outside for some reason, though it always seems eager to drink after a storm. Who has my knife?'

Nobody moved to return it.

'If you scrape off this inner layer,' Kaladin said, tapping at the rockbud shell, 'you can get to the dry portion. Now that the rain has stopped, I should be able to get us a fire going, assuming nobody has lost my tinder bag. We need to boil that grain, then dry it into cakes. They won't be tasty, but they'll keep. If you don't do something soon, your supplies *will* rot.'

He stood up and pointed. 'Since we're already here, we should be near enough the river that we can gather more water. It won't flow much longer with the end of the rains.

'Rockbud shells don't burn particularly well, so we'll want to harvest some real wood and dry it at the fire during the day. We can keep that one small, then do the cooking tomorrow night. In the dark, the smoke is less likely to reveal us, and we can shield the light in the trees. I just have to figure out how we're going to cook without any pots to boil the water.'

The parshmen stared at him. Then Khen finally pushed him away from the rockbud and took up the shard he'd been holding. Kaladin spotted his original captor standing near the rock where he himself had been sitting. The parshman held the rope Kaladin had cut, rubbing its sliced-through end with his thumb.

After a short conference, the parshmen dragged him to the trees he'd indicated, returned his knife – standing by with every cudgel they had – and demanded that he prove he could build a fire with wet wood.

He did just that.

18

DOUBLE VISION

You cannot have a spice described to you, but must taste it for yourself.

—From *Oathbringer*, preface

Shallan became Veil.

Stormlight made her face less youthful, more angular. Nose pointed, with a small scar on the chin. Her hair rippled from red to Alethi black. Making an illusion like this took a larger gem of Stormlight, but once it was going, she could maintain it for hours on just a smidgen.

Veil tossed aside the havah, instead pulling on trousers and a tight shirt, then boots and a long white coat. She finished with only a simple glove on the left hand. Veil, of course, wasn't in the least embarrassed at that.

There was a simple relief for Shallan's pain. There was an easy way to hide. Veil hadn't suffered as Shallan had – and she was tough enough to handle that sort of thing anyway. Becoming her was like setting down a terrible burden.

Veil threw a scarf around her neck, then slung a rugged satchel – acquired for Veil specifically – over her shoulder. Hopefully the conspicuous knife handle sticking out from the top would look natural, even intimidating.

The part at the back of her mind that was still Shallan worried about this. Would she look fake? She'd almost certainly missed some subtle clues encoded in her behavior, dress, or speech. These would indicate to the right people that Veil didn't have the hard-bitten experience she feigned.

Well, she would have to do her best and hope to recover from her inevitable mistakes. She tied another knife onto her belt, long, but not quite a sword, since Veil wasn't lighteyed. Fortunately. No lighteyed woman would be able to prance around so obviously armed. Some mores grew lax the farther you descended the social ladder.

'Well?' Veil asked, turning to the wall, where Pattern hung.

'Mmm . . .' he said. 'Good lie.'

'Thank you.'

'Not like the other.'

'Radiant?'

'You slip in and out of her,' Pattern said, 'like the sun behind clouds.'

'I just need more practice,' Veil said. Yes, that voice sounded excellent. Shallan *was* getting far better with sounds.

She picked Pattern up – which involved pressing her hand against the wall, letting him pass over to her skin and then her coat. With him humming happily, she crossed her room and stepped out onto the balcony. The first moon had risen, violet and proud Salas. She was the least bright of the moons, which meant it was mostly dark out.

Most rooms on the outside had these small balconies, but hers on the second level was particularly advantageous. It had steps down to the field below. Covered in furrows for water and ridges for planting rockbuds, the field also had boxes at the edges for growing tubers or ornamental plants. Each tier of the city had a similar one, with eighteen levels inside separating them.

She stepped down to the field in the darkness. How had anything ever grown up here? Her breath puffed out in front of her, and coldspren grew around her feet.

The field had a small access doorway back into Urithiru. Perhaps the subterfuge of not exiting through her room wasn't necessary, but Veil preferred to be careful. She wouldn't want guards or servants remarking on how Brightness Shallan went about during odd hours of the night.

Besides, who knew where Mraize and his Ghostbloods had operatives?

199

They hadn't contacted her since that first day in Urithiru, but she knew they'd be watching. She still didn't know what to do about them. They had admitted to assassinating Jasnah, which should be grounds enough to hate them. They also seemed to know things, important things, about the world.

Veil strolled through the corridor, carrying a small hand lamp for light, as a sphere would make her stand out. She passed evening crowds that kept the corridors of Sebarial's quarter as busy as his warcamp had been. Things never seemed to slow down here as much as they did in Dalinar's quarter.

The strangely mesmerizing strata of the corridors guided her out of Sebarial's quarter. The number of people in the hallways slackened. Just Veil and those lonely, endless tunnels. She felt as if she could sense the weight of the other levels of the tower, empty and unexplored, bearing down on her. A mountain of unknown stone.

She hurried on her way, Pattern humming to himself from her coat.

'I like him,' Pattern said.

'Who?' Veil said.

'The swordsman,' Pattern said. 'Mmm. The one you can't mate with yet.'

'Can we please stop talking about him that way?'

'Very well,' Pattern said. 'But I like him.'

'You hate his sword.'

'I have come to understand,' Pattern said, growing excited. 'Humans ... humans *don't care about the dead*. You build chairs and doors out of corpses! You *eat* corpses! You make clothing from the skins of corpses. Corpses are *things* to you.'

'Well, I guess that's true.' He seemed unnaturally excited by the revelation.

'It is grotesque,' he continued, 'but you all must *kill* and *destroy* to live. It is the way of the Physical Realm. So I should not hate Adolin Kholin for wielding a corpse!'

'You just like him,' Veil said, 'because he tells Radiant to respect the sword.'

'Mmm. Yes, very, very nice man. Wonderfully smart too.'

'Why don't you marry him, then?'

Pattern buzzed. 'Is that—'

'No that's not an option.'

'Oh.' He settled down into a contented buzz on her coat, where he appeared as a strange kind of embroidery.

After a short time walking, Shallan found she needed to say something more. 'Pattern. Do you remember what you said to me the other night, the first time . . . we became Radiant?'

'About dying?' Pattern asked. 'It may be the only way, Shallan. Mmm . . . You must speak truths to progress, but you will hate me for making it happen. So I can die, and once done you can—'

'No. No, *please* don't leave me.'

'But you hate me.'

'I hate myself too,' she whispered. 'Just . . . *please.* Don't go. Don't die.'

Pattern seemed pleased by this, as his humming increased – though his sounds of pleasure and his sounds of agitation could be similar. For the moment, Veil let herself be distracted by the night's quest. Adolin continued his efforts to find the murderer, but hadn't gotten far. Aladar was Highprince of Information, and his policing force and scribes were a resource – but Adolin wanted badly to do as his father asked.

Veil thought that perhaps both were looking in the wrong places. She finally saw lights ahead and quickened her pace, eventually stepping out onto a walkway around a large cavernous room that stretched up several stories. She had reached the Breakaway: a vast collection of tents lit by many flickering candles, torches, or lanterns.

The market had sprung up shockingly fast, in defiance of Navani's carefully outlined plans. Her idea had been for a grand thoroughfare with shops along the sides. No alleyways, no shanties or tents. Easily patrolled and carefully regulated.

The merchants had rebelled, complaining about lack of storage space, or the need to be closer to a well for fresh water. In reality, they wanted a larger market that was much harder to regulate. Sebarial, as Highprince of Commerce, had agreed. And despite having made a mess of his ledgers, he was sharp when it came to trade.

The chaos and variety of it excited Veil. Hundreds of people, despite the hour, attracting spren of a dozen varieties. Dozens upon dozens of tents of varied colors and designs. In fact, some weren't tents at all, but were better described as stands – roped-off sections of ground guarded by a few burly men with cudgels. Others were actual buildings. Small stone sheds that had been built inside this cavern, here since the days of the Radiants.

Merchants from all ten original warcamps mixed at the Breakaway. She passed three different cobblers in a row; Veil had never understood why merchants selling the same things congregated. Wouldn't it be better to set up where you wouldn't have competition literally next door?

She packed away her hand lamp, as there was plenty of light here from the merchant tents and shops, and sauntered along. Veil felt more comfortable than she had in those empty, twisted corridors; here, life had gained a foothold. The market grew like the snarl of wildlife and plants on the leeward side of a ridge.

She made her way to the cavern's central well: a large, round enigma that rippled with crem-free water. She'd never seen an actual well before – everyone normally used cisterns that refilled with the storms. The many wells in Urithiru, however, never ran out. The water level didn't even drop, despite people constantly drawing from them.

Scribes talked about the possibility of a hidden aquifer in the mountains, but where would the water come from? Snows at the tops of the peaks nearby didn't seem to melt, and rain fell very rarely.

Veil sat on the well's side, one leg up, watching the people who came and went. She listened to the women chatter about the Voidbringers, about family back in Alethkar, and about the strange new storm. She listened to the men worry about being pressed into the military, or about their darkeyed nahn being lowered, now that there weren't parshmen to do common work. Some lighteyed workers complained about supplies trapped back in Narak, waiting for Stormlight before they could be transferred here.

Veil eventually ambled off toward a particular row of taverns. *I can't interrogate too hard to get my answers,* she thought. *If I ask the wrong kind of questions, everyone will figure me for some kind of spy for Aladar's policing force.*

Veil. Veil didn't hurt. She was comfortable, confident. She'd meet people's eyes. She'd lift her chin in challenge to anyone who seemed to be sizing her up. Power was an illusion of perception.

Veil had her own kind of power, that of a lifetime spent on the streets knowing she could take care of herself. She had the stubbornness of a chull, and while she was cocky, that confidence was a power of its own. She got what she wanted and wasn't embarrassed by success.

The first bar she chose was inside a large battle tent. It smelled of spilled lavis beer and sweaty bodies. Men and women laughed, using overturned crates as tables and chairs. Most wore simple darkeyed clothing: laced shirts – no money or time for buttons – and trousers or skirts. A few men dressed after an older fashion, with a wrap and a loose filmy vest that left the chest exposed.

This was a low-end tavern, and likely wouldn't work for her needs. She'd need a place that was lower, yet somehow richer. More disreputable, but with access to the powerful members of the warcamp undergrounds.

Still, this seemed a good place to practice. The bar was made of stacked boxes and had some actual chairs beside it. Veil leaned against the 'bar' in what she hoped was a smooth way, and nearly knocked the boxes over. She stumbled, catching them, then smiled sheepishly at the bartender – an old darkeyed woman with grey hair.

'What do you want?' the woman asked.

'Wine,' Veil said. 'Sapphire.' The second most intoxicating. Let them see that Veil could handle the hard stuff.

'We got Vari, kimik, and a nice barrel of Veden. That one will cost you though.'

'Uh . . .' Adolin would have known the differences. 'Give me the Veden.' Seemed appropriate.

The woman made her pay first, with dun spheres, but the cost didn't seem outrageous. Sebarial wanted the liquor flowing – his suggested way to make sure tensions didn't get too high in the tower – and had subsidized the prices with low taxes, for now.

While the woman worked behind her improvised bar, Veil suffered beneath the gaze of one of the bouncers. Those didn't stay near the entrance, but instead waited here, beside the liquor and the money. Despite what Aladar's policing force would like, this place was not completely safe. If unexplained murders *had* been glossed over or forgotten, they would have happened in the Breakaway, where the clutter, worry, and press of tens of thousands of camp followers balanced on the edge of lawlessness.

The barkeep plunked a cup in front of Veil – a *tiny* cup, with a clear liquid in it.

Veil scowled, holding it up. 'You got mine wrong, barkeep; I ordered sapphire. What is this, water?'

The bouncer nearest Veil snickered, and the barkeep stopped in place, then looked her over. Apparently Shallan had already made one of those mistakes she'd been worried about.

'Kid,' the barkeep said, somehow leaning on the boxes near her and not knocking any over. 'That's the same stuff, just without the fancy infusions the lighteyes put in theirs.'

Infusions?

'You some kind of house servant?' the woman asked softly. 'Out for your first night on your own?'

'Of course not,' Veil said. 'I've done this a hundred times.'

'Sure, sure,' the woman replied, tucking a stray strand of hair behind her ear. It popped right back up. 'You certain you want that? I might have some wines back here done with lighteyed colors, for you. In fact, I know I've got a nice orange.' She reached to reclaim the cup.

Veil seized it and knocked the entire thing back in a single gulp. That proved to be one of the worst mistakes of her life. The liquid *burned,* like it was on fire! She felt her eyes go wide, and she started coughing and almost threw up right there on the bar.

That was wine? Tasted more like lye. What was wrong with these people? There was no sweetness to it at all, not even a hint of flavor. Just that burning sensation, like someone was scraping her throat with a scouring brush! Her face immediately grew warm. It hit her so fast!

The bouncer was holding his face, trying – and failing – not to laugh out loud. The barkeep patted Shallan on the back as she kept coughing. 'Here,' the woman said, 'let me get you something to chase that—'

'No,' Shallan croaked. 'I'm just happy to be able to drink this . . . again after so long. Another. Please.'

The barkeep seemed skeptical, though the bouncer was all for it – he'd settled down on the stool to watch Shallan, grinning. Shallan placed a sphere on the bar, defiant, and the barkeep reluctantly filled her cup again.

By now, three or four other people from nearby seats had turned to watch. Lovely. Shallan braced herself, then drank the wine in a long, extended gulp.

It wasn't any better the second time. She held for a moment, eyes watering, then let out an explosion of coughing. She ended up hunched over, shaking, eyes squeezed closed. She was pretty sure she let out a long squeak as well.

Several people in the tent clapped. Shallan looked back at the amused barkeep, her eyes watering. 'That was awful,' she said, then coughed. 'You *really* drink this dreadful liquid?'

'Oh, hon,' the woman said. 'That's not *nearly* as bad as they get.'

Shallan groaned. 'Well, get me another.'

'You sure—'

'Yes,' Shallan said with a sigh. She probably wasn't going to be establishing a reputation for herself tonight – at least not the type she wanted. But she could try to accustom herself to drinking this cleaning fluid.

Storms. She was already feeling lighter. Her stomach did *not* like what she was doing to it, and she shoved down a bout of nausea.

Still chuckling, the bouncer moved a seat closer to her. He was a younger man, with hair cut so short it stood up on end. He was as Alethi as they came, with a deep tan skin and a dusting of black scrub on his chin.

'You should try sipping it,' he said to her. 'Goes down easier in sips.'

'Great. That way I can savor the terrible flavor. So bitter! Wine is supposed to be sweet.'

'Depends on how you make it,' he said as the barkeep gave Shallan another cup. 'Sapphire can sometimes be distilled tallew, no natural fruit in it – just some coloring for accent. But they don't serve the really hard stuff at lighteyed parties, except to people who know how to ask for it.'

'You know your alcohol,' Veil said. The room shook for a moment before settling. Then she tried another drink – a sip this time.

'It comes with the job,' he said with a broad smile. 'I work a lot of fancy events for the lighteyes, so I know my way around a place with tablecloths instead of boxes.'

Veil grunted. 'They need bouncers at fancy lighteyed events?'

'Sure,' he said, cracking his knuckles. 'You just have to know how to "escort" someone out of the feast hall, instead of throwing them out. It's actually easier.' He cocked his head. 'But strangely, more dangerous at the same time.' He laughed.

Kelek, Veil realized as he scooted closer. *He's flirting with me.*

She probably shouldn't have found it so surprising. She'd come in alone, and while Shallan would never have described Veil as 'cute,' she wasn't ugly. She was kind of normal, if rugged, but she dressed well and obviously had money. Her face and hands were clean, her clothing – while not rich silks – a generous step up from worker garb.

Initially she was offended by his attention. Here she'd gone to all this trouble to make herself capable and hard as rocks, and the first thing she did was attract some guy? One who cracked his knuckles and tried to tell her how to drink her alcohol?

Just to spite him, she downed the rest of her cup in a single shot.

She immediately felt guilty for her annoyance at the man. Shouldn't she be flattered? Granted, Adolin *could* have destroyed this man in any conceivable way. Adolin even cracked his knuckles louder.

'So . . .' the bouncer said. 'Which warcamp you from?'

'Sebarial,' Veil said.

The bouncer nodded, as if he'd expected that. Sebarial's camp had been the most eclectic. They chatted a little longer, mostly with Shallan making the odd comment while the bouncer – his name was Jor – went off on various stories with many tangents. Always smiling, often boasting.

He wasn't too bad, though he didn't seem to care what she actually said, so long as it prompted him to keep talking. She drank some more of the terrible liquid, but found her mind wandering.

These people . . . they each had lives, families, loves, dreams. Some slumped at their boxes, lonely, while others laughed with friends. Some kept their clothing, poor though it was, reasonably clean – others were stained with crem and lavis ale. Several of them reminded her of Tyn, the way they talked with confidence, the way their interactions were a subtle game of one-upping each other.

Jor paused, as if expecting something from her. What . . . what had he been saying? Following him was getting harder, as her mind drifted.

'Go on,' she said.

He smiled, and launched into another story.

I'm not going to be able to imitate this, she thought, leaning against her box, *until I've lived it. No more than I could draw their lives without having walked among them.*

The barkeep came back with the bottle, and Shallan nodded. That last cup hadn't burned nearly as much as the others.

'You . . . sure you want more?' the bouncer asked.

Storms . . . she was starting to feel *really* sick. She'd had four cups, yes, but they were little cups. She blinked, and turned.

The room spun in a blur, and she groaned, resting her head on the table. Beside her, the bouncer sighed.

'I could have told you that you were wasting your time, Jor,' the barkeep said. 'This one will be out before the hour is done. Wonder what she's trying to forget . . .'

'She's just enjoying a little free time,' Jor said.

'Sure, sure. With eyes like those? I'm sure that's it.' The barkeep moved away.

'Hey,' Jor said, nudging Shallan. 'Where are you staying? I'll call you a palanquin to cart you home. You awake? You should get going before things go too late. I know some porters who can be trusted.'

'It's . . . not even late yet . . .' Shallan mumbled.

'Late enough,' Jor said. 'This place can get dangerous.'

'Yeaaah?' Shallan asked, a glimmer of memory waking inside of her. 'People get stabbed?'

'Unfortunately,' Jor said.

'You know of some . . . ?'

'Never happens here in this area, at least not yet.'

'Where? So I . . . so I can stay away . . .' Shallan said.

'All's Alley,' he said. 'Keep away from there. Someone got stabbed behind one of the taverns just last night there. They found her dead.'

'Real . . . real strange, eh?' Shallan asked.

'Yeah. You heard?' Jor shivered.

Shallan stood up to go, but the room upended about her, and she found herself slipping down beside her stool. Jor tried to catch her, but she hit the ground with a thump, knocking her elbow against the stone floor. She immediately sucked in a little Stormlight to help with the pain.

The cloud around her mind puffed away, and her vision stopped spinning. In a striking moment, her drunkenness simply vanished.

She blinked. *Wow.* She stood up without Jor's help, dusting off her coat and then pulling her hair back away from her face. 'Thanks,' she said, 'but that's exactly the information I need. Barkeep, we settled?'

The woman turned, then froze, staring at Shallan, pouring liquid into a cup until it overflowed.

Shallan picked up her cup, then turned it and shook the last drop into her mouth. 'That's good stuff,' she noted. 'Thanks for the conversation,

Jor.' She set a sphere on the boxes as a tip, pulled on her hat, then patted Jor fondly on the cheek before striding out of the tent.

'Stormfather!' Jor said from behind her. 'Did I just get played for a fool?'

It was still busy out, reminding her of Kharbranth, with its midnight markets. That made sense. Neither sun nor moon could penetrate to these halls; it was easy to lose track of time. Beyond that, while most people had been put immediately to work, many of the soldiers had free time without plateau runs to do any longer.

Shallan asked around, and managed to get pointed toward All's Alley. 'The Stormlight made me sober,' she said to Pattern, who had crawled up her coat and now dimpled her collar, folded over the top.

'Healed you of poison.'

'That will be useful.'

'Mmmm. I thought you'd be angry. You drank the poison on purpose, didn't you?'

'Yes, but the point wasn't to get drunk.'

He buzzed in confusion. 'Then why drink it?'

'It's complicated,' Shallan said. She sighed. 'I didn't do a very good job in there.'

'Of getting drunk? Mmm. You gave it a good effort.'

'As soon as I got drunk, as soon as I lost control, Veil slipped away from me.'

'Veil is just a face.'

No. Veil was a woman who didn't giggle when she got drunk, or whine, fanning her mouth when the drink was too hard for her. She never acted like a silly teenager. Veil hadn't been sheltered, practically locked away, until she went crazy and murdered her own family.

Shallan stopped in place, suddenly frantic. 'My brothers. Pattern, I didn't kill them, right?'

'What?' he said.

'I talked to Balat over spanreed,' Shallan said, hand to her forehead. 'But . . . I had Lightweaving then . . . even if I didn't fully know it. I could have fabricated that. Every message from him. My own memories . . .'

'Shallan,' Pattern said, sounding concerned. 'No. They live. Your brothers live. Mraize said he rescued them. They are on their way here. This isn't the lie.' His voice grew smaller. 'Can't you tell?'

She adopted Veil again, her pain fading. 'Yes. Of course I can tell.' She started forward again.

'Shallan,' Pattern said. 'This is . . . mmm . . . there is something wrong with these lies you place upon yourself. I don't understand it.'

'I just need to go deeper,' she whispered. 'I can't be Veil only on the surface.'

Pattern buzzed with a soft, anxious vibration – fast paced, high pitched. Veil hushed him as she reached All's Alley. A strange name for a tavern, but she had seen stranger. It wasn't an alley at all, but a big set of five tents sewn together, each a different color. It glowed dimly from within.

A bouncer stood out front, short and squat, with a scar running up his cheek, across his forehead, and onto his scalp. He gave Veil a critical looking-over, but didn't stop her as she sauntered – full of confidence – into the tent. It smelled worse than the other pub, with all these drunken people crammed together. The tents had been sewn to create partitioned-off areas, darkened nooks – and a few had tables and chairs instead of boxes. The people who sat at them didn't wear the simple clothing of workers, but instead leathers, rags, or unbuttoned military coats.

Both richer than the other tavern, Veil thought, *and lower at the same time.*

She rambled through the room, which – despite oil lamps on some tables – was quite dim. The 'bar' was a plank set across some boxes, but they'd draped a cloth over the middle. A few people waited for drinks; Veil ignored them. 'What's the strongest thing you've got?' she asked the barkeep, a fat man in a takama. She thought he might be lighteyed. It was too dim to tell for certain.

He looked her over. 'Veden saph, single barrel.'

'Right,' Veil said dryly. 'If I wanted water, I'd go to the well. Surely you've got something stronger.'

The barkeep grunted, then reached behind himself and took out a jug of something clear, with no label. 'Horneater white,' he said, thumping it down on the table. 'I have no idea what they ferment to make the stuff, but it takes paint off real nicely.'

'Perfect,' Veil said, clacking a few spheres onto the improvised counter. The others in line had been shooting her glares for ignoring the line, but at this their expressions turned to amusement.

The barkeep poured Veil a very small cup of the stuff and set it before her. She downed it in one gulp. Shallan trembled inside at the burning that followed – the immediate warmth to her cheeks and almost instant sense of nausea, accompanied by a tremor through her muscles as she tried to resist throwing up.

Veil was expecting all this. She held her breath to stifle the nausea, and *relished* the sensations. *No worse than the pains already inside,* she thought, warmth radiating through her.

'Great,' she said. 'Leave the jug.'

Those idiots beside the bar continued to gawk as she poured another cup of the Horneater white and downed it, feeling its warmth. She turned to inspect the tent's occupants. Who to approach first? Aladar's scribes had checked watch records for anyone else killed the same way as Sadeas, and they'd come up empty – but a killing in an alleyway might not get reported. She hoped that the people here would know of it regardless.

She poured some more of that Horneater drink. Though it was even fouler-tasting than the Veden saph, she found something strangely appealing about it. She downed the third cup, but drew in a tiny bit of Stormlight from a sphere in her pouch – just a smidge that instantly burned away and didn't make her glow – to heal herself.

'What are you looking at?' she said, eyeing the people in line at the bar.

They turned away as the bartender moved to put a stopper on the jug. Veil put her hand on top of it. 'I'm not done with that yet.'

'You are,' the bartender said, brushing her hand away. 'One of two things is going to happen if you continue like that. You'll either puke all over my bar, or you'll drop dead. You're not a Horneater; this *will* kill you.'

'That's my problem.'

'The mess is *mine*,' the barkeep said, yanking the jug back. 'I've seen your type, with that haunted look. You'll get yourself drunk, then pick a fight. I don't care what it is you want to forget; go find some other place to do it.'

Veil cocked an eyebrow. Getting kicked out of the most disreputable bar in the market? Well, at least her reputation wouldn't suffer here.

She caught the barkeep's arm as he pulled it back. 'I'm not here to tear your bar down, friend,' she said softly. 'I'm here about a murder. Someone who was killed here a few days back.'

The barkeep froze. 'Who are you? You with the guard?'

'Damnation, no!' Veil said. *Story. I need a cover story.* 'I'm hunting the man who killed my little sister.'

'And that has to do with my bar how?'

'I've heard rumors of a body found near here.'

'A grown woman,' the barkeep said. 'So not your sister.'

'My sister didn't die here,' Veil said. 'She died back in the warcamps; I'm just hunting the one who did it.' She hung on as the barkeep tried to pull away again. 'Listen. I'm not going to make trouble. I just need information. I hear there were . . . unusual circumstances about this death. This *rumored* death. The man who killed my sister, he has something strange about him. He kills in the same way every time. Please.'

The barkeep met her eyes. *Let him see,* Veil thought. *Let him see a woman with a hard edge, but wounds inside.* A story reflected in her eyes – a narrative she needed this man to believe.

'The one who did it,' the barkeep said softly, 'has already been dealt with.'

'I need to know if your murderer is the same one I've been hunting,' Veil said. 'I need details of the killing, however gruesome they may be.'

'I can't say anything,' the barkeep whispered, but he nodded toward one of the alcoves made from the stitched-together tents, where shadows indicated some people were drinking. 'They might.'

'Who are they?'

'Just your everyday, ordinary thugs,' the barkeep said. 'But they're the ones I pay to keep my bar out of trouble. If someone *had* disturbed this establishment in a way that risked the authorities shutting the place down – as that Aladar is so fond of doing – those are the people who would have taken care of said problem. I won't say more.'

Veil nodded in thanks, but didn't let go of his arm. She tapped her cup and cocked her head hopefully. The barkeep sighed and gave her one more hit of the Horneater white, which she paid for, then sipped as she walked away.

The alcove he'd indicated held a single table full of a variety of ruffians. The men wore the clothing of the Alethi upper crust: jackets and stiff uniform-style trousers, belts and buttoned shirts. Here, their jackets were undone, their shirts loose. Two of the women even wore the havah, though another was in trousers and a jacket, not too different from what

Veil wore. The whole group reminded her of Tyn in the way they lounged in an almost *deliberate* way. It took effort to look so indifferent.

There was an unoccupied seat, so Veil strolled right in and took it. The lighteyed woman across from her hushed a jabbering man by touching his lips. She wore the havah, but without a safehand sleeve – instead, she wore a glove with the fingers brazenly cut off at the knuckles.

'That's Ur's seat,' the woman said to Veil. 'When he gets back from the pisser, you'd best have moved on.'

'Then I'll be quick,' Veil said, downing the rest of her drink, savoring the warmth. 'A woman was found dead here. I think the murderer might have also killed someone dear to me. I've been told the murderer was "dealt with," but I need to know for myself.'

'Hey,' said a foppish man wearing a blue jacket, with slits in the outer layer to show yellow underneath. 'You're the one that was drinking the Horneater white. Old Sullik only keeps that jug as a joke.'

The woman in the havah laced her fingers before herself, inspecting Veil.

'Look,' Veil said, 'just tell me what the information will cost me.'

'One can't buy,' the woman said, 'what isn't for sale.'

'Everything is for sale,' Veil said, 'if you ask the right way.'

'Which you're not doing.'

'Look,' Veil said, trying to catch the woman's eyes. 'Listen. My kid sister, she—'

A hand fell on Shallan's shoulder, and she looked up to find an enormous Horneater man standing behind her. Storms, he had to be nearly seven feet tall.

'This,' he said, drawing out the *i* sound to an *e* instead, 'is my spot.'

He pulled Veil off the chair, tossing her backward to roll on the ground, her cup tumbling away, her satchel twisting and getting wound up in her arms. She came to a rest, blinking as the large man sat on the chair. She felt she could hear its soul groaning in protest.

Veil growled, then stood up. She yanked off her satchel and dropped it, then removed a handkerchief and the knife from inside. This knife was narrow and pointed, long but thinner than the one on her belt.

She picked up her hat and dusted it off before replacing it and strolling back up to the table. Shallan disliked confrontation, but Veil loved it.

'Well, well,' she said, resting her safehand on the top of the large

Horneater's left hand, which was lying flat on the tabletop. She leaned down beside him. 'You say it's your place, but I don't see it marked with your name.'

The Horneater stared at her, confused by the strangely intimate gesture of putting her safehand on his hand.

'Let me show you,' she said, removing her knife and placing the point onto the back of her hand, which was pressed against his.

'What is this?' he asked, sounding amused. 'You put on an act, being tough? I have seen men pretend—'

Veil rammed the knife down through her hand, through his, and into the tabletop. The Horneater screamed, whipping his hand upward, making Veil pull the knife out of both hands. The man toppled out of his chair as he scrambled away from her.

Veil settled down in it again. She took the cloth from her pocket and wrapped it around her bleeding hand. That would obscure the cut when she healed it.

Which she didn't do at first. It would need to be seen bleeding. Instead – a part of her surprised at how calm she remained – she retrieved her knife, which had fallen beside the table.

'You're crazy!' the Horneater said, recovering his feet, holding his bleeding hand. 'You're *ana'kai crazy*.'

'Oh wait,' Veil said, tapping the table with her knife. 'Look, I see your mark here, in blood. Ur's seat. I was wrong.' She frowned. 'But mine's here too. Suppose you can sit in my lap, if you want.'

'I'll throttle you!' Ur said, shooting a glare at the people in the main room of the tent, who had crowded around the entrance to this smaller room, whispering. 'I'll—'

'Quiet, Ur,' the woman in the havah said.

He sputtered. 'But Betha!'

'You think,' the woman said to Veil, 'assaulting my friends is going to make me *more* likely to talk?'

'Honestly, I just wanted the seat back.' Veil shrugged, scratching at the tabletop with her knife. 'But if you want me to start hurting people, I suppose I could do that.'

'You really are crazy,' Betha said.

'No. I just don't consider your little group a threat.' She continued scratching. 'I've tried being nice, and my patience is running thin.

It's time to tell me what I want to know before this turns ugly.'

Betha frowned, then glanced at what Veil had scratched into the tabletop. Three interlocking diamonds.

The symbol of the Ghostbloods.

Veil gambled that the woman would know what it meant. They seemed the type who would – small-time thugs, yes, but ones with a presence in an important market. Veil wasn't certain how secretive Mraize and his people were with their symbol, but the fact that they got it tattooed on their bodies indicated to her that it wasn't supposed to be terribly secret. More a warning, like cremlings who displayed red claws to indicate they were poisonous.

Indeed, the moment Betha saw the symbol, she gasped softly. 'We . . . we want nothing to do with your type,' Betha said. One of the men at the table stood up, trembling, and looked from side to side, as if expecting assassins to tackle him right then.

Wow, Veil thought. Even cutting the hand of one of their members hadn't provoked this strong a reaction.

Curiously though, one of the other women at the table – a short, younger woman wearing a havah – leaned forward, interested.

'The murderer,' Veil said. 'What happened to him?'

'We had Ur drop him off the plateau outside,' Betha said. 'But . . . how could this be a man *you* would be interested in? It was just Ned.'

'Ned?'

'Drunk, from Sadeas's camp,' said one of the men. 'Angry drunk; always got into trouble.'

'Killed his wife,' Betha said. 'Pity too, after she followed him all the way out here. Guess none of us had much choice, with that crazy storm. But still . . .'

'And this Ned,' Veil said, 'murdered his wife with a knife through the eye?'

'What? No, he strangled her. Poor bastard.'

Strangled? 'That's it?' Veil said. 'No knife wounds?'

Betha shook her head, seeming confused.

Stormfather, Veil thought. So it was a dead end? 'But I heard that the murder was strange.'

'No,' the standing man said, then settled back down beside Betha, knife out. He set it on the table, in front of them. 'We knew Ned would go too far at some point. Everyone did. I don't think any of us was surprised when, after she tried to drag him away from the tavern that night, he finally went over the edge.'

Literally, Shallan thought. *At least once Ur got hold of him.*

'It appears,' Veil said, standing up, 'that I have wasted your time. I will leave spheres with the barkeep; your tab is my debt, tonight.' She spared a glance for Ur, who hunched nearby and regarded her with a sullen expression. She waved her bloodied fingers at him, then made her way back toward the main tent room of the tavern.

She hovered just inside it, contemplating her next move. Her hand throbbed, but she ignored it. Dead end. Perhaps she'd been foolish to think she could solve in a few hours what Adolin had spent weeks trying to crack.

'Oh, don't look so sullen, Ur,' Betha said from behind, voice drifting out of the tent alcove. 'At least it was just your hand. Considering who that was, it could have been a *lot* worse.'

'But why was she so interested in Ned?' Ur said. 'Is she going to come back because I killed him?'

'She wasn't after him,' one of the other women snapped. 'Didn't you listen? Ain't nobody that cares Ned killed poor Rem.' She paused. 'Course, it could have been about the other woman he killed.'

Veil felt a shock run through her. She spun, striding back into the alcove. Ur whimpered, hunching down and holding his wounded hand.

'There was *another* murder?' Veil demanded.

'I . . .' Betha licked her lips. 'I was going to tell you, but you left so fast that—'

'Just talk.'

'We'd have let the watch take care of Ned, but he couldn't leave it at killing just poor Rem.'

'He killed another person?'

Betha nodded. 'One of the barmaids here. *That* we couldn't let pass. We protect this place, you see. So Ur had to take a long walk with Ned.'

The man with the knife rubbed his chin. 'Strangest thing, that he'd come back and kill a barmaid the next night. Left her body right around the corner from where he killed poor Rem.'

'He screamed the whole time we were taking him to his fall that he hadn't killed the second one,' Ur muttered.

'He did,' Betha said. 'That barmaid was strangled the exact same way as Rem, body dropped in the same position. Even had the marks of his ring scraping her chin like Rem did.' Her light brown eyes had a hollow cast to them, like she was staring at the body again, as it had been found. 'Exact same marks. Uncanny.'

Another double murder, Veil thought. *Storms. What does it mean?*

Veil felt dazed, though she didn't know if it was from drink or the unwelcome image of the strangled women. She went and gave the barkeep some spheres – probably too many – and hooked the jug of Horneater white with her thumb, then carted it out with her into the night.

19

THE SUBTLE ART
OF DIPLOMACY

THIRTY-ONE YEARS AGO

A candle flickered on the table, and Dalinar lit the end of his napkin in it, sending a small braid of pungent smoke into the air. Stupid decorative candles. What was the point? Looking pretty? Didn't they use spheres because they were better than candles for light?

At a glare from Gavilar, Dalinar stopped burning his napkin and leaned back, nursing a mug of deep violet wine. The kind you could smell from across the room, potent and flavorful. A feast hall spread before him, dozens of tables set on the floor of the large stone room. The place was far too warm, and sweat prickled on his arms and forehead. Too many candles maybe.

Outside the feast hall, a storm raged like a madman who'd been locked away, impotent and ignored.

'But how do you deal with highstorms, Brightlord?' Toh said to Gavilar. The tall, blond-haired Westerner sat with them at the high table.

'Good planning keeps an army from needing to be out during a storm except in rare situations,' Gavilar explained. 'Holdings are common in Alethkar. If a campaign takes longer than anticipated, we can split the army and retreat back to a number of these towns for shelter.'

'And if you're in the middle of a siege?' Toh asked.

'Sieges are rare out here, Brightlord Toh,' Gavilar said, chuckling.

'Surely there are cities with fortifications,' Toh said. 'Your famed Kholinar has majestic walls, does it not?' The Westerner had a thick accent and spoke in a clipped, annoying way. Sounded silly.

'You're forgetting about Soulcasters,' Gavilar said. 'Yes, sieges happen now and then, but it's very hard to starve out a city's soldiers while there are Soulcasters and emeralds to make food. Instead we usually break down the walls quickly, or – more commonly – we seize the high ground and use that vantage to pound the city for a while.'

Toh nodded, seeming fascinated. 'Soulcasters. We have not these things in Rira or Iri. Fascinating, fascinating ... And so many Shards here. Perhaps half the world's wealth of Blades and Plates, all contained in Vorin kingdoms. The Heralds themselves favor you.'

Dalinar took a long pull on his wine. Outside, thunder shook the bunker. The highstorm was in full force now.

Inside, servants brought out slabs of pork and lanka claws for the men, cooked in a savory broth. The women dined elsewhere, including, he'd heard, Toh's sister. Dalinar hadn't met her yet. The two Western lighteyes had arrived barely an hour before the storm hit.

The hall soon echoed with the sounds of people chatting. Dalinar tore into his lanka claws, cracking them with the bottom of his mug and biting out the meat. This feast seemed too polite. Where was the music, the laughter? The women? Eating in separate rooms?

Life had been different these last few years of conquest. The final four highprinces stood firm in their unified front. The once-frantic fighting had stalled. More and more of Gavilar's time was required by the administration of his kingdom – which was half as big as they wanted it to be, but still demanding.

Politics. Gavilar and Sadeas didn't make Dalinar play at it too often, but he still had to sit at feasts like this one, rather than dining with his men. He sucked on a claw, watching Gavilar talk to the foreigner. Storms. Gavilar actually looked regal, with his beard combed like that, glowing gemstones on his fingers. He wore a uniform of the newer style. Formal, rigid. Dalinar instead wore his skirtlike takama and an open overshirt that went down to midthigh, his chest bare.

Sadeas held court with a group of lesser lighteyes at a table across the hall. Every one of that group had been carefully chosen: men with uncertain loyalties. He'd talk, persuade, convince. And if he was worried, he'd find ways to eliminate them. Not with assassins, of course. They all found that sort of thing distasteful; it wasn't the Alethi way. Instead, they'd maneuver the man into a duel with Dalinar, or would position him at the front of an assault. Ialai, Sadeas's wife, spent an impressive amount of time cooking up new schemes for getting rid of problematic allies.

Dalinar finished the claws, then turned toward his pork, a succulent slab of meat swimming in gravy. The food *was* better at this feast. He just wished that he didn't feel so useless here. Gavilar made alliances; Sadeas dealt with problems. Those two could treat a feast hall like a battlefield.

Dalinar reached to his side for his knife so he could cut the pork. Except the knife wasn't there.

Damnation. He'd lent it to Teleb, hadn't he? He stared down at the pork, smelling its peppery sauce, his mouth watering. He reached to eat with his fingers, then thought to look up. Everyone else was eating primly, with utensils. But the servers had forgotten to bring him a knife.

Damnation again. He sat back, wagging his mug for more wine. Nearby, Gavilar and that foreigner continued their chat.

'Your campaign here *has* been impressive, Brightlord Kholin,' Toh said. 'One sees a glint of your ancestor in you, the great Sunmaker.'

'Hopefully,' Gavilar noted, 'my accomplishments won't be as ephemeral as his.'

'Ephemeral! He reforged Alethkar, Brightlord! You shouldn't speak so of one like him. You're his descendant, correct?'

'We all are,' Gavilar said. 'House Kholin, House Sadeas ... all ten princedoms. Their founders were his sons, you know. So yes, signs of his touch are here – yet his empire didn't last even a single generation past his death. Leaves me wondering what was wrong with his vision, his planning, that his great empire broke apart so quickly.'

The storm rumbled. Dalinar tried to catch the attention of a servant to request a dinner knife, but they were too busy scuttling about, seeing to the needs of other demanding feastgoers.

He sighed, then stood – stretching – and walked to the door, holding his empty mug. Lost in thought, he threw aside the bar on the door, then shoved open the massive wooden construction and stepped outside.

A sheet of icy rain suddenly washed over his skin, and wind blasted him fiercely enough that he stumbled. The highstorm was at its raging height, lightning blasting down like vengeful attacks from the Heralds.

Dalinar struck out into the storm, his overshirt whipping about him. Gavilar talked more and more about things like legacy, the kingdom, responsibility. What had happened to the fun of the fight, to riding into battle laughing?

Thunder crashed, and the periodic strikes of lightning were barely enough to see by. Still, Dalinar knew his way around well enough. This was a highstorm waystop, a place built to house patrolling armies during storms. He and Gavilar had been positioned at this one for a good four months now, drawing tribute from the nearby farms and menacing House Evavakh from just inside its borders.

Dalinar found the particular bunker he was looking for and pounded on the door. No response. So he summoned his Shardblade, slid the tip between the double doors, and sliced the bar inside. He pushed open the door to find a group of wide-eyed armed men scrambling into defensive lines, surrounded by fearspren, weapons held in nervous grips.

'Teleb,' Dalinar said, standing in the doorway. 'Did I lend you my belt knife? My favorite one, with the whitespine ivory on the grip?'

The tall soldier, who stood in the second rank of terrified men, gaped at him. 'Uh . . . your *knife*, Brightlord?'

'Lost the thing somewhere,' Dalinar said. 'I lent it to you, didn't I?'

'I gave it back, sir,' Teleb said. 'You used it to pry that splinter out of your saddle, remember?'

'Damnation. You're right. What *did* I do with that blasted thing?' Dalinar left the doorway and strode back out into the storm.

Perhaps Dalinar's worries had more to do with himself than they did Gavilar. The Kholin battles were so calculated these days – and these last months had been more about what happened off the battlefield than on it. It all seemed to leave Dalinar behind like the discarded shell of a cremling after it molted.

An explosive burst of wind drove him against the wall, and he stumbled, then stepped backward, driven by instincts he couldn't define. A large boulder slammed into the wall, then bounced away. Dalinar glanced and saw something luminous in the distance: a gargantuan figure that moved on spindly glowing legs.

Dalinar stepped back up to the feast hall, gave the whatever-it-was a rude gesture, then pushed open the door – throwing aside two servants who had been holding it closed – and strode back in. Streaming with water, he walked up to the high table, where he flopped into his chair and set down his mug. Wonderful. Now he was wet and he *still* couldn't eat his pork.

Everyone had gone silent. A sea of eyes stared at him.

'Brother?' Gavilar asked, the only sound in the room. 'Is everything . . . all right?'

'Lost my storming knife,' Dalinar said. 'Thought I'd left it in the other bunker.' He raised his mug and took a loud, lazy slurp of rainwater.

'Excuse me, Lord Gavilar,' Toh stammered. 'I . . . I find myself in need of refreshment.' The blond-haired Westerner stood from his place, bowed, and retreated across the room to where a master-servant was administering drinks. His face seemed even paler than those folk normally were.

'What's wrong with him?' Dalinar asked, scooting his chair closer to his brother.

'I assume,' Gavilar said, sounding amused, 'that people he knows don't casually go for strolls in highstorms.'

'Bah,' Dalinar said. 'This is a fortified waystop, with walls and bunkers. We needn't be scared of a little wind.'

'Toh thinks differently, I assure you.'

'You're grinning.'

'You may have just proven in one moment, Dalinar, a point I've spent a half hour trying to make politically. Toh wonders if we're strong enough to protect him.'

'Is that what the conversation was about?'

'Obliquely, yes.'

'Huh. Glad I could help.' Dalinar picked at a claw on Gavilar's plate. 'What does it take to get one of these fancy servants to get me a storming knife?'

'They're master-servants, Dalinar,' his brother said, making a sign by raising his hand in a particular way. 'The sign of need, remember?'

'No.'

'You really need to pay better attention,' Gavilar said. 'We aren't living in huts anymore.'

They'd never lived in huts. They were Kholin, heirs to one of the world's great cities – even if Dalinar had never seen the place before his twelfth year. He didn't like that Gavilar was buying into the story the rest of the kingdom told, the one that claimed their branch of the house had until recently been ruffians from the backwaters of their own princedom.

A gaggle of servants in black and white flocked to Gavilar, and he requested a new dining knife for Dalinar. As they split to run the errand, the doors to the women's feast hall opened, and a figure slipped in.

Dalinar's breath caught. Navani's hair glowed with the tiny rubies she'd woven into it, a color matched by her pendant and bracelet. Her face a sultry tan, her hair Alethi jet black, her red-lipped smile so knowing and clever. And a figure . . . a figure to make a man weep for desire.

His brother's wife.

Dalinar steeled himself and raised his arm in a gesture like the one Gavilar had made. A serving man stepped up with a springy gait. 'Bright-lord,' he said, 'I will see to your desires of course, though you might wish to know that the sign is off. If you'll allow me to demonstrate—'

Dalinar made a rude gesture. 'Is this better?'

'Uh . . .'

'Wine,' Dalinar said, wagging his mug. 'Violet. Enough to fill this three times at least.'

'And what vintage would you like, Brightlord?'

He eyed Navani. 'Whichever one is closest.'

Navani slipped between tables, followed by the squatter form of Ialai Sadeas. Neither seemed to care that they were the only lighteyed women in the room.

'What happened to the emissary?' Navani said as she arrived. She slid between Dalinar and Gavilar as a servant brought her a chair.

'Dalinar scared him off,' Gavilar said.

The scent of her perfume was heady. Dalinar scooted his chair to the side and set his face. Be firm, don't let her know how she warmed him, brought him to life like nothing else but battle.

Ialai pulled a chair over for herself, and a servant brought Dalinar's wine. He took a long, calming drink straight from the jug.

'We've been assessing the sister,' Ialai said, leaning in from Gavilar's other side. 'She's a touch vapid—'

'A *touch*?' Navani asked.

'—but I'm reasonably sure she's being honest.'

'The brother seems the same,' Gavilar said, rubbing his chin and inspecting Toh, who was nursing a drink near the bar. 'Innocent, wide-eyed. I think he's genuine though.'

'He's a sycophant,' Dalinar said with a grunt.

'He's a man without a home, Dalinar,' Ialai said. 'No loyalty, at the mercy of those who take him in. And he has only one piece he can play to secure his future.'

Shardplate.

Taken from his homeland of Rira and brought east, as far as Toh could get from his kinsmen – who were reportedly outraged to find such a precious heirloom stolen.

'He doesn't have the armor with him,' Gavilar said. 'He's at least smart enough not to carry it. He'll want assurances before giving it to us. Powerful assurances.'

'Look how he stares at Dalinar,' Navani said. 'You impressed him.' She cocked her head. 'Are you wet?'

Dalinar ran his hand through his hair. Storms. He hadn't been embarrassed to stare down the crowd in the room, but before her he found himself blushing.

Gavilar laughed. 'He went for a stroll.'

'You're kidding,' Ialai said, scooting over as Sadeas joined them at the high table. The bulbous-faced man settled down on her chair with her, the two of them sitting half on, half off. He dropped a plate on the table, piled with claws in a bright red sauce. Ialai attacked them immediately. She was one of the few women Dalinar knew who liked masculine food.

'What are we discussing?' Sadeas asked, waving away a master-servant with a chair, then draping his arm around his wife's shoulders.

'We're talking about getting Dalinar married,' Ialai said.

'What?' Dalinar demanded, choking on a mouthful of wine.

'That *is* the point of this, right?' Ialai said. 'They want someone who can protect them, someone their family will be too afraid to attack. But Toh and his sister, they'll want more than just asylum. They'll want to be part of things. Inject their blood into the royal line, so to speak.'

Dalinar took another long drink.

'You *could* try water sometime you know, Dalinar,' Sadeas said.

'I had some rainwater earlier. Everyone stared at me funny.'

Navani smiled at him. There wasn't enough wine in the world to prepare him for the gaze behind the smile, so piercing, so appraising.

'This could be what we need,' Gavilar said. 'It gives us not only the Shard, but the appearance of speaking for Alethkar. If people outside the kingdom start coming to me for refuge and treaties, we might be able to sway the remaining highprinces. We might be able to unite this country not through further war, but through sheer weight of *legitimacy*.'

A servant, at long last, arrived with a knife for Dalinar. He took it eagerly, then frowned as the woman walked away.

'What?' Navani asked.

'This little thing?' Dalinar asked, pinching the dainty knife between two fingers and dangling it. 'How am I supposed to eat a pork steak with *this*?'

'Attack it,' Ialai said, making a stabbing motion. 'Pretend it's some thick-necked man who has been insulting your biceps.'

'If someone insulted my biceps, I wouldn't attack him,' Dalinar said. 'I'd refer him to a physician, because *obviously* something is wrong with his eyes.'

Navani laughed, a musical sound.

'Oh, Dalinar,' Sadeas said. 'I don't think there's another person on Roshar who could have said that with a straight face.'

Dalinar grunted, then tried to maneuver the little knife into cutting the steak. The meat was growing cold, but still smelled delicious. A single hungerspren started flitting about his head, like a tiny brown fly of the type you saw out in the west near the Purelake.

'What defeated Sunmaker?' Gavilar suddenly asked.

'Hmm?' Ialai said.

'Sunmaker,' Gavilar said, looking from Navani, to Sadeas, to Dalinar. 'He united Alethkar. Why did he fail to create a lasting empire?'

'His kids were too greedy,' Dalinar said, sawing at his steak. 'Or too weak maybe. There wasn't one of them that the others would agree to support.'

'No, that's not it,' Navani said. 'They might have united, if the Sunmaker himself could have been bothered to *settle* on an heir. It's his fault.'

'He was off in the west,' Gavilar said. 'Leading his army to "further glory." Alethkar and Herdaz weren't enough for him. He wanted the whole world.'

'So it was his ambition,' Sadeas said.

'No, his greed,' Gavilar said quietly. 'What's the point of conquering if you can never sit back and enjoy it? Shubreth-son-Mashalan, Sunmaker, even the Hierocracy . . . they all stretched farther and farther until they collapsed. In all the history of mankind, has any conqueror decided they had enough? Has any man just said, 'This is good. This is what I wanted,' and gone home?'

'Right now,' Dalinar said, 'what I want is to eat my storming steak.' He held up the little knife, which was bent in the middle.

Navani blinked. 'How in the Almighty's tenth name did you do that?'

'Dunno.'

Gavilar stared with that distant, far-off look in his green eyes. A look that was becoming more and more common. 'Why are we at war, Brother?'

'This again?' Dalinar said. 'Look, it's not so complicated. Can't you remember how it was back when we started?'

'Remind me.'

'Well,' Dalinar said, wagging his bent knife. 'We looked at this place here, this kingdom, and we realized, "Hey, all these people have *stuff*." And we figured . . . hey, maybe *we* should have that stuff. So we took it.'

'Oh Dalinar,' Sadeas said, chuckling. 'You are a gem.'

'Don't you ever think about what it meant though?' Gavilar asked. 'A kingdom? Something grander than yourself?'

'That's foolishness, Gavilar. When people fight, it's about the stuff. That's it.'

'Maybe,' Gavilar said. 'Maybe. There's something I want you to listen to. The Codes of War, from the old days. Back when Alethkar meant something.'

Dalinar nodded absently as the serving staff entered with teas and fruit to close the meal; one tried to take his steak, and he growled at her. As she backed away, Dalinar caught sight of something. A woman peeking into the room from the other feast hall. She wore a delicate, filmy dress of pale yellow, matched by her blonde hair.

He leaned forward, curious. Toh's sister Evi was eighteen, maybe nineteen. She was tall, almost as tall as an Alethi, and small of chest. In fact, there was a certain sense of flimsiness to her, as if she were somehow less real than an Alethi. The same went for her brother, with his slender build.

But that *hair*. It made her stand out, like a candle's glow in a dark room.

She scampered across the feast hall to her brother, who handed her a drink. She tried to take it with her left hand, which was tied inside a small pouch of yellow cloth. The dress didn't have sleeves, strangely.

'She kept trying to eat with her safehand,' Navani said, eyebrow cocked.

Ialai leaned down the table toward Dalinar, speaking conspiratorially. 'They go about half-clothed out in the far west, you know. Rirans, Iriali, the Reshi. They aren't as inhibited as these prim Alethi women. I bet she's quite exotic in the bedroom. . . .'

Dalinar grunted. Then finally spotted a knife.

In the hand hidden behind the back of a server clearing Gavilar's plates.

Dalinar kicked at his brother's chair, breaking a leg off and sending Gavilar toppling to the ground. The assassin swung at the same moment, clipping Gavilar's ear, but otherwise missing. The wild swing struck the table, driving the knife into the wood.

Dalinar leaped to his feet, reaching over Gavilar and grabbing the assassin by the neck. He spun the would-be killer around and slammed him to the floor with a satisfying *crunch*. Still in motion, Dalinar grabbed the knife from the table and pounded it into the assassin's chest.

Puffing, Dalinar stepped back and wiped the rainwater from his eyes. Gavilar sprang to his feet, Shardblade appearing in his hand. He looked down at the assassin, then at Dalinar.

Dalinar kicked at the assassin to be sure he was dead. He nodded to himself, righted his chair, sat down, then leaned over and yanked the man's knife from his chest. A fine blade.

He washed it off in his wine, then cut off a piece of his steak and shoved it into his mouth. *Finally.*

'Good pork,' Dalinar noted around the bite.

Across the room, Toh and his sister were staring at Dalinar with looks that mixed awe and terror. He caught a few shockspren around them, like triangles of yellow light, breaking and re-forming. Rare spren, those were.

'Thank you,' Gavilar said, touching his ear and the blood that was dripping from it.

Dalinar shrugged. 'Sorry about killing him. You probably wanted to question him, eh?'

'It's no stretch to guess who sent him,' Gavilar said, settling down, waving away the guards who – belatedly – rushed to help. Navani clutched his arm, obviously shaken by the attack.

Sadeas cursed under his breath. 'Our enemies grow desperate. Cowardly. An assassin during a storm? An Alethi should be ashamed of such action.'

Again, everyone in the feast was gawking at the high table. Dalinar cut his steak again, shoving another piece into his mouth. What? He wasn't going to *drink* the wine he'd washed the blood into. He wasn't a barbarian.

'I know I said I wanted you free to make your own choice in regard to a bride,' Gavilar said. 'But . . .'

'I'll do it,' Dalinar said, eyes forward. Navani was lost to him. He needed to just storming accept that.

'They're timid and careful,' Navani noted, dabbing at Gavilar's ear with her napkin. 'It might take more time to persuade them.'

'Oh, I wouldn't worry about that,' Gavilar said, looking back at the corpse. 'Dalinar is nothing if not *persuasive*.'

*However, with a dangerous spice, you can be warned to taste lightly. I
would that your lesson may not be as painful as my own.*

—From *Oathbringer*, preface

ow this,' Kaladin said, 'isn't actually that serious a wound. I
know it looks deep, but it's often better to be cut deep by
a sharp knife than to be raggedly gouged by something
dull.'

He pressed the skin of Khen's arm together and applied the bandage to
her cut. 'Always use clean cloth you've boiled – rotspren love dirty cloth.
Infection is the real danger here; you'll spot it as red along the outsides
of the wound that grows and streaks. There will be pus too. Always wash
out a cut before binding it.'

He patted Khen's arm and took back his knife, which had caused the
offending laceration when Khen had been using it to cut branches off a
fallen tree for firewood. Around her, the other parshmen gathered the
cakes they'd dried in the sun.

They had a surprising number of resources, all things considered.
Several parshmen had thought to grab metal buckets during their raid
– which had worked as pots for boiling – and the waterskins were going
to be a lifesaver. He joined Sah, the parshman who had originally been

his captor, among the trees of their improvised camp. The parshman was lashing a stone axehead to a branch.

Kaladin took it from him and tested it against a log, judging how well it split the wood. 'You need to lash it tighter,' Kaladin said. 'Get the leather strips wet and really pull as you wrap it. If you aren't careful, it'll fall off on you midswing.'

Sah grunted, taking back the hatchet and grumbling to himself as he undid the lashings. He eyed Kaladin. 'You can go check on someone else, human.'

'We should march tonight,' Kaladin said. 'We've been in one spot too long. And break into small groups, like I said.'

'We'll see.'

'Look, if there's something wrong with my advice . . .'

'Nothing is wrong.'

'But—'

Sah sighed, looking up and meeting Kaladin's eyes. 'Where did a slave learn to give orders and strut about like a lighteyes?'

'My entire life was not spent as a slave.'

'I hate,' Sah continued, 'feeling like a child.' He started rewrapping the axehead, tighter this time. 'I hate being taught things that I should already know. Most of all, I hate needing your help. We ran. We escaped. Now what? You leap in, start telling us what to do? We're back to following Alethi orders again.'

Kaladin stayed silent.

'That yellow spren isn't any better,' Sah muttered. 'Hurry up. Keep moving. She tells us we're free, then with the very next breath berates us for not obeying quickly enough.'

They were surprised that Kaladin couldn't see the spren. They'd also mentioned to him the sounds they heard, distant rhythms, almost music.

' "Freedom" is a strange word, Sah,' Kaladin said softly, settling down. 'These last few months, I've probably been more "free" than at any time since my childhood. You want to know what I did with it? I stayed in the same place, serving another highlord. I wonder if men who use cords to bind are fools, since tradition, society, and momentum are going to tie us all down anyway.'

'I don't have traditions,' Sah said. 'Or society. But still, my "freedom" is that of a leaf. Dropped from the tree, I just blow on the wind and pretend I'm in charge of my destiny.'

'That was almost poetry, Sah.'

'I have no idea what that is.' He pulled the last lashing tight and held up the new hatchet.

Kaladin took it and buried it into the log next to him. 'Better.'

'Aren't you worried, human? Teaching us to make cakes is one thing. Giving us weapons is quite another.'

'A hatchet is a tool, not a weapon.'

'Perhaps,' Sah said. 'But with this same chipping and sharpening method you taught, I will eventually make a spear.'

'You act as if a fight is inevitable.'

Sah laughed. 'You don't think it is?'

'You have a choice.'

'Says the man with the brand on his forehead. If they're willing to do that to one of their *own*, what brutality awaits a bunch of thieving parshmen?'

'Sah, it *doesn't* have to come to war. You *don't* have to fight the humans.'

'Perhaps. But let me ask you this.' He set the axe across his lap. 'Considering what they did to me, why *wouldn't* I?'

Kaladin couldn't force out an objection. He remembered his own time as a slave: the frustration, powerlessness, anger. They'd branded him with *shash* because he was dangerous. Because he'd fought back.

Dared he demand this man do otherwise?

'They'll want to enslave us again,' Sah continued, taking the hatchet and hacking at the log next to him, starting to strip off the rough bark as Kaladin had instructed, so they could have tinder. 'We're money lost, and a dangerous precedent. Your kind will expend a fortune figuring out what changed to give us back our minds, and they'll find a way to reverse it. They'll strip from me my sanity, and set me to carrying water again.'

'Maybe . . . maybe we can convince them otherwise. I know good men among the Alethi lighteyes, Sah. If we talk to them, show them how you can talk and think – that you're like regular people – they'll listen. They'll agree to give you your freedom. That's how they treated your cousins on the Shattered Plains when they first met.'

Sah slammed the hatchet down into the wood, sending a chip fluttering into the air. 'And that's why we should be free now? Because we're acting like you? We deserved slavery before, when we were different? It's all right to dominate us when we won't fight back, but now it's not, because we can *talk*?'

'Well, I mean—'

'That's why I'm angry! Thank you for what you're showing us, but don't expect me to be happy that I need you for it. This just reinforces the belief within you, maybe even within myself, that your people should be the ones who decide upon our freedom *in the first place.*'

Sah stalked off, and once he was gone, Syl appeared from the underbrush and settled on Kaladin's shoulder, alert – watching for the Voidspren – but not immediately alarmed.

'I think I can sense a highstorm coming,' she whispered.

'What? Really?'

She nodded. 'It's distant still. A day or three.' She cocked her head. 'I suppose I could have done this earlier, but I didn't need to. Or know I wanted to. You always had the lists.'

Kaladin took a deep breath. How to protect these people from the storm? He'd have to find shelter. He'd . . .

I'm doing it again.

'I can't do this, Syl,' Kaladin whispered. 'I can't spend time with these parshmen, see their side.'

'Why?'

'Because Sah is right. This *is* going to come to war. The Voidspren will drive the parshmen into an army, and rightly so, after what was done to them. Our kind will have to fight back or be destroyed.'

'Then find the middle ground.'

'Middle ground only comes in war after lots of people have died – and only after the important people are worried they might actually lose. Storms, I shouldn't be here. I'm starting to want to defend these people! Teach them to fight. I don't dare – the only way I can fight the Voidbringers is to pretend there's a difference between the ones I have to protect and the ones I have to kill.'

He trudged through the underbrush and started helping tear down one of the crude tarp tents for the night's march.

21

SET UP TO FAIL

I am no storyteller, to entertain you with whimsical yarns.

—From *Oathbringer*, preface

A clamorous, insistent knocking woke Shallan. She still didn't have a bed, so she slept in a heap of red hair and twisted blankets.

She pulled one of these over her head, but the knocking persisted, followed by Adolin's annoyingly charming voice. 'Shallan? Look, this time I'm going to wait to come in until you're *really* sure I should.'

She peeked out at the sunlight, which poured through her balcony window like spilled paint. Morning? The sun was in the wrong place.

Wait . . . Stormfather. She'd spent the night out as Veil, then slept to the afternoon. She groaned, tossing off sweaty blankets, and lay there in just her shift, head pounding. There was an empty jug of Horneater white in the corner.

'Shallan?' Adolin said. 'Are you decent?'

'Depends,' she said, voice croaking, 'on the context. I'm decent at sleeping.'

She put hands over her eyes, safehand still wrapped in an improvised bandage. What had gotten into her? Tossing around the symbol of the Ghostbloods? Drinking herself silly? *Stabbing a man* in front of a gang of armed thugs?

Her actions felt like they'd taken place in a dream.

'Shallan,' Adolin said, sounding concerned. 'I'm going to peek in. Palona says you've been in here all day.'

She yelped, sitting up and grabbing the bedding. When he looked, he found her bundled there, a frizzy-haired head protruding from blankets – which she had pulled tight up to her chin. He looked perfect, of course. Adolin could look perfect after a storm, six hours of fighting, and a bath in cremwater. Annoying man. How *did* he make his hair so adorable? Messy in just the right way.

'Palona said you weren't feeling well,' Adolin said, pushing aside the cloth door and leaning in the doorway.

'Blarg.'

'Is it, um, girl stuff?'

'Girl stuff,' she said flatly.

'You know. When you . . . uh . . .'

'I'm aware of the biology, Adolin, thank you. Why is it that every time a woman is feeling a little odd, men are so quick to blame her cycle? As if she's suddenly unable to control herself because she has some pains. Nobody thinks that for men. "Oh, stay away from Venar today. He sparred too much yesterday, so his muscles are sore, and he's likely to *rip your head off*." '

'So it's our fault.'

'Yes. Like everything else. War. Famine. Bad hair.'

'Wait. Bad hair?'

Shallan blew a lock of it out of her eyes. 'Loud. Stubborn. Oblivious to our attempts to fix it. The Almighty gave us messy hair to prepare us for living with men.'

Adolin brought in a small pot of warm washwater for her face and hands. Bless him. And Palona, who had probably sent it with him.

Damnation, her hand ached. And her head. She remembered occasionally burning off the alcohol last night, but hadn't ever held enough Stormlight to completely fix the hand. And never enough to make her completely sober.

Adolin set the water down, perky as a sunrise, grinning. 'So what *is* wrong?'

She pulled the blanket up over her head and pulled it tight, like the hood of a cloak. 'Girl stuff,' she lied.

'See, I don't think men would blame your cycle nearly as much if you all didn't do the same. I've courted my share of women, and I once kept track. Deeli was once sick for womanly reasons four times in the same month.'

'We're very mysterious creatures.'

'I'll say.' He lifted up the jug and gave it a sniff. 'Is this *Horneater white*?' He looked to her, seeming shocked – but perhaps also a little impressed.

'Got a little carried away,' Shallan grumbled. 'Doing investigations about your murderer.'

'In a place serving Horneater moonshine?'

'Back alley of the Breakaway. Nasty place. Good booze though.'

'Shallan!' he said. 'You went alone? That's not safe.'

'Adolin, dear,' she said, finally pulling the blanket back down to her shoulders, 'I could *literally* survive being stabbed with a sword through the chest. I think I'll be fine with some ruffians in the market.'

'Oh. Right. It's kind of easy to forget.' He frowned. 'So . . . wait. You could survive all kinds of nasty murder, but you still . . .'

'Get menstrual cramps?' Shallan said. 'Yeah. Mother Cultivation can be hateful. I'm an all-powerful, Shardblade-wielding pseudo-immortal, but nature still sends a friendly reminder every now and then to tell me I should be getting around to having children.'

'No mating,' Pattern buzzed softly on the wall.

'But I shouldn't be blaming yesterday on that,' Shallan added to Adolin. 'My time isn't for another few weeks. Yesterday was more about psychology than it was about biology.'

Adolin set the jug down. 'Yeah, well, you might want to watch out for the Horneater wines.'

'It's not so bad,' Shallan said with a sigh. 'I can burn away the intoxication with a little Stormlight. Speaking of which, you don't have any spheres with you, do you? I seem to have . . . um . . . eaten all of mine.'

He chuckled. 'I have *one*. A single sphere. Father lent it to me so I could stop carrying a lantern everywhere in these halls.'

She tried to bat her eyelashes at him. She wasn't exactly sure how one did that, or why, but it seemed to work. At the very least, he rolled his eyes and handed over a single ruby mark.

She sucked in the Light hungrily. She held her breath so it wouldn't puff out when she breathed, and . . . suppressed the Light. She could do that, she'd found. To prevent herself from glowing or drawing attention. She'd done that as a child, hadn't she?

Her hand slowly reknit, and she let out a relieved sigh as the headache vanished as well.

Adolin was left with a dun sphere. 'You know, when my father explained that good relationships required investment, I don't think this is what he meant.'

'Mmm,' Shallan said, closing her eyes and smiling.

'Also,' Adolin added, 'we have the *strangest* conversations.'

'It feels natural to have them with you, though.'

'I think that's the oddest part. Well, you'll want to start being more careful with your Stormlight. Father mentioned he was trying to get you more infused spheres for practice, but there just aren't any.'

'What about Hatham's people?' she said. 'They left out lots of spheres in the last highstorm.' That had only been . . .

She did the math, and found herself stunned. It had been *weeks* since the unexpected highstorm where she'd first worked the Oathgate. She looked at the sphere between Adolin's fingers.

Those should all have gone dun by now, she thought. *Even the ones renewed most recently.* How did they have *any* Stormlight at all?

Suddenly, her actions the night before seemed even more irresponsible. When Dalinar had commanded her to practice with her powers, he probably hadn't meant practicing how to avoid getting too drunk.

She sighed, and – still keeping the blanket on – reached for the bowl of washing water. She had a lady's maid named Marri, but she kept sending her away. She didn't want the woman discovering that she was sneaking out or changing faces. If she kept on like that, Palona would probably assign the woman to other work.

The water didn't seem to have any scents or soaps applied to it, so Shallan raised the small basin and then took a long, slurping drink.

'I washed my feet in that,' Adolin noted.

'No you didn't.' Shallan smacked her lips. 'Anyway, thanks for dragging me out of bed.'

'Well,' he said, 'I have selfish reasons. I'm kind of hoping for some moral support.'

'Don't hit the message too hard. If you want someone to believe what you're telling them, come to your point gradually, so they're with you the entire time.'

He cocked his head.

'Oh, not *that* kind of moral,' Shallan said.

'Talking to you can be weird sometimes.'

'Sorry, sorry. I'll be good.' She sat as primly and attentively as she could, wrapped in a blanket with her hair sticking out like the snarls of a thornbush.

Adolin took a deep breath. 'My father finally persuaded Ialai Sadeas to speak with me. Father hopes she'll have some clues about her husband's death.'

'You sound less optimistic.'

'I don't like her, Shallan. She's strange.'

Shallan opened her mouth, but he cut her off.

'Not strange like you,' he said. 'Strange . . . bad strange. She's always weighing everything and everyone she meets. She's never treated me as anything other than a child. Will you go with me?'

'Sure. How much time do I have?'

'How much do you need?'

Shallan looked down at herself, huddled in her blankets, frizzy hair tickling her chin. 'A *lot*.'

'Then we'll be late,' Adolin said, standing up. 'It's not like her opinion of me could get any worse. Meet me at Sebarial's sitting room. Father wants me to take some reports from him on commerce.'

'Tell him the booze in the market is good.'

'Sure.' Adolin glanced again at the empty jug of Horneater white, then shook his head and left.

※

An hour later, Shallan presented herself – bathed, makeup done, hair somewhat under control – to Sebarial's sitting room. The chamber was larger than her room, but notably, the doorway out onto the balcony was enormous, taking up half the wall.

Everyone was out on the wide balcony, which overlooked the field below. Adolin stood by the railing, lost to some contemplation. Behind him, Sebarial and Palona lay on cots, their backs exposed to the sun, getting *massages*.

A flight of Horneater servants massaged, tended coal braziers, or stood dutifully with warmed wine and other conveniences. The air, particularly in the sun, wasn't as chilly as it had been most other days. It was almost pleasant.

Shallan found herself caught between embarrassment – this plump, bearded man wearing only a *towel* was the highprince – and outrage. She'd just taken a *cold* bath, pouring ladles of water on her own head while shivering. She'd considered that a luxury, as she hadn't been required to fetch the water herself.

'How is it,' Shallan said, 'that I am still sleeping on the floor, while you have cots *right here.*'

'Are you highprince?' Sebarial mumbled, not even opening his eyes.

'No. I'm a Knight Radiant, which I should think is higher.'

'I see,' he said, then groaned in pleasure at the masseuse's touch, 'and so you can pay to have a cot carried in from the warcamps? Or do you still rely on the stipend *I* give you? A stipend, I'll add, that was supposed to pay for your help as a scribe for my accounts – something I haven't seen in weeks.'

'She did save the world, Turi,' Palona noted from Shallan's other side. The middle-aged Herdazian woman also hadn't opened her eyes, and though she lay chest-down, her safehand was tucked only halfway under a towel.

'See, I don't think she saved it, so much as delayed its destruction. It's a *mess* out there, my dear.'

Nearby, the head masseuse – a large Horneater woman with vibrant red hair and pale skin – ordered a round of heated stones for Sebarial. Most of the servants were probably her family. Horneaters did like to be in business together.

'I will note,' Sebarial said, 'that this Desolation of yours is going to undermine years of my business planning.'

'You can't possibly blame me for that,' Shallan said, folding her arms.

'You did chase me out of the warcamps,' Sebarial said, 'even though they survived quite well. The remnants of those domes shielded them from the west. The big problem was the parshmen, but those have all cleared out now, marching toward Alethkar. So I plan to go back and reclaim my land there before others seize it.' He opened his eyes and glanced at Shallan. 'Your young prince didn't want to hear that – he worries I will stretch our forces too thin. But those warcamps are going to be vital for trade; we can't leave them completely to Thanadal and Vamah.'

Great. Another problem to think about. No wonder Adolin looked so distracted. He'd noted they'd be late to visiting Ialai, but didn't seem particularly eager to be on the move.

'You be a good Radiant,' Sebarial told her, 'and get those other Oath-gates working. I've prepared quite the scheme for taxing passage through them.'

'Callous.'

'Necessary. The only way to survive in these mountains will be to tax the Oathgates, and Dalinar knows it. He put me in charge of commerce. Life doesn't stop for a war, child. Everyone will still need new shoes, baskets, clothing, wine.'

'And we need massages,' Palona added. 'Lots of them, if we're going to have to live in this frozen wasteland.'

'You two are hopeless,' Shallan snapped, walking across the sunlit balcony to Adolin. 'Hey. Ready?'

'Sure.' She and Adolin struck out through the hallways. Each of the eight highprincedoms' armies in residence at the tower had been granted a quarter of the second or third level, with a few barracks on the first level, leaving most of that level reserved for markets and storage.

Of course, not even the first level had been completely explored. There were so many hallways and bizarre tangents – hidden sets of rooms tucked away behind everything else. Maybe eventually each highprince would rule his quarter in earnest. For now, they occupied little pockets of civilization within the dark frontier that was Urithiru.

Exploration on the upper levels had been completely halted, as they no longer had Stormlight to spare in working the lifts.

They left Sebarial's quarter, passing soldiers and an intersection with painted arrows on the floor leading to various places, such as the nearest privy. The guards' checkpoint didn't look like a barricade, but Adolin had pointed out the boxes of rations, the bags of grain, set in a specific way before the soldiers. Anyone rushing this corridor from the outside would get tangled in all of that, plus face pikemen beyond.

The soldiers nodded to Adolin, but didn't salute him, though one did bark an order to two men playing cards in a nearby room. The fellows stood up, and Shallan was startled to recognize them. Gaz and Vathah.

'Thought we'd take your guards today,' Adolin said.

My guards. Right. Shallan had a group of soldiers made up of deserters and despicable murderers. She didn't mind that part, being a despicable murderer herself. But she also had no idea what to do with them.

They saluted her lazily. Vathah, tall and scruffy. Gaz, short with a single brown eye, the other socket covered by a patch. Adolin had obviously already briefed them, and Vathah sauntered out to guard them in the front, while Gaz lingered behind.

Hoping they were far enough away not to hear, Shallan took Adolin by the arm.

'Do we *need* guards?' she whispered.

'Of course we do.'

'Why? You're a Shardbearer. I'm a Radiant. I think we'll be fine.'

'Shallan, being guarded isn't always about safety. It's about prestige.'

'I've got plenty. Prestige is practically leaking from my nose these days, Adolin.'

'That's not what I meant.' Adolin leaned down, whispering. 'This is for them. You don't need guards, maybe, but you do need an honor guard. Men to be *honored* by their position. It's part of the rules we play by – you get to be someone important, and they get to share in it.'

'By being useless.'

'By being part of what you're doing,' Adolin said. 'Storms, I forget how new you are to all this. What have you been doing with these men?'

'Letting them be, mostly.'

'What of when you need them?'

'I don't know if I will.'

'You will,' Adolin said. 'Shallan, you're their commander. Maybe not their military commander, as they're a civil guard, but it amounts to the same thing. Leave them idle, make them assume they're inconsequential, and you'll ruin them. Give them something important to do instead, work they'll be proud of, and they'll serve you with honor. A failed soldier is often one that has *been* failed.'

She smiled.

'What?'

'You sound like your father,' she said.

He paused, then looked away. 'Nothing wrong with that.'

'I didn't say there was. I like it.' She held his arm. 'I'll find something to do with my guards, Adolin. Something useful. I promise.'

Gaz and Vathah didn't seem to think the duty was all that important, from the way they yawned and slouched as they walked, holding out oil lamps, spears at their shoulders. They passed a large group of women carrying water, and then some men carrying lumber to set up a new privy. Most made way for Vathah; seeing a personal guard was a cue to step to the side.

Of course, if Shallan had really wanted to exude importance, she'd have taken a palanquin. She didn't mind the vehicles; she'd used them extensively in Kharbranth. Maybe it was the part of Veil inside of her, though, that made her resist Adolin whenever he suggested she order one. There was an independence to using her own feet.

They reached the stairwell up, and at the top, Adolin dug in his pocket for a map. The painted arrows weren't all finished up here. Shallan tugged his arm and pointed the way down a tunnel.

'How can you know that so easily?' he said.

'Don't you see how wide those strata are?' she asked, pointing to the wall of the corridor. 'It's this way.'

He tucked away his map and gestured for Vathah to lead the way. 'Do you really think I'm like my father?' Adolin said softly as they walked. There was a worried sense to his voice.

'You are,' she said, pulling his arm tight. 'You're just like him, Adolin. Moral, just, and capable.'

He frowned.

'What?'

'Nothing.'

'You're a terrible liar. You're worried you can't live up to his expectations, aren't you?'

'Maybe.'

'Well you have, Adolin. You have lived up to them in every way. I'm certain Dalinar Kholin couldn't hope for a better son, and . . . storms. That idea *bothers* you.'

'What? No!'

Shallan poked Adolin in the shoulder with her freehand. 'You're not telling me something.'

'Maybe.'

'Well, thank the Almighty for that.'

'Not . . . going to ask what it is?'

'Ash's eyes, no. I'd rather figure it out. A relationship needs *some* measure of mystery.'

Adolin fell silent, which was all well and good, because they were approaching the Sadeas section of Urithiru. Though Ialai had threatened to relocate back to the warcamps, she'd made no such move. Likely because there was no denying that this city was now the seat of Alethi politics and power.

They reached the first guard post, and Shallan's two guards pulled up close to her and Adolin. They exchanged hostile glares with the soldiers in forest-green-and-white uniforms as they were allowed past. Whatever Ialai Sadeas thought, her men had obviously made up their minds.

It was strange how much difference a few steps could make. In here, they passed far fewer workers or merchants, and far more soldiers. Men with dark expressions, unbuttoned coats, and unshaved faces of all varieties. Even the scribes were different – more makeup, but sloppier clothing.

It felt like they'd stepped from law into disorder. Loud voices echoed down hallways, laughing raucously. The stripes painted to guide the way were on the walls here rather than the floor, and the paint had been allowed to drip, spoiling the strata. They'd been smeared in places by men who had walked by, their coats brushing the still-wet paint.

The soldiers they passed all sneered at Adolin.

'They feel like gangs,' Shallan said softly, looking over her shoulder at one group.

'Don't mistake them,' Adolin said. 'They march in step, their boots are sturdy, and their weapons well maintained. Sadeas trained good soldiers. It's just that where Father used discipline, Sadeas used competition. Besides, here, looking too clean will get you mocked. You can't be mistaken for a Kholin.'

She'd hoped that maybe, now that the truth about the Desolation had been revealed, Dalinar would have an easier time of uniting the highprinces. Well, that obviously wasn't going to happen while these men blamed Dalinar for Sadeas's death.

They eventually reached the proper rooms and were ushered in to confront Sadeas's wife. Ialai was a short woman with thick lips and green eyes. She sat in a throne at the center of the room.

Standing beside her was Mraize, one of the leaders of the Ghostbloods.

22

THE DARKNESS WITHIN

I am no philosopher, to intrigue you with piercing questions.

—From *Oathbringer*, preface

Mraize. His face was crisscrossed by scars, one of which deformed his upper lip. Instead of his usual fashionable clothing, today he wore a Sadeas uniform, with a breastplate and a simple skullcap helm. He looked exactly like the other soldiers they'd passed, save for that face.

And the chicken on his shoulder.

A *chicken*. It was one of the stranger varieties, pure green and sleek, with a wicked beak. It looked much more like a predator than the bumbling things she'd seen sold in cages at markets.

But seriously. Who walked around with a pet chicken? They were for eating, right?

Adolin noted the chicken and raised an eyebrow, but Mraize didn't give any sign that he knew Shallan. He slouched like the other soldiers, holding a halberd and glaring at Adolin.

Ialai hadn't set out chairs for them. She sat with her hands in her lap, sleeved safehand beneath her freehand, lit by lamps on pedestals at either side of the room. She looked particularly vengeful by that unnatural flickering light.

'Did you know,' Ialai said, 'that after whitespines make a kill, they will eat, then hide near the carcass?'

'It's one of the dangers in hunting them, Brightness,' Adolin said. 'You assume that you're on the beast's trail, but it might be lurking nearby.'

'I used to wonder at this behavior until I realized the kill will attract scavengers, and the whitespine is not picky. The ones that come to feast on its leavings become another meal themselves.'

The implication of the conversation seemed clear to Shallan. *Why have you returned to the scene of the kill, Kholin?*

'We want you to know, Brightness,' Adolin said, 'that we take the murder of a highprince *very* seriously. We are doing everything we can to prevent this from happening again.'

Oh, Adolin . . .

'Of course you are,' Ialai said. 'The other highprinces are now too afraid to stand up to you.'

Yes, he'd walked right into that one. But Shallan didn't take over; this was Adolin's task, and he'd invited her for support, not to speak for him. Honestly, she wouldn't be doing much better. She'd just be making different mistakes.

'Can you tell us of anyone who might have had the opportunity and motive for killing your husband?' Adolin said. '*Other* than my father, Brightness.'

'So even you admit that—'

'It's strange,' Adolin snapped. 'My mother always said she thought you were clever. She admired you, and wished she had your wit. Yet here, *I* see no proof of that. Honestly, do you *really* think that my father would withstand Sadeas's insults for years – weather his betrayal on the Plains, suffer that dueling fiasco – only to *assassinate him* now? Once Sadeas was proven wrong about the Voidbringers, and my father's position is secure? We both know my father wasn't behind your husband's death. To claim otherwise is simple idiocy.'

Shallan started. She hadn't expected *that* from Adolin's lips. Strikingly, it seemed to her to be the *precise* thing he'd needed to say. Cut away the courtly language. Deliver the straight and earnest truth.

Ialai leaned forward, inspecting Adolin and chewing on his words. If there was one thing Adolin could convey, it was authenticity.

'Fetch him a chair,' Ialai said to Mraize.

'Yes, Brightness,' he said, his voice thick with a rural accent that bordered on Herdazian.

Ialai then looked to Shallan. 'And you. Make yourself useful. There are teas warming in the side room.'

Shallan sniffed at the treatment. She was no longer some inconsequential ward, to be ordered about. However, Mraize lurched off in the same direction she'd been told to go, so Shallan bore the indignity and stalked after him.

The next room was much smaller, cut out of the same stone as the others, but with a muted pattern of strata. Oranges and reds that blended together so evenly you could almost pretend the wall was all one hue. Ialai's people had been using it for storage, as evidenced by the chairs in one corner. Shallan ignored the warm jugs of tea heating on fabrials on the counter and stepped close to Mraize.

'What are you doing here?' she hissed at him.

His chicken chirped softly, as if in agitation.

'I'm keeping an eye on that one,' he said, nodding toward the other room. Here, his voice became refined, losing the rural edge. 'We have interest in her.'

'So she's not one of you?' Shallan asked. 'She's not a . . . Ghostblood?'

'No,' he said, eyes narrowing. 'She and her husband were too wild a variable for us to invite. Their motives are their own; I don't think they align to those of anyone else, human or listener.'

'The fact that they're crem didn't enter into it, I suppose.'

'Morality is an axis that doesn't interest us,' Mraize said calmly. 'Only loyalty and power are relevant, for morality is as ephemeral as the changing weather. It depends upon the angle from which you view it. You will see, as you work with us, that I am right.'

'I'm *not* one of you,' Shallan hissed.

'For one so insistent,' Mraize said, picking up a chair, 'you were certainly free in using our symbol last night.'

Shallan froze, then blushed furiously. So he knew about that? 'I . . .'

'Your hunt is worthy,' Mraize said. 'And you are allowed to rely upon our authority to achieve your goals. That is a benefit of your membership, so long as you do not abuse it.'

'And my brothers? Where are they? You promised to deliver them to me.'

'Patience, little knife. It has been but a few weeks since we rescued them. You will see my word fulfilled in that matter. Regardless, I have a task for you.'

'A task?' Shallan snapped, causing the chicken to chirp at her again. 'Mraize, I'm not going to do some task for you people. You *killed* Jasnah.'

'An enemy combatant,' Mraize said. 'Oh, don't look at me like that. You know full well what that woman was capable of, and what she got herself into by attacking us. Do you blame your wonderfully moral Blackthorn for what he did in war? The countless people *he* slaughtered?'

'Don't deflect your evils by pointing out the faults of others,' Shallan said. 'I'm not going to further your cause. I don't care how much you demand that I Soulcast for you, I'm not going to do it.'

'So quick to insist, yet you acknowledge your debt. One Soulcaster lost, destroyed. But we forgive these things, for missions undertaken. And before you object again, know that the task we require of you is one you're *already* undertaking. Surely you have sensed the darkness in this place. The ... wrongness.'

Shallan looked about the small room, flickering with shadows from a few candles on the counter.

'Your task,' Mraize said, 'is to secure this location. Urithiru must remain strong if we are to properly use the advent of the Voidbringers.'

'*Use* them?'

'Yes,' Mraize said. 'This is a power we will control, but we must not let either side gain dominance yet. Secure Urithiru. Hunt the source of the darkness you feel, and expunge it. This is your task. And for it I will give payment in information.' He leaned closer to her and spoke a single word. 'Helaran.'

He lifted the chair and walked out, adopting a more bumbling gait, stumbling and almost dropping the chair. Shallan stood there, stunned. Helaran. Her eldest brother had died in Alethkar – where he'd been for mysterious reasons.

Storms, what did Mraize know? She glared after him, outraged. How dare he tease with that name!

Don't focus on Helaran right now. Those were dangerous thoughts, and she could not become Veil now. Shallan poured herself and Adolin cups of tea, then grabbed a chair under her arm and awkwardly navigated back out. She sat down beside Adolin, then handed him a cup. She took a sip and smiled at Ialai, who glared at her, then directed Mraize to fetch a cup.

'I think,' Ialai said to Adolin, 'that if you honestly wish to solve this crime, you won't be looking at my husband's former enemies. Nobody had the opportunity or motives that you would find in your warcamp.'

Adolin sighed. 'We established that—'

'I'm not saying Dalinar did this,' Ialai said. She seemed calm, but she gripped the sides of her chair with white-knuckled hands. And her eyes ... makeup could not hide the redness. She'd been crying. She was truly upset.

Unless it was an act. *I could fake crying,* Shallan thought, *if I knew that someone was coming to see me, and if I believed the act would strengthen my position.*

'Then what *are* you saying?' Adolin asked.

'History is rife with examples of soldiers assuming orders when there were none,' Ialai said. 'I agree that Dalinar would never knife an old friend in dark quarters. His soldiers may not be so inhibited. You want to know who did this, Adolin Kholin? Look among your own ranks. I would wager the princedom that somewhere in the Kholin army is a man who thought to do his highprince a service.'

'And the other murders?' Shallan said.

'I do not know the mind of this person,' Ialai said. 'Maybe they have a taste for it now? In any case, I think we can agree this meeting serves no further purpose.' She stood up. 'Good day, Adolin Kholin. I hope you will share what you discover with me, so that my own investigator can be better informed.'

'I suppose,' Adolin said, standing. 'Who is leading your investigation? I'll send him reports.'

'His name is Meridas Amaram. I believe you know him.'

Shallan gaped. 'Amaram? *Highmarshal Amaram?*'

'Of course,' Ialai said. 'He is among my husband's most acclaimed generals.'

Amaram. He'd killed her brother. She glanced at Mraize, who kept his expression neutral. Storms, what did he know? She still didn't understand where Helaran had gotten his Shardblade. What had led him to clash with Amaram in the first place?

'Amaram is *here?*' Adolin asked. 'When?'

'He arrived with the last caravan and scavenging crew that you brought through the Oathgate. He didn't make himself known to the tower, but to me alone. We have been seeing to his needs, as he was caught out in a storm with his attendants. He assures me he will return to duty soon, and will make finding my husband's murderer a priority.'

'I see,' Adolin said.

He looked to Shallan, and she nodded, still stunned. Together they collected her soldiers from right inside the door, and left into the hallway beyond.

'Amaram,' Adolin hissed. 'Bridgeboy isn't going to be happy about this. They have a vendetta, those two.'

Not just Kaladin.

'Father originally appointed Amaram to refound the Knights Radiant,' Adolin continued. 'If Ialai has taken him in after he was so soundly discredited . . . The mere act of it calls Father a liar, doesn't it? Shallan?'

She shook herself and took a deep breath. Helaran was long dead. She would worry about getting answers from Mraize later.

'It depends on how she spins things,' she said softly, walking beside Adolin. 'But yes, she implies that Dalinar is at the least overly judgmental in his treatment of Amaram. She's reinforcing her side as an alternative to your father's rule.'

Adolin sighed. 'I'd have thought that without Sadeas, maybe it would get easier.'

'Politics is involved, Adolin – so by definition it can't be easy.' She took his arm, wrapping hers around it as they passed another group of hostile guards.

'I'm terrible at this,' Adolin said softly. 'I got so annoyed in there, I almost punched her. You watch, Shallan. I'll ruin this.'

'Will you? Because I think you're right about there being multiple killers.'

'What? Really?'

She nodded. 'I heard some things while I was out last night.'

'When you weren't staggering around drunk, you mean.'

'I'll have you know I'm a very graceful drunk, Adolin Kholin. Let's go . . .' She trailed off as a pair of scribes ran past in the hallway, heading toward Ialai's rooms at a shocking speed. Guards marched after them.

Adolin caught one by the arm, nearly provoking a fight as the man cursed at the blue uniform. The fellow, fortunately, recognized Adolin's face and held himself back, hand moving off the axe in a sling to his side.

'Brightlord,' the man said, reluctant.

'What is this?' Adolin said. He nodded down the hall. 'Why is everyone suddenly talking at that guard post farther along?'

'News from the coast,' the guard finally said. 'Stormwall spotted in New Natanan. The highstorms. They've returned.'

I am no poet, to delight you with clever allusions.

—From *Oathbringer*, preface

I don't got any meat to sell,' the old lighteyes said as he led Kaladin into the storm bunker. 'But your brightlord and his men can weather in here, and for cheap.' He waved his cane toward the large hollow building. It reminded Kaladin of the barracks on the Shattered Plains – long and narrow, with one small end pointed eastward.

'We'll need it to ourselves,' Kaladin said. 'My brightlord values his privacy.'

The elderly man glanced at Kaladin, taking in the blue uniform. Now that the Weeping had passed, it looked better. He wouldn't wear it to an officer's review, but he'd spent some good time scrubbing out the stains and polishing the buttons.

Kholin uniform in Vamah lands. It could imply a host of things. Hopefully one of them was not 'This Kholin officer has joined a bunch of runaway parshmen.'

'I can give you the whole bunker,' the merchant said. 'Was supposed to be renting it to some caravans out of Revolar, but they didn't show.'

'What happened?'

'Don't know,' he said. 'But it's storming strange, I'd say. Three caravans, with different masters and goods, all gone silent. Not even a runner to give me word. Glad I took ten percent up front.'

Revolar. It was Vamah's seat, the largest city between here and Kholinar.

'We'll take the bunker,' Kaladin said, handing over some dun spheres. 'And whatever food you can spare.'

'Not much, by an army's scale. Maybe a sack of longroots or two. Some lavis. Was expectin' one of those caravans to resupply me.' He shook his head, expression distant. 'Strange times, Corporal. That wrong-way storm. You reckon it will keep coming back?'

Kaladin nodded. The Everstorm had hit again the day before, its second occurrence – not counting the initial one that had only come in the far east. Kaladin and the parshmen had weathered this one, upon warning from the unseen spren, in an abandoned mine.

'Strange times,' the old man said again. 'Well, if you do need meat, there's been a nest of wild hogs rooting about in the ravine to the south of here. This is Highlord Cadilar's land though, so um. . . . Well, you just understand that.' If Kaladin's fictional 'brightlord' was traveling on the king's orders, they could hunt the lands. If not, killing another highlord's hogs would be poaching.

The old man spoke like a backwater farmer, light yellow eyes not-withstanding, but he'd obviously made something of himself running a waystop. A lonely life, but the money was probably quite good.

'Let's see what food I can find you here,' the old man said. 'Follow along. Now, you're *sure* a storm is coming?'

'I have charts promising it.'

'Well, bless the Almighty and Heralds for that, I suppose. Will catch some people surprised, but it will be nice to be able to work my spanreed again.'

Kaladin followed the man to a stone rootshed on the leeward edge of his home, and haggled – briefly – for three sacks of vegetables. 'One other thing,' Kaladin added. 'You can't watch the army arrive.'

'What? Corporal, it's my duty to see your people settled in—'

'My brightlord is a *very* private person. It's important nobody know of our passing. *Very important.*' He laid his hand on his belt knife.

The lighteyed man just sniffed. 'I can be trusted to hold my tongue, *soldier*. And don't threaten me. I'm sixth dahn.' He raised his chin, but when he hobbled back into his house, he shut the door tight and pulled closed the stormshutters.

Kaladin transferred the three sacks into the bunker, then hiked out to where he'd left the parshmen. He kept glancing about for Syl, but of course he saw nothing. The Voidspren was following him, hidden, likely to make sure he didn't do anything underhanded.

∴

They made it back right before the storm.

Khen, Sah, and the others had wanted to wait until dark – unwilling to trust that the old lighteyes wouldn't spy on them. But the wind had started blowing, and they'd finally believed Kaladin that a storm was imminent.

Kaladin stood by the bunker's doorway, anxious as the parshmen piled in. They'd picked up other groups in the last few days, led by unseen Voidspren that he was told darted away once their charges were delivered. Their numbers were now verging on a hundred, including the children and elderly. Nobody would tell Kaladin their end goal, only that the spren had a destination in mind.

Khen was last through the door; the large, muscled parshwoman lingered, as if she wanted to watch the storm. Finally she took their spheres – most of which they'd stolen from him – and locked the sack into the iron-banded lantern on the wall outside. She waved Kaladin through the door, then followed, barring it closed.

'You did well, human,' she said to Kaladin. 'I'll speak for you when we reach the gathering.'

'Thanks,' Kaladin said. Outside, the stormwall hit the bunker, making the stones shake and the very ground rattle.

The parshmen settled down to wait. Hesh dug into the sacks and inspected the vegetables with a critical eye. She'd worked the kitchens of a manor.

Kaladin settled with his back to the wall, feeling the storm rage outside. Strange, how he could hate the mild Weeping so much, yet feel a thrill when he heard thunder beyond these stones. That storm had tried its best to kill him on several occasions. He felt a kinship to it – but still a wariness. It was a sergeant who was too brutal in training his recruits.

The storm would renew the gems outside, which included not only spheres, but the larger gemstones he'd been carrying. Once renewed, he – well, the parshmen – would have a wealth of Stormlight.

He needed to make a decision. How long could he delay flying back to the Shattered Plains? Even if he had to stop at a larger city to trade his dun spheres for infused ones, he could probably make it in under a day.

He couldn't dally forever. What were they doing at Urithiru? What was the word from the rest of the world? The questions hounded him. Once, he had been happy to worry only about his own squad. After that, he'd been willing to look after a battalion. Since when had the state of the entire world become his concern?

I need to steal back my spanreed at the very least, and send a message to Brightness Navani.

Something flickered at the edge of his vision. Syl had come back? He glanced toward her, a question on his lips, and barely stopped the words as he realized his error.

The spren beside him was glowing yellow, not blue-white. The tiny woman stood on a translucent pillar of golden stone that had risen from the ground to put her even with Kaladin's gaze. It, like the spren herself, was the yellow-white color of the center of a flame.

She wore a flowing dress that covered her legs entirely. Hands behind her back, she inspected him. Her face was shaped oddly – narrow, but with large, childlike eyes. Like someone from Shinovar.

Kaladin jumped, which caused the little spren to smile.

Pretend you don't know anything about spren like her, Kaladin thought. 'Um. Uh . . . I can see you.'

'Because I want you to,' she said. 'You *are* an odd one.'

'Why . . . why do you want me to see you?'

'So we can talk.' She started to stroll around him, and at each step, a spike of yellow stone shot up from the ground and met her bare foot. 'Why are you still here, human?'

'Your parshmen took me captive.'

'Your mother teach you to lie like that?' she asked, sounding amused. 'They're less than a month old. Congratulations on fooling them.' She stopped and smiled at him. 'I'm a tad older than a month.'

'The world is changing,' Kaladin said. 'The country is in upheaval. I guess I want to see where this goes.'

She contemplated him. Fortunately, he had a good excuse for the bead of sweat that trickled down the side of his face. Facing a strangely intelligent, glowing yellow spren would unnerve anyone, not just a man with too many things to hide.

'Would you fight for us, deserter?' she asked.

'Would I be allowed?'

'My kind aren't *nearly* as inclined toward discrimination as yours. If you can carry a spear and take orders, then *I* certainly wouldn't turn you away.' She folded her arms, smiling in a strangely knowing way. 'The final decision won't be mine. I am but a messenger.'

'Where can I find out for certain?'

'At our destination.'

'Which is . . .'

'Close enough,' the spren said. 'Why? You have pressing appointments elsewhere? Off for a beard trim perhaps, or a lunch date with your grandmother?'

Kaladin rubbed at his face. He'd almost been able to forget about the hairs that prickled at the sides of his mouth.

'Tell me,' the spren asked, 'how did you know that there would be a highstorm tonight?'

'Felt it,' Kaladin said, 'in my bones.'

'Humans can*not* feel storms, regardless of the body part in question.'

He shrugged. 'Seemed like the right time for one, with the Weeping having stopped and all.'

She didn't nod or give any visible sign of what she thought of that comment. She merely held her knowing smile, then faded from his view.

24

MEN OF BLOOD
AND SORROW

I have no doubt that you are smarter than I am. I can only relate what happened, what I have done, and then let you draw conclusions.

—From *Oathbringer*, preface

D alinar remembered.

Her name had been Evi. She'd been tall and willowy, with pale yellow hair – not true golden, like the hair of the Iriali, but striking in its own right.

She'd been quiet. Shy, both she and her brother, for all that they'd been willing to flee their homeland in an act of courage. They'd brought Shardplate, and ...

That was all that had emerged over the last few days. The rest was still a blur. He could recall meeting Evi, courting her – awkwardly, since both knew it was an arrangement of political necessity – and eventually entering into a causal betrothal.

He didn't remember love, but he did remember attraction.

The memories brought questions, like cremlings emerging from their hollows after the rain. He ignored them, standing straight-backed with a line of guards on the field in front of Urithiru, suffering a bitter wind from the west. This wide plateau held some dumps of wood, as part of this space would probably end up becoming a lumberyard.

Behind him, the end of a rope blew in the wind, smacking a pile of wood again and again. A pair of windspren danced past, in the shapes of little people.

Why am I remembering Evi now? Dalinar wondered. *And why have I recovered only my first memories of our time together?*

He had always remembered the difficult years following Evi's death, which had culminated in his being drunk and useless on the night Szeth, the Assassin in White, had killed his brother. He assumed that he'd gone to the Nightwatcher to be rid of the pain at losing her, and the spren had taken his other memories as payment. He didn't know for certain, but that seemed right.

Bargains with the Nightwatcher were supposed to be permanent. Damning, even. So what was happening to him?

Dalinar glanced at his bracer clocks, strapped to his forearm. Five minutes late. Storms. He'd been wearing the thing barely a few days, and already he was counting minutes like a scribe.

The second of the two watch faces – which would count down to the next highstorm – still hadn't been engaged. A single highstorm had come, blessedly, carrying Stormlight to renew spheres. It seemed like so long since they'd had enough of that.

However, it would take until the next highstorm for the scribes to make guesses at the current pattern. Even then they could be wrong, as the Weeping had lasted far longer than it should have. Centuries – millennia – of careful records might now be obsolete.

Once, that alone would have been a catastrophe. It threatened to ruin planting seasons and cause famines, to upend travel and shipping, disrupting trade. Unfortunately, in the face of the Everstorm and the Voidbringers, it was barely third on the list of cataclysms.

The cold wind blew at him again. Before them, the grand plateau of Urithiru was ringed by ten large platforms, each raised about ten feet high, with steps up beside a ramp for carts. At the center of each one was a small building containing the device that—

With a bright flash, an expanding wave of Stormlight spread outward from the center of the second platform from the left. When the Light faded, Dalinar led his troop of honor guards up the wide steps to the top. They crossed to the building at the center, where a small group of people had stepped out and were now gawking at Urithiru, surrounded by awespren.

Dalinar smiled. The sight of a tower as wide as a city and as tall as a small mountain . . . well, there wasn't anything else like it in the world.

At the head of the newcomers was a man in burnt orange robes. Aged, with a kindly, clean-shaven face, he stood with his head tipped back and jaw lowered as he regarded the city. Near him stood a woman with silvery hair pulled up in a bun. Adrotagia, the head Kharbranthian scribe.

Some thought she was the true power behind the throne; others guessed it was that other scribe, the one they had left running Kharbranth in its king's absence. Whoever it was, they kept Taravangian as a figurehead – and Dalinar was happy to work through him to get to Jah Keved and Kharbranth. This man had been a friend to Gavilar; that was good enough for Dalinar. And he was more than glad to have at least one other monarch at Urithiru.

Taravangian smiled at Dalinar, then licked his lips. He seemed to have forgotten what he wanted to say, and had to glance at the woman beside him for support. She whispered, and he spoke loudly after the reminder.

'Blackthorn,' Taravangian said. 'It is an honor to meet you again. It has been too long.'

'Your Majesty,' Dalinar said. 'Thank you so much for responding to my call.' Dalinar had met Taravangian several times, years ago. He remembered a man of quiet, keen intelligence.

That was gone now. Taravangian had always been humble, and had kept to himself, so most didn't know he'd been intelligent once – before his strange illness five years ago, which Navani was fairly certain covered an apoplexy that had permanently wounded his mental capacities.

Adrotagia touched Taravangian's arm and nodded toward someone standing with the Kharbranthian guards: a middle-aged lighteyed woman wearing a skirt and blouse, after a Southern style, with the top buttons of the blouse undone. Her hair was short in a boyish cut, and she wore gloves on both hands.

The strange woman stretched her right hand over her head, and a Shardblade appeared in it. She rested it with the flat side against her shoulder.

'Ah yes,' Taravangian said. 'Introductions! Blackthorn, this is the newest Knight Radiant. Malata of Jah Keved.'

King Taravangian gawked like a child as they rode the lift toward the top of the tower. He leaned over the side far enough that his large Thaylen bodyguard rested a careful hand on the king's shoulder, just in case.

'So many levels,' Taravangian said. 'And this balcony. Tell me, Brightlord. What makes it move?'

His sincerity was so unexpected. Dalinar had been around Alethi politicians so much that he found honesty an obscure thing, like a language he no longer spoke.

'My engineers are still studying the lifts,' Dalinar said. 'It has to do with conjoined fabrials, they believe, with gears to modulate speed.'

Taravangian blinked. 'Oh. I meant . . . is this Stormlight? Or is someone pulling somewhere? We had parshmen do ours, back in Kharbranth.'

'Stormlight,' Dalinar said. 'We had to replace the gemstones with infused ones to make it work.'

'Ah.' He shook his head, grinning.

In Alethkar, this man would never have been able to hold a throne after the apoplexy struck him. An unscrupulous family would have removed him by assassination. In other families, someone would have challenged him for his throne. He'd have been forced to fight or abdicate.

Or . . . well, someone might have muscled him out of power, and acted like king in all but name. Dalinar sighed softly, but kept a firm grip on his guilt.

Taravangian wasn't Alethi. In Kharbranth – which didn't wage war – a mild, congenial figurehead made more sense. The city was *supposed* to be unassuming, unthreatening. It was a twist of luck that Taravangian had also been crowned king of Jah Keved, once one of the most powerful kingdoms on Roshar, following its civil war.

He would normally have had trouble keeping that throne, but perhaps Dalinar might lend him some support – or at least authority – through association. Dalinar certainly intended to do everything he could.

'Your Majesty,' Dalinar said, stepping closer to Taravangian. 'How well guarded is Vedenar? I have a great number of troops with too much idle time. I could easily spare a battalion or two to help secure the city. We can't afford to lose the Oathgate to the enemy.'

Taravangian glanced at Adrotagia.

She answered for him. 'The city is secure, Brightlord. You needn't fear. The parshmen made one push for the city, but there are still many Veden troops available. We fended the enemy off, and they withdrew eastward.'

Toward Alethkar, Dalinar thought.

Taravangian again looked out into the wide central column, lit from the sheer glass window to the east. 'Ah, how I wish this day hadn't come.'

'You sound as if you anticipated it, Your Majesty,' Dalinar said.

Taravangian laughed softly. 'Don't you? Anticipate sorrow, I mean? Sadness . . . loss . . .'

'I try not to hasten my expectations in either direction,' Dalinar said. 'The soldier's way. Deal with today's problems, then sleep and deal with tomorrow's problems tomorrow.'

Taravangian nodded. 'I remember, as a child, listening to an ardent pray to the Almighty on my behalf as glyphwards burned nearby. I remember thinking . . . surely the sorrows can't be past us. Surely the evils didn't actually end. If they had, wouldn't we be back in the Tranquiline Halls even now?' He looked toward Dalinar, and surprisingly there were tears in his pale grey eyes. 'I do not think you and I are destined for such a glorious place. Men of blood and sorrow don't get an ending like that, Dalinar Kholin.'

Dalinar found himself without a reply. Adrotagia gripped Taravangian on the forearm with a comforting gesture, and the old king turned away, hiding his emotional outburst. What had happened in Vedenar must have troubled him deeply – the death of the previous king, the field of slaughter.

They rode the rest of the way in silence, and Dalinar took the chance to study Taravangian's Surgebinder. She'd been the one to unlock – then activate – the Veden Oathgate on the other side, which she'd managed after some careful instructions from Navani. Now the woman, Malata, leaned idly against the side of the balcony. She hadn't spoken much during their tour of the first three levels, and when she looked at Dalinar, she always seemed to have a hint of a smile on her lips.

She carried a wealth of spheres in her skirt pocket; the light shone through the fabric. Perhaps that was why she smiled. He himself felt relieved to have Light at his fingertips again – and not only because it meant the Alethi Soulcasters could get back to work, using their emeralds to transform rock to grain to feed the hungry people of the tower.

Navani met them at the top level, immaculate in an ornate silver and black havah, her hair in a bun and stabbed through with hairspikes meant to resemble Shardblades. She greeted Taravangian warmly, then clasped hands with Adrotagia. After a greeting, Navani stepped back and let Teshav guide Taravangian and his little retinue into what they were calling the Initiation Room.

Navani herself drew Dalinar to the side. 'Well?' she whispered.

'He's as sincere as ever,' Dalinar said softly. 'But . . .'

'Dense?' she asked.

'Dear, *I'm* dense. This man has become an idiot.'

'You're not dense, Dalinar,' she said. 'You're rugged. Practical.'

'I've no illusions as to the thickness of my skull, gemheart. It's done right by me on more than one occasion – better a thick head than a broken one. But I don't know that Taravangian in his current state will be of much use.'

'Bah,' Navani said. 'We've more than enough clever people around us, Dalinar. Taravangian was always a friend to Alethkar during your brother's reign, and a little illness shouldn't change our treatment of him.'

'You're right, of course. . . .' He trailed off. 'There's an earnestness to him, Navani. And a melancholy I hadn't remembered. Was that always there?'

'Yes, actually.' She checked her own arm clock, like his own, though with a few more gemstones attached. Some kind of new fabrial she was tinkering with.

'Any news from Captain Kaladin?'

She shook her head. It had been days since his last check-in, but he'd likely run out of infused rubies. Now that the highstorms had returned, they'd expected something.

In the room, Teshav gestured to the various pillars, each representing an order of Knight Radiant. Dalinar and Navani waited in the doorway, separated from the rest.

'What of the Surgebinder?' Navani whispered.

'A Releaser. Dustbringer, though they don't like the term. She claims her spren told her that.' He rubbed his chin. 'I don't like how she smiles.'

'If she's truly a Radiant,' Navani said, 'can she be anything but trustworthy? Would the spren pick someone who would act against the best interests of the orders?'

Another question he didn't know the answer to. He'd need to see if he could determine whether her Shardblade was only that, or if it might be another Honorblade in disguise.

The touring group moved down a set of steps toward the meeting chamber, which took up most of the penultimate level and sloped down to the level below. Dalinar and Navani trailed after them.

Navani, he thought. *On my arm.* It still gave him a heady, surreal feeling. Dreamlike, as if this were one of his visions. He could vividly remember desiring her. Thinking about her, captivated by the way she talked, the things she knew, the look of her hands as she sketched – or, storms, as she did something as simple as raising a spoon to her lips. He remembered staring at her.

He remembered a specific day on a battlefield, when he had almost let his jealousy of his brother lead him too far – and was surprised to feel Evi slipping into that memory. Her presence colored the old, crusty memory of those war days with his brother.

'My memories continue to return,' he said softly as they paused at the door into the conference room. 'I can only assume that eventually it will all come back.'

'That shouldn't be happening.'

'I thought the same. But really, who can say? The Old Magic is said to be inscrutable.'

'No,' Navani said, folding her arms, getting a stern expression on her face – as if angry with a stubborn child. 'In each case I've looked into, the boon and curse both lasted until death.'

'Each case?' Dalinar said. 'How many did you find?'

'About three hundred at this point,' Navani said. 'It's been difficult to get any time from the researchers at the Palanaeum; everyone the world over is demanding research into the Voidbringers. Fortunately, His Majesty's impending visit here earned me special consideration, and I had some credit. They say it's best to patronize the place in person – at least Jasnah always said . . .'

She took a breath, steadying herself before continuing. 'In any case, Dalinar, the research is definitive. We haven't been able to find a *single* case where the effects of the Old Magic wore off – and it's not like people haven't tried over the centuries. Lore about people dealing with their curses, and seeking any cure for them, is practically its own *genre*. As my researcher said, "Old Magic curses aren't like a hangover, Brightness."'

She looked up at Dalinar, and must have seen the emotion in his face, for she cocked her head. 'What?' she asked.

'I've never had anyone to share this burden with,' he said softly. 'Thank you.'

'I didn't find anything.'

'It doesn't matter.'

'Could you at least confirm with the Stormfather again that his bond with you is absolutely, for sure *not* what's causing the memories to come back?'

'I'll see.'

The Stormfather rumbled. *Why would she want me to say more? I have spoken, and spren do not change like men. This is not my doing. It is not the bond.*

'He says it's not him,' Dalinar said. 'He's . . . annoyed at you for asking again.'

She kept her arms crossed. This was something she shared with her daughter, a characteristic frustration with problems she couldn't solve. As if she were disappointed in the facts for not arranging themselves more helpfully.

'Maybe,' she said, 'something was different about the deal you made. If you can recount your visit to me sometime – with as much detail as you can remember – I'll compare it to other accounts.'

He shook his head. 'There wasn't much. The Valley had a lot of plants. And . . . I remember . . . I asked to have my pain taken away, and she took memories too. I think?' He shrugged, then noticed Navani pursing her lips, her stare sharpening. 'I'm sorry. I—'

'It's not you,' Navani said. 'It's the Nightwatcher. Giving you a deal when you were probably too distraught to think straight, then erasing your memory of the details?'

'She's a spren. I don't think we can expect her to play by – or even understand – our rules.' He wished he could give her more, but even if he could dredge up something, this wasn't the time. They should be paying attention to their guests.

Teshav had finished pointing out the strange glass panes on the inner walls that seemed like windows, only clouded. She moved on to the pairs of discs on the floor and ceiling that looked something like the top and bottom of a pillar that had been removed – a feature of a number of rooms they'd explored.

Once that was done, Taravangian and Adrotagia returned to the top of the room, near the windows. The new Radiant, Malata, lounged in a seat near the wall-mounted sigil of the Dustbringers, staring at it.

Dalinar and Navani climbed the steps to stand by Taravangian. 'Breathtaking, isn't it?' Dalinar asked. 'An even better view than from the lift.'

'Overwhelming,' Taravangian said. 'So much space. We think . . . we think that we are the most important things on Roshar. Yet so much of Roshar is empty of us.'

Dalinar cocked his head. Yes . . . perhaps some of the old Taravangian lingered in there somewhere.

'Is this where you'll have us meet?' Adrotagia asked, nodding toward the room. 'When you've gathered all the monarchs, will this be our council chamber?'

'No,' Dalinar said. 'This seems too much like a lecture hall. I don't want the monarchs to feel as if they're being preached to.'

'And . . . when will they come?' Taravangian asked, hopeful. 'I am looking forward to meeting the others. The king of Azir . . . didn't you tell me there was a new one, Adrotagia? I know Queen Fen – she's very nice. Will we be inviting the Shin? So mysterious. Do they even have a king? Don't they live in tribes or something? Like Marati barbarians?'

Adrotagia tapped his arm fondly, but looked to Dalinar, obviously curious about the other monarchs.

Dalinar cleared his throat, but Navani spoke.

'So far, Your Majesty,' she said, 'you are the only one who has heeded our warning call.'

Silence followed.

'Thaylenah?' Adrotagia asked hopefully.

'We've exchanged communications on five separate occasions,' Navani said. 'In each one, the queen has dodged our requests. Azir has been even more stubborn.'

'Iri dismissed us almost outright,' Dalinar said with a sigh. 'Neither Marabethia nor Rira would respond to the initial request. There's no real government in the Reshi Isles or some of the middle states. Babatharnam's

Most Ancient has been coy, and most of the Makabaki states imply that they're waiting for Azir to make a decision. The Shin sent only a quick reply to congratulate us, whatever that means.'

'Hateful people,' Taravangian said. 'Murdering so many worthy monarchs!'

'Um, yes,' Dalinar said, uncomfortable at the king's sudden change in attitude. 'Our primary focus has been on places with Oathgates, for strategic reasons. Azir, Thaylen City, and Iri seem most essential. However, we've made overtures to everyone who will listen, Oathgate or no. New Natanan is being coy so far, and the Herdazians think I'm trying to trick them. The Tukari scribes keep claiming they will bring my words to their god-king.'

Navani cleared her throat. 'We actually got a reply from him, just a bit ago. Teshav's ward was monitoring the spanreeds. It's not exactly encouraging.'

'I'd like to hear it anyway.'

She nodded, and went to collect it from Teshav. Adrotagia gave him a questioning glance, but he didn't dismiss the two of them. He wanted them to feel they were part of an alliance, and perhaps they would have insights that would prove helpful.

Navani returned with a single sheet of paper. Dalinar couldn't read the script on it, but the lines seemed sweeping and grand – imperious.

'"A warning"' Navani read, ' "from Tezim the Great, last and first man, Herald of Heralds and bearer of the Oathpact. His grandness, immortality, and power be praised. Lift up your heads and hear, men of the east, of your God's proclamation.

' "None are Radiant but him. His fury is ignited by your pitiful claims, and your unlawful capture of his holy city is an act of rebellion, depravity, and wickedness. Open your gates, men of the east, to his righteous soldiers and deliver unto him your spoils.

' "Renounce your foolish claims and swear yourselves to him. The judgment of the final storm has come to destroy all men, and only his path will lead to deliverance. He deigns to send you this single mandate, and will not speak it again. Even this is far above what your carnal natures deserve." '

She lowered the paper.

'Wow,' Adrotagia said. 'Well, at least it's clear.'

Taravangian scratched at his head, brow furrowed, as if he didn't agree with that statement at all.

'I guess,' Dalinar said, 'we can cross the Tukari off our list of possible allies.'

'I'd rather have the Emuli anyway,' Navani said. 'Their soldiers might be less capable, but they're also . . . well, *not crazy*.'

'So . . . we are alone?' Taravangian said, looking from Dalinar to Adrotagia, uncertain.

'We are alone, Your Majesty,' Dalinar said. 'The end of the world has come, and still nobody will listen.'

Taravangian nodded to himself. 'Where do we attack first? Herdaz? My aides say it is the traditional first step for an Alethi aggression, but they also point out that if you could somehow take Thaylenah, you'd completely control the Straits and even the Depths.'

Dalinar listened to the words with dismay. It was the obvious assumption. So clear that even simpleminded Taravangian saw it. What else to make of Alethkar proposing a union? Alethkar, the great conquerors? Led by the Blackthorn, the man who had united his own kingdom by the sword?

It was the suspicion that had tainted every conversation with the other monarchs. *Storms*, he thought. *Taravangian didn't come because he believed in my grand alliance. He assumed that if he didn't, I wouldn't send my armies to Herdaz or Thaylenah – I'd send them to Jah Keved. To him.*

'We're not going to attack anyone,' Dalinar said. 'Our focus is on the Voidbringers, the true enemy. We will win the other kingdoms with diplomacy.'

Taravangian frowned. 'But—'

Adrotagia, however, touched him on the arm and quieted him. 'Of course, Brightlord,' she said to Dalinar. 'We understand.'

She thought he was lying.

And are you?

What would he do if nobody listened? How would he save Roshar without the Oathgates? Without resources?

If our plan to reclaim Kholinar works, he thought, *wouldn't it make* sense *to take the other gates the same way? Nobody would be able to fight both us and the Voidbringers. We could seize their capitals and force them – for their own good – to join our unified war effort.*

He'd been willing to conquer Alethkar for its own good. He'd been willing to seize the kingship in all but name, again for the good of his people.

How far would he go for the good of all Roshar? How far would he go to prepare them for the coming of that enemy? A champion with nine shadows.

I will unite instead of divide.

He found himself standing at that window beside Taravangian, staring out over the mountains, his memories of Evi carrying with them a fresh and dangerous perspective.

25

THE GIRL
WHO LOOKED UP

I will confess my murders before you. Most painfully, I have killed someone who loved me dearly.

—From *Oathbringer*, preface

The tower of Urithiru was a skeleton, and these strata beneath Shallan's fingers were veins that wrapped the bones, dividing and spreading across the entire body. But what did those veins carry? Not blood.

She slid through the corridors on the third level, in the bowels, away from civilization, passing through doorways without doors and rooms without occupants.

Men had locked themselves in with their light, telling themselves that they'd conquered this ancient behemoth. But all they had were outposts in the darkness. Eternal, waiting darkness. These hallways had *never* seen the sun. Storms that raged through Roshar never touched here. This was a place of eternal stillness, and men could no more conquer it than cremlings could claim to have conquered the boulder they hid beneath.

She defied Dalinar's orders that all were to travel in pairs. She didn't worry about that. Her satchel and safepouch were stuffed with new spheres recharged in the highstorm. She felt gluttonous carrying so many, breathing in the Light whenever she wished. She was as safe as a person could be, so long as she had that Light.

She wore Veil's clothing, but not yet her face. She wasn't truly exploring, though she did make a mental map. She just wanted to be in this place, sensing it. It could not be comprehended, but perhaps it could be *felt*.

Jasnah had spent years hunting for this mythical city and the information she'd assumed it would hold. Navani spoke of the ancient technology she was sure this place must contain. So far, she'd been disappointed. She'd cooed over the Oathgates, had been impressed by the system of lifts. That was it. No majestic fabrials from the past, no diagrams explaining lost technology. No books or writings at all. Just dust.

And darkness, Shallan thought, pausing in a circular chamber with corridors splitting out in seven different directions. She *had* felt the wrongness Mraize spoke of. She'd felt it the moment she'd tried to draw this place. Urithiru was like the impossible geometries of Pattern's shape. Invisible, yet grating, like a discordant sound.

She picked a direction at random and continued, finding herself in a corridor narrow enough that she could brush both walls with her fingers. The strata had an emerald cast here, an alien color for stone. A hundred shades of wrongness.

She passed several small rooms before entering a much larger chamber. She stepped into it, holding a diamond broam high for light, revealing that she was on a raised portion at the front of a large room with curving walls and rows of stone . . . benches?

It's a theater, she thought. *And I've walked out onto the stage.* Yes, she could make out a balcony above. Rooms like this struck her with their humanity. Everything else about this place was so empty and arid. Endless rooms, corridors, and caverns. Floors strewn with only the occasional bit of civilization's detritus, like rusted hinges or an old boot's buckle. Decayspren huddled like barnacles on ancient doors.

A theater was more *real.* More alive, despite the span of the epochs. She stepped into the center and twirled about, letting Veil's coat flare around her. 'I always imagined being up on one of these. When I was a child, becoming a player seemed the grandest job. To get away from home, travel to new places.' *To not have to be myself for at least a brief time each day.*

Pattern hummed, pushing out from her coat to hover above the stage in three dimensions. 'What is it?'

'It's a stage for concerts or plays.'

'Plays?'

'Oh, you'd like them,' she said. 'People in a group each pretend to be someone different, and tell a story together.' She strode down the steps at the side, walking among the benches. 'The audience out here watches.'

Pattern hovered in the center of the stage, like a soloist. 'Ah . . .' he said. 'A group lie?'

'A wonderful, wonderful lie,' Shallan said, settling onto a bench, Veil's satchel beside her. 'A time when people all imagine together.'

'I wish I could see one,' Pattern said. 'I could understand people . . . mmmm . . . through the lies they want to be told.'

Shallan closed her eyes, smiling, remembering the last time she'd seen a play at her father's. A traveling children's troupe come to entertain her. She'd taken Memories for her collection – but of course, that was now lost at the bottom of the ocean.

'The Girl Who Looked Up,' she whispered.

'What?' Pattern asked.

Shallan opened her eyes and breathed out Stormlight. She hadn't sketched this particular scene, so she used what she had handy: a drawing she'd done of a young child in the market. Bright and happy, too young to cover her safehand. The girl appeared from the Stormlight and scampered up the steps, then bowed to Pattern.

'There was a girl,' Shallan said. 'This was before storms, before memories, and before legends – but there was still a girl. She wore a long scarf to blow in the wind.'

A vibrant red scarf grew around the girl's neck, twin tails extending far behind her and flapping in a phantom wind. The players had made the scarf hang behind the girl using strings from above. It had seemed so real.

'The girl in the scarf played and danced, as girls do today,' Shallan said, making the child prance around Pattern. 'In fact, most things were the same then as they are today. Except for one big difference. The wall.'

Shallan drained an indulgent number of spheres from her satchel, then sprinkled the floor of the stage with grass and vines like from her homeland. Across the back of the stage, a wall grew as Shallan had imagined it. A high, terrible wall stretching toward the moons. Blocking the sky, throwing everything around the girl into shadow.

The girl stepped toward it, looking up, straining to see the top.

'You see, in those days, a wall kept out the storms,' Shallan said. 'It had existed for so long, nobody knew how it had been built. That did not bother them. Why wonder when the mountains began or why the sky was high? Like these things were, so the wall was.'

The girl danced in its shadow, and other people sprang up from Shallan's Light. Each was a person from one of her sketches. Vathah, Gaz, Palona, Sebarial. They worked as farmers or washwomen, doing their duties with heads bowed. Only the girl looked up at that wall, her twin scarf tails streaming behind her.

She approached a man standing behind a small cart of fruit, wearing Kaladin Stormblessed's face.

'Why is there a wall?' she asked the man selling fruit, speaking with her own voice.

'To keep the bad things out,' he replied.

'What bad things?'

'Very bad things. There is a wall. Do not go beyond it, or you shall die.'

The fruit seller picked up his cart and moved away. And still, the girl looked up at the wall. Pattern hovered beside her and hummed happily to himself.

'Why is there a wall?' she asked the woman suckling her child. The woman had Palona's face.

'To protect us,' the woman said.

'To protect us from what?'

'Very bad things. There is a wall. Do not go beyond it, or you shall die.'

The woman took her child and left.

The girl climbed a tree, peeking out the top, her scarf streaming behind her. 'Why is there a wall?' she called to the boy sleeping lazily in the nook of a branch.

'What wall?' the boy asked.

The girl thrust her finger pointedly toward the wall.

'That's not a wall,' the boy said, drowsy. Shallan had given him the face of one of the bridgemen, a Herdazian. 'That's just the way the sky is over there.'

'It's a *wall*,' the girl said. 'A giant wall.'

'It must be there for a purpose,' the boy said. 'Yes, it is a wall. Don't go beyond it, or you'll probably die.'

'Well,' Shallan continued, speaking from the audience, 'these answers did not satisfy the girl who looked up. She reasoned to herself, if the wall kept evil things out, then the space on this side of it should be safe.

'So, one night while the others of the village slept, she sneaked from her home with a bundle of supplies. She walked toward the wall, and indeed the land *was* safe. But it was also dark. Always in the shadow of that wall. No sunlight, ever, directly reached the people.'

Shallan made the illusion roll, like scenery on a scroll as the players had used. Only far, far more realistic. She had painted the ceiling with light, and looking up, you seemed to be looking only at an infinite sky – dominated by that wall.

This is . . . this is far more extensive than I've done before, she thought, surprised. Creationspren had started to appear around her on the benches, in the form of old latches or doorknobs, rolling about or moving end over end.

Well, Dalinar *had* told her to practice. . . .

'The girl traveled far,' Shallan said, looking back toward the stage. 'No predators hunted her, and no storms assaulted her. The only wind was the pleasant one that played with her scarf, and the only creatures she saw were the cremlings that clicked at her as she walked.

'At long last, the girl in the scarves stood before the wall. It was truly expansive, running as far as she could see in either direction. And its height! It reached almost to the Tranquiline Halls!'

Shallan stood and walked onto the stage, passing into a different land – an image of fertility, vines, trees, and grass, dominated by that terrible wall. It grew spikes from its front in bristling patches.

I didn't draw this scene out. At least . . . not recently.

She'd drawn it as a youth, in detail, putting her imagined fancies down on paper.

'What happened?' Pattern said. 'Shallan? I must know what happened. Did she turn back?'

'Of course she didn't turn back,' Shallan said. 'She *climbed*. There were outcroppings in the wall, things like these spikes or hunched, ugly statues. She had climbed the highest trees all through her youth. She could do this.'

The girl started climbing. Had her hair been white when she'd started? Shallan frowned.

Shallan made the base of the wall sink into the stage, so although the girl got higher, she remained chest-height to Shallan and Pattern.

'The climb took days,' Shallan said, hand to her head. 'At night, the girl who looked up would tie herself a hammock out of her scarf and sleep there. She picked out her village at one point, remarking on how small it seemed, now that she was high.

'As she neared the top, she finally began to fear what she would find on the other side. Unfortunately, this fear did not stop her. She was young, and questions bothered her more than fear. So it was that she finally struggled to the very top and stood to see the other side. The hidden side . . .'

Shallan choked up. She remembered sitting at the edge of her seat, listening to this story. As a child, when moments like watching the players had been the only bright spots in life.

Too many memories of her father, and of her mother, who had loved telling her stories. She tried to banish those memories, but they *wouldn't go*.

Shallan turned. Her Stormlight . . . she'd used up almost everything she'd pulled from her satchel. Out in the seats, a crowd of dark figures watched. Eyeless, just shadows, people from her memories. The outline of her father, her mother, her brothers and a dozen others. She couldn't create them, because she hadn't drawn them properly. Not since she'd lost her collection . . .

Next to Shallan, the girl stood triumphantly on the wall's top, her scarves and white hair streaming out behind her in a sudden wind. Pattern buzzed beside Shallan.

'. . . and on that side of the wall,' Shallan whispered, 'the girl saw steps.'

The back side of the wall was crisscrossed with enormous sets of steps leading down to the ground, so distant.

'What . . . what does it mean?' Pattern said.

'The girl stared at those steps,' Shallan whispered, remembering, 'and suddenly the gruesome statues on her side of the wall made sense. The spears. The way it cast everything into shadow. The wall did indeed hide something evil, something frightening. It was the people, like the girl and her village.'

The illusion started to break down around her. This was too ambitious for her to hold, and it left her strained, exhausted, her head starting to pound. She let the wall fade, claiming its Stormlight. The landscape vanished, then finally the girl herself. Behind, the shadowed figures in the seats started to evaporate. Stormlight streamed back to Shallan, stoking the storm inside.

'That's how it ended?' Pattern asked.

'No,' Shallan said, Stormlight puffing from her lips. 'She goes down, sees a perfect society lit by Stormlight. She steals some and brings it back. The storms come as a punishment, tearing down the wall.'

'Ah . . .' Pattern said, hovering beside her on the now-dull stage. 'So that's how the storms first began?'

'Of course not,' Shallan said, feeling tired. 'It's a lie, Pattern. A story. It doesn't mean anything.'

'Then why are you crying?'

She wiped her eyes and turned away from the empty stage. She needed to get back to the markets.

In the seats, the last of the shadowy audience members puffed away. All but one, who stood up and walked out the back doors of the theater. Startled, Shallan felt a sudden shock run through her.

That figure hadn't been one of her illusions.

She flung herself from the stage – landing hard, Veil's coat fluttering – and dashed after the figure. She held the rest of her Stormlight, a thrumming, violent tempest. She skidded into the hall outside, glad for sturdy boots and simple trousers.

Something shadowy moved down the corridor. Shallan gave chase, lips drawn to a sneer, letting Stormlight rise from her skin and illuminate her surroundings. As she ran, she pulled a string from her pocket and tied her hair back, becoming Radiant. Radiant would know what to do if she caught this person.

Can a person look that much like a shadow?

'Pattern,' she shouted, thrusting her right hand forward. Luminescent fog formed there, becoming her Shardblade. Light escaped her lips, transforming her more fully into Radiant. Luminescent wisps trailed behind her, and she felt it chasing her. She charged into a small round chamber and skidded to a stop.

A dozen versions of herself, from drawings she'd done recently, split around her and dashed through the room. Shallan in her dress, Veil in her coat. Shallan as a child, Shallan as a youth. Shallan as a soldier, a happy wife, a mother. Leaner here, plumper there. Scarred. Bright with excitement. Bloodied and in pain. They vanished after passing her, collapsing one after another into Stormlight that curled and twisted about itself before vanishing away.

Radiant raised her Shardblade in the stance Adolin had been teaching her, sweat dripping down the sides of her face. The room would have been dark but for the Light curling off her skin and passing through her clothing to rise around her.

Empty. She'd either lost her quarry in the corridors, or it had been a spren and not a person at all.

Or there was nothing there in the first place, a part of her worried. *Your mind is not trustworthy these days.*

'What was that?' Radiant said. 'Did you see it?'

No, Pattern thought to her. *I was thinking on the lie.*

She walked around the edge of the circular room. The wall was scored by a series of deep slots that ran from floor to ceiling. She could feel air moving through them. What was the purpose of a room like this? Had the people who had designed this place been mad?

Radiant noted faint light coming from several of the slots – and with it the sounds of people in a low, echoing clatter. The Breakaway market? Yes, she was in that region, and while she was on the third level, the market's cavern was a full four stories high.

She moved to the next slot and peered through it, trying to decide just where it let out. Was this—

Something moved in the slot.

A dark mass wriggled deep inside, squeezing between walls. Like goo, but with bits jutting out. Those were elbows, ribs, fingers splayed along one wall, each knuckle bending backward.

A spren, she thought, trembling. *It is some strange kind of spren.*

The thing twisted, head deforming in the tiny confines, and looked toward her. She saw eyes reflecting her light, twin spheres set in a mashed head, a distorted human visage.

Radiant pulled back with a sharp gasp, summoning her Shardblade again and holding it wardingly before herself. But what was she going to do? Hack her way through the stone to get to the thing? That would take forever.

Did she even want to reach it?

No. But she had to anyway.

The market, she thought, dismissing her Blade and darting back the way she'd come. *It's heading to the market.*

With Stormlight propelling her, Radiant dashed through corridors, barely noticing as she breathed out enough to transform her face into Veil's. She swerved through a network of twisted passages. This maze, these enigmatic tunnels, were not what she'd expected from the home of the Knights Radiant. Shouldn't this be a fortress, simple but grand – a beacon of light and strength in the dark times?

Instead it was a puzzle. Veil stumbled out of the back corridors into populated ones, then dashed past a group of children laughing and holding up chips for light and making shadows on the walls.

Another few turns took her out onto the balcony walk around the cavernous Breakaway market, with its bobbing lights and busy pathways. Veil turned left to see slots in the wall here. For ventilation?

The thing had come through one of these, but where had it gone after that? A scream rose, shrill and cold, from the floor of the market below. Cursing to herself, Veil took the steps at a reckless pace. Just like Veil. Running headlong into danger.

She sucked in her breath, and the Stormlight puffing around her pulled in, causing her to stop glowing. After a short dash, she found people gathering between two packed rows of tents. The stalls here sold various goods, many of which looked to be salvage from the more abandoned warcamps. More than a few enterprising merchants – with the tacit approval of their highprinces – had sent expeditions back to gather what they could. With Stormlight flowing and Renarin to help with the Oathgate, those had finally been allowed into Urithiru.

The highprinces had gotten first pick. The rest of their finds were heaped in the tents here, watched over by guards with long cudgels and short tempers.

Veil shoved her way to the front of the crowd, finding a large Horneater man cursing and holding his hand. *Rock,* she thought, recognizing the bridgeman though he wasn't in uniform.

His hand was bleeding. *Like it was stabbed right through the center,* Veil thought.

'What happened here?' she demanded, still holding her Light in to keep it from puffing out and revealing her.

Rock eyed her while his companion – a bridgeman she thought she'd seen before – wrapped his hand. 'Who are you to ask me this thing?'

Storms. She was Veil right now, but she didn't dare expose the ruse, especially not in the open. 'I'm on Aladar's policing force,' she said, digging in her pocket. 'I have my commission here . . .'

'Is fine,' Rock said, sighing, his wariness seeming to evaporate. 'I did nothing. Some person pulled knife. I did not see him well – long coat, and a hat. A woman in crowd screamed, drawing my attention. Then, this man, he attacked.'

'Storms. Who is dead?'

'Dead?' The Horneater looked to his companion. 'Nobody is dead. Attacker stabbed my hand, then ran. Was assassination attempt, maybe? Person got angry about rule of tower, so he attacked me, for being in Kholin guard?'

Veil felt a chill. *Horneater. Tall, burly.*

The attacker had chosen a man who looked very similar to the one she had stabbed the other day. In fact, they weren't far from All's Alley. Just a few 'streets' over in the market.

The two bridgemen turned to leave, and Veil let them go. What more could she learn? The Horneater had been targeted not because of anything he'd done, but because of how he looked. And the attacker had been wearing a coat and hat. Like Veil usually did . . .

'I thought I'd find you here.'

Veil started, then whirled around, hand going to her belt knife. The speaker was a woman in a brown havah. She had straight Alethi hair, dark brown eyes, bright red painted lips, and sharp black eyebrows almost certainly enhanced with makeup. Veil recognized this woman, who was shorter than she'd seemed while sitting down. She was one of the thieves that Veil had approached at All's Alley, the one whose eyes had lit up when Shallan had drawn the Ghostbloods' symbol.

'What did he do to you?' the woman asked, nodding toward Rock. 'Or do you just have a thing for stabbing Horneaters?'

'This wasn't me,' Veil said.

'I'm sure.' The woman stepped closer. 'I've been waiting for you to turn up again.'

'You should stay away, if you value your life.' Veil started off through the market.

The short woman scrambled after her. 'My name is Ishnah. I'm an excellent writer. I can take dictations. I have experience moving in the market underground.'

'You want to be my ward?'

'Ward?' The young woman laughed. 'What are we, lighteyes? I want to join you.'

The Ghostbloods, of course. 'We're not recruiting.'

'Please.' She took Veil by the arm. 'Please. The world is wrong now. Nothing makes sense. But you ... your group ... you know things. I don't want to be blind anymore.'

Shallan hesitated. She could understand that desire to do something, rather than just feeling the world tremble and shake. But the Ghostbloods were despicable. This woman would not find what she desired among them. And if she did, then she was not the sort of person that Shallan would want to add to Mraize's quiver.

'No,' Shallan said. 'Do the smart thing and forget about me and my organization.'

She pulled out of the woman's grip and hurried away through the bustling market.

26

BLACKTHORN UNLEASHED

TWENTY-NINE YEARS AGO

Incense burned in a brazier as large as a boulder. Dalinar sniffled as Evi threw a handful of tiny papers – each folded and inscribed with a very small glyph – into the brazier. Fragrant smoke washed over him, then whipped in the other direction as winds ripped through the warcamp, carrying windspren like lines of light.

Evi bowed her head before the brazier. She had strange beliefs, his betrothed. Among her people, simple glyphwards weren't enough for prayers; you needed to burn something more pungent. While she spoke of Jezrien and Kelek, she said their names strangely: Yaysi and Kellai. And she made no mention of the Almighty – instead she spoke of something called the One, a heretical tradition the ardents told him came from Iri.

Dalinar bowed his head for a prayer. *Let me be stronger than those who would kill me.* Simple and to the point, the kind he figured the Almighty would prefer. He didn't feel like having Evi write it out.

'The One watch you, near-husband,' Evi murmured. 'And soften your temper.' Her accent, to which he was now accustomed, was thicker than her brother's.

'Soften it? Evi, that's not the point of battle.'

'You needn't kill in anger, Dalinar. If you must fight, do it knowing that each death wounds the One. For we are all people in Yaysi's sight.'

'Yeah, all right,' Dalinar said.

The ardents didn't seem to mind that he was marrying someone half pagan. 'It is wisdom to bring her to Vorin truth,' Jevena – Gavilar's head ardent – had told him. Similar to how she'd spoken of his conquest. 'Your sword will bring strength and glory to the Almighty.'

Idly, he wondered what it would take to actually earn the ardents' displeasure.

'Be a man and not a beast, Dalinar,' Evi said, then pulled close to him, setting her head on his shoulder and encouraging him to wrap his arms around her.

He did so with a limp gesture. Storms, he could hear the soldiers snicker as they passed by. The Blackthorn, being consoled before battle? Publicly hugging and acting lovey?

Evi turned her head toward him for a kiss, and he presented a chaste one, their lips barely touching. She accepted that, smiling. And she did have a beautiful smile. Life would have been a lot easier for him if Evi would have just been willing to move along with the marriage. But her traditions demanded a long engagement, and her brother kept trying to get new provisions into the contract.

Dalinar stomped away. In his pocket he held another glyphward: one provided by Navani, who obviously worried about the accuracy of Evi's foreign script. He felt at the smooth paper, and didn't burn the prayer.

The stone ground beneath his feet was pocked with tiny holes – the pinpricks of hiding grass. As he passed the tents he could see it properly, covering the plain outside, waving in the wind. Tall stuff, almost as high as his waist. He'd never seen grass that tall in Kholin lands.

Across the plain, an impressive force gathered: an army larger than any they'd faced. His heart jumped in anticipation. After two years of political maneuvering, here they were. A real battle with a real army.

Win or lose, *this* was the fight for the kingdom. The sun was on its way up, and the armies had arrayed themselves north and south, so neither would have it in their eyes.

Dalinar hastened to his armorers' tent, and emerged a short time later in his Plate. He climbed carefully into the saddle as one of the grooms brought his horse. The large black beast wasn't fast, but it *could* carry a man in Shardplate. Dalinar guided the horse past ranks of soldiers – spearmen, archers, lighteyed heavy infantry, even a nice group of fifty cavalrymen under Ilamar, with hooks and ropes for attacking

Shardbearers. Anticipationspren waved like banners among them all.

Dalinar still smelled incense when he found his brother, geared up and mounted, patrolling the front lines. Dalinar trotted up beside Gavilar.

'Your young friend didn't show for the battle,' Gavilar noted.

'Sebarial?' Dalinar said. 'He's *not* my friend.'

'There's a hole in the enemy line, still waiting for him,' Gavilar said, pointing. 'Reports say he had a problem with his supply lines.'

'Lies. He's a coward. If he'd arrived, he'd have had to actually pick a side.'

They rode past Tearim, Gavilar's captain of the guard, who wore Dalinar's extra Plate for this battle. Technically that still belonged to Evi. Not Toh, but Evi herself, which was strange. What would a woman do with Shardplate?

Give it to a husband, apparently. Tearim saluted. He was capable with Shards, having trained, as did many aspiring lighteyes, with borrowed sets.

'You've done well, Dalinar,' Gavilar said as they rode past. 'That Plate will serve us today.'

Dalinar made no reply. Even though Evi and her brother had delayed such a painfully long time to even agree to the *betrothal*, Dalinar had done his duty. He just wished he felt more for the woman. Some passion, some true *emotion*. He couldn't laugh without her seeming confused by the conversation. He couldn't boast without her being disappointed in his bloodlust. She always wanted him to hold her, as if being alone for one *storming* minute would make her wither and blow away. And . . .

'Ho!' one of the scouts called from a wooden mobile tower. She pointed, her voice distant. 'Ho, there!'

Dalinar turned, expecting an advance attack from the enemy. But no, Kalanor's army was still deploying. It wasn't men that had attracted the scout's attention, but *horses*. A small herd of them, eleven or twelve in number, galloping across the battlefield. Proud, majestic.

'Ryshadium,' Gavilar whispered. 'It's rare they roam this far east.'

Dalinar swallowed an order to round up the beasts. Ryshadium? Yes . . . he could see the spren trailing after them in the air. Musicspren, for some reason. Made no storming sense. Well, no use trying to capture the beasts. They couldn't be held unless they chose a rider.

'I want you to do something for me today, Brother,' Gavilar said.

'Highprince Kalanor himself needs to fall. As long as he lives, there will be resistance. If he dies, his line goes with him. His cousin, Loradar Vamah, can seize power.'

'Will Loradar swear to you?'

'I'm certain of it,' Gavilar said.

'Then I'll find Kalanor,' Dalinar said, 'and end this.'

'He won't join the battle easily, knowing him. But he's a Shardbearer. And so . . .'

'So we need to force him to engage.'

Gavilar smiled.

'What?' Dalinar said.

'I'm simply pleased to see you talking of tactics.'

'I'm not an idiot,' Dalinar growled. He always paid attention to the tactics of a battle; he simply wasn't one for endless meetings and jaw wagging.

Though . . . even those seemed more tolerable these days. Perhaps it was familiarity. Or maybe it was Gavilar's talk of forging a dynasty. It was the increasingly obvious truth that this campaign – now stretching over many years – was no quick bash and grab.

'Bring me Kalanor, Brother,' Gavilar said. 'We need the Blackthorn today.'

'All you need do is unleash him.'

'Ha! As if anyone existed who could leash him in the first place.'

Isn't that what you've been trying to do? Dalinar thought immediately. *Marrying me off, talking about how we have to be 'civilized' now? Highlighting everything I do wrong as the things we must expunge?*

He bit his tongue, and they finished their ride down the lines. They parted with a nod, and Dalinar rode over to join his elites.

'Orders, sir?' asked Rien.

'Stay out of my way,' Dalinar said, lowering his faceplate. The Shardplate helm sealed closed, and a hush fell over the elites. Dalinar summoned Oathbringer, the sword of a fallen king, and waited. The enemy had come to stop Gavilar's continued pillage of the countryside; they would have to make the first move.

These last few months spent attacking isolated, unprotected towns had made for unfulfilling battles – but had also put Kalanor in a terrible position. If he sat back in his strongholds, he allowed more of his vassals to be destroyed. Already those started to wonder why they paid Kalanor taxes. A handful had preemptively sent messengers to Gavilar saying they would not resist.

The region was on the brink of flipping to the Kholins. And so, Highprince Kalanor had been forced to leave his fortifications to engage here. Dalinar shifted on his horse, waiting, planning. The moment came soon enough; Kalanor's forces started across the plain in a cautious wave, shields raised toward the sky.

Gavilar's archers released flights of arrows. Kalanor's men were well trained; they maintained their formations beneath the deadly hail. Eventually they met Kholin heavy infantry: a block of men so armored that it might as well have been solid stone. At the same time, mobile archer units sprang out to the sides. Lightly armored, they were *fast*. If the Kholins won this battle – and Dalinar was confident of victory – it would be because of the newer battlefield tactics they'd been exploring.

The enemy army found itself flanked – arrows pounding the sides of their assault blocks. Their lines stretched, the infantry trying to reach the archers, but that weakened the central block, which suffered a beating from the heavy infantry. Standard spearman blocks engaged enemy units as much to position them as to do them harm.

This all happened on the scale of the battlefield. Dalinar had to climb off his horse and send for a groom to walk the animal as he waited. Inside, Dalinar fought back the Thrill, which urged him to ride in immediately.

Eventually, he picked a section of Kholin troops who were faring poorly against the enemy block. Good enough. He remounted and kicked his horse into a gallop. This was the right moment. He could *feel* it. He needed to strike now, when the battle was pivoting between victory and loss, to draw out his enemy.

Grass wriggled and pulled back in a wave before him. Like subjects bowing. This might be the end, his final battle in the conquest of Alethkar. What happened to him after this? Endless feasts with politicians? A brother who refused to look elsewhere for battle?

Dalinar opened himself to the Thrill and drove away such worries. He struck the line of enemy troops like a highstorm hitting a stack of papers. Soldiers scattered before him, shouting. Dalinar laid about with his Shardblade, killing dozens on one side, then the other.

Eyes burned, arms fell limp. Dalinar breathed in the joy of the conquest, the narcotic beauty of destruction. None could stand before him; all were tinder and he the flame. The soldier block should have been able to band together and rush him, but they were too frightened.

And why shouldn't they be? People spoke of common men bringing down a Shardbearer, but surely that was a fabrication. A conceit intended to make men fight back, to save Shardbearers from having to hunt them down.

He grinned as his horse stumbled trying to cross the bodies piling around it. Dalinar kicked the beast forward, and it leaped – but as it landed, something gave. The creature screamed and collapsed, dumping him.

He sighed, shoving aside the horse and standing. He'd broken its back; Shardplate was not meant for such common beasts.

One group of soldiers tried a counterattack. Brave, but stupid. Dalinar felled them with broad sweeps of his Shardblade. Next, a lighteyed officer organized his men to come press and try to trap Dalinar, if not with their skill, then their weight of bodies. He spun among them, Plate lending him energy, Blade granting him precision, and the Thrill . . . the Thrill giving him *purpose*.

In moments like this, he could see why he had been created. He was wasted listening to men blab. He was wasted doing anything but *this:* providing the ultimate test of men's abilities, proving them, demanding their lives at the edge of a sword. He sent them to the Tranquiline Halls primed and ready to fight.

He was not a man. He was *judgment.*

Enthralled, he cut down foe after foe, sensing a strange rhythm to the fighting, as if the blows of his sword needed to fall to the dictates of some unseen beat. A redness grew at the edges of his vision, eventually covering the landscape like a veil. It seemed to shift and move like the coils of an eel, trembling to the beats of his sword.

He was furious when a calling voice distracted him from the fight.

'Dalinar!'

He ignored it.

'Brightlord Dalinar! Blackthorn!'

That voice was like a screeching cremling, playing its song inside his helm. He felled a pair of swordsmen. They'd been lighteyed, but their eyes had burned away, and you could no longer tell.

'Blackthorn!'

Bah! Dalinar spun toward the sound.

A man stood nearby, wearing Kholin blue. Dalinar raised his Shard-blade. The man backed away, raising hands with no weapon, still shouting Dalinar's name.

I know him. He's . . . Kadash? One of the captains among his elites. Dalinar lowered his sword and shook his head, trying to get the buzzing sound out of his ears. Only then did he see – really see – what surrounded him.

The dead. Hundreds upon hundreds of them, with shriveled coals for eyes, their armor and weapons sheared but their bodies eerily untouched. Almighty above . . . how many had he killed? He raised his hand to his helm, turning and looking about him. Timid blades of grass crept up among the bodies, pushing between arms, fingers, beside heads. He'd blanketed the plain so thoroughly with corpses that the grass had a diffi-cult time finding places to rise.

Dalinar grinned in satisfaction, then grew chill. A few of those bodies with burned eyes – three men he could spot – wore blue. His own men, bearing the armband of the elites.

'Brightlord,' Kadash said. 'Blackthorn, your task is accomplished!' He pointed toward a troop of horsemen charging across the plain. They car-ried the silver-on-red flag bearing a glyphpair of two mountains. Left no choice, Highprince Kalanor had committed to the battle. Dalinar had destroyed several companies on his own; only another Shardbearer could stop him.

'Excellent,' Dalinar said. He pulled off his helm and took a cloth from Kadash, using it to wipe his face. A waterskin followed. Dalinar drank the entire thing.

Dalinar tossed away the empty skin, his heart racing, the Thrill thrum-ming within. 'Pull back the elites. Do not engage unless I fall.' Dalinar pulled his helm back on, and felt the comforting tightness as the latches cinched it into place.

'Yes, Brightlord.'

'Gather those of us who . . . fell,' Dalinar said, waving toward the Kholin dead. 'Make certain they, and theirs, are cared for.'

'Of course, sir.'

Dalinar dashed toward the oncoming force, his Shardplate crunching against stones. He felt sad to have to engage a Shardbearer, instead of continuing his fight against the ordinary men. No more laying waste; he now had only one man to kill.

He could vaguely remember a time when facing lesser challenges hadn't sated him as much as a good fight against someone capable. What had changed?

His run took him toward one of the rock formations on the eastern side of the field – a group of enormous spires, weathered and jagged, like a row of stone stakes. As he entered the shadows, he could hear fighting from the other side. Portions of the armies had broken off and tried to flank each other by rounding the formations.

At their base, Kalanor's honor guard split, revealing the highprince himself on horseback. His Plate was overlaid with a silver coloring, perhaps steel or silver leaf. Dalinar had ordered his Plate buffed back to its normal slate grey; he'd never understood why people would want to 'augment' the natural majesty of Shardplate.

Kalanor's horse was a tall, majestic animal, brilliant white with a long mane. It carried the Shardbearer with ease. A Ryshadium. Yet Kalanor dismounted. He patted the animal fondly on the neck, then stepped forward to meet Dalinar, Shardblade appearing in his hand.

'Blackthorn,' he called. 'I hear you've been single-handedly destroying my army.'

'They fight for the Tranquiline Halls now.'

'Would that you had joined to lead them.'

'Someday,' Dalinar said. 'When I am too old and weak to fight here, I'll welcome being sent.'

'Curious, how quickly tyrants grow religious. It must be convenient to tell yourself that your murders belong to the Almighty instead.'

'They'd better not belong to him!' Dalinar said. 'I worked hard for those kills, Kalanor. The Almighty can't have them; he can merely credit them to me when weighing my soul!'

'Then let them weigh you down to Damnation itself.' Kalanor waved back his honor guard, who seemed eager to throw themselves at Dalinar. Alas, the highprince was determined to fight on his own. He swiped with his sword, a long, thin Shardblade with a large crossguard and glyphs down its length. 'If I kill you, Blackthorn, what then?'

'Then Sadeas gets a crack at you.'

'No honor on this battlefield, I see.'

'Oh, don't pretend you are any better,' Dalinar said. 'I know what you did to rise to your throne. You can't pretend to be a peacemaker now.'

'Considering what you did to the peacemakers,' Kalanor said, 'I'll count myself lucky.'

Dalinar leaped forward, falling into Bloodstance – a stance for someone who didn't care if he got hit. He was younger, more agile than his opponent. He counted on being able to swing faster, harder.

Strangely, Kalanor chose Bloodstance himself. The two clashed, bashing their swords against one another in a pattern that sent them twisting about in a quick shuffle of footings – each trying to hit the same section of Plate repeatedly, to open a hole to flesh.

Dalinar grunted, batting away his opponent's Shardblade. Kalanor was old, but skilled. He had an uncanny ability to pull back before Dalinar's strikes, deflecting some of the force of the impact, preventing the metal from breaking.

After furiously exchanging blows for several minutes, both men stepped back, a web of cracks on the left sides of their Plate leaking Stormlight into the air.

'It will happen to you too, Blackthorn,' Kalanor growled. 'If you do kill me, someone will rise up and take your kingdom from you. It will never last.'

Dalinar came in for a power swing. One step forward, then a twist all the way about. Kalanor struck him on the right side – a solid hit, but insignificant, as it was on the wrong side. Dalinar, on the other hand, came in with a sweeping stroke that hummed in the air. Kalanor tried to move with the blow, but this one had too much momentum.

The Shardblade connected, destroying the section of Plate in an explosion of molten sparks. Kalanor grunted and stumbled to the side, nearly tripping. He lowered his hand to cover the hole in his armor, which continued to leak Stormlight at the edges. Half the breastplate had shattered.

'You fight like you lead, Kholin,' he growled. 'Reckless.'

Dalinar ignored the taunt and charged instead.

Kalanor ran away, plowing through his honor guard in his haste, shoving some aside and sending them tumbling, bones breaking.

Dalinar almost caught him, but Kalanor reached the edge of the large rock formation. He dropped his Blade – it puffed away to mist – and sprang, grabbing hold of an outcropping. He started to climb.

He reached the base of the natural tower moments later. Boulders littered the ground nearby; in the mysterious way of the storms, this had probably been a hillside until recently. The highstorm had ripped most of it away, leaving this unlikely formation poking into the air. It would probably soon get blown down.

Dalinar dropped his Blade and leapt, snagging an outcropping, his fingers grinding on stone. He dangled before getting a footing, then proceeded to climb up the steep wall after Kalanor. The other Shardbearer tried to kick rocks down, but they bounced off Dalinar harmlessly.

By the time Dalinar caught up, they had climbed some fifty feet. Down below, soldiers gathered and stared, pointing.

Dalinar reached for his opponent's leg, but Kalanor yanked it out of the way and then – still hanging from the stones – summoned his Blade and began swiping down. After getting battered on the helm a few times, Dalinar growled and let himself slide down out of the way.

Kalanor gouged a few chunks from the wall to send them clattering at Dalinar, then dismissed his Blade and continued upward.

Dalinar followed more carefully, climbing along a parallel route to the side. He eventually reached the top and peeked over the edge. The summit of the formation was some flat-topped, broken peaks that didn't look terribly sturdy. Kalanor sat on one of them, Blade across one leg, his other foot dangling.

Dalinar climbed up a safe distance from his enemy, then summoned Oathbringer. Storms. There was barely enough room up here to stand. Wind buffeted him, a windspren zipping around to one side.

'Nice view,' Kalanor said. Though the forces had started out with equal numbers, below them were far more fallen men in silver and red strewn across the grassland than there were men in blue. 'I wonder how many kings get such prime seating to watch their own downfall.'

'You were never a king,' Dalinar said.

Kalanor stood and lifted his Blade, extending it in one hand, point toward Dalinar's chest. 'That, Kholin, is all tied up in bearing and assumption. Shall we?'

Clever, bringing me up here, Dalinar thought. Dalinar had the obvious edge in a fair duel – and so Kalanor brought random chance into the fight. Winds, unsteady footing, a plunge that would kill even a Shardbearer.

At the very least, this would be a novel challenge. Dalinar stepped forward carefully. Kalanor changed to Windstance, a more flowing, sweeping style of fighting. Dalinar chose Stonestance for the solid footing and straightforward power.

They traded blows, shuffling back and forth along the line of small peaks. Each step scraped chips off the stones, sending them tumbling down. Kalanor obviously wanted to draw out this fight, to maximize the time for Dalinar to slip.

Dalinar tested back and forth, letting Kalanor fall into a rhythm, then broke it to strike with everything he had, battering down in overhand blows. Each fanned something burning inside of Dalinar, a thirst that his earlier rampage hadn't sated. The Thrill wanted more.

Dalinar scored a series of hits on Kalanor's helm, backing him up to the edge, one step away from a fall. The last blow destroyed the helm entirely, exposing an aged face, clean-shaven, mostly bald.

Kalanor growled, teeth clenched, and struck back at Dalinar with unexpected ferocity. Dalinar met it Blade with Blade, then stepped forward to turn it into a shoving match – their weapons locked, neither with room to maneuver.

Dalinar met his enemy's gaze. In those light grey eyes, he *saw* something. Excitement, energy. A familiar bloodlust.

Kalanor felt the Thrill too.

Dalinar had heard others speak of it, this euphoria of the contest. The secret Alethi edge. But seeing it right there, in the eyes of a man trying to kill him, made Dalinar furious. He should not have to share such an intimate feeling with this man.

He grunted and – in a surge of strength – tossed Kalanor back. The man stumbled, then slipped. He instantly dropped his Shardblade and, in a frantic motion, managed to grab the rock lip as he fell.

Helmless, Kalanor dangled. The sense of the Thrill in his eyes faded to panic. 'Mercy,' he whispered.

'This *is* a mercy,' Dalinar said, then struck him straight through the face with his Shardblade.

Kalanor's eyes burned from grey to black as he dropped off the spire, trailing twin lines of black smoke. The corpse scraped rock before hitting far below, on the far side of the rock formation, away from the main army.

Dalinar breathed out, then sank down, wrung out. Shadows stretched long across the land as the sun met the horizon. It had been a fine fight. He'd accomplished what he'd wanted. He'd conquered all who stood before him.

And yet he felt empty. A voice within him kept saying, 'That's it? Weren't we promised more?'

Down below, a group in Kalanor's colors made for the fallen body. The honor guard had seen where their brightlord had fallen? Dalinar felt a spike of outrage. That was *his* kill, *his* victory. He'd won those Shards!

He scrambled down in a reckless half-climb. The descent was a blur; he was seeing red by the time he hit the ground. One soldier had the Blade; others were arguing over the Plate, which was broken and mangled.

Dalinar attacked, killing six in moments, including the one with the Blade. Two others managed to run, but they were slower than he was. Dalinar caught one by the shoulder, whipping him around and smashing him down into the stones. He killed the last with a sweep of Oathbringer.

More. Where were more? Dalinar saw no men in red. Only some in blue – a beleaguered set of soldiers who flew no flag. In their center, however, walked a man in Shardplate. Gavilar rested here from the battle, in a place behind the lines, to take stock.

The hunger inside of Dalinar grew. The Thrill came upon him in a rush, overwhelming. Shouldn't the strongest rule? Why should he sit back so often, listening to men *chat* instead of *war*?

There. There was the man who held what he wanted. A throne . . . a throne and more. The woman Dalinar *should* have been able to claim. A love he'd been forced to abandon, for what reason?

No, his fighting today was *not* done. This was *not* all!

He started toward the group, his mind fuzzy, his insides feeling a deep ache. Passionspren – like tiny crystalline flakes – dropped around him.

Shouldn't he have passion?

Shouldn't he be rewarded for all he had accomplished?

Gavilar was weak. He intended to give up his momentum and rest upon what *Dalinar* had won for him. Well, there was one way to make certain the war continued. One way to keep the Thrill alive.

One way for Dalinar to get everything he deserved.

He was running. Some of the men in Gavilar's group raised hands in welcome. Weak. No weapons presented against him! He could slaughter them all before they knew what had happened. They *deserved* it! Dalinar deserved to—

Gavilar turned toward him, pulling free his helm and smiling an open, honest grin.

Dalinar pulled up, stopping with a lurch. He stared at Gavilar, his *brother.*

Oh, Stormfather, Dalinar thought. *What am I doing?*

He let the Blade slip from his fingers and vanish. Gavilar strode up, unable to read Dalinar's horrified expression behind his helm. As a blessing, no shamespren appeared, though he should have earned a legion of them in that moment.

'Brother!' Gavilar said. 'Have you seen? The day is won! Highprince Ruthar brought down Gallam, winning Shards for his son. Talanor took a Blade, and I hear you finally drew out Kalanor. Please tell me he didn't escape you.'

'He ...' Dalinar licked his lips, breathing in and out. 'He is dead.' Dalinar pointed toward the fallen form, visible only as a bit of silvery metal shining amid the shadows of the rubble.

'Dalinar, you wonderful, *terrible* man!' Gavilar turned toward his soldiers. 'Hail the Blackthorn, men. Hail him!' Gloryspren burst around Gavilar, golden orbs that rotated around his head like a crown.

Dalinar blinked amid their cheering, and suddenly felt a shame so deep he wanted to crumple up. This time, a single spren – like a falling petal from a blossom – drifted down around him.

He had to do something. 'Blade and Plate,' Dalinar said to Gavilar urgently. 'I won them both, but I give them to you. A gift. For your children.'

'Ha!' Gavilar said. 'Jasnah? What would she do with Shards? No, no. You—'

'Keep them,' Dalinar pled, grabbing his brother by the arm. 'Please.'

'Very well, if you insist,' Gavilar said. 'I suppose you do already have Plate to give your heir.'

'If I have one.'

'You will!' Gavilar said, sending some men to recover Kalanor's Blade and Plate. 'Ha! Toh will have to agree, finally, that we can protect his line. I suspect the wedding will happen within the month!'

As would, likely, the official re-coronation where – for the first time in centuries – all ten highprinces of Alethkar would bow before a single king.

Dalinar sat down on a stone, pulling free his helm and accepting water from a young messenger woman. *Never again*, he swore to himself. *I give way for Gavilar in all things. Let him have the throne, let him have love.*

I must never be king.

I will confess my heresy. I do not back down from the things I have said, regardless of what the ardents demand.

—From *Oathbringer*, preface

The sounds of arguing politicians drifted to Shallan's ears as she sketched. She sat on a stone seat at the back of the large meeting room near the top of the tower. She'd brought a pillow to sit on, and Pattern buzzed happily on the little pedestal.

She sat with her feet up, thighs supporting her drawing pad, stockinged toes curling over the rim of the bench in front of her. Not the most dignified of positions; Radiant would be mortified. At the front of the auditorium, Dalinar stood before the glowing map that Shallan and he – somehow combining their powers – could create. He'd invited Taravangian, the highprinces, their wives, and their head scribes. Elhokar had come with Kalami, who was scribing for him lately.

Renarin stood beside his father in his Bridge Four uniform, looking uncomfortable – so basically, same as usual. Adolin lounged nearby, arms folded, occasionally whispering a joke toward one of the men of Bridge Four.

Radiant should be down there, engaging in this important discussion about the future of the world. Instead, Shallan drew. The light was just so *good* up here, with these broad glass windows. She was tired of feeling trapped in the dark hallways of the lower levels, always feeling that something was watching her.

She finished her sketch, then tipped it toward Pattern, holding the sketchbook with her sleeved safehand. He rippled up from his post to inspect her drawing: the slot obstructed by a mashed-up figure with bulging, inhuman eyes.

'Mmmm,' Pattern said. 'Yes, that is correct.'

'It has to be some kind of spren, right?'

'I feel I should know,' Pattern said. 'This ... this is a thing from long ago. Long, *long* ago ...'

Shallan shivered. 'Why is it here?'

'I cannot say,' Pattern replied. 'It is not a thing of us. It is of *him.*'

'An ancient spren of Odium. Delightful.' Shallan flipped the page over the top of her sketchbook and started on another drawing.

The others spoke further of their coalition, Thaylenah and Azir recurring as the most important countries to convince, now that Iri had made it completely clear they had joined the enemy.

'Brightness Kalami,' Dalinar was saying. 'The last report. It listed a large gathering of the enemy in Marat, was it?'

'Yes, Brightlord,' the scribe said from her position at the reading desk. 'Southern Marat. You hypothesized it was the low population of the region that induced the Voidbringers to gather there.'

'The Iriali have taken the chance to strike eastward, as they've always wanted to,' Dalinar said. 'They'll seize Rira and Babatharnam. Meanwhile, areas like Triax – around the southern half of central Roshar – continue to go dark.'

Brightness Kalami nodded, and Shallan tapped her lips with her drawing pencil. The question raised an implication. How could cities go completely dark? These days major cities – particularly ports – would have hundreds of spanreeds in operation. Every lighteyes or merchant wanting to watch prices or keep in contact with distant estates would have one.

Those in Kholinar had started working as soon as the highstorms returned – and then they'd been cut off one by one. Their last reports claimed that armies were gathering near the city. Then ... nothing. The enemy seemed to be able to locate spanreeds somehow.

At least they'd finally gotten word from Kaladin. A single glyph for time, implying they should be patient. He'd been unable to get to a town to find a woman to scribe for him, and just wanted them to know he was safe. Assuming someone else hadn't gotten the spanreed, and faked the glyph to put them off.

'The enemy is making a play for the Oathgates,' Dalinar decided. 'All of their motions, save for the gathering in Marat, indicate this. My instincts say that army is planning to strike back at Azir, or even to cross and try to assault Jah Keved.'

'I trust Dalinar's assessment,' Highprince Aladar added. 'If he believes this course to be likely, we should listen.'

'Bah,' said Highprince Ruthar. The oily man leaned against the wall across from the others, barely paying attention. 'Who cares what you say, Aladar? It's amazing you can even see, considering the place you've gone and stuck your head these days.'

Aladar spun and thrust his hand to the side in a summoning posture. Dalinar stopped him, as Ruthar must have known that he would. Shallan shook her head, letting herself instead be drawn farther into her sketching. A few creationspren appeared at the top of her drawing pad, one a tiny shoe, the other a pencil like the one she used.

Her sketch was of Highprince Sadeas, drawn without a specific Memory. She'd never wanted to add *him* to her collection. She finished the quick sketch, then flipped to a sketch of Brightlord Perel, the other man they'd found dead in the hallways of Urithiru. She'd tried to re-create his face without wounds.

She flipped back and forth between the two. *They do look similar*, Shallan decided. *Same bulbous features. Similar build.* Her next two pages were pictures of the two Horneaters. Those two looked roughly similar as well. And the two murdered women? Why would the man who strangled his wife confess to that murder, but then *swear* he hadn't killed the second woman? One was already enough to get you executed.

That spren is mimicking the violence, she thought. *Killing or wounding in the same way as attacks from previous days. A kind of . . . impersonation?*

Pattern hummed softly, drawing her attention. Shallan looked up to see someone strolling in her direction: a middle-aged woman with short black hair cut almost to the scalp. She wore a long skirt and a buttoning shirt with a vest. Thaylen merchant clothing.

'What is that you're sketching, Brightness?' the woman asked in Veden.

Hearing her own language so suddenly was strange to Shallan, and her mind took a moment to sort through the words. 'People,' Shallan said, closing her drawing pad. 'I enjoy figure drawing. You're the one who came with Taravangian. His Surgebinder.'

'Malata,' she said. 'Though I am not his. I came to him for convenience, as Spark suggested we might look to Urithiru, now that it has been redis-covered.' She surveyed the large auditorium. Shallan could see no sign of her spren. 'Do you suppose we really filled this entire chamber?'

'Ten orders,' Shallan said, 'with hundreds of people in most. Yes, I'd assume we could fill it – in fact, I doubt everyone belonging to the orders could fit in here.'

'And now there are four of us,' she said idly, eyeing Renarin, who stood stiff beside his father, sweating beneath the scrutiny as people occasion-ally glanced at him.

'Five,' Shallan said. 'There's a flying bridgeman out there somewhere – and those are only the ones of us gathered here. There are bound to be others like you, who are still looking for a way to reach us.'

'If they want to,' Malata said. 'Things don't have to be the way they were. Why should they? It didn't work out so well last time for the Radiants, did it?'

'Maybe,' Shallan said. 'But maybe this isn't the time to experiment either. The Desolation has started again. We could do worse than rely upon the past to survive this.'

'Curious,' the woman said, 'that we have only the word of a few stuffy Alethi about this entire "Desolation" business, eh sister?'

Shallan blinked at the casual way it was said, along with a wink. Malata smiled and sauntered back toward the front of the room.

'Well,' Shallan whispered, *'she's* annoying.'

'Mmm . . .' Pattern said. 'It will be worse when she starts destroying things.'

'Destroying?'

'Dustbringer,' Pattern said. 'Her spren . . . mmm . . . they like to break what is around them. They want to know what is inside.'

'Pleasant,' Shallan said, as she flipped back through her drawings. The thing in the crack. The dead men. This should be enough to present to

Dalinar and Adolin, which she planned to do today, now that she had her sketches done.

And after that?

I need to catch it, she thought. *I watch the market. Eventually someone will be hurt. And a few days later, this thing will try to copy that attack.*

Perhaps she could patrol the unexplored parts of the tower? Look for it, instead of waiting for it to attack?

The dark corridors. Each tunnel like a drawing's impossible line . . .

The room had grown quiet. Shallan shook out of her reverie and looked up to see what was happening: Ialai Sadeas had arrived at the meeting, carried in a palanquin. She was accompanied by a familiar figure: Meridas Amaram was a tall man, tan eyed, with a square face and solid figure. He was also a murderer, a thief, and a traitor. He had been caught trying to steal a Shardblade – proof that what Captain Kaladin said about him was true.

Shallan gritted her teeth, but found her anger . . . cool. Not gone. No, she would not forgive this man for killing Helaran. But the uncomfortable truth was that she didn't know why, or how, her brother had fallen to Amaram. She could almost hear Jasnah whispering to her: *Don't judge without more details.*

Below, Adolin had risen and stepped toward Amaram, right into the center of the illusory map, breaking its surface, causing waves of glowing Stormlight to ripple across it. He stared murder at Amaram, though Dalinar rested his hand on his son's shoulder, holding him back.

'Brightness Sadeas,' Dalinar said. 'I am glad you have agreed to join the meeting. We could use your wisdom in our planning.'

'I'm not here for your plans, Dalinar,' Ialai said. 'I'm here because it was a convenient place to find you all together. I've been in conference with my advisors back at our estates, and the consensus is that the heir, my nephew, is too young. This is no time for House Sadeas to be without leadership, so I've made a decision.'

'Ialai,' Dalinar said, stepping into the illusion beside his son. 'Let's talk about this. Please. I have an idea that, though untraditional, might—'

'Tradition is our ally, Dalinar,' Ialai said. 'I don't think you've ever understood that as you should. Highmarshal Amaram is our house's most decorated and well-regarded general. He is beloved of our soldiers, and known the world over. I name him regent and heir to the house title. He is, for all intents, Highprince Sadeas now. I would ask the king to ratify this.'

Shallan's breath caught. King Elhokar looked up from his seat, where he – seemingly – had been lost in thought. 'Is this legal?'

'Yes,' Navani said, arms folded.

'Dalinar,' Amaram said, stepping down several of the steps toward the rest of them at the bottom of the auditorium. His voice gave Shallan chills. That refined diction, that perfect face, that crisp uniform . . . this man was what every soldier aspired to be.

I'm not the only one who is good at playing pretend, she thought.

'I hope,' Amaram continued, 'our recent . . . friction will not prevent us from working together for the needs of Alethkar. I have spoken to Brightness Ialai, and I think I have persuaded her that our differences are secondary to the greater good of Roshar.'

'The greater good,' Dalinar said. 'You think you are one to speak about what is good?'

'Everything I've done is for the greater good, Dalinar,' Amaram said, his voice strained. '*Everything*. Please. I know you intend to pursue legal action against me. I will stand at trial, but let us postpone that until *after* Roshar has been saved.'

Dalinar regarded Amaram for an extended, tense moment. Then he finally looked to his nephew and nodded in a curt gesture.

'The throne acknowledges your act of regency, Brightness,' Elhokar said to Ialai. 'My mother will wish a formal writ, sealed and witnessed.'

'Already done,' Ialai said.

Dalinar met the eyes of Amaram across the floating map. 'Highprince,' Dalinar finally said.

'Highprince,' Amaram said back, tipping his head.

'Bastard,' Adolin said.

Dalinar winced visibly, then pointed toward the exit. 'Perhaps, son, you should take a moment to yourself.'

'Yeah. Sure.' Adolin pulled out of his father's grip, stalking toward the exit.

Shallan thought only a moment, then grabbed her shoes and drawing pad and hurried after him. She caught up to Adolin in the hallway outside, near where the palanquins for the women were parked, and took his arm.

'Hey,' she said softly.

He glanced at her, and his expression softened.

'You want to talk?' Shallan asked. 'You seem angrier about him than you were before.'

'No,' Adolin muttered, 'I'm just annoyed. We're finally rid of Sadeas, and now *that* takes his place?' He shook his head. 'When I was young, I used to look up to him. I started getting suspicious when I was older, but I guess part of me still wanted him to be like they said. A man above all the pettiness and the politics. A true soldier.'

Shallan wasn't certain what she thought of the idea of a 'true soldier' being the type who didn't care about politics. Shouldn't the *why* of what a man was doing be important to him?

Soldiers didn't talk that way. There was some ideal she couldn't quite grasp, a kind of cult of obedience – of caring only about the battlefield and the challenge it presented.

They walked onto the lift, and Adolin fished out a free gemstone – a little diamond not surrounded by a sphere – and placed it into a slot along the railing. Stormlight began to drain from the stone, and the balcony shook, then slowly began to descend. Removing the gem would tell the lift to stop at the next floor. A simple lever, pushed one way or the other, would determine whether the lift crawled upward or downward.

They descended past the top tier, and Adolin took up position by the railing, looking out over the central shaft with the window all along one side. They were starting to call it the atrium – though it was an atrium that ran up dozens upon dozens of floors.

'Kaladin's not going to like this,' Adolin said. 'Amaram as a highprince? The two of us spent weeks in jail because of the things that man did.'

'I think Amaram killed my brother.'

Adolin wheeled around to stare at her. '*What?*'

'Amaram has a Shardblade,' Shallan said. 'I saw it previously in the hands of my brother, Helaran. He was older than I am, and left Jah Keved years ago. From what I can gather, he and Amaram fought at some point, and Amaram killed him – taking the Blade.'

'Shallan . . . that Blade. You know where Amaram got that, right?'

'On the battlefield?'

'From *Kaladin*.' Adolin raised his hand to his head. 'The bridgeboy insisted that he'd saved Amaram's life by killing a Shardbearer. Amaram then killed Kaladin's squad and took the Shards for himself. That's basically the entire *reason* the two hate each other.'

Shallan's throat grew tight. 'Oh.'

Tuck it away. Don't think about it.

'Shallan,' Adolin said, stepping toward her. 'Why would your brother try to kill Amaram? Did he maybe know the highlord was corrupt? Storms! Kaladin didn't know any of that. Poor bridgeboy. Everyone would have been better off if he'd just let Amaram die.'

Don't confront it. Don't think about it.

'Yeah,' she said. 'Huh.'

'But how did your brother know?' Adolin said, pacing across the balcony. 'Did he say anything?'

'We didn't talk much,' Shallan said, numb. 'He left when I was young. I didn't know him well.'

Anything to get off this topic. For this was something she could still tuck away in the back of her brain. She did *not* want to think about Kaladin and Helaran. . . .

It was a long, quiet ride to the bottom floors of the tower. Adolin wanted to go visit his father's horse again, but she wasn't interested in standing around smelling horse dung. She got off on the second level to make her way toward her rooms.

Secrets. *There are more important things in this world,* Helaran had said to her father. *More important even than you and your crimes.*

Mraize knew something about this. He was withholding the secrets from her like sweets to entice a child to obedience. But all he wanted her to do was investigate the oddities in Urithiru. That was a good thing, wasn't it? She'd have done it anyway.

Shallan meandered through the hallways, following a path where Sebarial's workers had affixed some sphere lanterns to hooks on the walls. Locked up and filled with only the cheapest diamond spheres, they shouldn't be worth the effort to break into, but the light they gave was also rather dim.

She should have stayed above; her absence must have destroyed the illusion of the map. She felt bad about that. Was there a way she could learn to leave her illusions behind her? They'd need Stormlight to keep going. . . .

In any case, Shallan had needed to leave the meeting. The secrets this city hid were too engaging to ignore. She stopped in the hallway and dug out her sketchbook, flipping through pages, looking at the faces of the dead men.

Absently turning a page, she came across a sketch she didn't recall making. A series of twisting, maddening lines, scribbled and unconnected.

She felt cold. 'When did I draw this?'

Pattern moved up her dress, stopping under her neck. He hummed, an uncomfortable sound. 'I do not remember.'

She flipped to the next page. Here she'd drawn a rush of lines sweeping out from a central point, confused and chaotic, transforming to the heads of horses with the flesh ripping off, their eyes wide, equine mouths screaming. It was grotesque, nauseating.

Oh Stormfather . . .

Her fingers trembled as she turned to the next page. She'd scribbled it entirely black, using a circular motion, spiraling toward the center point. A deep void, an endless corridor, something terrible and unknowable at the end.

She snapped the sketchbook shut. 'What is happening to me?'

Pattern hummed in confusion. 'Do we . . . run?'

'Where.'

'Away. Out of this place. Mmmmm.'

'No.'

She trembled, part of her terrified, but she couldn't abandon those secrets. She had to have them, hold them, make them hers. She turned sharply in the corridor, taking a path away from her room. A short time later, she strode into the barracks where Sebarial housed his soldiers. There were plentiful spaces like this in the tower: vast networks of rooms with built-in stone bunks in the walls. Urithiru *had* been a military base; that much was evident from its ability to efficiently house tens of thousands of soldiers on the lower levels alone.

In the common room of the barracks, men lounged with coats off, playing with cards or knives. Her passing caused a stir as men gaped, then leaped to their feet, debating between buttoning their coats and saluting. Whispers of 'Radiant' chased her as she walked into a corridor lined with rooms, where the individual platoons bunked. She counted off doorways marked by archaic Alethi numbers etched into the stone, then entered a specific one.

She burst in on Vathah and his team, who sat inside playing cards by the light of a few spheres. Poor Gaz sat on the chamber pot in a corner privy, and he yelped, pulling closed the cloth on the doorway.

Guess I should have anticipated that, Shallan thought, covering her blush by sucking in a burst of Stormlight. She folded her arms and regarded the others as they – lazily – climbed to their feet and saluted. They were only twelve men now. Some had made their way to other jobs. A few others had died in the Battle of Narak.

She'd kind of been hoping that they would all drift away – if only so she wouldn't have to figure out what to do with them. She now realized that Adolin was right. That was a *terrible* attitude. These men were a re-source and, all things considered, had been remarkably loyal.

'I,' Shallan told them, 'have been an awful employer.'

'Don't know about that, Brightness,' Red said – she still didn't know how the tall, bearded man had gotten his nickname. 'The pay has come on time and you haven't gotten *too* many of us killed.'

'Oi got killed,' Shob said from his bunk, where he saluted – still lying down.

'Shut up, Shob,' Vathah said. 'You're not dead.'

'Oi'm dyin' this time, Sarge. Oi'm sure of it.'

'Then at least you'll be quiet,' Vathah said. 'Brightness, I agree with Red. You've done right by us.'

'Yes, well, the free ride is over,' Shallan said. 'I have work for you.'

Vathah shrugged, but some of the others looked disappointed. Maybe Adolin was right; maybe deep down, men like this did need something to do. They wouldn't have admitted that fact, though.

'I'm afraid it might be dangerous,' Shallan said, then smiled. 'And it will probably involve you getting a little drunk.'

Finally, I will confess my humanity. I have been named a monster, and do not deny those claims. I am the monster that I fear we all can become.

—From *Oathbringer*, preface

T

he decision has been made,"' Teshav read, ' "to seal off this Oathgate until we can destroy it. We realize this is not the path you wished for us to take, Dalinar Kholin. Know that the Prime of Azir considers you fondly, and looks forward to the mutual benefit of trade agreements and new treaties between our nations.

' "A magical portal into the very center of our city, however, presents too severe a danger. We will entertain no further pleas to open it, and suggest that you accept our sovereign will. Good day, Dalinar Kholin. May Yaezir bless and guide you."'

Dalinar punched his fist into his palm as he stood in the small stone chamber. Teshav and her ward occupied the writing podium and seat beside it, while Navani had been pacing opposite Dalinar. King Taravangian sat in a chair by the wall, hunched forward with hands clasped, listening with a concerned expression.

That was it then. Azir was out.

Navani touched his arm. 'I'm sorry.'

'There's still Thaylenah,' Dalinar said. 'Teshav, see if Queen Fen will speak with me today.'

'Yes, Brightlord.'

He had Jah Keved and Kharbranth from Taravangian, and New Natanan was responding positively. With Thaylenah, Dalinar could at least forge a unified Vorin coalition of all the Eastern states. That model might eventually persuade the nations of the west to join with them.

If anyone remained by then.

Dalinar started pacing again as Teshav contacted Thaylenah. He preferred little rooms like this one; the large chambers were a reminder of how enormous this place was. In a small room like this, you could pretend that you were in a cozy bunker somewhere.

Of course, even in a small chamber there were reminders that Urithiru wasn't normal. The strata on the walls, like the folds of a fan. Or the holes that commonly showed up at the tops of rooms, right where the walls met the ceiling. The one in this room couldn't help but remind him of Shallan's report. Was something in there, watching them? Could a *spren* really be murdering people in the tower?

It was nearly enough to make him pull out of the place. But where would they go? Abandon the Oathgates? For now, he'd quadrupled patrols and sent Navani's researchers searching for a possible explanation. At least until he could come up with a solution.

As Teshav wrote to Queen Fen, Dalinar stepped up to the wall, suddenly bothered by that hole. It was right by the ceiling, and too high for him to reach, even if he stood on a chair. Instead he breathed in Stormlight. The bridgemen had described using stones to climb walls, so Dalinar picked up a wooden chair and painted its back with shining light, using the palm of his left hand.

When he pressed the back of the chair against the wall, it stuck. Dalinar grunted, tentatively climbing up onto the seat of the chair, which hung in the air at about table height.

'Dalinar?' Navani asked.

'Might as well make use of the time,' he said, carefully balancing on the chair. He jumped, grabbing the edge of the hole by the ceiling, and pulled himself up to look down it.

It was three feet wide, and about one foot tall. It seemed endless, and he could feel a faint breeze coming out of it. Was that ... scraping he heard? A moment later, a mink slunk into the main tunnel from a shadowed crossroad, carrying a dead rat in its mouth. The tubular little animal twitched its snout toward him, then carried its prize away.

'Air *is* circulating through those,' Navani said as he hopped down off the chair. 'The method baffles us. Perhaps some fabrial we have yet to discover?'

Dalinar looked back up at the hole. Miles upon miles of even smaller tunnels threaded through the walls and ceilings of an already daunting system. And hiding in them somewhere, the thing that Shallan had drawn . . .

'She's replied, Brightlord!' Teshav said.

'Excellent,' Dalinar said. 'Your Majesty, our time is growing short. I'd like—'

'She's still writing,' Teshav said. 'Pardon, Brightlord. She says . . . um . . .'

'Just read it, Teshav,' Dalinar said. 'I'm used to Fen by now.'

' "Damnation, man. Are you ever going to leave me alone? I haven't slept a full night in weeks. The Everstorm has hit us twice now; we're barely keeping this city from falling apart." '

'I understand, Your Majesty,' Dalinar said. 'And am eager to send you the aid I promised. Please, let us make a pact. You've dodged my requests long enough.'

Nearby, the chair finally dropped from the wall and clattered to the floor. He prepared himself for another round of verbal sparring, of half promises and veiled meanings. Fen had been growing increasingly formal during their exchanges.

The spanreed wrote, then halted almost immediately. Teshav looked at him, grave.

' "No," ' she read.

'*Your Majesty*,' Dalinar said. 'This is not a time to forge on alone! Please. I beg you. Listen to me!'

' "You have to know by now," ' came the reply, ' "that this coalition is never going to happen. Kholin . . . I'm baffled, honestly. Your garnet-lit tongue and pleasant words make it seem like you really assume this will work.

' "Surely you see. A queen would have to be either stupid or desperate to let an Alethi army into the very center of her city. I've been the former at times, and I might be approaching the latter, but . . . storms, Kholin.

No. I'm not going to be the one who finally lets Thaylenah fall to you people. And on the off chance that you're sincere, then I'm sorry."'

It had an air of finality to it. Dalinar walked over to Teshav, looking at the inscrutable squiggles on the page that somehow made up the women's script. 'Can you think of anything?' he asked Navani as she sighed and settled down into a chair next to Teshav.

'No. Fen is stubborn, Dalinar.'

Dalinar glanced at Taravangian. Even he had assumed Dalinar's purpose was conquest. And who wouldn't, considering his history?

Maybe it would be different if I could speak to them in person, he thought. But without the Oathgates, that was virtually impossible.

'Thank her for her time,' Dalinar said. 'And tell her my offer remains on the table.'

Teshav started writing, and Navani looked to him, noting what the scribe hadn't – the tension in his voice.

'I'm fine,' he lied. 'I just need time to think.'

He strode from the room before she could object, and his guards outside fell into step behind him. He wanted some fresh air; an open sky always seemed so inviting. His feet didn't take him in that direction, however. He instead found himself roaming through the hallways.

What now?

Same as always, people ignored him unless he had a sword in his hand. Storms, it was like they *wanted* him to come in swinging.

He stalked the halls for a good hour, getting nowhere. Eventually, Lyn the messenger found him. Panting, she said that Bridge Four needed him, but hadn't explained why.

Dalinar followed her, Shallan's sketch a heavy weight in his mind. Had they found another murder victim? Indeed, Lyn led him to the section where Sadeas had been killed.

His sense of foreboding increased. Lyn led him to a balcony, where the bridgemen Leyten and Peet met him. 'Who was it?' he asked as he met them.

'Who . . .' Leyten frowned. 'Oh! It's not that, sir. It's something else. This way.'

Leyten led him down some steps onto the wide field outside the first level of the tower, where three more bridgemen waited near some rows of stone planters, probably for growing tubers.

'We noticed this by accident,' Leyten said as they walked among the planters. The hefty bridgeman had a jovial way about him, and talked to Dalinar – a highprince – as easily as he'd talk to friends at a tavern. 'We've been running patrols on your orders, watching for anything strange. And . . . well, Peet noticed something strange.' He pointed up at the wall. 'See that line?'

Dalinar squinted, picking out a gouge cut into the rock wall. What could score stone like that? It almost looked like . . .

He looked down at the planter boxes nearest them. And there, hidden between two of them, was a hilt protruding from the stone floor.

A Shardblade.

It was easy to miss, as the blade had sunk all the way down into the rock. Dalinar knelt beside it, then took a handkerchief from his pocket and used it to grab the hilt.

Even though he didn't touch the Blade directly, he heard a very distant whine, like a scream in the back of someone's throat. He steeled himself, then yanked the Blade out and set it across the empty planter.

The silvery Blade curved at the end almost like a fishhook. The weapon was even wider than most Shardblades, and near the hilt it rippled in wavelike patterns. He knew this sword, knew it intimately. He'd carried it for decades, since winning it at the Rift all those years ago.

Oathbringer.

He glanced upward. 'The killer must have dropped it out that window. It clipped the stone on its way down, then landed here.'

'That's what we figured, Brightlord,' Peet said.

Dalinar looked down at the sword. His sword.

No. Not mine at all.

He seized the sword, bracing himself for the screams. The cries of a dead spren. They weren't the shrill, painful shrieks he'd heard when touching other Blades, but more of a whimper. The sound of a man backed into a corner, thoroughly beaten and facing something terrible, but too tired to keep screaming.

Dalinar steeled himself and carried the Blade – a familiar weight – with the flat side against his shoulder. He walked toward a different entrance back into the tower city, followed by his guards, the scout, and the five bridgemen.

You promised to carry no dead Blade, the Stormfather thundered in his head.

'Calm yourself,' Dalinar whispered. 'I'm not going to bond it.'

The Stormfather rumbled, low and dangerous.

'This one doesn't scream as loudly as others. Why?'

It remembers your oath, the Stormfather sent. *It remembers the day you won it, and better the day you gave it up. It hates you – but less than it hates others.*

Dalinar passed a group of Hatham's farmers who had been trying, without success, to get some lavis polyps started. He drew more than a few looks; even at a tower populated by soldiers, highprinces, and Radiants, someone carrying a Shardblade in the open was an unusual sight.

'Could it be rescued?' Dalinar whispered as they entered the tower and climbed a stairway. 'Could we save the spren who made this Blade?'

I know of no way, the Stormfather said. *It is dead, as is the man who broke his oath to kill it.*

Back to the Lost Radiants and the Recreance – that fateful day when the knights had broken their oaths, abandoned their Shards, and walked away. Dalinar had witnessed that in a vision, though he still had no idea what had caused it.

Why? What had made them do something so drastic?

He eventually arrived at the Sadeas section of the tower, and though guards in forest green and white controlled access, they couldn't deny a highprince – particularly not Dalinar. Runners dashed before him to carry word. Dalinar followed them, using their path to judge if he was going in the right direction. He was; she was apparently in her rooms. He stopped at the nice wooden door, and gave Ialai the courtesy of knocking.

One of the runners he had chased here opened the door, still panting. Brightness Sadeas sat in a throne set in the center of the room. Amaram stood at her shoulder.

'Dalinar,' Ialai said, nodding her head to him like a queen greeting a subject.

Dalinar heaved the Shardblade off his shoulder and set it carefully on the floor. Not as dramatic as spearing it through the stones, but now that he could hear the weapon's screams, he felt like treating it with reverence.

He turned to go.

'Brightlord?' Ialai said, standing up. 'What is this in exchange for?'

'No exchange,' Dalinar said, turning back. 'That is rightfully yours. My guards found it today; the killer threw it out a window.'

She narrowed her eyes at him.

'I didn't kill him, Ialai,' Dalinar said wearily.

'I realize that. You don't have the bite left in you to do something like that.'

He ignored the gibe, looking to Amaram. The tall, distinguished man met his gaze.

'I *will* see you in judgment someday, Amaram,' Dalinar said. 'Once this is done.'

'As I said you could.'

'I wish that I could trust your word.'

'I stand by what I was forced to do, Brightlord,' Amaram said, stepping forward. 'The arrival of the Voidbringers only proves I was in the right. We need practiced Shardbearers. The stories of darkeyes gaining Blades are charming, but do you really think we have time for nursery tales now, instead of practical reality?'

'You murdered *defenseless men*,' Dalinar said through gritted teeth. 'Men who had saved your life.'

Amaram stooped, lifting Oathbringer. 'And what of the hundreds, even thousands, your wars killed?'

They locked gazes.

'I respect you greatly, Brightlord,' Amaram said. 'Your life has been one of grand accomplishment, and you have spent it seeking the good of Alethkar. But you – and take this with the respect I intend – are a *hypocrite*.

'You stand where you do because of a brutal determination to do what had to be done. It is because of that trail of corpses that you have the luxury to uphold some lofty, nebulous code. Well, it might make you feel better about your past, but morality is not a thing you can simply doff to put on the helm of battle, then put back on when you're done with the slaughter.'

He nodded his head in esteem, as if he hadn't just rammed a sword through Dalinar's gut.

Dalinar spun and left Amaram holding Oathbringer. Dalinar's stride down the corridors was so quick that his entourage had to scramble to keep up.

He finally found his rooms. 'Leave me,' he said to his guards and the bridgemen.

They hesitated, storm them. He turned, ready to lash out, but calmed himself. 'I don't intend to stray in the tower alone. I will obey my own laws. Go.'

They reluctantly retreated, leaving his door unguarded. He passed into his outer common room, where he'd ordered most of the furniture to be placed. Navani's heating fabrial glowed in a corner, near a small rug and several chairs. They finally had enough Stormlight to power it.

Drawn by the warmth, Dalinar walked up to the fabrial. He was surprised to find Taravangian sitting in one of the chairs, staring into the depths of the shining ruby that radiated heat into the room. Well, Dalinar *had* invited the king to use this common room when he wished.

Dalinar wanted nothing but to be alone, and he toyed with leaving. He wasn't sure that Taravangian had noticed him. But that warmth was so welcoming. There were few fires in the tower, and even with the walls to block wind, you always felt chilled.

He settled into the other chair and let out a deep sigh. Taravangian didn't address him, bless the man. Together they sat by that not-fire, staring into the depths of the gem.

Storms, how he had failed today. There would be no coalition. He couldn't even keep the Alethi highprinces in line.

'Not quite like sitting by a hearth, is it?' Taravangian finally said, his voice soft.

'No,' Dalinar agreed. 'I miss the popping of the logs, the dancing of flamespren.'

'It does have its own charm though. Subtle. You can see the Stormlight moving inside.'

'Our own little storm,' Dalinar said. 'Captured, contained, and channeled.'

Taravangian smiled, eyes lit by the ruby's Stormlight. 'Dalinar Kholin ... do you mind me asking you something? How do you know what is right?'

'A lofty question, Your Majesty.'

'Please, just Taravangian.'

Dalinar nodded.

'You have denied the Almighty,' Taravangian said.

'I—'

'No, no. I am not decrying you as a heretic. I do not care, Dalinar. I've questioned the existence of deity myself.'

'I feel there must be a God,' Dalinar said softly. 'My mind and soul rebel at the alternative.'

'Is it not our duty, as kings, to ask questions that make the minds and souls of other men cringe?'

'Perhaps,' Dalinar said. He studied Taravangian. The king seemed so contemplative.

Yes, there still is *some of the old Taravangian in there,* Dalinar thought. *We have misjudged him. He might be slow, but that doesn't mean he doesn't think.*

'I have felt warmth,' Dalinar said, 'coming from a place beyond. A light I can almost see. If there is a God, it was not the Almighty, the one who called himself Honor. He was a creature. Powerful, but still merely a creature.'

'Then how do you know what is right? What guides you?'

Dalinar leaned forward. He thought he could see something larger within the ruby's light. Something that moved like a fish in a bowl.

Warmth continued to bathe him. Light.

' "On my sixtieth day," ' Dalinar whispered, ' "I passed a town whose name shall remain unspoken. Though still in lands that named me king, I was far enough from my home to go unrecognized. Not even those men who handled my face daily – in the form of my seal imprinted upon their letters of authority – would have known this humble traveler as their king." '

Taravangian looked to him, confused.

'It's a quote from a book,' Dalinar said. 'A king long ago took a journey. His destination was this very city. Urithiru.'

'Ah . . .' Taravangian said. '*The Way of Kings*, is it? Adrotagia has mentioned that book.'

'Yes,' Dalinar said. ' "In this town, I found men bedeviled. There had been a murder. A hogman, tasked in protecting the landlord's beasts, had been assaulted. He lived long enough, only, to whisper that three of the other hogmen had gathered together and done the crime.

' "I arrived as questions were being raised, and men interrogated. You see, there were *four* other hogmen in the landlord's employ. Three of them had been responsible for the assault, and likely would have escaped suspicion had they finished their grim job. Each of the four loudly proclaimed that he was the one who had not been part of the cabal. No amount of interrogation determined the truth."'

Dalinar fell silent.

'What happened?' Taravangian asked.

'He doesn't say at first,' Dalinar replied. 'Throughout his book, he raises the question again and again. Three of those men were violent threats, guilty of premeditated murder. One was innocent. What do you do?'

'Hang all four,' Taravangian whispered.

Dalinar – surprised to hear such bloodthirst from the other man – turned. Taravangian looked sorrowful, not bloodthirsty at all.

'The landlord's job,' Taravangian said, 'is to prevent further murders. I doubt that what the book records actually happened. It is too neat, too simple a parable. Our lives are far messier. But assuming the story did occur as claimed, and there was absolutely no way of determining who was guilty . . . you have to hang all four. Don't you?'

'What of the innocent man?'

'One innocent dead, but three murderers stopped. Is it not the best good that can be done, and the best way to protect your people?' Taravangian rubbed his forehead. 'Stormfather. I sound like a madman, don't I? But is it not a particular madness to be charged with such decisions? It's difficult to address such questions without revealing our own hypocrisy.'

Hypocrite, Amaram accused Dalinar in his mind.

He and Gavilar hadn't used pretty justifications when they'd gone to war. They'd done as men did: they'd conquered. Only later had Gavilar started to seek validation for their actions.

'Why not let them all go?' Dalinar said. 'If you can't prove who is guilty – if you can't be *sure* – I think you should let them go.'

'Yes . . . one innocent in four is too many for you. That makes sense too.'

'No, *any* innocent is too many.'

'You say that,' Taravangian said. 'Many people do, but our laws *will* claim innocent men – for all judges are flawed, as is our knowledge. Eventually, you *will* execute someone who does not deserve it. This is the burden society must carry in exchange for order.'

'I hate that,' Dalinar said softly.

'Yes . . . I do too. But it's not a matter of morality, is it? It's a matter of thresholds. How many guilty may be punished before you'd accept one innocent casualty? A thousand? Ten thousand? A hundred? When you consider, all calculations are meaningless except one. Has more good been done than evil? If so, then the law has done its job. And so . . . I must hang all four men.' He paused. 'And I would weep, every night, for having done it.'

Damnation. Again, Dalinar reassessed his impression of Taravangian. The king was soft-spoken, but not slow. He was simply a man who liked to consider a great long time before committing.

'Nohadon eventually wrote,' Dalinar said, 'that the landlord took a modest approach. He imprisoned all four. Though the punishment should have been death, he mixed together the guilt and innocence, and determined that the *average* guilt of the four should deserve only prison.'

'He was unwilling to commit,' Taravangian said. 'He wasn't seeking justice, but to assuage his own conscience.'

'What he did was, nevertheless, another option.'

'Does your king ever say what he would have done?' Taravangian asked. 'The one who wrote the book?'

'He said the only course was to let the Almighty guide, and let each instance be judged differently, depending on circumstances.'

'So he too was unwilling to commit,' Taravangian said. 'I would have expected more.'

'His book was about his journey,' Dalinar said. 'And his questions. I think this was one he never fully answered for himself. I wish he had.'

They sat by the not-fire for a time before Taravangian eventually stood and rested his hand on Dalinar's shoulder. 'I understand,' he said softly, then left.

He was a good man, the Stormfather said.

'Nohadon?' Dalinar said.

Yes.

Feeling stiff, Dalinar rose from his seat and made his way through his rooms. He didn't stop at the bedroom, though the hour was growing late, and instead made his way onto his balcony. To look out over the clouds.

Taravangian is wrong, the Stormfather said. *You are not a hypocrite, Son of Honor.*

'I am,' Dalinar said softly. 'But sometimes a hypocrite is nothing more than a person who is in the process of changing.'

The Stormfather rumbled. He didn't like the idea of change.

Do I go to war with the other kingdoms, Dalinar thought, *and maybe save the world? Or do I sit here and pretend that I can do all this on my own?*

'Do you have any more visions of Nohadon?' Dalinar asked the Stormfather, hopeful.

I have shown you all that was created for you to see, the Stormfather said. *I can show no more.*

'Then I should like to rewatch the vision where I met Nohadon,' Dalinar said. 'Though let me go fetch Navani before you begin. I want her to record what I say.'

Would you rather I show the vision to her as well? the Stormfather asked. *She could record it herself that way.*

Dalinar froze. 'You can show the visions to *others*?'

I was given this leave: to choose those who would best be served by the visions. He paused, then grudgingly continued. *To choose a Bondsmith.*

No, he did not like the idea of being bonded, but it was part of what he'd been commanded to do.

Dalinar barely considered that thought.

The Stormfather could show the visions to *others*.

'Anyone?' Dalinar said. 'You can show them to anyone?'

During a storm, I can approach anyone I choose, the Stormfather said. *But you do not have to be in a storm, so you can join a vision in which I have placed someone else, even if you are distant.*

Storms! Dalinar bellowed a laugh.

What have I done? the Stormfather asked.

'You've just solved my problem!'

The problem from The Way of Kings?

'No, the greater one. I've been wishing for a way to meet with the other monarchs in person.' Dalinar grinned. 'I think that in a coming highstorm, Queen Fen of Thaylenah is going to have a quite remarkable experience.'

So sit back. Read, or listen, to someone who has passed between realms.

—From *Oathbringer,* preface

Veil prowled through the Breakaway market, hat pulled low, hands in her pockets. Nobody else seemed to be able to hear the beast that she did.

Regular shipments of supplies through Jah Keved via King Taravangian had set the market bustling. Fortunately, with a third Radiant capable of working the Oathgate now, less of Shallan's time was required.

Spheres that glowed again, and several highstorms as proof that that would persist, had encouraged everyone. Excitement was high, trading brisk. Drink flowed freely from casks emblazoned with the royal seal of Jah Keved.

Lurking within it all, somewhere, was a predator that only Veil could hear. She heard the thing in the silence between laughter. It was the sound of a tunnel extending into the darkness. The feel of breath on the back of your neck in a dark room.

How could they laugh while that void watched?

It had been a frustrating four days. Dalinar had increased patrols to almost ridiculous levels, but those soldiers weren't watching the right way. They were too easily seen, too disruptive. Veil had set her men to a more targeted surveillance in the market.

So far, they'd found nothing. Her team was tired, as was Shallan, who suffered from the long nights as Veil. Fortunately, Shallan wasn't doing anything particularly useful these days. Sword training with Adolin each day – more frolicking and flirting than useful swordplay – and the occasional meeting with Dalinar where she had nothing to add but a pretty map.

Veil though ... Veil hunted the hunter. Dalinar acted like a soldier: increased patrols, strict rules. He asked his scribes to find him evidence of spren attacking people in historical records.

He needed more than vague explanations and abstract ideas – but those were the very soul of art. If you could explain something perfectly, then you'd never *need* art. That was the difference between a table and a beautiful woodcutting. You could explain the table: its purpose, its shape, its nature. The woodcutting you simply had to experience.

She ducked into a tent tavern. Did it seem busier in here than on previous nights? Yes. Dalinar's patrols had people on edge. They were avoiding the darker, more sinister taverns in favor of ones with good crowds and bright lights.

Gaz and Red stood beside a pile of crates, nursing drinks and wearing plain trousers and shirts, not uniforms. She hoped they weren't too intoxicated yet. Veil pushed up to their position, crossing her arms on the boxes.

'Nothing yet,' Gaz said with a grunt. 'Same as the other nights.'

'Not that we're complaining,' Red added, grinning as he took a long pull on his drink. 'This is the kind of soldiering I can really get behind.'

'It's going to happen tonight,' Veil said. 'I can smell it in the air.'

'You said that last night, Veil,' Gaz said.

Three nights ago, a friendly game of cards had turned to violence, and one player had hit another over the head with a bottle. That often wouldn't have been lethal, but it had hit just right and killed the poor fellow. The perpetrator – one of Ruthar's soldiers – had been hanged the next day in the market's central square.

As unfortunate as the event had been, it was exactly what she'd been waiting for. A seed. An act of violence, one man striking the other. She'd mobilized her team and set them in the taverns near where the fight occurred. *Watch,* she'd said. *Someone will get attacked with a bottle, in exactly the same way. Pick someone who looks like the man who died, and watch.*

Shallan had done sketches of the murdered man, a short fellow with long drooping mustaches. Veil had distributed them; the men took her as no more than another employee.

Now . . . they waited.

'The attack *will* come,' Veil said. 'Who are your targets?'

Red pointed out two men in the tent who had mustaches and were of a similar height to the dead man. Veil nodded and dropped a few low-value spheres onto the table. 'Get something in you other than booze.'

'Sure, sure,' Red said as Gaz grabbed the spheres. 'But tell me, sweetness, don't you want to stay here with us a little longer?'

'Most men who have made a pass at me end up missing a finger or two, Red.'

'I'd still have plenty left to satisfy you, I promise.'

She looked back at him, then started snickering. 'That was a decently good line.'

'Thanks!' He raised his mug. 'So . . .'

'Sorry, not interested.'

He sighed, but raised his mug farther before taking a pull on it.

'Where did you come from, anyway?' Gaz said, inspecting her with his single eye.

'Shallan kind of sucked me up along the way, like a boat pulling flotsam into its wake.'

'She does that,' Red said. 'You think you're done. Living out the last light of your sphere, you know? And then suddenly, you're an honor guard to a storming *Knight Radiant,* and everyone's looking up to you.'

Gaz grunted. 'Ain't that true. Ain't that true. . . .'

'Keep watch,' Veil said. 'You know what to do if something happens.'

They nodded. They'd send one man to the meeting place, while the other tried to tail the attacker. They knew there might be something weird about the man they chased, but she hadn't told them everything.

Veil walked back to the meeting point, near a dais at the center of the market, close to the well. The dais looked like it had once held some kind of official building, but all that remained was the six-foot-high foundation with steps leading up to it on four sides. Here, Aladar's officers had set up central policing operations and disciplinary facilities.

She watched the crowds while idly spinning her knife in her fingers. Veil liked watching people. That she shared with Shallan. It was good to know how the two of them were different, but it was also good to know what they had in common.

Veil wasn't a true loner. She needed people. Yes, she scammed them on occasion, but she wasn't a thief. She was a lover of experience. She was at her best in a crowded market, watching, thinking, enjoying.

Now Radiant . . . Radiant could take people or leave them. They were a tool, but also a nuisance. How could they so often act *against* their own best interests? The world would be a better place if they'd all simply do what Radiant said. Barring that, they could at *least* leave her alone.

Veil flipped her knife up and caught it. Radiant and Veil shared efficiency. They liked seeing things done well, in the right way. They didn't suffer fools, though Veil could laugh at them, while Radiant simply ignored them.

Screams sounded in the market.

Finally, Veil thought, catching her knife and spinning. She came alert, eager, drawing in Stormlight. Where?

Vathah came barreling through the crowd, shoving aside a marketgoer. Veil ran to meet him.

'Details!' Veil snapped.

'It wasn't like you said,' he said. 'Follow me.'

The two took off back the way he'd come.

'It wasn't a bottle to the head.' Vathah said. 'My tent is near one of the buildings. The stone ones that were here in the market, you know?'

'And?' she demanded.

Vathah pointed as they drew close. You couldn't miss the tall structure beside the tent he and Glurv had been watching. At the top, a corpse dangled from an outcropping, hanged by the neck.

Hanged. *Storm it. The thing didn't imitate the attack with the bottle . . . it imitated the execution that followed!*

Vathah pointed. 'Killer dropped the person up there, leaving them to twitch. Then the killer *jumped* down. All that distance, Veil. How—'

'Where?' she demanded.

'Glurv is tailing,' Vathah said, pointing.

The two charged in that direction, shoving their way through the crowds. They eventually spotted Glurv up ahead, standing on the edge of the well, waving. He was a squat man with a face that always looked swollen, as if it were trying to burst through its skin.

'Man wearing all black,' he said. 'Ran straight toward the eastern tunnels!' He pointed toward where troubled marketgoers were peering down a tunnel, as if someone had just passed them in a rush.

Veil dashed in that direction. Vathah stayed with her longer than Glurv – but with Stormlight, she maintained a sprint no ordinary person could match. She burst into the indicated hallway and demanded to know if anyone had seen a man pass this way. A pair of women pointed.

Veil followed, heart beating violently, Stormlight raging within her. If she failed the chase, she'd have to wait for two more people to be assaulted – if it even happened again. The creature might hide, now that it knew she was watching.

She sprinted down this hallway, leaving behind the more populated sections of the tower. A few last people pointed down a tunnel at her shouted question.

She was beginning to lose hope as she reached the end of the hallway at an intersection, and looked one way, then the other. She glowed brightly to light the corridors for a distance, but she saw nothing in either.

She let out a sigh, slumping against the wall.

'Mmmm . . .' Pattern said from her coat. 'It's there.'

'Where?' Shallan asked.

'To the right. The shadows are off. The wrong pattern.'

She stepped forward, and something split out of the shadows, a figure that was jet black – though like a liquid or a polished stone, it reflected her light. It scrambled away, its shape *wrong*. Not fully human.

Veil ran, heedless of the danger. This thing might be able to hurt her – but the mystery was the greater threat. She *needed* to know these secrets.

Shallan skidded around a corner, then barreled down the next tunnel. She managed to follow the broken piece of shadow, but she couldn't quite catch it.

The chase led her deeper into the far reaches of the tower's ground floor, to areas barely explored, where the tunnels grew increasingly confusing. The air smelled of old things. Of dust and stone left alone for ages. The strata danced on the walls, the speed of her run making them seem to twist around her like threads in a loom.

The thing dropped to all fours, light from Shallan's glow reflecting off its coal skin. It ran, frantic, until it hit a turn in the tunnel ahead and *squeezed* into a hole in the wall, two feet wide, near the floor.

Radiant dropped to her knees, spotting the thing as it wriggled out the other side of the hole. *Not that thick,* she thought, standing. 'Pattern!' she demanded, thrusting her hand to the side.

She attacked the wall with her Shardblade, slicing chunks free, dropping them to the floor with a clatter. The strata ran all the way through the stone, and the pieces she carved off had a forlorn, broken beauty to them.

Engorged with Light, she shoved up against the sliced wall, finally breaking through into a small room beyond.

Much of its floor was taken up by the mouth of a pit. Circled by stone steps with no railing, the hole bored down through the rock into darkness. Radiant lowered her Shardblade, letting it slice into the rock at her feet. A hole. Like her drawing of spiraling blackness, a pit that seemed to descend into the void itself.

She released her Shardblade, falling to her knees.

'Shallan?' Pattern asked, rising up from the ground near where the Blade had vanished.

'We'll need to descend.'

'Now?'

She nodded. 'But first . . . first, go and get Adolin. Tell him to bring soldiers.'

Pattern hummed. 'You won't go alone, will you?'

'No. I promise. Can you make your way back?'

Pattern buzzed affirmatively, then zipped off across the ground, dimpling the floor of the rock. Curiously, the wall near where she'd broken in showed the rust marks and remnants of ancient hinges. So there was a secret door to get into this place.

Shallan kept her word. She was drawn toward that blackness, but she wasn't stupid. Well, mostly not stupid. She waited, transfixed by the pit, until she heard voices from the hallway behind her. *He can't see me in Veil's clothing!* she thought, and started to reawaken. How long had she been kneeling there?

She took off Veil's hat and long white coat, then hid them behind the debris. Stormlight enfolded her, painting the image of a havah over her trousers, gloved hand, and tight buttoned shirt.

Shallan. She was Shallan again – innocent, lively Shallan. Quick with a quip, even when nobody wanted to hear it. Earnest, but sometimes overeager. She could be that person.

That's you, a part of her cried as she adopted the persona. *That's the real you. Isn't it? Why do you have to paint that face over another?*

She turned as a short, wiry man in a blue uniform entered the room, grey dusting his temples. What was his name again? She'd spent some time around Bridge Four in the last few weeks, but still hadn't learned them all.

Adolin strode in next, wearing Kholin blue Shardplate, faceplate up, Blade resting on his shoulder. Judging from the sounds out in the hallway – and the Herdazian faces that peeked into the room – he had brought not only soldiers, but the *entirety* of Bridge Four.

That included Renarin, who clomped in after his brother, clad in slate-colored Shardplate. Renarin looked far less frail when fully armored, though his face didn't seem like a soldier's, even if he had stopped wearing his spectacles.

Pattern approached and tried to slide up her illusory dress, but then stopped, backing away and humming in pleasure at the lie. 'I found him!' he proclaimed. 'I found Adolin!'

'I see that,' Shallan said.

'He came at me,' Adolin said, 'in the training rooms, screaming that you'd found the killer. Said that if I didn't come, you'd probably – and I quote – "go do something stupid without letting me watch."'

Pattern hummed. 'Stupidity. Very interesting.'

'You should visit the Alethi court sometime,' Adolin said, stepping over to the pit. 'So . . .'

'We tracked the thing that has been assaulting people,' Shallan said. 'It killed someone in the market, then it came here.'

'The . . . thing?' one of the bridgemen asked. 'Not a person?'

'It's a spren,' Shallan whispered. 'But not like one I've ever seen. It's able to imitate a person for a time – but it eventually becomes something else. A broken face, a twisted shape . . .'

'Sounds like that girl you've been seeing, Skar,' one of the bridgemen noted.

'Ha ha,' Skar said dryly. 'How about we toss you in that pit, Eth, and see how far down this thing goes?'

'So this spren,' Lopen said, approaching the pit, 'it, sure, killed Highprince Sadeas?'

Shallan hesitated. No. It had killed Perel in copying the Sadeas murder, but someone *else* had murdered the highprince. She glanced at Adolin, who must have been thinking the same thing, for how solemn his expression was.

The spren was the greater threat – it had performed multiple murders. Still, it made her uncomfortable to acknowledge that her investigation hadn't taken them a single step closer to finding who had killed the highprince.

'We must have passed by this point a dozen times,' a soldier said from behind. Shallan started; that voice was *female*. Indeed, she'd mistaken one of Dalinar's scouts – the short woman with long hair – for another bridgeman, though her uniform was different. She was inspecting the cuts Shallan had made to get into this room. 'Don't you remember scouting right past that curved hallway outside, Teft?'

Teft nodded, rubbing his bearded chin. 'Yeah, you're right, Lyn. But why hide a room like this?'

'There's something down there,' Renarin whispered, leaning out over the pit. 'Something . . . ancient. You've felt it, haven't you?' He looked up at Shallan, then the others in the room. 'This place is weird; this whole tower is weird. You've noticed it too, right?'

'Kid,' Teft said, 'you're the expert on what's weird. We'll trust your word.'

Shallan looked with concern toward Renarin at the insult. He just grinned, as one of the other bridgemen slapped him on the back – Plate notwithstanding – while Lopen and Rock started arguing over who was truly the weirdest among them. In a moment of surprise, she realized that Bridge Four had actually assimilated Renarin. He might be the light-eyed son of a highprince, resplendent in Shardplate, but here he was just another bridgeman.

'So,' one of the men said, a handsome, muscled fellow with arms that seemed too long for his body, 'I assume we're heading down into this awful crypt of terror?'

'Yes,' Shallan said. She thought his name was Drehy.

'Storming lovely,' Drehy said. 'Marching orders, Teft?'

'That's up to Brightlord Adolin.'

'I brought the best men I could find,' Adolin said to Shallan. 'But I feel like I should bring an entire army instead. You sure you want to do this now?'

'Yes,' Shallan said. 'We have to, Adolin. And . . . I don't know that an army would make a difference.'

'Very well. Teft, give us a hefty rearguard. I don't fancy having something sneak up on us. Lyn, I want accurate maps – stop us if we get too far ahead of your drawing. I want to know my *exact* line of retreat. We go slowly, men. Be ready to perform a controlled, careful retreat if I command it.'

Some shuffling of personnel followed. Then the group finally started down the staircase, single file, Shallan and Adolin near the center of the pack. The steps jutted right from the wall, but were wide enough that people would be able to pass on their way up, so there was no danger of falling off. She tried to keep from brushing anyone, as it might disturb the illusion that she was wearing her dress.

The sound of their footsteps vanished into the void. Soon they were alone with the timeless, patient darkness. The light of the sphere lanterns the bridgemen carried didn't seem to stretch far in that pit. It reminded Shallan of the mausoleum carved into the hill near her manor, where ancient Davar family members had been Soulcast to statues.

Her father's body hadn't been placed there. They had lacked the funds to pay for a Soulcaster – and besides, they'd wanted to pretend he was alive. She and her brothers had burned the body, as the darkeyes did.

Pain . . .

'I have to remind you, Brightness,' Teft said from in front of her, 'you can't expect anything . . . extraordinary from my men. For a bit, some of us sucked up light and strutted about like we were Stormblessed. That stopped when Kaladin left.'

'It'll come back, gancho!' Lopen said from behind her. 'When Kaladin returns, we'll glow again good.'

'Hush, Lopen,' Teft said. 'Keep your voice down. Anyway, Brightness, the lads will do their best, but you need to know what – and what not – to expect.'

Shallan hadn't been expecting Radiant powers from them; she'd known about their limitation already. All she needed were soldiers. Eventually,

Lopen tossed a diamond chip into the hole, earning him a glare from Adolin.

'It might be down there waiting for us,' the prince hissed. 'Don't give it warning.'

The bridgeman wilted, but nodded. The sphere bounced as a visible pinprick below, and Shallan was glad to know that at least there was an end to this descent. She'd begun to imagine an infinite spiral, like with old Dilid, one of the ten fools. He ran up a hillside toward the Tranquiline Halls with sand sliding beneath his feet – running for eternity, but never making progress.

Several bridgemen let out audible sighs of relief as they finally reached the bottom of the shaft. Here, piles of splinters scattered at the edges of the round chamber, covered in decayspren. There had once been a banister for the steps, but it had fallen to the effects of time.

The bottom of the shaft had only one exit, a large archway more elaborate than others in the tower. Up above, almost everything was the same uniform stone – as if this whole tower had been carved in one go. Here, the archway was of separately placed stones, and the walls of the tunnel beyond were lined with bright mosaic tiles.

Once they entered the hall, Shallan gasped, holding up a diamond broam. Gorgeous, intricate pictures of the Heralds – made of thousands of tiles – adorned the ceiling, each in a circular panel.

The art on the walls was more enigmatic. A solitary figure hovering above the ground before a large blue disc, arms stretched to the side as if to embrace it. Depictions of the Almighty in his traditional form as a cloud bursting with energy and light. A woman in the shape of a tree, hands spreading toward the sky and becoming branches. Who would have thought to find pagan symbols in the home of the Knights Radiant?

Other murals depicted shapes that reminded her of Pattern, windspren . . . ten kinds of spren. One for each order?

Adolin sent a vanguard a short distance ahead, and soon they returned. 'Metal doors ahead, Brightlord,' Lyn said. 'One on each side of the hall.'

Shallan pried her eyes away from the murals, joining the main body of the force as they moved. They reached the large steel doors and stopped, though the corridor itself continued onward. At Shallan's prompting, the bridgemen tried them, but couldn't get them open.

'Locked,' Drehy said, wiping his brow.

Adolin stepped forward, sword in hand. 'I've got a key.'

'Adolin . . .' Shallan said. 'These are artifacts from another time. Valuable and precious.'

'I won't break them too much,' he promised.

'But—'

'Aren't we chasing a murderer?' he said. 'Someone who is likely to, say, hide in a locked room?'

She sighed, then nodded as he waved everyone back. She tucked her safehand, which had brushed him, back under her arm. It was so strange to feel like she was wearing a glove, but to see her hand as sleeved. Would it really have been so bad to let Adolin know about Veil?

A part of her panicked at the idea, so she let go of it quickly.

Adolin rammed his Blade through the door just above where the lock or bar would be, then swept it down. Teft tried the door, and was able to shove it open, hinges grinding loudly.

The bridgemen ducked in first, spears in hand. For all Teft's insistence that she wasn't to expect anything exceptional of them, they took point without orders, even though there were two Shardbearers at the ready.

Adolin rushed in after the bridgemen to secure the room, though Renarin wasn't paying much attention. He'd walked a few steps farther down the main corridor, and now stood still, staring deeper into the depths, sphere held absently in one gauntleted hand, Shardblade in the other.

Shallan stepped up hesitantly beside him. A cool breeze blew from behind them, as if being sucked into that darkness. The mystery lurked in that direction, the captivating depths. She could sense it more distinctly now. Not an evil really, but a *wrongness*. Like the sight of a wrist hanging from an arm after the bone is broken.

'What is it?' Renarin whispered. 'Glys is frightened, and won't speak.'

'Pattern doesn't know,' Shallan said. 'He calls it ancient. Says it's of the enemy.'

Renarin nodded.

'Your father doesn't seem to be able to feel it,' Shallan said. 'Why can we?'

'I . . . I don't know. Maybe—'

'Shallan?' Adolin said, looking out of the room, his faceplate up. 'You should see this.'

The wreckage inside the room was more decayed than most they'd found in the tower. Rusted clasps and screws clung to bits of wood. Decomposed heaps ran in rows, containing bits of fragile covers and spines.

A library. They'd finally found the books Jasnah had dreamed of discovering.

They were ruined.

With a sinking feeling, Shallan moved through the room, nudging at piles of dust and splinters with her toes, frightening off decayspren. She found some shapes of books, but they disintegrated at her touch. She knelt between two rows of fallen books, feeling lost. All that knowledge . . . dead and gone.

'Sorry,' Adolin said, standing awkwardly nearby.

'Don't let the men disturb this. Maybe . . . maybe there's something Navani's scholars can do to recover it.'

'Want us to search the other room?' Adolin asked.

She nodded, and he clanked off. A short time later, she heard hinges creak as Adolin forced open the door.

Shallan suddenly felt exhausted. If these books here were gone, then it was unlikely they'd find others better preserved.

Forward. She rose, brushing off her knees, which only reminded her that her dress wasn't real. *You aren't here for this secret anyway.*

She stepped out into the main hallway, the one with the murals. Adolin and the bridgemen were exploring the room on the other side, but a quick glance showed Shallan that it was a mirror of the one they'd left, furnished only with piles of debris.

'Um . . . guys?' Lyn, the scout, called. 'Prince Adolin? Brightness Radiant?'

Shallan turned from the room. Renarin had walked farther down the corridor. The scout had followed him, but had frozen in the hallway. Renarin's sphere illuminated something in the distance. A large mass that reflected the light, like glistening tar.

'We shouldn't have come here,' Renarin said. 'We can't fight this. Stormfather.' He stumbled backward. 'Stormfather . . .'

The bridgemen hastened into the hallway in front of Shallan, between her and Renarin. At a barked order from Teft, they made a formation spanning from one side of the main hallway to the other: a line of men holding spears low, with a second line behind holding more spears higher in an overhand grip.

Adolin burst out of the second library room, then gaped at the undulating shape in the distance. A living darkness.

That darkness seeped down the hallway. It wasn't fast, but there was an inevitability about the way it coated everything, flowing up the sides of the walls, onto the ceiling. On the ground, shapes split from the main mass, becoming figures that stepped as if from the surf. Creatures that had two feet and soon grew faces, with clothing that rippled into existence.

'She's here,' Renarin whispered. 'One of the Unmade. Re-Shephir . . . the Midnight Mother.'

'Run, Shallan!' Adolin shouted. 'Men, start back up the hall.'

Then – of course – he *charged* at the flood of things.

The figures . . . they look like us, Shallan thought, stepping back, farther from the line of bridgemen. There was one midnight creature that looked like Teft, and another that was a copy of Lopen. Two larger shapes seemed to be wearing Shardplate. Except they were made of shiny tar, their features blobby, imperfect.

The mouths opened, sprouting spiny teeth.

'Make a careful retreat, like the prince ordered!' Teft called. 'Don't get boxed in, men! Hold the line! Renarin!'

Renarin still stood out in front, holding forth his Shardblade: long and thin, with a waving pattern to the metal. Adolin reached his brother, then grabbed his arm and tried to tow him back.

He resisted. He seemed mesmerized by that line of forming monsters.

'Renarin! Attention!' Teft shouted. 'To the line!'

The boy's head snapped up at the command and he scrambled – as if he weren't the cousin of the king – to obey his sergeant's order. Adolin retreated with him, and the two fell into formation with the bridgemen. Together, they pulled backward through the main hall.

Shallan backed up, staying roughly twenty feet behind the formation. Suddenly, the enemy moved with a burst of speed. Shallan cried out, and the bridgemen cursed, turning spears as the main mass of darkness swept up along the sides of the corridor, covering the beautiful murals.

The midnight figures dashed forward, charging the line. An explosive, frantic clash followed, bridgemen holding formation and striking at creatures who suddenly began forming on the right and left, coming out of the blackness on the walls. The things bled vapor when struck, a darkness that hissed from them and dissipated into the air.

Like smoke, Shallan thought.

The tar swept down from the walls, surrounding the bridgemen, who circled to keep themselves from being attacked at the rear. Adolin and Renarin fought at the very front, hacking with Blades, leaving dark figures to hiss and gush smoke in pieces.

Shallan found herself separated from the soldiers, an inky blackness between them. There didn't seem to be a duplicate for her.

The midnight faces bristled with teeth. Though they thrust with spears, they did so awkwardly. They struck true now and then, wounding a bridgeman, who would pull back into the center of the formation to be hastily bandaged by Lyn or Lopen. Renarin fell into the center and started to glow with Stormlight, healing those who were hurt.

Shallan watched all this, feeling a numbing trance settle over her. 'I . . . know you,' she whispered to the blackness, realizing it was true. 'I know what you're doing.'

Men grunted and stabbed. Adolin swept before himself, Shardblade trailing black smoke from the creatures' wounds. He chopped apart dozens of the things, but new ones continued forming, wearing familiar shapes. Dalinar. Teshav. Highprinces and scouts, soldiers and scribes.

'You try to imitate us,' Shallan said. 'But you fail. You're a spren. You don't *quite* understand.'

She stepped toward the surrounded bridgemen.

'Shallan!' Adolin called, grunting as he cleaved three figures before him. 'Escape! Run!'

She ignored him, stepping up to the darkness. In front of her – at the closest point of the ring – Drehy stabbed a figure straight through the head, sending it stumbling back. Shallan seized its shoulders, spinning it toward her. It was Navani, a gaping hole in her face, black smoke escaping with a hiss. Even ignoring that, the features were off. The nose too big, one eye a little higher than the other.

It dropped to the floor, writhing as it deflated like a punctured wineskin.

Shallan strode right up to the formation. The things fled her, shying to the sides. Shallan had the distinct and terrifying impression that these things could have swept the bridgemen away at will – overwhelming them in a terrible black tide. But the Midnight Mother wanted to learn; she wanted to fight with spears.

If that was so, however, she was growing impatient. The newer figures forming up were increasingly distorted, more bestial, spiny teeth spilling from their mouths.

'Your imitation is pathetic,' Shallan whispered. 'Here. Let me show you how it's done.'

Shallan drew in her Stormlight, going alight like a beacon. Things screamed, pulling away from her. As she stepped around the formation of worried bridgemen – wading into the blackness at their left flank – figures extended from her, shapes growing from light. The people from her recently rebuilt collection.

Palona. Soldiers from the hallways. A group of Soulcasters she'd passed two days ago. Men and women from the markets. Highprinces and scribes. The man who had tried to pick up Veil at the tavern. The Horneater she'd stabbed in the hand. Soldiers. Cobblers. Scouts. Washwomen. Even a few kings.

A glowing, radiant force.

Her figures spread out to surround the beleaguered bridgemen like sentries. This new, glowing force drove the enemy monsters back, and the tar withdrew along the sides of the hall, until the path of retreat was open. The Midnight Mother dominated the darkness at the end of the hall, the direction they had not yet explored. It waited there, and did not recede farther.

The bridgemen relaxed, Renarin muttering as he healed the last few who had been hurt. Shallan's cohort of glowing figures moved forward and formed a line with her, between darkness and bridgemen.

The creatures formed again from the blackness ahead, growing more ferocious, like beasts. Featureless blobs with teeth sprouting from slit mouths.

'How are you doing this?' Adolin asked, voice ringing from within his helm. 'Why are they afraid?'

'Has someone with a knife – not knowing who you were – ever tried to threaten you?'

'Yeah. I just summoned my Shardblade.'

'It's a little like that.' Shallan stepped forward, and Adolin joined her. Renarin summoned his Blade and took a few quick steps to reach them, his Plate clicking.

The darkness pulled back, revealing that the hallway opened up into a room ahead. As she approached, Shallan's Stormlight illuminated a bowl-like chamber. The center was dominated by a heaving black mass that undulated and pulsed, stretching from floor to ceiling some twenty feet above.

The midnight beasts tested forward against her light, no longer seeming as intimidated.

'We have to choose,' Shallan said to Adolin and Renarin. 'Retreat or attack?'

'What do you think?'

'I don't know. This creature . . . she's been watching me. She's changed how I see the tower. I feel like I *understand* her, a connection I cannot explain. That can't be a good thing, right? Can we even trust what I think?'

Adolin raised his faceplate and smiled at her. Storms, that smile. 'Highmarshal Halad always said that to beat someone, you must first know them. It's become one of the rules we follow in warfare.'

'And . . . what did he say about retreat?'

' "Plan every battle as if you will inevitably retreat, but fight every battle like there is no backing down." '

The main mass in the chamber undulated, faces appearing from its tarry surface – pressing out as if trying to escape. There was something beneath the enormous spren. Yes, it was wrapped around a pillar that reached from the floor of the circular room to its ceiling.

The murals, the intricate art, the fallen troves of information . . . This place was important.

Shallan clasped her hands before herself, and the Patternblade formed in her palms. She twisted it in a sweaty grip, falling into the dueling stance Adolin had been teaching her.

Holding it immediately brought pain. Not the screaming of a dead spren. Pain inside. The pain of an Ideal sworn, but not yet overcome.

'Bridgemen,' Adolin called. 'You willing to give it another go?'

'We'll last longer than you will, gancho! Even with your fancy armor.'

Adolin grinned and slammed his faceplate down. 'At your word, Radiant.'

She sent her illusions in, but the darkness didn't shy before them as it had previously. Black figures attacked her illusions, testing to find that they weren't real. Dozens of these midnight men clogged the way forward.

'Clear the way for me to the thing in the center,' she said, trying to sound more certain than she felt. 'I need to get close enough to touch her.'

'Renarin, can you guard my back?' Adolin asked.

Renarin nodded.

Adolin took a deep breath, then charged into the room, bursting right through the middle of an illusion of his father. He struck at the first midnight man, chopping it down, then began sweeping around him in a frenzy.

Bridge Four shouted, rushing in behind him. Together, they began to form a path for Shallan, slaying the creatures between her and the pillar.

She walked through the bridgemen, a rank of them forming a spear line to either side of her. Ahead, Adolin pushed toward the pillar, Renarin at his back preventing him from being surrounded, bridgemen in turn pushing up along the sides to keep Renarin from being overwhelmed.

The monsters no longer bore even a semblance of humanity. They struck Adolin, too-real claws and teeth scraping his armor. Others clung to him, trying to weigh him down or find chinks in the Shardplate.

They know how to face men like him, Shallan thought, still holding her Shardblade in one hand. *Why then do they fear me?*

Shallan wove Light, and a version of Radiant appeared near Renarin. The creatures attacked it, leaving Renarin for a moment – unfortunately, most of her illusions had fallen, collapsing into Stormlight as they were disrupted again and again. She could have kept them going, she thought, with more practice.

Instead, she wove versions of herself. Young and old, confident and frightened. A dozen different Shallans. With a shock, she realized that several were pictures she'd lost, self-portraits she'd practiced with a mirror, as Dandos the Oilsworn had insisted was vital for an aspiring artist.

Some of her selves cowered; others fought. For a moment Shallan lost herself, and she even let Veil appear among them. She was those women, those girls, every one of them. And none of them were her. They were things she used, manipulated. Illusions.

'Shallan!' Adolin shouted, voice straining as Renarin grunted and ripped midnight men off him. 'Whatever you're going to do, do it now!'

She'd stepped up to the front of the column the soldiers had won for her, right near Adolin. She tore her gaze away from a child Shallan dancing among the midnight men. Before her, the main mass – coating the pillar in the center of the room – bubbled with faces that stretched against the surface, mouths opening to scream, then submerged like men drowning in tar.

'Shallan!' Adolin said again.

That pulsing mass, so terrible, but so *captivating*.

The image of the pit. The twisting lines of the corridors. The tower that couldn't be completely seen. This was why she'd come.

Shallan strode forward, arm out, and let the illusory sleeve covering her hand vanish. She pulled off her glove, stepped right up to the mass of tar and voiceless screams.

Then pressed her safehand against it.

Listen to the words of a fool.

—From *Oathbringer*, preface

Shallan was open to this thing. Laid bare, her skin split, her soul gaping wide. It could get *in*.

It was also open to her.

She felt its confused fascination with humankind. It remembered men – an innate understanding, much as newborn mink kits innately knew to fear the skyeel. This spren was not completely aware, not completely cognizant. She was a creation of instinct and alien curiosity, drawn to violence and pain like scavengers to the scent of blood.

Shallan knew Re-Shephir at the same time as the thing came to know her. The spren tugged and prodded at Shallan's bond with Pattern, seeking to rip it free and insert herself instead. Pattern clung to Shallan, and she to him, holding on for dear life.

She fears us, Pattern's voice buzzed in her head. *Why does she fear us?*

In her mind's eye, Shallan envisioned herself holding tightly to Pattern in his humanoid form, the two of them huddled down before the spren's attack. That image was all she could see at the moment, for the room – and everything in it – had dissolved to black.

This thing was ancient. Created long ago as a splinter of the soul of something even more terrible, Re-Shephir had been ordered to sow chaos, spawning horrors to confuse and destroy men. Over time, slowly, she'd become increasingly intrigued by the things she murdered.

Her creations had come to imitate what she saw in the world, but lacking love or affection. Like stones come alive, content to be killed or to kill with no attachment or enjoyment. No emotions beyond an overpowering curiosity, and that ephemeral attraction to violence.

Almighty above . . . it's like a creationspren. Only so, so wrong.

Pattern whimpered, huddled against Shallan in his shape of a man with a stiff robe and a moving pattern for a head. She tried to shield him from the onslaught.

Fight every battle . . . as if there is . . . no backing down.

Shallan looked into the depths of the swirling void, the dark spinning soul of Re-Shephir, the Midnight Mother. Then, growling, Shallan struck.

She didn't attack like the prim, excitable girl who had been trained by cautious Vorin society. She attacked like the frenzied child who had murdered her mother. The cornered woman who had stabbed Tyn through the chest. She drew upon the part of her that hated the way everyone assumed she was so nice, so sweet. The part of her that hated being described as *diverting* or *clever.*

She drew upon the Stormlight within, and pushed herself farther into Re-Shephir's essence. She couldn't tell if it was actually happening – if she was pushing her physical body farther into the creature's tar – or if this was all a representation of someplace else. A place beyond this room in the tower, beyond even Shadesmar.

The creature trembled, and Shallan finally saw the reason for its fear. It had been trapped. The event had happened recently in the spren's reckoning, though Shallan had the impression that in fact centuries upon centuries had passed.

Re-Shephir was terrified of it happening again. The imprisonment had been unexpected, presumed impossible. And it had been done by a Lightweaver like Shallan, who had *understood* this creature.

It feared her like an axehound might fear someone with a voice similar to that of its harsh master.

Shallan hung on, pressing herself against the enemy, but realization washed over her – the understanding that this thing was going to know her completely, discover each and every one of her secrets.

Her ferocity and determination wavered; her commitment began to seep away.

So she lied. She insisted that she wasn't afraid. She was *committed*. She'd always been that way. She would continue that way forever.

Power could be an illusion of perception. Even within yourself.

Re-Shephir broke. It screeched, a sound that vibrated through Shallan. A screech that remembered its imprisonment and feared something worse.

Shallan dropped backward in the room where they'd been fighting. Adolin caught her in a steel grip, going down on one knee with an audible crack of Plate against stone. She heard that echoing scream fading. Not dying. Fleeing, escaping, determined to get as far from Shallan as it could.

When she forced her eyes open, she found the room clean of the darkness. The corpses of the midnight creatures had dissolved. Renarin quickly knelt next to a bridgeman who had been hurt, removing his gauntlet and infusing the man with healing Stormlight.

Adolin helped Shallan sit up, and she tucked her exposed safehand under her other arm. Storms . . . she'd somehow kept up the illusion of the havah.

Even after all of that, she didn't want Adolin to know of Veil. She *couldn't*.

'Where?' she asked him, exhausted. 'Where did it go?'

Adolin pointed toward the other side of the room, where a tunnel extended farther down into the depths of the mountain. 'It fled in that direction, like moving smoke.'

'So . . . should we chase it down?' Eth asked, making his way carefully toward the tunnel. His lantern revealed steps cut into the stone. 'This goes down a long ways.'

Shallan could feel a change in the air. The tower was . . . different. 'Don't give chase,' she said, remembering the terror of that conflict. She was more than happy to let the thing run. 'We can post guards in this chamber, but I don't think she'll return.'

'Yeah,' Teft said, leaning on his spear and wiping sweat from his face. 'Guards seem like a very, *very* good idea.'

Shallan frowned at the tone of his voice, then followed his gaze, to look at the thing Re-Shephir had been hiding. The pillar in the exact center of the room.

It was set with thousands upon thousands of cut gemstones, most larger than Shallan's fist. Together, they were a treasure worth more than most kingdoms.

If they cannot make you less foolish, at least let them give you hope.

—From *Oathbringer,* preface

Throughout his youth, Kaladin had dreamed of joining the military and leaving quiet little Hearthstone. Everyone knew that soldiers traveled extensively and saw the world.

And he had. He'd seen dozens upon dozens of empty hills, weed-covered plains, and identical warcamps. Actual sights, though ... well, that was another story.

The city of Revolar was, as his hike with the parshmen had proven, only a few weeks away from Hearthstone by foot. He'd never visited. Storms, he'd never actually lived in a *city* before, unless you counted the warcamps.

He suspected most cities weren't surrounded by an army of parshmen as this one was.

Revolar was built in a nice hollow on the leeward side of a series of hills, the perfect spot for a little town. Except this was not a 'little town.' The city had sprawled out, filling in the areas between the hills, going up the leeward slopes – only leaving the tips completely bare.

He'd expected a city to look more organized. He'd imagined neat rows of houses, like an efficient warcamp. This looked more like a snarl of plants clumped in a chasm at the Shattered Plains. Streets running this way and that. Markets that poked out haphazardly.

Kaladin joined his team of parshmen as they wound along a wide roadway kept level with smoothed crem. They passed through thousands upon *thousands* of parshmen camped here, and more gathered by the hour, it seemed.

His, however, was the only group that carried stone-headed spears on their shoulders, packs of dried grain biscuits, and hogshide leather sandals. They tied their smocks with belts, and carried stone knives, hatchets, and tinder in waxed sleeves made from candles he'd traded for. He'd even begun teaching them to use a sling.

He probably shouldn't have shown them any of these things; that didn't stop him from feeling proud as he walked with them, entering the city.

Crowds thronged the streets. Where had all these parshmen come from? This was a force of at least forty or fifty thousand. He knew most people ignored parshmen ... and, well, he'd done the same. But he'd always had tucked into the back of his mind this idea that there weren't *that* many out there. Each high-ranking lighteyes owned a handful. And a lot of the caravaneers. And, well, even the less wealthy families from cities or towns had them. And there were the dockworkers, the miners, the water haulers, the packmen they used when building large projects....

'It's amazing,' Sah said from where he walked beside Kaladin, carrying his daughter on his shoulder to give her a better view. She clutched some of his wooden cards, holding them close like another child might carry a favorite stuffed doll.

'Amazing?' Kaladin asked Sah.

'Our own city, Kal,' he whispered. 'During my time as a slave, barely able to think, I still dreamed. I tried to imagine what it would be like to have my own home, my own life. Here it is.'

The parshmen had obviously moved into homes along the streets here. Were they running markets too? It raised a difficult, unsettling question. Where were all the humans? Khen's group walked deeper into the city, still led by the unseen spren. Kaladin spotted signs of trouble. Broken windows. Doors that no longer latched. Some of that would be from the Everstorm, but he passed a couple of doors that had obviously been hacked open with axes.

Looting. And ahead stood an inner wall. It was a nice fortification, right in the middle of the city sprawl. It probably marked the original city boundary, as decided upon by some optimistic architect.

Here, at long last, Kaladin found signs of the fight he'd expected during his initial trip to Alethkar. The gates to the inner city lay broken. The guardhouse had been burned, and arrowheads still stuck from some of the wood beams they passed. This was a conquered city.

But where had the humans been moved? Should he be looking for a prison camp, or a heaping pyre of burned bones? Considering the idea made him sick.

'Is this what it's about?' Kaladin said as they walked down a roadway in the inner city. 'Is this what you want, Sah? To conquer the kingdom? Destroy humankind?'

'Storms, I don't know,' he said. 'But I can't be a slave again, Kal. I *won't* let them take Vai and imprison her. Would you defend them, after what they did to you?'

'They're my people.'

'That's no excuse. If one of "your people" murders another, don't you put them in prison? What is a just punishment for enslaving my entire race?'

Syl soared past, her face peeking from a shimmering haze of mist. She caught his eye, then zipped over to a windowsill and settled down, taking the shape of a small rock.

'I . . .' Kaladin said. 'I don't know, Sah. But a war to exterminate one side or the other can't be the answer.'

'You can fight alongside us, Kal. It doesn't have to be about humans against parshmen. It can be nobler than that. Oppressed against the oppressors.'

As they passed the place where Syl was, Kaladin swept his hand along the wall. Syl, as they'd practiced, zipped up the sleeve of his coat. He could feel her, like a gust of wind, move up his sleeve then out his collar, into his hair. The long curls hid her, they'd determined, well enough.

'There are a *lot* of those yellow-white spren here, Kaladin,' she whispered. 'Zipping through the air, dancing through buildings.'

'Any signs of humans?' Kaladin whispered.

'To the east,' she said. 'Crammed into some army barracks and old parshman quarters. Others are in big pens, watched under guard. Kaladin . . . there's another highstorm coming today.'

'When?'

'Soon, maybe? I'm new to guessing this. I doubt anyone is expecting it. Everything has been thrown off; the charts will all be wrong until people can make new ones.'

Kaladin hissed slowly through his teeth.

Ahead, his team approached a large group of parshmen. Judging by the way they'd been organized into large lines, this was some kind of processing station for new arrivals. Indeed, Khen's band of a hundred was shuffled into one of the lines to wait.

Ahead of them, a parshman in full carapace armor – like a Parshendi – strolled down the line, holding a writing board. Syl pulled farther into Kaladin's hair as the Parshendi man stepped up to Khen's group.

'What towns, work camps, or armies do you all come from?' His voice had a strange cadence, similar to the Parshendi Kaladin had heard on the Shattered Plains. Some of those in Khen's group had hints of it, but nothing this strong.

The scribe parshman wrote down the list of towns Khen gave him, then noted their spears. 'You've been busy. I'll recommend you for special training. Send your captive to the pens; I'll write down a description here, and once you're settled, you can put him to work.'

'He ...' Khen said, looking at Kaladin. 'He is not our captive.' She seemed begrudging. 'He was one of the humans' slaves, like us. He wishes to join and fight.'

The parshman looked up in the air at nothing.

'Yixli is speaking for you,' Sah whispered to Kaladin. 'She sounds impressed.'

'Well,' the scribe said, 'it's not unheard of, but you'll have to get permission from one of the Fused to label him free.'

'One of the what?' Khen asked.

The parshman with the writing board pointed toward his left. Kaladin had to step out of the line, along with several of the others, to see a tall parshwoman with long hair. There was carapace covering her cheeks, running back along the cheekbones and into her hair. The skin on her arms prickled with ridges, as if there were carapace *under* the skin as well. Her eyes glowed red.

Kaladin's breath caught. Bridge Four had described these creatures to him, the strange Parshendi they'd fought during their push toward the center of the Shattered Plains. These were the beings who had summoned the Everstorm.

This one focused directly on Kaladin. There was something oppressive about her red gaze.

Kaladin heard a clap of thunder in the far distance. Around him, many of the parshmen turned toward it and began to mutter. Highstorm.

In that moment, Kaladin made his decision. He'd stayed with Sah and the others as long as he dared. He'd learned what he could. The storm presented a chance.

It's time to go.

The tall, dangerous creature with the red eyes – the Fused, they had called her – began walking toward Khen's group. Kaladin couldn't know if she recognized him as a Radiant, but he had no intention of waiting until she arrived. He'd been planning; the old slave's instincts had already decided upon the easiest way out.

It was on Khen's belt.

Kaladin sucked in the Stormlight, right from her pouch. He burst alight with its power, then grabbed the pouch – he'd need those gemstones – and yanked it free, the leather strap snapping.

'Get your people to shelter,' Kaladin said to the surprised Khen. 'A highstorm is close. Thank you for your kindness. No matter what you are told, know this: I do not wish to be your enemy.'

The Fused began to scream with an angry voice. Kaladin met Sah's betrayed expression, then launched himself into the air.

Freedom.

Kaladin's skin shivered with joy. Storms, how he'd missed this. The wind, the openness above, even the lurch in his stomach as gravity let go. Syl spun around him as a ribbon of light, creating a spiral of glowing lines. Gloryspren burst up about Kaladin's head.

Syl took on the form of a person just so she could glower at the little bobbing balls of light. 'Mine,' she said, swatting one of them aside.

About five or six hundred feet up, Kaladin changed to a half Lashing, so he slowed and hovered in the sky. Beneath, that red-eyed parshwoman was gesturing and screaming, though Kaladin couldn't hear her. Storms. He hoped this wouldn't mean trouble for Sah and the others.

He had an excellent view of the city – the streets filled with figures, now making for shelter in buildings. Other groups rushed to the city from all directions. Even after spending so much time with them, his first reaction was one of discomfort. So many parshmen together in one place? It was unnatural.

This impression bothered him now as it never would have before.

He eyed the stormwall, which he could see approaching in the far distance. He still had time before it arrived.

He'd have to fly up above the storm to avoid being caught in its winds. But then what?

'Urithiru is out there somewhere, to the west,' Kaladin said. 'Can you guide us there?'

'How would I do that?'

'You've been there before.'

'So have you.'

'You're a force of nature, Syl,' Kaladin said. 'You can feel the storms. Don't you have some kind of . . . location sense?'

'*You're* the one from this realm,' she said, batting away another glory-spren and hanging in the air beside him, folding her arms. 'Besides, I'm less a force of nature and more one of the raw powers of creation transformed by collective human imagination into a personification of one of their ideals.' She grinned at him.

'Where did you come up with *that*?'

'Dunno. Maybe I heard it somewhere once. Or maybe I'm just *smart*.'

'We'll have to make for the Shattered Plains, then,' Kaladin said. 'We can strike out for one of the larger cities in southern Alethkar, swap gemstones there, and hopefully have enough to hop over to the warcamps.'

That decided, he tied his gemstone pouch to his belt, then glanced down and tried to make a final estimate of troop numbers and parshman fortifications. It felt odd to not worry about the storm, but he'd just move up over it once it arrived.

From up here, Kaladin could see the great trenches cut into the stones to divert away floodwaters after a storm. Though most of the parshmen had fled for shelter, some remained below, craning necks and staring up at him. He read betrayal in their postures, though he couldn't even tell if these were members of Khen's group or not.

'What?' Syl asked, alighting on his shoulder.

'I can't help but feel a kinship to them, Syl.'

'They conquered the city. They're *Voidbringers*.'

'No, they're people. And they're *angry*, with good reason.' A gust of wind blew across him, making him drift to the side. 'I know that feeling. It burns in you, worms inside your brain until you forget everything but the injustice done to you. It's how I felt about Elhokar. Sometimes a world of rational explanations can become meaningless in the face of that all-consuming desire to *get what you deserve*.'

'You changed your mind about Elhokar, Kaladin. You saw what was right.'

'Did I? Did I find what was *right*, or did I just finally agree to see things the way you wanted?'

'Killing Elhokar *was* wrong.'

'And the parshmen on the Shattered Plains that I killed? Murdering them wasn't wrong?'

'You were protecting Dalinar.'

'Who was assaulting their homeland.'

'Because they killed his brother.'

'Which, for all we know, they did because they saw how King Gavilar and his people treated the parshmen.' Kaladin turned toward Syl, who sat on his shoulder, one leg tucked beneath her. 'So what's the difference, Syl? What is the difference between Dalinar attacking the parshmen, and these parshmen conquering that city?'

'I don't know,' she said softly.

'And why was it worse for me to *let* Elhokar be killed for his injustices than it was for me to actively kill parshmen on the Shattered Plains?'

'One is wrong. I mean, it just feels wrong. Both do, I guess.'

'Except one nearly broke my bond, while the other didn't. The bond isn't about what's right and wrong, is it, Syl. It's about what *you see* as right and wrong.'

'What *we* see,' she corrected. 'And about oaths. You swore to protect Elhokar. Tell me that during your time planning to betray Elhokar, you didn't – deep down – think you were doing something wrong.'

'Fine. But it's still about perception.' Kaladin let the winds blow him, feeling a pit open in his belly. 'Storms, I'd hoped ... I'd hoped you could tell me, give me an absolute *right*. For once, I'd like my moral code not to come with a list of exceptions at the end.'

She nodded thoughtfully.

'I'd have expected you to object,' Kaladin said. 'You're a ... what, embodiment of human perceptions of honor? Shouldn't you at least *think* you have all the answers?'

'Probably,' she said. 'Or maybe if there are answers, I should be the one who wants to find them.'

The stormwall was now fully visible: the great wall of water and refuse pushed by the oncoming winds of a highstorm. Kaladin had drifted along with the winds away from the city, so he Lashed himself eastward until they floated over the hills that made up the city's windbreak. Here, he spotted something he hadn't seen earlier: pens full of great masses of humans.

The winds blowing in from the east were growing stronger. However, the parshmen guarding the pens were just standing there, as if nobody had given them orders to move. The first rumblings of the highstorm had been distant, easy to miss. They'd notice it soon, but that might be too late.

'Oh!' Syl said. 'Kaladin, those people!'

Kaladin cursed, then dropped the Lashing holding him upward, which made him fall in a rush. He crashed to the ground, sending out a puff of glowing Stormlight that expanded from him in a ring.

'Highstorm!' he shouted at the parshman guards. 'Highstorm coming! Get these people to safety!'

They looked at him, dumbfounded. Not a surprising reaction. Kaladin summoned his Blade, shoving past the parshmen and leaping up onto the pen's low stone wall, for keeping hogs.

He held aloft the Sylblade. Townspeople swarmed to the wall. Cries of 'Shardbearer' rose.

'A highstorm is coming!' he shouted, but his voice was quickly lost in the tumult of voices. Storms. He had little doubt that the Voidbringers could handle a group of rioting townsfolk.

He sucked in more Stormlight, raising himself into the air. That quieted them, even drove them backward.

'Where did you shelter,' he demanded in a loud voice, 'when the last storms came?'

A few people near the front pointed at the large bunkers nearby. For housing livestock, parshmen, and even travelers during storms. Could those hold an entire town's worth of people? Maybe if they crowded in.

'Get moving!' Kaladin said. 'A storm will be here soon.'

Kaladin, Syl's voice said in his mind. *Behind you.*

He turned and found parshman guards approaching his wall with spears. Kaladin hopped down as the townspeople finally reacted, climbing the walls, which were barely chest high and slathered with smooth, hardened crem.

Kaladin took one step toward the parshmen, then swiped his Blade, separating their spearheads from the hafts. The parshmen – who had barely more training than the ones he'd traveled with – stepped back in confusion.

'Do you want to fight me?' Kaladin asked them.

One shook her head.

'Then see that those people don't trample each other in their haste to get to safety,' Kaladin said, pointing. 'And keep the rest of the guards from attacking them. This isn't a revolt. Can't you hear the thunder, and feel the wind picking up?'

He launched himself onto the wall again, then waved for the people to move, shouting orders. The parshman guards eventually decided that instead of fighting a Shardbearer, they'd risk getting into trouble for doing what he said. Before too long, he had an entire team of them prodding the humans – often less gently than he'd have liked – toward the storm bunkers.

Kaladin dropped down beside one of the guards, a female whose spear he'd sliced in half. 'How did this work the last time the storm hit?'

'We mostly left the humans to themselves,' she admitted. 'We were too busy running for safety.'

So the Voidbringers hadn't anticipated that storm's arrival either. Kaladin winced, trying not to dwell on how many people had likely been lost to the impact of the stormwall.

'Do better,' he said to her. 'These people are your charge now. You've seized the city, taken what you want. If you wish to claim any kind of moral superiority, treat your captives better than they did you.'

'Look,' the parshwoman said. 'Who *are* you? And why—'

Something large crashed into Kaladin, tossing him backward into the wall with a *crunch*. The thing had arms; a person who grasped for his throat, trying to strangle him. He kicked them off; their eyes trailed red.

A blackish-violet glow – like *dark Stormlight* – rose from the red-eyed parshman. Kaladin cursed and Lashed himself into the air.

The creature followed.

Another rose nearby, leaving a faint violet glow behind, flying as easily as he did. These two looked different from the one he'd seen earlier, leaner, with longer hair. Syl cried out in his mind, a sound like pain and surprise mixed. He could only assume that someone had run to fetch these, after he had taken to the sky.

A few windspren zipped past Kaladin, then began to dance playfully around him. The sky grew dark, the stormwall thundering across the land. Those red-eyed Parshendi chased him upward.

So Kaladin Lashed himself straight toward the storm.

It had worked against the Assassin in White. The highstorm was dangerous, but it was also something of an ally. The two creatures followed, though they overshot his elevation and had to Lash themselves back downward in a weird bobbing motion. They reminded him of his first experimentation with his powers.

Kaladin braced himself – holding to the Sylblade, joined by four or five windspren – and crashed through the stormwall. An unstable darkness swallowed him; a darkness that was often split by lightning and broken by phantom glows. Winds contorted and clashed like rival armies, so irregular that Kaladin was tossed by them one way, then the other. It took all his skill in Lashing to simply get going in the right direction.

He watched over his shoulder as the two red-eyed parshmen burst in. Their strange glow was more subdued than his own, and somehow gave off the impression of an *anti*-glow. A darkness that clung to them.

They were immediately disrupted, sent spinning in the wind. Kaladin smiled, then was nearly crushed by a boulder tumbling through the air. Sheer luck saved him; the boulder passed close enough that another few inches would have ripped off his arm.

Kaladin Lashed himself upward, soaring through the tempest toward its ceiling. 'Stormfather!' he yelled. 'Spren of storms!'

No response.

'Turn yourself aside!' Kaladin shouted into the churning winds. 'There are people below! Stormfather. You *must* listen to me!'

All grew still.

Kaladin stood in that strange space where he'd seen the Stormfather before – a place that seemed outside of reality. The ground was far beneath him, dim, slicked with rain, but barren and empty. Kaladin hovered in the air. Not Lashed; the air was simply solid beneath him.

WHO ARE YOU TO MAKE DEMANDS OF THE STORM, SON OF HONOR?

The Stormfather was a face as wide as the sky, dominating like a sunrise.

Kaladin held his sword aloft. 'I know you for what you are, Storm-father. A spren, like Syl.'

I AM THE MEMORY OF A GOD, THE FRAGMENT THAT REMAINS. THE SOUL OF A STORM AND THE MIND OF ETERNITY.

'Then surely with that soul, mind, and memory,' Kaladin said, 'you can find mercy for the people below.'

AND WHAT OF THE HUNDREDS OF THOUSANDS WHO HAVE DIED IN THESE WINDS BEFORE? SHOULD I HAVE HAD MERCY FOR THEM?

'Yes.'

AND THE WAVES THAT SWALLOW, THE FIRES THAT CONSUME? YOU WOULD HAVE THEM STOP?

'I speak only of you, and only today. Please.'

Thunder rumbled. And the Stormfather actually seemed to *consider* the request.

IT IS NOT SOMETHING I CAN DO, SON OF TANAVAST. IF THE WIND STOPS BLOWING, IT IS NOT A WIND. IT IS NOTHING.

'But—'

Kaladin dropped back into the tempest proper, and it seemed as if no time had passed. He ducked through the winds, gritting his teeth in frustration. Windspren accompanied him – he had two dozen now, a spinning and laughing group, each a ribbon of light.

He passed one of the glowing-eyed parshmen. The Fused? Did that term refer to all whose eyes glowed?

'The Stormfather really could be more helpful, Syl. Didn't he claim to be your father?'

It's complicated, she said in his mind. *He's stubborn though. I'm sorry.*

'He's callous,' Kaladin said.

He's a storm, Kaladin. As people over millennia have imagined him.

'He could choose.'

Perhaps. Perhaps not. I think what you're doing is like asking fire to please stop being so hot.

Kaladin zoomed down along the ground, quickly reaching the hills around Revolar. He had hoped to find that everyone was safe, but that was – of course – a frail hope. People were scattered across the pens and the ground near the bunkers. One of those bunkers still had the doors open, and a few men were trying – bless them – to gather the last people outside and carry them in.

Many were too far away. They huddled against the ground, holding to the wall or outcroppings of rock. Kaladin could barely make them out in flashes of lightning – terrified lumps alone in the tempest.

He had felt those winds. He'd been powerless before them, tied to the side of a building.

Kaladin . . . Syl said in his mind as he dropped.

The storm pulsed inside him. Within the highstorm, his Stormlight constantly renewed. It preserved him, had saved his life a dozen times over. That very power that had tried to kill him had been his salvation.

He hit the ground and dropped Syl, then seized the form of a young father clutching a son. He pulled them up, holding them secure, trying to run them toward the building. Nearby, another person – he couldn't see much of them – was torn away in a gust of wind and taken by the darkness.

Kaladin, you can't save them all.

He screamed as he grabbed another person, holding her tight and walking with them. They stumbled in the wind as they reached a cluster of people huddled together. Some two dozen or more, in the shadow of the wall around the pens.

Kaladin pulled the three he was helping – the father, the child, the woman – over to the others. 'You can't stay out here!' he shouted at them all. 'Together. You have to walk together, this way!'

With effort – winds howling, rain pelting like daggers – he got the group moving across the stony ground, arm in arm. They made good progress until a boulder crunched to the ground nearby, sending some of them huddling down in a panic. The wind rose, lifting some people up; only the clutching hands of the others kept them from blowing away.

Kaladin blinked away tears that mingled with the rain. He bellowed. Nearby, a flash of light illuminated a man being crushed as a portion of wall ripped away and towed his body off into the storm.

Kaladin, Syl said. *I'm sorry.*

'Being sorry isn't enough!' he yelled.

He clung with one arm to a child, his face toward the storm and its terrible winds. Why did it destroy? This tempest shaped them. Must it ruin them too? Consumed by his pain and feelings of betrayal, Kaladin surged with Stormlight and flung his hand forward as if to try to push back the wind itself.

A hundred windspren spun in as lines of light, twisting around his arm, wrapping it like ribbons. They surged with Light, then exploded outward in a blinding sheet, sweeping to Kaladin's sides and parting the winds around him.

Kaladin stood with his hand toward the tempest, and *deflected it*. Like a stone in a swift-moving river stopped the waters, he opened a pocket in the storm, creating a calm wake behind him.

The storm raged against him, but he held the point in a formation of windspren that spread from him like wings, diverting the storm. He managed to turn his head as the storm battered him. People huddled behind him, soaked, confused – surrounded by calm.

'Go!' he shouted. '*Go!*'

They found their feet, the young father taking his son back from Kaladin's leeward arm. Kaladin backed up with them, maintaining the windbreak. This group was only some of those trapped by the winds, yet it took everything Kaladin had to hold the tempest.

The winds seemed angry at him for his defiance. All it would take was one boulder.

A figure with glowing red eyes landed on the field before him. It advanced, but the people had finally reached the bunker. Kaladin sighed and released the winds, and the spren behind him scattered. Exhausted, he let the storm pick him up and fling him away. A quick Lashing gave him elevation, preventing him from being rammed into the buildings of the city.

Wow, Syl said in his mind. *What did you just do? With the storm?*

'Not enough,' Kaladin whispered.

You'll never be able to do enough to satisfy yourself, Kaladin. That was still wonderful.

He was past Revolar in a heartbeat. He turned, becoming merely another piece of debris on the winds. The Fused gave chase, but lagged behind, then vanished. Kaladin and Syl pushed out of the stormwall, then rode it at the front of the storm. They passed over cities, plains, mountains – never running out of Stormlight, for there was a source renewing them from behind.

They flew for a good hour like that before a current in the winds nudged him toward the south.

'Go that way,' Syl said, a ribbon of light.

'Why?'

'Just listen to the piece of nature incarnate, okay? I think Father wants to apologize, in his own way.'

Kaladin growled, but allowed the winds to channel him in a specific direction. He flew this way for hours, lost in the sounds of the tempest, until finally he settled down – half of his own volition, half because of the pressing winds. The storm passed – leaving him in the middle of a large, open field of rock.

The plateau in front of the tower city of Urithiru.

For I, of all people, have changed.

—From *Oathbringer*, preface

Shallan settled in Sebarial's sitting room. It was a strangely shaped stone chamber with a loft above – he sometimes put musicians there – and a shallow cavity in the floor, which he kept saying he was going to fill with water and fish. She was fairly certain he made claims like that just to annoy Dalinar with his supposed extravagance.

For now, they'd covered the hole with some boards, and Sebarial would periodically warn people not to step on them. The rest of the room was decorated lavishly. She was pretty sure she'd seen those tapestries in a monastery in Dalinar's warcamp, and they were matched by luxurious furniture, golden lamps, and ceramics.

And a bunch of splintery boards covering a pit. She shook her head. Then – curled up on a sofa with blankets heaped over her – she gladly accepted a cup of steaming citrus tea from Palona. She still hadn't been able to rid herself of the lingering chill she'd felt since her encounter with Re-Shephir a few hours back.

'Is there anything else I can get you?' Palona asked.

Shallan shook her head, so the Herdazian woman settled herself on a sofa nearby, holding another cup of tea. Shallan sipped, glad for the company. Adolin had wanted her to sleep, but the last thing she wanted was to be alone. He'd handed her over to Palona's care, then stayed with Dalinar and Navani to answer their further questions.

'So . . .' Palona said. 'What was it like?'

How to answer *that*? She'd touched the storming *Midnight Mother*. A name from ancient lore, one of the Unmade, princes of the Voidbringers. People sang about Re-Shephir in poetry and epics, describing her as a dark, beautiful figure. Paintings depicted her as a black-clad woman with red eyes and a sultry gaze.

That seemed to exemplify how little they really remembered about these things.

'It wasn't like the stories,' Shallan whispered. 'Re-Shephir is a spren. A vast, terrible spren who wants so *desperately* to understand us. So she kills us, imitating our violence.'

There was a deeper mystery beyond that, a wisp of something she'd glimpsed while intertwined with Re-Shephir. It made Shallan wonder if this spren wasn't merely trying to understand humankind, but rather searching for something *it itself had lost*.

Had this creature – in distant, distant time beyond memory – once been human?

They didn't know. They didn't know *anything*. At Shallan's first report, Navani had set her scholars searching for information, but their access to books here was still limited. Even with access to the Palanaeum, Shallan wasn't optimistic. Jasnah had hunted for years to find Urithiru, and even then most of what she'd discovered had been unreliable. It had simply been too many years.

'To think it was here, all this time,' Palona said. 'Hiding down there.'

'She was captive,' Shallan whispered. 'She eventually escaped, but that was centuries ago. She has been waiting here ever since.'

'Well, we should find where the others are held, and make sure *they* don't get out.'

'I don't know if the others were ever captured.' She'd felt isolation and loneliness from Re-Shephir, a sense of being torn away while the others escaped.

'So ...'

'They're out there, and always have been,' Shallan said. She felt exhausted, and her eyes were drooping in direct defiance of her insistence to Adolin that she was not *that* kind of tired.

'Surely we'd have discovered them by now.'

'I don't know,' Shallan said. 'They'll ... they'll just be normal to us. The way things have always been.'

She yawned, then nodded absently as Palona continued talking, her comments degenerating into praise of Shallan for acting as she had. Adolin had been the same way, which she hadn't minded, and Dalinar had been downright nice to her – instead of being his usual stern rock of a human being.

She didn't tell them how near she'd come to breaking, and how terrified she was that she might someday meet that creature again.

But ... maybe she did deserve some acclaim. She'd been a child when she'd left her home, seeking salvation for her family. For the first time since that day on the ship, watching Jah Keved fade behind her, she felt like she actually might have a handle on all of this. Like she might have found some stability in her life, some control over herself and her surroundings.

Remarkably, she *kind of* felt like an adult.

She smiled and snuggled into her blankets, drinking her tea and – for the moment – putting out of her mind that basically an entire troop of soldiers had seen her with her glove off. She was *kind of* an adult. She could deal with a little embarrassment. In fact, she was increasingly certain that between Shallan, Veil, and Radiant, she could deal with anything life could throw at her.

A disturbance outside made her sit up, though it didn't sound dangerous. Some chatter, a few boisterous exclamations. She wasn't terribly surprised when Adolin stepped in, bowed to Palona – he did have nice manners – and jogged over to her, his uniform still rumpled from having worn Shardplate over it.

'Don't panic,' he said. 'It's a good thing.'

'It?' she said, growing alarmed.

'Well, someone just arrived at the tower.'

'Oh, that. Sebarial passed the news; the bridgeboy is back.'

'Him? No, that's not what I'm talking about.' Adolin searched for words as voices approached, and several other people stepped into the room.

At their head was Jasnah Kholin.

THE END OF

Part One

INTERLUDES

⬧⬧

PUULI • ELLISTA • VENLI

PUULI

uuli the lighthouse keeper tried not to let everyone know how excited he was for this new storm.

It was truly tragic. Truly tragic. He told Sakin this as she wept. She had thought herself quite high and blessed when she'd landed her new husband. She'd moved into the man's fine stone hut in a prime spot for growing a garden, behind the northern cliffs of the town.

Puuli gathered scraps of wood blown eastward by the strange storm, and piled them in his little cart. He pulled it with two hands, leaving Sakin to weep for her husband. Up to three now, she was, all lost at sea. Truly tragic.

Still, he was excited for the storm.

He pulled his cart past other broken homes here, where they should have been sheltered west of the cliffs. Puuli's grandfather had been able to remember when those cliffs hadn't been there. Kelek himself had broken apart the land in the middle of a storm, making a new prime spot for homes.

Where would the rich people put their houses now?

And they did have rich people here in town, never mind what the travelers on the ocean said. Those would stop at this little port, on the crumbling eastern edge of Roshar, and shelter from storms in their cove alongside the cliffs.

Puuli pulled his cart past the cove. Here, one of the foreigner captains – with long eyebrows and tan skin, rather than the proper blue skin – was trying to make sense of her ruined ship. It had been rocked in the cove, struck by lightning, then smashed back against the stones. Now only the mast was visible.

Truly tragic, Puuli said. He complimented the captain on the mast though. It was a very nice mast.

Puuli picked up a few planks from the broken ship that had washed onto the shore of the cove, then threw them into his cart. Even if it had destroyed many a ship, Puuli was happy for this new storm. Secretly happy.

Had the time finally come, that his grandfather had warned of? The time of changes, when the men from the hidden island of the Origin at last came to reclaim Natanatan?

Even if not, this new storm brought him so much *wood*. Scraps of rockbuds, branches from trees. He gathered it all eagerly, piling his cart high, then pulled it past fishers in huddles, trying to decide how they'd survive in a world with storms from both directions. Fishers didn't sleep away the Weeping, like lazy farmers. They worked it, for there were no winds. Lots of bailing, but no winds. Until now.

A tragedy, he told Au-lam while helping him clear the refuse of his barn. Many of the boards ended up in Puuli's cart.

A tragedy, he agreed with Hema-Dak as he watched her children so she could run a broth to her sister, who was sick with the fever.

A tragedy, he told the Drummer brothers as he helped them pull a tattered sail from the surf and stretch it out on the rocks.

At last, Puuli finished his rounds and pulled his little cart up the long, twisting road toward Defiance. That was his name for the lighthouse. Nobody else called it that, because to them it was just the lighthouse.

At the top, he left out an offering of fruit for Kelek, the Herald who lived in the storm. Then he pulled his wagon into the room on the bottom floor. Defiance wasn't a tall lighthouse. He'd seen paintings of the sleek, fashionable ones down along Longbrow's Straits. Lighthouses for rich folks who sailed ships that didn't catch fish. Defiance was only two stories tall, and built squat like a bunker. But she had good stonework, and a buffer of crem on the outside kept her from leaking.

She'd stood for over a hundred years, and Kelek hadn't decided to knock her down. The Stormfather knew how important she was. Puuli carried a load of wet stormwood and broken boards up to the top of the lighthouse, where he set them out beside the fire – which burned low during the day – to dry. He dusted off his hands, then stepped up to the rim of the lighthouse. At night, the mirrors would shine the light right out through this hole.

He looked over the cliffs, to the east. His family was a lot like the lighthouse themselves. Squat, short, but powerful. And enduring.

They'll come with Light in their pockets, Grandfather had said. *They'll come to destroy, but you should watch for them anyway. Because they'll come from the Origin. The sailors lost on an infinite sea. You keep that fire high at night, Puuli. You burn it bright until the day they come.*

They'll arrive when the night is darkest.

Surely that was now, with a new storm. Darkest nights. A tragedy. And a sign.

ELLISTA

The Jokasha Monastery was ordinarily a very quiet place. Nestled in the forests on the western slopes of the Horneater Peaks, the monastery felt only rain at the passing of a highstorm. Furious rain, yes, but none of the terrible violence known in most parts of the world.

Ellista reminded herself every passing storm how lucky she was. Some ardents had fought half their lives to be transferred to Jokasha. Away from politics, storms, and other annoyances, at Jokasha you could simply *think*.

Usually.

'Are you *looking* at these numbers? Are your eyes *disconnected* from your brain?'

'We can't judge yet. Three instances are not enough!'

'Two data points to make a coincidence, three to make a sequence. The Everstorm travels at a consistent speed, unlike the highstorm.'

'You can't possibly say that! One of your data points, so highly touted, is from the original passing of the storm, which happened as an uncommon event.'

Ellista slammed her book closed and stuffed it into her satchel. She burst from her reading nook and gave a glare to the two ardents arguing in the hall outside, both wearing the caps of master scholars. They were so involved in their shouting match that they didn't even respond to the glare, though it had been one of her best.

She bustled from the library, entering a long hallway with sides open to the elements. Peaceful trees. A quiet brook. Humid air and mossy vines that popped and stretched as they lay out for the evening. Well, yes, a large swath of trees out there *had* been flattened by the new storm. But that was no reason for everyone to get upset! The rest of the world could worry. Here, at the central home of the Devotary of the Mind, she was supposed to be able to just read.

She set her things out at a reading desk near an open window. The humidity wasn't good for books, but weak storms went hand-in-hand with fecundity. You simply had to accept that. Hopefully those new fabrials to draw water from the air would—

'. . . Telling you, we're going to have to move!' a new voice echoed through the hallway. 'Look, the storm is going to ravage those woods. Before long, this slope will be barren, and the storm will be hitting us full force.'

'The new storm doesn't have that strong a wind factor, Bettam. It's *not* going to blow down the trees. Have you looked at my measurements?'

'I've disputed those measurements.'

'But—'

Ellista rubbed her temples. She wore her head shaved, like the other ardents. Her parents still joked that she'd joined the ardentia simply because she hated bothering with her hair. She tried earplugs, but could hear the arguing through them, so she packed up her things again.

Maybe the low building? She took the long set of steps outside, traveling down the slope along a forested path. Before arriving at the monastery for the first time, she'd had illusions about what it would be like to live among scholars. No bickering. No politicking. She hadn't found that to be true – but generally people left her alone. And so she was lucky to be here. She told herself that again as she entered the lower building.

It was basically a zoo. Dozens of people gathering information from spanreeds, talking to one another, buzzing with talk of this or that high-prince or king. She stopped in the doorway, took it all in for a moment, then turned on her heel and stalked back out.

Now what? She started back up the steps, but slowed. *It's probably the only route to peace . . .* she thought, looking out into the forest.

Trying not to think about the dirt, the cremlings, and the fact that something might drip on her head, she strode off into the forest. She didn't want to go too far, as who knew what might be out here? She chose a stump without *too* much moss on it and settled down among bobbing lifespren, book across her lap.

She could still hear ardents arguing, but they were distant. She opened her book, intent on finally getting something done today.

Wema spun away from Brightlord Sterling's forward advances, tucking her safehand to her breast and lowering her gaze from his comely locks. Such affection as to excite the unsavory mind could surely not satisfy her for an extended period, as though his attentions had at one time been fanciful delights to entertain her leisure hours, they now seemed to manifest his utmost impudence and greatest faults of character.

'What!' Ellista exclaimed, reading. 'No, you silly girl! He's finally pronounced his affection for you. Don't you dare turn away now.'

How could she accept this wanton justification of her once single-minded desires? Should she not, instead, select the more prudent choice, as advocated by the undeviating will of her uncle? Brightlord Vadam had an endowment of land upon the highprince's grace, and would have means to provide far beyond the satisfactions available to a simple officer, no matter how well regarded or what winds had graced his temperament, features, and gentle touch.

Ellista gasped. 'Brightlord *Vadam*? You little whore! Have you forgotten how he locked away your father?'

'Wema,' Brightlord Sterling intoned, 'it seems I have gravely misjudged your attentions. In this, I find myself deposited deep within an embarrassment of folly. I shall be away, to the Shattered Plains, and you shall not again suffer the torment of my presence.'

He bowed a true gentleman's bow, possessed of all proper refinement and deference. It was a supplication beyond what even a monarch could rightly demand, and in it Wema ascertained the true nature of Brightlord Sterling's regard. Simple, yet passionate. Respectful in deed. It lent great context to his earlier advance, which now appeared all at once to be a righteous division in otherwise sure armor, a window of vulnerability, rather than a model of avarice.

As he lifted the door's latch to forever make his exodus from her life, Wema surged with unrivaled shame and longing, twisted together not unlike two threads winding in a loom to construct a grand tapestry of desire.

'Wait!' Wema cried. 'Dear Sterling, wait upon my words.'

'Storms right you'd better wait, Sterling.' Ellista leaned closer to the book, flipping the page.

Decorum seemed a vain thing to her now, lost upon the sea that was her need to feel Sterling's touch. She rushed to him, and upon his arm pressed her ensleeved hand, which then she lifted to caress his sturdy jaw.

It was so warm out here in the forest. Practically sweltering. Ellista put her hand to her lips, reading with wide eyes, trembling.

Would that the window through that statuesque armor could still be located, and that a similar wound within herself might be found, to press against his own and offer passage deep within her soul. If only—

'Ellista?' a voice asked.

'Yip!' she said, bolting upright, snapping the book closed, and spun toward the sound. 'Um. Oh! Ardent Urv.' The young Siln ardent was tall, gangly, and obnoxiously loud at times. Except, apparently, when sneaking up on colleagues in the forest.

'What was that you were studying?' he asked.

'Important works,' Ellista said, then sat on the book. 'Nothing to mind yourself with. What is it you want?'

'Um ...' He looked down at her satchel. 'You were the last one to check out the transcriptions from Bendthel's collected Dawnchant? The old versions? I just wanted to check on your progress.'

Dawnchant. Right. They'd been working on that before this storm came, and everyone got distracted. Old Navani Kholin, in Alethkar, had somehow cracked the Dawnchant. Her story about visions was nonsense – the Kholin family was known for opaque politics – but her key was authentic, and had let them slowly work through the old texts.

363

Ellista started digging in her satchel. She came up with three musty codices and a sheaf of papers, the latter being the work she'd done so far.

Annoyingly, Urv settled on the ground beside her stump, taking the papers as she offered them. He laid his satchel across his lap and began reading.

'Incredible,' he said a few moments later. 'You've made more progress than I have.'

'Everyone else is too busy worrying about that storm.'

'Well, it *is* threatening to wipe out civilization.'

'An overreaction. Everyone always overreacts to every little gust of wind.'

He flipped through her pages. 'What's this section? Why take such care for where each text was found? Fiksin concluded that these Dawnchant books had all spread from a central location, and so there's nothing to learn by where they ended up.'

'Fiksin was a boot-licker, not a scholar,' Ellista said. 'Look, there's *easy* proof here that the same writing system was once used all across Roshar. I have references in Makabakam, Sela Tales, Alethela ... Not a diaspora of texts, but real evidence they wrote naturally in the Dawnchant.'

'Do you suppose they all spoke the same language?'

'Hardly.'

'But Jasnah Kholin's *Relic and Monument*?'

'Doesn't claim everyone spoke the same language, only that they wrote it. It's foolish to assume that everyone used the same language across hundreds of years and dozens of nations. It makes more sense that there was a codified *written* language, the language of scholarship, just like you'll find many undertexts written in Alethi now.'

'Ah ...' he said. 'And then a Desolation hit. ...'

Ellista nodded, showing him a later page in her sheaf of notes. 'This in-between, weird language is where people started using the Dawnchant script to *phonetically* transcribe their language. It didn't work so well.' She flipped two more pages. 'In this scrap we have one of the earliest emergences of the proto-Thaylo-Vorin glyphic radicals, and here is one showing a more intermediate Thaylen form.

'We've always wondered what happened to the Dawnchant. How could people forget how to read their own language? Well, it seems clear now. By the point this happened, the language had been moribund for millennia. They weren't speaking it, and hadn't been for generations.'

'Brilliant,' Urv said. He wasn't so bad, for a Siln. 'I've been translating what I can, but got stuck on the Covad Fragment. If what you've been doing here is correct, it might be because Covad isn't true Dawnchant, but a phonetic transcription of another ancient language. . . .'

He glanced to the side, then cocked his head. Was he looking at her—

Oh, no. It was just the book, which she was still sitting on.

'*An Accountability of Virtue.*' He grunted. 'Good book.'

'You've *read* it?'

'I have a fondness for Alethi epics,' he said absently, flipping through her pages. 'She really should have picked Vadam though. Sterling was a flatterer and a cadger.'

'Sterling is a noble and upright officer!' She narrowed her eyes. 'And *you* are just trying to get a rise out of me, Ardent Urv.'

'Maybe.' He flipped through her pages, studying a diagram she'd made of various Dawnchant grammars. 'I have a copy of the sequel.'

'There's a *sequel*?'

'About her sister.'

'The mousy one?'

'She is elevated to courtly attention and has to choose between a strapping naval officer, a Thaylen banker, and the King's Wit.'

'Wait. There are *three* different men this time?'

'Sequels always have to be bigger,' he said, then offered her the stack of pages back. 'I'll lend it to you.'

'Oh you will, will you? And what is the cost for this magnanimous gesture, Brightlord Urv?'

'Your help translating a stubborn section of Dawnchant. A particular patron of mine has a strict deadline upon its delivery.'

I-3

THE RHYTHM OF THE LOST

Venli attuned the Rhythm of Craving as she climbed down into the chasm. This wondrous new form, stormform, gave her hands a powerful grip, allowing her to hang hundreds of feet in the air, yet never fear that she would fall.

The chitin plating under her skin was far less bulky than that of the old warform, but at the same time nearly as effective. During the summoning of the Everstorm, a human soldier had struck her directly across the face. His spear had cut her cheek and across the bridge of her nose, but the mask of chitin armor underneath had deflected the weapon.

She continued to climb down the wall of stone, followed by Demid, her once-mate, and a group of her loyal friends. In her mind she attuned the Rhythm of Command – a similar, yet more powerful version of the Rhythm of Appreciation. Every one of her people could hear the rhythms – beats with some tones attached – yet she no longer heard the old, common ones. Only these new, superior rhythms.

Beneath her the chasm opened, where water from highstorms had carved a bulge. She eventually reached the bottom, and the others dropped around her, each landing with a thumping crunch. Ulim moved down the stone wall; the spren usually took the form of rolling lightning, moving across surfaces.

At the bottom, he formed from lightning into a human shape with odd eyes. Ulim settled on a patch of broken branches, arms folded, his long hair rippling in an unseen wind. She wasn't certain why a spren sent by Odium himself would look human.

'Around here somewhere,' Ulim said, pointing. 'Spread out and search.'

Venli set her jaw, humming to the Rhythm of Fury. Lines of power rippled up her arms. 'Why should I continue to obey your orders, spren? You should obey *me*.'

The spren ignored her, which further stoked her anger. Demid, however, placed his hand on her shoulder and squeezed, humming to the Rhythm of Satisfaction. 'Come, look with me this way.'

She curtailed her humming and turned south, joining Demid, picking her way through debris. Crem buildup had smoothed the floor of the chasm, but the storm had left a great deal of refuse.

She attuned the Rhythm of Craving. A quick, violent rhythm. 'I should be in charge, Demid. Not that spren.'

'You are in charge.'

'Then why haven't we been told anything? Our gods have returned, yet we've barely seen them. We sacrificed greatly for these forms, and to create the glorious true storm. We . . . we lost how many?'

Sometimes she thought about that, in strange moments when the new rhythms seemed to retreat. All of her work, meeting with Ulim in secret, guiding her people toward stormform. It had been about *saving* her people, hadn't it? Yet of the tens of thousands of listeners who had fought to summon the storm, only a fraction remained.

Demid and she had been scholars. Yet even scholars had gone to battle. She felt at the wound on her face.

'Our sacrifice was worthwhile,' Demid told her to the Rhythm of Derision. 'Yes, we have lost many, but humans sought our extinction. At least this way some of our people survived, and now we have great power!'

He was right. And, if she was being honest, a form of power was what she had always wanted. And she'd achieved one, capturing a spren in the storm within herself. That hadn't been one of Ulim's species, of course – lesser spren were used for changing forms. She could occasionally feel the pulsing, deep within, of the one she'd bonded.

In any case, this transformation had given her great power. The good of her people had always been secondary to Venli; now was a late time to be having a bout of conscience.

She resumed humming to Craving. Demid smiled and gripped her shoulder again. They'd shared something once, during their days in mate-form. Those silly, distracting passions were not ones they currently felt, nor were they something that any sane listener would desire. But the memories of them did create a bond.

They picked through the refuse, passing several fresh human corpses, smashed into a cleft in the rock. Good to see those. Good to remember that her people had killed many, despite their losses.

'Venli!' Demid said. 'Look!' He scrambled over a log from a large wooden bridge that was wedged in the center of the chasm. She followed, pleased by her strength. She would probably always remember Demid as the gangly scholar he had been before this change, but she doubted either of them would ever willingly return. Forms of power were simply too intoxicating.

Once across the log, she could see what Demid had spotted: a figure slumped by the wall of the chasm, helmeted head bowed. A Shardblade – shaped like frozen flames – rose from the ground beside her, rammed into the stone floor.

'Eshonai! Finally!' Venli leaped from the top of the log, landing near Demid.

Eshonai looked exhausted. In fact, she wasn't moving.

'Eshonai?' Venli said, kneeling beside her sister. 'Are you well? Eshonai?' She gripped the Plated figure by the shoulders and lightly shook it.

The head rolled on its neck, limp.

Venli felt cold. Demid solemnly lifted Eshonai's faceplate, revealing dead eyes set in an ashen face.

Eshonai . . . no . . .

'Ah,' Ulim's voice said. 'Excellent.' The spren approached across the stone wall, like crackling lightning moving through the stone. 'Demid, your hand.'

Demid obediently raised his hand, palm up, and Ulim shot across from the wall to the hand, then formed into his human shape, standing on the perch. 'Hmmm. Plate looks completely drained. Broken along the back, I see. Well, it's said to regrow on its own, even now that it is separated from its master from so long ago.'

'The . . . Plate,' Venli said softly, numb. 'You wanted the Plate.'

'Well, the Blade too, of course. Why else would we be hunting a corpse? You . . . Oh, you thought she was *alive*?'

'When you said we needed to find my sister,' Venli said, 'I thought . . .'

'Yes, looks like she drowned in the storm's floodwaters,' Ulim said, making a sound like a tongue clicking. 'Rammed the sword into the stone, held on to it to stay in place, but couldn't breathe.'

Venli attuned the Rhythm of the Lost.

It was one of the old, inferior rhythms. She hadn't been able to find those since transforming, and she had no idea how she happened upon this one. The mournful, solemn tone felt distant to her.

'Eshonai ...?' she whispered, and nudged the corpse again. Demid gasped. Touching the bodies of the fallen was taboo. The old songs spoke of days when humans had hacked apart listener corpses, searching for gemhearts. Leave the dead to peace instead; it was their way.

Venli stared into Eshonai's dead eyes. *You were the voice of reason,* Venli thought. *You were the one who argued with me. You ... you were supposed to keep me grounded.*

What do I do without you?

'Well, let's get that Plate off, kids,' Ulim said.

'Show respect!' Venli snapped.

'Respect for what? It's for the best that this one died.'

'For the best?' Venli said. 'For the *best*?' She stood, confronting the little spren on Demid's outstretched palm. 'That is my sister. She is one of our greatest warriors. An inspiration, and a martyr.'

Ulim rolled his head in an exaggerated way, as if perturbed – and bored – by the chastisement. How *dare* he! He was merely a spren. He was to be her *servant*.

'Your sister,' Ulim said, 'didn't undergo the transformation properly. She resisted, and we'd have eventually lost her. She was never dedicated to our cause.'

Venli attuned the Rhythm of Fury, speaking in a loud, punctuating sequence. 'You will not say such things. You are spren! You are to serve.'

'And I do.'

'Then you must obey me!'

'You?' Ulim laughed. 'Child, how long have you been fighting your little war against the humans? Three, four years?'

'Six years, spren,' Demid said. 'Six long, bloody years.'

'Well, do you want to guess how long *we've* been fighting this war?' Ulim asked. 'Go ahead. Guess. I'm waiting.'

Venli seethed. 'It doesn't matter—'

'Oh, but it does,' Ulim said, his red figure electrifying. 'Do you know how to lead armies, Venli? *True* armies? Supply troops across a battlefront that spans hundreds of miles? Do you have memories and experiences that span eons?'

She glared at him.

'Our leaders,' Ulim said, 'know exactly what they're doing. Them I obey. But *I* am the one who escaped, the spren of redemption. I don't have to listen to you.'

'I will be a queen,' Venli said to Spite.

'If you survive? Maybe. But your sister? She and the others sent that assassin to kill the human king *specifically* to keep us from returning. Your people are traitors – though your personal efforts do you justice, Venli. You may be blessed further, if you are wise. Regardless, get that armor off your sister, shed your tears, and get ready to climb back up. These plateaus are crawling with men who stink of Honor. We must be away and see what your ancestors need us to do.'

'Our ancestors?' Demid said. 'What do the dead have to do with this?'

'Everything,' Ulim replied, 'seeing as they're the ones in charge. Armor. *Now.*' He zipped to the wall as a tiny streak of lightning, then moved off.

Venli attuned Derision at the way she'd been treated, then – defying taboos – helped Demid remove the Shardplate. Ulim returned with the others and ordered them to gather up the armor.

They hiked off, leaving Venli to bring the Blade. She lifted it from the stone, then lingered, regarding her sister's corpse – which lay there in only padded underclothing.

Venli felt something stir inside her. Again, distantly, she was able to hear the Rhythm of the Lost. Mournful, slow, with separated beats.

'I . . .' Venli said. 'Finally, I don't have to listen to you call me a fool. I don't have to worry about you getting in the way. I can do what I want.'

That terrified her.

She turned to go, but paused as she saw something. What was that small spren that had crept out from beneath Eshonai's corpse? It looked like a small ball of white fire; it gave off little rings of light and trailed a streak behind it. Like a comet.

'What are you?' Venli demanded to Spite. 'Shoo.'

She hiked off, leaving her sister's corpse there at the bottom of the chasm, stripped and alone. Food for either a chasmfiend or a storm.

PART

TWO

New Beginnings Sing

SHALLAN • JASNAH • DALINAR •
BRIDGE FOUR

from the east

from the west

The city is incredibly huge! A chasmfiend's back would not reach the fourth floor.

cutaway

Panatham

Rall Elorim

Shinovar

Akinah

Azimir

Kurth

Vedenar

Kholinar

Natak

Thaylen City

33

A LECTURE

Dearest Cephandrius,
I received your communication, of course.

J asnah was alive.

Jasnah Kholin was *alive.*

Shallan was supposed to be recovering from her ordeal, never mind that the bridgemen had handled the fighting. All she'd done was grope an eldritch spren. Still, she spent the next day holed up in her room sketching and thinking.

Jasnah's return sparked something in her. Shallan had once been more analytical in her drawing, including notes and explanations with the sketches. Lately she'd only been doing pages and pages of twisted images.

Well, she'd been trained as a scholar, hadn't she? She shouldn't just draw; she should analyze, extrapolate, speculate. So, she addressed herself to fully recording her experiences with the Unmade.

Adolin and Palona visited her separately, and even Dalinar came to check on her while Navani clicked her tongue and asked after her health. Shallan endured their company, then eagerly returned to her drawing. There were so many questions. Why exactly had she been able to drive the thing away? What was the meaning of its creations?

Hanging over her research, however, was a single daunting fact. Jasnah was alive.

Storms . . . Jasnah was alive.

That changed *everything*.

Eventually, Shallan couldn't remain locked up any longer. Though Navani mentioned Jasnah was planning to visit her later in the evening, Shallan washed and dressed, then threw her satchel over her shoulder and went searching for the woman. She had to know *how* Jasnah had survived.

In fact, as Shallan stalked the hallways of Urithiru, she found herself increasingly perturbed. Jasnah claimed to always look at things from a logical perspective, but she had a flair for the dramatic to rival any storyteller. Shallan well remembered that night in Kharbranth when Jasnah had lured thieves in, then dealt with them in stunning – and brutal – fashion.

Jasnah didn't want to merely prove her points. She wanted to drive them right into your skull, with a flourish and a pithy epigram. Why hadn't she written via spanreed to let everyone know she had survived? Storms, where had she *been* all this time?

A few inquiries led Shallan back to the pit with its spiraling stairs. Guards in sharp Kholin blue confirmed that Jasnah was below, so Shallan started trudging down those steps again, and was surprised to find that she felt no anxiety at the descent. In fact . . . the oppressive feelings she'd felt since they'd arrived at the tower seemed to have evaporated. No more fear, no more formless sense of wrongness. The thing she'd chased away had been its cause. Somehow, its aura had pervaded the entire tower.

At the base of the stairs, she found more soldiers. Dalinar obviously wanted this place well guarded; she certainly couldn't complain about that. These let her pass without incident, save a bow and a murmur of 'Brightness Radiant.'

She strode down the muraled hallway, the sphere lanterns set along the base of the walls making it pleasingly bright. Once she'd passed the empty library rooms to either side, she heard voices drifting toward her from ahead. She stepped up into the room where she'd faced the Midnight Mother, and got her first good look at the place when it *wasn't* covered in writhing darkness.

The crystal pillar at the center really was something incredible. It wasn't a single gemstone, but a myriad of them fused together: emerald, ruby, topaz, sapphire . . . All ten varieties seemed to have been melted into a single thick pillar, twenty feet tall. Storms ... what would it look like if all those gems were somehow *infused*, rather than dun as they were at the moment?

A large group of guards stood at a barricade near the other side of the room, looking down into the tunnel where the Unmade had vanished. Jasnah rounded the giant pillar, freehand resting on the crystal. The princess wore red, lips painted to match, hair up and run through with swordlike hairspikes with rubies on the pommels.

Storms. She was perfect. A curvaceous figure, tan Alethi skin, light violet eyes, and not a hint of aberrant color to her jet-black hair. Making Jasnah Kholin as beautiful as she was brilliant was one of the most unfair things the Almighty had ever done.

Shallan hesitated in the doorway, feeling much as she had upon seeing Jasnah for the first time in Kharbranth. Insecure, overwhelmed, and – if she was honest – incredibly envious. Whatever ordeals Jasnah had been through, she looked no worse for wear. That was remarkable, considering that the last time Shallan had seen Jasnah, the woman had been lying unconscious on the floor while a man rammed a knife through her chest.

'My mother,' Jasnah said, hand still on the pillar, not looking toward Shallan, 'thinks this must be some kind of incredibly intricate fabrial. A logical assumption; we've always believed that the ancients had access to great and wonderful technology. How else do you explain Shardblades and Shardplate?'

'Brightness?' Shallan said. 'But ... Shardblades aren't fabrials. They're spren, transformed by the bond.'

'As are fabrials, after a manner of speaking,' Jasnah said. 'You do know how they're made, don't you?'

'Only vaguely,' Shallan said. This was how their reunion went? A lecture? *Fitting.*

'You capture a spren,' Jasnah said, 'and imprison it inside a gemstone crafted for the purpose. Artifabrians have found that specific stimuli will provoke certain responses in the spren. For example, flamespren give off heat – and by pressing metal against a ruby with a flamespren trapped inside, you can increase or decrease that heat.'

'That's ...'

'Incredible?'

'*Horrible*,' Shallan said. She'd known some of this, but to contemplate it directly appalled her. 'Brightness, we're *imprisoning* spren?'

'No worse than hitching a wagon to a chull.'

'Sure, if in order to get a chull to pull a wagon, you first had to lock it in a box forever.'

Pattern hummed softly from her skirts in agreement.

Jasnah just cocked an eyebrow. 'There are spren and there are spren, child.' She rested her fingers on the pillar again. 'Do a sketch of this for me. Be certain to get the proportions and colors right, if you please.'

The careless presumption of the command hit Shallan like a slap in the face. What was she, some servant to be given orders?

Yes, a part of her affirmed. *That's* exactly *what you are. You're Jasnah's ward.* The request wasn't at all unusual in that light, but compared to how she had grown accustomed to being treated, it was . . .

Well, it wasn't worth taking offense at, and she should accept that. Storms, when had she grown so touchy? She took out her sketchpad and got to work.

'I was heartened to hear that you had made it here on your own,' Jasnah said. 'I . . . apologize for what happened on *Wind's Pleasure*. My lack of foresight caused the deaths of many, and doubtless hardship for you, Shallan. Please accept my regret.'

Shallan shrugged, sketching.

'You've done *very* well,' Jasnah continued. 'Imagine my amazement when I reached the Shattered Plains, only to discover that the warcamp had already relocated to this tower. What you have accomplished is brilliant, child. We will need to speak further, however, about the group that again tried to assassinate me. The Ghostbloods will almost certainly start targeting you, now that you've begun progressing toward your final Ideals.'

'You're sure it was the Ghostbloods that attacked the ship?'

'Of course I am.' She glanced at Shallan, lips turning down. 'Are you certain you are well enough to be about, child? You seem uncharacteristically reserved.'

'I'm fine.'

'You're displeased because of the secrets I kept.'

'We all need secrets, Brightness. I know this more than anyone. But it would have been nice if you had let us know you were alive.' *Here I was assuming I could handle things on my own – assuming I'd have to handle things on my own. But all that time, you were on your way back to toss everything into the air again.*

'I only had the opportunity upon reaching the warcamps,' Jasnah said, 'and there decided that I couldn't risk it. I was tired and unprotected. If the Ghostbloods wished to finish me off, they could have done so at their leisure. I determined that a few more days of everyone believing I was dead would not greatly increase their distress.'

'But how did you even survive in the first place?'

'Child, I'm an Elsecaller.'

'Of course. An Elsecaller, Brightness. A thing you never explained; a word which no one but the most dedicated scholar of the esoteric would recognize! That explains it perfectly.'

Jasnah smiled for some reason.

'All Radiants have an attachment to Shadesmar,' Jasnah said. 'Our spren originate there, and our bond ties us to them. But my order has special control over moving between realms. I was able to shift to Shadesmar to escape my would-be assassins.'

'And that helped with the knife in your storming chest?'

'No,' Jasnah said. 'But surely by now you've learned the value of a little Stormlight when it comes to bodily wounds?'

Of course she had, and she could probably have guessed all of this. But for some reason she didn't want to accept that. She wanted to remain annoyed at Jasnah.

'My true difficulty was not escaping, but *returning*,' Jasnah said. 'My powers make it easy to transfer to Shadesmar, but getting back to this realm is no small feat. I had to find a transfer point – a place where Shadesmar and our realm touch – which is far, far more difficult than one might assume. It's like . . . going downhill one way, but uphill to get back.'

Well, perhaps her return would take some pressure off Shallan. Jasnah could be 'Brightness Radiant' and Shallan could be . . . well, whatever she was.

'We will need to converse further,' Jasnah said. 'I would hear the exact story, from your perspective, of the discovery of Urithiru. And I assume you have sketches of the transformed parshmen? That will tell us much. I . . . believe I once disparaged the usefulness of your artistic skill. I now find reason to call myself foolish for that presumption.'

'It's fine, Brightness,' Shallan said with a sigh, still sketching the pillar. 'I can get you those things, and there *is* a lot to talk about.' But how much of it would she be able to say? How would Jasnah react, for instance, to finding that Shallan had been dealing with the Ghostbloods?

It's not like you're really a part of their organization, Shallan thought to herself. *If anything, you're using them for information.* Jasnah might find that admirable.

Shallan still wasn't eager to broach the topic.

'I feel lost . . .' Jasnah said.

Shallan looked up from her sketchbook to find the woman regarding the pillar again, speaking softly, as if to herself.

'For years I was at the very forefront of all this,' Jasnah said. 'One short stumble, and I find myself scrambling to stay afloat. These visions that my uncle is having . . . the refounding of the Radiants in my absence . . .

'That Windrunner. What do you think of him, Shallan? I find him much as I imagined his order, but I have only met him once. It has all come so quickly. After years of struggling in the shadows, everything coming to light – and despite my years of study – I understand so very little.'

Shallan continued her sketch. It was nice to be reminded that, for all their differences, there were occasional things that she and Jasnah shared.

She just wished that ignorance weren't at the top of the list.

I noticed its arrival immediately, just as I noticed your many intrusions into my land.

I t is time, the Stormfather said.

All went dark around Dalinar, and he entered a place between his world and the visions. A place with a black sky and an infinite floor of bone-white rock. Shapes made of smoke seeped through the stone ground, then rose around him, dissipating. Common things. A chair, a vase, a rockbud. Sometimes people.

I HAVE HER. The Stormfather's voice shook this place, eternal and vast. THE THAYLEN QUEEN. MY STORM HITS HER CITY NOW.

'Good,' Dalinar said. 'Please give her the vision.'

Fen was to see the vision with the Knights Radiant falling from the sky, come to deliver a small village from a strange and monstrous force. Dalinar wanted her to see the Knights Radiant firsthand, as they had once been. Righteous, protecting.

WHERE SHALL I PUT HER? the Stormfather asked.

'The same place you put me my first time,' Dalinar said. 'In the home. With the family.'

AND YOU?

'I'll observe, then talk to her after.'

YOU MUST BE PART OF EVENTS, the Stormfather said, sounding

stubborn. You must take the role of someone. This is how it works.

'Fine. Pick someone. But if possible, make Fen see me as myself, and let me see her.' He felt at the side sword he wore at his belt. 'And can you let me keep this? I'd rather not have to fight with a poker again.'

The Stormfather rumbled in annoyance, but did not object. The place of endless white stone faded.

'What was that place?' Dalinar asked.

It is no place.

'But everything else in these visions is real,' Dalinar said. 'So why is it that—'

It is no place, the Stormfather insisted firmly.

Dalinar fell silent, letting himself be taken by the vision.

I imagined it, the Stormfather said more softly, as if he were admitting something embarrassing. All things have a soul. A vase, a wall, a chair. And when a vase is broken, it might die in the Physical Realm, but for a time its soul remembers what it was. So all things die twice. Its final death is when men forget it was a vase, and think only of the pieces. I imagine the vase floating away then, its form dissolving into the nothingness.

Dalinar had never heard anything so philosophical from the Stormfather. He hadn't imagined it was possible that a spren – even a mighty one of the highstorms – could dream in such a way.

Dalinar found himself hurtling through the air.

Flailing his arms, he shouted in panic. First moon's violet light bathed the ground far below. His stomach lurched and his clothes flapped in the wind. He continued yelling until he realized that he wasn't actually getting closer to the ground.

He *wasn't* falling, he was *flying*. The air was rushing against the top of his head, not his face. Indeed, now he saw that his body was glowing, Stormlight streaming off him. He didn't feel like he was holding it though – no raging inside his veins, no urge to action.

He shielded his face from the wind and looked forward. A Radiant flew ahead, resplendent in blue armor that glowed, the light brightest at the edges and in the grooves. The man was looking back at Dalinar, doubtless because of his cries.

Dalinar saluted him to indicate he was all right. The armored man nodded, looking forward again.

He's a Windrunner, Dalinar thought, piecing it together. *I've taken the place of his companion, a female Radiant.* He'd seen these two in the vision before; they were flying to save the village. Dalinar wasn't moving under his own power – the Windrunner had Lashed the female Radiant into the sky, as Szeth had done to Dalinar during the Battle of Narak.

It was still difficult to accept that he wasn't falling, and a sinking feeling persisted in the pit of his stomach. He tried to focus on other things. He was wearing an unfamiliar brown uniform, though he was glad to note that he had his side sword as requested. But why didn't he have on Shardplate? In the vision, the woman had worn a set that glowed amber. Was this the result of the Stormfather trying to make him look like himself to Fen?

Dalinar still didn't know why Radiant Plate glowed, while modern Shardplate did not. Was the ancient Plate 'living' somehow, like Radiant Blades lived?

Perhaps he could find out from that Radiant ahead. He had to ask his questions carefully, however. Everyone would see Dalinar as the Radiant he had replaced, and if his questions were uncharacteristic, that tended only to confuse people, rather than get him answers.

'How far away are we?' Dalinar asked. The sound was lost in the wind, so he shouted it more loudly, drawing the attention of his companion.

'Not long now,' the man shouted back, voice echoing inside his helm, which glowed blue – most strongly at the edges and across the eye slit.

'I think something might be wrong with my armor!' Dalinar shouted to him. 'I can't make my helm retract!'

In response, the other Radiant made his vanish. Dalinar caught sight of a puff of Light or mist.

Beneath the helm, the man had dark skin and curly black hair. His eyes glowed blue. 'Retract your helm?' he shouted. 'You haven't summoned your armor yet; you had to dismiss it so I could Lash you.'

Oh, Dalinar thought. 'I mean earlier. It wouldn't vanish when I wanted it to.'

'Talk to Harkaylain then, or to your spren.' The Windrunner frowned. 'Will this be a problem for our mission?'

'I don't know,' Dalinar shouted. 'But it distracted me. Tell me again how we know where to go, and what we know of the things we're going to fight?' He winced at how awkward that sounded.

'Just be ready to back me up against the Midnight Essence, and use Regrowth on any wounded.'

'But—'

You will find difficulty getting useful answers, Son of Honor, the Stormfather rumbled. *These do not have souls or minds. They are re-creations forged by Honor's will, and do not have the memories of the real people.*

'Surely we can learn things,' Dalinar said under his breath.

They were created to convey only certain ideas. Further pressing will merely reveal the thinness of the facade.

This brought up memories of the fake city Dalinar had visited in his first vision, the destroyed version of Kholinar that was more prop than reality. But there *had* to be things he could learn, things that Honor might not have intended, but had included by chance.

I need to get Navani and Jasnah in here, he thought. *Let them pick at these re-creations.*

Last time in this vision, Dalinar had taken the place of a man named Heb: a husband and father who had defended his family with only a fireplace poker for a weapon. He remembered his frantic struggle with a beast of oily, midnight skin. He had fought, bled, agonized. He'd spent what seemed like an eternity trying – and eventually failing – to protect his wife and daughter.

Such a personal memory. False though it was, he had *lived* it. In fact, seeing the small town ahead – in the lait created by a large ridge of rock – made emotions well up inside Dalinar. It was a painful irony that he should have such vivid feelings about this place, these people, when his memories of Evi were still so shadowy and confused.

The Windrunner slowed Dalinar by grabbing his arm. They drew to a stop in midair, hovering above the rocky flats outside the village.

'There.' The Windrunner pointed to the field around the town, where weird black creatures were swarming. About the size of an axehound, they had oily skin that reflected the moonlight. While they moved on all sixes, they were like no natural animal. They had spindly legs like a crab's, but a bulbous body and a sinuous head, featureless except for a slit of a mouth bristling with black teeth.

Shallan had faced the source of these things deep beneath Urithiru.

Dalinar had slept a little less secure each night since, knowing that one of the Unmade had been hidden in the bowels of the tower. Were the other eight similarly lurking nearby?

'I'll go down first,' the Windrunner said, 'and draw their attention. You make for the town and help the people there.' The man pressed his hand against Dalinar. 'You'll drop in about thirty seconds.'

The man's helm materialized, then he plunged toward the monsters. Dalinar remembered that descent from the vision – like a falling star come to rescue Dalinar and the family.

'How,' Dalinar whispered to the Stormfather. 'How do we get the armor?'

Speak the Words.

'Which words?'

You will know or you will not.

Great.

Dalinar saw no sign of Taffa or Seeli – the family he'd protected – below. In his version they'd been out here, but their flight had been his doing. He couldn't be sure how the vision had played out this time.

Storms. He hadn't planned this very well, had he? In his mind's eye, he'd anticipated getting to Queen Fen and helping her along, making sure she wasn't in too much danger. Instead, he'd wasted time flying here.

Stupid. He needed to learn to be more specific with the Stormfather.

Dalinar began to descend in a controlled float. He had some idea of how the Windrunner Surges worked together, but he was impressed nonetheless. Just as he touched down, the feeling of lightness left him and the Stormlight rising from his skin puffed away. This left him as much less of a target in the darkness than the other Radiant, who glowed like a brilliant blue beacon, sweeping about himself with a grand Shardblade as he fought the Midnight Essence.

Dalinar crept through the town, his common side sword feeling frail compared to a Shardblade – but at least it wasn't an iron poker. Some of the creatures scrambled by on the main thoroughfare, but Dalinar hid beside a boulder until they passed.

He easily identified the proper house, which had a small barn out back, nestled against the stone cliff that sheltered the town. He crept up, and found that the barn wall had been ripped open. He remembered hiding in there with Seeli, then fleeing as a monster attacked.

The barn was empty, so he headed for the house, which was much finer. Made of crem bricks, and larger, though it seemed only one family lived in it. For a house this big, that would be an oddity, wouldn't it? Space was at a premium in laits.

Some of his assumptions obviously didn't hold in this era. In Alethkar, a fine wooden mansion would be a symbol of wealth. Here, however, many of the other houses were of wood.

Dalinar slipped into the house, feeling increasingly worried. Fen's real body couldn't be harmed by what happened in the vision, but she could still feel pain. So while the injuries might not be real, her anger at Dalinar certainly would be. He could ruin any chance of her listening to him.

She's already given up on listening, he assured himself. Navani agreed – this vision couldn't make things worse.

He felt in his uniform's pocket, and was pleased to find some gemstones. A Radiant would have Stormlight. He took out a small diamond the size of a pebble and used its white light to inspect the room. The table had been overturned, chairs scattered. The door hung open and creaked softly in a breeze.

There was no sign of Queen Fen, but Taffa's body lay facedown near the hearth. She wore a single-piece brown dress, now in tatters. Dalinar sighed, sheathing his sword and kneeling to gently touch her back in a spot unraked by monster claws.

It's not real, he told himself, *not now. This woman lived and died thousands of years ago.*

It still hurt to see her. He walked to the swinging door and stepped outside into the night, where howls and cries rang out from the town.

He strode quickly down the roadway, feeling a sense of urgency. No . . . not just urgency, impatience. Seeing Taffa's corpse had changed something. He was not a confused man trapped in a nightmare, as he'd feared when first visiting this place. Why was he sneaking? These visions belonged to *him*. He should not fear their contents.

One of the creatures scuttled out of the shadows. Dalinar drew in Stormlight as it leaped and bit at his leg. Pain flared up his side, but he ignored it, and the wound reknit. He glanced down as the creature lunged again, with similar lack of results. It scurried backward a few paces, and he could sense *confusion* in its posture. This was not how its prey was supposed to act.

'You don't eat the corpses,' Dalinar said to it. 'You kill for pleasure, don't you? I often think of how spren and man are so different, but this we share. We can both murder.'

The unholy thing came at him again, and Dalinar seized it in both hands. The body felt springy to the touch, like a wineskin filled to bursting. He painted the writhing monster with Stormlight and spun, hurling it toward a nearby building. The creature hit the wall back-first and stuck there several feet above the ground, legs scrambling.

Dalinar continued on his way. He simply cut through the next two creatures that came for him. Their disjointed bodies twitched, black smoke leaking from the carcasses.

What is that light? It danced in the night ahead, growing stronger. Harsh, orange, flooding the end of the street.

He didn't remember a fire from before. Were homes burning? Dalinar approached, and found a *bonfire*, flickering with flamespren, built of furniture. It was surrounded by dozens of people holding brooms and crude picks: men and women alike, armed with whatever they could find. Even an iron poker or two.

Judging by the fearspren gathered around them, the townspeople were terrified. They managed some semblance of ranks anyway – with children at the center, nearer the fires – as they frantically defended themselves from the midnight monsters. A figure near the fire commanded from the top of a box. Fen's voice had no accent; to Dalinar, her shouts seemed to be in perfect Alethi, though – in the strange way of these visions – everyone present was actually speaking and thinking in an ancient language.

How did she manage this so quickly? Dalinar wondered, mesmerized by the fighting townsfolk. Some of them fell in bloody, screaming heaps, but others pinned down the monsters and stabbed open their backs – sometimes with kitchen knives – to deflate them.

Dalinar remained on the outskirts of the battle until a dramatic figure in glowing blue swept down upon the scene. The Windrunner made short work of the remaining creatures.

At the end, he saved a glare for Dalinar. 'What are you doing standing there? Why haven't you helped?'

'I—'

'We'll have words about this when we return!' he shouted, pointing toward one of the fallen. 'Go, help the wounded!'

Dalinar followed the gesture, but walked toward Fen instead of the wounded. Some of the townspeople huddled and wept, though others exulted in survival, cheering and holding up their improvised weapons. He'd seen these aftereffects of a battle before. The welling up of emotions came in a variety of ways.

The bonfire's heat caused Dalinar's brow to sweat. Smoke churned in the air, reminding him of the place he'd been before he'd fully entered this vision. He'd always loved the warmth of an actual fire, dancing with flamespren, so eager to burn themselves out and die.

Fen was over a foot shorter than Dalinar, with an oval face, yellow eyes, and white Thaylen eyebrows she kept curled to hang down beside her cheeks. She did not braid her grey hair like an Alethi woman would have, but instead let it fall down to cover her shoulders. The vision had given her a simple shirt and trousers to wear – the costume of the man she'd replaced – though she'd found a glove for her safehand.

'Now the Blackthorn himself shows up?' she said. 'Damnation, this is a strange dream.'

'Not quite a dream, Fen,' Dalinar said, looking back toward the Radiant, who had charged a small group of midnight monsters coming down the street. 'I don't know if I have time to explain.'

'I can slow it down,' one of the villagers said in the Stormfather's voice.

'Yes, please,' Dalinar said.

Everything stopped. Or . . . slowed greatly. The bonfire's flames shimmered lethargically, and the people slowed to a crawl.

Dalinar was unaffected, as was Fen. He sat down on a box beside the one Fen stood on, and she hesitantly settled down next to him. 'A *very* strange dream.'

'I assumed I was dreaming myself, when I saw the first vision,' Dalinar said. 'When they kept happening, I was forced to acknowledge that no dream is this crisp, this logical. In no dream could we be having this conversation.'

'In every dream I've experienced, what happened felt natural at the time.'

'Then you will know the difference when you wake. I can show many more of these visions to you, Fen. They were left for us by . . . a being with some interest in helping us survive the Desolations.' Best not to get into his heresy at the moment. 'If one isn't persuasive enough, I understand. I'm dense enough that I didn't trust them for months.'

'Are they all this . . . invigorating?'

Dalinar smiled. 'This was the most powerful of them, to me.' He looked to her. 'You did better than I did. I worried only about Taffa and her daughter, but just ended up getting them surrounded by monsters anyway.'

'I let the woman die,' Fen said softly. 'I ran with the child, and let the thing kill her. Used her almost as bait.' She looked to Dalinar, eyes haunted. 'What was your purpose in this, Kholin? You imply you have power over these visions. Why did you trap me in this one?'

'Honestly, I just wanted to talk to you.'

'Send me a storming letter.'

'In person, Fen.' He nodded toward the gathered townspeople. 'You did *this*. You organized the town, pitted them against the enemy. It's remarkable! You expect me to accept that you will turn your back on the world in a similar moment of need?'

'Don't be dense. My kingdom is suffering. I'm seeing to my people's needs; I'm not turning my back on anyone.'

Dalinar looked to her and pursed his lips, but said nothing.

'Fine,' she snapped. 'Fine, Kholin. You want to dig into it for real? Tell me this. You *really* expect me to believe that the storming *Knights Radiant* are back and that the Almighty chose *you* – a tyrant and a murderer – to lead them?'

In response, Dalinar stood up and drew in Stormlight. His skin began glowing with luminescent smoke, drifting from his body. 'If you wish proof, I can persuade you. Incredible though it seems, the Radiants *have* returned.'

'And of the second part? Yes, there is a new storm, and perhaps new manifestations of power. Fine. What I don't accept is that you, Dalinar Kholin, have been told by the Almighty to lead us.'

'I have been commanded to unite.'

'A mandate from God – the *very* same argument the Hierocracy used for seizing control of the government. What about Sadees, the Sunmaker? He claimed he had a calling from the Almighty too.' She stood and walked among the people of the town – who stood as if frozen, barely moving. She turned and swept a hand back toward Dalinar. 'Now here *you* are, saying the same things in the same way – not quite threats, but insistent. Let us join forces! If we don't, the world is doomed.'

Dalinar felt his patience slipping. He clenched his jaw, forced himself to be calm, and rose. 'Your Majesty, you're being irrational.'

'Am I? Oh, let me storming reconsider, then. All I need to do is let the storming *Blackthorn himself* into my city, so he can take control of my armies!'

'What would you have me *do?*' Dalinar shouted. 'Would you have me watch the world crumble?'

She cocked her head at his outburst.

'Maybe you're right, and I am a tyrant! Maybe letting my armies into your city is a terrible risk. But maybe you don't have good options! Maybe all the good men are dead, so all you have is me! Spitting into the storm isn't going to change that, Fen. You can risk *possibly* being conquered by the Alethi, or you can *definitely* fall to the Voidbringer assault alone!'

Curiously, Fen crossed her arms and raised her left hand to her chin, inspecting Dalinar. She didn't seem the least bit fazed by his shouting.

Dalinar stepped past a squat man who was slowly – as if through tar – turning toward where they'd once been seated. 'Fen,' Dalinar said. 'You don't like me. Fine. You tell me *to my face* that trusting me is worse than a Desolation.'

She studied him, aged eyes thoughtful. What was wrong? What had he said?

'Fen,' he tried again. 'I—'

'Where was this passion earlier?' she asked. 'Why didn't you speak like this in your letters to me?'

'I . . . Fen, I was being *diplomatic.*'

She sniffed. 'That made it sound like I was talking to a committee. It's what one always assumes anyway, when communicating via spanreed.'

'So?'

'So compared to that, it's good to hear some honest shouting.' She eyed the people standing around them. 'And this is *exceptionally* creepy. Can we get away from this?'

Dalinar found himself nodding, mostly to buy some time to think. Fen seemed to think his anger was . . . a good thing? He gestured at a path through the crowd and Fen joined him, walking away from the bonfire.

'Fen,' he said, 'you say you expected to talk to a committee through the spanreed. What's wrong with that? Why would you want me to *shout* at you instead?'

'I don't want you to shout at me, Kholin,' she said. 'But storms, man. Don't you know what has been said about you these last few months?'

'No.'

'You've been the hottest topic on the spanreed informant networks! Dalinar Kholin, the Blackthorn, has gone mad! He claims to have killed the Almighty! One day he refuses to fight, then the next day he marches his armies off on an insane quest into the Shattered Plains. He says he's going to enslave the Voidbringers!'

'I didn't say—'

'Nobody expects every report to be true, Dalinar, but I had extremely good information claiming you'd lost your mind. Refounding the Knights Radiant? Raving about a Desolation? You seized the throne of Alethkar in all but title, but refused to fight the other highprinces, and instead ran your armies off into the Weeping. Then you told everyone a new storm was coming. That was enough to convince me that you really *were* mad.'

'But then the storm came,' Dalinar said.

'But then the storm came.'

The two walked down the quiet street, light from behind flooding across them, making their shadows lengthen. To their right, a calm blue light shone between buildings – the Radiant, who fought monsters in slowed time.

Jasnah could probably learn something from these buildings, with their old architecture. These people wearing unfamiliar clothing. He'd have expected everything in the past to be crude, but it wasn't. The doors, the buildings, the clothing. It was well made, just . . . lacking something he couldn't define.

'The Everstorm proved I wasn't mad?' Dalinar asked.

'It proved that *something* was happening.'

Dalinar suddenly stopped. 'You think I'm working *with* them! You think that explains my behavior, my foreknowledge. You think I've been acting erratically because I've been in *contact* with the Voidbringers!'

'All I knew,' Fen said, 'was that the voice on the other end of the spanreed was *not* the Dalinar Kholin I'd expected. The words were too polite, too calm, to be trusted.'

'And now?' Dalinar asked.

Fen turned. 'Now . . . I'll consider. Can I see the rest of it? I want to know what happens to the little girl.'

Dalinar followed her gaze and saw – for the first time – little Seeli sitting, huddled with some other children near the fire. She had a haunted cast to her eyes. He could imagine her horror as Fen ran away, Taffa – the child's mother – screaming as she was ripped apart.

Seeli suddenly lurched into motion, turning her head to stare with a hollow gaze at a woman who knelt beside her, offering something to drink. The Stormfather had restored the vision's normal speed.

Dalinar backed up, letting Fen rejoin the people and experience the end of the vision. As he folded his arms to watch, he noted a shimmering in the air beside him.

'We'll want to send her more of these,' Dalinar said to the Stormfather. 'We can only be served by more people knowing the truths the Almighty left behind. Can you bring in only one person per storm, or can we accelerate that somehow? And can you bring two people into two different visions at once?'

The Stormfather rumbled. *I do not like to be ordered about.*

'And you prefer the alternative? Letting Odium win? How far will your pride push you, Stormfather?'

It is not pride, the Stormfather said, sounding stubborn. *I am not a man. I do not bend or cower. I do what is in my nature, and to defy that is pain.*

The Radiant finished off the last of the midnight creatures and stepped up to the gathered people, then looked at Fen. 'Your upbringing might be humble, but your talent for leadership is impressive. I have rarely seen a man – king or commander – organize people for defense as well as you did here today.'

Fen cocked her head.

'No words for me, I see,' the knight said. 'Very well. But should you wish to learn true leadership, come to Urithiru.'

Dalinar turned to the Stormfather. 'That's almost exactly what the knight said to me last time.'

By design, certain things always happen in the visions, the Stormfather replied. *I do not know Honor's every intention, but I know he wished you to interact with Radiants and know that men could join them.*

'All who resist are needed,' the Radiant said to Fen. 'Indeed, any who have a desire to fight should be compelled to come to Alethela. We can teach you, help you. If you have the soul of a warrior, that passion could destroy you, unless you are guided. Come to us.'

The Radiant strode off, then Fen jumped as Seeli stood up and started talking to her. The girl's voice was too quiet for Dalinar to hear, but he could guess what was happening. At the end of each vision, the Almighty himself spoke through one of the people, passing along wisdom that – at first – Dalinar had assumed was interactive.

Fen seemed troubled by what she heard. As well she should be. Dalinar remembered the words.

This is important, the Almighty had said. *Do not let strife consume you. Be strong. Act with honor, and honor will aid you.*

Except Honor was dead.

At the end of it, Fen turned toward Dalinar, her eyes measuring.

She still does not trust you, the Stormfather said.

'She wonders if I created this vision with the power of the Voidbringers. She no longer thinks I'm mad, but she does continue to wonder if I've joined the enemy.'

So you've failed again.

'No,' Dalinar said. 'Tonight she listened. And I think she'll end up taking the gamble of coming to Urithiru.'

The Stormfather rumbled, sounding confused. *Why?*

'Because,' Dalinar said, 'I know how to talk to her now. She doesn't want polite words or diplomatic phrases. She wants me to be myself. I'm fairly certain that's something I can deliver.'

You think yourself so clever, but my eyes are not those of some petty noble, to be clouded by a false nose and some dirt on the cheeks.

Someone bumped Sigzil's cot, waking him from a dream. He yawned, and Rock's breakfast bell began ringing in the next room.

He'd been dreaming in Azish. He'd been back home, studying for the governmental service tests. Passing would have qualified him to enter a real school, with a shot at becoming a clerk to someone important. Only, in the dream, he'd been panicked to realize he'd forgotten how to read.

After so many years away, thinking of his mother tongue felt strange. He yawned again, settling on his cot, back to the stone wall. They had three small barracks and a common room in the center.

Out there, everyone pushed, ramble-scramble, up to the breakfast table. Rock had to shout at them – yet again – to organize themselves. Months in Bridge Four, now apprentice Knights Radiant, and the lot of them *still* couldn't figure out how to line up properly. They wouldn't last a day in Azir, where queuing in an orderly way wasn't only expected, it was practically a mark of *national pride*.

Sigzil rested his head against the wall, remembering. He'd been the first from his family in generations with a real shot at passing the exams. A silly dream. Everyone in Azir *talked* about how even the humblest man could become Prime, but the son of a laborer had so little time to study.

He shook his head, then washed with a basin of water he'd fetched the night before. He took a comb to his hair, and inspected himself in a polished length of steel. His hair was growing far too long; the tight black curls had a tendency to stick straight out.

He set out a sphere to use its light for a shave – he had acquired his own razor. Soon after he started, however, he nicked himself. He sucked in a breath at the pain, and his sphere winked out. What . . .

His skin started glowing, letting off a faint luminescent smoke. Oh, right. Kaladin was back.

Well, that was going to solve *so* many problems. He got out another sphere, and did his best not to eat this one as he finished shaving. Afterward, he pressed his hand against his forehead. Once, he'd had slave brands there. The Stormlight had healed those, though his Bridge Four tattoo remained.

He rose and put on his uniform. Kholin blue, sharp and neat. He slid his new hogshide notebook into his pocket, then stepped out into the common room – and stopped short as Lopen's face swung *down* right in front of him. Sigzil almost slammed into the Herdazian, who was stuck by the bottoms of his feet to the storming *ceiling*.

'Hey,' Lopen said, bowl of morning porridge held upside down – or, well, right-side up, but upside down to Lopen – in front of him. The Herdazian tried to take a bite, but the porridge slipped off his spoon and splatted to the ground.

'Lopen, what are you *doing*?'

'Practicing. I've got to show them how good I am, hooch. It's like with women, only it involves sticking yourself to the ceiling and learning not to spill food on the heads of people you like.'

'Move, Lopen.'

'Ah, you have to ask the right way. I'm not one-armed anymore! I can't be shoved around. Say, do you know how to get *two armed* Herdazians to do what you want?'

'If I did, we wouldn't be having this conversation.'

'Well, you take away both of their spears, obviously.' He grinned. A few feet away, Rock laughed with a loud 'Ha!'

Lopen wiggled his fingers at Sigzil, as if to taunt him, fingernails glistening. Like all Herdazians, he had fingernails that were dark brown and hard as crystal. A bit reminiscent of carapace.

He still had a tattoo on his head too. Though so far only a few of Bridge Four had learned to draw in Stormlight, each of those had kept their tattoos. Only Kaladin was different; his tattoo had melted off once he took in Stormlight, and his scars refused to heal.

'Remember that one for me, hooch,' Lopen said. He never would explain what 'hooch' meant, or why he used it only to refer to Sigzil. 'I'll need, sure, lots and lots of new jokes. Also sleeves. Twice as many of those, except on vests. Then the same number.'

'How did you even manage to get up there, so you could stick your feet . . . no, don't start. I don't actually want to know.' Sigzil ducked under Lopen.

The men were still scrambling for food, laughing and shouting in complete disarray. Sigzil shouted to get their attention. 'Don't forget! The captain wanted us up and ready for inspection by second bell!'

Sigzil could barely be heard. Where was Teft? They actually listened when he gave orders. Sigzil shook his head, weaving his way toward the door. Among his people, he was of average height – but he'd gone and moved among the *Alethi*, who were practically giants. So here, he was a few inches shorter than most.

He slipped out into the hallway. The bridge crews occupied a sequence of large barracks on the tower's first floor. Bridge Four were gaining Radiant powers, but there were hundreds more men in the battalion who were still ordinary infantry. Perhaps Teft had gone to inspect the other crews; he'd been given responsibility for training them. Hopefully it wasn't the other thing.

Kaladin bunked in his own small suite of rooms at the end of the hallway. Sigzil made his way there, going over his scribbles in the notebook. He used Alethi glyphs, as was acceptable for a man out here, and had never learned their actual writing system. Storms, he'd been away so long, the dream was probably right. He might have trouble writing in the Azish script.

What would life be like if he hadn't turned into a failure and a disappointment? If he'd passed the tests, instead of getting into trouble, needing to be rescued by the man who had become his master?

The list of problems first, he decided, reaching Kaladin's door and knocking.

'Come!' the captain's voice said from inside.

Sigzil found Kaladin doing morning push-ups on the stone floor. His blue jacket was draped over a chair.

'Sir,' Sigzil said.

'Hey, Sig,' Kaladin said, grunting as he continued his push-ups. 'Are the men up and mustered?'

'Up, yes,' Sigzil said. 'When I left them, they seemed bordering on a food fight, and only half were in uniform.'

'They'll be ready,' Kaladin said. 'Was there something you wanted, Sig?'

Sigzil settled down in the chair next to Kaladin's coat and opened his notebook. 'A lot of things, sir. Not the least of which is the fact that you should have a real scribe, not . . . whatever I am.'

'You're my clerk.'

'A poor one. We've a full battalion of fighting men with only four lieu-tenants and no official scribes. Frankly, sir, the bridge crews are a mess. Our finances are in shambles, requisition orders are piling up faster than Leyten can deal with them, and there's an entire host of problems requir-ing an officer's attention.'

Kaladin grunted. 'The fun part of running an army.'

'Exactly.'

'That was sarcasm, Sig.' Kaladin stood up and wiped his brow with a towel. 'All right. Go ahead.'

'We'll start with something easy,' Sigzil said. 'Peet is now officially betrothed to the woman he's been seeing.'

'Ka? That's wonderful. Maybe she could help you with scribe duties.'

'Perhaps. I believe that you were looking into requisitioning housing for men with families?'

'Yeah. That was before the whole mess with the Weeping, and the expedition onto the Shattered Plains, and . . . And I should go back to Dalinar's scribes about it, shouldn't I?'

'Unless you expect the married couples to share a bunk in the standard barracks, then I'd say that yes, you should.' Sigzil looked to the next page in his book. 'I believe that Bisig is close to being betrothed as well.'

'Really? He's so quiet. I never know what's going on behind those eyes of his.'

'Not to mention Punio, who I found out recently is *already* married. His wife drops off food for him.'

'I thought that was his sister!'

'He wanted to fit in, I believe,' Sigzil said. 'His broken Alethi already makes that hard. And then there's the matter of Drehy . . .'

'What matter?'

'Well, he's been courting a man, you see . . .'

Kaladin threw on his coat, chuckling. 'I *did* know about that one. You only now noticed?'

Sigzil nodded.

'It's Dru he's been seeing, still? From the district quartermaster's offices?'

'Yes, sir.' Sigzil looked down. 'Sir, I . . . Well, it's just that . . .'

'Yes?'

'Sir, Drehy hasn't filled out the proper forms,' Sigzil said. 'If he wants to court another man, he needs to apply for social reassignment, right?'

Kaladin rolled his eyes. So, there were no forms for that in Alethkar.

Sigzil couldn't say he was surprised, as the Alethi didn't have proper procedures for anything. 'Then how do you apply for social reassignment?'

'We don't.' Kaladin frowned. 'Is this really that big a problem to you, Sig? Maybe—'

'Sir, it's not this specifically. Right now, there are four religions represented in Bridge Four.'

'Four?'

'Hobber follows the Passions, sir. Four, even if you don't count Teft, who I can't figure out rightly. And now there's all this talk of Brightlord Dalinar claiming the Almighty is dead, and . . . Well, I feel responsible, sir.'

'For Dalinar?' Kaladin frowned.

'No, no.' He took a deep breath. There had to be a way to explain this. What would his master do?

'Now,' Sigzil said, scrambling at an idea, 'everybody knows that Mishim – the third moon – is the most clever and wily of the moons.'

'All right . . . And this is relevant, why?'

'Because of a story,' Sigzil said. 'Hush. Uh, I mean, please listen, sir. You see, there are three moons, and the third moon is the cleverest. And she doesn't want to be in the sky, sir. She wants to escape.

'So one night, she tricked the queen of the Natan people – this was a long time ago, so they were still around. I mean, they're still around now, but they were more around then, sir. And the moon tricked her, and then they traded places until they stopped. And now the Natan people have blue skin. Does that make sense?'

Kaladin blinked. 'I have no idea what you just said.'

'Um, well,' Sigzil said. 'It's obviously fanciful. Not the real reason that the Natan people have blue skin. And, um . . .'

'It was supposed to explain something?'

'It's how my master always did things,' Sigzil said, looking at his feet. 'He'd tell a story anytime someone was confused, or when people were angry at him. And, well, it changed everything. Somehow.' He looked to Kaladin.

'I suppose,' Kaladin said slowly, 'that maybe you feel . . . like a moon. . . .'

'No, not really.' It was about responsibility, but he had really not explained it well. Storms. Master Hoid had named him a full Worldsinger, and here he couldn't even tell a story straight.

Kaladin clapped him on the shoulder. 'It's all right, Sig.'

'Sir,' Sigzil said. 'The other men don't have any *direction*. You've given them purpose, a reason to be good men. They *are* good men. But in some ways, it was easy when we were slaves. What do we do if not all the men manifest the ability to draw in Stormlight? What is our place in the army? Brightlord Kholin released us from guard duty, as he said he wanted us practicing and training as Radiants instead. But what *is* a Knight Radiant?'

'We'll need to figure it out.'

'And if the men need guidance? If they need a moral center? Someone has to talk to them when they're doing something wrong, but the ardents ignore us, since they associate us with the things Brightlord Dalinar is saying and doing.'

'You think you can be the one to guide the men instead?' Kaladin asked.

'Someone should, sir.'

Kaladin waved for Sigzil to follow him out into the corridor. Together they started walking toward the Bridge Four barracks, Sigzil holding out a sphere for light.

'I don't mind if you want to be something like our unit's ardent,' Kaladin said. 'The men like you, Sig, and they put a lot of stock in what you have to say. But you should try to understand what they want out of life, and respect that, rather than projecting onto them what you think they *should* want out of life.'

'But sir, some things are just *wrong*. You know what Teft has gotten into, and Huio, he's been visiting the prostitutes.'

'That's not forbidden. Storms, I've had some sergeants who suggested it as the key to a healthy mind in battle.'

'It's wrong, sir. It's imitating an oath without the commitment. Every major religion agrees to this, except the Reshi, I suppose. But they're pagans even among *pagans*.'

'Your master teach you to be this judgmental?'

Sigzil stopped short.

'I'm sorry, Sig,' Kaladin said.

'No, he said the same thing about me. All the time, sir.'

'I give you permission to sit down with Huio and explain your worries,' Kaladin said. 'I won't forbid you from expressing your morals – I'd encourage it. Just don't present your beliefs as our code. Present them as *yours*, and make a good argument. Maybe the men will listen.'

Sigzil nodded, hurrying to catch up. To cover his embarrassment – more at completely failing to tell the right story than anything else – he dug into his notebook. 'That does raise another issue, sir. Bridge Four is down to twenty-eight members, after our losses during the first Everstorm. Might be time for some recruitment.'

'Recruitment?' Kaladin said. He cocked his head.

'Well, if we lose any more members—'

'We *won't*,' Kaladin said. He always thought that.

'—or, even if we don't, we're down from the thirty-five or forty of a good bridge crew. Maybe we don't need to keep that number, but a good active unit should always be watching for people to recruit.

'What if someone else in the army has been displaying the right attitude to be a Windrunner? Or, more pointedly, what if our men start swearing oaths and bonding their own spren? Would we dissolve Bridge Four, and let each man be their own Radiant?'

The idea of dissolving Bridge Four seemed to pain Kaladin almost as much as the idea of losing men in battle. They walked in silence for a short time. They weren't going to the Bridge Four barracks after all; Kaladin had taken a turn deeper into the tower. They passed a water wagon, pulled by laborers to deliver water from the wells to the officers' quarters. Normally that would be parshman work.

'We should at least put out a call for recruitment,' Kaladin finally said, 'though honestly I can't think of how I'll cull hopefuls down to a manageable number.'

'I'll try to come up with some strategies, sir,' Sigzil said. 'If I might ask, where are we . . .' He trailed off as he saw Lyn hurrying down the hallway toward them. She carried a diamond chip in her palm for light, and wore her Kholin uniform, her dark Alethi hair pulled back in a tail.

She drew up when she saw Kaladin, then saluted him smartly. 'Just the man I was looking for. Quartermaster Vevidar sends word that "your unusual request has been fulfilled," sir.'

'Excellent,' Kaladin said, marching through the hallway past her. Sigzil shot her a look as she fell in with him, and she shrugged. She didn't know what the unusual request was, only that it had been fulfilled.

Kaladin eyed Lyn as they walked. 'You're the one who has been helping my men, right? Lyn, was it?'

'Yes, sir!'

'In fact, it seems you've been making excuses to run messages to Bridge Four.'

'Um, yes, sir.'

'Not afraid of the "Lost Radiants" then?'

'Frankly, sir, after what I saw on the battlefield, I'd rather be on your side than bet on the opposition.'

Kaladin nodded, thoughtful as he walked. 'Lyn,' he finally said, 'how would you like to join the Windrunners?'

The woman stopped in place, jaw dropping. 'Sir?' She saluted. 'Sir, I'd *love* that! Storms!'

'Excellent,' Kaladin said. 'Sig, can you get her our ledgers and accounts?'

Lyn's hand drooped from her brow. 'Ledgers? Accounts?'

'The men will also need letters written to family members,' Kaladin said. 'And we should probably write a history of Bridge Four. People will be curious, and a written account will save me from having to explain it all the time.'

'Oh,' Lyn said. 'A scribe.'

'Of course,' Kaladin said, turning back toward her in the hallway, frowning. 'You're a woman, aren't you?'

'I thought you were asking . . . I mean, in the highprince's visions, there were women who were Knights Radiant, and with Brightness Shallan . . .' She blushed. 'Sir, I didn't join the scouts because I liked sitting around staring at ledgers. If that's what you're offering, I'll have to pass.'

Her shoulders fell, and she wouldn't meet Kaladin's eyes. Sigzil found, strangely, that he wanted to punch his captain. Not hard, mind you. Just a gentle 'wake up' punch. He couldn't remember feeling that way with Kaladin since the time the captain had woken him up that first morning, back in Sadeas's warcamp.

'I see,' Kaladin said. 'Well . . . we're going to have tryouts to join the order proper. I suppose I could extend you an invitation. If you'd like.'

'Tryouts?' she said. 'For real positions? Not just doing accounts? Storms, I'm in.'

'Speak with your superior, then,' Kaladin said. 'I haven't devised the proper test yet, and you'd need to pass it before you could be let in. Either way, you'd need clearance to change battalions.'

'Yes, sir!' she said, and bounded off.

Kaladin watched her go, then grunted softly.

Sigzil – without even thinking about it – mumbled, 'Did your master teach you to be that insensitive?'

Kaladin eyed him.

'I have a suggestion, sir,' Sigzil continued. 'Try to understand what people want out of life, and respect that, rather than projecting onto them what you think they *should*—'

'Shut it, Sig.'

'Yes, sir. Sorry, sir.'

They continued on their way, and Kaladin cleared his throat. 'You don't have to be so formal with me, you know.'

'I know, sir. But you're a lighteyes now, and a Shardbearer and . . . well, it feels right.'

Kaladin stiffened, but didn't contradict him. In truth, Sigzil had always felt . . . awkward trying to treat Kaladin like any other bridgeman. Some of the others could do it – Teft and Rock, Lopen in his own strange way. But Sigzil felt more comfortable when the relationship was set out and clear. Captain and his clerk.

Moash had been the closest to Kaladin, but he wasn't in Bridge Four any longer. Kaladin hadn't said what Moash had done, only that he had 'removed himself from our fellowship.' Kaladin got stiff and unresponsive whenever Moash's name was mentioned.

'Anything else on that list of yours?' Kaladin asked as they passed a guard patrol in the hallway. He received crisp salutes.

Sigzil looked through his notebook. 'Accounts and the need for scribes . . . Code of morals for the men . . . Recruitment . . . Oh, we're still going to need to define our place in the army, now that we're no longer bodyguards.'

'We're still bodyguards,' Kaladin said. 'We just protect anyone who needs it. We have bigger problems, in that storm.'

It had come again, a third time, this event proving that it was even more regular than the highstorms. Right around every nine days. Up high as they were, its passing was only a curiosity – but throughout the world, each new arrival strained already beleaguered cities.

'I realize that, sir,' Sigzil said. 'But we still have to worry about procedure. Here, let me ask this. Are we, as Knights Radiant, still an Alethi military organization?'

'No,' Kaladin said. 'This war is bigger than Alethkar. We're for all mankind.'

'All right, then what's our chain of command? Do we obey King Elhokar? Are we still his subjects? And what dahn or nahn are we in society? You're a Shardbearer in Dalinar's court, aren't you?'

'Who pays the wages of Bridge Four? What about the other bridge crews? If there is a squabble over Dalinar's lands in Alethkar, can he call you – and Bridge Four – up to fight for him, like a normal liege-vassal relationship? If not, then can we still expect him to pay us?'

'Damnation,' Kaladin breathed.

'I'm sorry, sir. It—'

'No, they're good questions, Sig. I'm lucky to have you to ask them.' He clasped Sigzil on the shoulder, stopping in the hallway just outside the quartermaster's offices. 'Sometimes I wonder if you're wasted in Bridge Four. You should've been a scholar.'

'Well, that wind blew past me years ago, sir. I . . .' He took a deep breath. 'I failed the exams for government training in Azir. I wasn't good enough.'

'Then the exams were stupid,' Kaladin said. 'And Azir lost out, because they missed the chance to have you.'

Sigzil smiled. 'I'm glad they did.' And . . . strangely, he felt it was true. A nameless weight he'd been carrying seemed to slide off his back.

'Honestly, I feel like Lyn. I don't want to be huddled over a ledger when Bridge Four takes to the air. I want to be first into the sky.'

'I think you'll have to fight Lopen for that distinction,' Kaladin said with a chuckle. 'Come on.' He strode into the quartermaster's office, where a group of waiting guardsmen immediately made space for him. At the counter, a beefy soldier with rolled-up sleeves searched through boxes and crates, muttering to himself. A stout woman – presumably his wife – inspected requisition forms. She nudged the man and pointed at Kaladin.

'Finally!' the quartermaster said. 'I'm tired of having these here, drawing everyone's eyes and making me sweat like a spy with too many spren.'

He shuffled over to a pair of large black sacks in the corner that, best that Sigzil could tell, weren't drawing any eyes at all. The quartermaster hefted them and glanced at the scribe, who double-checked a few forms, then nodded, presenting them for Kaladin to stamp with his captain's seal. Paperwork done, the quartermaster handed a sack to Kaladin and another to Sigzil.

They clinked when moved, and were surprisingly heavy. Sigzil undid the ties and glanced into his.

A flood of green light, powerful as sunlight, shone out over him. Emeralds. The large type, not in spheres, probably cut from the gemhearts of chasmfiends hunted on the Shattered Plains. In a moment, Sigzil realized that the guards filling the room weren't here to get something from the quartermaster. They were here to protect this wealth.

'That's the royal emerald reserve,' the quartermaster said. 'Held for emergency grain, renewed with Light in the storm this morning. How you talked the highprince into letting you take it is beyond me.'

'We're only borrowing them,' Kaladin said. 'We'll have them back before evening arrives. Though be warned, some will be dun. We'll need to check them out tomorrow again. And the day after that . . .'

'I could buy a *princedom* for that much,' the quartermaster said with a grunt. 'What in Kelek's name do you need them for?'

Sigzil, however, had already guessed. He grinned like a fool. 'We're going to practice being Radiant.'

HERO

TWENTY-FOUR YEARS AGO

Dalinar cursed as smoke billowed out of the fireplace. He shoved his weight against the lever and managed to budge it, reopening the chimney flue. He coughed, backing up and waving smoke away from his face.

'We are going to need to see that replaced,' Evi said from the sofa where she was doing needlework.

'Yeah,' Dalinar said, thumping down to the floor before the fire.

'At least you got to it quickly. Today we will not need to scrub the walls, and the life will be as white as a sun at night!'

Evi's native idioms didn't always translate well into Alethi.

The fire's heat was welcome, as Dalinar's clothing was still damp from the rains. He tried to ignore the ever-present sound of the Weeping's rain outside, instead watching a pair of flamespren dance along one of the logs. These seemed vaguely human, with ever-shifting figures. He followed one with his eyes as it leaped toward the other.

He heard Evi rise, and thought she might be off to seek the privy again. She instead settled down next to him and took his arm, then sighed in contentment.

'That can't be comfortable,' Dalinar said.

'And yet you are doing it.'

'I'm not the one who is . . .' He looked at her belly, which had begun to round.

Evi smiled. 'My condition does not make me so frail that I risk *breaking* by sitting on the floor, beloved.' She pulled his arm tighter. 'Look at them. They play so eagerly!'

'It's like they're sparring,' Dalinar said. 'I can almost see the little blades in their hands.'

'Must everything be fighting to you?'

He shrugged.

She leaned her head on his arm. 'Can't you just enjoy it, Dalinar?'

'Enjoy what?'

'Your life. You went through so much to make this kingdom. Can't you be satisfied, now that you've won?'

He stood up, pulling his arm from her grip, and crossed the chamber to pour himself a drink.

'Don't think I haven't noticed the way you act,' Evi said. 'Perking up whenever the king speaks of the smallest conflict beyond our borders. Having the scribes read to you of great battles. Always talking about the next duel.'

'I'm not to have that much longer,' Dalinar grumbled, then took a sip of wine. 'Gavilar says it's foolish to endanger myself, says someone is bound to try to use one of those duels as a ploy against him. I'll have to get a champion.' He stared at his wine.

He'd never had a high opinion of dueling. It was too fake, too sanitized. But at least it was something.

'It's like you're dead,' Evi said.

Dalinar looked over at her.

'It's like you only live when you can fight,' she continued. 'When you can kill. Like a blackness from old stories. You live only by taking lives from others.'

With that pale hair and light golden skin, she was like a glowing gemstone. She was a sweet, loving woman who deserved better than the treatment he gave her. He forced himself to go back and sit down beside her.

'*I* still think the flamespren are playing,' she said.

'I've always wondered,' Dalinar said. 'Are they *made* of fire themselves? It looks like they are, and yet what of emotion spren? Are angerspren then *made* of anger?'

Evi nodded absently.

'And what of gloryspren?' Dalinar said. 'Made of glory? What *is* glory? Could gloryspren appear around someone who is delusional, or perhaps very drunk – who only *thinks* they've accomplished something great, while everyone else is standing around mocking them?'

'A mystery,' she said, 'sent by Shishi.'

'But don't you ever wonder?'

'To what end?' Evi said. 'We will know eventually, when we return to the One. No use troubling our minds now about things we cannot understand.'

Dalinar narrowed his eyes at the flamespren. That one *did* have a sword. A miniature Shardblade.

'This is why you brood so often, husband,' Evi said. 'It isn't healthy to have a stone curdling in your stomach, still wet with moss.'

'I . . . What?'

'You must not think such strange thoughts. Who put such things into your mind anyway?'

He shrugged, but thought of two nights before, staying up late and drinking wine beneath the rain canopy with Gavilar and Navani. She'd talked and talked about her research into spren, and Gavilar had simply grunted, while making notations in glyphs on a set of his maps. She'd spoken with such passion and excitement, and Gavilar had ignored her.

'Enjoy the moment,' Evi told him. 'Close your eyes and contemplate what the One has given you. Seek the peace of oblivion, and bask in the joy of your own sensation.'

He closed his eyes as she suggested, and tried to simply enjoy being here with her. 'Can a man actually change, Evi? Like those spren change?'

'We are all different aspects of the One.'

'Then can you change from one aspect to another?'

'Of course,' Evi said. 'Is not your own doctrine about transformation? About a man being Soulcast from crass to glorious?'

'I don't know if it's working.'

'Then petition the One,' she said.

'In prayer? Through the ardents?'

'No, silly. Yourself.'

'In *person*?' Dalinar asked. 'Like, at a temple?'

'If you wish to meet the One in person, you must travel to the Valley,' she said. 'There you can speak with the One, or to his avatar, and be granted—'

'The Old Magic,' Dalinar hissed, opening his eyes. 'The Nightwatcher. Evi, don't say things like that.' Storms, her pagan heritage popped up at the strangest times. She could be talking good Vorin doctrine, then out came something like *that*.

Fortunately, she spoke of it no more. She closed her eyes and hummed softly. Finally, a knock came at the outer door to his rooms.

Hathan, his room steward, would answer that. Indeed, Dalinar heard the man's voice outside, and that was followed by a light rap on the chamber door. 'It is your brother, Brightlord,' Hathan said through the door.

Dalinar leaped, opening the door and passing the short master-servant. Evi followed, trailing along with one hand touching the wall, a habit of hers. They passed open windows that looked down upon a sodden Kholinar, flickering lanterns marking where people moved through the streets.

Gavilar waited in the sitting room, dressed in one of those new suits with the stiff jacket and buttons up the sides of the chest. His dark hair curled to his shoulders, and was matched by a fine beard.

Dalinar hated beards; they got caught in your helm. He couldn't deny its effect on Gavilar though. Looking at Gavilar in his finery, one didn't see a backwater thug – a barely civilized warlord who had crushed and conquered his way to the throne. No, this man was a *king*.

Gavilar rapped a set of papers against the palm of his hand.

'What?' Dalinar asked.

'Rathalas,' Gavilar said, shoving the papers toward Evi as she entered.

'Again!' Dalinar said. It had been years since he'd visited the Rift, that giant trench where he'd won his Shardblade.

'They're demanding your Blade back,' Gavilar said. 'They claim that Tanalan's heir has returned, and deserves the Shard, as you never won it in a true contest.'

Dalinar felt cold.

'Now, I know this to be patently false,' Gavilar said, 'because when we fought at Rathalas all those years ago, you said you *dealt* with the heir. You *did* deal with the heir, did you not, Dalinar?'

He remembered that day. He remembered darkening that doorway, the Thrill pulsing inside him. He remembered a weeping child holding a Shardblade. The father, lying broken and dead behind. That soft voice, pleading.

The Thrill had vanished in a moment.

'He was a child, Gavilar,' Dalinar said, his voice hoarse.

'Damnation!' Gavilar said. 'He's a descendant of the old regime. That was . . . storms, that was a decade ago. He's old enough to be a threat! The whole city is going into rebellion, the entire *region*. If we don't act, the whole Crownlands could break off.'

Dalinar smiled. The emotion shocked him, and he quickly stifled the grin. But surely . . . surely someone would need to go and rout the rebels.

He turned and caught sight of Evi. She was beaming at him, though he'd have expected her to be indignant at the idea of more wars. Instead, she stepped up to him and took his arm. 'You spared the child.'

'I . . . He could barely lift the Blade. I gave him to his mother, and told her to hide him.'

'Oh, Dalinar.' She pulled him close.

He felt a swelling of pride. Ridiculous, of course. He had endangered the kingdom – how would people react if they knew the Blackthorn himself had broken before a crisis of conscience? They'd laugh.

In that moment, he didn't care. So long as he could be a hero to this woman.

'Well, I suppose rebellion was to be expected,' Gavilar said as he stared out the window. 'It's been years since the formal unification; people are going to start asserting their independence.' He raised his hand toward Dalinar, turning. 'I know what you want, Brother, but you'll have to forbear. I'm not sending an army.'

'But—'

'I can nip this thing with politics. We can't have a show of force be our *only* method of maintaining unity, or Elhokar will spend his entire life putting out fires after I'm gone. We need people to start thinking of Alethkar as a unified kingdom, not separate regions always looking for an advantage against one another.'

'Sounds good,' Dalinar said.

It wasn't going to happen, not without the sword to remind them. For once, however, he was fine not being the one to point that out.

You mustn't worry yourself about Rayse. It is a pity about Aona and Skai, but they were foolish – violating our pact from the very beginning.

Numuhukumakiaki'aialunamor had always been taught that the first rule of warfare was to know your enemy. One might assume that such lessons weren't terribly relevant in his life anymore. Fortunately, making a good stew was a lot like going to war.

Lunamor – called Rock by his friends, on account of their thick, low-lander tongues being incapable of proper speech – stirred his cauldron with an enormous wooden spoon the size of a longsword. A fire burned rockbud husks underneath, and a playful windspren whipped at the smoke, making it blow across him no matter where he stood.

He had placed the cauldron on a plateau of the Shattered Plains, and – beautiful lights and fallen stars – he was surprised to discover that he had *missed* this place. Who would have thought he could become fond of this barren, windswept flatland? His homeland was a place of extremes: bitter ice, powdery snow, boiling heat, and blessed humidity.

Down here, everything was so . . . moderate, and the Shattered Plains were the worst of all. In Jah Keved he'd found vine-covered valleys. In Alethkar they had fields of grain, rockbuds spreading endlessly like the bubbles of a boiling cauldron. Then the Shattered Plains. Endless empty plateaus with barely anything growing on them. Strangely, he loved them.

Lunamor hummed softly as he stirred with two hands, churning the stew and keeping the bottom from burning. When the smoke wasn't in his face – this cursed, too-thick wind had too much air to behave properly – he could smell the scent of the Shattered Plains. An . . . open scent. The scent of a high sky and baking stones, but spiced by the hint of life in the chasms. Like a pinch of salt. Humid, alive with the odors of plants and rot intermingling.

In those chasms, Lunamor had found himself again after a long time being lost. Renewed life, renewed purpose.

And stew.

Lunamor tasted his stew – using a fresh spoon of course, as he wasn't a barbarian like some of these lowlander cooks. The longroots still had further to cook before he could add the meat. Real meat, from finger crabs he'd spent all night shelling. Couldn't cook that too long, or it got rubbery.

The rest of Bridge Four stood arrayed on the plateau, listening to Kaladin. Lunamor had set up so that his back was toward Narak, the city at the center of the Shattered Plains. Nearby, one of the plateaus flashed as Renarin Kholin worked the Oathgate. Lunamor tried not to be distracted by that. He wanted to look out westward. Toward the old warcamps.

Not much longer now to wait, he thought. *But don't dwell on that. The stew needs more crushed limm.*

'I trained many of you in the chasms,' Kaladin said. The men of Bridge Four had been augmented by some members of the other bridge crews, and even a couple of soldiers that Dalinar had suggested for training. The group of five scout women was surprising, but who was Lunamor to judge?

'I could train people in the spear,' Kaladin continued, 'because I myself had been trained in the spear. What we're attempting today is different. I barely understand how I learned to use Stormlight. We're going to have to stumble through this together.'

'It's all good, gancho,' Lopen called. 'How hard can it be to learn how to fly? Skyeels do it all the time, and they are ugly and stupid. Most bridgemen are only one of those things.'

Kaladin stopped in line near Lopen. The captain seemed in good spirits today, for which Lunamor took credit. He had, after all, made Kaladin's breakfast.

'The first step will be to speak the Ideal,' Kaladin said. 'I suspect a few of you have already said it. But for the rest, if you wish to be a squire to the Windrunners, you will need to swear it.'

They began belting out the words. Everyone knew the right ones by now. Lunamor whispered the Ideal.

Life before death. Strength before weakness. Journey before destination.

Kaladin handed Lopen a pouch full of gemstones. 'The real test, and proof of your squireship, will be learning to draw Stormlight into yourselves. A few of you have learned it already—'

Lopen started glowing immediately.

'—and they will help the rest learn. Lopen, take First, Second, and Third Squads. Sigzil, you've got Fourth, Fifth, and Sixth. Peet, don't think I haven't seen you glowing. You take the other bridgemen, and Teft, you take the scouts and . . .'

Kaladin looked around. 'Where is Teft?'

He was only just noticing? Lunamor loved their captain, but he got distracted sometimes. Maybe airsickness.

'Teft didn't come back to the barracks last night, sir,' Leyten called, looking uncomfortable.

'Fine. I'll help the scouts. Lopen, Sigzil, Peet, talk your squads through how to draw in Stormlight. Before the day is done, I want everyone on this plateau glowing like they swallowed a lantern.'

They broke up, obviously eager. Translucent red streamers rose from the stone, whipping as if in the wind, one end connected to the ground. Anticipationspren. Lunamor gave them the sign of respect, hand to his shoulder, then his forehead. These were lesser gods, but still holy. He could see their true shapes beyond the streamers, a faint shadow of a larger creature at the bottom.

Lunamor handed off his stirring to Dabbid. The young bridgeman didn't talk, and hadn't since Lunamor had helped Kaladin pull him from the battlefield. He could stir though, and run waterskins. He had become something of an unofficial mascot for the team, as he'd been the first bridgeman that Kaladin had saved. When bridgemen passed Dabbid, they gave a subtle salute.

Huio was on kitchen duty with Lunamor today, as was becoming more common. Huio requested it, and the others avoided it. The squat, beefy Herdazian man was humming softly to himself as he stirred the shiki, a brownish Horneater drink that Lunamor had chilled overnight in metal bins on the plateau outside Urithiru.

Strangely, Huio took a handful of lazbo from a pot and sprinkled it into the liquid.

'What are you doing, crazy man!' Lunamor bellowed, stomping up. 'Lazbo? In drink? That thing is spicy powder, airsick lowlander!'

Huio said something in Herdazian.

'Bah!' Lunamor said. 'I do not speak this crazy language you use. Lopen! Come here and talk to this cousin you have! He is ruining our drinks!'

Lopen, however, was gesturing wildly at the sky and talking about how he'd stuck himself to the ceiling earlier.

Lunamor grunted and looked back at Huio, who proffered a spoon dripping with liquid.

'Airsick fool,' Lunamor said, taking a sip. 'You will ruin . . .'

Blessed gods of sea and stone. That was *good*. The spice added just the right *kick* to the chilled drink, combining flavors in a completely unexpected – yet somehow complementary – way.

Huio smiled. 'Bridge Four!' he said in thickly accented Alethi.

'You are lucky man,' Lunamor said, pointing. 'I will not kill you today.' He took another sip, then gestured with the spoon. 'Go do this thing to other bins of shiki.'

Now, where was Hobber? The lanky, gap-toothed man couldn't be *too* far away. That was one advantage of having an assistant chef who could not walk; he usually stayed where you put him.

'Watch me now, carefully!' Lopen said to his group, Stormlight puffing from his mouth as he spoke. 'All right. Here it is. I, the Lopen, will now fly. You may applaud as you feel is appropriate.'

He jumped up, then crashed back to the plateau.

'Lopen!' Kaladin called. 'You're supposed to be helping the others, not showing off!'

'Sorry, gon!' Lopen said. He quivered on the ground, his face pressed to the stone, and didn't rise.

'Did you . . . did you stick yourself to the *ground*?' Kaladin asked.

'Just part of the plan, gon!' Lopen called back. 'If I am to become a delicate cloud upon the sky, I must first convince the ground that I am not abandoning her. Like a worried lover, sure, she must be comforted and reassured that I will return following my dramatic and regal ascent to the sky.'

'You're not a king, Lopen,' Drehy said. 'We've been over this.'

'Of course I am not. I am a *former* king. You are obviously one of the stupid ones I mentioned earlier.'

Lunamor grunted in amusement and rounded his little cooking station toward Hobber, who he now remembered was peeling tubers by the side of the plateau. Lunamor slowed. Why was Kaladin kneeling before Hobber's stool, holding out . . . a gemstone?

Ahhh . . . Lunamor thought.

'I had to *breathe* to draw it in,' Kaladin explained softly. 'I'd been doing it unconsciously for weeks, maybe months, before Teft explained the truth to me.'

'Sir,' Hobber said, 'I don't know if . . . I mean, sir, I'm no Radiant. I was never that good with the spear. I'm barely a passable cook.'

Passable was a stretch. But he was earnest and helpful, so Lunamor was happy to have him. Besides, he needed a job he could do sitting. A month back, the Assassin in White had swept through the king's palace at the warcamps, trying to kill Elhokar – and the attack had left Hobber with dead legs.

Kaladin folded the gemstone in Hobber's fingers. 'Just try,' the captain said softly. 'Being a Radiant isn't so much about your strength or skill, but about your heart. And yours is the best of all of us.'

The captain seemed intimidating to many outsiders. A perpetual storm for an expression, an intensity that made men wilt when it turned on them. But there was also an astonishing tenderness to this man. Kaladin gripped Hobber on the arm, and almost seemed to be tearing up.

Some days, it seemed you couldn't break Kaladin Stormblessed with all the stones on Roshar. Then one of his men would get wounded, and you'd see him crack.

Kaladin headed back toward the scouts he'd been helping, and Lunamor jogged to catch up. He bowed to the little god who rode on the bridge captain's shoulder, then asked, 'You think Hobber can do this thing, Kaladin?'

'I'm sure he can. I'm sure *all* of Bridge Four can, and perhaps some of these others.'

'Ha!' Lunamor said. 'Finding a smile on your face, Kaladin Stormblessed, is like finding lost sphere in your soup. Surprising, yes, but very nice too. Come, I have drink you must try.'

'I need to get back to—'

'Come! Drink you must try!' Lunamor guided him to the big pot of shiki and poured him a cup.

Kaladin slurped it down. 'Hey, that's pretty good, Rock!'

'Is not my recipe,' Lunamor said. 'Huio has changed this thing. I now have to either promote him or push him off side of plateau.'

'Promote him to what?' Kaladin asked, getting himself another cup.

'To airsick lowlander,' Lunamor said, 'second class.'

'You might be too fond of that term, Rock.'

Nearby, Lopen talked to the ground, against which he was still pressed. 'Don't worry, dear one. The Lopen is vast enough to be possessed by many, many forces, both terrestrial and celestial! I *must* soar to the air, for if I were to remain only on the ground, surely my growing magnitude would cause the land to crack and break.'

Lunamor looked to Kaladin. 'I am fond of term, yes. But only because this thing has astounding number of applications among you.'

Kaladin grinned, sipping his shiki and watching the men. Farther along the plateau, Drehy suddenly raised his long arms and called out, 'Ha!' He was glowing with Stormlight. Bisig soon followed. That should fix his hand – he too had been injured by the Assassin in White.

'This *will* work, Rock,' Kaladin said. 'The men have been close to the power for months now. And once they have it, they'll be able to heal. I won't have to go into battle worrying which of you I'll lose.'

'Kaladin,' Lunamor said softly. 'This thing we have begun, it is still war. Men will die.'

'Bridge Four will be protected by their power.'

'And the enemy? They will not have power?' He stepped closer. 'Surely I do not wish to dampen Kaladin Stormblessed when he is optimistic, but nobody is ever perfectly safe. This is sad truth, my friend.'

'Maybe,' Kaladin admitted. He got a distant look on his face. 'Your people only let younger sons go to war, right?'

'Only tuanalikina, fourth son and younger, can be wasted in war. First, second, and third sons are too valuable.'

'Fourth son and younger. So hardly ever.'

'Ha! You do not know the size of Horneater families.'

'Still, it has to mean fewer men dying in battle.'

'Peaks are different place,' Lunamor said, smiling at Sylphrena as she rose off Kaladin's shoulder and started dancing on the nearby winds. 'And not just because we have right amount of air for brains to work. To attack another peak is costly and difficult, requiring much preparation and time. We speak of this thing more than we do him.'

'It sounds nice.'

'You will visit with me someday!' Lunamor said. 'You and all Bridge Four, as you are family now.'

'Ground,' Lopen insisted, 'I *will* still love you. I'm not attracted to anyone the way I am to you. Whenever I leave, I'll come right back!'

Kaladin glanced at Lunamor.

'Perhaps,' Lunamor noted, 'when that one is away from too much toxic air, he will be less . . .'

'Lopen?'

'Though upon consideration, this thing would be sad.'

Kaladin chuckled, handing Lunamor his cup. Then he leaned in. 'What happened to your brother, Rock?'

'My two brothers are well, so far as I know.'

'And the third brother?' Kaladin said. 'The one who died, moving you from fourth to third, and making you a cook instead of a soldier? Don't deny it.'

'Is sad story,' Lunamor said. 'And today is not day for sad stories. Today is day for laughter, stew, flight. These things.'

And hopefully . . . hopefully something even grander.

Kaladin patted him on the shoulder. 'If you ever need to talk, I'm here.'

'That is good to know. Though today, I believe someone else wishes to talk.' Lunamor nodded toward someone crossing a bridge onto their plateau. A figure in a stiff blue uniform, with a silver circlet on his head. 'The king has been eager to speak with you. Ha! Asked us several times if we knew when you would return. As if we are appointment keepers for our glorious flying leader.'

'Yes,' Kaladin said. 'He came to see me the other day.' Kaladin braced himself visibly, setting his jaw, then walked to the king, who had just marched onto the plateau, trailed by a cluster of guards from Bridge Eleven.

Lunamor positioned himself working on the soup where he could listen, as he was curious.

'Windrunner,' Elhokar said, nodding to Kaladin. 'It seems you are right, your men have had their powers restored. How soon will they be ready?'

'They're in fighting shape already, Your Majesty. But to master their powers . . . well, I can't say, honestly.'

Lunamor sipped his soup and didn't turn toward the king, but stirred and listened.

'Have you given thought to my request?' Elhokar said. 'Will you fly me to Kholinar, so we can reclaim the city?'

'I'll do as my commander tells me.'

'No,' Elhokar said. 'I'm asking you, personally. Will you come? Will you help me reclaim our homeland?'

'Yes,' Kaladin said softly. 'Give me some time, a few weeks at least, to train my men. I'd prefer to bring a few squire Windrunners with us – and if we're lucky, I might be able to leave a full Radiant behind to lead if something happens to me. But either way . . . yes, Elhokar. I'll go with you to Alethkar.'

'Good. We have some time, as Uncle wishes to try contacting people in Kholinar using his visions. Perhaps twenty days? Can you train your squires in that time?'

'I'll have to, Your Majesty.'

Lunamor glanced at the king, who folded his arms, watching the Windrunners, prospective and current. He seemed to have come not just to speak with Kaladin, but to watch the training. Kaladin walked back to the scouts – his god following in the air after him – so Lunamor brought the king something to drink. Then he hesitated beside the bridge that Elhokar had crossed to reach this plateau.

Their old bridge, from the bridge runs, had been repurposed for moving people around these plateaus closest to Narak. Permanent bridges were still being reconstructed. Lunamor patted the wood. They'd thought this lost, but a salvage party had discovered it wedged in a chasm a short distance away. Dalinar had agreed to have it hauled up, at Teft's request.

Considering what it had been through, the old bridge was in good shape. It was made of tough wood, Bridge Four was. He looked beyond it, and was unsettled by the sight of the next plateau over – or the rubble of it. A stump of a plateau, made of broken rock that extended only twenty feet or so from the chasm floor. Rlain said that had been an ordinary plateau, before the meeting of Everstorm and highstorm at the Battle of Narak.

During that terrible cataclysm when storms met, entire plateaus had been ripped up and shattered. Though the Everstorm had returned several times, the two storms had not again met over a populated area. Lunamor patted the old bridge, then shook his head, walking back toward his cooking station.

They could have trained at Urithiru, perhaps, but none of the bridgemen had complained at coming here. The Shattered Plains were far better than the lonesome plain before the tower. This place was just as barren, but it was also *theirs*.

They also hadn't questioned when Lunamor had decided to bring along his cauldrons and supplies to make lunch. It was inefficient, true, but a hot meal would make up for it – and beyond that, there was an unspoken rule. Though Lunamor, Dabbid, and Hobber didn't participate in the training or sparring, they were still Bridge Four. They went where the others went.

He had Huio add the meat – with a strict charge to *ask* before changing any spices. Dabbid continued to stir placidly. He seemed content, though it was hard to tell with that one. Lunamor washed his hands in a pot, then got to work on the bread.

Cooking *was* like warfare. You had to know your enemy – though his 'enemies' in this contest were his friends. They came to each meal expecting greatness, and Lunamor fought to prove himself time and time again. He waged war with breads and soups, sating appetites and satisfying stomachs.

As he worked, hands deep within the dough, he could hear his mother's humming. Her careful instructions. Kaladin was wrong; Lunamor hadn't *become* a cook. He'd always been one, since he could toddle up the stepstool to the counter and stick his fingers in the sticky dough. Yes, he'd once trained with a bow. But soldiers needed to eat, and nuatoma guards each did several jobs, even guards with his particular heritage and blessings.

He closed his eyes, kneading and humming his mother's song to a beat he could almost, barely, just *faintly* hear.

A short time later, he heard soft footsteps crossing the bridge behind.

Prince Renarin stopped beside the cauldron, his duty of transferring people through the Oathgate finished for now. On the plateau, more than a third of Bridge Four had figured out how to draw in Stormlight, but none of the newcomers had managed it, despite Kaladin's coaching.

Renarin watched with flushed cheeks. He'd obviously run to get here once released from his other duty, but now he was hesitant. Elhokar had set up to watch near some rocks, and Renarin stepped toward him, as if sitting at the side and watching was his place too.

'Hey!' Lunamor said. 'Renarin!'

Renarin jumped. The boy wore his blue Bridge Four uniform, though his seemed somehow . . . neater than the others.

'I could use some help with this bread,' Lunamor said.

Renarin smiled immediately. All the youth ever wanted was to be treated like the rest of them. Well, that attitude benefited a man. Lunamor would have the highprince himself kneading dough, if he could get away with it. Dalinar seemed like he could use a good session of making bread.

Renarin washed his hands, then sat on the ground across from Lunamor and followed his lead. Lunamor ripped off a piece of dough about as wide as his hand, flattened it, then slapped it against one of the large stones he'd put to warm by the fire. The dough stuck to the stone, where it would cook until one peeled it off.

Lunamor didn't push Renarin to talk. Some people you wanted to press, draw them out. Others you wanted to let move at their own pace. Like the difference between a stew you brought to a boil and one you kept at a simmer.

But where is his god? Lunamor could see all spren. Prince Renarin had bonded one, except Lunamor had never been able to spot it. He bowed when Renarin wasn't looking, just in case, and made a sign of reverence to the hidden god.

'Bridge Four is doing well,' Renarin finally said. 'He'll have them all drinking Stormlight soon.'

'Likely so,' Lunamor said. 'Ha! But they have much time until they catch up to you. Truthwatcher! Is good name. More people should watch truth, instead of lies.'

Renarin blushed. 'I . . . I suppose it means I can't be in Bridge Four anymore, doesn't it?'

'Why not?'

'I'm a different order of Radiant,' Renarin said, eyes down as he formed a perfectly round piece of dough, then carefully set it onto a stone.

'You have power to heal.'

'The Surges of Progression and Illumination. I'm not sure how to make the second one work though. Shallan has explained it seven times, but I can't create even the smallest illusion. Something's wrong.'

'Still, only healing for now? This thing will be very useful to Bridge Four!'

'I can't *be* Bridge Four anymore.'

'That is nonsense. Bridge Four is not Windrunners.'

'Then what is it?'

'It is us,' Lunamor sad. 'It is me, it is them, it is you.' He nodded toward Dabbid. 'That one, he will never hold spear again. He will not fly, but he is Bridge Four. I am forbidden to fight, but I am Bridge Four. And you, you might have fancy title and different powers.' He leaned forward. 'But I know Bridge Four. And you, Renarin Kholin, are Bridge Four.'

Renarin smiled widely. 'But Rock, don't you ever worry that you aren't the person everyone thinks you are?'

'Everyone thinks I am loud, insufferable lout!' Lunamor said. 'So to be something else would not be bad thing.'

Renarin chuckled.

'You think this about yourself?' Lunamor said.

'Maybe,' Renarin said, making another perfectly round piece of dough. 'I don't know *what* I am most days, Rock, but I seem to be the only one. Since I could walk, everyone was saying, "Look how bright he is. He should be an ardent."'

Lunamor grunted. Sometimes, even if you were loud and insufferable, you knew when not to say anything.

'Everyone thinks it's *so obvious*. I have a mind for figures, don't I? Yes, join the ardents. Of course, nobody *says* I'm much less of a man than my brother, and nobody points out that it *sure* would be nice for the succession if the sickly, strange younger brother were safely tucked away in a monastery.'

'When you say these things, you are *almost* not bitter!' Lunamor said. 'Ha! Much practice must have been required.'

'A lifetime.'

'Tell me,' Lunamor said. 'Why do you wish to be man who fights, Renarin Kholin?'

'Because it's what my father always wanted,' Renarin said immediately. 'He may not realize it, but it's there, Rock.'

Lunamor grunted. 'Perhaps this is stupid reason, but it is reason, and I can respect that. But tell me, why do you *not* want to become ardent or stormwarden?'

'Because everyone assumes I will be!' Renarin said, slapping bread down on the heated stones. 'If I go and do it, I'm giving in to what they all say.' He looked for something to fidget with, and Lunamor tossed him more dough.

'I think,' Lunamor said, 'your problem is different than you say. You claim you are not the person everyone thinks you are. Maybe you worry, instead, that you *are* that person.'

'A sickly weakling.'

'No,' Lunamor said, leaning in. 'You can be you without this being bad thing. You can admit you act and think differently from your brother, but can learn not to see this as flaw. It is just Renarin Kholin.'

Renarin started kneading the dough furiously.

'Is good,' Lunamor said, 'that you learn to fight. Men do well learning many different skills. But men also do well using what the gods have given them. In the Peaks, a man may not have such choices. Is privilege!'

'I suppose. Glys says . . . Well, it's complicated. I could talk to the ardents, but I'm hesitant to do anything that would make me stand out from the other bridgemen, Rock. I'm already the oddest one in this bunch.'

'Is that so?'

'Don't deny it, Rock. Lopen is . . . well, Lopen. And you're obviously . . . um . . . you. But *I'm* still the strange one. I've always been the strangest one.'

Lunamor slapped dough onto a rock, then pointed toward where Rlain – the Parshendi bridgeman they used to call Shen – sat on a rock near his squad, watching quietly as the others laughed at Eth having accidentally stuck a stone to his hand. He wore warform, and so was taller and stronger he had been before – but the humans seemed to have completely forgotten that he was there.

'Oh,' Renarin said. 'I don't know if he counts.'

'This thing is what everyone always tells him,' Lunamor said. 'Over and over again.'

Renarin stared for a long time while Lunamor continued to make bread. Finally, Renarin stood up and dusted off his uniform, walked across the stone plateau, and settled down beside Rlain. Renarin fidgeted and didn't say anything, but Rlain seemed to appreciate the company anyway.

Lunamor smiled, then finished the last of the bread. He rose and set up the shiki drink with a stack of wooden cups. He took another drink himself, then shook his head and glanced at Huio, who was harvesting the bread. The Herdazian man was glowing faintly – clearly, he'd already learned how to draw in Stormlight.

Airsick Herdazian. Lunamor raised a hand and Huio tossed him a flatbread, which Lunamor bit. He chewed the warm bread, thoughtful. 'More salt in the next batch?'

The Herdazian just kept harvesting the bread.

'You do think they need more salt, don't you?' Lunamor said.

Huio shrugged.

'Add more salt to that batch that I've started mixing,' Lunamor said. 'And do not look so self-satisfied. I may still throw you off side of plateau.'

Huio smiled and kept working.

The men soon started coming over for something to drink. They grinned, thumped Lunamor on the back, told him he was a genius. But of course, none remembered that he had tried serving them shiki once before. They had mostly left it in the cauldron, opting for beer instead.

That day they hadn't been hot, sweaty, and frustrated. Know your enemy. Out here, with the right drink, he was a little god unto himself. Ha! A god of cool drinks and friendly advice. Any chef worth his spoons learned to talk, because cooking was an art – and art was subjective. One man could love an ice sculpture while another thought it boring. It was the same with food and drink. It did not make the food broken, or the person broken, to not be liked.

He chatted with Leyten, who was still shaken by their experience with the dark god below Urithiru. Powerful god that had been, and very vengeful. There were legends of such things in the Peaks; Lunamor's great-great-great-grandfather had met with one while traveling the third divide. Excellent and important story, which Lunamor did not share today.

He calmed Leyten, commiserated with him. The thick-bodied armorer was a fine man, and could talk as loudly as Lunamor sometimes. Ha! You could hear him two plateaus away, which Lunamor liked. What was the point of a little voice? Weren't voices for being heard?

Leyten went back to his practice, but others had their worries. Skar was the best spearman among them – particularly now that Moash had left – but was feeling self-conscious at not having drawn in Stormlight. Lunamor asked Skar to show him what he'd learned, and – after Skar's instruction – Lunamor actually managed to draw some in himself. To his delight and surprise.

Skar left with a spring to his step. Another man would have felt worse, but Skar was a teacher at heart. The short man still hoped that Lunamor would someday choose to fight. He was the only one of the bridgemen who actively spoke out about Lunamor's pacifism.

Once the men had been thoroughly watered, Lunamor found himself looking out across the plateaus for some sign of movement in the distance. Well, best to keep busy with the meal. The stew was perfect – he was pleased to have been able to get the crabs. So much of what everyone ate in the tower was of Soulcast grain or meat, neither of which was very appetizing. The flatbread had cooked up nicely, and he'd even been able to concoct a chutney last night. Now he just had to . . .

Lunamor almost stumbled into his own cauldron as he saw what was assembling on the plateau to his left. *Gods!* Strong gods, like Sylphrena. Glowing a faint blue, they clustered around a tall spren woman, who had long hair streaming behind her. She had taken the shape of a person, human sized, and wore an elegant gown. The others swirled about in the air, though their focus was obviously the practicing bridgemen and hopefuls.

'Uma'ami tukuma mafah'liki . . .' Lunamor started, hastily making the signs of respect. Then, to be sure, he got down on his knees and bowed. He had never seen so many in one place. Even his occasional meeting with an afah'liki in the Peaks did not hit him as hard as this.

What was the proper offering? He could not give only bows for such a sight as this. But bread and stew? Mafah'liki would not want bread and stew.

'You,' a feminine voice said beside him, 'are so wonderfully respectful, it borders on being silly.'

Lunamor turned to find Sylphrena sitting on the side of his cauldron, in her small and girlish shape, legs crossed and hanging over the edge.

He made the sign again. 'They are your kin? Is this woman at their front your nuatoma, ali'i'kamura?'

'Kind of maybe sort of halfway,' she said, cocking her head. 'I can barely remember a voice ... her voice, Phendorana, reprimanding me. I got in *so* much trouble for searching out Kaladin. Yet here they are! They won't speak to me. I think they assume that if they do, they'd have to admit to me they were wrong.' She leaned forward, grinning. 'And they absolutely hate being wrong.'

Lunamor nodded solemnly.

'You're not as brown as you were,' Sylphrena said.

'Yes, my tan is fading,' Lunamor said. 'Too much time indoors, mafah'liki.'

'Humans can change colors?'

'Some more than others,' Lunamor said, holding up his hand. 'Some from other peaks are pale, like Shin, though my peak has always been more bronze.'

'You look like somebody washed you *way* too much,' Sylphrena said. 'They took a scrub brush to you, and rubbed your skin off! And that's why your hair is red, because you got so sore!'

'These are wise words,' Lunamor said. He wasn't sure why yet. He'd have to ponder them.

He fished in his pocket for the spheres that he had on him, which weren't many. Still, he arranged each one in its own bowl and then approached the assemblage of spren. There had to be two dozen or more of them! Kali'kalin'da!

The other bridgemen couldn't see the gods, of course. He wasn't sure what Huio or Hobber thought of him walking reverently across the plateau, then bowing himself and arranging the bowls with their spheres as offerings. When he looked up, the ali'i'kamura – the most important god here – was studying him. She rested her hand over one of the bowls and drew out the Stormlight. Then she left, turning into a streak of light and zipping away.

The others remained, a mottled collection of clouds, ribbons, people, bunches of leaves, and other natural objects. They flitted overhead, watching the practicing men and women.

Sylphrena crossed the air to stand beside Lunamor's head.

'They are looking,' Lunamor whispered. 'This thing *is* happening. Not just bridgemen. Not just squires. Radiants, as Kaladin wishes.'

'We'll see,' she said, then huffed softly before zipping away as a ribbon of light herself.

Lunamor left the bowls in case any of the others wished to partake of his offering. At his cook station, he stacked up the flatbread, intending to give the plates to Hobber to hold and distribute. Only, Hobber didn't respond to his request. The lanky man sat on his little stool, leaning forward, his hand in a tight fist that glowed from the gemstone inside. The cups he'd been washing lay in an ignored stack beside him.

Hobber's mouth moved – whispering – and he stared at that glowing fist in the same way a man might stare at the tinder in his firepit on a very cold night, surrounded by snow. Desperation, determination, prayer.

Do it, Hobber, Lunamor thought, stepping forward. *Drink it in. Make it yours.* Claim *it*.

Lunamor felt an energy to the air. A moment of focus. Several windspren turned toward Hobber, and for a heartbeat Lunamor thought that everything else faded. Hobber became one man alone in a darkened place, fist glowing. He stared, unblinking, at that sign of power. That sign of *redemption*.

The light in Hobber's fist went out.

'Ha!' Lunamor shouted. 'HA!'

Hobber jumped in surprise. His jaw dropped and he stared at the now-dun gemstone. Then he held up his hand, gawking at the luminescent smoke that rose from it. 'Guys?' he called. 'Guys, *guys*!'

Lunamor stepped back as the bridgemen left their stations and came rushing over. 'Give him your gemstones!' Kaladin called. 'He's going to need a lot! Pile them up!'

Bridgemen scrambled to give Hobber their emeralds, and he drew in more and more Stormlight. Then the light suddenly dampened. 'I can feel them again!' Hobber cried. 'I can feel my toes!'

He tentatively reached out for support. Drehy under one arm, Peet under the other, Hobber slipped off his stool and stood up. He grinned with a gap-toothed expression, and almost fell over – his legs obviously weren't very strong. Drehy and Peet righted him, but he forced them back, to let him stand precariously on his own.

The men of Bridge Four waited only briefly before pressing in with cries of excitement. Joyspren swirled around the group, like a sweeping gust of blue leaves. Amid them, Lopen shoved in close and made the Bridge Four salute.

It seemed to mean something special, coming from him. Two arms. One of the first times Lopen had been able to make the salute. Hobber saluted back, grinning like a boy who'd just hit his first center shot with the bow.

Kaladin stepped up beside Lunamor, Sylphrena on his shoulder. 'It *will* work, Rock. This will protect them.'

Lunamor nodded, then by habit checked toward the west as he'd been doing all day. This time he spotted something.

It looked like a plume of smoke.

·:·

Kaladin flew to check it out. Lunamor, along with the rest of them, followed along on the ground, carrying their mobile bridge.

Lunamor ran at the center front of the bridge. It smelled of memories. The wood, the stain used to seal it. The sounds of several dozen men grunting and breathing in the enclosed spaces. The slapping of feet on plateau. Mixed exhaustion and terror. An assault. Arrows flying. Men dying.

Lunamor had known what might happen when he chose to come down from the Peaks with Kef'ha. No nuatoma from the Peaks had ever yet won a Shardblade or Shardplate from the Alethi or Vedens they challenged. Still, Kef'ha had determined the cost was worth the risk. At worst he had thought he would end up dead, and his family would become servants to a wealthy lowlander.

They hadn't anticipated the cruelty of Torol Sadeas, who had murdered Kef'ha without a proper duel, killed many of Lunamor's family who resisted, and seized his property.

Lunamor roared, charging forward, and his skin started to glow with the power of the Stormlight from his pouch and the spheres he had collected before leaving. He seemed to be carrying the bridge all on his own, towing the others.

Skar called out a marching song, and Bridge Four thundered the words. Bridge Four had grown strong enough to carry the bridge long distances without difficulty, but this day put those previous runs to shame. They ran at a sprint the entire distance, vibrant with Stormlight, Lunamor calling the commands as Kaladin or Teft had once done. When they reached a chasm, they practically tossed the bridge across. When they picked it up on the other side, it seemed light as a reed.

It felt like they'd barely started going before they neared the source of the smoke: a beleaguered caravan crossing the plains. Lunamor threw his weight against the bridge's outer support rods, pushing it across the chasm, then he charged over. Others followed. Dabbid and Lopen unhooked shields and spears from the side of the bridge and tossed one to each bridgeman as they passed. They fell into squads, and the men who normally followed Teft fell in behind Lunamor, though he had – of course – refused the spear Lopen tried to toss him.

Many of the caravan wagons had been transporting lumber from the forests outside the warcamps, though some were piled high with furniture. Dalinar Kholin spoke of repopulating his warcamp, but the two highprinces who remained behind had been encroaching on the land – quietly, like eels. For now, it was best to scavenge what they could and bring it to Urithiru.

The caravan had been using Dalinar's large, wheeled bridges to cross chasms. Lunamor passed one of these, lying on its side, broken. Three of the large lumber wagons near it had been set afire, making the air acrid with smoke.

Kaladin floated overhead, holding his brilliant Shardspear. Lunamor squinted through the smoke in the direction Kaladin was looking, and made out figures streaking away through the sky.

'Voidbringer attack,' Drehy muttered. 'We should have guessed they'd start raiding our caravans.'

Lunamor didn't care at the moment. He pushed his way through weary caravan guards and frightened merchants hiding under wagons. There were bodies everywhere; the Voidbringers had killed dozens. Lunamor searched through the mess, trembling. Was that red hair on a corpse? No, that was blood soaking a headscarf. And that . . .

That other body wasn't human – it had marbled skin. A brilliant white arrow stuck from its back, fletched with goose feathers. An Unkalaki arrow.

Lunamor looked to the right, where someone had piled up furniture in a heap, almost like a fortification. A head poked up over the top, a stout woman with a round face and a deep red braid. She stood up tall and raised a bow toward Lunamor. Other faces peeked out from behind the furniture. Two youths, a boy and a girl, both around sixteen. Younger faces from there. Six in total.

Lunamor dashed toward them and found himself blubbering, tears streaming down his cheeks as he crawled up the outside of their improvised fortification.

His family, at long last, had arrived at the Shattered Plains.

.·.

'This is Song,' Lunamor said, pulling the woman close, one arm around her shoulders. 'Is best woman in all the Peaks. Ha! We made snow forts as childs, and hers was always best. I should have known to find her in castle, even if it was made of old chairs!'

'Snow?' Lopen asked. 'How do you make forts out of snow? I've heard all about this stuff – it's like frost, right?'

'Airsick lowlander.' Lunamor shook his head, moving to the twins. He put one hand on each of their shoulders. 'Boy is Gift. Girl is Cord. Ha! When I left, Gift was short like Skar. Now he is nearly my height!'

He struggled to keep the pain from his voice. It had been almost a year. So long. Originally, his intent had been to bring them as soon as possible, but then everything had gone wrong. Sadeas, the bridge crews . . .

'Next son is Rock, but not same kind of Rock as me. This is . . . um . . . smaller Rock. Third son is Star. Second daughter is Kuma'tiki – is kind of shell, you do not have him here. Last daughter is another Song. Beautiful Song.' He stooped down beside her, smiling. She was only four, and she shied away from him. She didn't remember her father. It broke his heart.

Song – Tuaka'li'na'calmi'nor – put her hand on his back. Nearby, Kaladin introduced Bridge Four, but only Gift and Cord had been taught lowlander languages, and Cord spoke only Veden. Gift managed a passable greeting in Alethi.

Little Song sought her mother's legs. Lunamor blinked away tears, though they were not completely sad tears. His family was *here*. His first saved wages had paid for the message, sent by spanreed to the Peaks message station. That station was still a week's travel from his home, and from there, traveling down from the slopes and crossing Alethkar took months.

Around them the caravan was finally limping into motion. This was the first chance Lunamor had found to introduce his family, as Bridge Four had spent the last half hour trying to help the wounded. Then, Renarin had arrived with Adolin and two companies of troops – and for all Renarin's worries about not being useful, his healing had saved several lives.

Tuaka rubbed Lunamor's back, then knelt down beside him, pulling their daughter close with one arm, Lunamor with the other. 'It was a long journey,' she said in Unkalaki, 'and longest at the end, when those things came from the sky.'

'I should have come to the warcamps,' Lunamor said. 'To escort you.'

'We're here now,' she said. 'Lunamor, what happened? Your note was so terse. Kef'ha is dead, but what happened to you? Why so long without word?'

He bowed his head. How could he explain this? The bridge runs, the cracks in his soul. How could he explain that the man she'd always said was so strong had wished to die? Had been a coward, had given up, near the end?

'What of Tifi and Sinaku'a?' she asked him.

'Dead,' he whispered. 'They raised weapons in vengeance.'

She put her hand to her lips. She wore a glove on her safehand, in deference to silly Vorin traditions. 'Then you—'

'I am a chef now,' Lunamor said, firm.

'But—'

'I cook, Tuaka.' He pulled her close again. 'Come, let us take the children to safety. We will reach the tower, which you will like – it is like the Peaks, almost. I will tell you stories. Some are painful.'

'Very well. Lunamor, I have stories too. The Peaks, our home . . . something is wrong. Very wrong.'

He pulled back and met her eyes. They'd call her darkeyed down here, though he found infinite depth, beauty, and light in those deep brown-green eyes.

'I will explain when we are safe,' she promised, picking up little Beautiful Song. 'You are wise to usher us forward. Wise as ever.'

'No, my love,' he whispered. 'I am a fool. I would blame the air, but

I was a fool above too. A fool to ever let Kef'ha leave on this errand of stupidity.'

She walked the children across the bridge. He watched, and was glad to hear Unkalaki again, a proper language. Glad that the other men did not speak it. For if they did, they might have picked out the lies that he had told them.

Kaladin stepped up, clapping him on the shoulder. 'I'm going to assign your family my rooms, Rock. I've been slow in getting family quarters for the bridgemen. This will light a fire under me. I'll get us an assignment, and until then I'll bunk with the rest of the men.'

Lunamor opened his mouth to object, then thought better of it. Some days, the more honorable thing was to take a gift without complaint. 'Thank you,' he said. 'For the rooms. For other things, my captain.'

'Go walk with your family, Rock. We can handle the bridge without you today. We have Stormlight.'

Lunamor rested his fingers on the smooth wood. 'No,' he said. 'It will be a privilege to carry him one last time, for my family.'

'One last time?' Kaladin said.

'We take to the skies, Stormblessed,' Lunamor said. 'We will walk no more in coming days. This is the end.' He looked back toward a subdued Bridge Four group, who seemed to sense that what he said was true. 'Ha! Do not look so sad. I left great stew back near city. Hobber will probably not ruin it before we return. Come! Pick up our bridge. The last time, we march not toward death, but toward full stomachs and good songs!'

Despite his urging, it was a solemn, respectful group who lifted the bridge. They were slaves no longer. Storms, in their pockets they carried riches! It glowed fiercely, and soon their skin did as well.

Kaladin took his place at the front. Together they carried the bridge on one final run – reverently, as if it were the bier of a king, being taken to his tomb for his eternal rest.

Your skills are admirable, but you are merely a man. You had your chance to be more, and refused it.

Dalinar entered the next vision in the middle of a fight.

He had learned his lesson; he didn't intend to mire another person in an unexpected battle. This time he intended to find a safe point, *then* bring people in.

That meant appearing as he had many months ago: holding a spear in sweaty hands, standing on a forlorn and broken plate of rock, surrounded by men in primitive clothing. They wore wraps of rough-spun lavis fibers and sandals of hogshide, and carried spears with bronze heads. Only the officer wore armor: a mere leather jerkin, not even properly hardened. It had been cured, then cut roughly into the shape of a vest. It proved no help against an axe to the face.

Dalinar roared, indistinctly remembering his first time in this vision. It had been one of the very earliest, when he still discounted them as nightmares. Today, he intended to tease out its secrets.

He charged the enemy, a group of men in similarly shoddy clothing. Dalinar's companions had backed themselves up to the edge of a cliff. If they didn't fight now, they'd be pushed off onto a steep incline that eventually ended in a sheer drop and a plummet of some fifty or sixty feet to the bottom of a valley.

Dalinar rammed into the enemy group trying to push his men off the cliff. He wore the same clothing as the others, carried their weapons, but had brought one oddity: a pouch full of gemstones tucked at his waist.

He gutted one enemy with his spear, then shoved the fellow toward the others: thirty or so men with ragged beards and callous eyes. Two tripped over their dying friend, which protected Dalinar's flank for a moment. He seized the fallen man's axe, then attacked to his left.

The enemy resisted, howling. These men weren't well trained, but any fool with a sharpened edge could be dangerous. Dalinar cut, slashed, laid about himself with the axe – which was well balanced, a good weapon. He was confident he could beat this group.

Two things went wrong. First, the other spearmen didn't support him. Nobody filled in behind to protect him from being surrounded.

Second, the wild men didn't flinch.

Dalinar had come to rely on the way soldiers pulled away when they saw him fighting. He depended on their discipline to fail – even when he hadn't been a Shardbearer, he'd counted on his ferocity, his sheer *momentum*, to win fights.

Turned out, the momentum of one man – no matter how skilled or determined – amounted to little when running into a stone wall. The men before him didn't bend, didn't panic, didn't so much as quiver as he killed four of them. They struck at him with increased ferocity. One even laughed.

In a flash, his arm was chopped by an axe he didn't even see, then he was shoved over by the rush of the attackers. Dalinar hit the ground, stunned, looking with disbelief at the stump of his left forearm. The pain seemed a disconnected thing, distant. Only a single painspren, like a hand made of sinew, appeared by his knees.

Dalinar felt a shattering, humbling sense of his own mortality. Was this what every veteran felt, when he finally fell on the battlefield? This bizarre, surreal sense of both disbelief and long-buried resignation?

Dalinar set his jaw, then used his good hand to pull free the leather strap he was using for a belt. Holding one end in his teeth, he wrapped it around the stump of his arm right above the elbow. The cut wasn't bleeding too badly yet. Took a moment for a wound like this to bleed; the body constricted blood flow at first.

Storms. This blow had gone clean through. He reminded himself that this wasn't his actual flesh exposed to the air. That it wasn't his own bone there, like the center ring of a hunk of pork.

Why not heal yourself as you did in the vision with Fen? the Stormfather asked. *You have Stormlight.*

'Cheating,' Dalinar said with a grunt.

Cheating? the Stormfather said. *Why in Damnation would that be cheating? You made no oath.*

Dalinar smiled to hear a fragment of God cursing. He wondered if the Stormfather was picking up bad habits from him. Ignoring the pain as best he could, Dalinar seized his axe in one hand and stumbled to his feet. Ahead of him, his squad of twelve fought desperately – and poorly – against the frantic enemy assault. They'd backed right to the edge of the cliff. With the towering rock formations all around, this place almost felt like a chasm, though it was considerably more open.

Dalinar wavered, and almost collapsed again. Storm it.

Just heal yourself, the Stormfather said.

'I used to be able to shrug off things like this.' Dalinar looked down at his missing arm. Well, perhaps nothing as bad as this.

You're old, the Stormfather said.

'Maybe,' Dalinar said, steadying himself, his vision clearing. 'But they made a mistake.'

Which is?

'They turned their backs on *me*.'

Dalinar charged again, wielding the axe in one hand. He dropped two of the enemy, punching through to his men. 'Down!' he shouted to them. 'We can't fight them up here. Skid down the incline to that ledge below! We'll try to find a way to climb down from there!'

He jumped off the cliff and hit the incline in motion. It was a reckless maneuver, but storms, they'd never survive up above. He slid down the stone, staying on his feet as he approached the sheer drop into the valley. A final small ledge of stone gave him a place to lurch to a stop.

Other men slid down around him. He dropped his axe and seized one man, keeping him from falling all the way off the ledge to his doom. He missed two others.

In all, seven men managed to stop around him. Dalinar puffed out, feeling light-headed again, then looked down over the side of their current perch. At least fifty feet to the bottom of the canyon.

His fellows were a broken, ragged group of men, bloodied and afraid. Exhaustionspren shot up nearby, like jets of dust. Above, the wild men clustered around the edge, looking down longingly, like axehounds contemplating the food on the master's table.

'Storms!' The man Dalinar had saved slumped down. 'Storms! They're dead. Everyone's dead.' He wrapped his arms around himself.

Looking about him, Dalinar counted only one man besides himself who had kept his weapon. The tourniquet he'd made was letting blood seep out.

'We win this war,' Dalinar said softly.

Several others looked to him.

'We *win*. I've seen it. Our platoon is one of the last still fighting. While we may yet fall, the war itself is being won.'

Above, a figure joined the wild men: a creature a good head taller than the others, with fearsome carapace armor of black and red. Its eyes glowed a deep crimson.

Yes . . . Dalinar remembered that creature. In this vision before, he'd been left for dead up above. This figure had walked past: a monster from a nightmare, he'd assumed, dredged from his subconscious, similar to the beings he fought on the Shattered Plains. Now he recognized the truth. That was a Voidbringer.

But there had been no Everstorm in the past; the Stormfather confirmed that. So where had those things come from, back during this time?

'Form up,' Dalinar commanded. 'Get ready!'

Two of the men listened, scrambling over to him. Honestly, two out of seven was more than he'd expected.

The cliff face shook as if something huge had struck it. And then the stones nearby *rippled*. Dalinar blinked. Was the blood loss causing his vision to waver? The stone face seemed to shimmer and undulate, like the surface of a pond that had been disturbed.

Someone grabbed the rim of their ledge from below. A figure resplendent in Shardplate – each piece visibly glowing an amber color at its edges despite the daylight – hauled itself onto their ledge. The imposing figure stood even larger than other men wearing Shardplate.

'Flee,' the Shardbearer commanded. 'Get your men to the healers.'

'How?' Dalinar asked. 'The cliff—'

Dalinar started. The cliff had handholds now.

The Shardbearer pressed his hand against the incline leading up toward the Voidbringer, and again the stone seemed to writhe. Steps formed in the rock, as if it were made of wax that could flow and be shaped. The Shardbearer extended his hand to the side, and a massive, glowing hammer appeared there.

He charged upward toward the Voidbringer.

Dalinar felt the rock, which was firm to his touch. He shook his head, then ushered his men to start climbing down.

The last one looked at the stump of his arm. 'How are you going to follow, Malad?'

'I'll manage,' Dalinar said. 'Go.'

The man left. Dalinar was growing more and more fuzzy-headed. Finally, he relented and drew in some Stormlight.

His arm regrew. First the cut healed, then the flesh expanded outward like a budding plant. In moments he wriggled his fingers, awed. He'd shrugged off a *lost arm* like a stubbed toe. The Stormlight cleared his head, and he took a deep, refreshed breath.

The sounds of fighting came from above, but even craning his neck, he couldn't see much – though a body did roll down the incline, then slip off the ledge.

'Those are humans,' Dalinar said.

Obviously.

'I never put it together before,' Dalinar said. 'There were men who fought *for* the Voidbringers?'

Some.

'And that Shardbearer I saw? A Herald?'

No. Merely a Stoneward. That Surge that changed the stone is the other you may learn, though it may serve you differently.

Such a contrast. The regular soldiers looked so primitive, but that Surgebinder . . .

With a shake of his head, Dalinar climbed down, using the handholds in the rock face. Dalinar spotted his fellows joining a large group of soldiers farther down the canyon. Shouts and whoops of joy echoed against the walls from that direction. It was as he vaguely remembered: The war had been won. Only pockets of the enemy still resisted. The larger bulk of the army was starting to celebrate.

'All right,' Dalinar said. 'Bring in Navani and Jasnah.' He eventually planned to show this vision to the young emperor of Azir, but first he wanted to prepare. 'Put them somewhere close to me, please. Let them keep their own clothing.'

Nearby, two men stopped in place. A mist of glowing Stormlight obscured their forms, and when the mist faded, Navani and Jasnah stood there, wearing havahs.

Dalinar jogged over to them. 'Welcome to my madness, ladies.'

Navani turned about, craning her neck to stare up at the tops of the castle-like rock formations. She glanced toward a group of soldiers who limped past, one man helping his wounded companion and calling for Regrowth. 'Storms!' Navani whispered. 'It feels so real.'

'I did warn you,' Dalinar said. 'Hopefully you don't look *too* ridiculous back in the rooms.' Though he had become familiar enough with the visions that his body no longer acted out what he was doing in them, that wouldn't be so for Jasnah, Navani, or any of the monarchs he brought in.

'What is that woman doing?' Jasnah asked, curious.

A younger woman met the limping men. A Radiant? She had the look about her, though she wasn't armored. It was more her air of confidence, the way she settled them down and took something glowing from the pouch at her belt.

'I remember this,' Dalinar said. 'It's one of those devices I mentioned from another vision. The ones that provide Regrowth, as they call it. Healing.'

Navani's eyes widened, and she beamed like a child who had been given a plate full of sweets for Middlefest. She gave Dalinar a quick hug, then hurried over to watch. She stepped right up to the side of the group, then waved impatiently for the Radiant to continue.

Jasnah turned to look around the canyon. 'I know of no place in our time of this description, Uncle. This seems like the stormlands, from those formations.'

'Maybe it's lost somewhere in the Unclaimed Hills?'

'That, or it's been so long the rock formations have weathered away completely.' She narrowed her eyes at a group of people who came through the canyon, carrying water to the soldiers. Last time, Dalinar had stumbled down into the canyon just in time to meet them and get a drink.

You're needed above, one had told him, pointing up the shallow slope along the side of the canyon opposite where he had been fighting.

'That clothing,' Jasnah said softly. 'Those weapons . . .'

'We've gone back to ancient times.'

'Yes, Uncle,' Jasnah said. 'But didn't you tell me this vision comes at the end of the Desolations?'

'From what I remember of it, yes.'

'So the vision with the Midnight Essence happened before this, chronologically. Yet you saw steel, or at least iron, in that one. Remember the poker?'

'I'm not likely to forget.' He rubbed his chin. 'Iron and steel then, but men wielding crude weapons here, of copper and bronze. As if they didn't know how to Soulcast iron, or at least not how to forge it properly, despite it being a later date. Huh. That *is* odd.'

'This is confirmation of what we've been told, but which I could never quite believe. The Desolations were so terrible they destroyed learning and progress and left behind a broken people.'

'The orders of Radiants were supposed to stop that,' Dalinar said. 'I learned it in another vision.'

'Yes, I read that one. All of them, actually.' She looked to him then, and smiled.

People were always surprised to see emotion from Jasnah, but Dalinar considered that unfair. She did smile – she merely reserved the expression for when it was most genuine.

'Thank you, Uncle,' she said. 'You have given the world a grand gift. A man can be brave in facing down a hundred enemies, but coming into these – and recording them rather than hiding them – was bravery on an entirely different level.'

'It was mere stubbornness. I refused to believe I was mad.'

'Then I bless your stubbornness, Uncle.' Jasnah pursed her lips in thought, then continued more softly. 'I'm worried about you, Uncle. What people are saying.'

'You mean my heresy?' Dalinar said.

'I'm less worried about the heresy itself, and more how you're dealing with the backlash.'

Ahead of them, Navani had somehow bullied the Radiant into letting her look at the fabrial. The day was stretching toward late afternoon, the

435

canyon falling into shadow. But this vision was a long one, and he was content to wait upon Navani. He settled down on a rock.

'I don't deny God, Jasnah,' he said. 'I simply believe that the being we call the Almighty was never actually God.'

'Which is the wise decision to make, considering the accounts of your visions.' Jasnah settled down beside him.

'You must be happy to hear me say that,' he said.

'I'm happy to have someone to talk to, and I'm certainly happy to see you on a journey of discovery. But am I happy to see you in pain? Am I happy to see you forced to abandon something you held dear?' She shook her head. 'I don't mind people believing what works for them, Uncle. That's something nobody ever seems to understand – I have no stake in their beliefs. I don't need *company* to be *confident*.'

'How do you suffer it, Jasnah?' Dalinar said. 'The things people say about you? I see the lies in their eyes before they speak. Or they will tell me, with utter sincerity, things I have reportedly said – even though I deny them. They refuse my own word against the rumors about me!'

Jasnah stared out across the canyon. More men were gathering at the other end, a weak, beleaguered group who were only now discovering they were the victors in this contest. A large column of smoke rose in the distance, though he couldn't see the source.

'I wish I had answers, Uncle,' Jasnah said softly. 'Fighting makes you strong, but also callous. I worry I have learned too much of the latter and not enough of the former. But I can give you a warning.'

He looked toward her, raising his eyebrows.

'They will try,' Jasnah said, 'to define you by something you are not. Don't let them. I can be a scholar, a woman, a historian, a Radiant. People will still try to classify me by the thing that makes me an outsider. They want, ironically, the thing I *don't* do or believe to be the prime marker of my identity. I have always rejected that, and will continue to do so.'

She reached over and put her freehand on his arm. 'You are not a heretic, Dalinar Kholin. You are a king, a Radiant, and a father. You are a man with complicated beliefs, who does not accept everything you are told. *You* decide how you are defined. Don't surrender that to them. They will gleefully take the chance to define you, if you allow it.'

Dalinar nodded slowly.

'Regardless,' Jasnah said, standing. 'This is probably not the best occasion for such a conversation. I realize we can replay this vision at will, but the number of storms in which we can do it will be limited. I should be exploring.'

'Last time, I went that way,' Dalinar said, pointing up the slope. 'I'd like to see what I saw again.'

'Excellent. We'd best split to cover more ground. I will go in the other direction, then we can meet afterward and compare notes.' She took off down the slope toward the largest gathering of men.

Dalinar stood up and stretched, his earlier exertion still weighing on him. A short time later Navani returned, mumbling explanations of what she'd seen under her breath. Teshav sat with her in the waking world, and Kalami with Jasnah, recording what they said – the only way to take notes in one of these visions.

Navani took his arm in hers and looked after Jasnah, a fond smile on her lips. No, none would think Jasnah emotionless if they'd witnessed that tearful reunion between mother and daughter.

'How did you ever mother that one?' Dalinar asked.

'Mostly without letting her realize she was being mothered,' Navani said. She pulled him close. 'That fabrial is wonderful, Dalinar. It's like a Soulcaster.'

'In what way?'

'In that I have no idea how it works! I think . . . I think something is wrong with the way we've been viewing the ancient fabrials.' He looked to her, and she shook her head. 'I can't explain yet.'

'Navani . . .' he prodded.

'No,' she said stubbornly. 'I need to present my ideas to the scholars, see if what I'm thinking even makes sense, and then prepare a report. That's the short of it, Dalinar Kholin. So be patient.'

'I probably won't understand half of what you say anyway,' he grumbled.

He didn't immediately start them up in the direction he'd gone before. Last time he'd been prompted by someone in the vision. He'd acted differently this time. Would the same prompting still come?

He had to wait only a short time until an officer came running up to them.

'You there,' the man said. 'Malad-son-Zent, isn't that your name? You're promoted to sergeant. Head to base camp three.' He pointed up the incline. 'Up over that knob there, down the other side. Hop to it!' He spared a frown for Navani – to his eyes, the two of them didn't belong standing in such a familial pose – but then charged off without another word.

Dalinar smiled.

'What?' Navani said.

'These are set experiences that Honor wanted me to have. Though there's freedom in them, I suspect that the same information will be conveyed no matter what I do.'

'So, do you want to disobey?'

Dalinar shook his head. 'There are some things I need to see again – now that I understand this vision is accurate, I know better questions to ask.'

They started up the incline of smooth rock, walking arm in arm. Dalinar felt unexpected emotions start to churn within him, partially due to Jasnah's words. But this was something deeper: a welling of gratitude, relief, even love.

'Dalinar?' Navani asked. 'Are you well?'

'I'm just . . . thinking,' he said, trying to keep his voice even. 'Blood of my fathers . . . it's been nearly half a year, hasn't it? Since all this started? All that time, I came to these alone. It's just good to share the burden, Navani. To be able to show this to you, and to know for once – absolutely and certainly – that what I'm seeing isn't merely in my own mind.'

She pulled him close again, walking with her head on his shoulder. Far more affectionate in public than Alethi propriety would sanction, but hadn't they thrown that out the window long ago? Besides, there was nobody to see – nobody real, anyway.

They crested the slope, then passed several blackened patches. What could burn rock like that? Other sections looked like they'd been broken by an impossible weight, while yet others had strangely shaped holes ripped in them. Navani stopped them beside a particular formation, only knee high, where the rock rippled in a strange little symmetrical pattern. It looked like liquid, frozen midflow.

Cries of pain echoed through these canyons and across the open plain of rock. Looking out over the ridge, Dalinar found the main battlefield. Stretching into the distance were corpses. Thousands of them, some in piles. Others slaughtered in heaps while pressed against walls of stone.

'Stormfather?' Dalinar said, addressing the spren. 'This *is* what I told Jasnah it was, isn't it? Aharietiam. The Last Desolation.'

That is what it was called.

'Include Navani in your responses,' Dalinar requested.

AGAIN, YOU MAKE DEMANDS OF ME. YOU SHOULD NOT DO THIS. The voice rumbled in the open air, and Navani jumped.

'Aharietiam,' Dalinar said. 'This isn't how songs and paintings depict the final defeat of the Voidbringers. In them, it's always some grand conflict, with tremendous monsters clashing against brave lines of soldiers.'

MEN LIE IN THEIR POETRY. SURELY YOU KNOW THIS.

'It just . . . seems so like any other battlefield.'

AND THAT ROCK BEHIND YOU?

Dalinar turned toward it, then gasped, realizing something he'd mistaken for a boulder was actually a giant skeletal face. A mound of rubble they'd passed was actually one of those *things* he'd seen in a different vision. A stone monster that ripped its way out of the ground.

Navani stepped up to it. 'Where are the parshmen?'

'Earlier, I fought against humans,' Dalinar said.

THEY WERE RECRUITED TO THE OTHER SIDE, the Stormfather said. I THINK.

'You think?' Dalinar demanded.

DURING THESE DAYS, HONOR STILL LIVED. I WAS NOT YET FULLY MYSELF. MORE OF A STORM. LESS INTERESTED IN MEN. HIS DEATH CHANGED ME. MY MEMORY OF THAT TIME IS DIFFICULT TO EXPLAIN. BUT IF YOU WOULD SEE PARSHMEN, YOU NEED BUT LOOK ACROSS THAT FIELD.

Navani joined Dalinar at the ridge, looking out over the plain of corpses below. 'Which ones?' Navani asked.

YOU CAN'T TELL?

'Not from this distance.'

MAYBE HALF OF THOSE ARE WHAT YOU'D CALL PARSHMEN.

Dalinar squinted, but still couldn't make out which were human and which were not. He led Navani down the ridge, then across a plain. Here, the corpses intermingled. Men in their primitive clothing. Parshmen corpses that bled orange blood. This was a warning he should have recognized, but hadn't been able to put together his first time in the vision.

He'd thought he was seeing a nightmare of their fight on the Shattered Plains.

He knew the path to take, one that led him and Navani across the field of corpses, then into a shadowed recess beneath a tall rocky spire. The light had caught on the rocks here, intriguing him. Before, he thought he'd wandered into this place by accident, but in truth the entire vision had pointed him at this moment.

Here, they found nine Shardblades rammed into the stone. Abandoned. Navani put her gloved safehand to her mouth at the sight – nine beautiful Blades, each a treasure, simply left here? Why and how?

Dalinar stepped through the shadows, rounding the nine Blades. This was another image he'd misunderstood when living this vision the first time. These weren't just Shardblades.

'Ash's eyes,' Navani said, pointing. 'I recognize that one, Dalinar. It's the one . . .'

'The one that killed Gavilar,' Dalinar said, stopping beside the plainest Blade, long and thin. 'The weapon of the Assassin in White. It's an Honorblade. They all are.'

'This is the day that the Heralds made their final ascension to the Tranquiline Halls!' Navani said. 'To lead the battle there instead.'

Dalinar turned to the side, to where he glimpsed the air shimmering. The Stormfather.

'Only . . .' Navani said. 'This wasn't actually the end. Because the enemy came back.' She walked around the ring of swords, then paused by an open spot in the circle. 'Where is the tenth Blade?'

'The stories are wrong, aren't they?' Dalinar said to the Stormfather. 'We didn't defeat the enemy for good, as the Heralds claimed. They *lied*.'

Navani's head snapped up, her eyes focused on Dalinar.

I LONG BLAMED THEM, the Stormfather said, FOR THEIR LACK OF HONOR. IT IS . . . DIFFICULT FOR ME TO LOOK PAST OATHS BROKEN. I HATED THEM. NOW, THE MORE I COME TO KNOW MEN, THE MORE I SEE HONOR IN THOSE POOR CREATURES YOU NAME HERALDS.

'Tell me what happened,' Dalinar said. 'What *really* happened?'

ARE YOU READY FOR THIS STORY? THERE ARE PARTS YOU WILL NOT LIKE.

'If I have accepted that God is dead, I can accept the fall of his Heralds.'

Navani settled down on a nearby stone, face pale.

IT STARTED WITH THE CREATURES YOU NAME VOIDBRINGERS, the Stormfather said, voice rumbling and low, distant. Introspective? As I SAID, MY VIEW OF THESE EVENTS IS DISTORTED. I DO REMEMBER THAT ONCE, LONG BEFORE THE DAY YOU'RE SEEING NOW, THERE WERE MANY SOULS OF CREATURES WHO HAD BEEN SLAIN, ANGRY AND TERRIBLE. THEY HAD BEEN GIVEN GREAT POWER BY THE ENEMY, THE ONE CALLED ODIUM. THAT WAS THE BEGINNING, THE START OF DESOLATIONS.

FOR WHEN THESE DIED, THEY REFUSED TO PASS ON.

'That's what is happening now,' Dalinar said. 'The parshmen, they're transformed by these things in the Everstorm. Those things are ...' He swallowed. 'The souls of their dead?'

THEY ARE THE SPREN OF PARSHMEN LONG DEAD. THEY ARE THEIR KINGS, THEIR LIGHTEYES, THEIR VALIANT SOLDIERS FROM LONG, LONG AGO. THE PROCESS IS NOT EASY ON THEM. SOME OF THESE SPREN ARE MERE FORCES NOW, ANIMALISTIC, FRAGMENTS OF MINDS GIVEN POWER BY ODIUM. OTHERS ARE MORE ... AWAKE. EACH RE-BIRTH FURTHER INJURES THEIR MINDS.

THEY ARE REBORN USING THE BODIES OF PARSHMEN TO BECOME THE FUSED. AND EVEN BEFORE THE FUSED LEARNED TO COMMAND THE SURGES, MEN COULD NOT FIGHT THEM. HUMANS COULD NEVER WIN WHEN THE CREATURES THEY KILLED WERE REBORN EACH TIME THEY WERE SLAIN. AND SO, THE OATHPACT.

'Ten people,' Dalinar said. 'Five male, five female.' He looked at the swords. 'They stopped this?'

THEY GAVE THEMSELVES UP. AS ODIUM IS SEALED BY THE POWERS OF HONOR AND CULTIVATION, YOUR HERALDS SEALED THE SPREN OF THE DEAD INTO THE PLACE YOU CALL DAMNATION. THE HER-ALDS WENT TO HONOR, AND HE GAVE THEM THIS RIGHT, THIS OATH. THEY THOUGHT IT WOULD END THE WAR FOREVER. BUT THEY WERE WRONG. HONOR WAS WRONG.

'He was like a spren himself,' Dalinar said. 'You told me before – Odium too.'

HONOR LET THE POWER BLIND HIM TO THE TRUTH – THAT WHILE SPREN AND GODS CANNOT BREAK THEIR OATHS, MEN CAN AND WILL. THE TEN HERALDS WERE SEALED UPON DAMNATION, TRAPPING THE VOIDBRINGERS THERE. HOWEVER, IF ANY ONE OF THE TEN AGREED

TO BEND HIS OATH AND LET VOIDBRINGERS PAST, IT OPENED A FLOOD. THEY COULD ALL RETURN.

'And that started a Desolation,' Dalinar said.

THAT STARTED A DESOLATION, the Stormfather agreed.

An oath that could be bent, a pact that could be undermined. Dalinar could see what had happened. It seemed so obvious. 'They were tortured, weren't they?'

HORRIBLY, BY THE SPIRITS THEY TRAPPED. THEY COULD SHARE THE PAIN BECAUSE OF THEIR BOND – BUT EVENTUALLY, SOMEONE ALWAYS YIELDED.

ONCE ONE BROKE, ALL TEN HERALDS RETURNED TO ROSHAR. THEY FOUGHT. THEY LED MEN. THEIR OATHPACT DELAYED THE FUSED FROM RETURNING IMMEDIATELY, BUT EACH TIME AFTER A DESOLATION, THE HERALDS RETURNED TO DAMNATION TO SEAL THE ENEMY AGAIN. TO HIDE, FIGHT, AND FINALLY WITHSTAND TOGETHER.

THE CYCLE REPEATED. AT FIRST THE RESPITE BETWEEN DESOLATIONS WAS LONG. HUNDREDS OF YEARS. NEAR THE END, DESOLATIONS CAME SEPARATED BY FEWER THAN TEN YEARS. THERE WAS LESS THAN ONE YEAR BETWEEN THE LAST TWO. THE SOULS OF THE HERALDS HAD WORN THIN. THEY BROKE ALMOST AS SOON AS THEY WERE CAUGHT AND TORTURED IN DAMNATION.

'Which explains why things look so bad this time,' Navani whispered from her seat. 'Society had suffered Desolation after Desolation, separated by short intervals. Culture, technology ... all broken.'

Dalinar knelt and rubbed her shoulder.

'It is not so bad as I feared,' she said. 'The Heralds, they *were* honorable. Perhaps not as divine, but I may even like them more, to know they were once just normal men and women.'

THEY WERE BROKEN PEOPLE, the Stormfather said. BUT I CAN START TO FORGIVE THEM, AND THEIR SHATTERED OATHS. IT MAKES ... SENSE TO ME NOW AS IT NEVER DID BEFORE. He sounded surprised.

'The Voidbringers who did this,' Navani said. 'They are the ones that are returning now. Again.'

THE FUSED, THE SOULS OF THE DEAD FROM LONG AGO, THEY *LOATHE* YOU. THEY ARE NOT RATIONAL. THEY HAVE BECOME PERMEATED WITH HIS ESSENCE, THE ESSENCE OF PURE HATRED. THEY WILL

SEE THIS WORLD DESTROYED IN ORDER TO DESTROY MANKIND. AND YES, THEY HAVE RETURNED.

'Aharietiam,' Dalinar said, 'was not really the end. It was just another Desolation. Except something changed for the Heralds. They left their swords?'

AFTER EACH DESOLATION, THE HERALDS RETURNED TO DAMNATION, the Stormfather said. IF THEY DIED IN THE FIGHTING, THEY WENT THERE AUTOMATICALLY. AND THOSE WHO SURVIVED WENT BACK WILLINGLY AT THE END. THEY HAD BEEN WARNED THAT IF ANY LINGERED, IT COULD LEAD TO DISASTER. BESIDES, THEY NEEDED TO BE TOGETHER, IN DAMNATION, TO SHARE THE BURDEN OF TORTURE IF ONE WAS CAPTURED. BUT THIS TIME, AN ODDITY OCCURRED. THROUGH COWARDICE OR LUCK, THEY AVOIDED DEATH. NONE WERE KILLED IN BATTLE – EXCEPT ONE.

Dalinar looked to the open spot in the ring.

THE NINE REALIZED, the Stormfather said, THAT ONE OF THEM HAD NEVER BROKEN. EACH OF THE OTHERS, AT SOME POINT, HAD BEEN THE ONE TO GIVE IN, TO START THE DESOLATION TO ESCAPE THE PAIN. THEY DETERMINED THAT PERHAPS THEY DIDN'T ALL NEED TO RETURN.

THEY DECIDED TO STAY HERE, RISKING AN ETERNAL DESOLATION, BUT HOPING THAT THE ONE THEY LEFT IN DAMNATION WOULD ALONE BE ENOUGH TO HOLD IT ALL TOGETHER. THE ONE WHO WASN'T MEANT TO HAVE JOINED THEM IN THE FIRST PLACE, THE ONE WHO WAS NOT A KING, SCHOLAR, OR GENERAL.

'Talenelat,' Dalinar said.

THE BEARER OF AGONIES. THE ONE ABANDONED IN DAMNATION. LEFT TO WITHSTAND THE TORTURES ALONE.

'Almighty above,' Navani whispered. 'How long has it been? Over a thousand years, right?'

FOUR AND A HALF THOUSAND YEARS, the Stormfather said. FOUR AND A HALF MILLENNIA OF TORTURE.

Silence settled over the little alcove, which was adorned with silvery Blades and lengthening shadows. Dalinar, feeling weak, sat down on the ground beside Navani's rock. He stared at those Blades, and felt a sudden irrational hatred for the Heralds.

It was foolish. As Navani had said, they *were* heroes. They'd spared humanity the assaults for great swaths of time, paying with their own sanity. Still, he hated them. For the man they had left behind.

The man . . .

Dalinar leaped to his feet. 'It's *him*!' he shouted. 'The madman. He really *is* a Herald!'

He finally broke, the Stormfather said. He has joined the nine, who still live. In these millennia none have ever died and returned to Damnation, but it doesn't matter as it once did. The Oathpact has been weakened almost to annihilation, and Odium has created his own storm. The Fused do not return to Damnation when killed. They are reborn in the next Everstorm.

Storms. How could they defeat that? Dalinar looked again at that empty spot among the swords. 'The madman, the Herald, he came to Kholinar with a Shardblade. Shouldn't that have been his Honorblade?'

Yes. But the one delivered to you is not it. I do not know what happened.

'I need to speak with him. He . . . he was at the monastery, when we marched. Wasn't he?' Dalinar needed to ask the ardents, to see who had evacuated the madmen.

'Is this what caused the Radiants to rebel?' Navani asked. 'Are these secrets what sparked the Recreance?'

No. That is a deeper secret, one I will not speak.

'Why?' Dalinar demanded.

Because were you to know it, you would abandon your oaths as the ancient Radiants did.

'I wouldn't.'

Wouldn't you? the Stormfather demanded, his voice growing louder. Would you swear it? Swear upon an unknown? These Heralds swore they would hold back the Voidbringers, and what happened to them?

There is not a man alive who has not broken an oath, Dalinar Kholin. Your new Radiants hold in their hands the souls and lives of my children. No. I will not let you do as your predecessors did. You know the important parts. The rest is irrelevant.

Dalinar drew in a deep breath, but contained his anger. In a way, the

Stormfather was right. He couldn't know how this secret would affect him or his Radiants.

He'd still rather know it. He felt as if he were walking about with a headsman following, planning to claim his life at any moment.

He sighed as Navani stood and walked to him, taking his arm. 'I'll need to try to do sketches from memory of each of those Honorblades – or better, send Shallan to do it. Perhaps we can use the drawings to locate the others.'

A shadow moved at the entrance to this little alcove, and a moment later a young man stumbled in. He was pale of skin, with strange, wide Shin eyes and brown hair that had a curl to it. He could have been one of any number of Shin men Dalinar had seen in his own time – they were still ethnically distinct, despite the passing of millennia.

The man fell to his knees before the wonder of the abandoned Honorblades. But a moment later, the man looked to Dalinar, and then spoke with the Almighty's voice. 'Unite them.'

'Was there nothing you could do for the Heralds?' Dalinar asked. 'Was there nothing their God could do to prevent this?'

The Almighty, of course, couldn't answer. He had died fighting this thing they faced, the force known as Odium. He had, in a way, given his own life to the same cause as the Heralds.

The vision faded.

Though fashion elites in Liafor have presented more daring
designs in past folios, they've found there is no quicker way
to influence Alethi and Veden styles than through subtle
changes over time in the traditional Vorin havah.

*No good can come of two **S**hards settling in one location. It was agreed that we would not interfere with one another, and it disappoints me that so few of the **S**hards have kept to this original agreement.*

S hallan can take notes for us,' Jasnah said.

Shallan looked up from her notebook. She'd settled against the tile-covered wall, sitting on the floor in her blue havah, and had intended to spend the meeting doing sketches.

It had been over a week since her recovery and subsequent meeting with Jasnah at the crystal pillar. Shallan was feeling better and better, and at the same time less and less like herself. What a surreal experience it was, following Jasnah around as if nothing had changed.

Today, Dalinar had called a meeting of his Radiants, and Jasnah had suggested the basement rooms of the tower because they were so well secured. She was incredibly worried about being spied upon.

The rows of dust had been removed from the library floor; Navani's flock of scholars had carefully catalogued every splinter. The emptiness served only to underscore the absence of the information they'd hoped to find.

Now everyone was looking at her. 'Notes?' Shallan asked. She'd barely been following the conversation. 'We could call for Brightness Teshav....'

So far, it was a small group. The Blackthorn, Navani, and their core

Surgebinders: Jasnah, Renarin, Shallan, and Kaladin Stormblessed, the flying bridgeman. Adolin and Elhokar were away, visiting Vedenar to survey the military capacities of Taravangian's army. Malata was working the Oathgate for them.

'No need to call in another scribe,' Jasnah said. 'We covered shorthand in your training, Shallan. I'd see how well you've retained the skill. Be fastidious; we will need to report to my brother what we determine here.'

The rest of them had settled into a group of chairs except for Kaladin, who stood leaning against the wall. Looming like a thundercloud. He had killed Helaran, her brother. The emotion of that peeked out, but Shallan smothered it, stuffing it into the back of her mind. Kaladin wasn't to be blamed for that. He'd just been defending his brightlord.

She stood up, feeling like a chastened child. The weight of their stares prodded her to walk over and take a seat beside Jasnah with her pad open and pencil ready.

'So,' Kaladin said. 'According to the Stormfather, not only is the Almighty dead, but he condemned ten people to an eternity of torture. We call them Heralds, and they're not only traitors to their oaths, they're probably also mad. We had one of them in our custody – likely the maddest of the lot – but we lost him in the turmoil of getting everyone to Urithiru. In short, everyone who might have been able to help us is crazy, dead, a traitor, or some combination of the three.' He folded his arms. 'Figures.'

Jasnah glanced at Shallan. She sighed, then recorded a summary of what he'd said. Even though it was *already* a summary.

'So what do we do with this knowledge?' Renarin said, leaning forward with his hands clasped.

'We *must* curb the Voidbringer assault,' Jasnah said. 'We can't let them secure too great a foothold.'

'The parshmen aren't our enemies,' Kaladin said softly.

Shallan glanced at him. There *was* something about that wavy dark hair, that grim expression. Always serious, always solemn – and so *tense*. Like he had to be strict with himself to contain his passion.

'Of course they're our enemies,' Jasnah said. 'They're in the process of *conquering the world*. Even if your report indicates they aren't as immediately destructive as we feared, they are still an enormous threat.'

'They just want to live better lives,' Kaladin said.

'I can believe,' Jasnah said, 'that the common parshmen have such a simple motive. But their leaders? They *will* pursue our extinction.'

'Agreed,' Navani said. 'They were born out of a twisted thirst to destroy humankind.'

'The parshmen are the key,' Jasnah said, shuffling through some pages of notes. 'Looking over what you discovered, it seems that all parshmen can bond with ordinary spren as part of their natural life cycle. What we've been calling "Voidbringers" are instead a combination of a parshman with some kind of hostile spren or spirit.'

'The Fused,' Dalinar said.

'Great,' Kaladin said. 'Fine. Let's fight *them*, then. Why do the common folk have to get crushed in the process?'

'Perhaps,' Jasnah said, 'you should visit my uncle's vision and see for yourself the consequences of a soft heart. Firsthand witness of a Desolation might change your perspective.'

'I've seen war, Brightness. I'm a soldier. Problem is, Ideals have expanded my focus. I can't help but see the common men among the enemy. They're *not* monsters.'

Dalinar raised a hand to stop Jasnah's reply. 'Your concern does you credit, Captain,' Dalinar said. 'And your reports have been exceptionally timely. Do you honestly see a chance for an accommodation here?'

'I . . . I don't know, sir. Even the common parshmen are furious at what was done to them.'

'I can't afford to stay my hand from war,' Dalinar said. 'Everything you say is right, but it is also nothing new. I have never gone to battle where some poor fools on either side – men who didn't want to be there in the first place – weren't going to bear the brunt of the pain.'

'Maybe,' Kaladin said, 'that should make you reconsider those other wars, rather than using them to justify this one.'

Shallan's breath caught. It didn't seem the sort of thing you said to the Blackthorn.

'Would that it were so simple, Captain.' Dalinar sighed loudly, looking . . . weathered to Shallan. 'Let me say this: If we can be certain of one thing, it is the morality of defending our homeland. I don't ask you to go to war idly, but I *will* ask you to protect. Alethkar is besieged. The men doing it might be innocents, but they are controlled by those who are evil.'

Kaladin nodded slowly. 'The king has asked my help in opening the Oathgate. I've agreed to give it to him.'

'Once we secure our homeland,' Dalinar said, 'I promise to do something I'd never have contemplated before hearing your reports. I'll seek to negotiate; I'll see if there is some way out of this that doesn't involve smashing our armies together.'

'Negotiate?' Jasnah said. 'Uncle, these creatures are crafty, ancient, and angry. They spent *millennia* torturing the Heralds just to return and seek our destruction.'

'We'll see,' Dalinar said. 'Unfortunately, I haven't been able to contact anyone in the city with the visions. The Stormfather has found Kholinar to be a "dark spot" to him.'

Navani nodded. 'That seems, unfortunately, to coordinate with the failure of the spanreeds in the city. Captain Kaladin's report confirms what our last notes from the city said: The enemy is mobilizing for an assault on the capital. We can't know what the city's status will be once our strike force arrives. You might have to infiltrate an occupied city, Captain.'

'Please send that it isn't so,' Renarin whispered, eyes down. 'How many would have died on those walls, fighting nightmares . . .'

'We need more information,' Jasnah said. 'Captain Kaladin, how many people can you take with you to Alethkar?'

'I plan to fly at the front of a storm,' Kaladin said. 'Like I did returning to Urithiru. It's a bumpy ride, but maybe I can fly over the top of the winds. I need to test it. Anyway, I think I could bring a small group.'

'You won't need a large force,' Dalinar said. 'You, a few of your best squires. I'd send Adolin with you too, so you have another Shardbearer in an emergency. Six, perhaps? You, three of your men, the king, Adolin. Get past the enemy, sneak into the palace, and activate the Oathgate.'

'Pardon if this is out of line,' Kaladin said, 'but Elhokar himself is the odd one. Why not just send me and Adolin? The king will probably slow us down.'

'The king needs to go for personal reasons. Will there be a problem between you?'

'I'll do what is right, regardless of my feelings, sir. And . . . I might be beyond those feelings anyway, now.'

'This is too small,' Jasnah mumbled.

Shallan started, then glanced at her. 'Too small?'

'Not ambitious enough,' Jasnah said more firmly. 'By the Stormfather's explanation, the Fused are immortal. Nothing stops their rebirth now that the Heralds have failed. *This* is our real problem. Our enemy has a near-endless supply of parshman bodies to inhabit, and judging by what the good captain has confirmed through experience, these Fused can access some kind of Surgebinding. How do we fight against that?'

Shallan looked up from her notepad, glancing toward the others in the room. Renarin still leaned forward, hands clasped, eyes on the floor. Navani and Dalinar were sharing a look. Kaladin continued to lean against the wall, arms folded, but he shifted his posture, uncomfortable.

'Well,' Dalinar finally said. 'We'll have to take this one goal at a time. First Kholinar.'

'Pardon, Uncle,' Jasnah said. 'While I don't disagree with that first step, now is not the time to think only of the immediate future. If we are to avoid a Desolation that breaks society, then we'll need to use the past as our guide and make a *plan.*'

'She's right,' Renarin whispered. 'We're facing something that killed the Almighty himself. We fight terrors that break the minds of men and ruin their souls. We can't think small.' He ran his hands through his hair, which was marked by less yellow than his brother's. 'Almighty. We have to think big – but can we take it all in without going mad ourselves?'

Dalinar took a deep breath. 'Jasnah, you have a suggestion of where to start this plan?'

'Yes. The answer is obvious. We need to find the Heralds.'

Kaladin nodded in agreement.

'Then,' Jasnah added, 'we need to kill them.'

'*What?*' Kaladin demanded. 'Woman, are you insane?'

'The Stormfather laid it out,' Jasnah said, unperturbed. 'The Heralds made a pact. When they died, their souls traveled to Damnation and trapped the spirits of the Voidbringers, preventing them from returning.'

'Yeah. Then the Heralds were *tortured* until they *broke.*'

'The Stormfather said their pact was weakened, but did not say it was destroyed,' Jasnah said. 'I suggest that we at least see if one of them is willing to return to Damnation. Perhaps they can still prevent the spirits of the enemy from being reborn. It's either that, or we completely exterminate the parshmen so that the enemy has no hosts.' She met Kaladin's eyes. 'In the face of such an atrocity, I would consider the sacrifice of one or more Heralds to be a small price.'

'Storms!' Kaladin said, standing up straight. 'Have you no sympathy?'

'I have plenty, bridgeman. Fortunately, I temper it with logic. Perhaps you should consider acquiring some at a future date.'

'Listen, *Brightness*,' Kaladin began. 'I—'

'Enough, Captain,' Dalinar said. He gave Jasnah a glance. Both fell quiet, Jasnah without so much as a peep. Shallan had never seen her respond to someone with the respect she gave Dalinar.

'Jasnah,' Dalinar said. 'Even if the pact of the Heralds still holds, we can't know that they'd stay in Damnation – or the mechanics for locking away the Voidbringers there. That said, locating them seems like an excellent first step; they must know much that can greatly assist us. I will leave it to you, Jasnah, to plan out how to accomplish that.'

'What . . . what of the Unmade?' Renarin said. 'There will be others, like the creature we found down here.'

'Navani has been researching them,' Dalinar said.

'We need to go even farther, Uncle,' Jasnah said. 'We need to watch the movements of the Voidbringers. Our only hope is to defeat their armies so soundly that even if their leaders are constantly reborn, they lack the manpower to overwhelm us.'

'Protecting Alethkar,' Kaladin said, 'doesn't have to mean completely crushing the parshmen and—'

'If you wish, Captain,' Jasnah snapped, 'I can get you some mink kits to cuddle while the adults plan. None of us *want* to talk about this, but that does not make it any less *inevitable*.'

'I'd love that,' Kaladin responded. 'In turn, I'll get you some eels to cuddle. You'll feel right at home.'

Jasnah, curiously, smiled. 'Let me ask this, Captain. Do you think ignoring the movement of Voidbringer troops would be wise?'

'Probably not,' he admitted.

'And do you think, perhaps, that you could train your squire Windrunners to fly up high and scout for us? If spanreeds are proving unreliable these days, we'll need another method of watching the enemy. I'd happily cuddle skyeels, as you offer, if your team would be willing to spend some time *imitating* them.'

Kaladin looked to Dalinar, who nodded appreciatively.

'Excellent,' Jasnah said. 'Uncle, your coalition of monarchs is a superb idea. We need to pen the enemy in and prevent them from overrunning all of Roshar. If . . .'

She trailed off. Shallan paused, looking at the doodle she'd been doing. Actually, it was a bit more complex than a doodle. It was . . . kind of a full sketch of Kaladin's face, with passionate eyes and a determined expression. Jasnah had noticed a creationspren in the form of a small gemstone that had appeared on the top of her page, and Shallan blushed, shooing it away.

'Perhaps,' Jasnah said, glancing at Shallan's sketchbook, 'we could do with a short break, Uncle.'

'If you wish,' he said. 'I could use something to drink.'

They broke up, Dalinar and Navani chatting softly as they went to check with the guards and servants in the main hallway. Shallan watched them go with a sense of longing, as she felt Jasnah loom over her.

'Let us chat,' Jasnah said, nodding toward the far end of the long, rectangular room.

Shallan sighed, closed her notebook, and followed Jasnah to the other end, near a pattern of tiles on the wall. This far from the spheres brought for the meeting, the lighting was dim.

'May I?' Jasnah said, holding out her hand for Shallan's notebook.

She relinquished it.

'A fine depiction of the young captain,' Jasnah said. 'I see . . . three lines of notes here? After you were pointedly instructed to take the minutes.'

'We should have sent for a scribe.'

'We had a scribe. To take notes is not a lowly task, Shallan. It is a service you can provide.'

'If it's not a lowly task,' Shallan said, 'then perhaps you should have done it.'

Jasnah closed the sketchpad and fixed Shallan with a calm, level stare. The type that made Shallan squirm.

'I remember,' Jasnah said, 'a nervous, desperate young woman. Frantic to earn my goodwill.'

Shallan didn't reply.

'I understand,' Jasnah said, 'that you have enjoyed independence. What you accomplished here is *remarkable*, Shallan. You even seem to have earned my uncle's trust – a challenging task.'

'Then maybe we can just call the wardship finished, eh?' Shallan said. 'I mean, I'm a full Radiant now.'

'Radiant, yes,' Jasnah said. 'Full? Where's your armor?'

'Um ... armor?'

Jasnah sighed softly, opening up the sketchpad again. 'Shallan,' she said in a strangely ... comforting tone. 'I'm impressed. I *am* impressed, truly. But what I've heard of you recently is troubling. You've ingratiated yourself with my family, and made good on the causal betrothal to Adolin. Yet here you are with wandering eyes, as this sketch testifies.'

'I—'

'You skip meetings that Dalinar calls,' Jasnah continued, soft but immovable. 'When you do go, you sit at the back and barely pay attention. He tells me that half the time, you find an excuse to slip out early.

'You investigated the presence of an Unmade in the tower, and frightened it off basically alone. Yet you never explained how you found it when Dalinar's soldiers could not.' She met Shallan's eyes. 'You've always hidden things from me. Some of those secrets were very damaging, and I find myself unwilling to believe you don't have others.'

Shallan bit her lip, but nodded.

'That was an invitation,' Jasnah said, 'to talk to me.'

Shallan nodded again. *She* wasn't working with the Ghostbloods. That was Veil. And Jasnah didn't need to know about Veil. Jasnah *couldn't* know about Veil.

'Very well,' Jasnah said with a sigh. 'Your wardship is not finished, and won't be until I'm convinced that you can meet minimum requirements of scholarship – such as taking shorthand notes during an important conference. Your path as a Radiant is another matter. I don't know that I can guide you; each order was distinctive in its approach. But as a young man will not be excused from his geography lessons simply because he has achieved competence with the sword, I will not release you from your duties to me simply because you have discovered your powers as a Radiant.'

Jasnah handed back the sketchpad and walked toward the ring of chairs. She settled next to Renarin, prodding him gently to speak with her. He looked up for the first time since the meeting had begun and nodded, saying something Shallan couldn't hear.

'Mmmm ...' Pattern said. 'She is wise.'

'That's perhaps her most infuriating feature,' Shallan said. 'Storms. She makes me feel like a child.'

'Mmm.'

'Worst part is, she's probably right,' Shallan said. 'Around her, I *do* act more like a child. It's like part of me wants to let her take care of everything. And I hate, hate, *hate* that about myself.'

'Is there a solution?'

'I don't know.'

'Perhaps . . . act like an adult?'

Shallan put her hands to her face, groaning softly and rubbing her eyes with her fingers. She'd basically asked for that, hadn't she? 'Come on,' she said, 'let's go to the rest of the meeting. As much as I want an excuse to get out of here.'

'Mmm . . .' Pattern said. 'Something about this room . . .'

'What?' Shallan asked.

'Something . . .' Pattern said in his buzzing way. 'It has memories, Shallan.'

Memories. Did he mean in Shadesmar? She'd avoided traveling there – that was at least one thing in which she'd listened to Jasnah.

She made her way back to her seat, and after a moment's thought, slipped Jasnah a quick note. *Pattern says this room has memories. Worth investigating in Shadesmar?*

Jasnah regarded the note, then wrote back.

I've found that we should not ignore the offhand comments of our spren. Press him; I will investigate this place. Thank you for the suggestion.

The meeting started again, and now turned to discussion of specific kingdoms around Roshar. Jasnah was most keen on getting the Shin to join them. The Shattered Plains held the easternmost of the Oathgates, and that was already under Alethi control. If they could gain access to the one farthest to the west, they could travel the breadth of Roshar—From the entry point of the highstorms to the entry point of the Everstorms – in a heartbeat.

They didn't talk tactics too specifically; that was a masculine art, and Dalinar would want his highprinces and generals to discuss the battle-fields. Still, Shallan didn't fail to notice the tactical terms Jasnah used now and then.

In things like this, Shallan had difficulty understanding the woman. In some ways, Jasnah seemed fiercely masculine. She studied whatever she pleased, and she talked tactics as easily as she talked poetry. She could be aggressive, even cold – Shallan had seen her straight-up *execute* thieves who had tried to rob her. Beyond that . . . well, it probably was best not to speculate on things with no meaning, but people *did* talk. Jasnah had turned down every suitor for her hand, including some very attractive and influential men. People wondered. Was she perhaps simply not interested?

All of this should have resulted in a person who was decidedly unfeminine. Yet Jasnah wore the finest makeup, and wore it well, with shadowed eyes and bright red lips. She kept her safehand covered, and preferred intricate and fetching styles of braids from her hairdresser. Her writings and her mind made her the very model of Vorin femininity.

Next to Jasnah, Shallan felt pale, stupid, and completely lacking in curves. What would it be like, to be so confident? So beautiful, yet so unconstrained, all at once? Surely, Jasnah Kholin had far fewer problems in life than Shallan. At the very least, she *created* far fewer for herself than Shallan did.

It was about this point that Shallan realized she'd missed a good fifteen minutes of the meeting, and had again lapsed in her note-taking. Blushing furiously, she huddled up on her chair and did her best to remain focused for the rest of the meeting. At the end, she presented a sheet of formal shorthand to Jasnah.

The woman looked it over, then cocked a perfectly shaped eyebrow at the line at the center where Shallan had grown distracted. *Dalinar said some stuff here,* the line read. *It was very important and useful, so I'm sure you remember it without needing a reminder.*

Shallan smiled apologetically and shrugged.

'Please write this out in longhand,' Jasnah said, handing it back. 'Have a copy sent to my mother and to my brother's head scribe.'

Shallan took it as a dismissal and rushed away. She felt like a student who had just been released from lessons, which angered her. At the same time, she wanted to run off and immediately do as Jasnah had asked, to renew her mistress's faith in her, which angered her even *more*.

She ran up the steps out of the tower's basement, using Stormlight to prevent fatigue. The different sides within her clashed, snapping at each other. She imagined months spent under Jasnah's watchful care, training to become a mousy scribe as her father had always wanted.

She remembered the days in Kharbranth, when she'd been so uncertain, so timid. She couldn't return to that. She *wouldn't*. But what to do instead?

When she finally reached her rooms, Pattern was buzzing at her. She tossed aside her sketchpad and satchel, digging out Veil's coat and hat. Veil would know what to do.

However, pinned to the inside of Veil's coat was a sheet of paper. Shallan froze, then looked around the room, suddenly anxious. Hesitantly, she unpinned the sheet and unfolded it.

The top read:

You have accomplished the task we set out for you. You have investigated the Unmade, and not only learned something of it, but also frightened it away. As promised, here is your reward.

The following letter explains the truth about your deceased brother, Nan Helaran, acolyte of the Radiant order of the Skybreakers.

As for Uli Da, it was obvious from the outset that she was going to be a problem. Good riddance.

Tここ here are at least two major institutions on Roshar, other than ourselves, which presaged the return of the Voidbringers and the Desolations, the letter read.

You are familiar with the first of these, the men who call themselves the Sons of Honor. The old king of Alethkar – the Blackthorn's brother, Gavilar Kholin – was a driving force in their expansion. He brought Meridas Amaram into their fold.

As you no doubt discovered upon infiltrating Amaram's mansion in the warcamps, the Sons of Honor explicitly worked for the return of the Desolations. They believed that only the Voidbringers would cause the Heralds to show themselves – and they believed that a Desolation would restore both the Knights Radiant and the classical strength of the Vorin church. King Gavilar's efforts to rekindle the Desolations are likely the true reason he was assassinated. Though there were many in the palace that night who had reason to see him dead.

A second group who knew the Desolations might return are the Skybreakers. Led by the ancient Herald Nalan'Elin – often simply called Nale – the Skybreakers are the only order of Radiants that did not betray its oaths during the Recreance. They have maintained a continuous clandestine line from ancient days.

Nale believed that men speaking the Words of other orders would hasten the return of the Voidbringers. We do not know how this could possibly be true, but as a Herald, Nale has access to knowledge and understanding beyond us.

You should know that the Heralds are no longer to be seen as allies to man. Those that are not completely insane have been broken. Nale himself is ruthless, without pity or mercy. He has spent the last two decades – perhaps much longer – dealing with anyone close to bonding a spren. Sometimes he recruited these people, bonding them to highspren and making them Skybreakers. Others he eliminated. If the person had already bonded a spren, then Nale usually went in person to dispatch them. If not, he sent a minion.

A minion like your brother Helaran.

Your mother had intimate contact with a Skybreaker acolyte, and you know the result of that relationship. Your brother was recruited because Nale was impressed with him. Nale may also have learned, through means we do not understand, that a member of your house was close to bonding a spren. If this is true, they came to believe that Helaran was the one they wanted. They recruited him with displays of great power and Shards.

Helaran had not yet proved himself worthy of a spren bond. Nale is exacting with his recruits. Likely, Helaran was sent to kill Amaram as a test – either that or he took it upon himself as a way of proving his worthiness for knighthood.

It is also possible that the Skybreakers knew someone in Amaram's army was close to bonding a spren, but I believe it likelier that the attack on Amaram was simply a strike against the Sons of Honor. From our spying upon the Skybreakers, we have records showing the only member of Amaram's army to have bonded a spren was long since eliminated.

The bridgeman was not, so far as we understand, known to them. If he had been, he would certainly have been killed during his months as a slave.

It ended there. Shallan sat in her room, lit only by the faintest sphere. Helaran, a Skybreaker? And King Gavilar, working with Amaram to bring back the Desolations?

Pattern buzzed with concern on her skirts and moved up onto the page, reading the letter. She whispered the words again to herself, to memorize them, for she knew she couldn't keep this letter. It was too dangerous.

'Secrets,' Pattern said. 'There are lies in this letter.'

So many questions. Who else had been there on the night Gavilar had died, as the letter hinted? And what about this reference to another Surgebinder in Amaram's army? 'He's dangling tidbits in front of me,' Shallan said. 'Like a man on the docks who has a trained kurl that will dance and wave its arms for fish.'

'But . . . we want those tidbits, don't we?'

'That's why it works.' Storm it.

She couldn't deal with this at the moment. She took a Memory of the page. It wasn't a particularly efficient method in regards to text, but it would work in a pinch. Then she stuffed the letter in a basin of water and washed off the ink, before shredding it and wadding it into a ball.

From there, she changed into her coat, trousers, and hat, and snuck from the rooms as Veil.

◆◆

Veil found Vathah and some of his men playing at pieces in their barracks common room. Though this was for Sebarial's soldiers, she saw men in blue uniforms as well – Dalinar had ordered his men to spend time with the soldiers of his allies, to help foster a sense of comradery.

Veil's entrance drew glances, but not stares. Women were allowed in such common rooms, though few came. Little sounded less appealing to a woman being courted than, 'Hey, let's go sit in the barracks common room and watch men grunt and scratch themselves.'

She sauntered over to where Vathah and his men had set up at a round wooden table. Furniture was finally trickling down to the ordinary men; Shallan even had a bed now. Veil settled down in a seat and leaned back, tipping the chair so it clicked against the stone wall. This large common room reminded her of a wine cellar. Dark, unadorned, and filled with a variety of unusual stenches.

'Veil,' Vathah said, nodding to her. Four of them were playing at this table: Vathah, one-eyed Gaz, lanky Red, and Shob. The latter wore a glyphward wrapped around one arm and sniffled periodically.

Veil leaned her head back. 'I seriously need something to drink.'

'I've got an extra mug or two on my ration,' Red said cheerfully.

Veil eyed him to see if he was hitting on her again. He was smiling, but otherwise didn't seem to be making a pass. 'Right kind of you, Red,' Veil said, digging out a few chips and tossing them to him. He tossed over his requisition chit, a little piece of metal with his number stamped on it.

A short time later she was back in her place, nursing some lavis beer.

'Tough day?' Vathah said, lining up his pieces. The small stone bricks were about the size of a thumb, and the men each had ten of them that they arranged facedown. The betting started soon after. Apparently, Vathah was the mink for this round.

'Yeah,' she replied. 'Shallan's been an even bigger pain than usual.'

The men grunted.

'It's like she can't decide who she is, you know?' Veil continued. 'One moment she's cracking jokes like she's sitting in a knitting circle with old ladies – the next she's staring at you with that hollow gaze. The one that makes you think her soul has gone vacant . . .'

'She's a strange one, our mistress,' Vathah agreed.

'Makes you want to do things,' Gaz said with a grunt. 'Things you never thought you'd do.'

'Yeah,' Glurv said from the next table over. 'I got a medal. *Me.* For helping find that mess hiding in the basement. Old Kholin himself sent it down for me.' The overweight soldier shook his head, bemused – but he *was* wearing the medal. Pinned right to his collar.

'It was fun,' Gaz admitted. 'Going out carousing, but feeling like we were doing something. That's what she promised us, you know? Making a difference again.'

'The difference I want to make,' Vathah said, 'is filling my pouch with your spheres. You men betting or not?'

The four players all tossed in some spheres. Pieces was one of those games that the Vorin church grudgingly allowed, as it involved no randomization. Dice, drawing from a deck of cards, even shuffling up the pieces – betting on such things was like trying to guess the future. And that was so deeply wrong, thinking of it made Veil's skin crawl. She wasn't even particularly religious, not like Shallan was.

People wouldn't play games like those in the official barracks. Here, they played guessing games. Vathah had arranged nine of his pieces in a triangle shape; the tenth one he set to the side and flipped over as the seed. It, like the hidden nine, was marked with the symbol of one of the

Alethi princedoms. In this case, the seed was Aladar's symbol, in the form of a chull.

The goal was to arrange your ten pieces in a pattern identical to his, even though they were facedown. You'd guess which were which through a series of questions, peeks, and inferences. You could force the mink to reveal pieces just to you, or to everyone, based on certain other rules.

In the end, someone called and everyone flipped over their pieces. The one with the most matches to the mink's pattern was declared winner, and claimed the pot. The mink got a percentage, based on certain factors, such as the number of turns it took before someone called.

'What do you think?' Gaz asked, as he tossed a few chips into the bowl at the center, buying the right to peek at one of Vathah's tiles. 'How long will Shallan go this time before she remembers we're here?'

'Long time, I hope,' Shob said. 'Oi think Oi might be comin' down with somethin'.'

'So all is normal, Shob,' Red said.

'It's big this time,' Shob said. 'Oi think Oi might be turnin' into a *Voidbringer*.'

'A Voidbringer,' Veil said flatly.

'Yeah, look at this rash.' He pulled back the glyphward, exposing his upper arm. Which looked perfectly normal.

Vathah snorted.

'Eh!' Shob said. 'Oi'm likely to die, Sarge. You mark me, Oi'm likely to die.' He moved around a few of his tiles. 'If Oi do, give my winnings to dem orphans.'

'Them orphans?' Red asked.

'You know, orphans.' Shob scratched his head. 'There's orphans, right? Somewhere? Orphans that need food? Give them mine after I die.'

'Shob,' Vathah said, 'with the way justice plays out in this world, I can guarantee you'll outlive the rest of us.'

'Ah, that's nice,' Shob said. 'Right nice, Sarge.'

The game progressed only a few rounds before Shob started flipping over his tiles.

'Already!' Gaz said. 'Shob, you cremling. Don't do it yet! I don't even have two lines!'

'Too late,' Shob said.

Red and Gaz reluctantly started flipping their tiles.

'Sadeas,' Shallan said absently. 'Bethab, Ruthar, Roion, Thanadal, Kholin, Sebarial, Vamah, Hatham. With Aladar as the seed.'

Vathah gaped at her, then flipped the tiles over, revealing them exactly as she'd said. 'And you didn't even get any peeks ... Storms, woman. Remind me never to play pieces with you.'

'My brothers always said the same thing,' she said as he split the pot with Shob, who had gotten them all right but three.

'Another hand?' Gaz asked.

Everyone looked at his bowl of spheres, which was almost empty.

'I can get a loan,' he said quickly. 'There's some fellows in Dalinar's guard who said—'

'Gaz,' Vathah said.

'But—'

'Seriously, Gaz.'

Gaz sighed. 'Guess we can play for ends, then,' he said, and Shob eagerly got out some drops of glass shaped roughly like spheres, but without gemstones at the center. Fake money for gambling without stakes.

Veil was enjoying her mug of beer more than she'd expected. It was refreshing to sit here with these men and not have to worry about all Shallan's problems. Couldn't that girl just *relax*? Let it all blow past her?

Nearby some washwomen entered, calling that laundry pickup would be in a few minutes. Vathah and his men didn't stir – though by Veil's estimation, the very clothing they were wearing could use a good scrub.

Unfortunately, Veil couldn't completely ignore Shallan's problems. Mraize's note proved how useful he could be, but she had to be careful. He obviously wanted a mole among the Knights Radiant. *I need to turn this around on him. Learn what he knows.* He'd told her what the Skybreakers and the Sons of Honor had been up to. But what about Mraize and his cohorts? What was *their* objective?

Storms, did she dare try to double-cross him? Did she really have the experience, or the training, to attempt something like that?

'Hey, Veil,' Vathah said as they prepped for another game. 'What do you think? Has the brightness already forgotten about us again?'

Veil shook herself out of her thoughts. 'Maybe. She doesn't seem to know what to do with you lot.'

'She's not the first,' Red said – he was the next mink, and carefully arranged his tiles in a specific order, facedown. 'I mean, it's not like we're *real* soldiers.'

'Our crimes are forgiven,' Gaz said with a grunt, squinting his single eye at the seed tile that Red turned over. 'But forgiven ain't forgotten. No military will take us on, and I don't blame them. I'm just glad those storming bridgemen haven't strung me up by my toes.'

'Bridgemen?' Veil asked.

'He's got a history with them,' Vathah noted.

'I used to be their storming sergeant,' Gaz said. 'Did everything I could to get them to run those bridges faster. Nobody likes their sergeant though.'

'I'm sure you were the *perfect* sergeant,' Red said with a grin. 'I'll bet you really looked out for them, Gaz.'

'Shut your cremhole,' Gaz grumbled. 'Though I do wonder. If I'd been a little less hard on them, do you think maybe I'd be out on that plateau right now, practicing like the lot of them do? Learning to fly . . .'

'You think *you* could be a Knight Radiant, Gaz?' Vathah said, chuckling.

'No. No, I guess I don't.' He eyed Veil. 'Veil, you tell the brightness. We ain't good men. Good men, they'll find something useful to do with their time. We, on the other hand, might do the opposite.'

'The opposite?' Zendid said from the next table over, where a few of the others continued to drink. 'Opposite of useful? I think we're already there, Gaz. And we've been there forever.'

'Not me,' Glurv said. 'I've got a *medal*.'

'I *mean*,' Gaz said, 'we might get into trouble. I *liked* being useful. Reminded me of back when I first joined up. You tell her, Veil. Tell her to give us something to do other than gambling and drinking. Because to be honest, I ain't very good at either one.'

Veil nodded slowly. A washwoman idled by, messing with a sack of laundry. Veil tapped her finger on her cup. Then she stood and seized the washwoman by the dress and hauled her backward. The woman shouted, dropping her pile of clothing as she stumbled, nearly falling.

Veil shoved her hand into the woman's hair, pushing away the wig of mottled brown and black. Underneath, the woman's hair was pure Alethi black, and she wore ashes on her cheeks, as if she'd been doing hard labor.

'You!' Veil said. This was the woman from the tavern at All's Alley. What had her name been? Ishnah?

Several nearby soldiers had leapt up with alarmed expressions at the woman's outcry. *Every one of those is a soldier from Dalinar's army*, Veil noted, suppressing a roll of her eyes. Kholin troops did have a habit of assuming that nobody could take care of themselves.

'Sit,' Veil said, pointing at the table. Red hastily pulled up another chair.

Ishnah settled herself, holding the wig to her chest. She blushed deeply, but maintained some measure of poise, meeting the eyes of Vathah and his men.

'You are getting to be an annoyance, woman,' Veil said, sitting.

'Why do you assume I'm here because of you?' Ishnah said. 'You're jumping to conclusions.'

'You showed an unhealthy fascination with my associates. Now I find you in disguise, eavesdropping on my conversations?'

Ishnah raised her chin. 'Maybe I'm just trying to prove myself to you.'

'With a disguise I saw through the moment I glanced at you?'

'You didn't catch me last time,' Ishnah said.

Last time?

'You talked about where to get Horneater lager,' Ishnah said. 'Red insisted it was nasty. Gaz loves it.'

'Storms. How long have you been spying on me?'

'Not long,' Ishnah said quickly, in direct contradiction to what she'd just said. 'But I can assure you, *promise it,* that I'll be more valuable to you than these rancid buffoons. Please, at least let me try.'

'Buffoons?' Gaz said.

'Rancid?' Shob said. 'Oh, that's just moi boils, miss.'

'Walk with me,' Veil said, standing up. She strode away from the table. Ishnah scrambled to her feet and followed. 'I wasn't *really* trying to spy on you. But how else was I—'

'Quiet,' Veil said. She stopped at the doorway to the barracks, far enough from her men that they couldn't hear. She folded her arms, leaning against the wall by the door and looking back at them.

Shallan had trouble with follow-through. She had good intentions and grand plans, but she got diverted too easily by new problems, new adventures. Fortunately, Veil could pick up a few of those loose threads.

These men had proven that they were loyal, and they wanted to be useful. A woman could be given much less than that to work with.

'The disguise was well done,' she said to Ishnah. 'Next time, rough up your freehand some more. The fingers gave you away; they aren't the fingers of a laborer.'

Ishnah blushed, balling her freehand into a fist.

'Tell me what you can do, and why I should care,' Veil said. 'You have two minutes.'

'I ...' Ishnah took a deep breath. 'I was trained as a spy for House Hamaradin. In Vamah's court? I know information gathering, message coding, observation techniques, and how to search a room without revealing what I've done.'

'So? If you're so useful, what happened?'

'Your people happened. The Ghostbloods. I'd heard of them, whispered of by Brightlady Hamaradin. She crossed them somehow, and then ...' She shrugged. 'She ended up dead, and everyone thought it might have been one of us who did it. I fled and ended up in the underground, working for a petty gang of thieves. But I could be so much more. Let me prove it to you.'

Veil crossed her arms. A spy. That could be useful. Truth was, Veil herself didn't have much actual training – only what Tyn had showed her and what she'd learned on her own. If she was going to dance with the Ghostbloods, she'd need to be better. Right now, she didn't even know what it was she didn't know.

Could she get some of that from Ishnah? Somehow get some training without revealing that Veil wasn't as skilled as she pretended to be?

An idea began to take form. She didn't trust this woman, but then she didn't need to. And if her former brightlady really *had* been killed by the Ghostbloods, perhaps there was a secret to learn there.

'I have some important infiltrations planned,' Veil said. 'Missions where I need to gather information of a sensitive nature.'

'I can help!' Ishnah said.

'What I really need is a support team, so I don't have to go in alone.'

'I can find people for you! Experts.'

'I wouldn't be able to trust them,' Veil said, shaking her head. 'I need someone I know is loyal.'

'Who?'

Veil pointed at Vathah and his men.

Ishnah's expression fell. 'You want to turn *those men* into *spies*?'

'That, and I want you to prove to me what you can do by showing it to those men.' *And hopefully I can pick up something too.* 'Don't look so daunted. They don't need to be true spies. They just need to know enough about my work to support me and keep watch.'

Ishnah raised her eyebrows skeptically, watching the men. Shob was, obligingly, picking his nose.

'That's a little like saying you want me to teach hogs to talk – with promises it will be easy, as they only need to speak Alethi, not Veden or Herdazian.'

'This is the chance I'm offering, Ishnah. Take it, or agree to stay away from me.'

Ishnah sighed. 'All right. We'll see. Just don't blame me if the pigs don't end up talking.'

Regardless, this is not your concern. You turned your back on divinity.
If Rayse becomes an issue, he will be dealt with.
And so will you.

Teft woke up. Unfortunately.

His first sensation was pain. Old, familiar pain. The throbbing behind his eyes, the raw biting needles of his burned fingers, the stiffness of a body that had outlived its usefulness. Kelek's breath . . . had he *ever* been useful?

He rolled over, groaning. No coat, only a tight undershirt soiled from lying on the ground. He was in an alleyway between tents in the Breakaway market. The high ceiling vanished into the darkness. From just beyond the alleyway came the bright sounds of people chatting and haggling.

Teft stumbled to his feet, and was halfway through relieving himself against some empty boxes before he realized what he was doing. There were no highstorms in here to wash the place out. Besides, he wasn't some drunkard who wallowed in filth and pissed in alleys. Was he?

That thought immediately reminded him of the deeper pain. A pain beyond the pounding in his head or the ache of his bones. The pain that was with him always, like a persistent ringing, cutting deep to his core. This pain had awakened him. The pain of *need*.

No, he wasn't just some drunkard. He was far, far worse.

He stumbled out of the alleyway, trying to smooth his hair and beard. Women he passed held safehands to mouths and noses, looking away as if embarrassed for him. Perhaps it was a good thing he'd lost his coat – storms help him if anyone recognized who he was. He'd shame the entire crew.

You're already a shame to the crew, Teft, and you know it, he thought. *You're a godless waste of spit.*

He eventually found his way to the well, where he slouched in a line behind some others. Once at the water, he fell down on his knees, then used a trembling hand to fish out a drink with his tin cup. Once he tasted the cool water, his stomach immediately cramped, rejecting it even though he was parched. This always happened after a night on the moss, so he knew to ride the nausea and the cramps, hoping he could keep the water down.

He slumped, holding his stomach, frightening the people in line behind him. Out in the crowd – there was always at least a small crowd near the well – some men in uniforms shoved through. Forest green. Sadeas's men.

They ignored the lines, then filled their buckets. When a man in Kholin blue objected, Sadeas's soldiers got right up in his face. The Kholin soldier finally backed down. Good lad. They didn't need *another* brawl starting between Sadeas's men and other soldiers.

Teft dipped his cup again, the pain from his previous sip fading. This well seemed deep. Rippling water on top, and a deep blackness below.

He almost threw himself in. If he woke up in Damnation tomorrow, would he still feel that itching need inside? That would be a fitting torment. Voidbringers wouldn't even have to flay his soul – all they'd need to do was tell him he'd never feel sated again, and then they could watch him squirm.

Reflected in the waters of the well, a face appeared over his shoulder. A woman with pale white skin, glowing faintly, and hair that hovered around her head like clouds.

'You leave me alone,' he said, slapping his hand into the water. 'You just . . . you just go find someone who cares.'

He stumbled back to his feet, finally getting out of the way so someone else could take a spot. Storms, what hour was it? Those women with buckets were ready to draw water for the day. The drunken nighttime crowds had been replaced by the enterprising and industrious.

He'd been out all night again. Kelek!

Returning to the barracks would be the smart thing to do. But could he face them like this? He wandered through the market instead, eyes down.

I'm getting worse, a piece of him realized. The first month in Dalinar's employ, he'd been able to resist for the most part. But he'd had money again, after so long as a bridgeman. Having money was dangerous.

He'd functioned, only mossing an evening here, an evening there. But then Kaladin had left, and this tower, where everything had felt so wrong ... Those monsters of darkness, including one that had looked just like Teft.

He'd needed the moss to deal with that. Who wouldn't? He sighed. When he looked up, he found that spren standing in front of him.

Teft ... she whispered. *You've spoken oaths. ...*

Foolish, stupid oaths, spoken when he'd hoped that being Radiant would remove the cravings. He turned away from her and found his way to a tent nestled among the taverns. Those were closed for the morning, but this place – it had no name and didn't need one – was open. It was always open, just like the ones back in Dalinar's warcamp had been, just like the ones in Sadeas's warcamp. They were harder to find in some places than others. But they were always there, nameless but still known.

The tough-looking Herdazian man sitting at the front waved him in. It was dim inside, but Teft found his way to a table and slumped down. A woman in tight clothing and a glove with no fingers brought him a little bowl of firemoss. They didn't ask for payment. They all knew that he wouldn't have any spheres on him today, not after his binge last night. But they *would* make sure to get paid eventually.

Teft stared at the little bowl, loathing himself. And yet the scent of it made his longing multiply tenfold. He let out a whimpering groan, then seized the firemoss and ground it between his thumb and forefinger. The moss let off a small plume of smoke, and in the dim light, the center of the moss glowed like an ember.

It hurt, of course. He'd worn through his calluses last night, and now rubbed the moss with raw, blistering fingers. But this was a sharp, present pain. A good kind of pain. Merely physical, it was a sign of life.

It took a minute before he felt the effects. A washing away of his pains, followed by a strengthening of his resolve. He could remember long ago that the firemoss had done more to him – he remembered euphoria, nights spent in a dizzy, wonderful daze, where everything around him seemed to make sense.

These days, he needed the moss to feel normal. Like a man scrambling up wet rocks, he could barely reach where everyone else was standing before he slowly started sliding back down. It wasn't euphoria he craved anymore; it was the mere capacity to keep on going.

The moss washed away his burdens. Memories of that dark version of himself. Memories of turning his family in as heretics, even though they'd been right all along. He was a wretch and a coward, and didn't deserve to wear the symbol of Bridge Four. He'd as good as betrayed that spren already. She'd best have fled.

For a moment he could give that all up to the firemoss.

Unfortunately, there was something broken in Teft. Long ago he'd gone to the moss at the urgings of other men in his squad in Sadeas's army. They could rub the stuff and get some benefit, like a man chewed ridgebark when on guard duty to stay awake. A little firemoss, a little relaxation, and then they moved on with their lives.

Teft didn't work that way. Burdens shoved aside, he *could* have gotten up and gone back to the bridgemen. He could have started his day.

But storms, a few more minutes sounded so nice. He kept going. He went through three bowls before a garish light made him blink. He pulled his face off the table where – to his shame – he'd drooled a puddle. How long had it been, and what was that terrible, awful light?

'Here he is,' Kaladin's voice said as Teft blinked. A figure knelt beside the table. 'Oh, Teft . . .'

'He owes us for three bowls,' said the den's keeper. 'One garnet broam.'

'Be glad,' an accented voice growled, 'we do not rip off pieces of your body and pay you with those.'

Storms. Rock was here too? Teft groaned, turning away. 'Don't see me,' he croaked. 'Don't . . .'

'Our establishment is perfectly legal, Horneater,' the den keeper said. 'If you assault us, be assured we *will* bring the guard and they *will* defend us.'

'Here's your blood money, you eel,' Kaladin said, pushing the light toward them. 'Rock, can you get him?'

Large hands took Teft, surprisingly gentle with their touch. He was crying. Kelek . . .

'Where's your coat, Teft?' Kaladin asked from the darkness.

'I sold it,' Teft admitted, squeezing his eyes shut against the shame-spren that drifted down around him, in the shape of flower petals. 'I sold my own storming coat.'

Kaladin fell silent, and Teft let Rock carry him from the den. Halfway back, he finally managed to scrounge up enough dignity to complain about Rock's breath and make them let him walk on his own feet – with a little support under the arms.

.·.

Teft envied better men than he. They didn't have the itch, the one that went so deep that it stung his soul. It was persistent, always with him, and couldn't ever be scratched. Despite how hard he tried.

Kaladin and Rock set him up in one of the barrack rooms, private, wrapped in blankets and with a bowl of Rock's stew in his hands. Teft made the proper noises, the ones they expected. Apologies, promises he would tell them if he was feeling the need again. Promises that he'd let them help him. Though he couldn't eat the stew, not yet. It would be another day before he could keep anything down.

Storms, but they were good men. Better friends than he deserved. They were all growing into something grand, while Teft . . . Teft just stayed on the ground, looking up.

They left him to get some rest. He stared at the stew, smelling the familiar scent, not daring to eat it. He'd go back to work before the day was out, training bridgemen from the other crews. He *could* function. He could go for days, pretending that he was normal. Storms, he'd balanced everything in Sadeas's army for years before taking one step too far, missing duty one too many times, and landing himself in the bridge crews as punishment.

Those months running bridges had been the only time in his adult life when he hadn't been dominated by the moss. But even back then, when he'd been able to afford a little alcohol, he'd known that eventually he'd find his way back. The liquor wasn't ever enough.

Even as he braced himself to go to work for the day, one nagging thought overshadowed his mind. A shameful thought.

I'm not going to get any more moss for a while, am I?

That sinister knowledge hurt him more than anything. He was going to have to go a few excruciating days feeling like half a man. Days when he couldn't feel anything but his own self-loathing, days living with the shame, the memories, the glances of other bridgemen.

Days without any storming help whatsoever.

That terrified him.

Cephandrius, bearer of the First Gem.
    You must know better than to approach us by relying upon presumption of past relationship.

Inside the increasingly familiar vision, Dalinar carefully nocked an arrow, then released, sending a black-fletched missile into the back of the wildman. The man's screech was lost in the cacophony of battle. Ahead, men fought frantically as they were pushed backward toward the edge of a cliff.

Dalinar methodically nocked a second arrow, then loosed. This arrow hit as well, lodging in a man's shoulder. The man dropped his axe midswing, causing him to miss the young, dark-skinned youth lying on the ground. The boy was barely into his teens; the awkwardness hadn't left him yet, and he had limbs that seemed too long, a face that was too round, too childlike. Dalinar might have let him run messages, but not hold a spear.

The lad's age hadn't prevented him from being named Prime Aqasix Yanagawn the First, ruler of Azir, emperor of greater Makabak.

Dalinar had perched on some rocks, bow in hand. While he didn't intend to repeat his mistake of letting Queen Fen manage all on her own in a vision, he also didn't want Yanagawn to slip through it without challenge or stress. There was a reason that the Almighty had often put

Dalinar in danger in these visions. He'd needed a visceral understanding of what was at stake.

He felled another enemy who got close to the boy. The shots weren't difficult from his vantage near the fight; he had some training with the bow – though his archery in recent years had been with so-called Shardbows, fabrial bows crafted with such a heavy draw weight that only a man in Shardplate could use them.

It was strange, experiencing this battle for the third time. Though each repetition played out slightly differently, there were certain familiar details. The scents of smoke and moldy, inhuman blood. The way that man below fell after losing an arm, screaming the same half-prayer, half-condemnation of the Almighty.

With Dalinar's bowmanship, the band of defenders lasted against the enemy until that Radiant climbed up over the edge of the cliff, glowing in Shardplate. Emperor Yanagawn sat down as the other soldiers rallied around the Radiant and pushed the enemy backward.

Dalinar lowered his bow, reading the terror in the youth's trembling figure. Other men spoke of getting the shakes when a fight was over – the horror of it catching up with them.

The emperor finally stumbled to his feet, using the spear like a staff. He didn't notice Dalinar, didn't even question why some of the bodies around him had arrows in them. This boy was no soldier, though Dalinar hadn't expected him to be one. From his experience, Azish generals were too pragmatic to want the throne. It involved too much pandering to bureaucrats and, apparently, dictating essays.

The youth started down a path away from the cliff, and Dalinar followed. Aharietiam. The people who lived through this had thought it the end of the world. Surely they assumed they'd soon return to the Tranquiline Halls. How would they respond to the information that – after four millennia – mankind still hadn't been allowed back into heaven?

The boy stopped at the bottom of the twisting path, which led into the valley between rock formations. He watched wounded men limp by, supported by friends. Moans and shouts rose in the air. Dalinar intended to step up and start explaining about these visions, but the boy strode out to walk beside some wounded men, chatting with them.

Dalinar followed, curious, catching fragments of the conversation. *What happened here? Who are you? Why were you fighting?*

The men didn't have many answers. They were wounded, exhausted, trailed by painspren. They did find their way to a larger group though, in the direction Jasnah had gone during Dalinar's previous visit to this vision.

The crowd had gathered around a man standing on a large boulder. Tall and confident, the man was in his thirties, and he wore white and blue. He had an Alethi feel to him, except ... not quite. His skin was a shade darker, and something was faintly off about his features.

Yet there was something ... familiar about the man.

'You must spread the word,' the man proclaimed. 'We have won! At long last, the Voidbringers are defeated. This is not my victory, or that of the other Heralds. It is *your* victory. You have done this.'

Some of the people shouted in triumph. Too many others stood silent, staring with dead eyes.

'I will lead the charge for the Tranquiline Halls,' the man shouted. 'You will not see me again, but think not on that now! You have won your peace. Revel in it! Rebuild. Go now, help your fellows. Carry with you the light of your Herald king's words. We are victorious, at long last, over evil!'

Another round of shouts, more energetic this time.

Storms, Dalinar thought, feeling a chill. This was Jezerezeh'Elin himself, Herald of Kings. The greatest among them.

Wait. Did the king have *dark* eyes?

The group broke up, but the young emperor remained, staring at the place where the Herald had stood. Finally, he whispered, 'Oh, Yaezir. King of the Heralds.'

'Yes,' Dalinar said, stepping up beside him. 'That *was* him, Your Excellency. My niece visited this vision earlier, and she wrote that she thought she'd spotted him.'

Yanagawn grabbed Dalinar by the arm. 'What did you say? You know me?'

'You are Yanagawn of Azir,' Dalinar said. He nodded his head in a semblance of a bow. 'I am Dalinar Kholin, and I apologize that our meeting must take place under such irregular circumstances.'

The youth's eyes widened. 'I see Yaezir himself first, and now my enemy.'

'I am *not* your enemy.' Dalinar sighed. 'And this is no mere dream, Your Excellency. I—'

'Oh, I know it's not a dream,' Yanagawn said. 'As I am a Prime raised to the throne miraculously, the Heralds may choose to speak through me!' He looked about. 'This day we are living through, it is the Day of Glory?'

'Aharietiam,' Dalinar said. 'Yes.'

'Why did they place you here? What does it mean?'

'They didn't place me here,' Dalinar said. 'Your Excellency, *I* instigated this vision, and *I* brought you into it.'

Skeptical, the boy folded his arms. He wore the leather skirt provided by the vision. He'd left his bronze-tipped spear leaning against a rock nearby.

'Have you been told,' Dalinar asked, 'that I am considered mad?'

'There are rumors.'

'Well, this was my madness,' Dalinar said. 'I suffered visions during the storms. Come. See.'

He led Yanagawn to a better view of the large field of the dead, which spread out from the mouth of the canyon. Yanagawn followed, then his face grew ashen at the sight. Finally, he strode down onto the larger battlefield, moving among the corpses, moans, and curses.

Dalinar walked beside him. So many dead eyes, so many faces twisted in pain. Lighteyed and dark. Pale skin like the Shin and some Horneaters. Dark skin like the Makabaki. Many that could have been Alethi, Veden, or Herdazian.

There were other things, of course. The giant broken stone figures. Parshmen wearing warform, with chitin armor and orange blood. One spot they passed had a whole heap of strange cremlings, burned and smoking. Who would have taken the time to pile up a thousand little crustaceans?

'We fought together,' Yanagawn said.

'How else could we have resisted?' Dalinar said. 'To fight the Desolation alone would be madness.'

Yanagawn eyed him. 'You wanted to talk to me without the viziers. You wanted me alone! And you can just ... you just show me whatever will strengthen your argument!'

'If you accept that I have the power to show you these visions,' Dalinar said, 'would that not in itself imply that you should listen to me?'

'The Alethi are dangerous. Do you know what happened the *last* time the Alethi were in Azir?'

'The Sunmaker's rule was a long time ago.'

'The viziers have talked about this,' Yanagawn said. 'They told me *all* about it. It started the same way back then, with a warlord uniting the Alethi tribes.'

'Tribes?' Dalinar said. 'You'd compare us to the nomads that roam Tu Bayla? Alethkar is one of the most cultured kingdoms on Roshar!'

'Your code of law is barely thirty years old!'

'Your Excellency,' Dalinar said, taking a deep breath, 'I doubt this line of conversation will be relevant. Look around us. Look and *see* what the Desolation will bring.'

He swept his hand across the awful view, and Yanagawn's temper cooled. It was impossible to feel anything but sorrow when confronted by so much death.

Eventually, Yanagawn turned and started back the way they'd come. Dalinar joined him, hands clasped behind.

'They say,' Yanagawn whispered, 'that when the Sunmaker rode out of the passes and into Azir, he had one unexpected problem. He conquered my people too quickly, and didn't know what to do with all of his captives. He couldn't leave a fighting population behind him in the towns. There were thousands upon thousands of men he needed to murder.

'Sometimes he'd simply assign the work to his soldiers. Every man was to kill thirty captives – like a child who had to find an armload of firewood before being allowed to play. In other places the Sunmaker declared something arbitrary. Say that every man with hair beyond a certain length was to be slaughtered.

'Before he was struck down with disease by the Heralds, he murdered *ten percent* of the population of Azir. They say Zawfix was filled with the bones, blown by highstorms into piles as tall as the buildings.'

'I am *not* my ancestor,' Dalinar said softly.

'You revere him. The Alethi all but worship Sadees. You carry his storming *Shardblade*.'

'I gave that away.'

They stopped at the edge of the battlefield. The emperor had grit, but didn't know how to carry himself. He walked with shoulders slumped, and his hands kept reaching for pockets his antiquated clothing didn't have. He was of low birth – though in Azir, they didn't properly revere eye color. Navani had once told him it was because there weren't enough people in Azir with light eyes.

The Sunmaker himself had used this to justify conquering them.

'I am not my ancestor,' Dalinar repeated. 'But I do share much with him. A youth of brutality. A lifetime spent at war. I have one advantage he did not.'

'Which is?'

Dalinar met the young man's eyes. 'I've lived long enough to see the consequences of what I've done.'

Yanagawn nodded slowly.

'Yeah,' a voice piped up. 'You're *old*.'

Dalinar turned, frowning. That had sounded like a young girl. Why would there be a girl on the battlefield?

'I didn't expect you to be so old,' the girl said. She sat perched cross-legged on a large boulder nearby. 'And you're not really that black. They call you Blackthorn, but you're really more like . . . Dark-tan-thorn. Gawx is more black than you are, and even *he's* pretty brownish.'

The young emperor, remarkably, burst into an enormous grin. 'Lift! You're back!' He started climbing up the boulder, heedless of decorum.

'Not quite back,' she said. 'Got sidetracked. But I'm close now.'

'What happened in Yeddaw?' Yanagawn said, eager. 'You barely gave me any kind of explanation!'

'Those people *lie* about their food.' She narrowed her eyes at Dalinar as the young emperor slipped down the boulder, then tried to climb up another side.

This is not possible, the Stormfather said in Dalinar's mind. *How did she come here?*

'You didn't bring her in?' Dalinar said softly.

No. This is not possible! How . . . ?

Yanagawn finally attained the top of the boulder and gave the younger girl a hug. She had long dark hair, pale white eyes, and tan skin, though she likely wasn't Alethi – the face was too round. Reshi, perhaps?

'He's trying to convince me I should trust him,' Yanagawn said, pointing at Dalinar.

'Don't,' she said. 'He's got too nice a butt.'

Dalinar cleared his throat. '*What?*'

'Your butt is too nice. Old guys shouldn't have tight butts. It means you spend *waaay* too much time swinging a sword or punching people. You should have an old flabby butt. Then I'd trust you.'

'She . . . has a thing about butts,' Yanagawn said.

'No I don't,' the girl said, rolling her eyes. 'If someone thinks I'm strange for talking about butts, it's usually because they're jealous, 'cuz I'm the only one *without* something rammed up mine.' She narrowed her eyes at Dalinar, then took the emperor by the arm. 'Let's go.'

'But—' Dalinar said, raising his hand.

'See, you're learning.' She grinned at him.

Then she and the emperor vanished.

The Stormfather rumbled in frustration. *That woman! This is a creation specifically meant to defy my will!*

'Woman?' Dalinar asked, shaking his head.

That child is tainted by the Nightwatcher.

'Technically, so am I.'

This is different. This is unnatural. She goes too far. The Stormfather rumbled his discontent, refusing to speak to Dalinar further. He seemed genuinely upset.

In fact, Dalinar was forced to sit and wait until the vision finished. He spent the time staring out over that field of the dead, haunted equally by the future and the past.

You have spoken to one who cannot respond. We, instead, will take your communication to us – though we know not how you located us upon this world.

Moash picked at the mush that Febrth called a 'stew.' It tasted like crem.

He stared at the flamespren in their large cookfire, trying to warm himself as Febrth – a Thaylen man with striking Horneater red hair – argued with Graves. The fire's smoke curled into the air, and the light would be visible for miles across the Frostlands. Graves didn't care; he figured that if the Everstorm hadn't cleared the bandits out of the area, two Shardbearers would be more than enough to deal with any who remained.

Shardblades can't stop an arrow in the back, Moash thought, feeling exposed. *And neither can Plate, if we're not wearing it.* His armor, and that of Graves, lay bundled in their wagon.

'Look, that is the Triplets,' Graves said, waving toward a rock formation. 'It's *right here* on the map. We go west now.'

'I've been this way before,' Febrth said. 'We must continue south, you see. Then east.'

'The map—'

'I have no need for your maps,' Febrth said, folding his arms. 'The Passions guide me.'

'The Passions?' Graves said, throwing his hands up. 'The *Passions*? You're supposed to have abandoned such superstitions. You belong to the Diagram now!'

'I can do both,' Febrth said solemnly.

Moash stuffed another spoonful of 'stew' into his mouth. Storms, he hated it when Febrth took a turn cooking. And when Graves took a turn. And when Fia took a turn. And . . . well, the stuff Moash himself cooked tasted like spiced dishwater. None of them could cook worth a dun chip. Not like Rock.

Moash dropped his bowl, letting the mush slop over the side. He grabbed his coat off a tree branch and stalked out into the night. The cold air felt strange on his skin after so long in front of the fire. He hated how cold it was down here. Perpetual winter.

The four of them had suffered through the storms hiding in the cramped, reinforced bottom of their wagon, which they'd chained to the ground. They'd frightened away rogue parshmen with their Shardblades – they hadn't been nearly as dangerous as he'd worried. But that new storm . . .

Moash kicked at a rock, but it was frozen to the ground and he just stubbed his toe. He cursed, then glanced over his shoulder as the argument ended in shouts. He'd once admired how refined Graves seemed. That had been before spending weeks crossing a barren landscape together. The man's patience had frayed to threads, and his refinement didn't matter much when they were all eating slop and pissing behind hills.

'So how lost are we?' Moash asked as Graves joined him in the darkness outside camp.

'Not lost at all,' Graves said, 'if that idiot would actually *look* at a *map*.' He glanced at Moash. 'I've told you to get rid of that coat.'

'Which I'll do,' Moash said, 'when we're not crawling across winter's own frozen backside.'

'At least take the patch off. It might give us away, if we meet someone from the warcamps. Rip it off.' Graves turned on his heel and walked back toward camp.

Moash felt at the Bridge Four patch on his shoulder. It brought memories. Joining Graves and his band, who had been planning to kill King Elhokar. An assassination attempt once Dalinar was away, marching toward the center of the Shattered Plains.

Facing off against Kaladin, wounded and bleeding.

You. Will. Not. Have. Him.

Moash's skin had gone clammy from the cold. He slid his knife from his side sheath – he still wasn't used to being able to carry one that long. A knife that was too big could get you into trouble as a darkeyes.

He wasn't darkeyed anymore. He was one of them.

Storms, he *was* one of them.

He cut the stitches on the Bridge Four patch. Up one side, then down the other. How simple it was. It would be harder to remove the tattoo he'd gotten with the others, but that he'd had placed on his shoulder, not his forehead.

Moash held up the patch, trying to catch the firelight for a last look, and then couldn't bring himself to throw it away. He walked back and settled by the fire. Were the others sitting around Rock's stewpot somewhere? Laughing, joking, betting on how many mugs of ale Lopen could drink? Ribbing Kaladin, trying to get him to crack a smile?

Moash could almost hear their voices, and he smiled, imagining that he was there. Then, he imagined Kaladin telling them what Moash had done.

He tried to kill me, Kaladin would say. *He betrayed everything. His oath to protect the king, his duty to Alethkar, but most importantly us.*

Moash sagged, patch in his fingers. He should throw that thing in the fire.

Storms. He should throw *himself* in the fire.

He looked up toward the skies, toward both Damnation and the Tranquiline Halls. A group of starspren quivered above.

And beside them, something moving in the sky?

Moash shouted, throwing himself backward off his perch as four Voidbringers descended upon the little camp. They smashed into the ground, wielding long, sinuous swords. Not Shardblades – those were Parshendi weapons.

One creature struck where Moash had been sitting an instant before. Another creature stabbed Graves straight through the chest, then yanked the weapon free and beheaded him with a backhand swipe.

Graves's corpse tumbled and his Shardblade materialized, clanging to the ground. Febrth and Fia didn't have a chance. Other Voidbringers struck them down, spilling their blood in this cold, forgotten land.

The fourth Voidbringer came for Moash, who threw himself into a roll. The creature's sword slammed down near him, hitting rock, the blade throwing sparks.

Moash rolled to his feet, and Kaladin's training – drilled into him through hours and hours spent at the bottom of a chasm – took over. He danced away, putting his back to the wagon, as his Shardblade fell into his fingers.

The Voidbringer rounded the fire toward him, light glittering from her taut, muscular body. These weren't like the Parshendi he'd seen on the Shattered Plains. They had deep red eyes and red-violet carapace, some of which framed their faces. The one facing him had a swirling pattern to her skin, three different colors mixing. Red, black, white.

Dark light, like inverse Stormlight, clung to each of them. Graves had spoken of these creatures, calling their return merely one of many events predicted by the inscrutable 'Diagram.'

Moash's foe came for him, and he lashed out with his Blade, driving her back. She seemed to *glide* as she moved, feet barely touching the ground. The other three ignored him, instead picking through the camp, inspecting the bodies. One soared in a graceful leap onto the wagon and began digging in the items there.

His opponent tried again, carefully sweeping her long, curved sword at him. Moash shied back, Shardblade gripped with both hands, trying to intercept her weapon. His motions seemed clumsy compared to the graceful power of this creature. She slipped to the side, clothing rippling in the wind, breath visible in the cold air. She wasn't taking chances against a Shardblade, and didn't strike as Moash stumbled.

Storms. This weapon was just too clunky. Six feet long, it was hard to angle right. Yes, it could cut through anything, but he needed to actually *hit* for that to matter. It had been much easier to wield the thing wearing Plate. Without it, he felt like a child holding an adult's weapon.

The Voidbringer smiled. Then she struck with blurring speed. Moash stepped back, swinging, forcing her to twist to the side. He took a long cut up the arm, but his move prevented her from impaling him.

His arm flared with pain and he grunted. The Voidbringer regarded him confidently, knowingly. He was dead. Maybe he should simply let it happen.

The Voidbringer working in the cart said something eager, excited.

He'd found the Shardplate. He kicked other items while digging it free, and something rolled out the back of the wagon, thumping against the stone. A spear.

Moash looked down at his Shardblade, the wealth of nations, the most valuable possession a man could own.

Who am I kidding? he thought. *Who did I ever think I was kidding?*

The Voidbringer woman launched into an attack, but Moash dismissed his Shardblade and dashed away. His attacker was so surprised that she hesitated, and Moash had time to dive for the spear, rolling to his feet. Holding the smooth wood in his hand, a familiar weight, Moash snapped easily into his stance. The air suddenly smelled damp and faintly rotten – he remembered the chasms. Life and death together, vines and rot.

He could almost hear Kaladin's voice. *You can't fear a Shardblade. You can't fear a lighteyes on horseback. They kill with fear first and the sword second.*

Stand your ground.

The Voidbringer came for him, and Moash stood his ground. He turned her aside by catching her weapon on the haft of the spear. Then he thrust the butt end of the spear up underneath her arm as she came in for a backhand.

The Voidbringer gasped in surprise as Moash executed a takedown he'd practiced a thousand times in the chasms. He swung the butt of his spear at her ankles and swept her legs out from under her. He began to follow with a classic twist and thrust, to stab down through her chest.

Unfortunately, the Voidbringer didn't fall. She caught herself in the air, hovering instead of collapsing. Moash noticed in time, and pulled out of his maneuver to block her next attack.

The Voidbringer glided backward, then dropped to the ground in a prowling crouch, sword held to the side. She then leaped forward and grabbed Moash's spear as he tried to use it to ward her off. Storms! She gracefully pulled herself close to him, inside his reach. She smelled of wet clothing and of the alien, moldy scent he associated with the Parshendi.

She pressed her hand against Moash's chest, and that dark light transferred from her to him. Moash felt himself grow lighter.

Fortunately, Kaladin had tried this on him too.

Moash seized the Voidbringer with one hand, holding on to the front of her loose shirt, as his body tried to fall into the air.

His sudden pull jerked her off balance, even lifted her a few inches. He yanked her up toward him with one hand while pushing his spearhead down against the rocky ground. That sent the two of them spinning in the air, hovering.

She cried out in an alien tongue. Moash dropped his spear and grabbed his knife. She tried to shove him away, Lashing him again, stronger this time. He grunted, but hung on, and got his knife up and rammed it into her chest.

Orange Parshendi blood poured around his hand, spraying into the cold night as they continued to spin in the air. Moash hung on tight and pushed the knife farther.

She didn't heal, as Kaladin would have. Her eyes stopped glowing, and the dark light vanished.

The body grew limp. A short time later, the force pulling Moash upward ran out. He dropped the five feet to the ground, her body cushioning his fall.

Orange blood coated him, steaming in the chill air. He seized his spear again, fingers slick with blood, and pointed it at the three remaining Voidbringers, who regarded him with stunned expressions.

'Bridge Four, you bastards,' Moash growled.

Two of the Voidbringers turned toward the third, the other woman, who looked Moash up and down.

'You can probably kill me,' Moash said, wiping a hand on his clothes to improve his grip. 'But I'll take one of you with me. At least one.'

They didn't seem angry that he'd killed their friend. Storms though, did things like these even *have* emotions? Shen had often just sat around staring. He locked eyes with the woman at the center. Her skin was white and red, not a bit of black in it. The paleness of that white reminded him of the Shin, who always looked sickly to Moash.

'You,' she said in accented Alethi, 'have passion.'

One of the others handed her Graves's Shardblade. She held it up, inspecting it by the firelight. Then she rose into the air. 'You may choose,' she said to him. 'Die here, or accept defeat and give up your weapons.'

Moash clung to the spear in the shadow of that figure, her clothing rippling in the air. Did they think he'd actually trust them?

But then . . . did he really think he could stand against three of them?

With a shrug, he tossed aside the spear. He summoned his Blade. After all those years dreaming of one of these, he'd finally received one.

Kaladin had given it to him. And what good had come of it? He obviously couldn't be trusted with such a weapon.

Setting his jaw, Moash pressed his hand to the gemstone, and willed the bond to break. The gemstone at its pommel flashed, and he felt an icy coolness wash through him. Back to being a darkeyes.

He tossed the Blade to the ground. One of the Voidbringers took it. Another flew off, and Moash was confused as to what was happening. A short time later, that one returned with six more. Three attached ropes to the Shardplate bundles, then flew off, hauling the heavy armor into the air after them. Why not Lash it?

Moash thought for a moment they were actually going to leave him there, but finally two others grabbed him – one arm each – and hauled him into the air.

We are indeed intrigued, for we thought it well hidden. Insignificant among our many realms.

Veil lounged in a tavern tent with her men. Her boots up on a table, chair tipped back, she listened to the life bubbling around her. People drinking and chatting, others strolling the path outside, shouting and joking. She enjoyed the warm, enveloping buzz of fellow humans who had turned this tomb of rock into something alive again.

It still daunted her to contemplate the size of the tower. How had anyone *built* a place this big? It could gobble up most cities Veil had seen without having to loosen its belt.

Well, best not to think about that. You needed to sneak low, beneath all the questions that distracted scribes and scholars. That was the only way to get anything useful done.

Instead she focused on the people. Their voices blended together, and collectively they became a faceless crowd. But the grand thing about people was that you could also choose to focus on particular faces, really see them, and find a wealth of stories. So many people with so many lives, each a separate little mystery. Infinite detail, like Pattern. Look close at his fractal lines, and you'd realize each little ridge had an entire architecture of its own. Look close at a given person, and you'd see their uniqueness – see that they didn't quite match whatever broad category you'd first put them in.

'So . . .' Red said, talking to Ishnah. Veil had brought three of her men today, with the spy woman to train them. So Veil could listen, learn, and try to judge if this woman was trustworthy – or if she was some kind of plant.

'This is great,' Red continued, 'but when do we learn the stuff with the knives? Not that I'm eager to kill anyone. Just . . . you know . . .'

'I know what?' Ishnah asked.

'Knives are deevy,' Red said.

'Deevy?' Veil asked, opening her eyes.

Red nodded. 'Deevy. You know. Incredible, or neat, but in a smooooth way.'

'Everyone knows that knives are deevy,' Gaz added.

Ishnah rolled her eyes. The short woman wore her havah with hand covered, and her dress had a light touch of embroidery. Her poise and dress indicated she was a darkeyed woman of relatively high social standing.

Veil drew more attention, and not just because of her white jacket and hat. It was the attention of men assessing whether they wanted to approach her, which they didn't do with Ishnah. The way she carried herself, the prim havah, kept them back.

Veil sipped her drink, enjoying the wine.

'You've heard lurid stories, I'm sure,' Ishnah said. 'But espionage is not about knives in alleys. I'd barely know what to do with myself if I had to stab someone.'

The three men deflated.

'Espionage,' Ishnah continued, 'is about the careful gathering of information. Your task is to observe, but to not *be* observed. You must be likable enough that people talk to you, but not so interesting that they remember you.'

'Well, Gaz is out,' Red said.

'Yeah,' Gaz said, 'it's a curse to be so storming interesting.'

'Would you two shut up?' Vathah said. The lanky soldier had leaned in, cup of cheap wine left untouched. 'How?' he asked. 'I'm tall. Gaz has one eye. We'll be remembered.'

'You need to learn to channel attention toward superficial traits you can change, and away from traits you cannot. Red, if *you* wore an eye patch, that detail would stick in their minds. Vathah, I can teach you how to slouch so your height isn't noticeable – and if you add an unusual accent, people will describe you by that. Gaz, I could put you in a tavern and have you lie on the table in a feigned drunken stupor. Nobody will notice the eye patch; they'll ignore you as a drunkard.

'That is beside the point. We must begin with observation. If you are to be useful, you need to be able to make quick assessments of a location, memorize details, and be able to report back. Now, close your eyes.'

They reluctantly did so, Veil joining them.

'Now,' Ishnah said. 'Can any of you describe the tavern's occupants? Without looking, mind you.'

'Uh . . .' Gaz scratched at his eye patch. 'There's a cute one at the bar. She might be Thaylen.'

'What color is her blouse?'

'Hm. Well, it's low cut, and she's grown some nice rockbuds . . . uh . . .'

'There's this really ugly guy with an eye patch,' Red said. 'Short, annoy-ing type. Drinks your wine when you aren't looking.'

'Vathah?' Ishnah asked. 'What about you?'

'I think there were some guys at the bar,' he said. 'They were in . . . Sebarial uniforms? And maybe half the tables were occupied. I couldn't say by who.'

'Better,' Ishnah said. 'I didn't expect you to be able to do this. It's human nature to ignore these things. I'll train you though, so that—'

'Wait,' Vathah said. 'What about Veil? What does she remember?'

'Three men at the bar,' Veil said absently. 'Older man with whitening hair, and two soldiers, probably related, judging by those hooked noses. The younger one is drinking wine; the older one is trying to pick up the woman Gaz noticed. She's not Thaylen, but she's wearing Thaylen dress with a deep violet blouse and a forest-green skirt. I don't like the pairing, but she seems to. She's confident, used to playing with the attention of men. But I think she came here looking for someone, because she's ignor-ing the soldier and keeps glancing over her shoulder.

'The barkeep is an older man, short enough that he stands on boxes when he fills orders. I bet he hasn't been a barkeep long. He hesitates when someone orders, and he has to glance over the bottles, reading their glyphs before he finds the right one. There are three barmaids – one is on break – and fourteen customers other than us.' She opened her eyes. 'I can tell you about them.'

'Won't be necessary,' Ishnah said as Red clapped softly. 'Very impressive, Veil, though I should note that there are *fifteen* other customers, not fourteen.'

Veil started, then glanced around the tent room again, counting – as she'd done in her head just a moment ago. Three at that table . . . four over there . . . two women standing together by the door . . .

And a woman she'd missed, nestled into a chair by a small table at the back of the tent. She wore simple clothing, a skirt and blouse of Alethi peasant design. Had she intentionally chosen clothing that blended in with the white of the tent and brown of the tables? And what was she doing there?

Taking notes, Veil thought with a spike of alarm. The woman had carefully hidden a little notebook in her lap. 'Who is she?' Veil hunkered down. 'Why is she watching us?'

'Not us specifically,' Ishnah said. 'There will be dozens like her in the market, moving like rats, gathering what information they can. She might be independent, selling tidbits she finds, but likely she's employed by one of the highprinces. That's the job I used to do. I'd guess from the people she's watching that she's been told to gather a report on the mood of the troops.'

Veil nodded and listened intently as Ishnah started training the men in memory tricks. She suggested they should learn glyphs, and use some ploy – like making marks on their hands – to help them keep track of information. Veil had heard of some of these tricks, including the one Ishnah talked about, the so-called mind museum.

Most interesting were Ishnah's tips on how to tell what was relevant to report, and how to find it. She talked about listening for the names of highprinces and for common words used as stand-ins for more important matters, and about how to listen for someone who had just the right amount of drink in them to say things they shouldn't. Tone, she said, was key. You could sit five feet from someone sharing important secrets, but miss it because you were focused on the argument at the next table over.

The state she described was almost meditative – sitting and letting your ears take in everything, your mind latching on to only certain conversations. Veil found it fascinating. But after about an hour of training, Gaz complained that his head felt like he'd had four bottles already. Red was nodding, and the way his eyes were crossed made him seem completely overwhelmed.

Vathah though . . . he'd closed his eyes and was reeling off descriptions of everyone in the room to Ishnah. Veil grinned. For as long as she'd known the man, he'd gone about each of his duties as if he had a boulder tied to his back. Slow to move, quick to find a place to sit down and rest. Seeing this enthusiasm from him was encouraging.

In fact, Veil was so engaged, she completely missed how much time had passed. When she heard the market bells she cursed softly. 'I'm a storming fool.'

'Veil?' Vathah asked.

'I've got to get going,' she said. 'Shallan has an appointment.' Who would have thought that bearing an ancient, divine mantle of power and honor would involve so many meetings?

'And she can't make it without you?' Vathah said.

'Storms, have you *watched* that girl? She'd forget her feet if they weren't stuck on. Keep practicing! I'll meet up with you later.' She pulled on her hat and went dashing through the Breakaway.

❖

A short time later, Shallan Davar – now safely tucked back into a blue havah – strolled through the hallway beneath Urithiru. She was pleased with the work that Veil was doing with the men, but storms, did she have to drink so much? Shallan burned off practically an entire *barrel's* worth of alcohol to clear her head.

She took a deep breath, then stepped into the former library room. Here she found not only Navani, Jasnah, and Teshav, but a host of ardents and scribes. May Aladar, Adrotagia from Kharbranth . . . there were even three *stormwardens,* the odd men with the long beards who liked to predict the weather. Shallan had heard that they would occasionally use the blowing of the winds to foretell the future, but they never offered such services openly.

Being near them made Shallan wish for a glyphward. Veil didn't keep any handy, unfortunately. *She* was basically a heretic, and thought about religion as often as she did seasilk prices in Rall Elorim. At least Jasnah had the backbone to pick a side and announce it; Veil would simply shrug and make some wisecrack. It—

'Mmmm . . .' Pattern whispered from her skirt. 'Shallan?'

Right. She'd been just standing in the doorway, hadn't she? She walked in, unfortunately passing Janala, who was acting as Teshav's assistant. The pretty young woman stood with her nose perpetually in the air, and was the type of person whose very enunciation made Shallan's skin crawl.

The woman's arrogance was what Shallan didn't like – not, of course, that Adolin had been courting Janala soon before meeting Shallan. She had once tried to avoid Adolin's former romantic partners, but . . . well, that was like trying to avoid soldiers on a battlefield. They were just kind of everywhere.

A dozen conversations buzzed through the room: talk about weights and measures, the proper placement of punctuation, and the atmospheric variations in the tower. Once she'd have given anything to be in a room like this. Now she was constantly late to the meetings. What had changed?

I know how much a fraud I am, she thought, hugging the wall, passing a pretty young ardent discussing Azish politics with one of the storm-wardens. Shallan had barely perused those books that Adolin had brought her. On her other side, Navani was talking fabrials with an engineer in a bright red havah. The woman nodded eagerly. 'Yes, but how to stabilize it, Brightness? With the sails underneath, it will want to spin over, won't it?'

Shallan's proximity to Navani had offered ample opportunity to study fabrial science. Why hadn't she? As it enveloped her – the ideas, the questions, the logic – she suddenly felt she was drowning. Overwhelmed. Everyone in this room knew so much, and she felt insignificant compared to them.

I need someone who can handle this, she thought. *A scholar. Part of me can become a scholar. Not Veil, or Brightness Radiant. But someone—*

Pattern started humming on her dress again. Shallan backed to the wall. No, this . . . this was *her,* wasn't it? Shallan had always wanted to be a scholar, hadn't she? She didn't need another persona to deal with this. Right?

. . . Right?

The moment of anxiety passed, and she breathed out, forcing herself to steady. Eventually she pulled a pad of paper and a charcoal pencil out of her satchel, then sought out Jasnah and presented herself.

Jasnah cocked an eyebrow. 'Late again?'

'Sorry.'

'I intended to ask your help understanding some of the translations we're receiving from the Dawnchant, but we haven't time before my mother's meeting starts.'

'Maybe I could help you—'

'I have a few items to finish up. We can speak later.'

An abrupt dismissal, but nothing more than Shallan had come to expect. She walked over to a chair beside the wall and sat down. 'Surely,' she said softly, 'if Jasnah had *known* that I'd just confronted a deep insecurity of mine, she'd have shown some empathy. Right?'

'Jasnah?' Pattern asked. 'I do not think you are paying attention, Shallan. She is not very empathetic.'

Shallan sighed.

'*You're* empathetic though!'

'The pathetic part, at least.' She steeled herself. 'I belong here, Pattern, don't I?'

'Mmm. Yes, of course you do. You'll want to sketch them, right?'

'The classic scholars didn't just draw. The Oilsworn knew mathematics – he *created* the study of ratios in art. Galid was an inventor, and her designs are still used in astronomy today. Sailors couldn't find longitude at sea until the arrival of her clocks. Jasnah's a historian – and more. That's what I want.'

'Are you sure?'

'I think so.' Problem was, Veil wanted to spend her days drinking and laughing with the men, practicing espionage. Radiant wanted to practice with the sword and spend time around Adolin. What did Shallan want? And did it matter?

Eventually Navani called the meeting to order, and people took seats. Scribes on one side of Navani, ardents from a variety of devotaries on the other – and far from Jasnah. As the stormwardens settled down farther around the ring of seats, Shallan noticed Renarin standing in the doorway. He shuffled, peeking in, but not entering. When several scholars turned toward him, he stepped backward, as if their stares were physically forcing him out.

'I . . .' Renarin said. 'Father said I could come . . . just listen maybe.'

'You're more than welcome, Cousin,' Jasnah said. She nodded for

Shallan to get him a stool, so she did – and didn't even protest being ordered about. She *could* be a scholar. She'd be the best little ward ever.

Head down, Renarin rounded the ring of scholars, keeping a white-knuckled grip on a chain hung from his pocket. As soon as he sat, he started pulling the chain between the fingers of one hand, then the other.

Shallan did her best to take notes, and *not* stray into sketching people instead. Fortunately, the proceedings were more interesting than usual. Navani had most of the scholars here working on trying to understand Urithiru. Inadara reported first – she was a wizened scribe who reminded Shallan of her father's ardents – explaining that her team had been trying to ascertain the meaning of the strange shapes of the rooms and tunnels in the tower.

She went on at length, talking of defensive constructions, air filtration, and the wells. She pointed out groupings of rooms that were shaped oddly, and of the bizarre murals they'd found, depicting fanciful creatures.

When she eventually finished, Kalami reported on her team, who were convinced that certain gold and copper metalworks they'd found embedded in walls were fabrials, but they didn't seem to do anything, even with gems attached. She passed around drawings, then moved on to explaining the efforts – failed so far – they'd taken to try to infuse the gemstone pillar. The only working fabrials were the lifts.

'I suggest,' interrupted Elthebar, head of the stormwardens, 'that the ratio of the gears used in the lift machinery might be indicative of the nature of those who built it. It is the science of digitology, you see. You can judge much about a man by the width of his fingers.'

'And this has to do with gears . . . how?' Teshav asked.

'In every way!' Elthebar said. 'Why, the fact that you don't know this is a *clear* indication that you are a scribe. Your writing is pretty, Brightness. But you must give more heed to *science*.'

Pattern buzzed softly.

'I never have liked him,' Shallan whispered. 'He acts nice around Dalinar, but he's quite mean.'

'So . . . which attribute of his are we totaling and how many people are in the sample size?' Pattern asked.

'Do you think, maybe,' Janala said, 'we are asking the wrong questions?'

Shallan narrowed her eyes, but checked herself, suppressing her jealousy. There was no need to hate someone simply because they'd been close to Adolin.

It was just that something felt ... *off* about Janala. Like many women at court, her laughter sounded rehearsed, contained. Like they used it as a seasoning, rather than actually feeling it.

'What do you mean, child?' Adrotagia asked Janala.

'Well, Brightness, we talk about the lifts, the strange fabrial column, the twisting hallways. We try to understand these things merely from their designs. Maybe instead we should figure out the tower's needs, and then work backward to determine how these things might have met them.'

'Hmmm,' Navani said. 'Well, we know that they grew crops outside. Did some of these wall fabrials provide heat?'

Renarin mumbled something.

Everyone in the room looked at him. Not a few seemed surprised to hear him speak, and he shrank back.

'What was that, Renarin?' Navani asked.

'It's not like that,' he said softly. 'They're not fabrials. They're *a* fabrial.'

The scribes and scholars shared looks. The prince ... well, he often incited such reactions. Discomforted stares.

'Brightlord?' Janala asked. 'Are you perhaps secretly an artifabrian? Studying engineering by night, reading the women's script?'

Several of the others chuckled. Renarin blushed deeply, lowering his eyes farther.

You'd never laugh like that at any other man of his rank, Shallan thought, feeling her cheeks grow hot. The Alethi court could be severely polite – but that didn't mean they were nice. Renarin always had been a more acceptable target than Dalinar or Adolin.

Shallan's anger was a strange sensation. On more than one occasion, she'd been struck by Renarin's oddness. His presence at this meeting was just another example. Was he thinking of finally joining the ardents? And he did that by simply showing up at a meeting for scribes, as if he were one of the women?

At the same time, how *dare* Janala embarrass him?

Navani started to say something, but Shallan cut in. 'Surely, Janala, you didn't just try to *insult* the son of the *highprince*.'

'What? No, no of course I didn't.'

'Good,' Shallan said. 'Because, if you *had* been trying to insult him, you did a terrible job. And I've heard that you're very clever. So full of wit, and charm, and . . . other things.'

Janala frowned at her. '. . . Is that flattery?'

'We weren't talking of your chest, dear. We're speaking of your mind! Your wonderful, brilliant mind, so keen that it's never been sharpened! So quick, it's still running when everyone else is done! So dazzling, it's never failed to leave everyone in awe at the things you say. So . . . um . . .'

Jasnah was glaring at her.

'. . . Hmm . . .' Shallan held up her notebook. 'I took notes.'

'Could we have a short break, Mother?' Jasnah asked.

'An excellent suggestion,' Navani said. 'Fifteen minutes, during which everyone should consider a list of requirements this tower would have, if it were to somehow become self-sufficient.'

She rose, and the meeting broke up into individual conversations again.

'I see,' Jasnah said to Shallan, 'that you still use your tongue like a bludgeon rather than a knife.'

'Yeah.' Shallan sighed. 'Any tips?'

Jasnah eyed her.

'You heard what she said to Renarin, Brightness!'

'And Mother was about to speak to her about it,' Jasnah said, 'discreetly, with a judicious word. Instead, you threw a dictionary at her head.'

'Sorry. She gets on my nerves.'

'Janala is a fool, just bright enough to be proud of the wits she has, but stupid enough to be unaware of how outmatched they are.' Jasnah rubbed her temples. 'Storms. This is why I never take wards.'

'Because they give you so much trouble.'

'Because I'm bad at it. I have scientific evidence of that fact, and you are but the latest experiment.' Jasnah shooed her away, rubbing her temples.

Shallan, feeling ashamed, walked to the side of the room, while everyone else got refreshments.

'Mmmm!' Pattern said as Shallan leaned against the wall, notebook held closer to her chest. 'Jasnah doesn't seem angry. Why are you sad?'

'Because I'm an idiot,' Shallan said. 'And a fool. And . . . because I don't *know* what I *want*.' Hadn't it been only a week or two ago that she'd innocently assumed she had it figured out? Whatever 'it' was?

'I can see him!' said a voice to her side.

Shallan jumped and turned to find Renarin staring at her skirt and the pattern there, which blended into her embroidery. Distinct if you knew to look, but easy to miss.

'He doesn't turn invisible?' Renarin said.

'He says he can't.'

Renarin nodded, then looked up at her. 'Thank you.'

'For?'

'Defending my honor. When Adolin does that, someone usually gets stabbed. Your way was pleasanter.'

'Well, nobody should take that tone with you. They wouldn't *dare* do it to Adolin. And besides, you're right. This place *is* one big fabrial.'

'You feel it too? They keep talking about this device or that device, but that's wrong, isn't it? That's like taking the parts of a cart, without realizing you've got a cart in the first place.'

Shallan leaned in. 'That *thing* that we fought, Renarin. It could stretch its tendrils all the way up to the very top of Urithiru. I felt its wrongness wherever I went. That gemstone at the center is tied to everything.'

'Yes, this isn't only a collection of fabrials. It's many fabrials put together to make one *big* fabrial.'

'But what does it do?' Shallan asked.

'It does being a city.' He frowned. 'Well, I mean, it bees a city. . . . It does what the city is. . . .'

Shallan shivered. 'And the Unmade was running it.'

'Which let us discover this room and the fabrial column,' Renarin said. 'We might not have accomplished that without it. Always look on the bright side.'

'Logically,' Shallan said, 'the bright side is the only side you can look on, because the other side is dark.'

Renarin laughed. It brought to mind how her brothers would laugh at what she said. Maybe not because it was the most hilarious thing ever spoken, but because it was good to laugh. That reminded her of what Jasnah had said, though, and Shallan found herself glancing at the woman.

'I know my cousin is intimidating,' Renarin whispered to her. 'But you're a Radiant too, Shallan. Don't forget that. We could stand up to her if we wanted to.'

'Do we want to?'

Renarin grimaced. 'Probably not. So often, she's right, and you just end up feeling like one of the ten fools.'

'True, but . . . I don't know if I can stand being ordered around like a child again. I'm starting to feel crazy. What do I do?'

Renarin shrugged. 'I've found the best way to avoid doing what Jasnah says is to not be around when she's looking for someone to give orders to.'

Shallan perked up. That made a lot of sense. Dalinar would need his Radiants to go do things, right? She needed to get away, just until she could figure things out. Go somewhere . . . like on that mission to Kholinar? Wouldn't they need someone who could sneak into the palace and activate the device?

'Renarin,' she said, 'you're a genius.'

He blushed, but smiled.

Navani called the meeting together again, and they sat to continue discussing fabrials. Jasnah tapped Shallan's notebook and she did a better job of taking the minutes, practicing her shorthand. It wasn't nearly as irksome now, as she had an exit strategy. An escape route.

She was appreciating that when she noticed a tall figure striding through the door. Dalinar Kholin cast a shadow, even when he wasn't standing in front of the light. Everyone immediately hushed.

'Apologies for my tardiness.' He glanced at his wrist, and the forearm timepiece that Navani had given him. 'Please don't stop because of me.'

'Dalinar?' Navani asked. 'You've never attended a meeting of scribes before.'

'I just thought I should watch,' Dalinar said. 'Learn what this piece of my organization is doing.' He settled down on a stool outside the ring. He looked like a warhorse trying to perch on a stand meant for a show pony.

They started up again, everyone obviously self-conscious. She'd have thought that Dalinar would know to stay away from meetings like this, where women and scribes . . .

Shallan cocked her head as she saw Renarin glance at his father. Dalinar responded with a raised fist.

He came so Renarin wouldn't feel awkward, Shallan realized. *It can't be improper or feminine for the prince to be here if the storming Blackthorn decides to attend.*

She didn't miss the way that Renarin actually raised his eyes to watch the rest of the proceedings.

45

A REVELATION

As the waves of the sea must continue to surge, so must our will continue resolute.

Alone.

The Voidbringers carried Moash to Revolar, a city in central Alethkar. Once there, they dropped him outside the city and shoved him toward a group of lesser parshmen.

His arms ached from being carried. Why hadn't they used their powers to Lash him upward and make him lighter, as Kaladin would have?

He stretched his arms, looking around. He'd been to Revolar many times, working a regular caravan to Kholinar. Unfortunately, that didn't mean he'd seen much of the city. Every city of size had a little huddle of buildings on the outskirts for people like him: modern-day nomads who worked caravans or ran deliveries. The people of the eaves, some had called them. Men and women who hovered close enough to civilization to get out of the weather when it turned bad, but who never really belonged.

From the looks of things, Revolar had quite the eaves culture now – too much of one. The Voidbringers seemed to have taken over the entire storming place, exiling the humans to the outskirts.

The Voidbringers left him without a word, despite having lugged him all this distance. The parshmen who took custody of him here looked like a hybrid between Parshendi warriors and the normal, docile parshmen he'd known from many a caravan run. They spoke perfect Alethi as they shoved him toward a group of humans in a little pen.

Moash settled in to wait. Looked like the Voidbringers had patrols scouting the area, grabbing human stragglers. Eventually, the parshmen herded him and the others toward one of the large storm bunkers outside the city – used for housing armies or multiple caravans during highstorms.

'Don't make trouble,' a parshwoman said, specifically eyeing Moash. 'Don't fight, or you'll be killed. Don't run, or you'll be beaten. You're the slaves now.'

Several of the humans – homesteaders, from the looks of it – started weeping. They clutched meager bundles, which parshmen searched through. Moash could read the signs of their loss in their reddened eyes and ragged possessions. The Everstorm had wiped out their farm. They'd come to the big city looking for refuge.

He had nothing on him of value, not any longer, and the parshmen let him go in before the others. He walked into the bunker, feeling a surreal sense of . . . abandonment? He'd spent the trip here alternately assuming he'd be executed or interrogated. Instead, they'd made a common slave of him? Even in Sadeas's army, he'd never technically been a slave. Assigned to bridge runs, yes. Sent to die. But he'd never worn the brands on his forehead. He felt at the Bridge Four tattoo under his shirt, on his left shoulder.

The vast, high-ceilinged storm bunker was shaped like a huge stone loaf. Moash ambled through it, hands stuffed in his coat pockets. Huddled groups of people regarded him with hostility, even though he was just another refugee.

He'd always been met with hostility, no matter where he storming went. A youth like him, too big and obviously too confident for a darkeyes, had been considered a threat. He'd joined the caravans to give himself something productive to do, encouraged by his grandparents. They'd been murdered for their kindly ways, and Moash . . . he'd spent his life putting up with looks like that.

A man on his own, a man you couldn't control, was dangerous. He was *inherently frightening*, just because of who he was. And nobody would ever let him in.

Except Bridge Four.

Well, Bridge Four had been a special case, and he'd failed that test.

Graves had been right to tell him to cut the patch off. *This* was who he really was. The man everyone looked at with distrust, pulling their children tight and nodding for him to move along.

He stalked down the middle of the structure, which was so wide it needed pillars to hold up the ceiling. Those rose like trees, Soulcast right into the rock below. The edges of the building were crowded with people, but the center was kept clear and patrolled by armed parshmen. They'd set up stations with wagons as perches, where parshmen were addressing crowds. Moash went over to one.

'In case we missed any,' the parshman shouted, 'experienced farmers should report to Bru at the front end of the chamber. He will assign you a plot of land to work. Today, we also need workers to carry water in the city, and more to clear debris from the last storm. I can take twenty of each.'

Men started calling out their willingness, and Moash frowned, leaning toward a man nearby. 'They offer us work? Aren't we slaves?'

'Yeah,' the man said. 'Slaves who don't eat unless they work. They let us choose what we want to do, though it's not much of a storming choice. One kind of drudgery or another.'

With a start, Moash realized that the man had pale green eyes. Yet he still raised his hand and volunteered to carry water – something that had once been parshman work. Well, that was a sight that couldn't help but brighten a man's day. Moash shoved hands back in pockets and continued through the room, checking each of the three stations where parshmen offered jobs.

Something about these parshmen and their perfect Alethi unsettled him. The Voidbringers were what he'd expected, with their alien accents and dramatic powers. But the ordinary parshmen – many of them looked like Parshendi now, with those taller builds – seemed almost as bewildered at their reversal in fortune as the humans were.

Each of the three stations dealt with a different category of labor. The one at the far end was looking for farmers, women with sewing skill, and cobblers. Food, uniforms, boots. The parshmen were preparing for war. Asking around, Moash learned they'd already grabbed the smiths, fletchers, and armorers – and if you were found hiding skill in any of these three, your whole family would be put on half rations.

The middle station was for basic labor. Hauling water, cleaning, cooking food. The last station was the most interesting to Moash. This was for hard labor.

He lingered here, listening to a parshman ask for volunteers to pull wagons of supplies with the army when it marched. Apparently, there weren't enough chulls to move wagons for what was coming.

Nobody raised their hands for this one. It sounded like ghastly work, not to mention the fact that it would mean marching toward battle.

They'll need to press the people into this, Moash thought. *Maybe they can round up some lighteyes and make them trudge across the rock like beasts of burden.* He'd like to see that.

As he left this last station, Moash spotted a group of men with long staffs, leaning against the wall. Sturdy boots, waterskins in holsters tied to their thighs, and a walking kit sewn into the trousers on the other side. He knew from experience what that would carry. A bowl, spoon, cup, thread, needle, patches, and some flint and tinder.

Caravaneers. The long staffs were for slapping chull shells while walking beside them. He'd worn an outfit like that many times, though many of the caravans he'd worked had used parshmen to pull wagons instead of chulls. They were faster.

'Hey,' he said, strolling over to the caravaneers. 'Is Guff still around?'

'Guff?' one of the caravaneers said. 'Old wheelwright? Half a reed tall? Bad at cussing?'

'That's him.'

'I think he's over there,' the young man said, pointing with his staff. 'In the tents. But there ain't work, friend.'

'The shellheads are marching,' Moash said, thumbing over his shoulder. 'They'll need caravaneers.'

'Positions are full,' another of the men said. 'There was a fight to see who got those jobs. Everyone else will be pulling wagons. Don't draw too much attention, or they'll slap a harness on you. Mark my words.'

They smiled in a friendly way to Moash, and he gave them an old caravaneers' salute – close enough to a rude gesture that everyone else mistook it – and strode in the direction they'd pointed. Typical. Caravaneers were a big family – and, like a family, prone to squabbling.

The 'tents' were really some sections of cloth that had been stretched from the wall to poles driven into buckets of rocks to keep them steady. That made a kind of tunnel along the wall here, and underneath, a lot of older people coughed and sniffled. It was dim, with only the occasional chip on an overturned box giving light.

He picked out the caravaneers by their accents. He asked after Guff – who was one of the men he'd known back in the day – and was allowed to penetrate deeper along the shadowy tent tunnel. Eventually, Moash found old Guff sitting right in the middle of the tunnel, as if to keep people from going farther. He had been sanding a piece of wood – an axle, by the looks of it.

He squinted as Moash stepped up. 'Moash?' he said. 'Really? What storming storm brought you here?'

'You wouldn't believe me if I told you,' Moash said, squatting down beside the old man.

'You were on Jam's caravan,' Guff said. 'Off to the Shattered Plains; gave you all up for dead. Wouldn't have bet a dun chip on you returning.'

'A wise enough bet,' Moash said. He hunched forward, resting his arms on his knees. In this tunnel, the buzz of people outside seemed a distant thing, though only cloth separated them.

'Son?' Guff asked. 'Why you here, boy? What do you want?'

'I just need to be who I was.'

'That makes as much sense as the storming Stormfather playing the flute, boy. But you wouldn't be the first to go off to those Plains and come back not all right. No you wouldn't. That's the Stormfather's storming own truth, that storming is.'

'They tried to break me. Damnation, they did break me. But then he made me again, a new man.' Moash paused. 'I threw it all away.'

'Sure, sure,' Guff said.

'I always do that,' Moash whispered. 'Why must we always take something precious, Guff, and find ourselves *hating* it? As if by being pure, it reminds us of just how little we deserve it. I held the spear, and I stabbed myself with it. . . .'

'The spear?' Guff asked. 'Boy, you a storming soldier?'

Moash looked at him with a start, then stood up, stretching, showing his patchless uniform coat.

Guff squinted in the darkness. 'Come with me.' The old wheelwright rose – with difficulty – and set his piece of wood on his chair. He led Moash with a rickety gait farther into the cloth tunnel, and they entered a portion of the tented area that was more roomlike, the far corner of the large bunker. Here, a group of maybe a dozen people sat in furtive conversation, chairs pulled together.

A man at the door grabbed Guff by the arm as he shuffled in. 'Guff? You're supposed to be on guard, fool man.'

'I'm storming on storming guard, you pisser,' Guff said, shaking his arm free. 'The bright wanted to know if we found any soldiers. Well I found a storming soldier, so storm off.'

The guard turned his attention to Moash, then flicked his eyes to Moash's shoulder. 'Deserter?'

Moash nodded. It was true in more ways than one.

'What's this?' One of the men stood up, a tall fellow. Something about his silhouette, that bald head, that cut of clothing . . .

'Deserter, Brightlord,' the guard said.

'From the Shattered Plains,' Guff added.

The highlord, Moash realized. *Paladar.* Vamah's kinsman and regent, a notoriously harsh man. In years past, he had nearly run the city to the ground, driving away many darkeyes who had the right of travel. Not a caravan had passed when someone hadn't complained about Paladar's greed and corruption.

'From the Shattered Plains, you say?' Paladar said. 'Excellent. Tell me, deserter, what news is there from the highprinces? Do they know of my plight here? Can I expect aid soon?'

They put him in charge, Moash thought, spotting other lighteyes. They wore fine clothing – not silks of course, but well-trimmed uniforms. Exceptional boots. There was food aplenty set out at the side of this chamber, while those outside scrounged and did heavy labor.

He'd begun to hope . . . But of course that had been stupid. The arrival of the Voidbringers hadn't cast the lighteyes down; the few Moash had seen outside were merely the sacrifices. The fawning darkeyes at the periphery confirmed this. Soldiers, guards, some favored merchants.

To *Damnation* with them! They'd been given a chance to escape from the lighteyes, and it had only made them *more eager* to be servants! In that moment – surrounded by the pettiness that was his own kind – Moash had a revelation.

He wasn't broken. *All* of them were broken. Alethi society – lighteyed and dark. Maybe all of humankind.

'Well?' the regent demanded. 'Speak up, man!'

Moash remained silent, overwhelmed. He wasn't the exception, always ruining what he was given. Men like *Kaladin* were the exception – the very, very rare exception.

These people proved it. There was *no reason* to obey lighteyes. They had no power, no authority. Men had taken opportunity and cast it to the crem.

'I . . . I think there's something wrong with him, Brightlord,' the guard said.

'Yeah,' Guff added. 'Should maybe have mentioned, he's storming strange in the head now, storming pisser.'

'Bah!' the regent said, pointing at Moash. 'Have that one thrown out. We haven't time for foolishness if we are to restore my place!' He pointed at Guff. 'Have *that one* beaten, and post a competent guard next time, Ked, or you'll be next!'

Old Guff cried out as they seized him. Moash just nodded. Yes. Of course. That was what they would do.

The guards took him under the arms and dragged him to the side of the tent. They parted the cloth and hauled him out. They passed a frazzled woman trying to divide a single piece of flatbread between three young, crying children. You could probably hear their weeping from the brightlord's tent, where he had a stack of bread piled high.

The guards threw him back out into the 'street' that ran down the middle of the large bunker. They told him to stay away, but Moash barely heard. He picked himself up, dusted himself off, then walked to the third of the work stations – the one seeking hard laborers.

There, he volunteered for the most difficult job they had, pulling wagons of supplies for the Voidbringer army.

Did you expect anything else from us? We need not suffer the interference of another. Rayse is contained, and we care not for his prison.

Skar the bridgeman ran up one of the ramps outside Urithiru, breath puffing in the cold air as he silently counted his steps to maintain focus. The air was thinner up here at Urithiru, and that made running harder, though he really only noticed it outside.

He wore full marching pack and gear: rations, equipment, helmet, jerkin, and a shield tied to the back. He carried his spear, and even had some greaves stuck to his legs, held in place by the shape of the metal. All of that weighed almost as much as he did.

He finally hit the top of the Oathgate platform. Storms, but the center building looked farther away than he remembered. He tried to pick up his pace anyway, and jogged for all he was worth, the pack clinking. Finally – sweating, breath growing ragged – he reached the control building and dashed inside. He pulled to a stop, dropping his spear and resting his hands on his knees, gasping for breath.

Most of Bridge Four waited here, some glowing with Stormlight. Of them all, Skar was the only one who – despite two weeks of practice – still hadn't figured out how to draw it in. Well, except for Dabbid and Rlain.

Sigzil checked the clock they'd been allocated by Navani Kholin, a device the size of a small box. 'That was about ten minutes,' he said. 'Just under.'

Skar nodded, wiping his brow. He'd run over a mile from the center of the market, then crossed the plateau and charged the ramp. Storms. He'd pushed himself too hard.

'How long,' he said, gasping, 'how long did it take Drehy?' The two had set out together.

Sigzil glanced at the tall, muscled bridgeman who still glowed with residual Stormlight. 'Under six minutes.'

Skar groaned, sitting down.

'The baseline is equally important, Skar,' Sigzil said, marking glyphs in his notebook. 'We need to know a normal man's abilities to make comparisons. Don't worry though. I'm sure you'll figure out Stormlight soon.'

Skar flopped backward, looking up. Lopen was walking around on the ceiling of the room. Storming Herdazian.

'Drehy, you used a quarter of a Basic Lashing, by Kaladin's terminology?' Sigzil continued, still making notes.

'Yeah,' Drehy said. 'I . . . I know the precise amount, Sig. Strange.'

'Which made you half as heavy as usual, when we put you on the scale back in the rooms. But *why* does a quarter Lashing make you half as heavy? Shouldn't it make you twenty-five percent as heavy?'

'Does it matter?' Drehy asked.

Sigzil looked at him as if he were crazy. 'Of course it does!'

'I want to try a Lashing at an angle next,' Drehy said. 'See if I can make it feel like I'm running downhill, no matter which direction I go. Might not need it. Holding Stormlight . . . it made me feel like I could run forever.'

'Well, it's a new record . . .' Sigzil mumbled, still writing. 'You beat Lopen's time.'

'Did he beat mine?' Leyten called from the side of the small room where he was inspecting the tiling on the floor.

'You stopped for food on the way, Leyten,' Sigzil said. 'Even *Rock* beat your time, and he was skipping like a girl the last third.'

'Was Horneater dance of victory,' Rock said from near Leyten. 'Is very manly.'

'Manly or not, it threw off my test,' Sigzil said. 'At least Skar is willing to pay attention to proper procedure.'

Skar remained lying on the ground as the others chatted – Kaladin was supposed to come and transport them to the Shattered Plains, and Sigzil had decided to run some tests. Kaladin, as usual, was late.

Teft sat down next to Skar, inspecting him with dark green eyes with bags underneath. Kaladin had named the two of them lieutenants, along with Rock and Sigzil, but their roles had never really settled into that ranking. Teft was the perfect definition of a platoon sergeant.

'Here,' Teft said, handing over a chouta – meatballs wrapped in flatbread, Herdazian style. 'Leyten brought food. Eat something, lad.'

Skar forced himself to sit up. 'I'm not that much younger than you, Teft. I'm hardly a lad.'

Teft nodded to himself, chewing on his own chouta. Finally, Skar started into his. It was good, not spicy like a lot of Alethi food, but still good. Flavorful.

'Everyone keeps telling me that I'll "get it soon,"' Skar said. 'But what if I don't? There won't be room in the Windrunners for a lieutenant who has to walk everywhere. I'll end up cooking lunch with Rock.'

'Ain't nothing wrong with being on the support team.'

'Pardon, Sarge, but *storm that*! Do you know how long I waited to hold a spear?' Skar picked up the weapon from beside his pack and laid it across his lap. 'I'm good at it. I can fight. Only . . .'

Lopen left the ceiling, rotating to get his legs under him and floating gently to the floor. He laughed as Bisig in turn tried flying up to the ceiling and crashed headfirst into it. Bisig hopped to his feet, looking down at them all, embarrassed. But what did he have to be embarrassed about? He was standing on the ceiling!

'You were in the military before,' Teft guessed.

'No, but not for lack of trying. You heard of the Blackcaps?'

'Aladar's personal guards.'

'Let's just say they didn't think much of my application.'

Yes, we let darkeyes in. But not runts.

Teft grunted, chewing on his chouta.

'Said they might reconsider if I equipped myself,' Skar said. 'Do you know how much armor costs? I was a stupid rocksplitter with visions of battlefield glory.'

It used to be they'd never speak about their pasts. That had changed, though Skar couldn't specify exactly when. It came out, as part of the catharsis of having become something greater.

Teft was an addict. Drehy had struck an officer. Eth had been caught planning to desert with his brother. Even simple Hobber had been part of a drunken brawl. Knowing Hobber, he'd probably only gone along with what his squad was doing, but a man had ended up dead.

'You'd think,' Teft said, 'that our high and mighty leader would have gotten here by now. I swear, Kaladin acts more like a lighteyes every day.'

'Don't let *him* hear you say that,' Skar said.

'I'll say what I want,' Teft snapped. 'If that boy's not going to come, maybe I should be going. I have things to do.'

Skar hesitated, glancing up at Teft.

'Not *that*,' Teft growled. 'I've barely touched the stuff in days. You'd think a man had never had a wild night out, the way you're all treating me.'

'Didn't say a thing, Teft.'

'Knowing what we've suffered, it's insane to think that we *wouldn't* need something to get us through the day. The moss isn't the problem. It's the storming world going all crazy. That's the problem.'

'Sure is, Teft.'

Teft eyed him, then studied his chouta roll intently. 'So ... how long have the men known? I mean, did anyone ...'

'Not long,' Skar said quickly. 'Nobody's even thinking about it.'

Teft nodded, and didn't see through the lie. Truth was, most of them had noticed Teft sneaking off to grind a little moss now and then. It wasn't uncommon in the army. But doing what he'd done – missing duty, selling his uniform, ending up in an alley – that was different. It was the sort of thing that could get you discharged, at best. At worst ... well, it might get you assigned to bridge duty.

Trouble was, they weren't common soldiers anymore. They weren't lighteyes either. They were something strange, something that nobody understood.

'I don't want to talk about this,' Teft said. 'Look, weren't we discussing how to get you to glow? *That's* the problem at hand.'

Before he could press further, Kaladin Stormblessed finally deigned to arrive, bringing with him the scouts and hopefuls from other bridge crews who had been trying to draw in Stormlight. So far, nobody except men from Bridge Four had managed it, but that included a few that had never actually run bridges: Huio and Punio – Lopen's cousins – and men like Koen from the old Cobalt Guard, who had been recruited into Bridge Four a couple months back. So there was still hope that others could manage it.

Kaladin had brought roughly thirty people *beyond* those who had already been training with the team. Judging by their uniform patches, this thirty had come from other divisions – and some were lighteyed. Kaladin had mentioned asking General Khal to round up the most promising potential recruits from throughout the Alethi army.

'All here?' Kaladin said. 'Good.' He strode to the side of the single-roomed control building, a sack of glowing gemstones slung over his shoulder. His magnificent Shardblade appeared in his hand, and he slid it into the keyhole in the chamber wall.

Kaladin engaged the ancient mechanism, pushing the sword – and the entire inner wall, which could rotate – toward a specific point marked by murals. The floor began to glow, and outside, Stormlight rose in a swirl around the entire stone plateau.

Kaladin locked the Blade into place at the mark on the floor designating the Shattered Plains. When the glow faded, they'd come to Narak.

Sigzil left his pack and armor leaning against the wall, and strode out. Best they could determine, the entire stone top of the platform had come with them, swapping places with the one that had been out here.

At the platform edge, a group of people climbed across a ramp to meet them. A short Alethi woman named Ristina counted out the bridgemen and soldiers as they passed, marking on her ledger.

'Took you long enough, Brightlord,' she noted to Kaladin – whose eyes glowed faintly blue. 'The merchants were beginning to complain.'

It took Stormlight to power the device – some of the gemstones in Kaladin's sack would have been drained by the process – but curiously, it didn't take much more to swap two groups than it did to travel one way. So they tried to run the Oathgates when they had people on both sides wanting to exchange places.

'Tell the merchants when they next come through,' Kaladin said, 'that the Knights Radiant are not their doormen. They'll want to accustom themselves to waiting, unless they find a way to swear the oaths themselves.'

Ristina smirked and wrote it down, as if she were going to pass on that exact message. Skar smiled at that. Nice to see a scribe with a sense of humor.

Kaladin led the way through the city of Narak, once a Parshendi stronghold, now an increasingly important human waystop between the warcamps and Urithiru. The buildings here were surprisingly sturdy: well constructed of crem and carved greatshell carapace. Skar had always assumed the Parshendi to be like the nomads who roved between Azir and Jah Keved. He imagined Parshendi who were wild and ferocious, without civilization, hiding in caves for storms.

Yet here was a well-built, carefully laid-out city. They'd found a building full of artwork of a style that baffled the Alethi scribes. Parshman *art*. They'd been painting even while they fought a war. Just like ... well, just like ordinary people.

He glanced at Shen – no, Rlain, it was hard to remember – walking with spear to his shoulder. Skar forgot he was there most of the time, and that made him ashamed. Rlain was as much a member of Bridge Four as anyone else, right? Would he rather have been painting than fighting?

They passed sentry posts full of Dalinar's soldiers, along with many in red and light blue. Ruthar's colors. Dalinar was putting some of the other soldiers to work, trying to prevent more dustups between soldiers from different princedoms. Without the fighting on the Shattered Plains to keep them focused, the men were getting restless.

They passed a large group of soldiers practicing with bridges on a nearby plateau. Skar couldn't hold back a grin as he saw their black uniforms and helms. Plateau runs had been started again, but with more structure, and the spoils were shared equally among the highprinces.

Today, it was the Blackcaps' turn. Skar wondered if any of them would recognize him. Probably not, even if he *had* caused quite a ruckus among them. There had been only one logical way to get the equipment he needed for his application: He'd stolen it from the Blackcap quartermaster.

Skar had thought they would praise his ingenuity. He was so eager to be a Blackcap that he'd go to great lengths to join them, right?

Wrong. His reward had been a slave brand and eventual sale to Sadeas's army.

He brushed his fingers across the scars on his forehead. Stormlight had healed the brands of the other men – they'd covered them all up with tattoos anyway – but it seemed another little dig, dividing him from the others. Right now, he was the only fighting man in Bridge Four who still had his slave brand.

Well, him and Kaladin, whose scars wouldn't heal for some reason.

They reached the training plateau, crossing the old Bridge Four, which was held in place with some Soulcast rock guideposts. Kaladin called a meeting of the officers as several of Rock's children set up a water station. The tall Horneater seemed beyond enthused to have his family working with him.

Skar joined Kaladin, Sigzil, Teft, and Rock. Though they stood close, there was a conspicuous gap where Moash should have been. It felt so wrong to have a member of Bridge Four completely unaccounted for, and Kaladin's silence on the topic hung over them like an executioner's axe.

'I'm worried,' Kaladin said, 'that nobody practicing with us has begun breathing Stormlight.'

'It's only been two weeks, sir,' Sigzil said.

'True, but Syl thinks several "feel right," though she won't tell me who, as she says it would be wrong.' Kaladin gestured toward the newcomers. 'I asked Khal to send me another batch of hopefuls because I figured the more people we had, the better our chances of finding new squires.' He paused. 'I didn't specify they couldn't be lighteyed. Perhaps I should have.'

'Don't see why, sir,' Skar said, pointing. 'That's Captain Colot – good man. He helped us explore.'

'Just wouldn't feel right, having lighteyed men in Bridge Four.'

'Other than you?' Skar asked. 'And Renarin. And, well, any of us who earn our own Blades, and maybe Rock, who I *think* might have been lighteyed among his people, even if he has dark—'

'Fine, Skar,' Kaladin said. 'Point made. Anyway, we don't have a lot of time left before I leave with Elhokar. I'd like to push the recruits harder, see if they're likely to be able to swear the oaths. Any thoughts?'

'Shove them off edge of plateau,' Rock said. 'Those who fly, we let in.'

'Any *serious* suggestions?' Kaladin asked.

'Let me run them through some formations,' Teft said.

'A good idea,' Kaladin said. 'Storms, I wish we knew how the Radiants used to handle expansion. Were there recruitment drives, or did they just wait until someone attracted a spren?'

'That wouldn't make them a squire though,' Teft said, rubbing his chin. 'But a full Radiant, right?'

'A valid point,' Sigzil said. 'We have no proof that we squires are a step *toward* becoming full Radiants. We might always be your support team – and in that case, it's not individual skill that matters, but your decision. Maybe that of your spren. You choose them, they serve under you, and then they start drawing in Stormlight.'

'Yeah,' Skar said, uncomfortable.

They all glanced at him.

'The first of you that says something placating,' Skar said, 'gets a fist in the face. Or the stomach, if I can't reach your storming stupid Horneater face.'

'Ha!' Rock said. 'You could hit my face, Skar. I have seen you jump very high. Almost, you seem as tall as regular person when you do that.'

'Teft,' Kaladin said, 'go ahead and run those potential recruits through formations. And tell the rest of the men to watch the sky; I'm worried about more raids on the caravans.' He shook his head. 'Something about those raids doesn't add up. The warcamps' parshmen, by all reports, have marched to Alethkar. But why would those Fused keep harrying us? They won't have the troops to take advantage of any supply problems they cause.'

Skar shared a glance with Sigzil, who shrugged. Kaladin talked like this sometimes, differently from the rest of them. He'd trained them in formations and the spear, and they could proudly call themselves soldiers. But they'd only *actually* fought a few times. What did they know of things like strategy and battlefield tactics?

They broke, Teft jogging off to drill the potential recruits. Kaladin set Bridge Four to studying their flying. They practiced landings, and then did sprints in the air, zipping back and forth in formation, getting used to changing directions quickly. It was a little distracting, seeing those glowing lines of light shoot through the sky.

Skar attended Kaladin as he observed the recruits doing formations. The lighteyes didn't voice a single complaint about being filed into ranks with darkeyes. Kaladin and Teft ... well, all of them really ... had a tendency to act as if every lighteyed man was in some way regal. But there were far, far more of them who did normal jobs – though granted, they got paid better for those jobs than a darkeyed man did.

Kaladin watched, then glanced at the Bridge Four men in the sky. 'I wonder, Skar,' he said. 'How important are formations going to be for us, going forward? Can we devise new ones to use in flying? Everything changes when your enemy can attack from all sides. . . .'

After about an hour, Skar went for water, and enjoyed some good-natured ribbing from the others, who landed to grab something to drink. He didn't mind. What you had to watch out for was when Bridge Four *didn't* torment you.

The others took off a short time later, and Skar watched them go, launching into the sky. He took a long draught of Rock's current refreshment – he called it tea, but it tasted like boiled grain – and found himself feeling useless. Were these people, these new recruits, going to start glowing and take his place in Bridge Four? Would he be shuffled off to other duties, while someone else laughed with the crew and got ribbed for their height?

Storm it, he thought, tossing aside his cup. *I hate feeling sorry for myself.* He hadn't sulked when the Blackcaps had turned him down, and he wouldn't sulk now.

He was fishing in his pocket for gemstones, determined to practice some more, when he spotted Lyn sitting on a rock nearby, watching the recruits run formations. She was slouching, and he read frustration in her posture. Well, he knew *that* feeling.

Skar shouldered his spear and sauntered over. The four other scout women had gone to the water station; Rock let out a bellowing laugh at what one of them said.

'Not joining in?' Skar asked, nodding toward the new recruits marching past.

'I don't know formations, Skar. I've never done drills – never even held a storming spear. I ran messages and scouted the Plains.' She sighed. 'I didn't pick it up fast enough, did I? He's gone and gotten some new people to test, since I failed.'

'Don't be stupid,' Skar said, sitting beside her on the large rock. 'You're not being forced out. Kaladin just wants to have as many potential re-cruits as possible.'

She shook her head. 'Everyone knows that we're in a new world now – a world where rank and eye color don't matter. Something glorious.' She looked up at the sky, and the men training there. 'I want to be part of it, Skar. So *badly.*'

'Yeah.'

She looked at him, and probably saw it in his eyes. That same emotion. 'Storms. I hadn't even thought, Skar. Must be worse for you.'

He shrugged and reached into his pouch, taking out an emerald as big as his thumb. It shone fiercely, even in the bright daylight. 'You ever hear about the first time Captain Stormblessed drew in Light?'

'He told us. That day, after he knew he could do it because Teft told him. And—'

'Not that day.'

'You mean while he was healing,' she said. 'After the highstorm where he was strung up.'

'Not that day either,' Skar said, holding up the gemstone. Through it, he saw men running formations, and imagined them carrying a bridge. 'I was there, second row. Bridge run. Bad one. We were charging the plateau, and a lot of Parshendi had set up. They dropped most of the first row, all but Kaladin.

'That exposed me, right beside him, second row. In those days, you didn't have good odds, running near the front. The Parshendi wanted to take down our bridge, and they focused their shots on us. On me. I knew I was dead. I *knew* it. I saw the arrows coming, and I breathed a last prayer, hoping the next life wouldn't be quite so bad.

'Then ... then the arrows moved, Lyn. They storming *swerved toward Kaladin.*' He turned the emerald over, and shook his head. 'There's a special Lashing you can do, which makes things curve in the air. Kaladin painted the wood above his hands with Stormlight and drew the arrows toward him, instead of me. That's the first time I can say I knew something special was happening.' He lowered the gemstone and pressed it into her hand. 'Back then, Kaladin did it without even knowing what he was doing. Maybe we're just trying too hard, you know?'

'But it doesn't make sense! They say you have to suck it in. What does that even mean?'

'No idea,' Skar said. 'They each describe it differently, and it's breaking my brain trying to figure it out. They talk about a sharp intake of breath – only, not really for breathing.'

'Which is perfectly clear.'

'Tell me about it,' Skar said, tapping the gemstone in her palm. 'It worked best for Kaladin when he didn't stress. It was harder when he focused on *making* it happen.'

'So I'm supposed to accidentally but deliberately breathe something in without breathing, but not try too hard at it?'

'Doesn't it just make you want to string the lot of them up in the storms? But their advice is all we got. So . . .'

She looked at the stone, then held it close to her face – that didn't seem to be important, but what could it hurt – and breathed in. Nothing happened, so she tried again. And again. For a solid ten minutes.

'I don't know, Skar,' she finally said, lowering the stone. 'I keep thinking, maybe I don't belong here. If you haven't noticed, none of the women have managed this. I kind of forced my way among you all, and nobody asked—'

'Stop,' he said, taking the emerald and holding it before her again. 'Stop right there. You want to be a Windrunner?'

'More than anything,' she whispered.

'Why?'

'Because I want to soar.'

'Not good enough. Kaladin, he wasn't thinking about being left out, or how great it would be to fly. He was thinking about saving the rest of us. Saving *me*. Why do *you* want to be in the Windrunners?'

'Because I want to help! I want to do something other than stand around, waiting for the enemy to come to us!'

'Well, you have a chance, Lyn. A chance nobody has had for ages, a chance in millions. Either you seize it, and in so doing decide you're worthy, or you leave and give up.' He pressed the gemstone back down into her hand. 'But if you leave, you don't get to complain. As long as you keep trying, there's a chance. When you give up? That's when the dream dies.'

She met his eyes, closed her fist around the gemstone, and breathed in with a sharp, distinct breath.

Then started glowing.

She yelped in surprise and opened her hand to find the gemstone within dun. She looked at him in awe. 'What did you do?'

'Nothing,' Skar said. Which was the problem. Still, he found he couldn't be jealous. Maybe this was his lot, helping others become Radiants. A trainer, a facilitator?

Teft saw Lyn glowing, then dashed over and started cursing – but they were 'good' Teft curses. He grabbed her by the arm and towed her toward Kaladin.

Skar took in a long, satisfied breath. Well, that was two he'd helped so far, counting Rock. He . . . he could live with that, couldn't he?

He strolled over to the drink station and got another cup. 'What is this foul stuff, Rock?' he asked. 'You didn't mistake the washing water for tea, did you?'

'Is old Horneater recipe,' he said. 'Has proud tradition.'

'Like skipping?'

'Like formal war dance,' he said. 'And hitting annoying bridgemen on head for not showing proper respect.'

Skar turned around and leaned one hand on the table, watching Lyn's enthusiasm as her squad of scouts ran up to her. He felt good about what he'd done – strangely good. Excited, even.

'I think I'm going to have to get used to smelly Horneaters, Rock,' Skar said. 'I'm thinking of joining your support team.'

'You think I will let *you* anywhere near cook pot?'

'I might not ever learn to fly.' He squished the part of him that whimpered at that. 'I need to come to terms with the fact. So, I'll have to find another way to help out.'

'Ha. And the fact that you are glowing with Stormlight right now is not at all consideration in decision?'

Skar froze. Then he focused on his hand, right in front of his face, holding a cup. Tiny wisps of Stormlight curled off it. He dropped the cup with a cry, digging from his pocket a couple of dun chips. He'd given his practice gemstone to Lyn.

He looked up at Rock, then grinned stupidly.

'I suppose,' Rock said, 'I can maybe have you wash dishes. Though you do keep throwing my cups on ground. Is not proper respect at all . . .'

He trailed off as Skar left him, running for the others and whooping with excitement.

Indeed, we admire his initiative. Perhaps if you had approached the correct one of us with your plea, it would have found favorable audience.

I am Talenel'Elin, Herald of War. The time of the Return, the Desolation, is near at hand. We must prepare. You will have forgotten much, following the destruction of the times past.

Kalak will teach you to cast bronze, if you have forgotten this. We will Soulcast blocks of metal directly for you. I wish we could teach you steel, but casting is so much easier than forging, and you must have something we can produce quickly. Your stone tools will not serve against what is to come.

Vedel can train your surgeons, and Jezrien will teach you leadership. So much is lost between Returns. I will train your soldiers. We should have time. Ishar keeps talking about a way to keep information from being lost following Desolations. And you have discovered something unexpected. We will use that. Surgebinders to act as guardians ... Knights ...

The coming days will be difficult, but with training, humanity *will* survive. You must bring me to your leaders. The other Heralds should join us soon.

I think I am late, this time. I think ... I fear, oh God, that I have failed. No. This is not right, is it? How long has it been? Where am I? I ... am

Talenel'Elin, Herald of War. The time of the Return, the Desolation, is near at hand. . . .

Jasnah trembled as she read the madman's words. She turned over the sheet, and found the next one covered in similar ideas, repeated over and over.

This couldn't be a coincidence, and the words were too specific. The abandoned Herald had come to Kholinar – and had been dismissed as a madman.

She leaned back in her seat and Ivory – full-sized, like a human – stepped over to the table. Hands clasped behind his back, he wore his usual stiff formal suit. The spren's coloring was jet black, both clothing and features, though something prismatic swirled on his skin. It was as if pure black marble had been coated in oil that glistened with hidden color. He rubbed his chin, reading the words.

Jasnah had rejected the nice rooms with balconies on the rim of Urithiru; those had such an obvious entrance for assassins or spies. Her small room at the center of Dalinar's section was far more secure. She had stuffed the ventilation openings with cloth. The airflow from the hallway outside was adequate for this room, and she wanted to make sure nobody could overhear her by listening through the shafts.

In the corner of her room, three spanreeds worked tirelessly. She had rented them at great expense, until she could acquire new ones of her own. They were paired with reeds in Tashikk that had been delivered to one of the finest – and most trustworthy – information centers in the princedom. There, miles and miles away, a scribe was carefully rewriting each page of her notes, which she had originally sent to them to keep safe.

'This speaker, Jasnah,' Ivory said, tapping the sheet she'd just read. Ivory had a clipped, no-nonsense voice. 'This one who said these words. This person *is* a Herald. Our suspicions are true. The Heralds *are,* and the fallen one still *is.*'

'We need to find him,' Jasnah said.

'We must search Shadesmar,' Ivory said. 'In this world, men can hide easily – but their souls shine out to us on the other side.'

'Unless someone knows how to hide them.'

Ivory looked toward the growing stack of notes in the corner; one of the pens had finished writing. Jasnah rose to change the paper; Shallan had rescued one of her trunks of notes, but two others had gone down with the sinking ship. Fortunately, Jasnah had sent off these backup copies.

Or did it matter? This sheet, encrypted by her cipher, contained lines and lines of information connecting the parshmen to the Voidbringers. Once, she'd slaved over each of these passages, teasing them from history. Now their contents were common knowledge. In one moment, all of her expertise had been wiped away.

'We've lost so much time,' she said.

'Yes. We must catch what we have lost, Jasnah. We *must*.'

'The enemy?' Jasnah asked.

'He stirs. He angers.' Ivory shook his head, kneeling beside her as she changed the sheets of paper. 'We are naught before him, Jasnah. He would destroy my kind and yours.'

The spanreed finished, and another started writing out the first lines of her memoirs, which she'd worked on intermittently throughout her life. She'd thrown aside a dozen different attempts, and as she read this latest one, she found herself disliking it as well.

'What do you think of Shallan?' she asked Ivory, shaking her head. 'The person she's become.'

Ivory frowned, lips drawing tight. His sharply chiseled features, too angular to be human, were like those of a roughed-out statue the sculptor had neglected to finish.

'She . . . is troubling,' he said.

'That much hasn't changed.'

'She is not stable.'

'Ivory, you think *all* humans are unstable.'

'Not you,' he said, lifting his chin. '*You* are like a spren. You think by facts. You change not on simple whims. You are as you *are*.'

She gave him a flat stare.

'Mostly,' he added. 'Mostly. But it *is*, Jasnah. Compared to other humans, you are practically a stone!'

She sighed, standing up and brushing past him, returning to her writing desk. The Herald's ravings glared at her. She settled down, feeling tired.

'Jasnah?' Ivory asked. 'Am I . . . in error?'

'I am not so much a stone as you think, Ivory. Sometimes I wish I were.'

522

'These words trouble you,' he said, stepping up to her again and resting his jet-black fingers on the paper. 'Why? You have read many troubling things.'

Jasnah settled back, listening to the three spanreeds scratching paper, writing out notes that – she feared – would mostly be irrelevant. Something stirred deep within her. Glimmers of memory from a dark room, screaming her voice ragged. A childhood illness nobody else seemed to remember, for all it had done to her.

It had taught her that people she loved could still hurt her.

'Have you ever wondered how it would feel to lose your sanity, Ivory?'

Ivory nodded. 'I have wondered this. How could I not? Considering what the ancient fathers are.'

'You call me logical,' Jasnah whispered. 'It's untrue, as I let my passions rule me as much as many. In my times of peace, however, my mind has always been the one thing I could rely upon.'

Except once.

She shook her head, picking up the paper again. 'I fear losing that, Ivory. It *terrifies* me. How would it have felt, to be these Heralds? To suffer your mind slowly becoming untrustworthy? Are they too far gone to know? Or are there lucid moments, where they strain and sort through memories . . . trying frantically to decide which are reliable and which are fabrications . . .'

She shivered.

'The ancient ones,' Ivory said again, nodding. He didn't often speak of the spren who had been lost during the Recreance. Ivory and his fellows had been mere children – well, the spren equivalent – at the time. They spent years, centuries, with no older spren to nurture and guide them. The inkspren were only now beginning to recover the culture and society they had lost when men abandoned their vows.

'Your ward,' Ivory said. 'Her spren. A Cryptic.'

'Which is bad?'

Ivory nodded. He preferred simple, straightforward gestures. You never saw Ivory shrug. 'Cryptics *are* trouble. They enjoy lies, Jasnah. Feast upon them. Speak one word untrue at a gathering, and seven cluster around you. Their humming fills your ears.'

'Have you warred with them?'

'One does not war with Cryptics, as one does honorspren. Cryptics have but one city, and do not wish to rule more. Only to listen.' He tapped the table. 'Perhaps this one is better, with the bond.'

Ivory was the only new-generation inkspren to form a Radiant bond. Some of his fellows would rather have killed Jasnah, instead of letting him risk what he had done.

The spren had a noble air about him, stiff-backed and commanding. He could change his size at will, but not his shape, except when fully in this realm, manifesting as a Shardblade. He had taken the name Ivory as a symbol of defiance. He was not what his kin said he was, and would not suffer what fate proclaimed.

The difference between a higher spren like him and a common emotion spren was in their ability to decide how to act. A living contradiction. Like human beings.

'Shallan won't listen to me any longer,' Jasnah said. 'She rebels against every little thing I tell her. These last few months on her own have changed the child.'

'She never obeyed well, Jasnah. That is who she *is*.'

'In the past, at least she pretended to care about my teaching.'

'But you have said, more humans should question their places in life. Did you not say that they too often accept presumed truth as fact?'

She tapped the table. 'You're right, of course. Wouldn't I rather have her straining against her boundaries, as opposed to happily living within them? Whether she obeys me or not is of little import. But I *do* worry about her ability to command her situation, rather than letting her impulses command her.'

'How do you change this, if it is?'

An excellent question. Jasnah searched through the papers on her small table. She'd been collecting reports from her informants in the warcamps – the ones who had survived – about Shallan. She'd truly done well in Jasnah's absence. Perhaps what the child needed was not more structure, but more challenges.

'All ten orders are again,' Ivory said from behind her. For years it had been only the two of them, Jasnah and Ivory. Ivory had been dodgy about giving odds on whether the other sapient spren would refound their orders or not.

However, he'd always said that he was certain that the honorspren – and therefore the Windrunners – would never return. Their attempts to rule Shadesmar had apparently not endeared them to the other races.

'Ten orders,' Jasnah said. 'All ended in death.'

'All but one,' Ivory agreed. 'They lived in death instead.'

She turned around, and he met her eyes with his own. No pupils, just oil shimmering above something deeply black.

'We must tell the others what we learned from Wit, Ivory. Eventually, this secret must be known.'

'Jasnah, *no*. It would be the end. Another Recreance.'

'The truth has not destroyed me.'

'You are special. No knowledge is that can destroy you. But the others . . .'

She held his eyes, then gathered the sheets stacked beside her. 'We shall see,' she said, then carried them to the table to bind them into a book.

But we stand in the sea, pleased with our domains. Leave us alone.

Moash grunted as he crossed the uneven ground, hauling a thick, knotted cord over his shoulder. Turned out, the Voidbringers had run out of wagons. Too many supplies to bring, and not enough vehicles.

At least, vehicles with wheels.

Moash had been assigned to a sledge – a cart with broken wheels that had been repurposed with a pair of long, steel skids. They'd put him first in the line pulling their rope. The parshman overseers had considered him the most enthusiastic.

Why wouldn't he be? The caravans moved at the slow pace of the chulls, which pulled roughly half the ordinary wagons. He had sturdy boots, and even a pair of gloves. Compared to bridge duty, this was a paradise.

The scenery was even better. Central Alethkar was far more fertile than the Shattered Plains, and the ground sprouted with rockbuds and the gnarled roots of trees. The sledge bounced and crunched over these, but at least he didn't have to carry the thing on his shoulders.

Around him, hundreds of men pulled wagons or sledges piled high with foodstuffs, freshly cut lumber, or leather made from hogshide or eelskin. Some of the workers had collapsed on their first day out of Revolar. The Voidbringers had separated these into two groups. The ones who had tried, but were genuinely too weak, had been sent back to the city. A few deemed to be faking had been whipped, then moved to sledges instead of wagons.

Harsh, but fair. Indeed, as the march continued, Moash was surprised at how well the human workers were treated. Though strict and unforgiving, the Voidbringers understood that to work hard, slaves needed good rations and plenty of time at night to rest. They weren't even chained up. Running away would be pointless under the watchful care of Fused who could fly.

Moash found himself enjoying these weeks hiking and pulling his sledge. It exhausted his body, quieted his thoughts, and let him fall into a calm rhythm. This was certainly far better than his days as a lighteyes, when he'd worried incessantly about the plot against the king.

It felt *good* to just be told what to do.

What happened at the Shattered Plains wasn't my fault, he thought as he hauled the sledge. *I was pushed into it. I can't be blamed.* These thoughts comforted him.

Unfortunately, he couldn't ignore their apparent destination. He'd walked this path dozens of times, running caravans with his uncle even when he'd been a youth. Across the river, straight southeast. Over Ishar's Field and cutting past the town of Inkwell.

The Voidbringers were marching to take Kholinar. The caravan included tens of thousands of parshmen armed with axes or spears. They wore what Moash now knew was called warform: a parshman form with carapace armor and a strong physique. They weren't experienced – watching their nightly training told him they were basically the equivalent of darkeyes scrounged from villages and pressed into the army.

But they were learning, and they had access to the Fused. Those zipped through the air or strode along beside carts, powerful and imperious – and surrounded by dark energy. There seemed to be different varieties, but each was intimidating.

Everything was converging on the capital. Should that bother him? After all, what had Kholinar ever done for him? It was the place where his grandparents had been left to die, cold and alone in a prison cell. It was where the blighted King Elhokar had danced and connived while good people rotted.

Did humankind even deserve this kingdom?

During his youth, he'd listened to traveling ardents who accompanied the caravans. He knew that long ago, humankind had *won*. Aharietiam, the final confrontation with the Voidbringers, had happened thousands of years ago.

What had they done with that victory? They'd set up false gods in the form of men whose eyes reminded them of the Knights Radiant. The life of men over the centuries had been nothing more than a long string of murders, wars, and thefts.

The Voidbringers had obviously returned because men had proven they couldn't govern themselves. That was why the Almighty had sent this scourge.

Indeed, the more he marched, the more Moash admired the Void-bringers. The armies were efficient, and the troops learned quickly. The caravans were well supplied; when an overseer saw that Moash's boots were looking worn, he had a new pair by evening.

Each wagon or sledge was given two parshman overseers, but these were told to use their whips sparingly. They were quietly trained for the position, and Moash heard the occasional conversation between an overseer – once a parshman slave – and an unseen spren who gave them directions.

The Voidbringers were smart, driven, and efficient. If Kholinar fell to this force, it would be no more than humankind deserved. Yes . . . perhaps the time for his people had passed. Moash had failed Kaladin and the others – but that was merely how men were in this debased age. He couldn't be blamed. He was a product of his culture.

Only one oddity marred his observations. The Voidbringers seemed so much better than the human armies he'd been part of . . . except for one thing.

There was a group of parshman slaves.

They pulled one of the sledges, and always walked apart from the humans. They wore workform, not warform – though otherwise they looked exactly like the other parshmen, with the same marbled skin. Why did this group pull a sledge?

At first, as Moash plodded across the endless plains of central Al-ethkar, he found the sight of them encouraging. It suggested that the Voidbringers could be egalitarian. Maybe there'd simply been too few men with the strength to pull these sledges.

Yet if that were so, why were these parshman sledge-pullers treated so poorly? The overseers did little to hide their disgust, and were allowed to whip the poor creatures without restriction. Moash rarely glanced in their direction without finding one of them being beaten, yelled at, or abused.

Moash's heart wrenched to see and hear this. Everyone else seemed to work so well together; everything else about the army seemed so perfect. Except this.

Who were these poor souls?

⁘

The overseer called a break, and Moash dropped his rope, then took a long pull on his waterskin. It was their twenty-first day of marching, which he only knew because some of the other slaves kept track. He judged the location as several days past Inkwell, in the final stretch toward Kholinar.

He ignored the other slaves and settled down in the shade of the sledge, which was piled high with cut timber. Not far behind them, a village burned. There hadn't been anyone in it, as word had run before them. Why had the Voidbringers burned it, but not others they'd passed? Perhaps it was to send a message – indeed, that smoke trail was ominous. Or perhaps it was to prevent any potential flanking armies from using the village.

As his crew waited – Moash didn't know their names, and hadn't bothered to ask – the parshman crew trudged past, bloodied and whipped, their overseers yelling them onward. They'd lagged behind. Pervasive cruel treatment led to a tired crew, which in turn led to them being forced to march to catch up when everyone else got a water break. That, of course, only wore them out and caused injuries – which made them lag farther behind, which made them get whipped . . .

That's what happened to Bridge Four, back before Kaladin, Moash thought. *Everyone said we were unlucky, but it was just a self-perpetuating downward spiral.*

Once that crew passed, trailing a few exhaustionspren, one of Moash's overseers called for his team to take up their ropes and get moving again. She was a young parshwoman with dark red skin, marbled only slightly with white. She wore a havah. Though it didn't seem like marching clothing, she wore it well. She had even done up the sleeve to cover her safehand.

'What'd they do, anyway?' he said as he took up his rope.

'What was that?' she asked, looking back at him. Storms. Save for that skin and the odd singsong quality to her voice, she could have been a pretty Makabaki caravan girl.

'That parshman crew,' he said. 'What did they do to deserve such rough treatment?'

He didn't actually expect an answer. But the parshwoman followed his gaze, then shook her head. 'They harbored a false god. Brought him into the very center among us.'

'The Almighty?'

She laughed. 'A *real* false god, a living one. Like our living gods.' She looked up as one of the Fused passed overhead.

'There are lots who think the Almighty is real,' Moash said.

'If that's the case, why are *you* pulling a sledge?' She snapped her fingers, pointing.

Moash picked up his rope, joining the other men in a double line. They merged with the enormous column of marching feet, scraping sledges, and rattling wheels. The Parshendi wanted to arrive at the next town before an impending storm. They'd weathered both types – highstorm and Everstorm – sheltering in villages along the way.

Moash fell into the sturdy rhythm of the work. It wasn't long until he was sweating. He'd grown accustomed to the colder weather in the east, near the Frostlands. It was strange to be in a place where the sun felt hot on his skin, and now the weather here was turning toward summer.

His sledge soon caught up to the parshman crew. The two sledges walked side by side for a time, and Moash liked to think that keeping pace with his crew could motivate the poor parshmen. Then one of them slipped and fell, and the entire team lurched to a stop.

The whipping began. The cries, the *crack* of leather on skin.

That's enough.

Moash dropped his rope and stepped out of the line. His shocked overseers called after him, but didn't follow. Perhaps they were too surprised.

He strode up to the parshman sledge, where the slaves were struggling to pull themselves back up and start again. Several had bloodied faces and backs. The large parshman who had slipped lay curled on the ground. His feet were bleeding; no wonder he'd had trouble walking.

Two overseers were whipping him. Moash seized one by the shoulder and pushed him back. 'Stop it!' he snapped, then shoved the other over-seer aside. 'Don't you see what you're doing? You're becoming like *us*.'

The two overseers stared at him, dumbfounded.

'You can't abuse each other,' Moash said. 'You *can't*.' He turned toward the fallen parshman and extended a hand to help him up, but from the corner of his eye he saw one of the overseers raise his arm.

Moash spun and caught the whip that cracked at him, snatching it from the air and twisting it around his wrist to gain leverage. Then he *yanked* it – pulling the overseer stumbling toward him. Moash smashed a fist into his face, slamming him backward to the ground.

Storms that hurt. He shook his hand, which had clipped carapace on the side as he'd connected. He glared at the other overseer, who yelped and dropped his whip, jumping backward.

Moash nodded once, then took the fallen slave by the arm and pulled him upright. 'Ride in the sledge. Heal those feet.' He took the parshman slave's place in line, and pulled the rope taut over his shoulder.

By now, his own overseers had gathered their wits and chased after him. They conferred with the two that he'd confronted, one nursing a bleeding cut around his eye. Their conversation was hushed, urgent, and punctuated by intimidated glances toward him.

Finally, they decided to let it be. Moash pulled the sledge with the parshmen, and they found someone to replace him on the other sledge. For a while he thought more would come of it – he even saw one of the overseers conferring with a Fused. But they didn't punish him.

No one dared to again raise a whip against the parshman crew the rest of the march.

49

BORN UNTO LIGHT

TWENTY-THREE YEARS AGO

Dalinar pressed his fingers together, then rubbed them, scraping the dry, red-brown moss against itself. The scratchy sound was unpleasantly similar to that of a knife along bone.

He felt the warmth immediately, like an ember. A thin plume of smoke rose from his callused fingers and struck below his nose, then parted around his face.

Everything faded: the raucous sound of too many men in one room, the musky smell of their bodies pressed together. Euphoria spread through him like sudden sunlight on a cloudy day. He released a protracted sigh. He didn't even mind when Bashin accidentally elbowed him.

Most places, being highprince would have won him a bubble of space, but at the stained wooden table in this poorly lit den, social standing was irrelevant. Here, with a good drink and a little help pressed between his fingers, he could finally relax. Here nobody cared how presentable he was, or if he drank too much.

Here, he didn't have to listen to reports of rebellion and imagine himself out on those fields, solving problems the direct way. Sword in hand, Thrill in his heart . . .

He rubbed the moss more vigorously. Don't think about war. Just live in the moment, as Evi always said.

Havar returned with drinks. The lean, bearded man studied the overcrowded bench, then set the drinks down and hauled a slumped drunk out of his spot. He squeezed in beside Bashin. Havar was lighteyed, good family too. He'd been one of Dalinar's elites back when that had meant something, though now he had his own land and a high commission. He was one of the few who didn't salute Dalinar so hard you could hear it.

Bashin though ... well, Bashin was an odd one. Darkeyed of the first nahn, the portly man had traveled half the world, and encouraged Dalinar to go with him to see the other half. He still wore that stupid, wide-brimmed floppy hat.

Havar grunted, passing down the drinks. 'Squeezing in beside you, Bashin, would be far easier if you didn't have a gut that stretched to next week.'

'Just trying to do my duty, Brightlord.'

'Your duty?'

'Lighteyes need folks to obey them, right? I'm making certain that you got *lots* to serve you, at least by weight.'

Dalinar took his mug, but didn't drink. For now, the firemoss was doing its job. His wasn't the only plume rising in the dim stone chamber.

Gavilar hated the stuff. But then, Gavilar *liked* his life now.

In the center of the dim room, a pair of parshmen pushed tables aside, then started setting diamond chips on the floor. Men backed away, making space for a large ring of light. A couple of shirtless men pushed their way through the crowd. The room's general air of clumsy conversation turned to one of roaring excitement.

'Are we going to bet?' Havar asked.

'Sure,' Bashin replied. 'I'll put three garnet marks on the shorter one.'

'I'll take that bet,' Havar said, 'but not for the money. If I win, I want your hat.'

'Deal! Ha! So you're finally going to admit how dashing it is?'

'Dashing? Storms, Bashin. I'm going to do you a favor and *burn* the thing.'

Dalinar sat back, mind dulled by the firemoss.

'Burn my hat?' Bashin said. 'Storms, Havar. That's harsh. Just because you envy my dashing profile.'

'The only thing dashing about that hat is how it makes women run the other way.'

'It's *exotic*. From the *west*. Everyone knows fashion comes from the west.'

'Yeah, from Liafor and Yezier. Where did you get that hat again?'

'The Purelake.'

'Ah, that bastion of culture and fashion! Are you going shopping in Bavland next?'

'Barmaids don't know the difference,' Bashin grumbled. 'Anyway, can we just watch the match? I'm looking forward to winning those marks off you.' He took a drink, but fingered his hat anxiously.

Dalinar closed his eyes. He felt as if he could drift off, maybe get some sleep without worrying about Evi, or dreaming of war. . . .

In the ring, bodies *smacked* against each other.

That sound – the grunts of exertion as the wrestlers tried to push each other from the ring – reminded him of the battle. Dalinar opened his eyes, dropped the moss, and leaned forward.

The shorter wrestler danced out of the other's grip. They revolved around one another, crouched, hands at the ready. When they locked again, the shorter man pushed his opponent off balance. *Better stance,* Dalinar thought. *Kept himself low. That taller fellow has gotten by too long on his strength and size. He's got terrible form.*

The two strained, backing toward the edge of the ring, before the taller man managed to trip them both. Dalinar stood up as others, ahead of him, raised their hands and cheered.

The contest. The fight.

That led me to almost kill Gavilar.

Dalinar sat back down.

The shorter man won. Havar sighed, but rolled a few glowing spheres to Bashin. 'Double or nothing on the next bout?'

'Nah,' Bashin said, hefting the marks. 'This should be enough.'

'For what?'

'To bribe a few influential young dandies into trying hats like mine,' Bashin said. 'I tell you, once word gets out, *everyone* is going to be wearing them.'

'You're an idiot.'

'So long as I'm a fashionable one.'

Dalinar reached to the floor and picked up the firemoss. He tossed it onto the table and stared at it, then took a pull from his mug of wine.

The next wrestling match started, and he winced as the two competitors collided. Storms. Why did he keep putting himself into situations like this?

'Dalinar,' Havar said. 'Any word yet on when we're going to the Rift?'

'The Rift?' Bashin asked. 'What about it?'

'Are you dense?' Havar said.

'No,' Bashin said, 'but I might be *drunk*. What's up with the Rift?'

'Rumor is they want to set up their own highprince,' Havar said. 'Son of the old one, what was his name . . .'

'Tanalan,' Dalinar said. 'But we are not going to be visiting the Rift, Havar.'

'Surely the king can't—'

'*We* won't be going,' Dalinar said. 'You've got men to train. And I . . .' Dalinar drank more wine. 'I'm going to be a father. My brother can handle the Rift with diplomacy.'

Havar leaned back, flippantly dropping his mug to the table. 'The king can't politic his way past open rebellion, Dalinar.'

Dalinar closed his fist around the firemoss, but didn't rub it. How much of his interest in the Rift was his duty to protect Gavilar's kingdom, and how much was his craving to feel the Thrill again?

Damnation. He felt like half a man these days.

One of the wrestlers had shoved the other from the ring, disturbing the line of lights. The loser was declared, and a parshman carefully reset the ring. As he did so, a master-servant stepped up to Dalinar's table.

'Pardon, Brightlord,' he whispered. 'But you should know. The feature match will have to be canceled.'

'What?' Bashin said. 'What's wrong? Makh isn't going to fight?'

'Pardon,' the master-servant repeated. 'But his opponent has stomach problems. The match must be canceled.'

Apparently, news was spreading through the room. The crowd manifested their disapproval with boos and curses, shouts, and spilled drinks. A tall, bald man stood at the side of the ring, bare-chested. He argued with several of the lighteyed organizers, pointing at the ring, angerspren boiling on the floor around him.

To Dalinar, this racket sounded like the calls of battle. He closed his eyes and breathed it in, finding a euphoria far superior to the firemoss. Storms. He should have gotten drunker. He was going to slip.

Might as well be quick about it then. He tossed aside the firemoss and stood, then pulled off his shirt.

'Dalinar!' Havar said. 'What are you doing?'

'Gavilar says I need to have more concern for our people's sorrows,' Dalinar said, stepping up onto the table. 'Seems like we've got a room full of sorrow here.'

Havar gaped, jaw dropping.

'Bet on me,' Dalinar said. 'For old times' sake.' He leaped off the table on the other side, then shoved through the crowd. 'Someone tell that man he has a challenger!'

Silence spread from him like a bad smell. Dalinar found himself at the edge of the ring in a completely quiet room, packed with once-rowdy men both lighteyed and dark. The wrestler – Makh – stepped back, his dark green eyes wide, angerspren vanishing. He had a powerful build, arms that bulged like they were overstuffed. Word was, he'd never been defeated.

'Well?' Dalinar said. 'You wanted a fight and I need a workout.'

'Brightlord,' the man said. 'This was to be a freeform bout, all hits and holds allowed.'

'Excellent,' Dalinar said. 'What? You worried about injuring your highprince? I promise you clemency for anything done to me.'

'Hurting *you*?' the man said. 'Storms, that's not what I'm afraid of.' He shivered visibly, and a Thaylen woman – perhaps his manager – smacked him on the arm. She thought he'd been rude. The wrestler only bowed and backed away.

Dalinar turned about the room, confronted by a sea of faces that suddenly seemed very uncomfortable. He'd broken some kind of rule here.

The gathering dissolved, parshmen retrieving spheres from the ground. It seemed Dalinar had been too hasty to judge rank unimportant here. They'd suffered him as an observer, but he was not to participate.

Damnation. He growled softly as he stalked to his bench, those angerspren following him on the floor. He took his shirt from Bashin with a swipe of the hand. Back with his elites, any man – from the lowest spearman to the highest captains – would have sparred or wrestled with him. Storms, he'd faced the *cook* several times, much to the amusement of everyone involved.

He sat down and pulled on his shirt, stewing. He'd ripped the buttons free in removing it so quickly. The room fell silent as people continued to leave, and Dalinar just sat there, tense – his body still expecting the fight that would never come. No Thrill. Nothing to fill him.

Soon, he and his friends were alone in the room, surveying empty tables, abandoned cups, and spilled drinks. The place somehow smelled even worse now than it had when crowded with men.

'Probably for the best, Brightlord,' Havar said.

'I want to be among soldiers again, Havar,' Dalinar whispered. 'I want to be marching again. Best sleep a man can get is after a long march. And, Damnation, I want to *fight*. I want to face someone who won't pull their punches because I'm a highprince.'

'Then let's *find* such a fight, Dalinar!' Havar said. 'Surely the king will let us go. If not to the Rift, then to Herdaz or one of the isles. We can bring him land, glory, honor!'

'That wrestler,' Dalinar said, 'there was ... something to his words. He was certain I would hurt him.' Dalinar drummed his fingers on the table. 'Was he scared off because of my reputation in general, or is there something more specific?'

Bashin and Havar shared a look.

'When?' Dalinar asked.

'Tavern fight,' Havar said. 'Two weeks back? Do you remember it?'

Dalinar remembered a haze of monotony broken by light, a burst of color in his life. Emotion. He breathed out. 'You told me everyone was fine.'

'They lived,' Havar said.

'One ... of the brawlers you fought will never walk,' Bashin admitted. 'Another had to have his arm removed. A third babbles like a child. His brain doesn't work anymore.'

'That's far from *fine*,' Dalinar snapped.

'Pardon, Dalinar,' Havar said. 'But when facing the Blackthorn, that's as good as one can expect.'

Dalinar crossed his arms on the table, grinding his teeth. The firemoss wasn't working. Yes, it gave him a quick rush of euphoria, but that only made him want the greater headiness of the Thrill. Even now he felt on edge – he had the urge to smash this table and everything in the room. He'd been so ready for the fight; he'd surrendered to the temptation, and then had the pleasure stolen from him.

He felt all the shame of losing control, but none of the satisfaction of actually getting to fight.

Dalinar seized his mug, but it was empty. Stormfather! He threw it and stood up, wanting to scream.

He was fortunately distracted by the back door to the wrestling den inching open, revealing a familiar pale face. Toh wore Alethi clothing now, one of the new suits that Gavilar preferred, but it fit him poorly. He was too spindly. No man would ever mistake Toh – with that overcautious gait and wide-eyed innocence – for a soldier.

'Dalinar?' he asked, looking over the spilled drinks and the locked sphere lamps on the walls. 'The guards said I could find you here. Um . . . was this a party?'

'Ah, Toh,' Havar said, lounging back in his seat. 'How could it have been a party without you?'

Toh's eyes flicked toward the chunk of firemoss on the ground nearby. 'I'll never understand what you see in these places, Dalinar.'

'He's just getting to know the common people, Brightlord,' Bashin said, pocketing the firemoss. 'You know us darkeyed types, always wallowing in depravity. We need good role models to—'

He cut off as Dalinar raised his hand. He didn't need underlings to cover for him. 'What is it, Toh?'

'Oh!' the Riran man said. 'They were going to send a messenger, but I wanted to deliver the news. My sister, you see. It's a little early, but the midwives aren't surprised. They say it's natural when—'

Dalinar gasped, like he'd been punched in the stomach. *Early. Midwives. Sister.*

He charged for the door, and didn't hear the rest of what Toh said.

⁙

Evi looked like she'd fought in a battle.

He'd seen that expression on the faces of soldiers many times: that sweaty brow, that half-dazed, drowsy look. Exhaustionspren, like jets in the air. These were the mark of a person pushed past the limits of what they thought they could do.

She bore a smile of quiet satisfaction. A look of victory. Dalinar pushed past doting surgeons and midwives, stepping up to Evi's bed. She held out a limp hand. Her left hand, which was wrapped only in a thin envelope that ended at the wrist. It would have been a sign of intimacy, to an Alethi. But Evi still preferred that hand.

'The baby?' he whispered, taking the hand.

'A son. Healthy and strong.'

'A son. I . . . I have a son?' Dalinar dropped to his knees beside the bed. 'Where is he?'

'Being washed, my lord,' said one of the midwives. 'He will be returned shortly.'

'Torn buttons,' Evi whispered. 'You've been fighting again, Dalinar?'

'Just a small diversion.'

'That's what you say each time.'

Dalinar squeezed her hand through the envelope, too elated to prickle at the chastisement. 'You and Toh came here to Alethkar because you wanted someone to protect you. You *sought out* a fighter, Evi.'

She squeezed his hand back. A nurse approached with a bundle in her arms and Dalinar looked up, stunned, unable to rise.

'Now,' the woman said, 'many men are apprehensive at first when—'

She cut off as Dalinar found his strength and seized the child from her arms. He held the boy aloft in both hands, letting out a whooping laugh, gloryspren bursting around him as golden spheres.

'My son!' he said.

'My lord!' the nurse said. 'Be careful!'

'He's a Kholin,' Dalinar said, cradling the child. 'He's made of hardy stuff.' He looked down at the boy, who – red faced – wiggled and thrashed with his tiny fists. He had shockingly thick hair, black and blond mixed. Good coloring. Distinctive.

May you have your father's strength, Dalinar thought, rubbing the child's face with his finger, *and at least some of your mother's compassion, little one.*

Looking into that face, swelling with joy, Dalinar finally understood. *This* was why Gavilar thought so much about the future, about Alethkar, about crafting a kingdom that would last. Dalinar's life so far had stained him crimson and thrashed his soul. His heart was so crusted over with crem, it might as well have been a stone.

But this boy . . . he could rule the princedom, support his cousin the king, and live a life of honor.

'His name, Brightlord?' asked Ishal, an aged ardent from the Devotary of Purity. 'I would burn the proper glyphwards, if it pleases you.'

'Name ...' Dalinar said. 'Adoda.' Light. He glanced toward Evi, who nodded in agreement.

'Without a suffix, my lord? Adodan? Adodal?'

'Lin,' Dalinar whispered. Born unto. 'Adolin.' A good name, traditional, full of meaning.

With regret, Dalinar surrendered the child to the nurses, who returned him to his mother, explaining that it was important to train the baby to suckle as soon as possible. Most in the room began to file out to offer privacy, and as they did, Dalinar caught sight of a regal figure standing at the back. How had he missed Gavilar there?

Gavilar took him by the arm and gave him a good thump on the back as they left the chamber. Dalinar was so dazed he barely felt it. He needed to celebrate – buy drinks for every man in the army, declare a holiday, or just run through the city whooping for joy. He was a father!

'An excellent day,' Gavilar said. 'A *most* excellent day.'

'How do you contain it?' Dalinar said. 'This *excitement*?'

Gavilar grinned. 'I let the emotion be my reward for the work I have done.'

Dalinar nodded, then studied his brother. 'What?' Dalinar said. 'Something is wrong.'

'Nothing.'

'Don't lie to me, Brother.'

'I don't want to ruin your wonderful day.'

'Wondering will ruin it more than anything you could say, Gavilar. Out with it.'

The king mulled, then nodded toward Dalinar's den. They crossed the main chamber, passing furniture that was far too showy – colorful, with floral patterns and plush cushions. Evi's taste was partially to blame, though it was also just ... life, these days. His *life* was plush.

The den was more to his liking. A few chairs, a hearth, a simple rug. A cabinet with various exotic and potent wines, each in a distinctive bottle. They were the type it was almost a shame to drink, as it spoiled the display.

'It's your daughter,' Dalinar guessed. 'Her lunacy.'

'Jasnah is fine, and recovering. It's not that.' Gavilar frowned, his expression dangerous. He'd agreed to a crown after much debate – Sunmaker hadn't worn one, and the histories said Jezerezeh'Elin refused them as well. But people did love symbols, and most Western kings wore crowns.

Gavilar had settled upon a black iron circlet. The more Gavilar's hair greyed, the easier the crown was to see.

A servant had set a fire in the hearth, though it was burning low, only a single flamespren crawling along the embers.

'I am failing,' Gavilar said.

'What?'

'Rathalas. The Rift.'

'But I thought—'

'Propaganda,' Gavilar said. 'Intended to quiet critical voices in Kholinar. Tanalan is raising an army and settling into his fortifications. Worse, I think the other highprinces are encouraging him. They want to see how I handle this.' He sneered. 'There's talk I've grown soft over the years.'

'They're wrong.' Dalinar had seen it, these months living with Gavilar. His brother had *not* grown soft. He was still as eager for conquest as ever; he simply approached it differently. The clash of words, the maneuvering of princedoms into positions where they were forced to obey.

The fire's embers seemed to pulse like a heartbeat. 'Do you ever wonder about the time when this kingdom was truly great, Dalinar?' Gavilar asked. 'When people looked to the Alethi. When kings sought their advice. When we were . . . Radiant.'

'Traitors,' Dalinar said.

'Does the act of a single generation negate many generations of domination? We revere the Sunmaker when his reign lasted but the blink of an eye – yet we ignore the centuries the Radiants led. How many Desolations did they defend mankind?'

'Um . . .' The ardents talked about this in prayers, didn't they? He tried a guess. 'Ten?'

'A meaningless number,' Gavilar said, waving his fingers. 'The histories just say "ten" because it sounds significant. Either way, I have failed in my diplomatic efforts.' He turned toward Dalinar. 'It is time to show the kingdom that we are not soft, Brother.'

Oh no. Hours ago, he would have leaped in excitement. But after seeing that child . . .

You'll be anxious again in a few days, Dalinar told himself. *A man can't change in a moment.*

'Gavilar,' he whispered, 'I'm worried.'

'You're still the Blackthorn, Dalinar.'

'I'm not worried about whether I can win battles.' Dalinar stood, throwing back his chair in his haste. He found himself pacing. 'I'm like an animal, Gavilar. Did you hear about the bar fight? Storms. I can't be trusted around people.'

'You are what the Almighty made you.'

'I'm telling you, I'm dangerous. Sure, I can crush this little rebellion, bathe Oathbringer in some blood. Great. Wonderful. Then what? I come back here and lock myself in a cage again?'

'I . . . might have something that will help.'

'Bah. I've tried living a quiet life. I can't live through endless politics, like you can. I need more than *just words*!'

'You've merely been trying to restrain yourself – you've tried casting out the bloodthirst, but you haven't replaced it with anything else. Go do what I command, then return and we can discuss further.'

Dalinar stopped near his brother, then took a single purposeful step into his shadow. *Remember this. Remember you serve him.* He would never return to that place that had almost led him to attack this man.

'When do I ride for the Rift?' Dalinar asked.

'You don't.'

'But you just said—'

'I'm sending you to battle, but not against the Rift. Our kingdom suffers threats from abroad. There is a new dynasty threatening us from Herdaz; a Reshi house has gained power there. And the Vedens have been raiding Alethkar in the southwest. They're claiming it's bandits, but the forces are too organized. It's a test to see how we react.'

Dalinar nodded slowly. 'You want me to go fight on our borders. Remind everyone we're still capable of employing the sword.'

'Exactly. This is a dangerous time for us, Brother. The highprinces question. Is a united Alethkar worth the trouble? Why bow before a king? Tanalan is the manifestation of their questions, but he has been careful not to stray into outright rebellion. If you attack him, the other highprinces could unite behind the rebels. We could shatter the kingdom and have to start all over.

'I will not allow that. I *will* have a unified Alethkar. Even if I have to hit the highprinces so hard, they are forced to *melt* together from the heat of it. They need to remember that. Go to Herdaz first, then Jah Keved. Remind everyone *why* they fear you.'

Gavilar met Dalinar's eyes. No ... he was not soft. He thought like a king now. He sought the long term, but Gavilar Kholin was as determined as ever.

'It will be done,' Dalinar said. Storms, this day had been a tempest of emotion. Dalinar stalked toward the door. He wanted to see the child again.

'Brother?' Gavilar said.

Dalinar turned back and regarded Gavilar, who was bathed by the bleeding light of a fire reaching its end.

'Words *are* important,' Gavilar said. 'Much more than you give them credit for being.'

'Perhaps,' Dalinar said. 'But if they were all-powerful, you wouldn't need my sword, would you?'

'Perhaps. I can't help feeling words *would* be enough, if only I knew the right ones to say.'

We also instruct that you should not return to Obrodai. We have claimed that world, and a new avatar of our being is beginning to manifest there.

She is young yet, and – as a precaution – she has been instilled with an intense and overpowering dislike of you.

To Dalinar, flying felt much like being on a ship in the ocean.

There was something profoundly disconcerting about being out on the ocean, subject to the winds and currents. Men didn't control the waves, they merely set out and prayed that the ocean didn't decide to consume them.

Flying alongside Captain Kaladin provoked some of the same emotions in Dalinar. On one hand, the view over the Shattered Plains was magnificent. He felt he could almost see the pattern to it that Shallan mentioned.

On the other hand, this kind of travel was deeply unnatural. Winds buffeted them, and if you moved your hands or arched your back in the wrong way, you were sent in a different direction from everyone else. Kaladin had to constantly zip back and forth, righting one of them that got blown off-course. And if you looked down, and paused to consider exactly how high up you were . . .

Well, Dalinar was not a timid man, but he was still glad of Navani's hand in his.

On his other side flew Elhokar, and beyond him were Kadash and a pretty young ardent who served as one of Navani's scholars. The five of them were escorted by Kaladin and ten of his squires. The Windrunners had been training steadily for three weeks now, and Kaladin had finally – after practicing by flying groups of soldiers back and forth to the war-camps – agreed to treat Dalinar and the king to a similar trip.

It is like being on a ship, Dalinar thought. What would it feel like to be up here during a highstorm? That was how Kaladin planned to get Elhokar's team to Kholinar – fly them at the leading edge of a storm, so his Stormlight was continually renewed.

You're thinking of me, the Stormfather sent. *I can feel it.*

'I'm thinking of how you treat ships,' Dalinar whispered, his physical voice lost to the winds – yet his meaning carried, unhampered, to the Stormfather.

Men should not be upon the waters during a storm, he replied. *Men are not of the waves.*

'And the sky? Are men of the sky?'

Some are. He said this grudgingly.

Dalinar could only imagine how terrible it must be to be a sailor out at sea during a storm. He had taken only short coastwise trips by ship.

No, wait, he thought. *There was one, of course. A trip to the Valley . . .*

He barely remembered that voyage, though he could not blame that solely upon the Nightwatcher.

Captain Kaladin swooped over. He was the only one who seemed truly in control of his flying. Even his men flew more like dropped rocks than skyeels. They lacked his finesse, his *control.* Though the others could help if something went wrong, Kaladin had been the only one Lashing Dalinar and the others. He said he wanted practice, for the eventual flight to Kholinar.

Kaladin touched Elhokar, and the king started to slow. Kaladin then moved down the line, slowing each in turn. He then swept them up so they were close enough to speak. His soldiers stopped and floated nearby.

'What's wrong?' Dalinar asked, trying to ignore that he was hanging hundreds of feet in the sky.

'Nothing's wrong,' Kaladin said, then pointed.

With the wind in his eyes, Dalinar had failed to spot the warcamps: ten craterlike circles arrayed along the northwestern edge of the Shattered Plains. From up here, it was obvious they had once been domes. The way their walls curved, like cupping fingers from underneath.

Two of the camps were still fully occupied, and Sebarial had set up forces to lay claim to the nearby forest. Dalinar's own warcamp was less populated, but had a few platoons of soldiers and some workers.

'We arrived so quickly!' Navani said. Her hair was a wind-tousled mess, much of it having escaped her careful braid. Elhokar hadn't fared much better – his hair sprayed out from his face like waxed Thaylen eyebrows. The two ardents, of course, were bald and didn't have such worries.

'Quick indeed,' Elhokar said, redoing a few buttons of his uniform. 'This is most promising for our mission.'

'Yeah,' Kaladin said. 'I still want to test it more in front of a storm.' He took the king by the shoulder, and Elhokar started to drift downward.

Kaladin sent them each down in turn, and when his feet finally touched stone again, Dalinar heaved a sigh of relief. They were only one plateau over from the warcamp, where a soldier at a watchpost waved to them with eager, exaggerated movements. Within minutes, a troop of Kholin soldiers had surrounded them.

'Let's get you inside the walls, Brightlord,' their captainlord said, hand on the pommel of his sword. 'The shellheads are still active out here.'

'Have they attacked this close to the camps?' Elhokar asked, surprised.

'No, but that doesn't mean they won't, Your Majesty.'

Dalinar wasn't so worried, but said nothing as the soldiers ushered him and the others into the warcamp where Brightness Jasalai – the tall, stately woman Dalinar had put in charge of the camp – met and accompanied them.

After spending so much time in the alien hallways of Urithiru, walking through this place – which had been Dalinar's home for five years – was relaxing. Part of that was finding the warcamp mostly intact; it had weathered the Everstorm quite well. Most of the buildings were stone bunkers, and that western rim of the former dome had provided a solid windbreak.

'My only worry,' he told Jasalai after a short tour, 'is about logistics. This is a long march from Narak and the Oathgate. I fear that by dividing our forces among Narak, here, and Urithiru, we're increasing our vulnerability to an attack.'

'That is true, Brightlord,' the woman said. 'I endeavor only to provide you with options.'

Unfortunately, they would probably need this place for farming operations, not to mention the lumber. Plateau runs for gemhearts couldn't sustain the tower city's population forever, particularly in the face of Shallan's assessment that they had likely hunted chasmfiends near to extinction.

Dalinar glanced at Navani. She thought they should found a new kingdom here, on and around the Shattered Plains. Import farmers, retire older soldiers, start production here on a much larger scale than they'd ever tried before.

Others disagreed. There was a reason the Unclaimed Hills weren't densely inhabited. It would be a harsh life here – rockbuds grew smaller, crops would be less productive. And founding a new kingdom during a Desolation? Better to protect what they had. Alethkar could probably feed Urithiru – but that depended on Kaladin and Elhokar recovering the capital.

Their tour ended with a meal at Dalinar's bunker, in his former sitting room, which looked bare now that most of the furniture and rugs had been removed to Urithiru.

After the meal, he found himself standing by the window, feeling oddly out of place. He'd left this warcamp only ten weeks ago, but the place was at once deeply familiar and also no longer his.

Behind him, Navani and her scribe ate fruit as they chatted quietly over some sketches that Navani had done.

'Oh, but I think that the others need to experience that, Brightness!' the scribe said. 'The flight was *remarkable*. How fast do you think we were going? I believe we might have attained a speed that no human has reached since the Recreance. Think about that, Navani! Surely we were faster than the fastest horse or ship.'

'Focus, Rushu,' Navani said. 'My sketch.'

'I don't think this math is right, Brightness. No, that sail will never stand.'

'It's not meant to be completely accurate,' Navani said. 'Just a concept. My question is, can it work?'

'We'll need more reinforcement. Yes, more reinforcement for certain. And then the steering mechanism . . . definitely work to do there. This *is* clever though, Brightness. Falilar needs to see it; he will be able to say whether or not it can be built.'

Dalinar glanced away from the window, catching Navani's eye. She smiled. She always claimed that she wasn't a scholar, but a patron of scholars. She said her place was to encourage and guide the real scientists. Anyone who saw the light in her eyes as she took out another sheet and sketched her idea further knew she was being too modest.

She began another sketch, but then stopped and glanced to the side, where she'd set out a spanreed. The ruby was blinking.

Fen! Dalinar thought. The queen of Thaylenah had asked that, in this morning's highstorm, Dalinar send her into the vision of Aharietiam, which she knew about from the published accounts of Dalinar's visions. He'd reluctantly sent her alone, without supervision.

They'd been waiting for her to speak of the event, to say anything. In the morning, she hadn't replied to their requests for a conversation.

Navani prepared the spanreed, then set it writing. It scribbled for only a brief moment.

'That was short,' Dalinar said, stepping toward her.

'Only one word,' Navani said. She looked up at him. 'Yes.'

Dalinar heaved out a long breath. She was willing to visit Urithiru. *Finally!*

'Tell her we'll send her a Radiant.' He left the window, watching as she replied. In her sketchpad, he caught sight of some kind of shiplike contraption, but with the sail on the *bottom*. What in the world?

Fen seemed content to leave the conversation there, and Navani returned to her discussion of engineering, so Dalinar slipped from the room. He passed through his bunker, which felt hollow. Like the rind of a fruit with the pulp scooped out. No servants scuttling back and forth, no soldiers. Kaladin and his men had gone off somewhere, and Kadash was probably at the camp monastery. He'd been keen to get there, and Dalinar had been gratified by his willingness to fly with Kaladin.

They hadn't spoken much since their confrontation in the sparring room. Well, perhaps seeing the Windrunners' power firsthand would improve Kadash's opinion of the Radiants.

Dalinar was surprised – and secretly pleased – to find that no guards had been posted at the bunker's back door. He slipped out alone and headed to the warcamp monastery. He wasn't looking for Kadash; he had another purpose.

He soon arrived at the monastery, which looked like most of the warcamp – a collection of buildings with the same smooth, rounded construction. Crafted from the air by Alethi Soulcasters. This place had a few small, hand-built buildings of cut stone, but they looked more like bunkers than places of worship. Dalinar had never wanted his people to forget that they were at war.

He strolled through the campus and found that without a guide, he didn't know his way among the nearly identical structures. He stopped in a courtyard between buildings. The air smelled of wet stone from the highstorm, and a nice group of shalebark sculptures rose to his right, shaped like stacks of square plates. The only sound was water dripping from the eaves of the buildings.

Storms. He should know his way around his own monastery, shouldn't he? *How often did you actually visit here, during all the years in the warcamps?* He'd meant to come more often, and talk to the ardents in his chosen devotary. There had always been something more pressing, and besides, the ardents stressed that he didn't *need* to come. They had prayed and burned glyphwards on his behalf; that was why highlords owned ardents.

Even during his darkest days of war, they'd assured him that in pursuing his Calling – by leading his armies – he served the Almighty.

Dalinar stooped into a building that had been divided into many small rooms for prayers. He walked down a hallway until he stepped through a storm door into the atrium, which still smelled faintly of incense. It seemed insane that the ardents would be angry with him now, after training him his whole life to do as he wished. But he'd upset the balance. Rocked the boat.

He moved among braziers filled with wet ash. Everyone liked the system they had. The lighteyes got to live without guilt or burden, always confident that they were active manifestations of God's will. The darkeyes got free access to training in a multitude of skills. The ardents got to pursue scholarship. The best of them lived lives of service. The worst lived lives of indolence – but what else were important lighteyed families going to do with unmotivated children?

A noise drew his attention, and he left the courtyard and looked into a dark corridor. Light poured from a room at the other end, and Dalinar was not surprised to find Kadash inside. The ardent was moving some ledgers and books from a wall safe into a pack on the floor. On a desk nearby, a spanreed scribbled.

Dalinar stepped into the room. The scarred ardent jumped, then relaxed when he saw it was Dalinar.

'Do we need to have this conversation again, Dalinar?' he asked, turning back to his packing.

'No,' Dalinar said. 'I didn't actually come looking for you. I want to find a man who lived here. A madman who claimed to be one of the Heralds.'

Kadash cocked his head. 'Ah, yes. The one who had a Shardblade?'

'All of the other patients at the monastery are accounted for, safe at Urithiru, but he vanished somehow. I was hoping to see if his room offered any clues to what became of him.'

Kadash looked at him, gauging his sincerity. Then the ardent sighed, rising. 'That's a different devotary from mine,' he said, 'but I have occupancy records here. I should be able to tell you which room he was in.'

'Thank you.'

Kadash looked through a stack of ledgers. 'Shash building,' he finally said, pointing absently out the window. 'That one right there. Room thirty-seven. Insah ran the facility; her records will list details of the madman's treatment. If her departure from the warcamp was anything like mine, she'll have left most of her paperwork behind.' He gestured toward the safe and his packing.

'Thank you,' Dalinar said. He moved to leave.

'You . . . think the madman was actually a Herald, don't you?'

'I think it's likely.'

'He spoke with a rural Alethi accent, Dalinar.'

'And he looked Makabaki,' Dalinar replied. 'That alone is an oddity, wouldn't you say?'

'Immigrant families are not so uncommon.'

'Ones with Shardblades?'

Kadash shrugged.

'Let's say I could actually find one of the Heralds,' Dalinar said. 'Let's say we could confirm his identity, and you accepted that proof.

'Would you believe him if he told you the same things I have?'

Kadash sighed.

'Surely you'd want to know if the Almighty were dead, Kadash,' Dalinar said, stepping back into the room. 'Tell me you wouldn't.'

'You know what it would mean? It would mean there is no spiritual basis for your rule.'

'I know.'

'And the things you did in conquering Alethkar?' Kadash said. 'No divine mandate, Dalinar. Everyone accepts what you did because your victories were proof of the Almighty's favor. Without him . . . then what are you?'

'Tell me, Kadash. Would you *really* rather not know?'

Kadash looked at the spanreed, which had stopped writing. He shook his head. 'I don't know, Dalinar. It certainly would be easier.'

'Isn't that the problem? What has any of this ever required of men like me? What has it required of *any* of us?'

'It required you to be what you are.'

'Which is self-fulfilling,' Dalinar said. 'You were a swordsman, Kadash. Would you have gotten better without opponents to face? Would you have gotten stronger without weights to lift? Well, in Vorinism, we've spent *centuries* avoiding the opponents and the weights.'

Again, Kadash glanced at the spanreed.

'What is it?' Dalinar asked.

'I left most of my spanreeds behind,' Kadash explained, 'when I went with you toward the center of the Shattered Plains. I took only the spanreed linked to an ardent transfer station in Kholinar. I thought that would be enough, but it no longer works. I've been forced to use intermediaries in Tashikk.'

Kadash lifted a box onto the desk and opened it. Inside were five more spanreeds, with blinking rubies, indicating that someone had been trying to contact Kadash.

'These are links to the leaders of Vorinism in Jah Keved, Herdaz, Kharbranth, Thaylenah, and New Natanan,' Kadash said, counting them off. 'They had a meeting via reeds today, discussing the nature of the Desolation and the Everstorm. And perhaps you. I mentioned I was going to recover my own spanreeds today. Apparently, their meeting has made them all very eager to question me further.'

He let the silence hang between them, measured out by the five blinking red lights.

'What of the one that is writing?' Dalinar asked.

'A line to the Palanaeum and the heads of Vorin research there. They've been working on the Dawnchant, using the clues Brightness Navani gave them from your visions. What they've sent me are relevant passages from ongoing translations.'

'Proof,' Dalinar said. 'You wanted solid proof that what I've been seeing is real.' He strode forward, grabbing Kadash by the shoulders. 'You waited for that reed first, before answering the leaders of Vorinism?'

'I wanted all the facts in hand.'

'So you know that the visions are real!'

'I long ago accepted that you weren't mad. These days, it's more a question of who might be influencing you.'

'Why would the Voidbringers give me these visions?' Dalinar said. 'Why would they grant us great powers, like the one that flew us here? It's not rational, Kadash.'

'Neither is what you're saying about the Almighty.' He held up a hand to cut off Dalinar. 'I *don't* want to have this argument again. Before, you asked me for proof that we are following the Almighty's precepts, right?'

'All I asked for and all I want is the truth.'

'We have it already. I'll show you.'

'I look forward to it,' Dalinar said, walking to the door. 'But Kadash? In my painful experience, the truth may be simple, but it is rarely *easy*.'

Dalinar crossed to the next building over and counted down the rooms. Storms, this building felt like a prison. Most of the doors hung open, revealing uniform chambers beyond: each had one tiny window, a slab for a bed, and a thick wooden door. The ardents knew what was best for the sick – they had access to all the world's latest research in all fields – but was it really necessary to lock madmen away like this?

Number thirty-seven was still bolted shut. Dalinar rattled the door, then threw his shoulder against it. Storms, it was thick. Without thinking he put his hand to the side and tried summoning his Shardblade. Nothing happened.

What are you doing? the Stormfather demanded.

'Sorry,' Dalinar said, shaking his hand out. 'Habit.'

He crouched down and tried peeking under the door, then called out, suddenly horrified by the idea that they might have simply left the man in here to starve. That couldn't have happened, could it?

'My powers,' Dalinar said, rising. 'Can I use them?'

Binding things? the Stormfather said. *How would that open a door? You are a Bondsmith; you bring things together, you do not divide them.*

'And my other Surge?' Dalinar said. 'That Radiant in the vision made stone warp and ripple.'

You are not ready. Besides, that Surge is different for you than it is for a Stoneward.

Well, from what Dalinar could see underneath the door, there seemed to be light in this room. Perhaps it had a window to the outside he could use.

On his way out, he poked through the ardent chambers until he found an office like Kadash's. He didn't find any keys, though the desk still had pens and ink sitting on it. They'd left in haste, so there was a good chance the wall safe contained records – but of course, Dalinar couldn't get in. Storms. He missed having a Shardblade.

He rounded the outside of the building to check the window, then immediately felt silly for spending so much time trying to get through the door. Somebody else had already cut a hole in the stone out here, using the distinctive, clean slices of a Shardblade.

Dalinar stepped inside, picking his way around the broken remnants of the wall, which had fallen inward – indicating that the Shardbearer had cut from the outside. He found no madman. The ardents had likely seen this hole and moved on with their evacuation. News of the strange hole must not have filtered up to the lead ardents.

He didn't find anything to indicate where the Herald had gone, but at least he knew a Shardbearer was involved. Someone powerful had wanted into this room, which lent even more credence to the madman's claims of being a Herald.

So who had taken him? Or had they done something to him instead? What happened to a Herald's body when they died? Could someone else have come to the same conclusion that Jasnah had?

As he was about to leave, Dalinar spotted something on the ground beside the bed. He knelt down, shooed away a cremling, and picked up a small object. It was a dart, green with yellow twine wrapped around it.

He frowned, turning it over in his fingers. Then he looked up as he heard someone distantly calling his name.

He found Kaladin out in the monastery courtyard, calling for him. Dalinar approached, then handed him the little dart. 'Ever seen anything like this before, Captain?'

Kaladin shook his head. He sniffed at the tip, then raised his eyebrows. 'That's poison on the tip. Blackbane derived.'

'Are you sure?' Dalinar asked, taking the dart back.

'Very. Where did you find it?'

'In the chamber that housed the Herald.'

Kaladin grunted. 'You need more time for your search?'

'Not much,' Dalinar said. 'Though it would help if you'd summon your Shardblade. . . .'

A short time later, Dalinar handed Navani the records he'd taken from the ardent's safe. He dropped the dart in a pouch and handed it over as well, warning her about the poisoned tip.

One by one, Kaladin sent them into the sky, where his bridgemen caught them and used Stormlight to stabilize them. Dalinar was last, and as Kaladin reached for him, he took the captain by the arm.

'You want to practice flying in front of a storm,' Dalinar said. 'Could you get to Thaylenah?'

'Probably,' Kaladin said. 'If I Lashed myself southward as fast as I can go.'

'Go, then,' Dalinar said. 'Take someone with you to test flying another person in front of a storm, if you want, but get to Thaylen City. Queen Fen is willing to join us, and I want that Oathgate active. The world has been turning before our very noses, Captain. Gods and Heralds have been warring, and we were too focused on our petty problems to even notice.'

'I'll go next highstorm,' Kaladin said, then sent Dalinar soaring up into the air.

51

FULL CIRCLE

*This is all we will say at this time. If you wish more, seek these waters
in person and overcome the tests we have created.*

Only in this will you earn our respect.

The parshmen of Moash's new sledge crew didn't like him. That
didn't bother him. Lately, he didn't much like himself.

He didn't expect or need their admiration. He knew what it
felt like to be beaten down, despised. When you'd been treated as they
had, you didn't trust someone like Moash. You asked yourself what *he* was
trying to get from you.

After a few days of pulling their sledge, the landscape began to change.
The open plains became cultivated hills. They passed great sweeping
wards – artificial stone ridges built by planting sturdy wooden barricades
to collect crem during storms. The crem would harden, slowly building
up a mound on the stormward side. After a few years, you raised the top
of the barricade.

They took generations to grow to useful sizes, but here – around the
oldest, most populated centers of Alethkar – they were common. They
looked like frozen waves of stone, stiff and straight on the western side,
sloping and smooth on the other side. In their shadows, vast orchards
spread in rows, most of the trees cultivated to grow no more than the
height of a man.

The western edge of those orchards was ragged with broken trees. Barriers would need to be erected to the west as well, now.

He expected the Fused to burn the orchards, but they didn't. During a water break, Moash studied one of them – a tall woman who hovered a dozen feet in the air, toes pointed downward. Her face was more angular than those of the parshmen. She resembled a spren the way she hung there, an impression accented by her flowing clothing.

Moash leaned back against his sledge and took a pull on his waterskin. Nearby, an overseer watched him and the parshmen of his crew. She was new; a replacement for the one he'd punched. A few more of the Fused passed on horses, trotting the beasts with obvious familiarity.

That variety doesn't fly, he thought. *They can raise the dark light around themselves, but it doesn't give them Lashings. Something else.* He glanced back at the one nearest him, the one hovering. *But that type almost never walks. It's the same kind that captured me.*

Kaladin wouldn't have been able to stay aloft as long as these did. He'd run out of Stormlight.

She's studying those orchards, Moash thought. *She looks impressed.*

She turned in the air and soared off, long clothing rippling behind her. Those overlong robes would have been impractical for anyone else, but for a creature who almost always flew, the effect was mesmerizing.

'This isn't what it was supposed to be like,' Moash said.

Nearby, one of the parshmen of his crew grunted. 'Tell me about it, human.'

Moash glanced at the man, who had settled down in the shade of their lumber-laden sledge. The parshman was tall, with rough hands, mostly dark skin marbled with lines of red. The others had called him 'Sah,' a simple Alethi darkeyes name.

Moash nodded his chin toward the Voidbringers. 'They were supposed to sweep in relentlessly, destroying everything in their path. They are *literally* incarnations of destruction.'

'And?' Sah asked.

'And that one,' Moash said, pointing toward the flying Voidbringer, 'is pleased to find these orchards here. They only burned a few towns. They seem intent on keeping Revolar, working it.' Moash shook his head. 'This was supposed to be an apocalypse, but you don't *farm* an apocalypse.'

Sah grunted again. He didn't seem to know any more about this than

Moash did, but why should he? He'd grown up in a rural community in Alethkar. Everything he knew about history and religion, he'd have heard filtered through the human perspective.

'You shouldn't speak so casually about the Fused, human,' Sah said, standing up. 'They're dangerous.'

'Don't know about that,' Moash said as two more passed overhead. 'The one I killed went down easy enough, though I don't think she was expecting me to be able to fight back.'

He handed his waterskin to the overseer as she came around for them; then he glanced at Sah, who was staring at him, slack-jawed.

Probably shouldn't have mentioned killing one of their gods, Moash thought, walking to his place in line – last, closest to the sledge, so he stared at a sweaty parshman back all day.

They started up again, and Moash expected another long day's work. These orchards meant Kholinar itself was a little over a day's hike away at an easy pace. He figured the Voidbringers would push them hard to reach the capital by nightfall.

He was surprised, then, when the army diverged from the direct route. They wove between some hillsides until they reached a town, one of the many suburbs of Kholinar. He couldn't recall the name. The tavern had been nice, and welcoming to caravaneers.

Clearly there were other Voidbringer armies moving through Alethkar, because they'd obviously seized this city days – if not weeks – ago. Parshmen patrolled it, and the only humans he saw were already working the fields.

Once the army arrived, the Voidbringers surprised Moash again by selecting some of the wagon-pullers and setting them free. They were the weaklings, the ones who had fared worst on the road. The overseers sent them trudging toward Kholinar, which was still too far off to see.

They're trying to burden the city with refugees, Moash thought. *Ones that aren't fit to work or fight anymore.*

The main bulk of the army moved into the large storm bunkers in this suburb. They wouldn't attack the city immediately. The Voidbringers would rest their armies, prepare, and besiege.

In his youth, he'd wondered why there weren't any suburbs closer than a day's walk from Kholinar. In fact, there was nothing between its walls and here, only empty flats – even the hills there had been mined down centuries ago. The purpose was clear to him now. If you wanted to lay siege to Kholinar, this was the closest you could put your army. You couldn't camp in the city's shadow; you'd be swept away by the first storm.

In the town, the supply sledges were split, some sent down one street – which looked hauntingly empty to him – while his went down another. They actually passed the tavern he'd preferred, the Fallen Tower; he could see the glyph etched into the leeward stone.

Finally his crew was called to a halt, and he let go of the rope, stretching his hands and letting out a relieved sigh. They'd been sent to a large open ground near some warehouses, where parshmen were cutting lumber.

A lumberyard? he thought, then felt stupid. After hauling wood all this way, what else would he expect?

Still ... a lumberyard. Like those back in the warcamps. He started laughing.

'Don't be so jovial, human,' spat one of the overseers. 'You're to spend the next few weeks working here, building siege equipment. When the assault happens, *you'll* be at the front, running a ladder toward Kholinar's infamous walls.'

Moash laughed even harder. It consumed him, shook him; he couldn't stop. He laughed helplessly until, short of breath, he dizzily lay back on the hard stone ground, tears leaking down the sides of his face.

·:·

We have investigated this woman, Mraize's newest letter to Shallan read.

> Ishnah has overinflated her importance to you. She was indeed involved in espionage for House Hamaradin, as she told you, but she was merely an assistant to the true spies.
>
> We have determined that she is safe to allow close to you, though her loyalties should not be trusted too far. If you eliminate her, we will help cover up the disappearance, at your request. But we have no objection to you retaining her services.

Shallan sighed, settling back in her seat, where she waited outside King Elhokar's audience chamber. She'd found this paper unexpectedly in her satchel.

So much for hoping Ishnah had information about the Ghostbloods she could use. The letter practically boiled with possessiveness. They would 'allow' Ishnah to be close to her? Storms, they acted like they owned her already.

She shook her head, then rummaged in her satchel, taking out a small sphere pouch. It would look unremarkable to anyone inspecting it – for they wouldn't know that she'd transformed it with a small but simple illusion. Though it appeared violet, it was actually white.

The interesting thing about it was not the illusion itself, but how she was powering it. She'd practiced before with attaching an illusion to Pattern, or to a location, but she'd always needed to power it with her own Stormlight. This one, however, she'd attached to a sphere inside the pouch.

She was going on four hours now with the Lightweaving needing no extra Stormlight from her. She'd needed only to create it, then affix it to the sphere. Slowly, the Light had been draining from the sapphire mark – just like a fabrial draining its gemstone. She'd even left the pouch alone in her rooms when going out, and the illusion had still been in place when she'd returned.

This had begun as an experiment on how she could help Dalinar create his illusory maps of the world, then leave them for him, without her having to remain in the meeting. Now, however, she was seeing all *kinds* of possible applications.

The door opened, and she dropped the pouch back into her satchel. A master-servant ushered a few merchants out of the king's presence; then the servant bowed to Shallan, waving her in. She stepped hesitantly into the audience chamber: a room with a fine blue and green rug and stuffed with furniture. Diamonds shone from lamps, and Elhokar had ordered the walls painted, obscuring the strata.

The king himself, in a blue Kholin uniform, was unrolling a map onto a large table at the side of the room. 'Was there another, Helt?' he asked the master-servant. 'I thought I was done for the . . .' He trailed off as he turned. 'Brightness Shallan! Were you waiting out there? You could have seen me immediately!'

'I didn't want to be a bother,' Shallan said, stepping over to him as the master-servant prepared refreshment.

The map on the table showed Kholinar, a grand city, which seemed every bit as impressive as Vedenar. Papers in a pile beside it looked to have the final reports from spanreeds in the city, and a wizened ardent sat near them, ready to read for the king or take notes at his request.

'I think we're almost ready,' the king said, noting her interest. 'The delay has been nearly insufferable, but requisite, I'm sure. Captain Kaladin did want to practice flying other people before bringing my royal person. I can respect that.'

'He's asked me to fly with him above the storm to Thaylen City,' Shallan said, 'to open the Oathgate there. He's overly worried about dropping people – but if he does that to me, I'll have Stormlight of my own, and should survive the fall.'

'Excellent,' Elhokar said. 'Yes, a fine solution. But then, you didn't come here to talk about this. What is your request of me?'

'Actually,' Shallan said. 'Could I talk to you in private for a moment, Your Majesty?'

He frowned, but then ordered his people to step out into the hallway. When two guards from Bridge Thirteen hesitated, the king was firm. 'She's a Knight Radiant,' he said. 'What do you think is going to happen to me?'

They filed out, leaving the two of them beside Elhokar's table. Shallan took a deep breath.

Then changed her face.

Not to that of Veil or Radiant – not one of her *secrets* – but instead to an illusion of Adolin. It was still surprisingly uncomfortable for her to do it in front of someone. She'd still been telling most people that she was of the Elsecallers, like Jasnah, so they wouldn't know of her ability to become other people.

Elhokar jumped. 'Ah,' he said. 'Ah, that's right.'

'Your Majesty,' Shallan said, changing her face and body to look like that of a cleaning woman she'd sketched earlier, 'I'm worried that your mission will not be as simple as you think.'

The letters out of Kholinar – the last ones they'd gotten – were frightened, worried things. They spoke of riots, of darkness, of spren taking form and hurting people.

Shallan changed her face to that of a soldier. 'I've been preparing a team of spies,' she explained. 'Specializing in infiltration and information gathering. I've been keeping my focus quiet, for obvious reasons. I would like to offer my services for your mission.'

'I'm not certain,' Elhokar said, hesitantly, 'if Dalinar would want me taking *two* of his Radiants away from him.'

'I'm not accomplishing much for him sitting around here,' Shallan said, still wearing the soldier's face. 'Besides. Is it his mission? Or is it yours?'

'My mission,' the king said. Then hesitated. 'But let's not fool ourselves. If he didn't want you to go . . .'

'I am not his subject,' she said. 'Nor yours, yet. I'm my own woman. You tell me. What happens if you get to Kholinar, and the Oathgate is held by the enemy? Are you going to let the bridgeman just fight his way in? Or might there be a better option?'

She changed her face to that of a parshwoman she had from her older sketches.

Elhokar nodded, walking around her. 'A team, you say. Of spies? Interesting . . .'

⁘

A short time later, Shallan left the room carrying – tucked into her safepouch – a formal royal request to Dalinar for Shallan's aid on the mission. Kaladin had said he felt comfortable bringing six people, other than a few bridgemen, who could fly on their own.

Adolin and Elhokar would leave room for four others. She tucked Elhokar's request into her safepouch, beside the letter from Mraize.

I just need to be away from this place, Shallan thought. *I need to be away from them, and from Jasnah, at least until I can figure out what I want.*

A part of her knew what she was doing. It was getting harder to hide things in the back of her mind and ignore them, now that she'd spoken Ideals. Instead she was fleeing.

But she *could* help the group going to Kholinar. And it *did* feel exciting, the idea of going to the city and finding the secrets there. She wasn't *only* running. She'd also be helping Adolin reclaim his home.

Pattern hummed from her skirts, and she hummed along with him.

52

AFTER HIS FATHER

EIGHTEEN AND A HALF YEARS AGO

Dalinar plodded back into camp, so tired he suspected only the energy of his Plate was keeping him upright. Each muggy breath inside his helm fogged the metal, which – as always – went somewhat transparent from the inside when you engaged the visor.

He'd crushed the Herdazians – sending them back to start a civil war, securing the Alethi lands to the north and claiming the island of Akak. Now he'd moved southward, to engage the Vedens at the border. Herdaz had taken far longer than Dalinar had expected. He'd been out on campaign a total of four years now.

Four glorious years.

Dalinar walked straight to his armorers' tent, picking up attendants and messengers along the way. When he ignored their questions, they trailed after him like cremlings eyeing a greatshell's kill, waiting for their moment to snatch a tidbit.

Inside the tent, he extended his arms to the sides and let the armorers start the disassembly. Helm, then arms, revealing the gambeson he wore for padding. The helm's removal exposed sweaty, clammy skin that made the air feel too cold. The breastplate was cracked along the left side, and the armorers buzzed, discussing the repair. As if they had to do something other than merely give the Plate Stormlight and let it regrow itself.

Eventually, all that remained were his boots, which he stepped out of, maintaining a martial posture by pure force of will. The support of his Plate removed, exhaustionspren began to shoot up around him like jets of dust. He stepped over to a set of travel cushions and sat down, reclining against them, sighing, and closing his eyes.

'Brightlord?' one of the armorers asked. 'Um . . . that's where we set—'

'This is now my audience tent,' Dalinar said, not opening his eyes. 'Take what is absolutely essential and leave me.'

The clanking of armor stopped as the workers digested what he'd said. They left in a whispering rush, and nobody else bothered him for a blissful five minutes – until footfalls sounded nearby. Tent flaps rustled, then leather scrunched as someone knelt beside him.

'The final battle report is here, Brightlord.' Kadash's voice. Of course it would be one of his storming officers. Dalinar had trained them far too well.

'Speak,' Dalinar said, opening his eyes.

Kadash had reached middle age, maybe two or three years older than Dalinar. He now had a twisting scar across his face and head from where a spear had hit him.

'We completely routed them, Brightlord,' Kadash said. 'Our archers and light infantry followed with an extended harry. We slew, by best count, two thousand – nearly half. We could have gotten more if we'd boxed them in to the south.'

'Never box in an enemy, Kadash,' Dalinar said. 'You want them to be able to retreat, or they'll fight you worse for it. A rout will serve us better than an extermination. How many people did we lose?'

'Barely two hundred.'

Dalinar nodded. Minimal losses, while delivering a devastating blow.

'Sir,' Kadash said. 'I'd say this raiding group is done for.'

'We've still got many more to dig out. This will last years yet.'

'Unless the Vedens send in an entire army and engage us in force.'

'They won't,' Dalinar said, rubbing his forehead. 'Their king is too shrewd. It isn't full-on war he wants; he only wanted to see if any contested land had suddenly become uncontested.'

'Yes, Brightlord.'

'Thank you for the report. Now get out of here and post some storming guards at the front so I can rest. Don't let anyone in, not even the Nightwatcher herself.'

'Yes, sir.' Kadash crossed the tent to the flaps. 'Um ... sir, you were incredible out there. Like a tempest.'

Dalinar just closed his eyes and leaned back, fully determined to fall asleep in his clothing.

Sleep, unfortunately, refused to come. The report set his mind to considering implications.

His army had only one Soulcaster, for emergencies, which meant supply trains. These borderlands were expansive, hilly, and the Vedens had better generals than the Herdazians. Defeating a mobile enemy was going to be hard in such circumstances, as this first battle proved. It would take planning, maneuvering, and skirmish after skirmish to pin the various groups of Vedens down and bring them into proper battle.

He yearned for those early days, when their fights had been more rowdy, less coordinated. Well, he wasn't a youth anymore, and he'd learned in Herdaz that he no longer had Gavilar to do the hard parts of this job. Dalinar had camps to supply, men to feed, and logistics to work out. This was almost as bad as being back in the city, listening to scribes talk about sewage disposal.

Save for one difference: Out here, he had a reward. At the end of all the planning, the strategy, and the debates with generals, came the Thrill.

In fact, through his exhaustion, he was surprised to find that he could sense it still. Deep down, like the warmth of a rock that had known a recent fire. He was *glad* that the fighting had dragged on all these years. He was *glad* that the Herdazians had tried to seize that land, and that now the Vedens wanted to test him. He was *glad* that other highprinces weren't sending aid, but waiting to see what he could accomplish on his own.

Most of all, he was glad that – despite today's important battle – the conflict was not over. Storms, he loved this feeling. Today, hundreds had tried to bring him down, and he'd left them ashen and broken.

Outside his tent, people demanding his attention were turned away one after another. He tried not to feel pleasure each time. He would answer their questions eventually. Just ... not now.

Thoughts finally released their grip on his brain, and he dipped toward slumber. Until one unexpected voice jerked him out of it and sent him bolting upright.

That was Evi.

He leapt to his feet. The Thrill surged again within him, drawn out of its own slumber. Dalinar ripped open the tent's front flaps and gaped at the blonde-haired woman standing outside, wearing a Vorin havah – but with sturdy walking boots sticking out below.

'Ah,' Evi said. 'Husband.' She looked him up and down, and her expression soured, lips puckering. 'Has no person seen fit to order him a bath? Where are his grooms, to see him undressed properly?'

'Why are you here?' Dalinar demanded. He hadn't intended to roar it, but he was so tired, so shocked . . .

Evi leaned backward before the outburst, eyes opening wide.

He briefly felt a spike of shame. But why should he? This was his warcamp – here he was the Blackthorn. This was the place where his domestic life should have no purchase on him! By coming here, she invaded that.

'I . . .' Evi said. 'I . . . Other women are at the camp. Other wives. It is common, for women to go to war. . . .'

'Alethi women,' Dalinar snapped, 'trained to it from childhood and acquainted with the ways of warfare. We spoke of this, Evi. We – ' He halted, looking at the guards. They shuffled uncomfortably.

'Come inside, Evi,' Dalinar said. 'Let's discuss this in private.'

'Very well. And the children?'

You brought our children to the battlefront? Storms, she didn't even have the sense to leave them at the town the army was using as a long-term command post?

'I—'

'In,' Dalinar said, pointing at the tent.

Evi wilted, then scuttled to obey, cringing as she passed him. Why had she come? Hadn't he just been back to Kholinar to visit? That had been . . . recent, he was sure. . . .

Or maybe not so recent. He did have several letters from Evi that Teleb's wife had read to him, with several more waiting to be read. He dropped the flaps back into position and turned toward Evi, determined not to let his frayed patience rule him.

'Navani said I should come,' Evi said. 'She said it was shameful that you have waited so long between visits. Adolin has gone over a year without seeing you, Dalinar. And little Renarin has never even *met* his father.'

'Renarin?' Dalinar said, trying to work out the name. He hadn't picked that. 'Rekher . . . no, Re . . .'

'Re,' Evi said. 'From my language. Nar, after his father. In, to be born unto.'

Stormfather, that was a butchering of the language. Dalinar fumbled, trying to work through it. Nar meant 'like unto.'

'What does 'Re' mean in your language?' Dalinar asked, scratching his face.

'It has no meaning,' Evi said. 'It is simply the name. It means our son's name, or him.'

Dalinar groaned softly. So the child's name was 'Like one who was born unto himself.' Delightful.

'You didn't answer,' Evi pointed out, 'when I asked after a name via spanreed.'

How had Navani and Ialai allowed this travesty of a name? Storms . . . knowing those two, they'd probably encouraged it. They were always trying to get Evi to be more forceful. He moved to get something to drink, but then remembered that this wasn't actually his tent. There wasn't anything in here to drink but armor oil.

'You shouldn't have come,' Dalinar said. 'It is dangerous out here.'

'I wish to be a more Alethi wife. I want you to *want* me to be with you.'

He winced. 'Well, you still should not have brought the children.' Dalinar slumped down into the cushions. 'They are heirs to the princedom, assuming this plan of Gavilar's with the Crownlands and his own throne works out. They need to remain safe in Kholinar.'

'I thought you'd want to see them,' Evi said, stepping up to him. Despite his harsh words, she unbuckled the top of his gambeson to get her hands under it, and began rubbing his shoulders.

It felt wonderful. He let his anger melt away. It *would* be good to have a wife with him, to scribe as was proper. He just wished that he didn't feel so guilty at seeing her. He was not the man she wanted him to be.

'I hear you had a great victory today,' Evi said softly. 'You do service to the king.'

'You'd have hated it, Evi. I killed hundreds of people. If you stay, you'll have to listen to war reports. Accounts of deaths, many at my hand.'

She was silent for a time. 'Could you not . . . let them surrender to you?'

'The Vedens aren't here to surrender. They're here to test us on the battlefield.'

'And the individual men? Do they care for such reasoning as they die?'

'What? Would you like me to stop and ask each man to surrender as I prepare to strike him down?'

'Would that—'

'No, Evi. That wouldn't work.'

'Oh.'

He stood up, suddenly anxious. 'Let's see the boys, then.'

Leaving his tent and crossing the camp was a slog, his feet feeling like they'd been encased in blocks of crem. He didn't dare slouch – he always tried to present a strong image for the men and women of the army – but he couldn't help that his padded garb was wrinkled and stained with sweat.

The land here was lush compared to Kholinar. The thick grass was broken by sturdy stands of trees, and tangled vines draped the western cliff faces. There were places farther into Jah Keved where you couldn't take a step without vines writhing under your feet.

The boys were by Evi's wagons. Little Adolin was terrorizing one of the chulls, perched atop its shell and swinging a wooden sword about, showing off for several of the guards – who dutifully complimented his moves. He'd somehow assembled 'armor' from strings and bits of broken rockbud shell.

Storms, he's grown, Dalinar thought. When last he'd seen Adolin, the child had still looked like a toddler, stumbling through his words. Little over a year later, the boy spoke clearly – and dramatically – as he described his fallen enemies. They were, apparently, evil flying chulls.

He stopped when he saw Dalinar, then he glanced at Evi. She nodded, and the child scrambled down from the chull – Dalinar was certain he'd fall at three different points. He got down safely, walked over.

And saluted.

Evi beamed. 'He asked the best way to talk to you,' she whispered. 'I told him you were a general, the leader of all the soldiers. He came up with that on his own.'

Dalinar squatted down. Little Adolin immediately shied back, reaching for his mother's skirts.

'Afraid of me?' Dalinar asked. 'Not unwise. I'm a dangerous man.'

'Daddy?' the boy said, holding to the skirt with one white-knuckled hand – but not hiding.

'Yes. Don't you remember me?'

Hesitantly, the motley-haired boy nodded. 'I remember you. We talk about you every night when we burn prayers. So you will be safe. Fighting bad men.'

'I'd prefer to be safe from the good ones too,' Dalinar said. 'Though I will take what I am offered.' He stood up, feeling ... what? Shame to not have seen the boy as often as he should have? Pride at how the boy was growing? The Thrill, still squirming deep down. How had it not dissipated since the battle?

'Where is your brother, Adolin?' Dalinar asked.

The boy pointed toward a nurse who carried a little one. Dalinar had expected a baby, but this child could nearly walk, as evidenced by the nurse putting him down and watching fondly as he toddled a few steps, then sat, trying to grab blades of grass as they pulled away.

The child made no sounds. He just stared, solemn, as he tried to grip blade after blade. Dalinar waited for the excitement he'd felt before, upon meeting Adolin for the first time ... but storms, he was just so *tired*.

'Can I see your sword?' Adolin asked.

Dalinar wanted nothing more than to sleep, but he summoned the Blade anyway, driving it into the ground with the edge pointed away from Adolin. The boy's eyes grew wide.

'Mommy says I can't have my Plate yet,' Adolin said.

'Teleb needs it. You can have it when you come of age.'

'Good. I'll need it to win a Blade.'

Nearby, Evi clicked her tongue softly, shaking her head.

Dalinar smiled, kneeling beside his Blade and resting his hand on the small boy's shoulder. 'I'll win you one in war, son.'

'No,' Adolin said, chin up. 'I want to win my own. Like you did.'

'A worthy goal,' Dalinar said. 'But a soldier needs to be willing to accept help. You mustn't be hardheaded; pride doesn't win battles.'

The boy cocked his head, frowning. 'Your head isn't hard?' He rapped his knuckles against his own.

Dalinar smiled, then stood up and dismissed Oathbringer. The last embers of the Thrill finally faded. 'It's been a long day,' he told Evi. 'I need to rest. We'll discuss your role here later.'

Evi led him to a bed within one of her stormwagons. Then, at last, Dalinar was able to sleep.

My Friend,

The secrets uncovered infiltrating the Calligraphers Guild are more mundane than expected. I prefer bloodstains to inkstains any day, so next time send me somewhere I'm more likely to die from wounds than from handcramps. By Purity's Eye, if you ask me to draw another glyph...

The darkest secret of the guild is that the phonemes within a glyph can sometimes be deciphered. (Sorry to shatter your theories of dark rites and ancient moon dances.) But glyphs aren't pronounced or read. They're memorized, and they change over time till the original collection of phonograms is almost unrecognizable. Take, for instance, the glyph for storm: "zeras."

Old   Middle   Modern

high "kecheh" storm "zeras"   eternal "kalad" storm "zeras"

Highstorm "kezeras"   Everstorm "kalazeras"

> Glyphpairs are slightly more common than single glyphs. Less used are 3 glyphs in a row.

> Glyphs have simplified versions for small writing

Contrast "zeras" with a glyph in its infancy: "zatalef," a bat-like cephalopod the Alethi hadn't encountered until their recent conquests in Akak.

The glyph's phonemes are apparent as well as the glyph's resemblance to the actual creature.

Even older than "zeras" are the glyphs used in the First Oath of the Knights Radiant. These resemble more the complex, unreadable glyphs representing the orders of knights than they do any middle or modern Alethi glyphs.

javani   tebel   tsameth

I suspect these were borrowed from an earlier source and incorporated into an already developing Alethi glyph lexicon.

This supports the claim that Alethi glyphs were adopted from older scripts likely descended from Dawnchant and might explain the two sets of phonemes used in glyph creation: Standard and Calligraphic.

katef   tebel   kadulek

mehlak   tebel   mevizh

Glyphmakers use both, the phonemes rotated, flipped, and distorted to fit the calligrapher's vision. Next page: The Calligraphic Phoneme set.

Friend,
Your letter is most intriguing, even revelatory.

The ancient Siln dynasty in Jah Keved had been founded after the death of King NanKhet. No contemporary accounts survived; the best they had dated from two centuries later. The author of that text – Natata Ved, often called Oileyes by her contemporaries – insisted that her methods were rigorous, although by modern standards, historical scholarship had been in its infancy.

Jasnah had long been interested in NanKhet's death, because he'd ruled for only three months. He'd succeeded to the throne when the previous king, his brother NanHar, had taken ill and died while on campaign in what would become modern Triax.

Remarkably, during the brief span of his reign, NanKhet survived *six* assassination attempts. The first had come from his sister, who had wanted to place her husband on the throne. After surviving poisoning, NanKhet had put them both to death. Soon after, their son had tried to kill him in his bed. NanKhet, apparently a light sleeper, struck down his nephew with his own sword.

NanKhet's cousin tried next – that attack left NanKhet blinded in one eye – and was followed by another brother, an uncle, and finally NanKhet's own son. At the end of three exasperating months, according to Oileyes, 'The great, but weary, NanKhet called for an accounting of all his household. He gathered them together at a grand feast, promising the delights of distant Aimia. Instead, when all were assembled, NanKhet had them executed one by one. Their bodies were burned in a grand pyre, upon which was cooked the meat for the feast that he ate alone, at a table set for two hundred.'

Natata Oileyes was known to have had a passion for the dramatic. The text sounded almost delighted when she'd explained how he'd died by choking on the food at that very feast, alone with nobody to help him.

Similar tales repeated themselves throughout the long history of the Vorin lands. Kings fell, and their brothers or sons took the throne. Even a pretender of no true lineage would usually claim kinship through oblique and creative genealogical justifications.

Jasnah was simultaneously fascinated and worried by these accounts. Thoughts about them were unusually present in her mind as she made her way into Urithiru's basement. Something in her readings the night before had lodged this particular story in her brain.

She soon peeked into the former library beneath Urithiru. Both rooms – one on either side of the hallway that led to the crystal pillar – were filled with scholars now, occupying tables carried down by squads of soldiers. Dalinar had sent expeditions down the tunnel the Unmade had used to flee. The scouts reported a long network of caverns.

Following a stream of water, they'd marched for days, and eventually located an exit into the mountain foothills of Tu Fallia. It was nice to know that, in a pinch, there was another way out of Urithiru – and a potential means of supply other than through the Oathgates.

They maintained guards in the upper tunnels, and for now it seemed safe enough in the basement. Therefore, Navani had transformed the area into a scholarly institute designed to solve Dalinar's problems and to provide an edge in information, technology, and pure research. Concentrationspren rippled in the air like waves overhead – a rarity in Alethkar, but common here – and logicspren darted through them, like tiny stormclouds.

Jasnah couldn't help but smile. For over a decade, she'd dreamed of uniting the best minds of the kingdom in a coordinated effort. She'd been ignored; all anyone had wanted to discuss was her lack of belief in their god. Well, they were focused now. Turned out that the end of the world had to actually *arrive* before people would take it seriously.

Renarin was there, standing near the corner, watching the work. He'd been joining the scholars with some regularity, but he still wore his uniform with the Bridge Four patch.

You can't spend forever floating between worlds, Cousin, she thought. *Eventually you'll need to decide where you want to belong.* Life was so much harder, but potentially so much more fulfilling, when you found the courage to choose.

The story of the old Veden king, NanKhet, had taught Jasnah something troubling: Often, the greatest threat to a ruling family was its own members. Why were so many of the old royal lines such knots of murder, greed, and infighting? And what made the few exceptions different?

She'd grown adept at protecting her family against danger from without, carefully removing would-be deposers. But what could she do to protect it from within? In her absence, already the monarchy trembled. Her brother and her uncle – who she knew loved each other deeply – ground their wills against one another like mismatched gears.

She would *not* have her family implode. If Alethkar was going to survive the Desolation, they'd need committed leadership. A stable throne.

She entered the library room and walked to her writing stand. It was in a position where she could survey the others and have her back to a wall.

She unpacked her satchel, setting up two spanreed boards. One of the reeds was blinking early, and she twisted the ruby, indicating she was ready. A message came back, writing out, *We will begin in five minutes.*

She passed the time scrutinizing the various groups in the room, reading the lips of those she could see, absently taking notes in shorthand. She moved from conversation to conversation, gleaning a little from each one and noting the names of the people who spoke.

—*tests confirm something is different here. Temperatures are distinctly lower on other nearby peaks of the same elevation*—

—*we have to assume that Brightlord Kholin is not going to return to the faith. What then?*—

—*don't know. Perhaps if we could find a way to conjoin the fabrials, we could imitate this effect*—

—*the boy could be a powerful addition to our ranks. He shows interest in numerology, and asked me if we can truly predict events with it. I will speak with him again*—

That last one was from the stormwardens. Jasnah tightly pursed her lips. 'Ivory?' she whispered.

'I will watch them.'

He left her side, shrunken to the size of a speck of dust. Jasnah made a note to speak to Renarin; she would not have him wasting his time with a bunch of fools who thought they could foretell the future based on the curls of smoke from a snuffed candle.

Finally, her spanreed woke up.

I have connected Jochi of Thaylenah and Ethid of Azir for you, Brightness. Here are their passcodes. Further entries will be strictly their notations.

Excellent, Jasnah wrote back, authenticating the two passcodes. Losing her spanreeds in the sinking of the *Wind's Pleasure* had been a huge setback. She could no longer directly contact important colleagues or informants. Fortunately, Tashikk was set up to deal with these kinds of situations. You could always buy new reeds connected to the princedom's infamous information centers.

You could reach anyone, in practice, so long as you trusted an intermediary. Jasnah had one of those she'd personally interviewed – and whom she paid good money – to ensure confidentiality. The intermediary would burn her copies of this conversation afterward. The system was as secure as Jasnah could make it, all things considered.

Jasnah's intermediary would now be joined by two others in Tashikk. Together, the three would be surrounded by six spanreed boards: one each for receiving comments from their masters, and one each to send back the entire conversation in real time, including the comments from the other two. That way, each conversant would be able to see a constant stream of comments, without having to stop and wait before replying.

Navani talked of ways to improve the experience – of spanreeds that could be adjusted to connect to different people. That was one area of scholarship, however, that Jasnah did not have time to pursue.

Her receiving board started to fill with notes written by her two colleagues.

Jasnah, you live! Jochi wrote. *Back from the dead. Remarkable!*

I can't believe you ever thought she was dead, Ethid replied. *Jasnah Kholin? Lost at sea? Likelier we'd find the Stormfather dead.*

Your confidence is comforting, Ethid, Jasnah wrote on her sending board.

A moment later, those words were copied by her scribe into the common spanreed conversation.

Are you at Urithiru? Jochi wrote. *When can I visit?*

As soon as you're willing to let everyone know you aren't female, Jasnah wrote back. Jochi – known to the world as a dynamic woman of distinctive philosophy – was a pen name for a potbellied man in his sixties who ran a pastry shop in Thaylen City.

Oh, I'm certain your wonderful city has need of pastries, Jochi wrote back jovially.

Can we please discuss your silliness later? Ethid wrote. *I have news.* She was a scion – a kind of religious order of scribe – at the Azish royal palace.

Well stop wasting time then! Jochi wrote. *I love news. Goes excellently with a filled doughnut . . . no, no, a fluffy brioche.*

The news? Jasnah just wrote, smiling. These two had studied with her under the same master – they were Veristitalians of the keenest mind, regardless of how Jochi might seem.

I've been tracking a man we are increasingly certain is the Herald Nakku, the Judge, Ethid wrote. *Nalan, as you call him.*

Oh, are we sharing nursery tales now? Jochi asked. *Heralds? Really, Ethid?*

If you haven't noticed, Ethid wrote, *the Voidbringers are back. Tales we dismissed are worth a second look, now.*

I agree, Jasnah wrote. *But what makes you think you've found one of the Heralds?*

It's a combination of many things, she wrote. *This man attacked our palace, Jasnah. He tried to kill some thieves – the new Prime is one of them, but keep that in your sleeve. We're doing what we can to play up his common roots while ignoring the fact that he was intent on robbing us.*

Heralds alive and trying to kill people, Jochi wrote. *And here I thought my news about a sighting of Axies the Collector was interesting.*

There's more, Ethid wrote. *Jasnah, we've got a Radiant here. An Edge-dancer. Or . . . we had one.*

Had one? Jochi wrote. *Did you misplace her?*

She ran off. She's just a kid, Jasnah. Reshi, raised on the streets.

I think we may have met her, Jasnah wrote. *My uncle encountered someone interesting in one of his recent visions. I'm surprised you let her get away from you.*

Have you ever tried to hold on to an Edgedancer? Ethid wrote back. *She chased after the Herald to Tashikk, but the Prime says she is back now – and avoiding me. In any case, something's wrong with the man I think is Nalan, Jasnah. I don't think the Heralds will be a resource to us.*

I will provide you with sketches of the Heralds, Jasnah said. *I have drawings of their true faces, provided by an unexpected source. Ethid, you are right about them. They aren't going to be a resource; they're broken. Have you read the accounts of my uncle's visions?*

I have copies somewhere, Ethid wrote. *Are they real? Most sources agree that he's . . . unwell.*

He's quite well, I assure you, Jasnah wrote. *The visions are related to his order of Radiants. I will send you the latest few; they have relevance to the Heralds.*

Storms, Ethid wrote. *The Blackthorn is actually a Radiant? Years of drought, and now they're popping up like rockbuds.*

Ethid did not think highly of men who earned their reputations through conquest, despite having made the study of such men a cornerstone of her research.

The conversation continued for some time. Jochi, growing uncharacteristically solemn, spoke directly of the state of Thaylenah. It had been hit hard by the repeated coming of the Everstorm; entire sections of Thaylen City were in ruin.

Jasnah was most interested in the Thaylen parshmen who had stolen the ships that had survived the storm. Their exodus – combined with Kaladin Stormblessed's interactions with the parshmen in Alethkar – was painting a new picture of what and who the Voidbringers were.

The conversation moved on as Ethid transcribed an interesting account she'd discovered in an old book discussing the Desolations. From there, they spoke of the Dawnchant translations, in particular those by some ardents in Jah Keved who were ahead of the scholars at Kharbranth.

Jasnah glanced through the library room, seeking out her mother, who was sitting near Shallan to discuss wedding preparations. Renarin still lurked at the far side of the room, mumbling to himself. Or perhaps to his spren? She absently read his lips.

—it's coming from in here, Renarin said. *Somewhere in this room—*

Jasnah narrowed her eyes.

Ethid, she wrote, *weren't you going to try to construct drawings of the spren tied to each order of Radiant?*

I've gotten quite far, actually, she wrote back. *I saw the Edgedancer spren personally, after demanding a glimpse.*

What of the Truthwatchers? Jasnah wrote.

Oh! I found a reference to those, Jochi wrote. *The spren reportedly looked like light on a surface after it reflects through something crystalline.*

Jasnah thought for a moment, then briefly excused herself from the conversation. Jochi said he needed to go find a privy anyway. She slipped off her seat and crossed the room, passing near Navani and Shallan.

'I don't want to push you at all, dear,' Navani was saying. 'But in these uncertain times, surely you wish for stability.'

Jasnah stopped, freehand resting idly on Shallan's shoulder. The younger woman perked up, then followed Jasnah's gaze toward Renarin.

'What?' Shallan whispered.

'I don't know,' Jasnah said. 'Something odd . . .'

Something about the way the youth was standing, the words he had spoken. He still looked wrong to her without his spectacles. Like a different person entirely.

'Jasnah!' Shallan said, suddenly tense. 'The doorway. Look!'

Jasnah sucked in Stormlight at the girl's tone and turned away from Renarin, toward the room's doorway. There, a tall, square-jawed man had darkened the opening. He wore Sadeas's colors, forest green and white. In fact, he *was* Sadeas now, at least its regent.

Jasnah would always know him as Meridas Amaram.

'What's *he* doing here?' Shallan hissed.

'He's a highprince,' Navani said. 'The soldiers aren't going to forbid him without a direct command.'

Amaram fixated on Jasnah with regal, light tan eyes. He strode toward her, exuding confidence, or was it conceit? 'Jasnah,' he said when he drew close. 'I was told I could find you here.'

'Remind me to find whoever told you,' Jasnah said, 'and have them hanged.'

Amaram stiffened. 'Could we speak together more privately, just for a moment?'

'I think not.'

'We need to discuss your uncle. The rift between our houses serves nobody. I wish to bridge that chasm, and Dalinar listens to you. Please, Jasnah. You can steer him properly.'

'My uncle knows his own mind on these matters, and doesn't require me to "steer" him.'

'As if you haven't been doing so already, Jasnah. Everyone can see that he has started to share your religious beliefs.'

'Which would be incredible, since I don't *have* religious beliefs.'

Amaram sighed, looking around. 'Please,' he said. 'Private?'

'Not a chance, Meridas. Go. Away.'

'We were close once.'

'My father *wished* us to be close. Do not mistake his fancies for fact.'

'Jasnah—'

'You really should leave before somebody gets hurt.'

He ignored her suggestion, glancing at Navani and Shallan, then stepping closer. 'We thought you were *dead*. I needed to see for myself that you are well.'

'You have seen. Now leave.'

Instead, he gripped her forearm. 'Why, Jasnah? *Why* have you always denied me?'

'Other than the fact that you are a detestable buffoon who achieves only the lowest level of mediocrity, as it is the best your limited mind can imagine? I can't possibly think of a reason.'

'Mediocre?' Amaram growled. 'You insult my mother, Jasnah. You know how hard she worked to raise me to be the best soldier this kingdom has ever known.'

'Yes, from what I understand, she spent the seven months she was with child entertaining each and every military man she could find, in the hopes that something of them would stick to you.'

Meridas's eyes widened, and his face flushed deeply. To their side, Shallan audibly gasped.

'You godless *whore*,' Amaram hissed, releasing her. 'If you weren't a woman . . .'

'If I weren't a woman, I suspect we wouldn't be having this conversation. Unless I were a pig. Then you'd be doubly interested.'

He thrust his hand to the side, stepping back, preparing to summon his Blade.

Jasnah smiled, holding her freehand toward him, letting Stormlight curl and rise from it. 'Oh, please do, Meridas. Give me an excuse. I dare you.'

He stared at her hand. The entire room had gone silent, of course. He'd forced her to make a spectacle. His eyes flicked up to meet hers; then he spun and stalked from the room, shoulders hunched as if trying to shrug away the eyes – and the snickers – of the scholars.

He will be trouble, Jasnah thought. *Even more than he has been.* Amaram genuinely thought he was Alethkar's only hope and salvation, and had a keen desire to prove it. Left alone, he'd rip the armies apart to justify his inflated opinion of himself.

She'd speak with Dalinar. Perhaps the two of them could devise something to keep Amaram safely occupied. And if that didn't work, she *wouldn't* speak to Dalinar about the other precaution she would take. She'd been out of touch for a long time, but she was confident there would be assassins for hire here, ones who knew her reputation for discretion and excellent pay.

A high-pitched sound came from beside her, and Jasnah glanced to find Shallan sitting perkily on her seat, making an excited noise in the back of her throat and clapping her hands together quickly, the sound muffled by her clothed safehand.

Wonderful.

'Mother,' Jasnah said, 'might I speak for a moment with my ward?'

Navani nodded, her eyes lingering on the doorway where Amaram had exited. Once, she'd pushed for the union between them. Jasnah didn't blame her; the truth of Amaram was difficult to see, and had been even more so in the past, when he'd been close to Jasnah's father.

Navani withdrew, leaving Shallan alone at the table stacked with reports.

'Brightness!' Shallan said as Jasnah sat. 'That was incredible!'

'I let myself be pushed into abundant emotion.'

'You were so *clever!*'

'And yet, my first insult was not to attack *him,* but the moral reputation of his *female relative.* Clever? Or simply the use of an obvious bludgeon?'

'Oh. Um ... Well ...'

'Regardless,' Jasnah cut in, wishing to avoid further conversation about Amaram, 'I've been thinking about your training.'

Shallan stiffened immediately. 'I've been very busy, Brightness.

However, I'm sure I'll be able to get to those books you assigned me very soon.'

Jasnah rubbed her forehead. This girl . . .

'Brightness,' Shallan said, 'I think I might have to request a leave from my studies.' Shallan spoke so quickly the words ran into one another. 'His Majesty says he needs me to go with him on the expedition to Kholinar.'

Jasnah frowned. Kholinar? 'Nonsense. They'll have the Windrunner with them. Why do they need you?'

'The king is worried they might need to sneak into the city,' Shallan said. 'Or even through the middle of it, if it's occupied. We can't know how far the siege has progressed. If Elhokar has to reach the Oathgate without being recognized, then my illusions will be invaluable. I have to go. It's so inconvenient. I'm sorry.' She took a deep breath, eyes wide, as if afraid that Jasnah would snap at her.

This girl.

'I'll speak with Elhokar,' Jasnah said. 'I feel that might be extreme. For now, I want you to do drawings of Renarin's and Kaladin's spren, for scholarly reasons. Bring them to me for . . .' She trailed off. 'What *is* he doing?'

Renarin stood near the far wall, which was covered in palm-size tiles. He tapped a specific one, and somehow made it pop *out*, like a drawer.

Jasnah stood, throwing back her chair. She strode across the room, Shallan scampering along behind her.

Renarin glanced at them, then held up what he'd found in the small drawer. A ruby, long as Jasnah's thumb, cut into a strange shape with holes drilled in it. What on Roshar? She took it from him and held it up.

'What is it?' Navani said, shouldering up beside her. 'A fabrial? No metal parts. What is that shape?'

Jasnah reluctantly surrendered it to her mother.

'So many imperfections in the cut,' Navani said. 'That will cause it to lose Stormlight quickly. It won't even hold a charge for a day, I bet. And it will vibrate something fierce.'

Curious. Jasnah touched it, infusing the gemstone with Stormlight. It started glowing, but not nearly as brightly as it should have. Navani was, of course, right. It vibrated as Stormlight curled off it. Why would anyone spoil a gem with such a twisted cut, and why hide it? The small drawer was latched with a spring, but she couldn't see how Renarin had gotten it undone.

'Storms,' Shallan whispered as other scholars crowded around. 'That's a pattern.'

'A pattern?'

'Buzzes in sequence . . .' Shallan said. 'My spren says he thinks this is a code. Letters?'

'Music of language,' Renarin whispered. He drew in Stormlight from some spheres in his pocket, then turned and pressed his hands against the wall, sending a surge of Stormlight through it that extended from his palms like twin ripples on the surface of a pond.

Drawers slid open, one behind each white tile. A hundred, two hundred . . . each revealing gemstones inside.

The library had decayed, but the ancient Radiants had obviously anticipated that.

They'd found another way to pass on their knowledge.

54

AN ANCIENT
SINGER'S NAME

I would have thought, before attaining my current station, that a deity could not be surprised.

Obviously, this is not true. I can be surprised. I can perhaps even be naive, I think.

'm just asking,' Khen grumbled, 'how this is any better. We were slaves under the Alethi. Now we're slaves under the Fused. Great. It does me so much good to know that our misery is now at the hands of our own people.' The parshwoman set her bundle down with a rattling thump.

'You'll get us in trouble again, talking like that,' Sah said. He dropped his bundle of wooden poles, then walked back the other way.

Moash followed, passing rows of humans and parshmen turning the poles into ladders. These, like Sah and the rest of his team, would soon be carrying those ladders into battle, facing down a storm of arrows.

What a strange echo of his life months ago in Sadeas's warcamp. Except here he'd been given sturdy gloves, a nice pair of boots, and three solid meals a day. The only thing wrong with the situation – other than the fact that he and the others would soon be charging a fortified position – was that he had too much free time.

The workers hauled stacks of wood from one part of the lumberyard to the next, and were occasionally assigned to saw or chop. But there wasn't enough to keep them busy. That was a very bad thing, as he'd learned on the Shattered Plains. Give condemned men too much time and they'd start to ask questions.

'Look,' Khen said, walking next to Sah just ahead, 'at least tell me you're *angry*, Sah. Don't tell me you think we *deserve* this.'

'We harbored a spy,' Sah muttered.

A spy that, Moash had quickly learned, had been none other than *Kaladin Stormblessed*.

'Like a bunch of slaves should be able to spot a spy?' Khen said. 'Really? Shouldn't the *spren* have been the one to spot him? It's like they wanted something to pin on us. Like it's ... it's a ...'

'Like it's a setup?' Moash asked from behind.

'Yeah, a setup,' Khen agreed.

They did that a lot, forgetting words. Or ... maybe they were simply trying the words out for the first time.

Their accent was so similar to that of many of the bridgemen who had been Moash's friends.

Let go, Moash, something deep within him whispered. *Give up your pain. It's all right. You did what was natural.*

You can't be blamed. Stop carrying that burden.

Let go.

They each picked up another bundle and began walking back. They passed the carpenters who were making the ladder poles. Most of these were parshmen, and one of the Fused walked among their ranks. He was a head taller than the parshmen, and was a subspecies that grew large portions of carapace armor in wicked shapes.

The Fused stopped, then explained something to one of the working parshmen. The Fused made a fist, and dark violet energy surrounded his arm. Carapace grew there into the shape of a saw. The Fused sawed, carefully explaining what he did. Moash had seen this before. Some of these monsters from the void were *carpenters*.

Out beyond the lumberyards, parshman troops practiced close-order drill and received basic weapon training. Word was that the army intended to assault Kholinar within weeks. That was ambitious, but they didn't have time for an extended siege. Kholinar had Soulcasters to make food, while the Voidbringer operations in the country would take months to get going. This Voidbringer army would soon eat itself out of supplies, and would have to divide up to forage. Better to attack, use overwhelming numbers, and seize the Soulcasters for themselves.

Every army needed someone to run at the front and soak up arrows. Well organized or not, benevolent or not, the Voidbringers couldn't avoid that. Moash's group wouldn't be trained; they were really only waiting until the assault so they could run in front of more valuable troops.

'We were set up,' Khen repeated as they walked. 'They knew they had too few humans strong enough to run the first assault. They need some of us in there, so they found a *reason* to toss us out to die.'

Sah grunted.

'Is that all you're going to say?' Khen demanded. 'Don't you care what our *own gods* are doing to us?'

Sah slammed his bundle to the ground. 'Yes, I *care*,' Sah snapped. 'You think I haven't been asking the same questions? Storms! They took my daughter, Khen! They ripped her away from me and sent me off to die.'

'Then what do we do?' Khen asked, her voice growing small. 'What do we *do*?'

Sah looked around at the army moving and churning, preparing for war. Overwhelming, enveloping, like its own kind of storm – in motion and inexorable. The sort of thing that picked you up and carried you along.

'I don't know,' Sah whispered. 'Storms, Khen. I don't know anything.'

I do, Moash thought. But he couldn't find the will to say anything to them. Instead, he found himself annoyed, angerspren boiling up around him. He felt frustrated both at himself and at the Voidbringers. He slammed his bundle down, but then stalked off, out of the lumberyard.

An overseer yelped loudly and scuttled after him – but she didn't stop him, and neither did the guards he passed. He had a reputation.

Moash strode through the city, tailed by the overseer, searching for one of the flying type of Fused. They seemed to be in charge, even of the other Fused.

He couldn't find one, so he settled for approaching one of the other subspecies: a malen that sat near the city's cistern, where rainwater collected. The creature was of the heavily armored type, with no hair, the carapace encroaching across his cheeks.

Moash strode right up to the creature. 'I need to talk to someone in charge.'

Behind him, Moash's overseer gasped – perhaps only now realizing that whatever it was Moash was up to, it could get her in serious trouble.

The Fused regarded him and grinned.

'Someone in charge,' Moash repeated.

The Voidbringer laughed, then fell backward into the water of the cistern, where he floated, staring at the sky.

Great, Moash thought. *One of the crazy ones.* There were many of those.

Moash stalked away, but didn't get much farther into the town before something dropped from the sky. Cloth fluttered in the air, and in the middle of it floated a creature with skin that matched the black and red clothing. He couldn't tell if it was malen or femalen.

'Little human,' the creature said with a foreign accent, 'you are passionate and interesting.'

Moash licked his lips. 'I need to talk to someone in charge.'

'You *need* nothing but what we give you,' the Fused said. 'But your *desire* is to be granted. Lady Leshwi will see you.'

'Great. Where can I find her?'

The Fused pressed its hand against his chest and smiled. Dark Void-light spread from its hand across Moash's body. Both of them rose into the air.

Panicking, Moash clutched at the Fused. Could he get the creature into a chokehold? *Then* what? If he killed it up here, he'd drop to his own death.

They rose until the town looked like a tiny model: lumberyard and parade ground on one side, the single prominent street down the center. To the right, the man-made ward provided a buffer against the high-storms, creating a shelter for trees and the citylord's mansion.

They ascended even farther, the Fused's loose clothes fluttering. Though the air was warm at ground level, up here it was quite chilly, and Moash's ears felt odd – dull, as if they were stuffed with cloth.

Finally, the Fused slowed them to a hovering stop. Though Moash tried to hold on, the Fused shoved him to the side, then zoomed away in a flaring roil of cloth.

Moash drifted alone above the expansive landscape. His heart thundered, and he regarded that drop, realizing something. He did *not* want to die.

He forced himself to twist and look about him. He felt a surge of hope as he found he was drifting toward another Fused. A woman who hovered in the sky, wearing robes that must have extended a good ten feet below her, like a smear of red paint. Moash drifted right up beside her, getting so close that she was able to reach out and stop him.

He resisted grabbing that arm and hanging on for dear life. His mind was catching up to what was happening – she wanted to meet him, but in a realm where she belonged and he did not. Well, he would contain his fear.

'Moash,' the Fused said. Leshwi, the other had called her. She had a face that was all three Parshendi colors: white, red, and black, marbled like paint swirled together. He had rarely seen someone who was all three colors before, and this was one of the most transfixing patterns he'd seen, almost liquid in its effect, her eyes like pools around which the colors ran.

'How do you know my name?' Moash asked.

'Your overseer told me,' Leshwi said. She had a distinct serenity about her as she floated with feet down. The wind up here tugged at the ribbons she wore, pushing them backward in careless ripples. There were no windspren in sight, oddly. 'Where did you get that name?'

'My grandfather named me,' Moash said, frowning. This was not how he'd anticipated this conversation going.

'Curious. Do you know that it is one of our names?'

'It is?'

She nodded. 'How long has it drifted on the tides of time, passing from the lips of singers to men and back, to end up here, on the head of a human slave?'

'Look, you're one of the leaders?'

'I'm one of the Fused who is sane,' she said, as if it were the same thing.

'Then I need to—'

'You're bold,' Leshwi said, eyes forward. 'Many of the singers we left here are not. We find them remarkable, considering how long they were abused by your people. But still, they are not bold enough.'

She looked to him for the first time during the conversation. Her face was angular, with long flowing parshman hair – black and crimson, thicker than that of a human. Almost like thin reeds or blades of grass. Her eyes were a deep red, like pools of shimmering blood.

'Where did you learn the Surges, human?' she asked.

'The Surges?'

585

'When you killed me,' she said, 'you were Lashed to the sky – but you responded quickly, with familiarity. I will say, without guile, that I was furious to be caught so unaware.'

'Wait,' Moash said, cold. 'When I *killed* you?'

She regarded him, unblinking, with those ruby eyes.

'You're the same one?' Moash asked. *That pattern of marbled skin . . .* he realized. *It's the same as the one I fought.* But the features were different.

'This is a new body offered to me in sacrifice,' Leshwi said. 'To bond and make my own, as I have none.'

'You're some kind of spren?'

She blinked but did not reply.

Moash started to drop. He felt it in his clothes, which lost their power to fly first. He cried out, reaching toward the Fused woman, and she seized him by the wrist and injected him with more Voidlight. It surged across his body, and he hovered again. The violet darkness retreated, visible again only as faint periodic crackles on her skin.

'My companions spared you,' she said to him. 'Brought you here, to these lands, as they thought I might wish personal vengeance once reborn. I did not. Why would I destroy that which had such passion? Instead I watched you, curious to see what you did. I saw you help the singers who were pulling the sledges.'

Moash took a deep breath. 'Can you tell me, then, why you treat your own so poorly?'

'Poorly?' she said, sounding amused. 'They are fed, clothed, and trained.'

'Not all of them,' Moash said. 'You had those poor parshmen working as slaves, like humans. And now you're going to throw them at the city walls.'

'Sacrifice,' she said. 'Do you think an empire is built without sacrifice?' She swept her arm across the landscape before them.

Moash's stomach turned over; he'd briefly been able to fixate only on her and forget exactly how *high* he was. Storms . . . this land was big. He could see extensive hills, plains, grass, trees, and stone in all directions.

And in the direction she gestured, a dark line on the horizon. Kholinar?

'I breathe again because of their sacrifices,' Leshwi said. 'And this world will be ours, because of sacrifice. Those who fall will be sung of, but their blood is ours to demand. If they survive the assault, if they prove themselves, then they will be honored.' She looked to him again. 'You fought for them during the trip here.'

'Honestly, I expected you to have me killed for that.'

'If you were not killed for striking down one of the Fused,' she said, 'then why would you be killed for striking one of our lessers? In both cases, human, you proved your passion and earned your right to succeed. Then you bowed to authority when presented, and earned your right to continue to live. Tell me. *Why* did you protect those slaves?'

'Because you need to be unified,' Moash said. He swallowed. 'My people don't deserve this land. We're broken, ruined. Incapable.'

She cocked her head. A cool wind played with her clothing. 'And are you not angered that we took your Shards?'

'They were first given me by a man I betrayed. I . . . don't deserve them.'

No. Not you. It's not your fault.

'You aren't angry that we conquer you?'

'No.'

'Then what *does* anger you? What is your passionate fury, Moash, the man with an ancient singer's name?'

Yes, it was there. Still burning. Deep down.

Storm it, Kaladin had been protecting a *murderer*.

'Vengeance,' he whispered.

'Yes, I understand.' She looked at him, smiling in what seemed to him a distinctly sinister way. 'Do you know why *we* fight? Let me tell you. . . .'

⁖

A half hour later as evening approached, Moash walked the streets of a conquered town. By himself. Lady Leshwi had ordered that Moash be left alone, freed.

He walked with his hands in the pockets of his Bridge Four coat, remembering the frigid air up above. He still felt chilled, even though down here it was muggy and warm.

This was a nice town. Quaint. Little stone buildings, plants growing at the backs of every house. On his left, that meant cultivated rockbuds and bushes burst from around doors – but to his right, facing the storm, there were only blank stone walls. Not even a window.

The plants smelled of civilization to him. A sort of civic perfume that you didn't get out in the wilds. They barely quivered as he passed, though lifespren bobbed at his presence. The plants were accustomed to people on the streets.

He finally stopped at a low fence surrounding pens holding the horses the Voidbringers had captured. The animals munched cut grass the parshmen had thrown to them.

Such strange beasts. Hard to care for, expensive to keep. He turned from the horses and looked out over the fields toward Kholinar. She'd said he could leave. Join the refugees making for the capital. Defend the city.

What is your passionate fury?

Thousands of years being reborn. What would it be like? Thousands of years, and they'd never given up.

Prove yourself . . .

He turned and made his way back to the lumberyard, where the workers were packing up for the day. There was no storm projected tonight, and they wouldn't have to secure everything, so they worked with a relaxed, almost jovial air. All save for his crew, who – as usual – gathered by themselves, ostracized.

Moash seized a bundle of ladder rods off a pile. The workers there turned to object, but cut off when they saw who it was. He untied the bundle and, upon reaching the crew of unfortunate parshmen, tossed a length of wood to each one.

Sah caught his and stood up, frowning. The others mimicked him.

'I can train you with those,' Moash said.

'Sticks?' Khen asked.

'Spears,' Moash said. 'I can teach you to be soldiers. We'll probably die anyway. Storm it, we'll probably never make it to the top of the walls. But it's something.'

The parshmen looked at one another, holding rods that could mimic spears.

'I'll do it,' Khen said.

Slowly, the others nodded in agreement.

*I am the least equipped, of all, to aid you in this endeavor. I am find-
ing that the powers I hold are in such conflict that the most simple of
actions can be difficult.*

Rlain sat on the Shattered Plains alone and listened to the rhythms.
Enslaved parshmen, deprived of true forms, weren't able to
hear the rhythms. During his years spent as a spy, he'd adopted
dullform, which heard them weakly. It had been so hard to be apart from
them.

They weren't quite true songs; they were beats with hints of tonality
and harmony. He could attune one of several dozen to match his mood,
or – conversely – to help alter his mood.

His people had always assumed the humans were deaf to the rhythms,
but he wasn't convinced. Perhaps it was his imagination, but it seemed
that sometimes they responded to certain rhythms. They'd look up at a
moment of frenzied beats, eyes getting a far-off look. They'd grow agitated and shout in time, for a moment, to the Rhythm of Irritation, or
whoop right on beat with the Rhythm of Joy.

It comforted him to think that they might someday learn to hear the
rhythms. Perhaps then he wouldn't feel so alone.

He currently attuned the Rhythm of the Lost, a quiet yet violent
beat with sharp, separated notes. You attuned it to remember the fallen,

and that felt the correct emotion as he sat here outside Narak, watching humans build a fortress from what used to be his home. They set a watchpost atop the central spire, where the Five had once met to discuss the future of his people. They turned homes into barracks.

He was not offended – his own people had repurposed the ruins of Stormseat into Narak. No doubt these stately ruins would outlast the Alethi occupation, as they had the listeners. That knowledge did not prevent him from mourning. His people were gone, now. Yes, parshmen had awakened, but they were not listeners. No more than Alethi and Vedens were the same nationality, simply because most had similar skin tones.

Rlain's people were gone. They had fallen to Alethi swords or had been consumed by the Everstorm, transformed into incarnations of the old listener gods. He was, as far as he knew, the last.

He sighed, pulling himself to his feet. He swung a spear to his shoulder, the spear they *let* him carry. He loved the men of Bridge Four, but he was an oddity, even to them: the parshman they allowed to be armed. The potential Voidbringer they had decided to trust, and wasn't he just so lucky.

He crossed the plateau to where a group of them trained under Teft's watchful eye. They didn't wave to him. They often seemed surprised to find him there, as if they'd forgotten he was around. But when Teft did notice him, the man's smile was genuine. They were his friends. It was merely . . .

How could Rlain be so fond of these men, yet at the same time want to slap them?

When he and Skar had been the only two who couldn't draw Stormlight, they'd encouraged Skar. They'd given him pep talks, told him to keep trying. They had believed in him. Rlain, though . . . well, who knew what would happen if he could use Stormlight? Might it be the first step in turning him into a monster?

Never mind that he'd told them you had to open yourself to a form to adopt it. Never mind that he had the power to *choose* for himself. Though they never spoke it, he saw the truth in their reactions. As with Dabbid, they thought it best that Rlain remain without Stormlight.

The parshman and the insane man. People you couldn't trust as Windrunners.

Five bridgemen launched into the air, Radiant and steaming with

Light. Some of the crew trained while another group patrolled with Kaladin, checking on caravans. A third group – the ten other newcomers that had learned to draw in Stormlight – trained with Peet a few plateaus over. That group included Lyn and all *four* of the other scouts, along with four men from other bridge crews, and a single lighteyed officer. Colot, the archer captain.

Lyn had slid into Bridge Four's comradery easily, as had a couple of the bridgemen. Rlain tried not to feel jealous that they almost seemed more a part of the team than he did.

Teft led the five in the air through a formation while the four others strolled toward Rock's drink station. Rlain joined them, and Yake slapped him on the back, pointing toward the next plateau over, where the bulk of the hopefuls continued to train.

'That group can barely hold a spear properly,' Yake said. 'You ought to go show them how a *real* bridgeman does a kata, eh, Rlain?'

'Kalak help them if they have to fight those shellheads,' Eth added, taking a drink from Rock. 'Um, no offense, Rlain.'

Rlain touched his head, where he had carapace armor – distinctively thick and strong, as he held warform – covering his skull. It had stretched out his Bridge Four tattoo, which had transferred to the carapace. He had protrusions on his arms and legs too, and people always wanted to feel those. They couldn't believe they actually grew from his skin, and somehow thought it was appropriate to try to peek underneath.

'Rlain,' Rock said. 'Is okay to throw things at Eth. He has hard head too, almost like he has shell.'

'It's all right,' Rlain said, because that was what they expected him to say. He accidentally attuned Irritation, though, and the rhythm laced his words.

To cover his embarrassment, he attuned Curiosity and tried Rock's drink of the day. 'This is good! What is in it?'

'Ha! Is water I boiled cremlings in, before serving them last night.'

Eth spurted out his mouthful of drink, then looked at the cup, aghast.

'What?' Rock said. 'You ate the cremlings easily!'

'But this is . . . like their *bathwater*,' Eth complained.

'Chilled,' Rock said, 'with spices. Is good taste.'

'Is bathwater,' Eth said, imitating Rock's accent.

Teft led the other four in a streaking wave of light overhead. Rlain looked up, and found himself attuning Longing before he stomped it out. He attuned Peace instead. Peace, yes. He could be peaceful.

'This isn't working,' Drehy said. 'We can't storming patrol the entirety of the Shattered Plains. More caravans are going to get hit, like that one last night.'

'The captain says it's strange for those Voidbringers to keep raiding like this,' Eth said.

'Tell that to the caravaneers from yesterday.'

Yake shrugged. 'They didn't even burn much; we got there before the Voidbringers had time to do much more than frighten everyone. I'm with the captain. It's strange.'

'Maybe they're testing our abilities,' Eth said. 'Seeing what Bridge Four can really do.'

They glanced at Rlain for confirmation.

'Am . . . am I supposed to be able to answer?' he asked.

'Well,' Eth said. 'I mean . . . storms, Rlain. They're your kinsmen. Surely you know something about them.'

'You can guess, right?' Yake said.

Rock's daughter refilled his cup for him, and Rlain looked down at the clear liquid. *Don't blame them*, he thought. *They don't know. They don't understand.*

'Eth, Yake,' Rlain said carefully, 'my people did everything we could to separate ourselves from those creatures. We went into hiding long ago, and swore we would never accept forms of power again.

'I don't know what changed. My people must have been tricked somehow. In any case, these Fused are as much my enemies as they are yours – *more*, even. And no, I can't say what they will do. I spent my entire life trying to avoid thinking of them.'

Teft's group came crashing down to the plateau. For all his earlier difficulty, Skar had quickly taken to flight. His landing was the most graceful of the bunch. Hobber hit so hard he yelped.

They jogged over to the watering station, where Rock's eldest daughter and son began giving them drinks. Rlain felt sorry for the two; they barely spoke Alethi, though the son – oddly – was Vorin. Apparently, monks came from Jah Keved to preach the Almighty to the Horneaters, and Rock let his children follow any god they wanted. So it was that the pale-skinned young Horneater wore a glyphward tied to his arm and burned prayers to the Vorin Almighty instead of making offerings to the Horneater spren.

Rlain sipped his drink and wished Renarin were here; the quiet, lighteyed man usually made a point of speaking with Rlain. The others jabbered excitedly, but didn't think to include him. Parshmen were invisible to them – they'd been brought up that way.

And yet, he loved them because they *did* try. When Skar bumped him – and was reminded that he was there – he blinked, then said, 'Maybe we should ask Rlain.' The others immediately jumped in and said he didn't want to talk about it, giving a kind of Alethi version of what he'd told them earlier.

He belonged here as much as he did anywhere else. Bridge Four was his family, now that those from Narak were gone. Eshonai, Varanis, Thude . . .

He attuned the Rhythm of the Lost and bowed his head. He had to believe that his friends in Bridge Four could feel a hint of the rhythms, for otherwise how would they know how to mourn with true pain of soul?

Teft was getting ready to take the other squad into the air when a group of dots in the sky announced the arrival of Kaladin Stormblessed. He landed with his squad, including Lopen, who juggled an uncut gemstone the size of a man's head. They must have found a chrysalis from a beast of the chasms.

'No sign of Voidbringers today,' Leyten said, turning over one of Rock's buckets and using it as a seat. 'But storms . . . the Plains sure do seem smaller when you're up there.'

'Yeah,' Lopen said. 'And *bigger*.'

'Smaller and bigger?' Skar asked.

'Smaller,' Leyten said, 'because we can cross them so fast. I remember plateaus that felt like they took *years* to cross. We zip past those in an eyeblink.'

'But then you get up high,' Lopen added, 'and you realize how wide this place is – sure, how much of it we never even explored – and it just seems . . . big.'

The others nodded, eager. You had to read their emotion in their expressions and the way they moved, not in their voices. Maybe that was why emotion spren came so often to humans, more often than to listeners.

Without the rhythms, men needed help understanding one another.

'Who's on the next patrol?' Skar asked.

'None for today,' Kaladin said. 'I have a meeting with Dalinar. We'll leave a squad in Narak, but . . .'

Soon after he left through the Oathgate, everyone would slowly start to lose their powers. They'd be gone in an hour or two. Kaladin had to be relatively near – Sigzil had placed their maximum distance from him at around fifty miles, though their abilities started to fade somewhere around thirty miles.

'Fine,' Skar said. 'I was looking forward to drinking more of Rock's cremling juice anyway.'

'Cremling juice?' Sigzil said, drink halfway to his lips. Other than Rlain, Sigzil's dark brown skin was the most different from the rest of the crew – though the bridgemen didn't seem to care much about skin color. To them, only eyes mattered. Rlain had always found that strange, as among listeners, your skin patterns had at times been a matter of some import.

'So . . .' Skar said. 'Are we going to talk about Renarin?'

The twenty-eight men shared looks, many settling down around the barrel of Rock's drink as they once had around the cookfire. There were certainly a suspicious number of buckets to use as stools, as if Rock had planned for this. The Horneater himself leaned against the table he'd brought out for holding cups, a cleaning rag thrown over his shoulder.

'What about him?' Kaladin asked, frowning and looking around at the group.

'He's been spending a lot of time with the scribes studying the tower city,' Natam said.

'The other day,' Skar added, 'he was talking about what he's doing there. It sounded an *awful* lot like he was learning how to read.'

The men shifted uncomfortably.

'So?' Kaladin asked. 'What's the problem? Sigzil can read his own language. Storms, *I* can read glyphs.'

'It's not the same,' Skar said.

'It's feminine,' Drehy added.

'Drehy,' Kaladin said, 'you are *literally* courting a man.'

'So?' Drehy said.

'Yeah, what are you saying, Kal?' Skar snapped.

'Nothing! I just thought Drehy might empathize. . . .'

'That's hardly fair,' Drehy said.

'Yeah,' Lopen added. 'Drehy likes other guys. That's like . . . he wants to be even less around women than the rest of us. It's the *opposite* of feminine. He is, you could say, extra manly.'

'Yeah,' Drehy said.

Kaladin rubbed his forehead, and Rlain empathized. It was sad that humans were so burdened by always being in mateform. They were *always* distracted by the emotions and passions of mating, and had not yet reached a place where they could put that aside.

He felt embarrassed for them – they were simply too concerned about what a person should and shouldn't be doing. It was because they didn't have forms to change into. If Renarin wanted to be a scholar, let him be a scholar.

'I'm sorry,' Kaladin said, holding out his hand to calm the men. 'I wasn't trying to insult Drehy. But storms, men. We know that things are changing. Look at the lot of us. We're halfway to being lighteyes! We've already let five women into Bridge Four, and they'll be fighting with spears. Expectations are being upended – and *we're* the cause of it. So let's give Renarin a little leeway, shall we?'

Rlain nodded. Kaladin *was* a good man. For all his faults, he tried even more than the rest of them.

'I have thing to say,' Rock added. 'During last few weeks, how many of you have come to me, saying you feel you don't fit in with Bridge Four now?'

The plateau fell silent. Finally, Sigzil raised his hand. Followed by Skar. And several others, including Hobber.

'Hobber, you did not come to me,' Rock noted.

'Oh. Yeah, but I felt like it, Rock.' He glanced down. 'Everything's changing. I don't know if I can keep up.'

'I still have nightmares,' Leyten said softly, 'about what we saw in the bowels of Urithiru. Anyone else?'

'I have trouble Alethi,' Huio said. 'It makes me . . . embarrassing. Alone.'

'I'm scared of heights,' Torfin added. 'Flying up there is terrifying to me.'

A few glanced at Teft.

'What?' Teft demanded. 'You expect this to be a feeling-sharing party because the storming Horneater gave you a sour eye? Storm off. It's a miracle I'm not burning moss every moment of the day, having to deal with you lot.'

Natam patted him on the shoulder.

'And I will not fight,' Rock said. 'I know some of you do not like this. He makes me feel different. Not only because I am only one with proper beard in crew.' He leaned forward. 'Life *is* changing. We will all feel alone because of this, yes? Ha! Perhaps we can feel alone together.'

They all seemed to find this comforting. Well, except Lopen, who had snuck away from the group and for some reason was lifting up rocks on the other side of the plateau and looking underneath them. Even among humans, he was a strange one.

The men relaxed and started to chat. Though Hobber slapped Rlain on the back, it was the closest any of them came to asking how he felt. Was it childish of him to feel frustrated? They all thought they were alone, did they? Felt that they were outsiders? Did they *know* what it was like to be of an entirely different species? A species they were currently at war with – a species whose people had all been either murdered or corrupted?

People in the tower watched him with outright hatred. His friends didn't, but they sure did like to pat themselves on the back for that fact. *We understand that you're not like the others, Rlain. You can't help what you look like.*

He attuned Annoyance and sat there until Kaladin sent the rest of them off to train the aspiring Windrunners. Kaladin spoke softly with Rock, then turned and paused, seeing Rlain sitting there on his bucket.

'Rlain,' Kaladin said, 'why don't you take the rest of the day off?'

What if I don't want special accommodation because you feel sorry for me?

Kaladin squatted down beside Rlain. 'Hey. You heard what Rock said. I know how you feel. We can help you shoulder this.'

'Do you really?' Rlain said. 'Do you *actually* know how I feel, Kaladin Stormblessed? Or is that simply a thing that men say?'

'I guess it's a thing men say,' Kaladin admitted, then pulled over an upside-down bucket for himself. 'Can you tell me how it feels?'

Did he really want to know? Rlain considered, then attuned Resolve. 'I can try.'

56

ALWAYS WITH YOU

I am also made uncertain by your subterfuge. Why have you not made yourself known to me before this? How is it you can hide? Who are you truly, and how do you know so much about Adonalsium?

D alinar appeared in the courtyard of a strange fortress with a single towering wall of bloodred stones. It closed a large gap in a mountainous rock formation.

Around him, men carried supplies or otherwise made themselves busy, passing in and out of buildings constructed against the natural stone walls. Winter air made Dalinar's breath puff before him.

He held Navani's freehand on his left, and Jasnah's on his right. It had worked. His control over these visions was increasing beyond even what the Stormfather assumed possible. Today, by holding their hands, he had brought Navani and Jasnah in without a highstorm.

'Wonderful,' Navani said, squeezing his hand. 'That wall is as majestic as you described. And the people. Bronze weapons again, very little steel.'

'That armor is Soulcast,' Jasnah said, releasing his hand. 'Look at the fingermarks on the metal. That's burnished iron, not true steel, Soulcast from clay into that shape. I wonder . . . did access to Soulcasters retard their drive to learn smelting? Working steel is difficult. You can't simply melt it over a fire, like you can bronze.'

'So . . .' Dalinar asked, 'when are we?'

'Maybe two thousand years ago,' Jasnah said. 'Those are Haravingian swords, and see those archways? Late classical architecture, but washed out faux blue on the cloaks, rather than true blue dyes. Mix that with the language you spoke in – which my mother recorded last time – and I'm fairly certain.' She glanced at the passing soldiers. 'A multiethnic coalition here, like during the Desolations – but if I'm right, this is over two thousand years after Aharietiam.'

'They're fighting someone,' Dalinar said. 'The Radiants retreat from a battle, then abandon their weapons on the field outside.'

'Which places the Recreance a little more recently than Masha-daughter-Shaliv had it in her history,' Jasnah said, musing. 'From my reading of your vision accounts, this is the last chronologically – though it's difficult to place the one with you overlooking ruined Kholinar.'

'Who could they be fighting?' Navani asked as men atop the wall raised the alarm. Horsemen galloped out of the keep, off to investigate. 'This is well after the Voidbringers left.'

'It could be the False Desolation,' Jasnah said.

Dalinar and Navani both looked at her.

'A legend,' Jasnah said. 'Considered pseudohistorical. Dovcanti wrote an epic about it somewhere around fifteen hundred years ago. The claim is that some Voidbringers survived Aharietiam, and there were many clashes with them afterward. It's considered unreliable, but that's because many later ardents insist that no Voidbringers could have survived. I'm inclined to assume this is a clash with parshmen before they were somehow deprived of their ability to change forms.'

She looked to Dalinar, eyes alight, and he nodded. She strode off to collect whatever historical tidbits she could.

Navani took some instruments from her satchel. 'One way or another, I'm going to figure out where this "Feverstone Keep" is, even if I have to bully these people into drawing a map. Perhaps we could send scholars to this location and find clues about the Recreance.'

Dalinar made his way over to the base of the wall. It *was* a truly majestic structure, typical of the strange contrasts of these visions: a classical people, without fabrials or even proper metallurgy, accompanied by wonders.

A group of men piled down the steps from the top of the wall. They were trailed by His Excellency Yanagawn the First, Prime Aqasix of Azir.

While Dalinar had brought Navani and Jasnah by touch, he had asked the Stormfather to bring in Yanagawn. The highstorm currently raged in Azir.

The youth saw Dalinar and stopped. 'Do I have to fight today, Blackthorn?'

'Not today, Your Excellency.'

'I'm getting really tired of these visions,' Yanagawn said, descending the last few steps.

'That fatigue never leaves, Your Excellency. In fact, it has grown as I've begun to grasp the importance of what I have seen in vision, and the burden it puts upon me.'

'That *isn't* what I meant by tired.'

Dalinar didn't reply, hands clasped behind him as together they walked to the sally port, where Yanagawn watched events unfold outside. Radiants were crossing the open plain or flying down. They summoned their Blades, provoking concern from the watching soldiers.

The knights drove their weapons into the ground, then *abandoned* them. They left their armor as well. Shards of incalculable value, renounced.

The young emperor looked to be in no rush to confront them as Dalinar had been. Dalinar, therefore, took him by the arm and guided him out as the first soldiers opened the doors. He didn't want the emperor to get caught in the flood that would soon come, as men dashed for those Blades, then started killing one another.

As before in this vision, Dalinar felt as if he could hear the screaming deaths of the spren, the terrible sorrow of this field. It almost overwhelmed him.

'Why?' Yanagawn asked. 'Why did they just . . . give up?'

'We don't know, Your Excellency. This scene haunts me. There is so much I don't understand. Ignorance has become the theme of my rule.'

Yanagawn looked around, then scrambled for a tall boulder to climb, where he could better watch the Radiants. He seemed far more engaged by this than he had been by other visions. Dalinar could respect that. War was war, but this . . . this was something you never saw. Men willingly giving up their Shards?

And that *pain*. It pervaded the air like a terrible stench.

Yanagawn settled down on his boulder. 'So why show me this? You don't even know what it means.'

'If you're not going to join my coalition, I figure I should still give you as much knowledge as I can. Perhaps we will fall, and you will survive. Maybe your scholars can solve these puzzles when we cannot. And maybe you are the leader Roshar needs, while I am just an emissary.'

'You don't believe that.'

'I don't. I still want you to have these visions, just in case.'

Yanagawn fidgeted, playing with the tassels on his leather breastplate. 'I . . . don't matter as much as you think I do.'

'Pardon, Your Excellency, but you underestimate your importance. Azir's Oathgate will be vital, and you are the strongest kingdom of the west. With Azir at our side, many other countries will join with us.'

'I mean,' Yanagawn said, 'that *I* don't matter. Sure, Azir does. But I'm only a kid they put on the throne because they were afraid that assassin would come back.'

'And the miracle they're publishing? The proof from the Heralds that you were chosen?'

'That was Lift, not me.' Yanagawn looked down at his feet, swinging beneath him. 'They're training me to act important, Kholin, but I'm not. Not yet. Maybe not ever.'

This was a new face to Yanagawn. The vision today had shaken him, but not in the way Dalinar had hoped. *He's a youth,* Dalinar reminded himself. Life at his age was challenging anyway, without adding to it the stress of an unexpected accession to power.

'Whatever the reason,' Dalinar told the young emperor, 'you are Prime. The viziers have published your miraculous elevation to the public. You do have some measure of authority.'

He shrugged. 'The viziers aren't bad people. They feel guilty for putting me in this position. They give me education – kind of force it down my throat, honestly – and expect me to participate. But I'm *not* ruling the empire.

'They're scared of you. Very scared. More scared than they are of the assassin. He burned the emperors' eyes, but emperors can be replaced. You represent something far more terrible. They think you could destroy our entire culture.'

'No Alethi has to set foot on Azish stone,' Dalinar said. 'But come to me, Your Excellency. Tell them you've seen visions, that the Heralds want you to at least *visit* Urithiru. Tell them that the opportunities far outweigh the danger of opening that Oathgate.'

'And if this happens again?' Yanagawn asked, nodding toward the field of Shardblades. Hundreds of them sprouting from the ground, silvery, reflecting sunlight. Men were now pouring out of the keep, flooding toward those weapons.

'We will see that it doesn't. Somehow.' Dalinar narrowed his eyes. 'I don't know what caused the Recreance, but I can guess. They lost their vision, Your Excellency. They became embroiled in politics and let divisions creep among them. They forgot their purpose: protecting Roshar for its people.'

Yanagawn looked to him, frowning. 'That's harsh. You always seemed so respectful of the Radiants before.'

'I respect those who fought in the Desolations. These? I can sympathize. I too have on occasion let myself be distracted by small-minded pettiness. But respect? No.' He shivered. 'They killed their spren. They betrayed their oaths! They may not be villains, as history paints them, but in this moment they failed to do what was right and just. *They failed Roshar.*'

The Stormfather rumbled in the distance, agreeing with this sentiment.

Yanagawn cocked his head.

'What?' Dalinar asked.

'Lift doesn't trust you,' he said.

Dalinar glanced about, expecting her to appear as she had in the previous two visions he'd shown Yanagawn. There was no sign of the young Reshi girl that the Stormfather detested so much.

'It's because,' Yanagawn continued, 'you act so righteous. She says anyone who acts like you do is trying to hide something.'

A soldier strode up and spoke to Yanagawn in the Almighty's voice. 'They are the first.'

Dalinar stepped back, letting the young emperor listen as the Almighty gave his short speech for this vision. *These events will go down in history. They will be infamous. You will have many names for what happened here . . .*

The Almighty said the same words he had to Dalinar.

The Night of Sorrows will come, and the True Desolation. The Everstorm.

The men on the field full of Shards started to fight over the weapons. For the first time in history, men started slaughtering one another with dead spren. Finally, Yanagawn faded, vanishing from the vision. Dalinar closed his eyes, feeling the Stormfather draw away. Everything now dissolved . . .

Except it didn't.

Dalinar opened his eyes. He was still on the field before the looming, bloodred wall of Feverstone Keep. Men fought over Shardblades while some voices called for everyone to be patient.

Those who claimed a Shard this day would become rulers. It bothered Dalinar that the best men, the ones calling for moderation or raising concerns, would be rare among their numbers. They weren't aggressive enough to seize the advantage.

Why was he still here? Last time, the vision had ended before this.

'Stormfather?' he asked.

No reply. Dalinar turned around.

A man in white and gold stood there.

Dalinar jumped, scrambling backward. The man was old, with a wide, furrowed face and bone-white hair that swept back from his head as if blown by wind. Thick mustaches with a hint of black in them blended into a short white beard. He seemed to be Shin, judging by his skin and eyes, and he wore a golden crown in his powdery hair.

Those eyes . . . they were ancient, the skin surrounding them deeply creased, and they danced with joy as he smiled at Dalinar and rested a golden scepter on his shoulder.

Suddenly overwhelmed, Dalinar fell to his knees. 'I know you,' he whispered. 'You're . . . you're Him. God.'

'Yes,' the man said.

'Where have you been?' Dalinar said.

'I've always been here,' God said. 'Always with you, Dalinar. Oh, I've watched you for a long, long time.'

'Here? You're . . . not the Almighty, are you?'

'Honor? No, he truly is dead, as you've been told.' The old man's smile deepened, genuine and kindly. 'I'm the other one, Dalinar. They call me Odium.'

57

PASSION

If you would speak to me further, I request open honesty. Return to my lands, approach my servants, and I will see what I can do for your quest.

Odium.

Dalinar scrambled to his feet, lurching backward and seeking a weapon he didn't possess.

Odium. Standing in *front* of him.

The Stormfather had grown distant, almost vanished – but Dalinar could sense a faint emotion from him. A whine, like he was straining against something heavy?

No. No, that was a whimper.

Odium rested his golden scepter against the palm of his hand, then turned to regard the men fighting over Shardblades.

'I remember this day,' Odium said. 'Such *passion*. And such loss. Terrible for many, but glorious for others. You are wrong about why the Radiants fell, Dalinar. There was infighting among them, true, but no more than in other eras. They were honest men and women, with different views at times, but unified in their desire to do what was best.'

'What do you want of me?' Dalinar said, hand to his breast, breathing quickly. Storms. He wasn't ready.

Could he *ever* be ready for this moment?

Odium strolled over to a small boulder and settled down. He sighed in relief, like a man releasing a heavy burden, then nodded to the space next to him.

Dalinar made no move to sit.

'You have been placed in a difficult position, my son,' Odium said. 'You are the first to bond the Stormfather in his current state. Did you know that? You are deeply connected to the remnants of a god.'

'Whom you killed.'

'Yes. I'll kill the other one too, eventually. She's hidden herself somewhere, and I'm too . . . shackled.'

'You're a monster.'

'Oh, Dalinar. This from you of all people? Tell me you've never found yourself in conflict with someone you respect. Tell me you've never killed a man because you had to, even if – in a better world – he shouldn't deserve it?'

Dalinar bit back a retort. Yes, he'd done that. Too many times.

'I know you, Dalinar,' Odium said. He smiled again, a paternal expression. 'Come sit down. I won't devour you, or burn you away at a touch.'

Dalinar hesitated. *You need to hear what he says. Even this creature's lies can tell you more than a world of common truths.*

He walked over, then stiffly sat down.

'What do you know of us three?' Odium asked.

'Honestly, I wasn't even aware there *were* three of you.'

'More, in fact,' Odium said absently. 'But only three of relevance to you. Me. Honor. Cultivation. You speak of her, don't you?'

'I suppose,' Dalinar said. 'Some people identify her with Roshar, the spren of the world itself.'

'She'd like that,' Odium said. 'I wish I could simply let her have this place.'

'So do it. Leave us alone. Go away.'

Odium turned to him so sharply that Dalinar jumped. 'Is that,' Odium said quietly, 'an offer to release me from my bonds, coming from the man holding the remnants of Honor's name and power?'

Dalinar stammered. *Idiot. You're not some raw recruit. Pull yourself together.* 'No,' he said firmly.

'Ah, all right then,' Odium said. He smiled, a twinkle in his eyes. 'Oh, don't fret so. These things must be done properly. I *will* go if you release me, but only if you do it by Intent.'

'And what are the consequences of my releasing you?'

'Well, first I'd see to Cultivation's death. There would be . . . other consequences, as you call them, as well.'

Eyes burned as men swept about themselves with Shardblades, killing others who had mere moments before been their comrades. It was a frantic, insane brawl for power.

'And you can't just . . . leave?' Dalinar asked. 'Without killing anyone?'

'Well, let me ask you this in return. Why did you seize control of Alethkar from poor Elhokar?'

'I . . .' *Don't reply. Don't give him ammunition.*

'You knew it was for the best,' Odium said. 'You knew that Elhokar was weak, and the kingdom would suffer without firm leadership. You took control for the greater good, and it has served Roshar well.'

Nearby, a man stumbled toward them, limping out of the fray. His eyes burned as a Shardblade rammed through his back, protruding three feet out of his chest. He fell forward, eyes trailing twin lines of smoke.

'A man cannot serve two gods at once, Dalinar,' Odium said. 'And so, I cannot leave her behind. In fact, I cannot leave behind the Splinters of Honor, as I once thought I could. I can already see that going wrong. Once you release me, my transformation of this realm will be substantial.'

'You think you'll do better?' Dalinar wet his mouth, which had gone dry. 'Do better than others would, for this land? You, a manifestation of hatred and pain?'

'They call me Odium,' the old man said. 'A good enough name. It does have a certain *bite* to it. But the word is too limiting to describe me, and you should know that it is not all I represent.'

'Which is?'

He looked to Dalinar. '*Passion*, Dalinar Kholin. I am emotion incarnate. I am the soul of the spren and of men. I am lust, joy, hatred, anger, and exultation. I am glory and I am vice. I am the very thing that makes men *men*.

'Honor cared only for bonds. Not the *meaning* of bonds and oaths, merely that they were kept. Cultivation only wants to see transformation. Growth. It can be good or bad, for all she cares. The pain of men is nothing to her. Only I understand it. Only I *care*, Dalinar.'

I don't believe that, Dalinar thought. *I can't* believe *that.*

The old man sighed, then heaved himself to his feet. 'If you could see the result of Honor's influence, you would not be so quick to name me a god of anger. Separate the emotion from men, and you have creatures like Nale and his Skybreakers. *That* is what Honor would have given you.'

Dalinar nodded toward the terrible fray on the field before them. 'You said I was wrong about what caused the Radiants to abandon their oaths. What was it really?'

Odium smiled. 'Passion, son. Glorious, wondrous *passion*. Emotion. It is what defines men – though ironically you are poor vessels for it. It fills you up and breaks you, unless you find someone to share the burden.' He looked toward the dying men. 'But can you imagine a world without it? No. Not one I'd want to live in. Ask that of Cultivation, next time you see her. Ask what she'd want for Roshar. I think you'll find me to be the better choice.'

'Next time?' Dalinar said. 'I've never seen her.'

'Of course you have,' Odium said, turning and walking away. 'She simply robbed you of that memory. Her touch is not how I would have helped you. It stole a part of you away, and left you like a blind man who can't remember that he once had sight.'

Dalinar stood up. 'I offer you a challenge of champions. With terms to be discussed. Will you accept it?'

Odium stopped, then turned slowly. 'Do you speak for the world, Dalinar Kholin? Will you offer this for all Roshar?'

Storms. Would he? 'I . . .'

'Either way, I don't accept.' Odium stood taller, smiling in an unnervingly understanding way. 'I need not take on such a risk, for I know, Dalinar Kholin, that you will make the right decision. You will free me.'

'No.' Dalinar stood. 'You shouldn't have revealed yourself, Odium. I once feared you, but it is easier to fear what you don't understand. I've seen you now, and I can fight you.'

'You've seen me, have you? Curious.'

Odium smiled again.

Then everything went white. Dalinar found himself standing on a speck of nothingness that was the entire world, looking up at an eternal, all-embracing *flame.* It stretched in every direction, starting as red, moving to orange, then changing to blazing white.

Then somehow, the flames seemed to burn into a deep blackness, violet and angry.

This was something so terrible that it consumed light itself. It was hot. A radiance indescribable, intense heat and black fire, colored violet at the outside.

Burning.

Overwhelming.

Power.

It was the scream of a thousand warriors on the battlefield.

It was the moment of most sensual touch and ecstasy.

It was the sorrow of loss, the joy of victory.

And it *was* hatred. Deep, pulsing hatred with a pressure to turn all things molten. It was the heat of a thousand suns, it was the bliss of every kiss, it was the lives of all men wrapped up in one, defined by everything they felt.

Even taking in the smallest fraction of it terrified Dalinar. It left him tiny and frail. He knew if he drank of that raw, concentrated, liquid black fire, he'd be nothing in a moment. The entire planet of Roshar would puff away, no more consequential than the curling smoke of a snuffed-out candle.

It faded, and Dalinar found himself lying on the rock outside Feverstone Keep, staring upward. Above him, the sun seemed dim and cold. Everything felt frozen by contrast.

Odium knelt down beside him, then helped him rise to a seated position. 'There, there. That was a smidge too much, wasn't it? I had forgotten how overwhelming that could be. Here, take a drink.' He handed Dalinar a waterskin.

Dalinar looked at it, baffled, then up at the old man. In Odium's eyes, he could see that violet-black fire. Deep, deep within. The figure with whom Dalinar spoke was not the god, it was merely a face, a mask.

Because if Dalinar had to confront the true force behind those smiling eyes, he would go mad.

Odium patted him on the shoulder. 'Take a minute, Dalinar. I'll leave you here. Relax. It—' He cut off, then frowned, spinning. He searched the rocks.

'What?' Dalinar asked.

'Nothing. Just an old man's mind playing tricks on him.' He patted Dalinar on the arm. 'We'll speak again, I promise.'

He vanished in an eyeblink.

Dalinar collapsed backward, completely drained. Storms. Just . . . Storms.

'That guy,' a girl's voice said, 'is *creepy*.'

Dalinar shifted, sitting up with difficulty. A head popped up from behind some nearby rocks. Tan skin, pale eyes, long dark hair, lean, girlish features.

'I mean, old men are *all* creepy,' Lift said. 'Seriously. All wrinkly and "Hey, want some sweets?" and "Oh, listen to this boring story." I'm on to them. They can act nice all they want, but nobody gets old without ruining a whole buncha lives.'

She climbed over the rocks. She wore fine Azish clothing now, compared to the simple trousers and shirt from last time. Colorful patterns on robes, a thick overcoat and cap. 'Even as old people go, that one was extra creepy,' she said softly. 'What was that thing, tight-butt? Didn't smell like a real person.'

'They call it Odium,' Dalinar said, exhausted. 'And it is what we fight.'

'Huh. Compared to that, you're *nothing*.'

'Thank you?'

She nodded, as if it were a compliment. 'I'll talk to Gawx. You got good food at that tower city of yours?'

'We can prepare some for you.'

'Yeah, I don't care what you prepare. What do *you* eat? Is it good?'

'. . . Yes?'

'Not military rations or some such nonsense, right?'

'Not usually.'

'Great.' She looked at the place where Odium had vanished, then shivered visibly. 'We'll visit.' She paused, then poked him in the arm. 'Don't tell Gawx about that Odium thing, okay? He's got too many old people to worry about already.'

Dalinar nodded.

The bizarre girl vanished and, moments later, the vision finally faded.

THE END OF

Part Two

INTERLUDES

❖

KAZA • TARAVANGIAN • VENLI

The ship *First Dreams* crashed through a wave, prompting Kaza to cling tightly to the rigging. Her gloved hands already ached, and she was certain each new wave would toss her overboard.

She refused to go down below. This was *her* destiny. She was not a thing to be carted from place to place, not any longer. Besides, that dark sky – suddenly stormy, even though the sailing had been easy up until an hour ago – was no more disconcerting than her visions.

Another wave sent water crashing across the deck. Sailors scrambled and screamed, mostly hirelings out of Steen, as no rational crew would make this trip. Captain Vazrmeb stalked among them, shouting orders, while Droz – the helmsman – kept them on a steady heading. Into the storm. Straight. Into. The storm.

Kaza held tight, feeling her age as her arms started to weaken. Icy water washed over her, pushing back the hood of her robe, exposing her face – and its twisted nature. Most sailors weren't paying attention, though her cry *did* bring Vazrmeb's attention.

The only Thaylen on board, the captain didn't much match her image of the people. Thaylens, to her, were portly little men in vests – merchants with styled hair who haggled for every last sphere. Vazrmeb, however, was as tall as an Alethi, with hands wide enough to palm boulders and forearms large enough to lift them.

Over the crashing of waves, he yelled, 'Someone get that Soulcaster below deck!'

'No,' she shouted back at him. 'I stay.'

'I didn't pay a prince's ransom to bring you,' he said, stalking up to her, 'only to lose you over the side!'

'I'm not a thing to—'

'Captain!' a sailor shouted. '*Captain!*'

They both looked as the ship tipped over the peak of a huge wave, then teetered, before just kind of *falling* over the other side. Storms! Kaza's stomach practically squeezed up into her throat, and she felt her fingers sliding on the ropes.

Vazrmeb seized her by the side of her robe, holding her tight as they plunged into the water beyond the wave. For a brief terrifying moment, they seemed entombed in the chill water. As if the entire ship had sunk.

The wave passed, and Kaza found herself lying in a sodden heap on the deck, held by the captain. 'Storming fool,' he said to her. 'You're my secret weapon. You drown yourself when you're *not* in my pay, understand?'

She nodded limply. And then realized, with a shock, she'd been able to hear him easily. The storm . . .

Was gone?

Vazrmeb stood up straight, grinning broadly, his white eyebrows combed back into his long mane of dripping hair. All across the deck, the sailors who had survived were climbing to their feet, sopping wet and staring at the sky. It maintained its overcast gloom – but the winds had fallen completely still.

Vazrmeb bellowed out a laugh, sweeping back his long, curling hair. 'What did I tell you, men! That new storm came from Aimia! Now it has gone and escaped, leaving the riches of its homeland to be plundered!'

Everyone knew you didn't linger around Aimia, though everyone had different explanations why. Some rumors told of a vengeful storm here, one that sought out and destroyed approaching ships. The strange wind they'd encountered – which didn't match the timing of highstorm *or* Everstorm – seemed to support that.

The captain started shouting orders, getting the men back into position. They hadn't been sailing long, only a short distance out of Liafor, along the Shin coast, then westward toward this northern section of Aimia. They'd soon spotted the large main island, but had not visited it. Everyone knew that it was barren, lifeless. The treasures were on the hidden islands, supposedly lying in wait to enrich those willing to brave the winds and treacherous straits.

She cared less for that – what were riches to her? She had come because of another rumor, one spoken of only among her kind. Perhaps here, at last, she could find a cure for her condition.

Even as she righted herself, she felt in her pouch, seeking the comforting touch of her Soulcaster. *Hers,* no matter what the rulers of Liafor claimed. Had they spent their youths caressing it, learning its secrets? Had they spent their middle years in service, stepping – with each use – closer and closer to oblivion?

The common sailors gave Kaza space, refusing to look her in the eyes. She pulled her hood up, unaccustomed to the gaze of ordinary people. She'd entered the stage where her . . . disfigurements were starkly obvious.

Kaza was, slowly, becoming smoke.

Vazrmeb took the helm himself, giving Droz a break. The lanky man stepped down from the poop deck, noting her by the side of the ship. He grinned at her, which she found curious. She hadn't ever spoken to him. Now he sauntered over, as if intending to make *small talk.*

'So . . .' he said. 'Up on deck? Through *that*? You've got guts.'

She hesitated, considering this strange creature, then lowered her hood.

He didn't flinch, even though her hair, her ears, and now parts of her face were disintegrating. There was a hole in her cheek through which you could see her jaw and teeth. Lines of smoke rimmed the hole; the flesh seemed to be burning away. Air passed through it when she spoke, altering her voice, and she had to tip her head all the way back to drink anything. Even then, it dribbled out.

The process was slow. She had a few years left until the Soulcasting killed her.

Droz seemed intent on pretending nothing was wrong. 'I can't believe we got through that storm. You think it hunts ships, like the stories say?'

He was Liaforan like herself, with deep brown skin and dark brown eyes. What *did* he want? She tried to remember the ordinary passions of human life, which she'd begun to forget. 'Is it sex you want? . . . No, you are much younger than I am. Hmmm . . .' Curious. 'Are you frightened, and wishing for comfort?'

He started to fidget, playing with the end of a tied-off rope. 'Um . . . So, I mean, the prince sent you, right?'

'Ah.' So he knew that she was the prince's cousin. 'You wish to connect yourself to royalty. Well, I came on my own.'

'Surely he *let* you go.'

'Of course he didn't. If not for my safety, then for that of my device.' It *was* hers. She looked off across the too-still ocean. 'They locked me up each day, gave me comforts they assumed would keep me happy. They realized that at any moment, I could *literally* make walls and bonds turn to smoke.'

'Does . . . does it hurt?'

'It is blissful. I slowly connect to the device, and through it to Roshar. Until the day it will take me fully into its embrace.' She lifted a hand and pulled her black glove off, one finger at a time, revealing a hand that was disintegrating. Five lines of darkness, one rising from the tip of each finger. She turned it, palm toward him. 'I could show you. Feel my touch, and you can know. One moment, and then you will mingle with the air itself.'

He fled. Excellent.

The captain steered them toward a small island, poking from the placid ocean right where the captain's map had claimed it would be. It had dozens of names. The Rock of Secrets. The Void's Playground. So melodramatic. She preferred the old name for the place: Akinah.

Supposedly, there had once been a grand city here. But who would put a city on an island you couldn't approach? For, jutting from the ocean here were a set of strange rock formations. They ringed the entire island like a wall, each some forty feet tall, resembling spearheads. As the ship drew closer, the sea grew choppy again, and she felt a bout of nausea. She liked that. It was a *human* feeling.

Her hand again sought her Soulcaster.

That nausea mixed with a faint sense of hunger. Food was something she often forgot about these days, as her body needed less of it now. Chewing was annoying, with the hole in her cheek. Still, she liked the scents from whatever the cook was stirring up below. Perhaps the meal would calm the men, who seemed agitated about approaching the island.

Kaza moved to the poop deck, near the captain.

'Now you earn your keep, Soulcaster,' he said. 'And I'm justified in hauling you all the way out here.'

'I'm not a thing,' she said absently, 'to be used. I am a person. Those spikes of stone ... they were Soulcast there.' The enormous stone spear-heads were too even in a ring about the island. Judging by the currents ahead, some lurked beneath the waters as well, to rip up the hulls of approaching vessels.

'Can you destroy one?' the captain asked her.

'No. They are much larger than you indicated.'

'But—'

'I can make a hole in them, Captain. It is easier to Soulcast an entire object, but I am no ordinary Soulcaster. I have begun to see the dark sky and the second sun, the creatures that lurk, hidden, around the cities of men.'

He shivered visibly. Why should that have frightened him? She'd merely stated facts.

'We need you to transform the tips of a few under the waves,' he said. 'Then make a hole at least large enough for the dinghies to get in to the island beyond.'

'I will keep my word, but you must remember. I do not *serve* you. I am here for my own purposes.'

They dropped anchor as close to the spikes as they dared get. The spikes were even more daunting – and more obviously Soulcast – from here. *Each would have required several Soulcasters in concert,* she thought, standing at the prow of the ship as the men ate a hasty meal of stew.

The cook was a woman, Reshi from the looks of her, with tattoos all across her face. She pushed the captain to eat, claiming that if he went in hungry, he'd be distracted. Even Kaza took some, though her tongue no longer tasted food. It all felt like the same mush to her, and she ate with a napkin pressed to her cheek.

The captain drew anticipationspren as he waited – ribbons that waved in the wind – and Kaza could see the beasts beyond, the creatures that accompanied the spren.

The ship's four dinghies were cramped, with rowers and officers all together, but they made space for her at the front of one. She pulled up her hood, which still hadn't dried, and sat on her bench. What had the captain been planning to do if the storm hadn't stopped? Would he seriously have tried to use her and a dinghy to remove these spears in the middle of a tempest?

They reached the first spike, and Kaza carefully unwrapped her

Soulcaster, releasing a flood of light. Three large gemstones connected by chains, with loops for her fingers. She put it on, with the gemstones on the back of her hand. She sighed softly to feel the metal against her skin again. Warm, welcoming, a part of her.

She reached over the side into the chill water and pressed her hand against the tip of the stone spear – smoothed from years in the ocean. Light from the gemstones lit the water, reflections dancing across her robe.

She closed her eyes, and felt the familiar sensation of being drawn into the other world. Of another will reinforcing her own, something commanding and powerful, attracted by her request for aid.

The stone did not wish to change. It was content with its long slumber in the ocean. But ... yes, yes, it *remembered*. It had once been air, until someone had locked it into this shape. She could not make it air again; her Soulcaster had only one mode, not the full three. She did not know why.

Smoke, she whispered to the stone. *Freedom in the air. Remember?* She tempted it, picking at its memories of dancing free.

Yes ... freedom.

She nearly gave in herself. How *wonderful* would it be to no longer fear? To soar into infinity on the air? To be free of mortal pains?

The tip of the stone burst into smoke, sending an explosion of bubbles up around the dinghy. Kaza was shocked back into the real world, and a piece deep within her trembled. Terrified. She'd almost gone that time.

Smoke bubbles rattled the dinghy, which nearly upended. She should have warned them. Sailors muttered, but in the next dinghy over, the captain praised her.

She removed two more spear tips beneath the waves before finally reaching the wall. Here, the spearheadlike formations had been grown so close together, there was barely a handspan gap between them. It took three tries to get the dinghy close enough – as soon as they got into position, some turning of the waves would pull them away again.

Finally, the sailors managed to keep the dinghy steady. Kaza reached out with the Soulcaster – two of the three gems were almost out of Stormlight, and glowed only faintly. She should have enough.

She pressed her hand against the spike, then convinced it to become smoke. It was ... easy this time. She felt the explosion of wind from the transformation, her soul crying in delight at the smoke, thick and sweet. She breathed it in through the hole in her cheek while sailors coughed. She looked up at the smoke, drifting away. How wonderful it would be to join it. . . .

No.

The island proper loomed beyond that hole. Dark, like its stones had been stained by smoke themselves, it had tall rock formations along its center. They looked almost like the walls of a city.

The captain's dinghy pulled up to hers, and the captain transferred to her boat. His began to row backward.

'What?' she asked. 'Why is your boat heading back?'

'They claim to not be feeling well,' the captain said. Was he abnormally pale? 'Cowards. They won't have any of the prize, then.'

'Gemstones lay around just for the plucking here,' Droz added. 'Generations of greatshells have died here, leaving their hearts. We're going to be rich, rich men.'

As long as the secret was here.

She settled into her place at the prow of the boat as the sailors guided the three dinghies through the gap. The Aimians had known about Soulcasters. This was where you'd come to get the devices, in the old days. You'd come to the ancient island of Akinah.

If there was a secret of how to avoid death by the device she loved, she would find it here.

Her stomach began acting up again as they rowed. Kaza endured it, though she felt as if she were slipping into the other world. That wasn't an ocean beneath her, but deep black glass. And two suns in the sky, one that drew her soul toward it. Her shadow, to stretch out in the wrong direction . . .

Splash.

She started. One of the sailors had slipped from his boat into the water. She gaped as another slumped to the side, oar falling from his fingers.

'Captain?' She turned to find him with drooping eyes. He went limp, then fell backward, unconscious, knocking his head against the back seat of the boat.

The rest of the sailors weren't doing any better. The other two dinghies had begun to drift aimlessly. Not a single sailor seemed to be conscious.

My destiny, Kaza thought. *My choice.*

Not a thing to be carted from place to place, and ordered to Soulcast. Not a *tool*. A *person*.

She shoved aside an unconscious sailor and took the oars herself. It was difficult work. She was unaccustomed to physical labor, and her fingers had trouble gripping. They'd started to dissolve further. Perhaps a year or two for her survival was optimistic.

Still, she rowed. She fought the waters until she at long last got close enough to hop out into the water and feel rock beneath her feet. Her robes billowing up around her, she finally thought to check if Vazrmeb was alive.

None of the sailors in her dinghy were breathing, so she let the boat slip backward on the waves. Alone, Kaza fought through the surf and – finally – on hands and knees, crawled up onto the stones of the island.

There, she collapsed, drowsy. Why was she so sleepy?

She awoke to a small cremling scuttling across the rocks near her. It had a strange shape, with large wings and a head that made it look like an axehound. Its carapace shimmered with dozens of colors.

Kaza could remember a time when she'd collected cremlings, pinning them to boards and proclaiming she'd become a natural historian. What had happened to that girl?

She was transformed by necessity. Given the Soulcaster, which was always to be kept in the royal family. Given a charge.

And a death sentence.

She stirred, and the cremling scrambled away. She coughed, then began to crawl toward those rock formations. That city? Dark city of stone? She could barely think, though she did notice a gemstone as she passed it – a large uncut gemheart among the bleached white carapace leftovers of a dead greatshell. Vazrmeb had been right.

She collapsed again near the perimeter of the rock formations. They looked like large, ornate buildings, crusted with crem.

'Ah . . .' a voice said from behind her. 'I should have guessed the drug would not affect you as quickly. You are barely human anymore.'

Kaza rolled over and found someone approaching on quiet, bare feet. The cook? Yes, that was her, with the tattooed face.

'You . . .' Kaza croaked, 'you *poisoned* us.'

'After many warnings not to come to this place,' the cook said. 'It is rare I must guard it so . . . aggressively. Men must not again discover this place.'

'The gemstones?' Kaza asked, growing more drowsy. 'Or . . . is it something else . . . something . . . more . . .'

'I cannot speak,' the cook said, 'even to sate a dying demand. There are those who could pull secrets from your soul, and the cost would be the ends of worlds. Sleep now, Soulcaster. This is the most merciful end I could give.'

The cook began to hum. Pieces of her broke off. She crumbled to a pile of chittering little *cremlings* that moved out of her clothing, leaving it in a heap.

A hallucination? Kaza wondered as she drifted.

She was dying. Well, that was nothing new.

The cremlings began to pick at her hand, taking off her Soulcaster. No . . . she had one last thing to do.

With a defiant shout, she pressed her hand to the rocky ground beneath her and demanded it change. When it became smoke, she went with it.

Her choice.

Her destiny.

TARAVANGIAN

Taravangian paced in his rooms in Urithiru as two servants from the Diagram arranged his table, and fidgety Dukar – head of the King's Testers, who each wore a ridiculous stormwarden robe with glyphs all along the seams – set out the tests, though they needn't have bothered.

Today, Taravangian was a storming *genius*.

The way he thought, breathed, even moved, implicitly conveyed that today was a day of intelligence – perhaps not as brilliant as that single transcendent one when he'd created the Diagram, but he finally felt like himself after so many days trapped in the mausoleum of his own flesh, his mind like a master painter allowed only to whitewash walls.

Once the table was finished, Taravangian pushed a nameless servant aside and sat down, grabbing a pen and launching into the problems – starting at the second page, as the first was too simple – and flicking ink at Dukar when the idiot started to complain.

'Next page,' he snapped. 'Quickly, quickly. Let's not waste this, Dukar.'

'You still must—'

'Yes, yes. Prove myself not an idiot. The one day I'm not drooling and lying in my own waste, you tax my time with this idiocy.'

'You set—'

'It up. Yes, the irony is that you let the prohibitions instituted by my idiot self control my true self when it finally has opportunity to emerge.'

'You weren't an idiot when you—'

'Here,' Taravangian said, proffering the sheet of math problems to him. 'Done.'

'All but the last on this sheet,' Dukar said, taking it in cautious fingers. 'Do you want to try that one, or . . .'

'No need. I know I can't solve it; too bad. Make quick with the requisite formalities. I have work to do.'

Adrotagia had entered with Malata, the Dustbringer; they were growing in companionship as Adrotagia attempted to secure an emotional bond with this lesser Diagram member who had suddenly been thrust into its upper echelons, an event predicted by the Diagram – which explained that the Dustbringers would be the Radiants most likely to accept their cause, and at that Taravangian felt proud, for actually locating one of their number who could bond a spren had not, by any means, been an assured accomplishment.

'He's smart,' Dukar said to Mrall. The bodyguard was the final adjudicator of Taravangian's daily capacity – an infuriating check necessary to prevent his stupid side from ruining anything, but a mere annoyance when Taravangian was like this.

Energized.

Awake.

Brilliant.

'He's almost to the danger line,' Dukar said.

'I can see that,' Adrotagia said. 'Vargo, are you—'

'I feel perfect. Can't we be done with this? I can interact, and make policy decisions, and need no restrictions.'

Dukar nodded, reluctantly, in agreement. Mrall assented. Finally!

'Get me a copy of the Diagram,' Taravangian said, pushing past Adrotagia. 'And some music, something relaxing but not too slow. Clear the chambers of nonessential persons, empty the bedroom of furniture, and *don't* interrupt me.'

It took them a frustratingly long time to accomplish, almost half an hour, which he spent on his balcony, contemplating the large space for a garden outside and wondering how big it was. He needed measurements. . . .

'Your room is prepared, Your Majesty,' Mrall said.

'Thank you, Uscritic one, for your leave to go into my own bedroom. Have you been drinking salt?'

'. . . What?'

Taravangian strode through the small room beside the balcony and into his bedroom, then breathed deeply, pleased to find it completely empty of furniture – only four blank stone walls, no window, though it had a strange rectangular outcropping along the back wall, like a high step, which Maben was dusting.

Taravangian seized the maid by the arm and hauled her out, to where Adrotagia was bringing him a thick book bound in hogshide. A copy of the Diagram. Excellent. 'Measure the available gardening area of the stone field outside our balcony and report it to me.'

He carried the Diagram into the room, and then shut himself into blissful self-company, in which he arranged a diamond in each corner – a light to accompany that of his own spark, which shone in truth where others could not venture – and as he finished, a small choir of children started to sing Vorin hymns outside the room per his request.

He breathed in, out, bathed in light and encouraged by song, his hands to the sides; capable of *anything*, he was consumed by the satisfaction of his own working mind, unclogged and flowing freely for the first time in what seemed like ages.

He opened the Diagram. In it, Taravangian finally faced something greater than himself: a different version of himself.

The Diagram – which was the name for this book and for the organization that studied it – had not originally been written merely on paper, for on that day of majestic capacity, Taravangian had annexed every surface to hold his genius – from the cabinetry to the walls – and while so doing had invented new languages to better express ideas that had to be recorded, by necessity, in a medium less perfect than his thoughts. Even as the intellect he was today, the sight of that writing enforced humility; he leafed through pages packed with tiny scrawls, copied – spots, scratches, and all – from the original Diagram room, created during what felt like a different lifetime, as alien to him now as was the drooling idiot he sometimes became.

More alien. Everyone understood stupidity.

He knelt on the stones, ignoring his aches of body, reverently leafing through the pages. Then he slipped out his belt knife, and began to cut it up.

The Diagram had not been written on paper, and interacting with its transcription bound into codex form must necessarily have influenced their thinking, so to obtain true perspective – he now decided – he needed the flexibility of seeing the pieces, then arranging them in new ways, for his thoughts had not been locked down on that day and he should not perceive them as such today.

He was not as brilliant as he'd been on that day, but he didn't need to be. That day, he'd been God. Today, he could be God's prophet.

He arranged the cut-out pages, and found numerous new connections simply by how the sheets were placed next to each other – indeed, this page here *actually* connected to this page here . . . yes. Taravangian cut them both down the middle, dividing sentences. When he put the halves of separate pages beside one another, they made a more complete whole. Ideas he'd missed before seemed to rise from the pages like spren.

Taravangian did not believe in any religion, for they were unwieldy things, designed to fill gaps in human understanding with nonsensical explanations, allowing people to sleep well at night, granting them a false sense of comfort and control and preventing them from stretching further for true understanding, yet there was something strangely holy about the Diagram, the power of raw intelligence, the only thing man should worship, and oh how little most understood it – oh, how little they *deserved* it – in handling purity while corrupting it with flawed understanding and silly superstitions. Was there a way he could prevent any but the most intelligent from learning to read? That would accomplish so much good; it seemed insane that nobody had implemented such a ban, for while Vorinism forbade men to read, that merely prevented an arbitrary half of the population from handling information, when it was the stupid who should be barred.

He paced in the room, then noted a scrap of paper under the door; it contained the answer to his question about the size of the farming platform. He looked over the calculations, listening with half an ear to voices outside, almost overwhelmed by the singing children.

'Uscritic,' Adrotagia said, 'seems to refer to Uscri, a figure from a tragic poem written seventeen hundred years ago. She drowned herself after hearing her lover had died, though the truth was that he'd not died at all, and she misunderstood the report about him.'

'All right . . .' Mrall said.

'She was used in following centuries as an example of acting without information, though the term eventually came to simply mean "stupid." The salt seems to refer to the fact that she drowned herself in the sea.'

'So it was an insult?' Mrall asked.

'Using an obscure literary reference. Yes.' He could almost hear Adrotagia's sigh. Best to interrupt her before she thought on this further.

Taravangian flung open the door. 'Gum paste for sticking paper to this wall. Fetch it for me, Adrotagia.'

They'd put paper in a stack by the door without being asked, which surprised him, as they usually had to be ordered to do everything. He closed the door, then knelt and did some calculations relating to the size of the tower city. *Hmmmm . . .*

It provided a fine distraction, but he was soon drawn back to the true work, interrupted only by the arrival of his gum paste, which he used to begin sticking fragments of the Diagram to his walls.

This, he thought, arranging pages with numbers interspersing the text, pages they'd never been able to make sense of. *It's a list of what? Not code, like the other numbers. Unless . . . could this be shorthand for words?*

Yes . . . yes, he'd been too impatient to write the actual words. He'd numbered them in his head – alphabetically perhaps – so he could write quickly. Where was the key?

This is reinforcement, he thought as he worked, *of the Dalinar paradigm!* His hands shook with excitement as he wrote out possible interpretations. Yes . . . Kill Dalinar, or he will resist your attempts to take over Alethkar. So Taravangian had sent the Assassin in White, which – incredibly – had failed.

Fortunately, there were contingencies. *Here,* Taravangian thought, bringing up another scrap from the Diagram and gluing it to the wall beside the others. *The initial explanation of the Dalinar paradigm, from the catechism of the headboard, back side, third quadrant.* It had been written in meter, as a poem, and presaged that Dalinar would attempt to unite the world.

So if he looked to the second contingency . . .

Taravangian wrote furiously, seeing words instead of numbers, and – full of energy – for a time he forgot his age, his aches, the way his fingers trembled – sometimes – even when he wasn't so excited.

The Diagram hadn't seen the effect the second son, Renarin, would have – he was a completely wild element. Taravangian finished his notations, proud, and wandered toward the door, which he opened without looking up.

'Get me a copy of the surgeon's words upon my birth,' he said to those outside. 'Oh, and kill those children.'

The music trailed off as the children heard what he'd said. Musicspren flitted away.

'You mean, quiet them from singing,' Mrall said.

'Whatever. I'm perturbed by the Vorin hymns as a reminder of historic religious oppression of ideas and thought.'

Taravangian returned to his work, but a short time later a knock came at the door. He flung it open. 'I was not to be—'

'Interrupted,' Adrotagia said, proffering him a sheet of paper. 'The surgeon's words you requested. We keep them handy now, considering how often you ask for them.'

'Fine.'

'We need to talk, Vargo.'

'No we—'

She walked in anyway, then stopped, inspecting the cut-up pieces of the Diagram. Her eyes widened as she turned about. 'Are you . . .'

'No,' he said. 'I haven't become him again. But I *am* me, for the first time in weeks.'

'This *isn't* you. This is the monster you sometimes become.'

'I am not smart enough to be in the dangerous zone.' The zone where, annoyingly, they claimed he was *too* smart to be allowed to make decisions. As if intelligence were somehow a liability!

She unfolded a piece of paper from the pocket of her skirt. 'Yes, your daily test. You stopped on this page, claiming you couldn't answer the next question.'

Damnation. She'd seen it.

'If you'd answered,' she said, 'it would have proved you were intelligent enough to be dangerous. Instead, you decided you couldn't manage. A loophole we should have considered. You *knew* that if you finished the question, we'd restrict your decision-making for the day.'

'Do you know about Stormlight growth?' he said, brushing past her and taking one of the pages he'd written earlier.

'Vargo . . .'

'Calculating the total surface area for farming at Urithiru,' he said, 'and comparing it to the projected number of rooms that could be occupied, I have determined that even *if* food grew here naturally – as it would at the temperatures of your average fecund plain – it could not provide enough to sustain the entire tower.'

'Trade,' she said.

'I have trouble believing the Knights Radiant, always threatened with war, would build a fortress like this to be anything but self-sufficient. Have you read Golombi?'

'Of course I have, and you know it,' she said. 'You think they enhanced the growth by use of Stormlight-infused gemstones, providing light to darkened places?'

'Nothing else makes sense, does it?'

'The tests are inconclusive,' she said. 'Yes, spherelight inspires growth in a dark room, when candlelight cannot, but Golombi says that the results may have been compromised, and the efficiency is . . . Oh, bah! That's a distraction, Vargo. We were discussing what you've done to circumvent the rules *you yourself* set out!'

'When I was stupid.'

'When you were normal.'

'Normal is stupid, Adro.' He took her by the shoulders and firmly pushed her from the room. 'I won't make policy decisions, and I'll avoid ordering the murder of any further groups of melodic children. Fine? All right? Now leave me alone. You're stinking up the place with an air of contented idiocy.'

He shut the door, and – deep down – felt a glimmer of shame. Had he called Adrotagia, of all people, an idiot?

Well. Nothing to do about it now. She would understand.

He set to work again, cutting out more of the Diagram, arranging it, searching for any mentions of the Blackthorn, as there was too much in the book to study today, and he had to be *focused* on their current problem.

Dalinar lived. He was building a coalition. So what did Taravangian do now? Another assassin?

What is the secret? he thought, holding up sheets from the Diagram, finding one where he could see the words on the other side through the paper. Could that have been intentional? *What should I do? Please. Show me the way.*

He scribbled words on a page. Light. Intelligence. Meaning. He hung them on the wall to inspire him, but he couldn't help reading the surgeon's words – the words of a master healer who had delivered Taravangian through a cut in his mother's belly.

He had the cord wrapped around his neck, the surgeon had said. *The queen will know the best course, but I regret to inform her that while he lives, your son may have diminished capacity. Perhaps this is one to keep on outer estates, in favor of other heirs.*

The 'diminished capacity' hadn't appeared, but the reputation had chased Taravangian from childhood, so pervasive in people's minds that not a one had seen through his recent act of stupidity, which they'd attributed to a stroke or to simple senility. Or maybe, some said, that was the way he'd always been.

He'd overcome that reputation in magnificent ways. Now he'd save the world. Well, the part of the world that mattered.

He worked for hours, pinning up more portions of the Diagram, then scribbling on them as connections came to him, using beauty and light to chase away the shadows of dullness and ignorance, giving him answers – they were here, he merely needed to interpret them.

His maid finally interrupted him; the annoying woman was always bustling around, trying to make him do this or that, as if he didn't have more important concerns than soaking his feet.

'Idiot woman!' he shouted.

She didn't flinch, but walked forward and put a tray of food down beside him.

'Can't you see that my work here is important?' he demanded. 'I haven't time for food.'

She set out drink for him, then, infuriatingly, patted him on the shoulder. As she left, he noticed Adrotagia and Mrall standing right outside.

'I don't suppose,' he said to Mrall, 'you'd execute that maid if I demanded it?'

'We have decided,' the bodyguard said, 'that you are not allowed to make such decisions today.'

'To Damnation with you then. I almost have the answers anyway. We must not assassinate Dalinar Kholin. The time has passed for that. Instead, we must support his coalition. Then we force him to step down, so that I can take his place at the head of the monarchs.'

Adrotagia walked in and inspected his work. 'I doubt Dalinar will simply *give* leadership of the coalition to you.'

Taravangian rapped on a set of pages stuck to the wall. 'Look here. It should be clear, even to you. I foresaw this.'

'You've made *changes*,' Mrall said, aghast. 'To the Diagram.'

'Only little ones,' Taravangian said. 'Look, see the original writing here? I didn't change that, and it's clear. Our task now is to make Dalinar withdraw from leadership, take his place.'

'We don't kill him?' Mrall asked.

Taravangian eyed him, then turned and waved toward the other wall, with even more papers stuck to it. 'Killing him now would only raise suspicion.'

'Yes,' Adrotagia said, 'I see this interpretation of the headboard – we must push the Blackthorn so hard that he collapses. But we'll need secrets to use against him.'

'Easy,' Taravangian said, pushing her toward another set of notations on the wall. 'We send that Dustbringer's spren to spy. Dalinar Kholin *reeks* of secrets. We can break him, and I can take his place – as the coalition will see me as nonthreatening – whereupon we'll be in a position of power to negotiate with Odium – who will, by laws of spren and gods, be bound by the agreement made.'

'Can't we . . . *beat* Odium instead?' Mrall asked.

Muscle-bound idiot. Taravangian rolled his eyes, but Adrotagia – more sentimental than he was – turned and explained. 'The Diagram is clear, Mrall,' she said. 'This is the *purpose* of its creation. We cannot beat the enemy; so instead, we save whatever we can.'

'The only way,' Taravangian agreed. Dalinar would never accept this fact. Only one man would be strong enough to make that sacrifice.

Taravangian felt a glimmer of . . . something. Memory.

Give me the capacity to save us.

'Take this,' he said to Adrotagia, pulling down a sheet he'd annotated. 'This *will* work.'

She nodded, towing Mrall from the room as Taravangian knelt before the broken, ripped, sliced-up remnants of the Diagram.

Light and truth. Save what he could.

Abandon the rest.

Thankfully, he had been given that capacity.

THIS ONE IS MINE

Venli was determined to live worthy of power.

She presented herself with the others, a small group selected from the remaining listeners, and braced for the oncoming storm.

She didn't know if Ulim – or his phantom masters, the ancient listener gods – could read her mind. But if they could, they'd find that she was loyal.

This was war, and Venli among its vanguard. *She* had discovered the first Voidspren. *She* had discovered stormform. *She* had redeemed her people. *She* was blessed.

Today would prove it. Nine of them had been selected from among the two thousand listener survivors, Venli included. Demid stood beside her with a wide grin on his face. He loved to learn new things, and the storm was another adventure. They'd been promised something great.

See, Eshonai? Venli thought. *See what we can do, if you don't hold us back?*

'All right, yes, that's it,' Ulim said, rippling across the ground as vibrant red energy. 'Good, good. All in a line. Keep facing west.'

'Should we seek for cover before the storm, Envoy?' Melu asked to the Rhythm of Agony. 'Or carry shields?'

Ulim took the form of a small person before them. 'Don't be silly. This is *our* storm. You have nothing to fear.'

'And it will bring us power,' Venli said. 'Power beyond even that of stormform?'

'Great power,' Ulim said. 'You've been chosen. You're special. But you *must* embrace this. Welcome it. You have to *want* it, or the powers will not be able to take a place in your gemhearts.'

Venli had suffered so much, but this was her reward. She was done with a life spent wasting away under human oppression. She would never again be trapped, impotent. With this new power, she would always, *always* be able to fight back.

The Everstorm appeared from the west, returning as it had before. A tiny village in the near distance fell into the storm's shadow, then was illuminated by the striking of bright red lightning.

Venli stepped forward and hummed to Craving, holding her arms out to the sides. The storm wasn't like the highstorms – no stormwall of blown debris and cremwater. This was far more elegant. It was a billowing cloud of smoke and darkness, lightning breaking out on all sides, coloring it crimson.

She tipped her head back to meet the boiling, churning clouds, and was consumed by the storm.

Angry, violent darkness overshadowed her. Flecks of burning ash streamed past her on all sides, and she felt no rain this time. Just the beat of thunder. The storm's pulse.

Ash bit into her skin, and something crashed down beside her, rolling on the stones. A tree? Yes, a burning tree. Sand, shredded bark, and pebbles washed across her skin and carapace. She knelt down, eyes squeezed closed, arms protecting her face from the blown debris.

Something larger glanced off her arm, cracking her carapace. She gasped and dropped to the stone ground, curling up.

A pressure enveloped her, pushing at her mind, her soul. *Let Me In.*

With difficulty, she opened herself up to this force. This was just like adopting a new form, right?

Pain seared her insides, as if someone had set fire to her veins. She screamed, and sand bit her tongue. Tiny coals ripped at her clothing, singeing her skin.

And then, a voice.

WHAT IS THIS?

It was a warm voice. An ancient, paternal voice, kindly and enveloping. 'Please,' Venli said, gasping in breaths of smoky air. 'Please.'

YES, the voice said. CHOOSE ANOTHER. THIS ONE IS MINE.

The force that had been pushing against her retreated, and the pain stopped. Something else – something smaller, less domineering – took its place. She accepted this spren gladly, then whimpered in relief, attuned to Agony.

An eternity seemed to pass as she lay huddled before the storm. Finally, the winds weakened. The lightning faded. The thunder moved into the distance.

She blinked the grit from her eyes. Bits of cremstone and broken bark streamed from her as she moved. She coughed, then stood, looking at her ruined clothing and singed skin.

She no longer bore stormform. She'd changed to ... was this nimbleform? Her clothing felt large on her, and her body no longer bore its impressive musculature. She attuned the rhythms, and found they were still the new ones – the violent, angry rhythms that came with forms of power.

This wasn't nimbleform, but it also wasn't anything she recognized. She had breasts – though they were small, as with most forms outside of mateform – and long hairstrands. She turned about to see if the others were the same.

Demid stood nearby, and though his clothing was in tatters, his well-muscled body wasn't scored. He stood tall – far taller than her – with a broad chest and powerful stance. He seemed more like a statue than a listener. He flexed, eyes glowing red, and his body pulsed with a dark violet power – a glow that somehow evoked both light and darkness at once. It retreated, but Demid seemed pleased by his ability to invoke it.

What form was *that*? So majestic, with ridges of carapace poking through his skin along the arms and at the corners of the face. 'Demid?' she asked.

He turned toward Melu, who strode up in a similar form and said something in a language Venli didn't recognize. The rhythms were there though, and this was to Derision.

'Demid?' Venli asked again. 'How do you feel? What happened?'

He spoke again in that strange language, and his next words seemed to blur in her mind, somehow shifting until she understood them. '... Odium rides the very winds, like the enemy once did. Incredible. Aharat, is that you?'

'Yes,' Melu said. 'This ... this feels ... good.'

'Feel,' Demid said. 'It feels.' He took a long, deep breath. 'It feels.'

Had they gone mad?

Nearby, Mrun pulled himself past a large boulder, which had not been there before. With horror, Venli realized that she could see a broken arm underneath it, blood leaking out. In direct defiance of Ulim's promise of safety, one of them had been crushed.

Though Mrun had been blessed with a tall, imperious form like the others, he stumbled as he stepped away from the boulder. He grabbed the stone, then fell to his knees. His body coursing with that dark violet light, he groaned, muttering gibberish. Altoki approached from the other direction, standing low, teeth bared, her steps like those of a predator. When she drew closer, Venli could hear her whispering between bared teeth. 'High sky. Dead winds. Blood rain.'

'Demid,' Venli said to Destruction. 'Something has gone wrong. Sit down, wait. I will find the spren.'

Demid looked at her. 'You knew this corpse?'

'This corpse? Demid, why—'

'Oh no. Oh no. Oh *no*!' Ulim coursed across the ground to her. 'You – You aren't – Oh, bad, bad.'

'Ulim!' Venli demanded, attuning Derision and gesturing at Demid. 'Something is wrong with my companions. What have you brought upon us?'

'Don't talk to them, Venli!' Ulim said, forming into the shape of a little man. 'Don't point at them!'

Nearby, Demid was pooling dark violet power in his hand somehow, studying her and Ulim. 'It is you,' he said to Ulim. 'The Envoy. You have my respect for your work, spren.'

Ulim bowed to Demid. 'Please, grand of the Fused, see passion and forgive this child.'

'You should explain to her,' Demid said, 'so she does not . . . aggravate me.'

Venli frowned. 'What is—'

'Come with me,' Ulim said, rippling across the ground. Concerned, overwhelmed by her experience, Venli attuned Agony and followed. Behind, Demid and the others were gathering.

Ulim formed as a person again before her. 'You're lucky. He could have destroyed you.'

'Demid would never do that.'

'Unfortunately for you, your once-mate is *gone*. That's Hariel – and he has one of the worst tempers of all the Fused.'

'Hariel? What do you mean by . . .' She trailed off as the others spoke softly to Demid. They stood so tall, so haughty, and their mannerisms – all wrong.

Each new form changed a listener, down to their ways of thinking, even their temperament. Despite that, you were always you. Even storm-form hadn't changed her into someone else. Perhaps . . . she had become less empathetic, more aggressive. But she'd still been herself.

This was different. Demid didn't stand like her once-mate, or speak like him.

'No . . .' she whispered. 'You said we were opening ourselves up to a new spren, a new form!'

'I *said*,' Ulim hissed, 'that you were opening yourselves up. I didn't say what would enter. Look, your gods need bodies. It's like this every Return. You should be flattered.'

'Flattered to be *killed*?'

'Yeah, for the good of the race,' Ulim said. 'Those are the Fused: ancient souls reborn. What you have, apparently, is just another form of power. A bond with a lesser Voidspren, which puts you above common listeners – who have normal forms – but a step below the Fused. A *big* step.'

She nodded, then started to walk back toward the group.

'Wait,' Ulim said, rippling across the ground before her. 'What are you doing? What is *wrong* with you?'

'I'm going to send that soul out,' she said. 'Bring Demid back. He needs to know the consequences before he can choose such a drastic—'

'Back?' Ulim said. '*Back?* He's *dead*. As you should be. This is bad. What did you do? Resist, like that sister of yours?'

'Out of my way.'

'He'll kill you. I warned of his temper—'

'Envoy,' Demid said to Destruction, turning toward them. It wasn't his voice.

She attuned Agony. It *wasn't his voice.*

'Let her pass,' the thing with Demid's body said. 'I will speak with her.'

Ulim sighed. 'Bother.'

'You speak like a human, spren,' Demid said. 'Your service here was grand, but you use their ways, their language. I find that displeasing.'

Ulim rippled away across the stones. Venli stepped up to the group of Fused. Two still had trouble moving. They lurched, stumbled, fell to their knees. A different two wore smiles, twisted and wrong.

The listener gods were not completely sane.

'I regret the death of your friend, good servant,' Demid said with a deep voice, fully in sync with the Rhythm of Command. 'Though you are the children of traitors, your war here is to be commended. You faced our hereditary enemies and gave no quarter, even when doomed.'

'Please,' Venli said. 'He was precious to me. Can you return him?'

'He has passed into the blindness beyond,' Demid said. 'Unlike the witless Voidspren you bonded – which resides in your gemheart – my soul cannot share its dwelling. Nothing, not Regrowth or act of Odium, can restore him now.'

He reached out and took Venli by the chin, lifting her face, inspecting it. 'You were to bear a soul I have fought beside for thousands of years. She was turned away, and you were reserved. Odium has a purpose for you. Revel in that, and mourn not your friend's passing. Odium will bring vengeance at long last to those we fight.'

He let go of her, and she had to struggle to keep herself from collapsing. No. No, she would not show weakness.

But . . . Demid . . .

She put him out of her mind, like Eshonai before him. This was the path she had placed herself on from the moment she'd first listened to Ulim years ago, deciding that she would risk the return of her people's gods.

Demid had fallen, but she had been preserved. And Odium himself, god of gods, had a purpose for her. She sat down on the ground to wait as the Fused conversed in their strange language. As she waited, she noted something hovering near the ground a short distance away. A little spren that looked like a ball of light. Yes . . . she'd seen one of those near Eshonai. What was it?

It seemed agitated, and scooted across the stone closer to her. She instantly knew something – an instinctive truth, as sure as the storms and the sun. If the creatures standing nearby saw this spren, they would destroy it.

She slapped her hand down over the spren as the creature wearing

Demid's body turned toward her. She cupped the little spren against the stone, and attuned Abashment.

He didn't seem to notice what she'd done.

'Ready yourself to be carried,' he said. 'We must travel to Alethela.'

BRANDON SANDERSON is the author of, amongst others, the Mistborn books, the Reckoners novels and the epic fantasy that hit the *Sunday Times* Hardback Bestsellers list, The Stormlight Archive. He is currently working on new books in each of these series.

• • •

Chosen by Robert Jordan's family to complete Jordan's epic Wheel of Time Sequence, Brandon Sanderson has gone on to become an internationally bestselling author in his own right.

• • •

He lives with his family in Utah. Find out more on his website, www.brandonsanderson.com, or you can follow @brandsanderson on Twitter.

More from Brandon Sanderson . . .

• • •

MISTBORN

*What if the **Dark Lord** won?*

The epic fantasy that has taken readers across the world by storm with 150,000 Mistborn books sold in the UK alone.

FOR A THOUSAND YEARS THE ASH FELL.
THE MISTS RULED THE NIGHT.
THE LORD RULER OWNS THE WORLD.
YET SOMEHOW HOPE SURVIVES.

• • •

Praise for the **Mistborn** books

**'Highly recommended to anyone hungry for a good read'
Robin Hobb**

'Sanderson's saga of consequences offers complex characters and a compelling plot, asking hard questions about loyalty, faith and responsibility' *Publishers Weekly*

**'All the explosive action and adventure any
fan could want'** *Locus*

WARBREAKER

Brandon Sanderson

WARBREAKER is the story of two sisters – who happen to be princesses, the God King one of them has to marry, a lesser god, and an immortal trying to undo the mistakes he made hundreds of years ago.

Theirs is a world in which those who die in glory return as gods to live confined to a pantheon in Hallandren's capital city. A world transformed by BioChromatic magic, a power based on an essence known as *breath*. Using magic is arduous: breath can only be collected one unit at a time from individual people.

But the rewards are great: by using *breath* and drawing upon the colour in everyday objects, all manner of miracles and mischief can be performed.

Brandon Sanderson proves again that he is a master of what Tolkien called 'secondary creation,' the invention of whole worlds, complete with magics and myths all of their own.

• • •

'Anyone looking for a different and refreshing fantasy novel will be delighted by this exceptional tale of magic, mystery and the politics of divinity. *Warbreaker* might even take your breath away' Michael Moorcock

'A powerful tale of unpredictable loyalties, dark intrigue and dangerous magic . . . Sanderson melds complex, believable characters, a marvellous world and thoughtful, ironic humour into an extraordinary and highly entertaining story' *Publishers Weekly*

**'This is essential reading for fantasy fans'
*Library Journal***

'Sanderson is clearly a master of large-scale stories, splendidly depicting worlds as well as strong female characters' *Booklist*

THE RECKONERS

They say no one can kill a High Epic.

A new, action-packed thrill ride of a series, from
the No.#1 New York Times bestselling author of the
Mistborn trilogy and **The Way of Kings**

Ten years ago, Calamity came.
It was a burst in the sky that gave ordinary men
and women extraordinary powers. The awed public
started calling them Epics. But Epics are no friend of
man. With incredible gifts came the desire to rule.
And to rule man you must crush his wills.
Nobody fights the Epics... nobody but the Reckoners.

• • •

Praise for the **Reckoners** books:

ABOUT GOLLANCZ

Gollancz is the oldest SF publishing imprint in the world. Since being founded in 1927 Gollancz has continued to publish a focused selection of bestselling and award-winning authors. The front-list includes **Ben Aaronovitch**, **Joe Abercrombie**, **Charlaine Harris**, **Joanne Harris**, **Joe Hill**, **Alastair Reynolds**, **Patrick Rothfuss**, **Nalini Singh** and **Brandon Sanderson**.

As one of the largest Science Fiction and Fantasy imprints in the UK it is no surprise we have one of the most extensive backlists in the world. Find high-quality SF on Gateway written by such authors as **Philip K. Dick**, **Ursula Le Guin**, **Connie Willis**, **Sir Arthur C. Clarke**, **Pat Cadigan**, **Michael Moorcock** and **George R.R. Martin**.

We also have a strand of publishing in translation, which includes French, Polish and Russian authors. Gollancz is home to more award-winning authors than any other imprint, with names including **Aliette de Bodard**, **M. John Harrison**, **Paul McAuley**, **Sarah Pinborough**, **Pierre Pevel**, **Justina Robson** and many more.

The SF Gateway
More than 3,000 classic, rare and previously out-of-print SF novels at your fingertips.
www.sfgateway.com

The Gollancz Blog
Bringing you news from our worlds to yours. Stories, interviews, articles and exclusive extracts just for you!
www.gollancz.co.uk

GOLLANCZ
LONDON